FROM THE PAGES OF THE *HISTORIES*

"Men trust their ears less than their eyes." (1.8)

"When a woman puts off her tunic she puts off her modesty also." (1.8)

"In peace the sons bury their fathers, but in war the fathers bury their sons." (1.87)

They are wont to deliberate when drinking hard about the most important of their affairs, and whatever conclusion has pleased them, this on the next day, when they are sober, the master of the house where they happen to deliberate lays before them for discussion. If it pleases them when they are sober also, they adopt it, but if it does not please them, they let it go. Whatever they have had the first deliberation on when they are sober, they consider again when they are drinking. (1.133)

For great wrongs great also are the penalties which come from the gods. (2.120)

"To be envied is better than to be pitied." (3.52)

"Insolence is engendered in him by the good things which he possesses, and envy is implanted in man from the beginning; and having these two things, he has all vice." (3.80)

"The most valuable of all possessions is a friend who is a man of under-standing and also sincerely well-disposed." (5.24)

"God strikes with thunderbolts the creatures which stand above the rest and suffers them not to make a proud show; while those which are small do not provoke him to jealousy." (7.10)

"The hastening of any matter breeds disasters." (7.10)

"Misfortunes falling upon us and diseases disturbing our happiness make the time of life, though short indeed, seem long: thus, since life is full of trouble, death has become the most acceptable refuge for man." (7.46)

"Accidents will rule the men and not men the accidents." (7.49)

"Great power is in general gained by running great risks." (7.50)

These neither snow nor rain nor heat nor darkness of night prevents from accomplishing each one the task proposed to him, with the very utmost speed. (8.98)

"The power of the king is above that of a man and his arm is very long." (8.140)

"The most hateful grief of all human griefs is this, to have knowledge of the truth but no power over the event." (9.16)

"From lands which are not rugged men who are not rugged are apt to come forth." (9.122)

THE HISTORIES

Herodotus

With an Introduction and Notes
by Donald Lateiner

Translated by G. C. Macaulay and
Revised throughout by Donald Lateiner

George Stade
Consulting Editorial Director

ЛƁ

BARNES & NOBLE CLASSICS
NEW YORK

ℬ

BARNES & NOBLE CLASSICS

NEW YORK

Published by Barnes & Noble Books
122 Fifth Avenue
New York, NY 10011

www.barnesandnoble.com/classics

It is believed that Herodotus' *Histories* was first published, or recited, between 449 and 447 B.C.
G. C. Macaulay's English translation of the *Histories* first appeared in the United States in 1890.

Originally published in trade paperback format in 2004 by Barnes & Noble Classics
with new Introduction, Notes, Biography, Chronology, Note on the Text, Appendix,
Inspired By, Comments & Questions, and For Further Reading.
This hardcover edition published in 2005.

The Histories
ISBN 13: 978-1-59308-355-7
ISBN 10: 1-59308-355-6
LC Control Number 2004112687

Produced and published in conjunction with:
Fine Creative Media, Inc.
322 Eighth Avenue
New York, NY 10001
Michael J. Fine, President and Publisher

Printed in the United States of America
QM

1 3 5 7 9 10 8 6 4 2

FIRST PRINTING

HERODOTUS

Little information exists about the life of Herodotus, the Father of History, except what we can glean from his writing. In or around 484 B.C. he was born in Asia Minor in the Carian town of Halicarnassos (now Bodrum, Turkey), at that time a Greek city-state under the rule of the Persian Empire. His father was Greek; the family was a prominent one. Herodotus had a brother, Theodorus, and was related to an epic poet, Panyassis, whose works are lost. Panyassis took part in an uprising against the Persians in 457 B.C. It is thought that at this time Herodotus, perhaps because of his own support for the revolt, left Halicarnassos for the Ionian island of Samos.

Herodotus appears to have traveled widely. He first visited Susa and Babylon in Persia (modern Iran). After 460 B.C. he traveled to Egypt (as far south as modern Aswan), North Africa, the Greek islands and mainland, Scythia (parts of modern Ukraine, Russia, and Kazakhstan), and Colchis (modern Georgia). His modes of travel remain unclear, although his attention to commerce suggests he may have journeyed on merchant ships. Around 449 or 448, he probably would have composed some of the books of his *Histories* and perhaps began to "publish" his work in the manner of the time—that is, by reciting it.

Around 447 B.C. he went to Athens, led at the time by Pericles. In Athens, Herodotus would have associated with the orator Antiphon, the musician Damon, the philosophers Protagoras and Zeno, and the playwrights Euripides and Sophocles. There are late reports of Herodotus reading to an audience that included the young Thucydides, who later became the principal historian of the Peloponnesian War. But Herodotus was not a citizen of Athens, and it was difficult to become one. In 443 he joined a group of colonists setting out to found the colony of Thurii in southern Italy and became a citizen of that new town, where he most likely expanded and polished the *Histories*. He died in Thurii in 414 B.C.

The subject of Herodotus' *Histories* (in Greek the word means "inquiries") is the twenty years (499–479 B.C.) of war between Greece and Persia for domination of the Greek world. He broke new ground in looking to past events for the roots of the conflict and incorporating in his accounts surrounding information that shed light on the conduct of the war and the personalities of those who waged it. Unlike Homer, whose epics about the past were based on legend and myth, Herodotus also gathered evidence firsthand from personal accounts and from his observation of places, monuments, and works of art. Herodotus had an appreciation for a good story, and many fascinating tales are sprinkled throughout the *Histories*, including many the historian himself may not have fully believed.

Without Herodotus' *Histories,* we would have no written record of the pivotal historical events of the Greco-Persian Wars. In addition to that invaluable contribution, Herodotus has given us a lively compendium of ancient personalities and events that we can read for pleasure, amazement, and edification.

TABLE OF CONTENTS

List of Maps
ix

The World of Herodotus and the *Histories*
xi

Introduction by Donald Lateiner
xv

A Brief Note on the Text
xxxiii

Translator's Preface
xxxv

THE HISTORIES
1

Book I: Prologues, Croesus of Lydia, and Cyrus of Persia
3

Book II: Egypt: Geography, Customs, History, Tales
79

Book III: Persian Conquest of Egypt, Samos,
King Dareios of Persia
141

Book IV: Scythia and Dareios's Failure, North Africa
199

Book V: The Ionians Revolt, The Athenians Assist
259

Book VI: The Ionian Defeat, Sparta and Athens,
The Marathon Campaign
301

Book VII: Xerxes' Expedition into Greece,
Battle of Thermopylai
345

Book VIII: Battle of Artemision, Athens Abandoned,
Battle of Salamis
419

Book IX: Battles of Plataia and Mycale, Epilogues
462

Appendix: A Repertory of English Translations of Herodotus
503

Inspired by the *Histories*
505

Comments & Questions
509

For Further Reading
515

Index
523

LIST OF MAPS

Map 1. The Achaimenid empire.
page 190

Map 2. Greek and Phoenician trade in the period of
the Persian Wars.
page 242

Map 3. The battle of Marathon.
page 334

Map 4. Greece and the Aegean Sea.
page 356

Map 5. Thermopylai.
page 408

Map 6. The battle of Salamis.
page 439

Map 7. The battle of Plataea (Plataia).
page 468

Map 8. Mycale, Samos Strait, and Heraeum
(Sanctuary of Hera).
page 495

THE WORLD OF HERODOTUS
AND THE *HISTORIES*

560–   Croesus, wealthy king of Lydia, in Asia Minor, conquers coastal
547 B.C. Ionia, where many Hellenic communities have been established.

547   The Persian king Cyrus overthrows Croesus.

522   Dareios I usurps the Persian throne.

512   Dareios crosses the Bosporus and subdues Thrace (modern Turkey, northeastern Greece, and parts of Bulgaria).

c.500   Hecataios writes *Genealogies* and *Journey Around the Lands;* the
B.C.   first prose writing in Greece, *Genealogies* is an attempt to trace the mythological roots of several Greek families. Pythagoras, the influential mathematician and philosopher, dies around this time, and the philosopher Anaxagoras, the sculptor Phidias, and the future Athenian ruler Pericles are born. The Ionians attempt to overthrow their Persian rulers, in what is known as the Ionian Revolt.

499   Persia attacks the Greek island of Naxos in the Aegean Sea. The Ionians capture and burn Sardis, the Persian-controlled capital of Lydia.

497   Greece and Persia fight battles in Cyprus and adjoining sea territories.

496   The playwright Sophocles is born.

c.495   The philosopher Zeno, founder of the dialectic, is born.

494   Persia destroys Miletus, in Asia Minor, ending the Ionian Revolt and restoring Persian dominance over the Hellenic cities in Ionia.

c. 493 The tragedian Phrynichus writes and stages *Sack of Miletus,* a moment in Attic tragic history mentioned by Herodotus (6.21).

490   Persia invades Greece, and the Persian Wars begin; they will continue for more than forty years, with the heaviest, European-based fighting continuing until 479 B.C. The Athenians and Plataians win the battle of Marathon. The philosopher Empedocles is born.

486   Dareios dies. His son Xerxes succeeds him. The poet Anacreon dies.

c.484   Herodotus is born in Halicarnassos, a Greek colony in Caria, in Persian-controlled Asia Minor. The playwright Euripides is born.

481   Representatives from many Greek cities meet in Corinth, resolving to set aside their internal disputes and unite against the Persian invasion.

480   The Persians annihilate the troops of King Leonidas of Sparta at Thermopylai. Under the leadership of Xerxes, Persian troops severely damage and occupy Athens. Greek naval troops win a battle

	with the Persians in the straits of Salamis, near Athens; it is the first great naval conflict to be recorded in history. Buddha dies around this time.
479	The Greeks defeat the Persians by land at Plataia and by sea at Mycale. This year marks the end of the most intensive, European-based fighting of the Persian Wars; sporadic conflict occurs in Asia Minor until 449 B.C. Confucius dies.
478	An alliance of Greek cities under the leadership of Athens, known as the Delian League, is founded to avenge the destruction caused by Persia and to regain formerly Greek-owned cities under Persian control. Athens takes control of Byzantium.
475	Phrynichus' Persian War tragedy *Phoenissae* (*Phoenician Women*) is staged.
472	Aeschylus' dramatic tragedy *Persians* is staged.
470	Socrates is born.
468	The poet Simonides dies; he wrote and memorialized the Spartan expeditionary force that defended the pass at Thermopylai.
466	Greek troops under the Athenian Cimon defeat the Persians at the river Eurymedon.
c.465	Earthquakes rock Sparta. Xerxes is assassinated and succeeded by his son Artaxerxes.
c.464	Herodotus begins to travel around the known world.
461	Pericles begins his rise to power in Athens.
460	Hippocrates, the "Father of Medicine," is born. The philosopher Democritus is born. Thucydides, the historian of the Peloponnesian War, is born around this time.
458	Aeschylus stages his trilogy the *Oresteia*.
457	In Halicarnassos, a relative of Herodotus and perhaps the future historian himself take part in a revolt against Persian rule. Herodotus leaves Halicarnassos for the Ionian island of Samos.
456	Aeschylus dies.
454	Athens is defeated in Egypt.
c.450	Aristophanes is born.
449	The Greek navy defeats the Persians at Salamis, a city in Cyprus. The Persian Wars end with the Peace of Callias, in which Persia recognizes the independence of Greek cities, especially those of Asia Minor.
449–448	Herodotus perhaps begins to recite his *Histories*.
447	He travels to Athens, where he continues to recite his work.
443	Herodotus joins a group from Athens that founds the Hellenic colony of Thurii in southern Italy.
c.441	Sophocles' *Antigone* is staged; it contains scenes related to incidents in the *Histories*.
431	The Peloponnesian War between Athens and Sparta begins; it will be recorded by Herodotus' successor Thucydides. Euripides' *Medea* is staged.

429   Pericles dies.

c.428–   Plato is born.
427

425   Aristophanes' *The Archarnians* is staged; it parodies the opening
         of Herodotus' *Histories*.

424   Thucydides is exiled from Athens.

414   Herodotus dies in Thurii. (Many sources give 425 as the year he
         died; the date 414 is based on references by Aristophanes and on
         recent historiographical work showing Herodotus' awareness of
         and reflections on events that took place after 425.)

INTRODUCTION

The wrecked central figure of the novel *The English Patient* (1992) has nothing to establish his identity, in his Florentine World War II hospital, other than a battered and interleaved copy of the *Histories* of Herodotus. Throughout the novel, Herodotus is quoted, described, and used as an analogy for fascination with the desert, interest in love and war, and wisdom on human happenstance. Indeed, author Michael Ondaatje's acknowledgment makes clear that the character Almásy had in hand the very translation you now hold, George C. Macaulay's. The story of the Lydian king Candaules, his trusted spearman Gyges, and the king's wife (told at 1.8–12) parallels the tale of the erotic threesome featured in Ondaatje's novel.

"Herodotus sometimes writes for children and sometimes for philosophers," said the greatest of modern historians, Edward Gibbon (*The History of the Decline and Fall of the Roman Empire,* 1776–1788, chapter 24, note 54). Casual and serious readers alike have loved the first historian, the inventor of history, for his narrative genius and tragicomic view of human events, great and small. He has been equally criticized and damned by professional historians, ethnographers, and geographers for errors of fact and method, and even for his Greek. Cicero was not the first to call him "the father of lies." The German scholar Detlev Fehling (see "For Further Reading") actually avers that he never left Greece or perhaps even his Anatolian study, copying others' lies and travelers' tales, inventing claims of visits to exotic places and familiar monuments, and fabricating hundreds of alleged sources.

Whereas other ancient historians who followed his large footsteps narrowed their scope in terms of topic (Thucydides, Polybius, Sallust), time (Theopompus, Livy, Tacitus), or territory (the local historians, such as those of Athens, the Atthidographers, or the chroniclers of other *poleis*), Herodotus Homerically encompasses vast realms in topic, time, and territory. After leaving his birthplace, Halicarnassos on the western edge of Asia Minor (Anatolia, now roughly Turkey), he sailed on various voyages, perhaps as a merchant, south to Egypt, east to Sidon, north to the Hellespont and Black Sea, and west to Italy and Sicily. He then traveled inland in all these directions, although one cannot always separate his reports based on personal visits from what he heard or thought he heard, through interpreters who were sometimes comparatively informed and sometimes no better than local loungers eager to help a tourist. He saw the earth beneath his feet and existing structures at Delphi, Marathon, and Delos. He traveled to the edges of the known and unknown inhabited world in Egypt and Italy, and around the Black Sea. He heard about Spain, Babylon (in modern Iraq), Afghanistan, cold Britain, and the hot Sahara. This last region, described with wonder and some disparagement in the latter half of book IV, is crucial to the story of Ondaatje's protagonist in *The English Patient,* a Central European explorer of North Africa. Herodotus was his guide in those vast spaces, and he was never separated from this talisman, a kind of Bible for his restless search in life.

Herodotus—the inquirer, evaluator, and judge (a combination of the three is what "historian" means in Greek)—tells us what he observed. He saw pyramids, inscriptions, and other natural and artificial alterations of the environment. He heard facts and fictions from combatants, travelers, and survivors. He gathered legends and anecdotes from oral traditional tales. And he surmised certain things to be possible or probable from his own penetrating critiques of humans, their normal and odd behaviors, and their environment. Some of his alleged errors turn out to be misunderstandings of what he wrote. Some real errors (such as his disbelief [4.42] in the possibility of Phoenician circumnavigation of Africa) derive from his honest mistakes in a young and illiterate world without prose books—his was one of the first and certainly the most ambitious work of research to his day.

Notwithstanding the somewhat exceptional case of the Athenians and the unavailability of scribal records of the Eastern autocracies, his world possessed few public records, no libraries or databases, only many personal and parochial biases and foreign tongues. His sources and source materials include Egyptian, African, Persian, Phoenician, Scythian, Celtic, and Ethiopian as well as Greek information. For one exotic example, his account of gold-digging, furry giant ants in the northeastern corner of the Persian Empire (Pactyike; 3.102–105) may have misreported, through many intermediary sources, the habits of a larger animal. The large burrowing marmots of the Dansar plateau, which overlooks the Indus in Kashmir, may have given rise to Herodotus' bizarre account of mining insects; see Michel Peissel's *The Ants' Gold: The Discovery of the Greek El Dorado in the Himalayas* (1984) and an article by Marlise Simons ("Gold-Digging Ants' Mystery Seems Solved, After Bugging Scholars for Centuries"; *New York Times,* November 25, 1996). In "The Place of Herodotus in the History of Historiography," the eminent student of ancient historiography Arnaldo Momigliano wrote: "If we had to give an *a priori* estimate of . . . success in writing history by Herodotus' method, we should probably shake our heads in sheer despondency."

Life

Herodotus is a reclusive personality, despite the frequent intrusion of the pronoun "I" in his text. He generously tells us much about the claims of other men, many cities, and tribes about their origins and achievements but offers little about himself. He says nothing directly of his ethnicity or his family or his personality. His first sentence may report that his home-city was Halicarnassos, now in coastal southwestern Turkey (an ancient Dorian Greek colony), but another manuscript tradition reports Thurii (in coastal southern Italy, a recent Athenian colonial outpost in Herodotus' time) as his residence. His probable life span was from 484 to 414 B.C. (many sources give 425 as the year Herodotus died; the date 414 is based on references by Aristophanes and on recent historiographical work showing Herodotus' awareness of and reflections on events that took place after 425). His reticence trumps even his evidence when he parenthetically informs us (2.143) that, unlike Hecataios, his predecessor in touring Egyptian Thebes and reporting it, he did not recount his own genealogy to the antiquarian Egyptian priests. "The authorial I," the many first-person pronouns and verbs in his text—more than one thousand, according to Carolyn Dewald ("Narrative Surface and Authorial Voice in Herodotus' *Histories,*" pp. 147–170, and " 'I didn't give my own genealogy': Herodotus and the Authorial Personality," p. 271)—do not produce confessions or much self-revelation. Indeed, this story proves that pioneering Hecataios had made a fool of himself and his nation's supposed "history" in Egypt, and Herodotus did not imitate his Greek predecessor's historical shortsightedness. Other emphatic insertions of his views in the text are unexpected and infrequent: his polemical insistence on the historical reality of the Persian debate about possible forms of government—monarchy, oligarchy, and democracy (3.80), the fact that the Persians treated the Ionians gently and that their viceroys installed local democracies (6.42–43), the reality of the traitorous Marathon shield-signal (6.121–124), and his pleasant chortles at Athenian superstition (1.59) and at the Athenian democracy's political gullibility (5.97).

The great historiographer Felix Jacoby assiduously collected the references to Herodotus' travels and the objects he observed ("Herodot," cols. 247–281), but this does not add up to even a snapshot of the author. Other rare sources for information about his life are quite late—Hellenistic and Roman imperial—and not worth much credence. What they report is frequently no more than what one can extract or extrapolate from his text. Thucydides, who might have told us most (one anecdote reports him hearing with admiration the elder historian recite from his work), never mentions Herodotus by name. He barely notices any other prose writer, but he certainly alludes to Herodotus' results and his method, falsely minimizing the length of the earlier conflict between the Persians and the Greeks (1.23) and directly and obliquely criticizing the research methods by which Herodotus (and others, such as Hellanicos) had pursued their historical investigations. But very few historians met Thucydides' demanding standards.

Character of the Author

Herodotus was, to judge solely from his text, well traveled, urbane, tolerant, curious about everything, and able to find amusement and dismay in the foibles of his fellow men and women. Like Voltaire, he recognized the compromises that survival and prosperity demand. I think many people today would enjoy his open-minded company. He often noted how, for individuals and states, intention outpaces execution and how the law of unexpected consequences can deceive powerful people and nations. Scoundrels sometimes do good despite themselves, and heroes are not rarely humiliated by the unpredictable element in human life. This is not a philosophy—merely a historically observed reality.

Herodotus values the personally detached but politically and intellectually engaged persona of investigator that he has created. His self-effacing text more frequently offers the reader the impersonal presentation and the neutral observer than the subjective evaluator, but both voices are present. In the second book, on Egypt, he is lavish in applying superlatives such as "cleverest," "largest," "most expensive," "most worthy of seeing"—in part because wonderful Egypt invited such language and thinking.

History, as perceptive readers now more often recognize, is many different things. It is the vanished events of the past, what participants in those events "remember" or claim, and the preserved contemporary—and often intentionally false or misleading—records of those events. (Consider Octavian's [the emperor Augustus'] self-composed and finally, throughout three continents of the Roman Empire, imposed inscriptional autobiography, *Achievements of the Divinized Augustus*.) Finally, to keep the description of these issues relatively simple, we lump together here another historiographic category: all later records and historical accounts that are subject to ethnic or nationalist bias or the necessary misperceptions arising from the particular circumstances of even an honest, hypothetically unself-interested writer.

Political Views

One can confidently say that Herodotus did not admire the political organizations of the Eastern "hydraulic civilizations"(centralized bureaucracies based on complete control of essential water resources)—autocracies, tyrannies, and monarchies. Not that he was so foolish as to think, as we apparently do, that a form of government that is successful in the context of one economy and ecology and transport network could be easily transplanted to another. Direct Athenian democracy suggested to him both weaknesses (5.97) and strengths. The tightly controlled Spartan totalitarian state (with two kings, a small senate, and a nondebating soldier-assembly) both appealed and appalled. The other Greeks found it fascinating, but none were invited to live there, and few, if any, would have accepted such an invitation.

Herodotus saw the good in various government systems that permitted free expression (*isegorie*) and equal justice under law (*isonomie*). He was no ideologue for democracy, oligarchy, timocracy, or plutocracy. His reticence to speak about ahistorical religious beliefs and practices is explicit (see 2.3 and 9.65). He applies his experience-based relativism, which is clearest when he describes religious practices (3.38), equally to politics

(7.152), aesthetics, various ethnic customs (marriage, burial), and different belief-systems.

He describes noble peasants and brutal royals. The man who saved Greece (Themistocles) can also be portrayed as self-serving and even treasonous. Herodotus' Spartans are brave, suitably laconic (a word derived from their famous ethnic distrust of discourse), often late for battle, invincible but also unappreciative of their occasionally eccentric fellow citizens and their economically productive underclass, the helots. Herodotus finds admirable actions in autocrats and nasty faults among gentlefolk. Without the sometimes pseudo-objectivity of Thucydides or the selfless image of the self-propagandizing Julius Caesar (both employing the third person for their own presence in their narratives), Herodotus attains a real, because self-aware, objectivity. Some have blamed him for this evenhandedness, alleging excessive Athenian bias or pro-barbarian leaning—for example, Plutarch, who resented Herodotus' negative portrait of Plutarch's fellow Boeotians who joined the "national" enemy Xerxes' invading forces. The truth is not always attractive or likable.

Religious Conceptions

Many critics and other readers have found Herodotus to be a deeply religious chap, indeed even superstitious about the causes and outcome of the conflicts that he records (for example, Mikalson, *Herodotus and Religion in the Persian Wars,* p. 187). His avowed interest in the cults, spiritual beliefs, and beliefs about spirits manifested by his varied Greek, half-Greek, non-Greek, and "marginal" ethnic subjects is undeniable. This curiosity about ceremonies, oracles, omens, prophets, dreams, and divine attributes, however, does not define his own beliefs any more than a Methodist missionary or Roman Catholic priest on African assignment delimits or describes his own forms of spirituality when he records the allegedly magical practices of a Bantu witch. Divine interference is sometimes claimed by his characters or by his sources, but this ploy can be but a means to achieve patently fraudulent purposes— for example, Peisistratos' charade (1.59) or Dareios' "divinely sanctioned" accession (3.84–87). Herodotus himself on occasion observes a metaphysical *tisis* ("compensation" or "rebalancing"). This Heraclitan and Toynbeean principle evens out high and low, power and weakness over time, sometimes in the apparent service of justice, always reestablishing some equilibrium of forces. (Many people since, both the religiously inclined and secular humanists, have imagined the same cosmic dynamic in the defeat and death of the Nazi juggernaut of Adolf Hitler.) Herodotus' inquisitiveness about the world justly extends to the observable, human phenomena of religious practice. He keeps various mystery cults' secrets secret and truncates other inquiries that verge into nonhistorical issues—see, for example, 2.3, 2.51, 2.171, 3.98, 6.124, 7.185, 8.112, and 9.84.

Herodotus never describes the Greek gods interfering in human actions (as they do not infrequently in Homer's narratives), and this silence or search for natural and human causes is a large historical advance. No divinity or person, no status, caste, or culture holds the only key to cosmic power, earthly piety, or human virtue. Divine intentions appear in some of his speculations, but never without separate human independent agency. His powerful speculations redirected historical thought.

Physical Form of the Histories

An ancient "book" had no spine, since it existed in rolls or volumes rather than our codex format of bound pages. Further, it displayed no title page or ISBN number, and it carried a very high price tag. Each "book" had to be laboriously copied, written out by hand. Herodotus' magisterial first sentence names the author, the hometown, the work, and his several comprehensive purposes (see below; compare Flory, "Who Read Herodotus' *Histories*?"). The current division into nine books, named pointlessly after the nine Muses, an organization canonized in Egyptian Alexandria 300 or more years later, is most probably not the original. That first papyrus mega-text may have appeared in three times as many "books." Some divisions make little sense by our contemporary criteria (book 8 was divided from book 9 in mid-sentence in the original Greek, but some endings arrive at suitable pause points. The reader must imagine a stack of rolled papyrus manuscripts before conventions of titling, dividing, copying, and disseminating were established.

We do not know who were the first readers of the physically unwieldy text we call the *Histories* or the *History*. We do not know that the author himself gave it any title—other than the first sentence. Stewart Flory estimates (pp. 13–14) that the text would require 300 feet of papyrus divided into thirty rolls or volumes and an unknown number of marked divisions (not the nine "books" already known to the second-century comic essayist Lucian, who describes them in his *Herodotus* 1–2). Aristophanes perhaps alludes to the *Histories* in his next comedies *The Acharnians* (verses 68–92 and 523–528) and *The Birds* (verses 1124–1138), although the meanings of his comic swipe for evaluating Herodotus' reputation or notoriety are unclear. A steady reading aloud of the full text would take more than fifty hours—it is not, then, an entertainment for a crowd. All books were generally read aloud in antiquity, even by those perusing them alone, and Herodotus' Ionic Greek does roll sweetly off the tongue. The cumbersome whole could never have been memorized like the shorter and rhythmic *Iliad* or *Odyssey*. Plutarch and Dio Chrysostom mention legendary recitations, in whole or part, by the author of this heavily researched work at Olympia, Athens, and elsewhere. Such performances do not find a good parallel in tag-team Homeric epic recitations to the illiterate at panhellenic festivals, or in group-trained and polis-paid performances of Attic drama, or in brief solo lyric performances by musical stars.

Herodotus' astonishing product presumes significant Hellenic literacy
and a book trade. More books were documentary, however, than literary,
and more of the latter were poetry than prose, as Flory notes. Herodotus'
work was a "sport" in his own lifetime, thirty times longer than an Athenian tragedy, never performed, as the tragedies were in his day, for an
audience of 14,000 Athenians. It was accessible therefore only to the educated Athenian elite. It was never anyone's popular entertainment but a
challenging mental activity for the few erudite readers available. Standing
on the threshold of a wider spread of readers and literature, Herodotus invented a new kind and length of book, as well as a new access to the past.
He relates that political and cultural information to his present (see Flory)
and fleshed it out to mean something still worth reading for subsequent
generations, including ours.

Plan of the Histories

In brief, Herodotus wrote a series of ethnographies with interwoven history (of Persia, Sparta, Athens from about 560 to 490 B.C.) in the first four
books, the first half of the *Histories*. In the last five books, the second half,
the narrative becomes a more unified, more focused, generally continuous
account of a war between a jerry-rigged Greek alliance and a Persian Empire governed from the top down. Some of the ethnographies are very
short (the Auseans, at 4.180, a page), and some fill a book (the Egyptians,
all of book II, seventy-five pages) or a large part of one (the Scythians,
4.1–144; the Lydians, 1.6–94: 1.6–92 providing a history and 1.93–94 the
ethnographic particulars; and the Libyans—that is, all North Africans—
4.145–205 with interruptions). When the Persian commanders subjugate
various peoples for their empire, Herodotus describes the victims' national histories, such as they could be recovered, and their customs.
Herodotus' method is deliberate and habitual, although not one of those
later to be canonized by the differently organizing historical minds of
Thucydides, Ephorus, the Hellenistic Polybius, or the Roman Tacitus, or
modern historians such as Edward Gibbon, Leopold von Ranke, Arnold
Toynbee, or Steven Ambrose (as Robin Collingwood argues in *The Idea
of History*). Herodotus coordinated reams of facts and explanations in his
work in a way that remains vivid and convincing. When it can be tested, it
stands up remarkably well, in the West and in the East. The result was
no accident, as John Denniston (*Greek Prose Style*) and John Myres
(*Herodotus, Father of History*) realized. The first-time reader will puzzle
over Herodotus' ways of connecting topics or resuming one after an
"interruption"—for example, the Chinese-box or archaic Greek "ring
composition" technique of ABCBA (see Immerwahr, *Form and Thought
in Herodotus*). If attentive, however, the reader will soon become comfort-
able with the author's coherent and consistent modes of exposition, such
as prospective and retrospective "glosses" or pointers (see the insights of
Rosaria Munson in *Telling Wonders*).

Speech and Other Direct Quotation

Ancient texts did not have our convention of quotation marks for "direct speech"—that is, words quoted verbatim. Modern readers and historians understand quotation marks to indicate material spoken or written in precisely the form presented. Along with quotations, Herodotus supplies other reports, abstracts of speeches, and summarized views, which was presented in ancient texts in "indirect speech"—for example, "Churchill said that the English would fight on the beaches, etc." Modern translations of ancient texts employ quotation marks for ancient direct speech, but readers need to understand that the ancient historians employed different conventions. Ancient authors write what appear to be the very words in the original tenses of someone's remarks, and so they offer a lively reconstruction (following the speech-rich epic convention found in the texts of Homer's poems) of what "must" or "should" have been said. They do not thereby claim that they know that Xerxes or Leonidas ever said *exactly* what is reported—the *ipsissima verba* or very words.

Sources

Herodotus names many sources, literary, documentary, oral, and material. His accounts of Persian tribute and the Persian royal post (3.89–97 and 8.98—words from the latter are recorded in the stone architrave of Manhattan's old main Post Office), and the battle numbers and lineup of the Greeks who fought the Persians (8.43 for Salamis, 9.28 for Plataia) seem, because of their unexpected detail, to be based on written records. These documents can be archival records from Dareios' and Xerxes' palace at Persepolis; inscriptions on stone records and dedications (twenty of these—for example, in 2.106 and 4.91); legends and types on gold, silver, and other coins; some archaeological remains, such as extant and ruined structures (8.53); and more recent commemorative monuments (see 7.228 and 9.81; the latter describes the Serpent Column, still extant and for millennia on display in Istanbul). Some inscriptions were written in Greek and others in languages presumably unknown to Herodotus, including Egyptian, "Assyrian," as he styles them, and old Persian, the latter for the account of Dareios' rise to power, if Herodotus knew anything of the Behistun inscription (a massive rock-cut inscription and set of bas-reliefs extant still in Iran; relevant at 3.68–87) and did not merely hear of it from an oral informant. His literary sources include prose writers and poets. Among the first we count the geographer and mythographer Hecataios and perhaps the explorer and geographer Skylax (compare 4.44; see Drews, *The Greek Accounts of Eastern History,* and Luraghi's collection of essays *The Historian's Craft in the Age of Herodotus*). Among the second are Sappho, Pindar, and Aeschylus the tragedian, who perhaps fought the invader at Marathon and Salamis and then wrote the *Persians* (see Lateiner, *The Historical Method of Herodotus,* pp. 91–108).

Most of Herodotus' sources were certainly oral: individuals and groups with whom he spoke, such as descendants of the Spartans who died at Thermopylai (7.224), or acquaintances of participants in battle at Marathon or Salamis (Epizelos at 6.117 and Dicaios at 8.65). Herodotus pauses to note (2.99) when his sources for Egyptian information change from his own observation (*autopsy* is the Greek term) to hearsay. In between come eyewitness reports, an invaluable but slippery source for past events.

The impersonal voice presents hundreds of Hellenic and barbarian partisan and partial accounts, some preserved in writing (see Drews) but more collected from oral informants. More than two hundred sources are identified with some specifics (individuals sometimes by name, but more often "the Egyptians say," "the Samians claim," "it is said by the Persians," etc.). Sources are not rarely entirely anonymous (more than one hundred such citations). Specific informants are generally mentioned because they disagree. Some sources are cited for expert knowledge, others because of their presence at events where particular actions are disputed, such as what part the Corinthians played at the battle of Salamis (8.94). Herodotus both names some sources (unlike the suppressive Thucydides) and leaves their conflicting versions side by side within his text for the reader to decide among (for example, 3.122, 4.195, 6.75, 8.87, again unlike Thucydides' standard "magisterial" practice). The audience is able to form an independent opinion; it does not need to depend on the judgment of fallible observers or self-appointed authorities (for an extensive inventory, see Lateiner, pp. 84–90).

Citation itself may have been a Herodotean innovation. Among his unnamed sources—and perhaps we should think of these as his intellectual context—are nonhistorical writers and thinkers who influenced his *Histories*. These include the so-called pre-Socratic philosophers, the itinerant Sophists such as Protagoras, the Hippocratic medical writers, and other investigators working in scientific fields such as geology and climatology (as Rosalind Thomas has demonstrated in *Herodotus in Context*).

Herodotus weighs the conflicting accounts, judges them, and when the evidence permits, accepts one or none of them. Whether or not he explicitly selects one, or elements of several, among the *logoi* or accounts received—and he is more transparent about his procedure here than Thucydides and the rest of his alleged successors—he creates his own account from the congeries and from self-revealing silences. That narrator's account therefore encompasses the polyphony of his sources. Although managing the living historical tradition—including, excluding explicitly, ordering, sequencing, admitting a failure to find a dependable account, etc.—Herodotus does not suppress the data that he has excavated, the *histor*'s (investigator's) spadework. By telling the reader when he is supervising the sometimes rambunctious *logoi* (by means of metanarrative signposting—see, for example, 1.95, 2.43, 4.10–11, 4.30, 5.62, and 9.84; compare Munson, pp. 20–24 and 32–37, and Dewald, " 'I didn't give my own genealogy': Herodotus and the Authorial Personality," pp. 274–276), Herodotus preserves (or encourages us to believe that he preserves) the autonomy of future readers and investigators.

Nevertheless, Herodotus' lively mind seeps through his story—that
is, a narrator's persona emerges in the text, however true or untrue it
may be to the personality of the dead author. That persona can be com-
bative, dispensing praise and blame to other researchers as well as to the
veterans and politicos still fighting the last generation's battles. He admires clear thinkers and clever tricksters like the Halicarnassian queen
Artemisia; he (intermittently) defends the Athenian general and later
turncoat Themistocles, and he respects the exiled Spartan king Demaratos
(compare Boedeker, "The Two Faces of Demaratus"), an eloquent
Laconian.

Chronology

Herodotus, like other Greeks, considered certain mythical and legendary
events to be part of some recoverable history, the distant but real past—
for example, the Trojan War (2.145) and perhaps Minos and his navy
(3.122). However, he saw the need to treat those spectacular wars and
god-infected stories of heroic expeditions with a pinch of salt—or a chari-
otful. He distinguishes (unlike his predecessors and his contemporaries)
the mythical and even earlier historical pasts from the investigable past.
He divides the mythical heroes from the more dependably verifiable past
stretching back approximately one hundred years. For this era some reliable evidence and reports exist (although not necessarily reliable methods
for interpreting them). Since Herodotus worked without having chroni-
cles at hand for Greek or Near Eastern histories, some of his dates and
reigns are, not surprisingly, now known to be wrong. This applies not only
to early Egyptian dynasties but even to more recent events such as the
short reign incorrectly attributed to Cleomenes (5.48). His indications of
chronology are reasonably more precise the closer he comes to the events
of the recent past.

Geography

Hecataios (mentioned prominently at 2.143 and 6.137) wrote a *Trip around
the Earth,* by which he meant a circumnavigation of the Mediterranean.
Herodotus knew some areas better than others—for example, he knew the
eastern Mediterranean better than the western—but he would be considered a well-traveled researcher and historian even today (see Romm, *The
Edges of the Earth in Ancient Thought*). The Persian Empire and the
Athenian were fairly open to civilian travel for merchants, tourists, and
others who caused no trouble and brought drachmas along. If we believe
Herodotus, he went as far as Babylon in the east, far up the Nile in the
south, to the Crimea in the north, and to at least southern Italy in the west.

So-called "Digressions"

Herodotus speaks of additions and insertions in his work—for example, at 4.30, 7.5, 7.171, where they are usually mistranslated as "digressions." Therefore, we cannot claim that everything therein is equally integral to his *Histories,* but those critics are mistaken who think an account of the two military invasions of mainland Greece by Dareios and Xerxes were his only or principal theme. In fact, most who object to his catholic and inclusive comprehensiveness have failed to appreciate how for him history includes geography, ethnography, anthropology (see Hartog, *The Mirror of Herodotus;* Evans, *Herodotus: Explorer of the Past;* and Gould, *Herodotus*), economics, sociology, and cultural criticism. Since no one had conceived of, or delimited, the field of history before Herodotus, much less defined it (insofar as one can assert that it even now stands defined), Herodotus' themes and subjects may be said to include whatever Herodotus has provided us. He also alludes briefly to persons, places, and events that he has deliberately omitted, and he consciously suppresses various names and deeds (for example, at 1.14.4, 2.70.1, 4.43.8, 5.72.4, and 9.43.2). Only through presumption or inattentiveness would we assert that he did not control his materials or that he "could not resist a good story." The text proves repeatedly that he did.

Object of the Histories

Beyond the information in that magisterial and periodic first sentence, among the questions that Herodotus set out to answer are: (1) How have peoples (including the women) of Asia, Africa, and Europe organized themselves, and what have they accomplished and built? (2) How did the marginal Persians from the northeast of the known or "inhabited" world (*oikoumene*) come to rule the barbarian (that is, non-Greek) and much of the Greek world in sixty years? (3) How did the marginal and divided pesky Greeks occupying the northwest corner of the ancient "civilized" world defeat them, after richer, stronger, more populous autocratic national states fell like matchsticks or with a hollow thud? (4) What can we ever know of the always instantly vanishing past?

Herodotus supplements and curtails his reported *logoi* (accounts), to help the reader get situated and to fit them into his larger picture. He has discovered wildly heterogeneous information, collected and collated it, and now he guides the reader through it—sometimes correcting, sometimes asserting a contrarian view or wonderful fact (the "works great and marvelous" emphasized in his first sentence along with the perduring achievements)—without being able to explain all the occurrences adequately, or to his own satisfaction. Herodotus recognizes limits to what a historical investigator can prove; rarely is certainty attainable about past particulars, or even about contemporary natural history of fauna, flora, or exotic civilizations. Surviving traces of the past, such as tombs, dedications, and memorials, can preserve testimony "to my time" (*Histories* has more than one hundred examples of this phrase), but they can also mislead, intentionally or innocently.

Writing for his future readers, not only for those "insiders" who already know the stories, Herodotus "unobtrusively explains the background" (see Dewald's article " 'I didn't give my own genealogy,' " p. 286). He points out connections that are helpful and make him readable. He is the only Ionian historical author deemed worthy of preservation for later centuries of Greeks, and is thus useful to us still.

Methods of the Histories

Few readers looking for historical "facts" have appreciated the methodological sophistication of Herodotus' profoundly historical work. Based on an amazing experience and grasp of the heterogeneous Mediterranean world and its hinterland, and on hundreds, perhaps thousands, of interviews with survivors and descendants, Herodotus' *Histories* gives shape and meaning to a mini-world war that lasted, off and on, a good twenty-five years and sucked in every city and nation. The educated layman, less concerned with the accuracy of every specific detail, has never failed to find delight and instruction in Herodotus' variegated and serious contribution to countless questions about antiquity. The accuracy of even the accounts that have been impugned turns out to be greater with nearly every new discovery—lately, for example, excavations of the Athos Canal (7.22); see the *New York Times,* November 13, 2001, p. F5).

Merits

Let us here briefly summarize the merits and defects of the first historian, perhaps the last who followed his demanding but peculiar criteria.

Originality. No one had ever written a rational account of the past based on evidence before Herodotus did so. His architectural conception of building a narrative that combines many stories concerning many nations— a structure that culminates in the dynamic intersection of major historical internal pressures and external forces—is breathtaking. No one has yet written a better study of his one hundred years (approximately 575–475 B.C.) and more. No one probably ever will or could.

Veracity. Herodotus is astute at looking over the monuments and the land, at asking probing questions, and at recording what he heard from survivors and descendants. He then intelligently creates a narrative from conflicting evidence and accounts. While his considered opinions sometimes have been improved upon, the "liar school of Herodotus" has not convinced many others. Those detractors attempt to convict him of ingeniously making up his evidence as well as his history out of whole cloth while sitting in comfort, without ever having visited the sites or the informants that he claims to have examined. (Fehling argues that all his sources were invented and serve for bluff and ornament; Pritchett, in *The Liar School of Herodotus,* ably refutes him.)

Impartiality. Herodotus clearly thought the Hellenic victory was a good thing for Hellenic civilization. Yet he just as obviously admires societies in which intelligence and energy are rewarded, and in which justice and honest labor are respected. Thus he reports virtues and defects in both the Hellenes and the Persians, as well as in others. He is relatively free of national vanity, although he clearly admired the unexpected Hellenic alliance, the preservation of local independence, and the repulse of the Iranian military machine.

English historian Edward Creasy, author of *The Fifteen Decisive Battles of the World* (1851), allegedly opined that the battle of Marathon was more important for the history of Britain than the battle of Hastings. Except for Herodotus, no account of that day at Marathon would exist. Creasy was claiming that Western Civilization could not be imagined if the Athenians and Plataeans had not taken their unexpected and valiant stand in September of 490 B.C. If Creasy, with centuries of hindsight, thought that this battle was pivotal, Herodotus must be allowed to argue its importance for further Hellenic resistance (6.109, 6.112). The delicious fact that Herodotus has been charged by various authors with philo-Laconism and philo-Athenianism and philo-barbarism suggests his generosity to all these ethnic and political divisions. His admiration for yet other groups is evident on every page. Herodotus credits men and women of all nations for clever contrivances, institutions, inventions, and aphorisms. Although he speaks of barbarians, he does not usually weight that term negatively. Like the once Christian and still Hebrew and Mormon term "gentiles," "barbarian" indicates for his Hellenic group all those in the category of "other."

Defects

Herodotus has never lacked honest critics and hostile detractors, the latter sometimes motivated by envious malice. One can criticize his *Histories* for what he did not learn only after recognizing what he could not, in his situation, learn. Many of the following alleged "failings" seem venial once understood in the context of his and his contemporaries' limited resources for excavating the human past.

Diplomatic and Military Inexperience. Herodotus was never a politician or a general, so far as we know. He probably never experienced combat

even as an infantryman or oarsman. His accounts of negotiations and
battles often reflect the interpretations of the "man in the street" or
rank-and-file soldier rather than the strategic thinking of infantry and
naval commanders, although that planning would not have been very so-
phisticated. His simplified accounts of the battles of Lade, Marathon,
and Salamis suggest this limited perspective. His Victorian translator
George Rawlinson, brother of the early Assyriologist, praised his ability
to sift and weigh evidence when it was adequate (see Rawlinson's
lengthy introduction to the 1875 edition of his translation, pp. 69–112 of
the third edition, published in London by John Murray). In "On the Possibility of Reconstructing Marathon and Other Ancient Battles," Norman Whatley employs the battle of Marathon—chiefly Herodotus'
account, of course—to illustrate the pitfalls we face today when trying to
understand the means and ends of ancient hoplite warfare from the
available evidence.

Ignorance. Herodotus did not know the Persian, Egyptian, Phoenician, or
Accadian languages, or any African or Asiatic language. Nor did he claim
to know them. This linguistic ignorance rendered him liable to interpreters' errors, exaggerations, and desires to please. It is not to be confused with credulity, "an undue love of the marvelous in religion, nature,
or the habits of men," as Rawlinson would have it. Beyond language bar-
riers, Herodotus had no experts or encyclopedias to consult on the ad-
ministration of the Persian Empire, the extraction of oils and minerals, or
the cultivation of cotton. His access to information that we take for
granted was very limited, in Greece and more so beyond. His ability to
get many things right in so many fields of human activity (politics, economics, anthropology, religion, ecology, geography, etc.) is more astonishing than his demonstrable errors or failures to prosecute further his
varied researches.

Gullibility. Lacking access to whichever archives existed, to written
sources, and to proven methods for cross-checking informants, especially
those not speaking any or much Greek, Herodotus accepts accounts or explanations that leave us puzzled even when we cannot disprove specific
statements, such as the nature of the bleached skulls of soldiers slain at the
Pelusic mouth of the Nile and at Papremis (3.12). Like all men of his age,
he had (by our standards) no good maps, no works of reference, no tabu-
lar summaries of historical events, no agreed-upon calendar or chronolo-
gies, no libraries, and, of course, no previous historical narratives on which
he might enlarge or from which he might diverge.

Failure to Eliminate the Divine from History. Herodotus seeks human
explanation for all human events, but, even if reluctantly, he admits and
includes—more often than the rigorously and uniquely non-supernaturalist
Thucydides—other, supernatural and metaphysical explanations, such as the
rare appearances of Fate or Nemesis. Parallel human and trans-historical

explanations are left to coexist—uneasily, at least for us. Here the modern reader must remember (again) that Herodotus does not automatically endorse the statements that he reports, and that his characters must never be assumed to serve as his mouthpieces. Oracles, dreams, and reported visions need not be supernatural phenomena at all, and Thucydides himself reports the first of these, if usually to discredit them. Coincidences in time likewise may and do occur. Few historical (as opposed to anecdotal or legendary) narratives in Herodotus depend on supernatural agencies. Many stories or anecdotes are just that, excrescences on the historical narrative that lend historical depth or understanding to the motives of the men and nations involved. Fewer events are connected in any way to the divine; as Herodotus approaches recent events, some claimed miracles are rationalized; and in general Herodotus seeks out human explanations even where a divine cause is also appended. These facets of his *Histories,* unsatisfactory to us, must be kept in mind when reading his seductive text.

Historical Achievement

"The conversion of legend-writing into the science of history was not native to the Greek mind, it was a fifth-century invention, and Herodotus was the man who invented it" (Collingwood, p. 19). Every historian selects, omits, and organizes his or her data. It cannot be avoided. Every historian assesses the accuracy of what s/he hears and tries to present the accepted residue and explanations for it in a coherent, unified narrative. Every historian interprets that narrative by intrusive evaluations and hypothetical alternatives to what happened. Better historians "torture their evidence" (Thucydides' vivid image) to produce a substantial package in a convincing and lucid manner. This elegant publication demonstrates that the necessity, pleasure, and value of reading the considered narrative and explanations of a fifth-century Greek mind has not perished from a greedy and war-prone planet.

Literary Achievement

"Herodotus is an unaccountable phenomenon in the history of literature. . . . [His predecessors] the logographers . . . had no technique at all, but he had a technique at once effortless and adequate to any demands" (Denniston, p. 5). The dramatic power of Herodotus' style can be understood only from the experience that you are about to enjoy, in George Macaulay's remarkable translation. The power and style of the original derive from at least three literary paradigms: his most important literary predecessor, the epics of Homer; the development of literary intensity in contemporary Attic tragedy (Herodotus was reportedly a friend of Sophocles, with whom he shares discussion of several pressing issues); and the charm of traditional Indo-European and Near Eastern folktales.

In brief, "there was no Herodotus before Herodotus" (Momigliano, p. 129), and "Herodotus had no successors" (Collingwood, p. 29). He was one of a kind, *sui generis,* "a powerful eccentric" (according to translator David Grene; see "Appendix"), and no writer ever can compare himself to Herodotus in all his excellence. Thucydides consciously set forth to move historical prose and thinking in other directions, arguably further from and narrower than the available record, and some sheep tried to follow him. This dynamic was sharply focused on external and internal armed conflict and political decision making. It largely left out social context and economic patterns, and spiritual beliefs and sexual customs. Meanwhile the goats failed to imitate Herodotus' Shakespearian insightfulness and Tolstoyan inclusiveness.

Significance

An Oxford student once asked historian and geographer of the ancient world John Myres, "Sir, if Herodotus was such a fool as they say, why do we read him for Greats?" Many answers percolate, but here I offer only three:

Content. If we throw out the information and traditions of Herodotus' *Histories,* we know almost nothing of Greek history before the generation of Thucydides. That would require of us a great loss. Material objects—smaller artifacts, structures, and "ecofacts" such as bones and coprolites—alone cannot provide a historical account. The ever-expanding archaeological evidence for ancient Hellas is confused and nearly impenetrable (beyond pottery evolution and sequencing for column moldings) without some organizing, interpretive historical narrative. Robin Osborne's brave history of the prehistory and archaic Greek eras, *Greece in the Making, 1200–479 B.C.,* unintentionally demonstrates this truth. Osborne cannot dispense with the traditions and data that he gleans from Herodotus, despite his valid and minimizing statement (p. 5) that "no history of the archaic period was ever written." So, we are reminded not to expect more from Herodotus' work than what is promised. Herodotus accomplished what he set out to do: to save the great deeds, especially the recent ones, of Greeks and barbarians from the oblivion they would have suffered except for the intervention of his historical genius. Herodotus is an education.

Style. Those who affect to scorn Herodotus' intellect confess the power, beauty, and charm of the inventor and first master of Greek prose. The invention of Greek, that is, European, prose was a signal achievement and Herodotus' was the mind responsible. Our translator, George Macaulay, a longtime student and teacher of Greek at the Rugby School, captures with exquisite care and skill the sweep of Herodotus' sentences, their variety, their subtle and ironic evaluations of veracity and duplicity. Drama, pathos, descriptive accuracy, humor, and unexpected climax—all of these are common in the following pages. Tragedy and comedy mix and often are juxtaposed. The jolly comedy of Arion's double salvation barely precedes Solon's attempted compact lesson in humility for the haughty king Croesus and then the narrative of Croesus' tragic loss of his son, killed by the man he had purified, protected and befriended (1.23–45). The pivotal heroic battle and Athenian victory of Marathon soon yield attention to the comically greedy Athenian Alcmaion loaded down with Croesus' gold dust in his boots and ears, and to his unperturbed, imprudent descendant, the drunken Athenian Hippocleides, dancing away money and power while "hanging out" of his clothing, upside down on a tyrant's banquet table (6.125–136).

I never read the closing chapters of the battle of Thermopylai (7.223–225) without tears of admiration for the Spartans' humbling courage and the historian's quietly effective disposition of the facts, attitudes, and aftermath. The only other passages in Greek literature that regularly produce this affect on me are two. First, the equally sublime Homeric description of beggar Odysseus testing his bow and killing the offensive suitors (*Odyssey* 21.393–430) and, second, Plato's astonishing account of Socrates speaking his last quiet words to the Attic jurymen who unwisely condemned him and to those who admirably acquitted him (Plato *Apology* 38c–42a). Herodotus is a pleasure.

Intellectual Achievement. Herodotus invented historical reasoning and historical writing. He did not perfect them—nor have we—but he took more steps and made longer strides than perhaps any one successor. Thucydides' further achievement (ignoring his regressive tendencies) is unimaginable without the pioneer Herodotus, and that is credit enough. Collingwood argued that Herodotus was closer to an accurate conception of history than his sainted successor. Whether this be true or not, his progress in organizing narratives of the past and investing human ephemera with enduring significance render him one of the classics of intellectual experiment and historiographic progress. Herodotus changed the pastness of the past by creating a meaningful way to preserve it.

Idiosyncratic Herodotus chose to remain outside his edited *logoi*—what others said and what he then composed. Sometimes his own stories "forced" him in directions he had not contemplated. This historian rarely claims to be authoritative and univocal—a cautious stance that Thucydides, Polybius, Tacitus, and their imitators misunderstood and rejected. This attachment to modest claims, opinions, and tentative interpretation devalued Herodotus' *Histories* for subsequent scientistic, law-seeking historians. Unpersuaded that history is generally law-abiding, except in the longest term, Herodotus presents its instructive unpredictability. He preserves insightful accounts of men and communities who flexibly and alertly processed information and of others who dangerously neglected useful warning signs (natural or not), other helpful, historical *logoi*, and breaking events that discomfited their preconceptions. Autocrats such as Polycrates and Xerxes seem most susceptible to believing what they would like to be

so. Historical knowledge, such as it is, does not meet Hellenic philosophic
demands (the pre-Socratics', Socrates', Plato's, or Aristotle's). Herodotus'
journey left the highway of the eternal truth-seekers as he hacked his way
through jungles and deserts of historical instruction, humanist edification,
and entertaining enlightenment. Enjoy!

Donald Lateiner teaches humanities, history, and classics courses at Ohio
Wesleyan University in Delaware, Ohio, where he occupies the John
Wright Chair of Humanities and Greek. He holds degrees from the University of Chicago, Cornell University, and Stanford University. He was
the Thomas Day Seymour fellow for a year at the American School of
Classical Studies at Athens. He has taught the ancient Greek and Roman
world at the University of Pennsylvania, for Syracuse University in Florence, Italy, for Carleton College, and principally at Ohio Wesleyan. He has
guided student and alumni expeditions to Etruria and Rome, and to
Greece, Crete, and coastal Turkey. Lateiner teaches ancient languages, archaeology, ancient history, ancient literatures in translation, and world
folklore. He has published articles on Greek history, historiography, Attic
oratory, Latin lyric poetry, and Greek and Latin epic poetry and prose fiction. His published scholarly books include *The Historical Method of
Herodotus* (1989) and *Sardonic Smile: Nonverbal Behavior in Homeric Epic*
(1995). The Ohio Humanities Council awarded him the 2003 Bjornson
prize for his work in promoting appreciation of the cultural achievements
of the ancient past.

A BRIEF NOTE ON THE TEXT

I have generally retained Macaulay's accuracy in the ordering of the Greek text's phrases. I have altered many passive constructions to the active voice for tighter clauses, eliminated the archaic "thou" and "thee," etc. from the speeches, and removed other archaisms and obsolete words and repetitions that seem obtrusive in modern English. I have incorporated some of the author's endnotes into my footnotes and translated measurements into American terms. Nearly every statement that Herodotus presents has been subjected to doubt or denial, defense and further discussion. My footnotes represent the tip of this iceberg.

—Donald Lateiner, 2003

TRANSLATOR'S PREFACE

If a new translation of Herodotus does not justify itself,[*] it will hardly be justified in a preface; therefore the question whether it was needed may be left here without discussion. The aim of the translator has been above all things faithfulness—faithfulness to the manner of expression and to the structure of sentences, as well as to the meaning of the Author. At the same time it is conceived that the freedom and variety of Herodotus is not always best reproduced by such severe consistency of rendering as is perhaps desirable in the case of the Epic writers before and the philosophical writers after his time: nor again must his simplicity of thought and occasional quaintness be reproduced in the form of archaisms of language; and that not only because the affectation of an archaic style would necessarily be offensive to the reader, but also because in language Herodotus is not archaic. His style is the "best canon of the Ionic speech," marked, however, not so much by primitive purity as by eclectic variety. At the same time it is characterised largely by the poetic diction of the Epic and Tragic writers; and while the translator is free to employ all the resources of modern English, he must carefully retain this poetical colouring and by all means avoid the courtier phrase by which the style of Herodotus has too often been made "more noble."

As regards the text from which this translation has been made, it is based upon that of Stein's critical edition. On the other hand the conjectural emendations proposed by Stein have very seldom been adopted, and his text has been departed from in a large number of other instances also. I thought it right to examine the Medicean MS. myself in all those passages where questions about text arise which concern a translator, that is in nearly five hundred places altogether. I re-collated a large part of the third book in the MS. which is commonly referred to as F (*i.e.* Florentinus), called by Stein C, and I examined this MS. also in a certain number of other places.

For the orthography of proper names reference may be made to the note prefixed to the index. No consistent system has been adopted, and the result will therefore be open to criticism. The aim has been to avoid on the one hand the pedantry of seriously altering the form of those names which are fairly established in the English language, and on the other hand the absurdity of looking to Latin rather than to Greek for the orthography of the names which are not so established.

The index of proper names will, it is hoped, be found more complete

---

[*]The editor has abridged Macaulay's remarks and notes and provided many new ones in the text.

and accurate than those hitherto published. The best with which I was
acquainted I found to have so many errors and omissions that I was
compelled to do the work again from the beginning. In a collection of
more than ten thousand references there must be mistakes, but I trust they
will be found to be few.

My acknowledgments of obligation are due first to Dr. Stein, both for his
critical work and also for his most excellent commentary, which I have had
always by me. As to translations, I have had Rawlinson's before me while re-
vising my own work, and I have referred also occasionally to the translations of Littlebury (perhaps the best English version as regards style, but full
of gross errors), Taylor, and Larcher. In the second book I have also used the
version of B. R.[*]

---

[*]See "Appendix: A Repertory of English Translations of Herodotus" following
the endnotes.

THE HISTORIES

BOOK I

PROLOGUES, CROESUS OF LYDIA AND CYRUS OF PERSIA

THIS IS THE SHOWING forth of the Inquiry of Herodotus[*] of Halicarnassos so that neither the deeds of men may be forgotten by lapse of time, nor the works great and marvellous, which have been produced some by Hellenes and some by Barbarians, may lose their renown; and especially that the causes may be remembered for which these waged war with one another.

1. Those of the Persians who have knowledge of their stories declare that the Phenicians first began the quarrel. These, they say, came from that which is called the Erythraian Sea to this of ours;[†] and having settled in the land where they continue even now to dwell, set themselves at once to make long voyages by sea. And conveying merchandise of Egypt and of Assyria they arrived at other places and also at Argos; now Argos was at that time in all points the first of the States within that land which is now called Hellas.[‡] Phenicians arrived then at this land of Argos, and began to dispose of their ship's cargo. On the fifth or sixth day after they had arrived, when their goods had been almost all sold, there came down to the sea a great company of women, and among them the daughter of the king; and her name, as the Hellenes also agree, was Io the daughter of Inachos. These standing near to the stern of the ship were buying the wares that pleased them most, when suddenly the Phenicians, passing the word from one to another, made a rush upon them; and the greater part of the women escaped by flight, but Io and certain others were carried off. So they put them on board their ship, and immediately departed, sailing away to Egypt. **2.** In this manner the Persians report that Io came to Egypt, not agreeing therein with the Hellenes, and this they say was the first beginning of wrongs. Then after this, they say, certain Hellenes (but the name of the people they are not able to report) put in to the city of Tyre in Phenicia and carried off the king's daughter Europa—these would doubtless be Cretans—and so they were quits for the former injury. After this however the Hellenes, they say, were the authors of the second wrong; for they sailed in to Aia of Colchis and to the river Phasis with a ship of war, and from thence, after they had done the other business for which they came, they carried off the king's daughter Medea. The king of

---

[*]Herodotus was born c.484 B.C. and died c.414 B.C.
[†]The Erythraian Sea (which translates as "Red Sea") includes the Indian Ocean and the Persian Gulf; "this [sea] of ours" refers to the Mediterranean.
[‡]"Hellas" describes a shared blood and ideology rather than a bounded area; compare 8.144.

3

Colchis sent a herald to the land of Hellas and demanded satisfaction for
the abduction and to have his daughter back; but they answered that, as the
Barbarians had given them no satisfaction for the rape of Io the Argive, so
neither would they give satisfaction to the Barbarians for this.

3. In the next generation after this, they say, Alexander the son of
Priam, having heard of these things, desired to abduct a wife for himself
from Hellas, being fully assured that he would not be compelled to give
any satisfaction for this wrong, inasmuch as the Hellenes gave none for
theirs. So he carried off Helen, and the Hellenes resolved to send messengers first and to demand her back with satisfaction for the rape; and when
they put forth this demand, the others alleged to them the rape of Medea,
saying that the Hellenes were now desiring satisfaction to be given to
them by others, though they had given none themselves nor had surrendered the person when demand was made.

4. Up to this point, they say, nothing more had happened than the abduction of women on both sides; but after this the Hellenes were very
greatly to blame; for they set the first example of war, making an expedition into Asia before the Barbarians made any into Europe. Now they say
that in their judgment, though it is wrong to abduct women by force, it is
folly to take vengeance for their rape, and the wise course is to pay no regard when they have been abducted, since it is evident that they would
never be abducted if they were not themselves willing to go. And the Persians say that they, namely the people of Asia, when their women were
carried away by force, had considered it insignificant, but the Hellenes on
account of a woman of Lacedemon gathered together a great armament,
and then came to Asia and destroyed the dominion of Priam;* and that
from this time forward they had always considered the Hellenic race to be
their enemy. The Persians claim Asia and the Barbarian races which dwell
there as belonging to them; but Europe and the Hellenic race they consider to be parted off from them.

5. The Persians for their part say that things happened thus; and they
conclude that the beginning of their quarrel with the Hellenes was on account of the taking of Ilion. As regards Io the Phenicians do not agree with
the Persians in telling the tale thus; for they deny that they carried her off
to Egypt by violent means, and they say on the other hand that when they
were in Argos she enjoyed sex with the master of their ship, and perceiving that she was with child, she was ashamed to confess it to her parents,
and therefore sailed away with the Phenicians of her own will, for fear of
being found out. These are the tales told by the Persians and the Phenicians severally: and concerning these things I am not going to say that they
happened thus or some other way, but when I have pointed to the man
who first within my own knowledge began to commit wrong against the
Hellenes, I shall advance the story, giving an account of the cities of men,
small as well as great. Those which in old times were great have for the

*Herodotus parodies vacuous accounts of the causes for war; compare 2.118–120.

most part become small, while those that were in my own time great used to be small. Since I know that human prosperity never continues steadfast in the same place, I shall mention both equally.

6. Crœsus was Lydian by race, the son of Alyattes and ruler of the nations which dwell on this side of the river Halys; which river, flowing from the South between the Cappadocian Syrians and the Paphlagonians, runs out towards the North into that Sea called the Euxine. This Crœsus, first of all the Barbarians of whom we know, subdued certain of the Hellenes and forced them to pay tribute, while others he gained over and made them his friends. Those whom he subdued were the Ionians, the Aiolians, and the Dorians who dwell in Asia; and those whom he made his friends were the Lacedemonians. But before the reign of Crœsus all the Hellenes were free; for the expedition of the Kimmerians, which came upon Ionia before the time of Crœsus, was not a conquest of the cities but a plundering incursion only.

7. Now the supremacy which had belonged to the Heracleidai came to the family of Crœsus, called Mermnadai, in the following manner:—Candaules, whom the Hellenes call Myrsilos, was ruler of Sardis and a descendant of Alcaios, son of Heracles. Agron, the son of Ninos, the son of Belos, the son of Alcaios, was the first of the Heracleidai who became king of Sardis, and Candaules the son of Myrsos was the last; but those who were kings over this land before Agron, were descendants of Lydos the son of Atys, whence this whole nation was called Lydian, having been before called Meonian. From these the Heracleidai, descended from Heracles and the slave-girl of Iardanos, obtained the government, being charged with it by reason of an oracle; and they reigned for two-and-twenty generations of men, five hundred and five years, handing on the power from father to son, till the time of Candaules the son of Myrsos.

8. This Candaules then of whom I speak fell passionately in love with his own wife; and so, he deemed that his wife was fairer by far than all other women. To Gyges the son of Daskylos (for he of all his spearmen most pleased him), he used to entrust the more weighty of his affairs and also he praised to excess the beauty of his wife. After some time, since it was destined that evil should happen to Candaules, he said to Gyges: "Gyges, I think that you do not believe me when I tell you of the beauty of my wife, for it happens that men trust their ears less than their eyes. Figure out how to look upon her naked." But he cried out aloud and said: "Master, what word of unwisdom is this which you utter, bidding me look upon my mistress naked? When a woman puts off her tunic she puts off her modesty also. Moreover of old time those fair sayings have been found out by men, from which we ought to learn wisdom; and of these one is this,—that each man should look on his own.* I believe already indeed that she is of all women the fairest and I beg you not to ask of me that which it is not lawful

---

*A principle throughout the *Histories*.

for me to do." **9.** With such words as these he resisted, fearing lest some evil might come to him from this; but the king answered him thus: "Be of good courage, Gyges, and have no fear, either of me, that I am saying these words to test you, or of my wife, lest any harm may happen to you from her. For I will contrive it so from the first that she shall not even perceive that she has been seen by you. I will place you in the room where we sleep, behind the open door; and after I have gone in, my wife also will come to lie down. Now there is a seat near the entrance of the room, and upon this she will lay her garments as she takes them off one by one; and so you will be able to gaze upon her at full leisure. And when she goes from the chair to the bed and you shall be behind her back, then take care that she does not see you as you go through the door."

10. He then, since he could not avoid it, agreed. Candaules, when he considered that it was time to go to bed, led Gyges to the chamber; and at once the woman also appeared. Gyges looked upon her after she came in and as she laid down her garments; and when she had her back towards him, as she went to the bed, then he slipped away from his hiding-place and was leaving. And as he went out, the woman caught sight of him, and perceiving what her husband had done she did not cry out, though struck with shame, but she pretended she had not perceived the matter, meaning to avenge herself upon Candaules, since among the Lydians and also among most other Barbarians it is a shame even for a man to be seen naked.

11. At the time then she kept silence and made no outward sign; but as soon as day had dawned, she made ready those of the servants whom she perceived to be the most attached to herself, and after that she summoned Gyges. He then, not supposing that she knew anything, came upon her summons; for he had been accustomed before to attend whenever the queen summoned him. And when Gyges arrived, the woman said: "There are now two ways open to you, Gyges, and I give you the choice which of the two you prefer to take. Either you must slay Candaules and possess both me and the kingdom of Lydia, or you must yourself here on the spot be slain, so that you may not in future, by obeying Candaules in all things, see that which you should not. Either he must die who formed this design, or you who have looked upon me naked and done something taboo."

For a time then Gyges was amazed at these words, and afterwards he began to entreat her that she would not bind him by necessity to make such a choice. However, as he could not prevail with her, but saw that necessity was in truth set before him either to slay his master or to be himself slain by others, he chose to survive. He inquired further: "Since you compel me to take my master's life against my own will, let me hear from you also how we shall lay hands upon him." And she answered: "From that same place shall the attempt be, where he displayed me naked;* and we will lay hands upon him as he sleeps."

---

*Tit-for-tat revenge is noted frequently.

12. So after they had prepared the plot, when night came on, (for Gyges was not let go nor was there any way of escape for him, but he must either be slain himself or slay Candaules), he followed the woman to the bed-chamber; and she gave him a dagger and concealed him behind that very same door. Then afterwards, while Candaules was sleeping, Gyges came stealthily up to him and slew him, and he obtained both his wife and his kingdom. [Archilochos the Parian, who lived about that time, mentioned him in a trimeter iambic verse.]* **13.** He obtained the kingdom however† and was strengthened in it by means of the Oracle at Delphi; for when the Lydians were angry because of the fate of Candaules, and had risen in arms, a treaty was made between the followers of Gyges and the other Lydians to this effect, that if the Oracle should give answer that he was to be king of the Lydians, he should be king, and if not, he should give back the power to the sons of Heracles. So the Oracle gave answer, and Gyges accordingly became king. Yet the Pythian prophetess said this also, that vengeance for the Heracleidai should come upon the descendants of Gyges in the fifth generation. Of this oracle the Lydians and their kings made no account until it was in fact fulfilled.

14. Thus the Mermnadai obtained the government having driven out the Heracleidai. Gyges when he became ruler sent votive offerings to Delphi not a few, for of all the silver offerings at Delphi his are more in number than those of any other man; and besides the silver he offered a vast quantity of gold, and especially one offering which is more worthy of mention than the rest, namely six golden mixing-bowls, which are dedicated there as his gift. The weight of these is thirty talents,‡ and they stand in the treasury of the Corinthians, (though in truth this treasury does not belong to the State of the Corinthians, but is that of Kypselos the son of Aëtion).§ This Gyges was the first of the Barbarians within our knowledge who dedicated votive offerings at Delphi, except only Midas the son of Gordias king of Phrygia, who dedicated for an offering the royal throne on which he sat before all to decide causes; and this throne, a sight worth seeing, stands in the same place with the bowls of Gyges. This gold and silver which Gyges dedicated is called Gygian by the people of Delphi, after him who offered it.

Now Gyges also, like other Lydian rulers, as soon as he became king, led an army against Miletos and Smyrna, and he took the lower part of the town of Colophon. No other great deed did he do in his reign, which lasted eight-and-thirty years, therefore we will pass him by with no further mention, **15,** and I will speak now of Ardys the son of Gyges, who became king after Gyges. He took Prienē and made an invasion against Miletos; and

---

*Bracketed passages are deemed to be additions inserted later and not by the author's hand.
†Gyges became king c.716 B.C.; he appears in Assyrian documents.
‡Approximately 342 pounds of gold.
§At 5.92 we hear more of this tyrant.

while he was ruling over Sardis, the Kimmerians driven from their abodes by the nomad Scythians came to Asia and took Sardis except the citadel.

16. Now when Ardys had been king for nine-and-forty years, Sadyattes his son succeeded to his kingdom, and reigned twelve years; and after him Alyattes. This last made war against Kyaxares the descendant of Deïokes and against the Medes,* and he drove the Kimmerians out of Asia, and he took Smyrna which had been founded from Colophon, and made an invasion against Clazomenai. From this he returned not as he desired, but with great loss.

During his reign however he performed other deeds very worthy of mention as follows:—**17.** He made war against Miletos, having received this war as an inheritance from his father who used to invade their land and besiege Miletos in the following manner:—whenever there were ripe crops upon the land, then he led an army in, making his march to the sound of pipes and harps and flutes both of male and female tone. When he came to the Milesian land, he neither pulled down the houses that were in the fields, nor set fire to them nor tore off their doors, but let them stand as they were; the trees however and the crops that were upon the land he destroyed, and then departed by the way he came because the men of Miletos had command of the sea, so that it was of no use for his army to blockade them. He abstained from pulling down the houses so that the Milesians might have places to dwell in while they sowed and tilled the land, and by the means of their labour he might have something to pillage when he made his invasion.

18. Thus he continued to war with them for eleven years; and in the course of these years the Milesians suffered two great defeats, once when they fought a battle in the district of Limeneion in their own land, and again in the plain of the Maiander. Now for six of the eleven years Sadyattes the son of Ardys was still ruler of the Lydians, the same who was wont to invade the land of Miletos at harvest time. Sadyattes began the war but for the five years which followed the war was carried on by Alyattes the son of Sadyattes, who received it as an inheritance from his father (as I have already said) and applied himself to it earnestly. And none of the Ionians helped Miletos in this war except only the men of Chios. These came to their aid to pay back like with like, for the Milesians had formerly assisted the Chians throughout their war with the people of Erythrai.

19. Then in the twelfth year of the war, when standing grain was being burnt by the army of the Lydians, something like this happened:—as soon as the grain was kindled, it was driven by a violent wind and set fire to the temple of Athenē surnamed Assessos; and the temple burnt down to the ground. No one paid attention then; but afterwards when the army had returned to Sardis, Alyattes fell sick, and as his sickness lasted long, he sent messengers to inquire of the Oracle at Delphi, either being advised to do so, or because he himself thought it best to inquire of the god concerning

---

*In 1.72–130, we will hear more of the Medes. They are central for those sixty chapters (along with Lydia, the Lydians, and their conflict).

his sickness. But when these arrived at Delphi, the Pythian prophetess said that she would give them no answer, until they should restore the temple of Athenē which they had burnt at Assessos in the land of Miletos.

20. Thus much I know by the report of the people of Delphi; but the Milesians add to this that Periander the son of Kypselos, being a special guest-friend of Thrasybulos the then despot of Miletos, heard of the oracle which had been given to Alyattes, and sending a messenger told Thrasybulos, in order that he might have knowledge of it beforehand and plan as the case required. This is the story told by the Milesians. **21.** And Alyattes, when this answer was reported to him, sent a herald immediately to Miletos, desiring to make a truce with Thrasybulos and the Milesians for so long as he should be building the temple. He then was dispatched to Miletos; and Thrasybulos in the meantime being clearly informed and knowing what Alyattes meant to do, contrived this device:—he gathered together in the market-place all the store of provisions which was found in the city, both his own and that which belonged to private persons; and he proclaimed to the Milesians that on his signal they should all begin to drink and make merry with one another. **22.** This Thrasybulos did and thus proclaimed to the public so that the herald from Sardis, seeing a vast quantity of provisions carelessly piled up, and the people feasting, might report this to Alyattes. That in fact happened; for when the herald returned to Sardis after seeing this and delivering to Thrasybulos the commands entrusted to him by the king of Lydia, the peace came about, as I am informed, entirely because of this. For Alyattes, who thought that there was a great famine in Miletos and that the people had been worn down to the extreme of misery, heard from the herald, when he returned from Miletos, the opposite to his expectation. And after this the peace was made between them on condition of being guest-friends and allies to one another, and Alyattes built two temples to Athenē at Assessos in place of one, and himself recovered from his sickness. The war between Alyattes and the Milesians and Thrasybulos went thus.

23. As for Periander,* the man who gave information about the oracle to Thrasybulos, he was the son of Kypselos, and despot of Corinth. In his life, say the Corinthians, (and with them agree the Lesbians), a very great marvel happened to him. Arion of Methymna was carried ashore at Tainaron upon a dolphin's back. This man was a harper second to none of those who then lived, and the first, so far as we know, who composed a dithyramb, naming it so† and teaching it to a chorus at Corinth. **24.** This Arion, they say, who for the most part of his time stayed with Periander, conceived a desire to sail to Italy‡ and Sicily; and after he had there acquired large sums of money, he wished to return again to Corinth. He set forth therefore from Taras, and as he trusted Corinthians more than other

---

*Periander reigned at Corinth 625–585 B.C.; see 3.48–53.

†Type of hymn to honor the ecstatic god Dionysos.

‡Herodotus uses the name "Italy" for the southern part of the peninsula.

men, he hired a ship with a crew of Corinthians. These, the story says, when out in the open sea, formed a plot to cast Arion overboard and so seize his wealth; and he figuring this out entreated them, offering them his wealth and asking them to grant him his life. However he did not prevail upon them, but the men who were conveying him bade him either slay himself there, that he might receive burial on the land, or leap out then and there into the sea. So Arion being driven to extremes entreated them that, since they were so minded, they would allow him to take his stand in full minstrel's garb upon the deck of the ship and sing; and he promised to put himself to death after he had sung. They then, well pleased to think that they should hear the best of all minstrels upon earth, drew back from the stern towards the middle of the ship; and he put on the full minstrel's garb and took his lyre, and standing on the deck performed the Orthian measure.* Then when he ended, he threw himself into the sea just as he was, in his full minstrel's garb; and they went on sailing away to Corinth. But him, they say, a dolphin supported on its back and brought him to shore at Tainaron. When he had come to land he proceeded to Corinth with his minstrel's garb and he related all that had been done. Periander doubting of his story kept Arion under guard and would let him go nowhere, while he kept careful watch for those who had conveyed him. When these came, he called them and inquired of them if they had any report to make of Arion; and when they said that he was safe in Italy and that they had left him at Taras faring well, Arion suddenly jumped out before them in the same guise as when he made his leap from the ship. Struck with amazement they were no longer able to deny when they were questioned. This is the tale told by the Corinthians and Lesbians alike, and there is at Tainaron a little votive offering of Arion namely a bronze figure of a man upon a dolphin's back.

25. Alyattes the Lydian, when he had thus waged war against the Milesians, afterwards died, having reigned seven-and-fifty years. This king, when he recovered from his sickness, dedicated a votive offering at Delphi (being the second of his house who had so done), namely a great mixing-bowl of silver with a welded iron stand, a sight worth seeing above all the offerings at Delphi and the work of Glaucos the Chian, who first discovered the art of welding iron.

26. After Alyattes was dead Crœsus† the son of Alyattes at the age of thirty-five received the kingdom. He (as I said) fought against the Hellenes and of them he attacked the Ephesians first. The Ephesians then, being besieged by him, dedicated their city to Artemis and tied a rope from the temple to the wall of the city. Now the distance between the ancient city, which was then being besieged, and the temple is eight-tenths of a mile. These, I say, were the first upon whom Crœsus laid hands, but afterwards he did the same to the other Ionian and Aiolian cities one by one,

---

*Type of shrill tune employed in religious ritual.
†Croesus reigned over the Lydians 560–547/6 B.C.

alleging against them various causes of complaint, and making serious charges against those in whose cases he could find serious grounds, while against others he charged trifling offences.

27. Then when the Hellenes in Asia had been conquered and forced to pay tribute, he determined next to build for himself ships and to lay hands upon those who dwelt in the islands. When all was prepared for his building of ships, they say that Bias of Prienē (or, according to another account, Pittacos of Mytilenē) came to Sardis, and being asked by Crœsus whether there was any new developments in Hellas, put a halt to his building of ships by saying: "O king," said he, "the men of the islands are hiring a troop of ten thousand horse, and with this they mean to march to Sardis and fight against you."

And Crœsus, supposing that what he reported was true, said: "May the gods put it into the minds of the dwellers in the islands to come with horses against the sons of the Lydians!" And he answered and said: "O king, I perceive that you earnestly desire to catch the men of the islands on the mainland riding upon horses; and it is not unreasonable that you should wish for this. But what else however do you think the men of the islands desire and have been praying for ever since the time they heard that you were about to build ships against them, than that they might catch the Lydians upon the sea, so as to take vengeance upon you for the Hellenes who dwell upon the mainland, whom you hold enslaved?" Crœsus, they say, was greatly pleased with this conclusion, and obeying his suggestion, for he judged him to speak suitably, he ceased building ships; and then he formed a friendship with the Ionians dwelling in the islands.

28. As time went on, nearly all those dwelling on this side the river Halys had been subdued, (for except the Kilikians and Lykians Crœsus subdued and kept under his rule all the nations, that is to say Lydians, Phrygians, Mysians, Mariandynoi, Chalybians, Paphlagonians, Thracians both Thynian and Bithynian, Carians, Ionians, Dorians, Aiolians, and Pamphylians). **29.** While he was still adding to his Lydian dominions, there came to Sardis, then at the height of its wealth, all the wise men of Hellas of that time, brought there for various reasons. One of them was Solon the Athenian, who after he had made laws for the Athenians at their bidding, left his native country for ten years and sailed away saying that he desired to visit various lands, in order that he might not be compelled to repeal any of his new laws. For of themselves the Athenians were not competent to do this, having bound themselves by solemn oaths to submit for ten years to the laws which Solon should establish for them.

30. So Solon, having left his native country for this reason and for the sake of seeing various lands, came to Amasis in Egypt, and also to Crœsus at Sardis. He was entertained as a guest by Crœsus in the king's palace; and afterwards, on the third or fourth day, at the bidding of Crœsus his servants led Solon round to see his treasuries; and they showed him all things, how great and magnificent they were.

After he had looked upon them all and examined them, when he had a suitable occasion, Crœsus asked him: "Athenian guest, we've heard a lot about you, both in regard to your intelligence and your wanderings, how in your search for intelligence you have traversed many lands to see them; now therefore I desire to ask you whether yet you have seen the man who is the most happy." He asked supposing that he himself was the happiest of men; but Solon, using no flattery but the truth only, said: "Yes, O king, Tellos the Athenian."

Crœsus, marvelling at that, asked him earnestly: "How do you judge Tellos to be the most happy?" And he said: "Tellos, in the first place, living while his native State was prosperous, had sons fair and good and saw from all of them children begotten and living to grow up; and secondly he had what with us is accounted wealth, and after his life a most glorious end. When a battle was fought by the Athenians at Eleusis against the neighbouring people, he brought up supports and routed the foe and there died by a most fair death; and the Athenians buried him publicly where he fell, and honoured him greatly."

31. So when Solon had moved Crœsus to inquire further by the story of Tellos, recounting how many points of happiness he had, the king asked again whom he had seen proper to be placed next, supposing that he himself would certainly obtain at least the second place. Crœsus, however, replied: "Cleobis and Biton, since these, who were of Argos by race, possessed a sufficiency of wealth and, in addition to this, great strength of body. Both had won equal prizes in the games, and the following tale is told of them:—There was a feast of Hera among the Argives and their mother needed to be borne in a car to the temple. But since their oxen did not come in time from the field, the young men, barred from all else by lack of time, submitted themselves to the yoke and drew the cart, their mother travelling in it; and so they brought it on for over five miles, and came to the temple. Then after they had been seen by the assembled crowd, their life came to a most excellent ending; and in this the deity declared that it was better for man to die than to continue to live.

The Argive men were standing round and extolling the strength of the young men, while the Argive women were extolling the mother who enjoyed such sons; and the mother rejoicing in the deed itself and in the report made of it, took her stand in front of the image of the goddess and prayed that she would give to Cleobis and Biton her sons, who had honoured her greatly, that gift which is best for man to receive. After this prayer, when they had sacrificed and feasted, the young men lay down to sleep within the temple itself, and never rose again, but were held by this death. And the Argives made statues in the likeness of them and dedicated them as offerings at Delphi, thinking that they had proved themselves most excellent."

32. Thus Solon assigned the second place for happiness to these. Crœsus was moved to anger and said: "Athenian guest, have you then so cast aside our prosperous state as worth nothing, that you prefer to us even men of private station?" And he said: "Crœsus, you are inquiring about human fortunes from one who well knows that the Deity is altogether envious and apt to disturb our lot. For in the course of long time a man may see many things which he would not desire to see, and suffer also many things which he would not desire to suffer. The limit of life for a man I lay down at seventy years. These seventy years give twenty-five thousand and two hundred days, not reckoning for any intercalated month. Then if every other one of these years shall be made longer by one month, that the seasons may be caused to come round at the due time of the year, the intercalated months will be in number five-and-thirty besides the seventy years; and of these months the days will be one thousand and fifty. Of all these days, being in number twenty-six thousand two hundred and fifty, which go to the seventy years, one day produces nothing at all which resembles what the next brings with it. Thus then, O Crœsus, man is altogether a creature of accident. As for you, I perceive that you are both great in wealth and king of many men, but what you asked me I cannot call you yet, until I learn that you have brought your life to a fair ending.* The very rich man is not at all to be accounted more happy than he who has but his subsistence from day to day, unless also the fortune go with him of ending his life well in possession of all things fair. For many very wealthy men are not happy, while many who have only a moderate living are fortunate. In truth the very rich man who is not happy has two advantages only as compared with the poor man who is fortunate, whereas this latter has many as compared with the rich man who is not happy. The rich man is able better to fulfil his desire, and also to endure a great calamity if it fall upon him; whereas the other has these advantages over him:—he is not indeed able equally with the rich man to endure a calamity or to fulfil his desire, but these his good fortune keeps away from him, while he is sound of limb, free from disease, untouched by suffering, the father of fair children and handsome himself. If in addition to this he shall end his life well, he is worthy to be called that which you seekest, namely a happy man; but before he comes to his end it is well to hold back and not to call him happy yet but only fortunate.

"Now to possess all these things together is impossible for one who is mere man, just as no single land suffices to supply all things for itself, but one thing it has and another it lacks, and the land that has the greatest number of things is the best. So also in the case of a man, no single person is complete in himself, for one thing he has and another he lacks; but whosoever of men continues to the end in possession of the greatest number of these things and then dies with grace, he is by me accounted worthy, O king, to receive this name. But we must for every thing examine the end and how it will turn out at the last, for to many God shows but a glimpse of happiness and then plucks them up by the roots and overturns them."

33. Thus saying he refused to gratify Crœsus, who sent him away as worthless. He thought him utterly a fool in that he passed over present good things and bade men look to the end of every matter.†

---

*Solon voices a Hellenic pessimism that will be ironically realized for Croesus.
†This warning against jumping to (wrong) conclusions is repeatedly ignored.

34. After Solon had departed, a great retribution from God came upon Crœsus, probably because he judged himself to be the happiest of all men. First there came and stood by him a dream, which showed to him the truth of the evils that were about to happen to his son. Now Crœsus had two sons, of whom one was deficient, seeing that he was deaf and dumb, while the other far surpassed his companions of the same age in all things and his name was Atys. The dream signified to Crœsus that he should lose Atys by the blow of an iron spear-point. When he rose up from sleep and considered the matter with himself, he was struck with fear on account of the dream. First he took for his son a wife; and whereas his son had been wont to lead the armies of the Lydians, he now no longer sent him forth anywhere on any such business; and the javelins and lances and all such things which men use for fighting he conveyed out of the men's apartments and piled them up in the inner bed-chambers, lest something hanging up might fall upon his son. **35.** Then while he was busy with the marriage of his son, a man came to Sardis under a misfortune and with hands not clean, a Phrygian by birth and of the royal house. This man came to the house of Crœsus, and according to the customs which prevail in that land, made request that he might gain purification; and Crœsus gave him cleansing. The manner of cleansing among the Lydians is the same almost as that which the Hellenes use. So when Crœsus had followed custom, he asked of him whence he came and who he was, saying: "Man, who are you, and from what region of Phrygia did you come to sit upon my hearth? And whom of men or women did you slay?" And he replied: "O king, I am the son of Gordias, the son of Midas, and I am called Adrastos. I slew my own brother against my will, and therefore am I here, having been driven forth by my father and deprived of all that I had." And Crœsus answered: "You are, as it chances, the offshoot of men who are our friends and you have come to friends, among whom you shall lack nothing so long as you remain in our land: and you will find it most profitable to bear this misfortune as lightly as you can." So he lived with Crœsus.

36. During this time on the Mysian Olympos a boar of monstrous size appeared. This, coming down from the mountain, ravaged the fields of the Mysians, and although the Mysians went out against it often, yet they could do it no hurt, but rather received hurt themselves from it. Finally messengers came from the Mysians to Crœsus and said: "O king, a boar of monstrous size has appeared in our land, which lays waste our fields; and we, desiring eagerly to take it, are not able. Therefore we ask you to send with us your son and also a chosen band of young men with dogs, that we may rid our land of it." Thus they made request, and Crœsus calling to mind the words of the dream responded: "Make no further mention of my son in this matter; for I will not send him with you, seeing that he is newly married and is concerned now with his marriage. But I will send with you chosen men of the Lydians and the whole number of my hunting dogs; and I will give command to those who go, to be as zealous as can be in helping you to rid your land of the wild beast."

37. Thus he made reply. While the Mysians were contenting themselves with this answer, there came in also the son of Crœsus, having heard of the Mysians' request. After Crœsus said that he would not send his son with them, the young man said: "My father, in times past the fairest and most noble part was allotted to us, to go out continually to wars and to the chase and so gain repute; but now you have debarred me from both of these, although you have not observed in me any cowardly or fainthearted spirit. And now with what face must I appear when I visit the market-place of the city? What kind of a man shall I be esteemed by the citizens, and what kind of a man shall I be esteemed by my newly-married wife? With what kind of a husband will she think that she is mated? Therefore either let me go to the hunt, or persuade me by reason that your plan is better for me."

38. And Crœsus answered: "My son, not because I have observed in you any spirit of cowardice or any other displeasing thing, do I act thus; but a vision in a dream came and stood by me in my sleep and told me that you will be short-lived, and that you will perish by a spear-point of iron. With thought of this vision therefore I both urged on this marriage for you, and I refuse now to send you upon this undertaking, guarding a hope that I may steal you from fate at least while I live, if by any means it be possible for me to do so. For you are, as it chances, my only son; the other I do not reckon as one, seeing that he is deficient in his hearing."

39. The young man replied: "It may well be forgiven, my father, that you should worry about me after having seen such a vision; but what you do not understand, and how the meaning of the dream has escaped you, it is right that I should expound. You say the dream declared that I should end my life by means of a spear-point of iron. Yet what hands has a boar, or what spear-point of iron, which you fear? If the dream had told you that I should end my life by a tusk, or any other thing which resembles that, it would be right for you doubtless to do as you are doing; but it said 'by a spear-point.' Since therefore our fight will not be with men, let me now go." **40.** Crœsus made answer: "My son, you somewhat prevail with me by your explanation of the dream; therefore, persuaded, I change my resolution and allow you to go to the hunt."

41. Crœsus then summoned Adrastos the Phrygian; and when he came, he addressed him thus: "Adrastos, when you were struck with a grievous misfortune (with which I reproach you not), I cleansed you, and I have received you into my house supplying all your costs. Now therefore, since having first received kindness from me you are bound to requite me with kindness, I ask you to protect my son who goes to the hunt, lest any evil robbers accost you on the way to do you harm. Besides this you too ought to go where you may become famous by your deeds, for it belongs to you as an inheritance from your fathers to do so, and moreover you have the strength for it."

42. Adrastos made answer: "O king, but for this I should not have been going to any such contest of valour; for first it is not fitting that one who is suffering such a misfortune as mine should seek the company of his fellows who are in prosperity, and secondly I have no desire for it; and for many reasons I should have kept myself away. But now, since you urge me, and I ought to gratify you (for I am bound to requite your kindness), I am ready to do this. Expect therefore that your son, whom you command me to protect, will return home to you unhurt, insofar as his guardian can help." **43.** When he had answered Crœsus, they afterwards set forth provided with chosen young men and with dogs. And when they were come to Mount Olympos, they tracked the animal; and having found it and taken their stand round in a circle, they were hurling against it their spears. Then the guest, he who had been cleansed of the manslaughter, whose name was Adrastos, hurling a spear at it missed the boar and struck the son of Crœsus. So he, struck by the spear-point, fulfilled the saying of the dream. And one man ran to report the event to Crœsus, and having come to Sardis he signified to him the combat and the fate of his son.

44. And Crœsus was very greatly disturbed by the death of his son, and was much the more moved to complaining by this, namely that his son was slain by the man whom he had himself cleansed of manslaughter. And being grievously troubled by the misfortune he called upon Zeus the Cleanser, protesting to him that which he had suffered from his guest, and he called moreover upon the Protector of Suppliants and the Guardian of Friendship, naming still the same god, and calling upon him as the Protector of Suppliants because when he received the guest into his house he had been fostering ignorantly the slayer of his son, and as the Guardian of Friendship because having sent him as a protector he had found him the worst of foes.

45. After this the Lydians came bearing the corpse, and behind it followed the slayer. Taking his stand before the corpse he delivered himself up to Crœsus, holding forth his hands and bidding the king slay him over the corpse, speaking of his former misfortune and saying that in addition to this he had now been the destroyer of the man who had cleansed him of it; and that life for him was no more worth living. But Crœsus hearing this pitied Adrastos, although he was himself suffering so great an evil of his own, and said: "Guest, I have already received from you all the satisfaction that is due, seeing that you condemn yourself to suffer death; and not you alone are the cause of this evil, except in so far as you were the instrument of it against your own will, but some one, as I suppose, of the gods, who also long ago signified to me that outcome." So Crœsus buried his son as was fitting; but Adrastos the son of Gordias, the son of Midas, he who had been the slayer of his own brother and the slayer also of the man who had cleansed him, when all men had departed and silence came round about the tomb, recognising that he was more grievously burdened by misfortune than all men of whom he knew, slew himself upon the grave.*

46. For two years then Crœsus remained quiet in great mourning, because he was deprived of his son. After this the overthrow of the rule of Astyages, the son of Kyaxares by Cyrus the son of Cambyses, and the growing greatness of the Persians caused Crœsus to cease from his mourning,

---

*This long Greek sentence (48 words) required 72 English words in translation, a one-third increase. Herodotus builds it to an inevitable climax.

and led him to think about cutting short the power of the Persians, if by any means he might, while yet it was in growth and before they should have become great.

So he then began to make trial of the Oracles, both those of the Hellenes and that in Libya, sending messengers to one place and another, some to go to Delphi, others to Abai of the Phokians, and others to Dodona; and some were sent to the shrine of Amphiaraos and to that of Trophonios,* others to Branchidai in the land of Miletos. These are the Oracles of the Hellenes to which Crœsus sent messengers for divination; and others he sent to the shrine of Ammon in Libya to inquire there. Now he was sending the messengers abroad to the end that he might try the Oracles and find out what knowledge they had, so that if they should be found to have knowledge of the truth, he might ask them secondly whether he should attempt to march against the Persians.

47. And to the Lydians whom he sent to make trial of the Oracles he gave this charge. From the day on which they set out from Sardis they should reckon up the number of the days following and on the hundredth day they should consult the Oracles, asking what Crœsus the son of Alyattes king of the Lydians chanced then to be doing. Whatever the Oracles should prophesy, this they should cause to be written down and bear it back to him. Now what the other Oracles prophesied is not by any reported, but at Delphi, so soon as the Lydians entered the sanctuary of the temple to consult the god and asked as they were commanded, the Pythian prophetess spoke thus in hexameter measure:†

> "But the number of sand I know, and the measure of drops in the
>   ocean;
> The dumb man I understand, and I hear the speech of the speechless:
> And there hath come to my soul the smell of a strong-shelled tortoise
> Boiling in caldron of bronze, and the flesh of a lamb mingled with it;
> Under it bronze is laid, it has bronze as clothing upon it."

48. When the Pythian prophetess had uttered this oracle, the Lydians caused the prophecy to be written down, and went away at once to Sardis. And when the rest also who had been sent round arrived there with the answers of the Oracles, then Crœsus unfolded the writings one by one and looked upon them. At first none of them pleased him, but when he heard that from Delphi, immediately he did worship to the god and accepted the answer, judging that the Oracle at Delphi was the only true one, because it

---

*North of Athens, over the Boeotian border.
†The "six foot verse" is the meter of the Homeric epics and much other ancient poetry as well as of most reported oracles. Scholars continue to wrangle over the degree of credence that Herodotus grants oracles and other divine channels. The reader will often note an indication that distances Herodotus from his report; compare 7.152.

had found out what he himself had done. For when he had sent to the several Oracles his messengers to consult the gods, keeping well in mind the appointed day he contrived the following device. He thought of something which it would be impossible to discover or to conceive of, and cutting up a tortoise and a lamb he boiled them together himself in a caldron of bronze, laying a cover of bronze over them.* **49.** This then was the answer given to Crœsus from Delphi; and as regards the answer of Amphiaraos, I cannot tell what he replied to the Lydians after they had done the customary things in his temple,† for there is no record of this any more than of the others, except only that Crœsus thought that he also possessed a true Oracle.

50. After this with great sacrifices he set about winning the favour of the god at Delphi. He offered three thousand of each kind of all the animals that are fit for sacrifice, and he heaped up couches overlaid with gold and silver, and cups of gold, and robes of purple, and tunics, making of them a great pyre, and this he burnt up, hoping by these means the more to win over the god to the Lydians. He proclaimed to all the Lydians that every one of them should make sacrifice with what each man had. And when he had finished the sacrifice, he melted down a vast quantity of gold, and of it he wrought ingots making them eighteen inches in length and nine in breadth, and in height three inches; and their number was one hundred and seventeen. Of these four were of pure gold weighing one hundred forty-five pounds each, and the others of electrum, gold alloyed with silver, weighing one hundred sixteen pounds. And he caused to be made also an image of a lion of pure gold weighing 580 pounds. This lion, when the temple at Delphi was burnt down, fell from off the ingots, for upon these it was set, and is placed now in the treasury of the Corinthians, weighing 377 pounds, for 203 pounds were melted from it.

51. So Crœsus having finished all these things sent them to Delphi, and these besides:—two mixing-bowls of great size, one of gold and the other of silver, of which the golden bowl was placed on the right hand as one enters the temple,‡ and the silver on the left, but the places of these also were changed after the temple was burnt down, and the golden bowl is now placed in the treasury of the people of Clazomenai, weighing 505 pounds, while the silver one is placed in the corner of the vestibule and holds 5,400 gallons (being filled with wine by the Delphians on the feast of the Theophania). The people of Delphi say this is the work of Theodoros the Samian, and, as I think, rightly, for it is evident to me that the workmanship is of no common kind. Moreover Crœsus sent four silver wine-jars, which stand in the treasury of the Corinthians, and two vessels for lustral water,

---

*Herodotus preserves many folktales in his *Histories;* the widely dispersed folktale motif of the "Sham Wise Man" who "knows" what he cannot know by accident in this situation is rejiggered for a theological proof.

†See 8.134 for the procedure. See 7.178 and 9.91 for other examples of omens accepted.

‡Credible evidence for Herodotus' visit to central Greece.

one of gold and the other of silver, of which the gold one is inscribed "from the Lacedemonians," who say that it is their offering. Therein however they do not speak rightly; for this also is from Crœsus, but one of the Delphians wrote the inscription upon it, desiring to gratify the Lacedemonians; and his name I know but I will not mention it. The boy through whose hand the water flows is from the Lacedemonians, but neither vessel for lustral water. And many other votive offerings Crœsus sent with these, not so distinguished, among which are certain round bowls of silver, and also a golden figure of a woman 4½ feet high, which the Delphians say is a statue of the baker of Crœsus. Moreover Crœsus dedicated the ornaments from his wife's neck and her decorated belts.

52. These things he sent to Delphi; and to Amphiaraos, having heard of his valour and of his evil fate, he dedicated a shield made of gold throughout, and a spear all of solid gold, the shaft being of gold also as well as the two points, which offerings were both remaining even to my time at Thebes in the temple of Ismenian Apollo.

53. To the Lydians who were to carry these gifts to the temples[*] Crœsus gave charge that they should also ask the Oracles this question: Whether Crœsus should march against the Persians, and if so, whether he should join with himself any army of men as his friends. And when the Lydians had arrived at the places to which they had been sent and had dedicated the votive offerings, they inquired of the Oracles: "Crœsus, king of the Lydians and of other nations, considering that these are the only true Oracles among men, presents to you gifts such as your revelations deserve, and asks you again now whether he shall march against the Persians, and if so, whether he shall ally himself to any army of men." They inquired thus, and the answers of both the Oracles agreed in one particular, declaring to Crœsus that if he should march against the Persians he should destroy a great empire. Further, they counselled him to find out the most powerful of the Hellenes and join these with himself as friends.

54. So when the answers were brought back and Crœsus heard them, he was delighted with the oracles, and expecting that he would certainly destroy the kingdom of Cyrus, he sent again to Pytho at Delphi, and presented to the men of Delphi, having ascertained the number of them, two staters[†] of gold for each man. In return for this the Delphians gave to Crœsus and to the Lydians precedence in consulting the Oracle and freedom from all payments, and the right to front seats at the games, with this privilege also for all time, that any one of them who wished should be allowed to become a citizen of Delphi. **55.** And having made presents to the men of Delphi, Crœsus consulted the Oracle the third time; for from the time when he learnt the truth of the Oracle, he made abundant use of it. He inquired whether his monarchy would endure for a long time. And the Pythian prophetess answered him:

---

*This sending was in 556 B.C.
†Each stater weighed about 2/3 ounce.

"But when it cometh to pass that a mule of the Medes shall be
    monarch,
Then by the pebbly Hermos, O Lydian delicate-footed,
Flee and stay not, and be not ashamed to be called a coward."

56. These lines when they came to him pleased Crœsus more than all the
rest, for he supposed that a mule would never be ruler of the Medes instead of a man, and accordingly that he himself and his heirs would never
cease from their rule. Then after this he thought about inquiring which
people of the Hellenes he should esteem the most powerful and gain over
to himself as friends. And he found that the Lacedemonians and the Athenians had the pre-eminence, the first of the Dorian and the others of the
Ionian race. For these were the most eminent races in ancient time, the
second being a Pelasgian and the first a Hellenic race. The one never migrated from its place in any direction, while the other was exceedingly
given to wandering; for in the reign of Deucalion this race dwelt in Pthio-
tis, and in the time of Doros the son of Hellen in the land lying below Ossa
and Olympos, which is called Histiaiotis; and when it was driven from Histiaiotis by the sons of Cadmos, it dwelt in Pindos and was called Makednian; and thence it moved afterwards to Dryopis, and from Dryopis it
came finally to Peloponnesus, and began to be called Dorian.
    57. What language however the Pelasgians used to speak I am not able
with certainty to say. But one must pronounce judging by those that still
remain of the Pelasgians who dwelt in the city of Creston above the Tyrsenians, and who were once neighbours of the race now called Dorian,
dwelling then in the land which is now called Thessaliotis, and also by
those that remain of the Pelasgians who settled at Plakia and Skylakē in
the region of the Hellespont, who before that had been settlers with the
Athenians, and of the natives of the various other towns which are really
Pelasgian, though they have lost the name. If one must pronounce judging
by these, the Pelasgians used to speak a Barbarian language.* If therefore
all the Pelasgian race was such as these, then the Attic race, being Pelasgian, at the same time when it changed and became Hellenic, unlearnt also
its language. For the people of Creston do not speak the same language
with any of those who dwell about them, nor yet do the people of Plakia,
but they speak the same language as each other. By this it is proved that
they still keep unchanged the form of language which they brought with
them when they migrated to these places. **58.** As for the Hellenic race, it
has used ever the same language, as I clearly perceive, since it first took its
rise; but since the time when it parted off feeble at first from the Pelasgian
race, setting forth from a small beginning it has increased to a great number of ethnic groups, and chiefly because many Barbarian races have been
added to it besides. Moreover it is true, as I think, of the Pelasgian race
also, that so far as it remained Barbarian it never made any great increase.

---

*For more information on these Pelasgians see 2.51 and 6.137.

59. Crœsus was informed about these races then that the Athenian was held subject and torn with faction by Peisistratos* the son of Hippocrates, who then was despot of the Athenians. A great marvel had occurred to Hippocrates, when as a private citizen he went to view the Olympic games. After he had offered the sacrifice, the caldrons which were standing upon the hearth, full of pieces of flesh and of water, boiled without fire under them and ran over. And Chilon the Lacedemonian, who chanced to be there and to have seen the marvel, advised Hippocrates first not to bring into his house a wife to bear him children, and secondly, if he happened to have one already, to dismiss her, and if he chanced to have a son, to disown him. When Chilon had thus recommended, Hippocrates, they say, was not willing to be persuaded and so there was born to him afterwards this Peisistratos. When the Athenians of the shore were at feud with those of the plain, Megacles the son of Alcmaion being leader of the first faction, and Lycurgos the son of Aristolaïdes of that of the plain, Peisistratos aimed at despotism for himself and gathered a third party. So then, having collected supporters and called himself leader of the men of the hills, he contrived this ruse:—he inflicted wounds upon himself and upon his mules, and then drove his car into the market-place, as if he had just escaped from his opponents, who, as he alleged, had desired to kill him when he was driving into the country. As a result he asked the commons for some protection from them, for before this he had gained reputation in his command against the Megarians, during which he took Nisaia and performed other signal service. And the commons of the Athenians being deceived gave him those men chosen from the dwellers in the city who became not indeed the [usual body-guard of] spear-men of Peisistratos but his club-men; for they followed him bearing wooden clubs. And these staged a coup with Peisistratos and obtained possession of the Acropolis. Then Peisistratos was ruler of the Athenians, not having disturbed the existing magistrates nor changed the ancient laws. He administered the State under the already established constitution, ordering it fairly and well.

60. However, no long time after this the followers of Megacles and those of Lycurgos joined together and drove him out.† Thus Peisistratos had obtained possession of Athens for the first time, and thus he lost the power before he had it very firmly rooted. But those who had driven out Peisistratos feuded with one another again. And Megacles, harassed by the factional strife, sent a message to Peisistratos asking whether he was willing to marry his daughter on condition of becoming despot. And Peisistratos having accepted the proposal and agreed to these terms, they contrived for his reestablishment a device the most simple by far, as I think, that ever was practised, considering at least that it was devised when the Hellenic race had been long marked off from the Barbarian as more clever and further removed from foolish simplicity, and devised against the Athenians

---

*Peisistratos became despot first in 560 B.C.
†Perhaps c.555 B.C.

who are accounted the first of the Hellenes in mental ability. In the deme of
Paiania there was a woman whose name was Phya, in height five feet nine
inches and also fair of form.* This woman they dressed in full armour and
mounted her in a chariot and showed her the most impressive bearing for
her part. Then they drove to the city, having sent on heralds to run before
them, who, when they arrived at the city, spoke as directed: "Athenians, receive with favour Peisistratos, whom Athenē herself, honouring him most
of all men, brings back to her Acropolis." So the heralds went about hither
and thither saying this, and at once the demes in the country round heard
a report that Athenē was bringing Peisistratos back, while at the same time
the men of the city, persuaded that the woman was the very goddess herself, were paying worship to the human creature and receiving Peisistratos.

61. So having received back the despotism in the manner which has
been said, Peisistratos according to the agreement made with Megacles
married the daughter of Megacles. Since he had already sons who were
young men, and as the descendants of Alcmaion were said to be under a
curse,† therefore not desiring that children should be born to him from his
newly-married wife, he slept with her not in the usual way. And at first the
woman kept this secret, but afterwards she told her mother, whether in answer to her inquiry or not I cannot tell; and the mother told her husband
Megacles. He then was very indignant that he should be dishonoured by
Peisistratos. So he proceeded to compose his quarrel with his factional ri-
vals. And when Peisistratos heard of the preparations against himself, he
departed from the land altogether and came to Eretria, where he deliberated together with his sons.‡ Hippias' advice having prevailed, that they
should endeavour to win back the despotism, they began to gather gifts of
money from those States which were under obligation for favours received. Many contributed great sums, but the Thebans surpassed the rest
in the giving of money. Then, not to make the story long, time elapsed and
at last everything was prepared for their return. Certain Argives came as
mercenaries from Peloponnesus, and a man of Naxos had come to them as
a volunteer, whose name was Lygdamis, and showed the greatest enthusi-
asm in providing both money and men.

62. So starting from Eretria after the lapse of ten years§ they returned;
and in Attica the first place of which they took possession was Marathon.
While they were encamping here, their partisans from the city came to
them, and also others flowed in from the various demes, to whom despotic
rule was more welcome than freedom. So these were gathering themselves
together; but the Athenians in the city, so long as Peisistratos was collecting

---

*Compare 5.12 for another tall, young beauty engaged in a fraud. The sham
Athene was not of great stature by modern standards.
†Herodotus explains this problem more fully at 5.70–71.
‡Peisistratos' second tyranny dates to 550–549 B.C.
§Peisistratos returned this second time in 538 B.C. for his third period of rule, ac-
cording to one chronology, but no firm dates survive.

the money, and afterwards when he took possession of Marathon, remained
unconcerned; but when they heard that he was marching from Marathon
towards the city, then they assembled to march against him. These then
were going in full force to fight against the returning exiles, and the forces
of Peisistratos, as they went towards the city starting from Marathon, met
them just when they came to the temple of Athenē Pallenis, and there encamped opposite to them. Then moved by divine impulse Amphilytos the
Acarnanian, a soothsayer, came into the presence of Peisistratos. He, approaching him, uttered an oracle in hexameter verse, saying:

> "But now the cast hath been made and the net hath been widely
>   extended,
> And in the night the tunnies will dart through the moon-lighted
>   waters."

63. This oracle he, being divinely inspired, uttered to him, and Peisistratos, having understood the oracle and having said that he accepted the
prophecy, led his army against the enemy. Now the Athenians from the
city were just at that time occupied with the morning meal, and some of
them after their meal, with games of dice or with sleep; and the forces of
Peisistratos fell upon the Athenians and put them to flight. Then as they
fled, Peisistratos devised a very skilful stratagem so that the Athenians
might not gather again into one body but might remain scattered abroad.
He mounted his sons on horseback and sent them before him; overtaking
the fugitives they repeated Peisistratos' instructions, bidding them be of
good cheer and that each man should depart to his own home.
   64. Thus he persuaded the Athenians and Peisistratos for the third time
obtained possession of Athens. He firmly rooted his despotism by many
foreign mercenaries and by much revenue of money, coming partly from
the land itself and partly from the region of the river Strymon, and also by
taking as hostages the sons of those Athenians who had remained in the
land and had not at once fled, and placing them in the island of Naxos. Peisistratos conquered Naxos by war and delivered it to Lygdamis. Besides
this he cleansed the island of Delos in obedience to the oracles; and his purification was of the following kind:—so far as the view from the temple
extended he dug up all the dead bodies which were buried and removed
them to another part of Delos. So Peisistratos was despot of the Athenians; but of the Athenians some had fallen in the battle, and others of them
with the Alcmaionids* were exiles from their native land.
   65. Such was the prevailing Athenian situation which Crœsus heard
about. He heard that the Lacedemonians had escaped from great evils
and had now got the better of the Tegeans in their war. For when Leon and
Hegesicles were kings of Sparta, the Lacedemonians, who had good success
in all their other wars, suffered disaster in that alone waged against the

---

*Megacles, and later Cleisthenes and Pericles, belonged to this powerful clan.

men of Tegea. Moreover in the times before this they had the worst customs of almost all the Hellenes, both in matters which concerned themselves alone and also because they had no dealings with strangers. But they made their change to a good constitution of laws thus:—Lycurgos, a Spartan of high repute, came to the Oracle at Delphi, and as he entered the sanctuary of the temple, the Pythian prophetess said at once:

> "Lo, thou art come, Lycurgos, to this rich shrine of my temple,
> Loved thou by Zeus and by all who possess the abodes of Olympos.
> Whether to call you a god, I doubt, in my voices prophetic,
> God or a man, but rather a god I think, Lycurgos."

Some say in addition to this that the Pythian prophetess also set forth to him the order of things which is now established for the Spartans; but the Lacedemonians themselves say that Lycurgos having become guardian of Leobotes his brother's son, who was king of the Spartans, brought this order from Crete. For as soon as he became guardian, he changed all the prevailing laws, and took measures that they should not transgress his institutions. After this Lycurgos established that which appertained to war, namely army companies and "Bands of Thirty," and Common Meals, and in addition to this the Ephors and the Senate.

66. Having changed thus, the Spartans had good laws; and to Lycurgos after he was dead they erected a shrine, and they pay him great worship. So then, as might be supposed, with a fertile land and with many men dwelling in it, they quickly shot up and became prosperous. They were not satisfied to keep still; but presuming that they were superior in strength to the Arcadians, they consulted the Oracle at Delphi respecting conquest of all Arcadia; and the Pythian prophetess answered thus:

> "The land of Arcadia thou askest; thou askest me much; I refuse it:
> Many there are in Arcadian land, stout men, eating acorns;
> These will prevent you from this: but I am not grudging towards thee;
> Tegea beaten with sounding feet I will give thee to dance in,
> And a fair plain I will give thee to measure with line and divide it."

When the Lacedemonians heard this reported, they held off from the other Arcadians, and marched against the Tegeans with fetters in their hands, trusting to a deceptive oracle and expecting that they would make slaves of the men of Tegea. But having been worsted in the encounter, those of them who were taken alive worked wearing the fetters which they themselves brought with them and "measured with line and divided" the plain of the Tegeans. And these fetters with which they had been bound were preserved safe even to my own time at Tegea, hanging around the temple of Athenē Alea.*

---

*Herodotus reports other dedications there at 9.70.

67. In the former war then I say they struggled against the Tegeans continually with ill success; but in the time of Crœsus and in the reign of Anaxandrides and Ariston at Lacedemon the Spartans had at length become victors in the war in the following manner:—As they continued to be always worsted in the war by the men of Tegea, they sent messengers to consult the Oracle at Delphi and inquired what god they should propitiate in order to subdue the men of Tegea in the war. The Pythian prophetess answered that they should bring back the bones of Orestes the son of Agamemnon. Then as they were not able to find the grave of Orestes, they sent men again to go to the god and to inquire about the spot where Orestes was laid. The messengers asked this, so the prophetess declared:

> "Tegea there is, in Arcadian land, in a smooth place founded;
>   Where there do blow two blasts by strong compulsion together;
>   Stroke too there is and stroke in return, and trouble on trouble.
>   There Agamemnon's son in the life-giving earth is reposing;
>   Him if thou bring with thee home, of Tegea thou shalt be protector."

When the Lacedemonians had heard this they remained equally far from finding it out, though they searched all places. Eventually Lichas, one of those Spartans who are called "Well-doers," discovered it. Now the "Well-doers" are the eldest of the citizens passing from the ranks of the "Horsemen," five in each year; and these are bound during that year in which they pass out from the "Horsemen," to allow themselves to be sent without rest to various places by the Spartan State.

68. Lichas then, being one of these, discovered it in Tegea by means both of good fortune and brains. For as there were at that time dealings under truce with the men of Tegea, he had come to a forge there and was looking at iron being wrought; and he wondered at what was being done. The smith therefore, perceiving that he marvelled at it, ceased from his work and said: "Surely, stranger of Lacedemon, if you had seen that which once I saw, you would have marvelled much, since now it falls out that you marvel so greatly at the working of this iron. I, desiring in this enclosure to make a well, hit in my digging upon a coffin ten and one-half feet in length. Not believing that ever there had been men larger than those of the present day, I opened it, and I saw that the dead body was equal in length to the coffin. After I had measured it, I filled in the earth over it again." He then thus told him of that which he had seen; and the other, having thought about it, conjectured that this was Orestes of the saying of the Oracle. He speculated thus:—whereas he saw that the smith had two pairs of bellows, he concluded that these were the winds spoken of, and that the anvil and the hammer were the stroke and the stroke in return, and that the iron which was being wrought was the trouble laid upon trouble, making comparison by the thought that iron has been discovered for the evil of mankind. Having thus conjectured he came back to Sparta and declared the whole matter to the Lacedemonians; and they brought a charge against him on a fictitious pretext and drove him into exile. So having come to Tegea, he told the smith of his evil fortune and endeavoured to hire from him the enclosure, but at first he would not allow him to have it. At length Lichas persuaded him and took up his abode there; and he dug up the grave and gathered together the bones and went with them away to Sparta. From that time, whenever they made trial of one another, the Lacedemonians had much the advantage in the war; and by now they had subdued to themselves the greater part of Peloponnesus besides.

69. Crœsus accordingly, informed of all these things, was sending messengers to Sparta with gifts in their hands to ask for an alliance, having commanded them to say: "Crœsus king of the Lydians and also of other nations sent us hither and says as follows: Lacedemonians, whereas the god by an oracle bade me join with myself the Hellene as a friend, therefore, since I am informed that you are the chiefs of Hellas, I invite you according to the oracle, desiring to be your friend and your ally without any guile and deceit." Thus did Crœsus announce to the Lacedemonians through his messengers; and the Lacedemonians, who themselves also had heard of the oracle given to Crœsus, were pleased at the coming of the Lydians and exchanged oaths of friendship and alliance. They were bound to Crœsus also by some services rendered to them even before this time; since the Lacedemonians had sent to Sardis and were buying gold there with purpose of using it for the image of Apollo which is now set up on Mount Thornax in the Lacedemonian land; and Crœsus, when they desired to buy it, gave it to them as a gift. **70.** For this reason therefore the Lacedemonians accepted the alliance, and also because he chose them as his friends, preferring them to all the other Hellenes. And not only were they ready themselves when he made his offer, but they caused a mixing-bowl to be made of bronze, covered outside with figures round the rim and able to hold 2,550 gallons. This they conveyed, desiring to give it as a gift in return to Crœsus. This bowl never came to Sardis for reasons of which two accounts are given:*—The Lacedemonians say that when the bowl was on its way to Sardis and came opposite the land of Samos, the men of Samos having heard of it sailed out with ships of war and seized it; but the Samians themselves say that the Lacedemonians who were conveying the bowl, finding that they were too late and hearing that Sardis had been taken and Crœsus was a prisoner, sold the bowl in Samos, and certain private persons bought it and dedicated it as a votive offering in the temple of Hera; and probably those who had sold it would say when they returned to Sparta that it had been seized from them by the Samians. **71.** So much for the mixing-bowl. Meanwhile Crœsus, mistaking the meaning of the oracle, was making a march into Cappadokia, expecting to overthrow Cyrus and the power of the Persians. While Crœsus was preparing to march against the Persians, one of the Lydians, who even before this time was thought to be a bright man but in consequence of this opinion

---

*Herodotus often preserves various versions and often identifies their ethnic sources.

got a very great name for wisdom among the Lydians, had advised Crœsus as follows, (the name of the man was Sandanis):—"King, you are preparing to march against men who wear breeches of leather, and the rest of their clothing is of leather also; and they eat food not such as they desire but such as they can obtain, dwelling in a land which is rugged; and moreover they make no use of wine but drink water; and no figs have they for dessert, nor any other good thing.* On the one hand, if you shall overcome, them, what will you take away from them, seeing they have nothing? and on the other hand, if you shall be overcome, consider how many good things you will lose; for once having tasted our good things, they will cling to them fast and it will not be possible to drive them away. I for my own part feel gratitude to the gods that they do not put it into the minds of the Persians to march against the Lydians." Thus he spoke, but he did not persuade Crœsus. The Persians before they subdued the Lydians had no luxury nor any good thing.

72. Now the Cappadokians are called Syrians by the Hellenes; and these Syrians, before the Persians had rule,† were subjects of the Medes, but at this time they were subjects of Cyrus. For the boundary between the Median empire and the Lydian was the river Halys; and this flows from the mountain-land of Armenia through the Kilikians, and afterwards, as it flows, it has the Matienians on the right hand and the Phrygians on the other side; then passing by these and flowing towards the North, it bounds on the one side the Cappadokian Syrians and on the left hand the Paphlagonians. Thus the river Halys cuts off from the rest almost all the lower parts of Asia by a line extending from the sea that is opposite Cyprus to the Euxine. And this tract is the neck‡ of the whole peninsula, the distance of the journey being such that five days suffice on the way by an unencumbered man.

73. Now Crœsus was marching into Cappadokia for the following reasons:—first because he desired to acquire the land in addition to his own possessions, and then especially because he had confidence in the oracle and wished to take vengeance on Cyrus for Astyages. For Cyrus the son of Cambyses had conquered Astyages and was keeping him in captivity, who was brother by marriage to Crœsus and king of the Medes. He had become the brother by marriage of Crœsus in this manner:—A horde of the nomad Scythians at feud with the rest withdrew and sought refuge in the land of the Medes. At this time the ruler of the Medes was Kyaxares the son of Phraortes, the son of Deïokes, who at first treated these Scythians well, being suppliants for his protection. Esteeming them very highly he delivered boys to them to learn their speech and the art of shooting with the bow. Then time went by, and the Scythians used to go out continually to the chase and always brought back something; till once it happened that they took nothing, and when they returned with empty hands Kyaxares

---

*The theme "rugged lands breed rugged men" also appears at 7.102 and 9.122.
†The rise of Persia begins at 1.108.
‡The shortest distance across Anatolia from north to south is 300 miles.

(being, as he showed here, quick to anger) dealt with them very harshly and insulted them. And they, when they had received this treatment from Kyaxares, considering that they had suffered indignity, planned to kill and to cut up one of the boys who were being instructed among them, and having dressed his flesh as they usually dressed the wild animals, to bear it to Kyaxares and give it to him, pretending that it was game taken in hunting; and when they had given it, their design was to make their way as quickly as possible to Alyattes the son of Sadyattes at Sardis. This then was done; and Kyaxares with the guests who ate at his table tasted of that meat, and the Scythians having so done became suppliants for the protection of Alyattes.

74. After this, seeing that Alyattes would not give up the Scythians when Kyaxares demanded them, there had arisen war between the Lydians and the Medes lasting five years; in which years the Medes often discomfited the Lydians and the Lydians often discomfited the Medes (and among others they fought also a battle by night). While they still carried on the war with equally balanced fortune, in the sixth year a battle took place in which, when the fight had begun, suddenly the day became night.* And this change of the day Thales the Milesian had foretold to the Ionians laying down as a limit this very year. The Lydians however and the Medes, when they saw that it had become night instead of day, ceased fighting and were much more eager for peace. And they who brought about the peace between them were Syennesis the Kilikian and Labynetos the Babylonian. These urged also the taking of the oath by them, and they brought about an interchange of marriages; for they decided that Alyattes should give his daughter Aryenis to Astyages the son of Kyaxares, seeing that without the compulsion of a strong tie agreements are apt not to hold strongly together. Now these nations observe the same ceremonies in taking oaths as the Hellenes, and in addition to them they make incision into the skin of their arms, and then lick up the blood of each other.

75. Cyrus had conquered this Astyages then, his mother's father, and made him prisoner for a reason which I shall clarify later in my history. This complaint Crœsus had against Cyrus when he sent to the Oracles to ask if he should march against the Persians; and when a deceptive answer had come back to him, he marched into the dominion of the Persians, supposing that the answer was favourable to himself. And when Crœsus came to the river Halys,† then, according to my account, he passed his army across by the existing bridges; but according to the account which prevails among the Hellenes, Thales the Milesian enabled him to pass his army across. For, say they, when Crœsus was at a loss how his army should pass over the river (since, they add, the bridges which now there are had not yet been built), Thales accompanying the army caused the river, which flowed then on the left hand of the army, to flow partly also on the right.

---

*This eclipse probably occurred on May 28 in 585 B.C.
†This war was probably fought in 546 B.C.

He did it thus:—beginning above the camp he proceeded to dig a deep channel, directing it in the form of a crescent moon, so that the river might take the camp there pitched in the rear, being turned aside from its ancient course by this way along the channel, and afterwards passing by the camp might fall again into its ancient course; so that as soon as the river was thus parted in two it became fordable by both branches. Some say even that the ancient course of the river was altogether dried up. But this tale I do not admit as true, for how then did they pass over the river as they went back?

76. And Crœsus, when he had passed over with his army, came to that place in Cappadokia which is called Pteria, (now Pteria is the strongest place in this country, and is situated [south] about in a line with the city of Sinopē on the Euxine). Here he encamped and ravaged the fields of the Syrians. Moreover he took the city of the Pterians, and sold the people into slavery, and he took also all the neighboring towns; and the Syrians, who were not guilty of any wrong, he forcibly removed from their homes.

Meanwhile Cyrus, having gathered his own forces and having taken up in addition to them all who dwelt in the region between, was coming to meet Crœsus. Before he began however to lead forth his army, he had sent heralds to the Ionians and tried to induce them to revolt from Crœsus; but the Ionians would not do as he said. Then when Cyrus was come and had encamped over against Crœsus, they tested one another's forces in the land of Pteria. After hard fighting, when many had fallen on both sides, at length, night having come on, they parted one from the other with no victory.

77. Thus the two armies contended with one another. Crœsus being ill satisfied with his own army's numbers (for the army which he had when he fought was far smaller than that of Cyrus), as Cyrus did not attempt to advance against him on the following day, marched back to Sardis. He intended to call the Egyptians to his help according to the oath which they had taken (for he had made alliance with Amasis king of Egypt before the alliance with the Lacedemonians), and to summon the Babylonians as well (for with these also an alliance had been concluded by him, Labynetos* being then despot of the Babylonians), and moreover to send a message to the Lacedemonians bidding them appear at a fixed time. After he had got all these together and had gathered his own army, his design was to let the winter go by and at the coming of spring to march against the Persians. So with these plans, as soon as he came to Sardis he proceeded to send heralds to his several allies to give them notice that by the fifth month from that time they should assemble at Sardis. The army which he had with him and which had fought with the Persians, an army which consisted of mercenary troops, he let go and disbanded altogether, never expecting that Cyrus, after having contended against him evenly, would after all march upon Sardis.

78. While Crœsus had these plans, the suburb of the city suddenly became full of serpents; and when these had appeared, the horses leaving off

---

*Nabonidus was the last Babylonian ruler; he was the son of Labynetos in 1.74.

the feed in their pastures came constantly thither and devoured them. When Croesus saw this he deemed it to be a portent, as indeed it was. He immediately despatched messengers to the dwelling of the Telmessians, who interpret omens.* The messengers who were sent to consult arrived there and learnt from the Telmessians what the portent meant to signify, but they did not succeed in reporting the answer to Croesus, for before they sailed back to Sardis Croesus had been taken prisoner. The Telmessians however gave decision thus: that an army speaking a foreign tongue was to be looked for by Croesus to invade his land, and that this when it came would subdue the native inhabitants; for they said that the serpent was born of the soil, while the horse was an enemy and a stranger. The men of Telmessos thus made answer to Croesus after he was already taken prisoner, not knowing as yet what had happened to Sardis and to Croesus himself.

79. Cyrus however, so soon as Croesus marched away after the battle fought in Pteria, having learnt that Croesus meant after he had marched away to disband his army, strategized that it was good for him to march as quickly as possible to Sardis, before the power of the Lydians should be again gathered together. So when he had resolved upon this, he did it without delay. He marched his army into Lydia with such speed that he himself first announced his coming to Croesus. Then Croesus, although he was stymied, since his affairs had fallen out altogether contrary to expectation, yet proceeded to lead forth the Lydians to battle. Now there was at this time no nation in Asia more courageous or stout in battle than the Lydian; and they fought on horseback carrying long spears, the men being excellent in horsemanship.

80. So the armies had met in that plain which is in front of the city of Sardis. This plain is wide and open, through which flow rivers (especially the river Hyllos) all rushing down to join the largest called Hermos, which flows from the mountain sacred to the [Phrygian] Mother surnamed "of [Mount] Dindymos" and runs out into the sea by the city of Phocaia. When Cyrus saw the Lydians being arrayed for battle, fearing their horsemen, he followed the suggestion of Harpagos a Mede:—all the camels which were in the train of his army carrying provisions and baggage he gathered together, and he took off their burdens and set men upon them provided with cavalry equipment. Having thus furnished them, he stationed them in front of the rest of the army towards the horsemen of Croesus; and after the camel-troop he ordered the infantry to follow; and behind the infantry he placed his whole force of cavalry. Then when all his men had been placed in their several positions, he charged them to spare none of the other Lydians, slaying all who might come in their way, but Croesus himself they were not to slay, not even if he should make resistance when he was being captured. Such was his charge. He set the camels opposite the horsemen because the horse has a fear of the camel and cannot endure either to see his form or to scent his smell. The trick then had been devised in order

---

*A Lycian coastal village in southwestern Anatolia.

that the cavalry of Crœsus might be useless, that very force wherewith the
Lydian king was expecting most to shine. And as they were coming together to battle, so soon as the horses scented the camels and saw them
they turned away back, and the hopes of Crœsus were at once dashed. The
Lydians however did not upon that act as cowards, but when they perceived the situation they leapt from their horses and fought with the Persians on foot. At length however, when many had fallen on either side, the
Lydians turned to flight; and having been driven within the wall they were
besieged by the Persians.

81. By these then a siege had been established. Crœsus, supposing that
the siege would last a long time, proceeded to send from the fortification
other messengers to his allies. For the former messengers were sent round
to give notice that they should assemble at Sardis by the fifth month, but
these he sent out to ask them to aid him as quickly as possible, because
Crœsus was being besieged. **82.** Sending then to his other allies he sent
also to Lacedemon. But these Spartans had themselves at this very time
(for so it had fallen out) a quarrel with the Argives about the district
called Thyrea. For this Thyrea, being part of the Argive possessions, the
Lacedemonians had cut off and taken for themselves. Now the whole region towards the west extending as far South as Malea was then possessed
by the Argives, both the parts situated on the mainland and also the island
of Kythera with the other islands. And when the Argives had come to save
their territory from being cut off from them, then the two sides came to a
parley together and agreed that three hundred should fight on each side,
and whichever side had the better in the fight that nation should possess
the disputed land. They agreed moreover that the main body of each army
should withdraw to their own country, and not stand by while the contest
was fought, fearing lest, if the armies were present, one side seeing their
countrymen suffering defeat should come to their support. Having made
this agreement they withdrew; and chosen men of both sides were left behind and engaged in fight with one another. So they fought and proved
themselves to be equally matched; and three were left at last of six hundred men, on the side of the Argives Alkenor and Chromios, and on the
side of the Lacedemonians Othryades. Only these were left alive when
night came on. So then the two men of the Argives, supposing that they
were the victors, set off to run to Argos, but the Lacedemonian Othryades,
after having stripped the corpses of the Argives and carried their arms to
his own camp, remained in his place.

On the next day both sides came thither to inquire about the result; and
for some time both claimed the victory for themselves, the one side saying
that more of them had remained alive, and the others declaring that these
had fled away, whereas their own man had stood his ground and had
stripped the corpses of the other party. At length by reason of this dispute
they fell upon one another and began to fight; and after many had fallen
on both sides, the Lacedemonians were the victors. The Argives then cut
their hair short, whereas formerly they were compelled by law to wear it
long, and they made a law with a curse attached to it, that from that time

forth no man of the Argives should grow long hair nor their women wear
ornaments of gold, until they should have won back Thyrea. The Lacedemonians however laid down for themselves the opposite law to this,
namely that they should wear long hair from that time forward, whereas
before that time they had not their hair long. And they say that the one
man who was left alive of the three hundred, namely Othryades, being
ashamed to return to Sparta when all his comrades had been slain, slew
himself there in Thyrea.[*]

83. Such was the situation at Sparta when the herald from Sardis arrived asking them to come to the assistance of Crœsus, who was being besieged. And they notwithstanding their own difficulties, so soon as they
heard the news from the herald, were eager to assist him; but when they
had completed their preparations and their ships were ready, another message reported that the fortification of the Lydians had been taken and that
Crœsus had been made prisoner. Then (and not before) they ceased from
their efforts, being grieved at the great calamity.

84. Now the taking of Sardis came about as follows:—Fourteen days after Crœsus began to be besieged, Cyrus made proclamation to his army,
sending horsemen round, that he would reward the man who should first
scale the wall. After this the army made an attempt; and when it failed and
after all the rest had ceased from the attack, a certain Mardian whose
name was Hyroiades attempted to approach on that side of the citadel
where no guard had been set. They had no fear that it would ever be taken
from that side, seeing that here the citadel is precipitous and unassailable.
To this part of the wall alone Meles also, formerly king of Sardis, did not
carry round the lion which his concubine bore to him, although the
Telmessians judged that if the lion should be carried round the wall, Sardis
would be safe from capture. Meles having carried it round the rest of the
wall, that is to say those parts of the citadel where the fortress was open to
attack, passed over this part as being unassailable and precipitous. (This
is a part of the citadel which is turned [South] towards Tmolos). So then
this Mardian Hyroiades, having seen on the day before how one of the
Lydians had descended on that side of the citadel to recover his helmet
which had rolled down from above, and had picked it up, took thought and
put his mind to work. Then he himself ascended first, and after him came
up others of the Persians. Many having thus attacked, Sardis was finally
taken and the whole city was given up to plunder.

85. Meanwhile Crœsus himself experienced this:—He had a son, of
whom I made mention before, who was presentable enough but deprived of speech. Now in his former time of prosperity Crœsus had done
everything possible for him, and besides the rest he had also sent messengers to Delphi to inquire concerning him. And the Pythian prophetess spoke:

---

[*]Spartan sole survivors faced a difficult future; compare 7.229–231 and 9.71,
Aristodemos' story.

"Lydian, master of many, much blind to destiny, Crœsus,
 Do not desire to hear in thy halls that voice that is prayed for,
 Voice of thy son; much better if this from thee were removèd,
 Since he shall first utter speech in an evil day of misfortune."

Now when the fortress was being taken, one of the Persians was about to slay Crœsus taking him for another; and Crœsus for his part, seeing him coming, cared nothing because of the misfortune upon him, and to him it was irrelevant whether he should be slain by the stroke. But this voiceless son, when he saw the Persian coming on, by reason of terror and affliction burst into utterance and said: "Man, slay not Crœsus." This son, I say, uttered voice then first, but after this he continued to speak for the rest of his life.

86. The Persians then had obtained possession of Sardis[*] and had taken Crœsus himself prisoner, after he had reigned fourteen years and had been besieged fourteen days, having fulfilled the oracle in that he had brought to an end his own great empire. So the Persians having taken him brought him before Cyrus. He piled up a great pyre and mounted Crœsus upon it bound in fetters, and along with him twice seven sons of Lydians, whether it was that he meant to dedicate this offering as first-fruits of his victory to some god, or whether he desired to fulfil a vow, or else had heard that Crœsus was a god-fearing man and so caused him to ascend the pyre because he wished to know if any one of the divine powers would save him, so that he should not be burnt alive.[†] He, they say, did this; but to Crœsus as he stood upon the pyre there came, although he was in such a bad way, a memory of the saying of Solon, how he had said with divine inspiration that no one of the living might be called happy. And when this thought occurred, they say that he sighed deeply and groaned aloud, having for long been silent, and three times he uttered the name of Solon. Cyrus bade the interpreters ask Crœsus who was this person on whom he called; and they came near and asked. And Crœsus for a time, it is said, kept silence when he was asked this, but afterwards under coercion he said: "One whom beyond great wealth I should have desired to converse with all despots." Then, since his words were unreadable to them, they asked again. Since they were persistent and gave him no peace, he told how once Solon an Athenian had come, and having inspected all his wealth had scoffed at it, with such and such words; and how all had turned out for him as Solon had said, not speaking at all especially about Crœsus himself, but with a view to the whole human race and especially those who seem to themselves to be happy men.

And while Crœsus related these things, already the pyre was lighted and the edges of it round about were burning. Then they say that Cyrus, hearing from the interpreters what Crœsus had said, changed his purpose and considered that he himself also was but a man, and that he was

---

*Cyrus took Sardis in 546 B.C.
†One of many royal experiments; compare 2.2.

delivering another man, who had been not inferior to himself in felicity, alive to the fire; and moreover he feared the requital, and reflected that nothing that men possessed was secure; therefore, they say, he ordered them to extinguish as quickly as possible the fire that was burning, and to bring down Crœsus and those with him from the pyre. They although trying were not able now to master the flames.

87. Then it is related by the Lydians that Crœsus, having learned how Cyrus had changed his mind, and seeing that every one was trying to put out the fire but that they no longer could check it, cried aloud entreating Apollo that if any gift had ever been given by him acceptable to the god, he would come to his aid and rescue him from the evil which was now upon him.

So he with tears entreated the god, and suddenly, they say, after clear sky and calm weather clouds gathered and a storm burst, and it rained with a very violent shower, and the pyre was extinguished. Then Cyrus, having perceived that Crœsus was a lover of the gods and a good man, caused him to be brought down from the pyre and asked him: "Crœsus, tell me who of all men was it who persuaded you to march upon my land and so to become an enemy to me instead of a friend?" and he said: "King, I did this to your good fortune and to my own misfortune, and the causer of this was the god of the Hellenes, who incited me to march with my army. For no one is so senseless as to choose of his own will war rather than peace, since in peace the sons bury their fathers, but in war the fathers bury their sons.* But it was pleasing, I suppose, to the divine powers that these things should happen."

88. So he spoke, and Cyrus loosed his bonds and caused him to sit near himself and paid to him much regard, and he himself marvelled and all who were about him at the sight of Crœsus. And Crœsus wrapt in thought was silent; but after a time, turning round and seeing the Persians plundering the city of the Lydians, he said: "King, must I say to you what I happen to think, or must I keep silent in my present fortune?" Then Cyrus bade him say boldly whatsoever he desired; and he asked him: "What business is this great multitude of men doing with so much eagerness?" and he said: "They are plundering your city and carrying away the wealth." And Crœsus answered: "Neither is it my city that they are plundering nor my wealth which they are carrying away; for I have no longer any property in these things: but it is your wealth that they are carrying and driving away."

89. And Cyrus was engaged by what Crœsus had said, and he caused all the rest to withdraw and asked Crœsus what he discerned for his advantage in these events. He said: "Since the gods gave me to you as a slave, I think it right if I discern anything more than others to signify it to you. The Persians, who are by nature high-spirited are without wealth. If therefore you allow them to carry off plunder and possess great wealth, then expect this result: whosoever gets possession of the largest share will lead an insurrection against you. Now therefore, if what I say suits you, do this:—set spearmen

---

*It is a misperception to imagine that the Greeks glorified war at all times.

of your guard to guard all the gates, and let these take away the things, and say to the men bearing them out of the city that they must first be tithed for Zeus: and thus you on the one hand will not be hated by them for taking away the things by force, and they on the other will willingly let the things go, admitting that you are doing that which is just."

90. Hearing this Cyrus was above measure pleased, because he thought that Crœsus advised well; and he commended him much and commanded the spearmen of his guard to complete what Crœsus had advised. After that he spoke to Crœsus: "Crœsus, since you are prepared, like the king you are, to do good deeds and speak good words, ask me for a gift, whatsoever you desire to receive at once." And he said: "Master, you will do me the greatest pleasure if you permit me to send to the god of the Hellenes, whom I honoured most of all gods, these fetters, and to ask him whether it is accounted by him right to deceive those who do well to him."

Then Cyrus asked him what accusation he made against the god, that he thus requested; and Crœsus repeated to him all that had been in his mind and the answers of the Oracles, and especially the votive offerings, and how he had been incited by the prophecy to march upon the Persians. Eventually he came back again* to the request that it might be permitted to him to make this reproach against the god.

And Cyrus laughed and said: "Not this only shall you obtain from me, Crœsus, but also whatsoever you may desire of me at any time." Then Crœsus sent certain of the Lydians to Delphi, enjoining them to lay the fetters upon the threshold of the temple and to ask the god whether he felt no shame that he had incited Crœsus by his prophecies to march upon the Persians, persuading him that he should bring to an end the empire of Cyrus, seeing that *these* were the first-fruits of spoil which he had won from it,—at the same time pointing to the fetters. This they were to ask, and moreover also whether it was thought right by the gods of the Hellenes to practise ingratitude.

91. When the Lydians came and repeated their message, it is related that the Pythian prophetess responded: "The fated destiny it is impossible even for a god to escape. And Crœsus paid the debt due for the sin of his fifth ancestor, who being one of the spearmen of the Heracleidai driven by the treachery of a woman, and having slain his master took possession of his royal dignity, which did not properly belong to him. And although Loxias† eagerly desired that the calamity of Sardis might come upon the sons of Crœsus and not upon Crœsus himself, it was not possible for him to draw the Destinies aside from their course; but so much as these granted he brought to pass, and gave it as a gift to Crœsus. He put off the taking of Sardis for three years; and let Crœsus be assured that he was taken prisoner later by these years than the fated time. Secondly, he assisted him when he

---

*Herodotus often ends an incident just where he began—a feature of archaic and oral styles called "ring-composition."
†A Delphic name for Apollo.

was about to be burnt. And as to the oracle which was given, Crœsus finds fault without good ground. Loxias told him beforehand that if he should march upon the Persians he should destroy a great empire. After hearing this, if he wished to take counsel well, he ought to have sent and asked further whether the god meant his own empire or that of Cyrus. Since he did not comprehend that which was uttered and did not ask again, let him pronounce himself to be the cause of that which followed. To him also when he consulted the Oracle for the last time Loxias said concerning a mule; but this also he failed to comprehend. Cyrus was in fact this mule, seeing that he was born of parents who were of two different races, his mother being of nobler descent and his father of less noble. She was a Median woman, daughter of Astyages the king of the Medes, but he was a Persian, one of a race subject to the Medes, and being inferior in all respects he was the husband of his royal mistress."

Thus the Pythian prophetess replied to the Lydians, and they brought the answer back to Sardis and reported it to Crœsus; and he acknowledged that the fault was his own and not that of the god. With regard then to the empire of Crœsus and the first conquest of Ionia, it happened thus.

92. Now Hellas possesses many other votive offerings made by Crœsus and not only those which have been mentioned: at Thebes of the Bœotians there is a tripod of gold, which he dedicated to the Ismenian Apollo; then at Ephesos there are the golden cows and the greater number of the pillars of the temple; and in the temple of Athenē Pronaia at Delphi a large golden shield. These still remained down to my own time, but others of his votive offerings have perished. The votive offerings of Crœsus at Branchidai of the Milesians were, as I am told, equal in weight and similar to those at Delphi. Now those which he sent to Delphi and to the temple of Amphiaraos he dedicated of his own goods and as first-fruits of the wealth inherited from his father; but the other offerings were made from the substance of a man who was his foe, who before Crœsus became king had opposed him and had joined in endeavouring to make Pantaleon ruler of the Lydians. Now Pantaleon was a son of Alyattes and a brother of Crœsus, but not by the same mother, for Crœsus was born to Alyattes of a Carian woman, but Pantaleon of an Ionian. And when Crœsus had gained possession of the kingdom by the gift of his father, he put to death the man who opposed him, drawing him upon the carding-comb. He then offered in the manner mentioned to those shrines which have been named his property, which even before that time he had vowed to dedicate. About his votive offerings let so much suffice.

93. The land of Lydia has no great store of marvels to be recorded as compared with other lands,* excepting the gold-dust which is carried down from Tmolos. But it has one work to show which is larger far than any other except only those of Egypt and Babylon. There is there the sepulchral

---

*Herodotus returns to the promise of his preface in the first ethnographic section of his *Histories*.

monument of Alyattes the father of Crœsus, of which the base is made of large stones and the rest of the monument is of piled up earth. And this was built by contributions of the traders, the artisans, and the whores there. There still existed to my own time five boundary-stones erected upon the monument above, on which were carved inscriptions telling how much of the work was done by each class; and upon measurement it was found that the whores' work was the greatest. For the daughters of the common people in Lydia practise prostitution one and all, to gather for themselves dowries, continuing this until the time when they marry; and the girls give themselves away in marriage. Now the circuit of the monument is three thousand eight hundred feet, and the breadth is thirteen hundred feet. And adjoining the monument is a great lake, which the Lydians say has a never-failing supply of water, and it is called the lake of Gyges. Such is the nature of this monument.

94. Now the Lydians have very nearly the same customs as the Hellenes, with the exception that they prostitute their female children; and they were the first of men, so far as we know, who struck and used coin of gold or silver; and also they were the first retail-traders. And the Lydians themselves say that the games which are now in use among them and among the Hellenes were also their invention.

These they say were invented among them at the same time as they colonised Tyrsenia,* and this is their account:—In the reign of Atys the son of Manes their king a grievous dearth came over the whole of Lydia; and the Lydians for a time continued to endure it, but afterwards, as it did not cease, they sought for remedies; and one devised one thing and another another thing. And then were discovered, they say, the ways of playing with dice and the knucklebones and the ball, and all the other games excepting draughts (for the discovery of this last is not claimed by the Lydians). These games they invented in response to the famine, and thus they used to do:—on one of the days they would play games all the time in order that they might not feel the want of food, and on the next they ceased from their games and had food. They went on like that for eighteen years. As however the evil did not slacken but pressed upon them ever more, their king divided the whole Lydian people into two parts, and he appointed by lot one part to remain and the other to go forth from the land. The king appointed himself to be over that part which had the lot to stay in the land, and his son to be over that which was departing; and the name of his son was Tyrsenos. So the one party of them, having obtained the lot to go forth from the land, went down to the sea at Smyrna and built ships for themselves, wherein they placed all their movable goods and sailed away to seek for means of living and a land to dwell in. After passing by many nations they came at last to the land of the Ombricans.† There they

---

*Lydian electrum coinage is the oldest known; Tyrsenia is what the Romans called Etruria in northern Italy.
†That is, Umbria, to the east of Etruria.

founded cities and dwell up to the present time and changing their name
they were called after the king's son who led them out from home, not
Lydians but Tyrsenians, taking the name from him. The Lydians then had
been made subject to the Persians.

95. After this our history proceeds to inquire about Cyrus, who he was
who destroyed the empire of Crœsus, and about the Persians, in what manner they obtained the hegemony of Asia. Following then the report of
some of the Persians,—those I mean who do not desire to glorify the history of Cyrus but to tell the true tale,—according to their report, I say, I
shall write although I could set forth also three other forms of the story.

The Assyrians ruled Upper Asia* for five hundred and twenty years,
and from them the Medes were the first to revolt. These having fought for
their freedom with the Assyrians proved themselves good men, and thus
they threw off the yoke of slavery and freed themselves; and after them the
other nations also did the same as the Medes. When all on the continent
were thus independent, they returned again to despotic rule in this way.

96. There appeared among the Medes a man of ability whose name was
Deïokes, and this man was the son of Phraortes. This Deïokes, having de-
veloped a lust for despotic power, did thus:—whereas the Medes dwelt in
separate villages, he, being even before that time a respected man in his
own village, set himself to practise just dealing much more and with
greater zeal than before; and this he did although there was much lawlessness throughout the whole of Media, and although he knew that injustice
is ever an enemy of justice. And the Medes of the same village, seeing his
habits, chose him for their judge. So he, since he was wooing power, was
upright and just, and doing thus he had no little praise from his fellow-
citizens, so that those of the other villages learning that Deïokes was a
man who more than all others gave decision rightly, whereas before this
they had been wont to suffer from unjust judgments, themselves also when
they heard it came gladly to Deïokes to have their causes determined, and
at last they trusted no one else.

97. Then, as more and more continually kept coming to him, because
men learnt that his decisions proved to accord with the truth, Deïokes perceiving that everything was referred to himself refused to sit in the place
where he formerly used to sit in public to determine causes, and said that
he would determine causes no more, for it was not profitable for him to
neglect his own affairs and to determine causes for his neighbours all day.
So then, since robbery and lawlessness prevailed even much more in the
villages than they did before, the Medes having assembled together considered with one another and spoke about the state in which they were:
and I suppose the friends of Deïokes spoke mostly to this effect: "Seeing

*Herodotus means the regions further inland than the coasts of the Mediter-
ranean. The Assyrians ruled longer than he notes here, from c.1400 to 612 B.C.,
the fall of Nineveh.

that we are not able to dwell in the land under the present order of things, let us set up a king from among ourselves, and thus the land will be well governed and we ourselves shall turn to labour, and shall not be ruined by lawlessness." By some such words as these they persuade themselves to have a king.

98. And when they at once proposed the question, whom they should set up to be king, Deïokes was repeatedly put forward and commended by every one, until at last they agreed that he should be their king.* And he bade them build for him a palace worthy of the royal dignity and strengthen him with a guard of spearmen. And the Medes did so. They built him a large and strong palace in that part of the land which he told them, and they allowed him to select spearmen from all the Medes. And when he had obtained the rule over them, he compelled the Medes to make one fortified city and pay chief attention to this, having less regard to the other cities. And as the Medes obeyed him in this also, he built large and strong walls, those which are now called Agbatana,† standing in concentric circles one within the other. And this wall is so contrived that one circle is higher than the next by the height of the battlements alone. And to some extent, I suppose, the nature of the ground, seeing that it is on a hill, assists towards this end; but much more was it produced by art. The circles are in all seven in number, and within the last circle are the royal palace and the treasure-houses. The largest of these walls is in size about equal to the circuit of the wall round Athens;‡ and of the first circle the battlements are white, of the second black, of the third crimson, of the fourth blue, of the fifth red: thus are the battlements of all the circles coloured with various tints, and the two last have their battlements overlaid one of them with silver and the other with gold.

99. These walls then Deïokes built for himself and round his own palace, and the people he commanded to dwell round about the wall. And after all was built, Deïokes established the rule, which he was the first to establish, ordaining that none should enter into the presence of the king, but they should deal with him always through messengers; and that the king should be seen by no one; and moreover that to laugh or to spit in his presence is unseemly, and this last for every one at all times. Now he surrounded himself with this pomp and state to the end that his fellows, who had been brought up with him and were of no meaner family nor behind him in manly virtue, might not be irritated by seeing him and make plots against him, but that being unseen by them he might be thought made from a different mould.

100. Having set these things in order and strengthened himself in his despotism, he was severe in preserving justice; and the people used to write down their causes and send them in to his presence, and he determined

---

*Deïokes was king of the Medes c.709 b.c.

†"Place of gathering," if this is Ekbatana, later Hamadan; in any case, the facts have been embellished.

‡Just under 7 miles, in that case.

the questions which were brought in to him and sent them out again. Thus he used to determine judgment of causes; and he also set in order this: if he heard that any one was behaving in an arrogant manner, he sent for him and punished him according as each act of wrong deserved, and he had watchers and listeners throughout all the land he ruled.

101. Deïokes then united the Median race alone, and was ruler. These are the tribes of the Medes: Busai, Paretakenians, Struchates, Arizantians, Budians, Magians: the tribes of the Medes are six in number.

102. Now the son of Deïokes was Phraortes, who when Deïokes was dead, having been king for three-and-fifty years, received the power in succession; and having received it he was not satisfied to be ruler of the Medes alone, but marched upon the Persians; and attacking them first before others, he made these first subject to the Medes. After this, being ruler of these two nations and both of them strong, he proceeded to subdue Asia going from one nation to another, until at last he marched against the Assyrians who dwelt at Nineveh, and who formerly had been rulers of the whole. At that time they were left without support because their allies had revolted from them, though at home they were prosperous. Phraortes marched against these, and was both himself slain, after he had reigned two-and-twenty years, and the greater part of his army was destroyed.

103. When Phraortes had brought his life to an end, Kyaxares* the son of Phraortes, the son of Deïokes, received the power. This king is said to have been yet much more warlike than his forefathers; and he first banded the men of Asia into separate divisions, that is to say, he first arrayed apart from one another the spearmen and the archers and the horsemen, for before that time they were all mingled together. This ruler fought with the Lydians when the day became night as they fought, and he also united under his rule the whole of Asia above or east of the river Halys. And having gathered together all his subjects he marched upon Nineveh to avenge his father, and also because he desired to conquer that city. And when he had fought a battle with the Assyrians and had defeated them, while he was settling into siege before Nineveh there came upon him a great army of Scythians, and their leader was Madyas the son of Protothyas, king of the Scythians. These had invaded Asia after driving the Kimmerians out of Europe, and in pursuit of them as they fled they had come to the land of Media.

104. Now from the Maiotian lake to the river Phasis and to the land of the Colchians is a journey of thirty days for an unencumbered traveller; and from Colchis it is not far to pass over to Media, for there is only one nation between them, the Saspeirians, and passing by this nation you are in Media. However the Scythians did not make their invasion by this way, but turned aside from it to go by the upper road, east of the Euxine Sea, which is much longer, keeping Mount Caucasus on their right hand. Then the Medes fought with the Scythians, and having been worsted in the battle they lost their power, and the Scythians ruled over all Asia. **105.** Thence

---

*He became king in 634 B.C.

they went on to invade Egypt; and when they were in Syrian Palestine, Psammetichos king of Egypt met them; and by gifts and entreaties he turned them from their purpose, so that they should not advance any further. As they retreated, when they came to the city of Ascalon in Syria, most of the Scythians passed through without doing any damage, but a few stayed behind and plundered the temple of Aphroditē Urania.* Now this temple, as I find by inquiry, is the most ancient of all temples which belong to this goddess; for the temple in Cyprus was founded from this, as the people of Cyprus themselves report, and it was the Phenicians who founded the temple in Kythera, coming from this land of Syria. These Scythians who had plundered the temple at Ascalon, and their descendants for ever, were smitten by the divinity with a woman's disease. The Scythians say that is why they were diseased, and that for this reason travellers who visit Scythia now, see among them the affliction of those who by Scythians are called *Enareës*.

106. For eight-and-twenty years then the Scythians were rulers of Asia, and by their aggression and reckless behaviour everything was ruined; for they exacted that amount of tribute from each people which they laid upon them, and apart from the tribute they rode about and carried off by force the possessions of each tribe. Then Kyaxares with the Medes, having invited the greater number of them to a banquet, made them drunk and slew them; and thus the Medes recovered their power, and had rule over the same nations as before; and they also took Nineveh,—the manner how it was taken I shall set forth in another history,†—and made the Assyrians subject to them excepting only the land of Babylon.

107. After this Kyaxares died, having reigned forty years including those years during which the Scythians had rule, and Astyages son of Kyaxares received from him the kingdom.‡

To him was born a daughter whom he named Mandanē; and in his sleep it seemed to him that she pissed urine enough to fill his city and also to flood the whole of Asia. This dream he delivered to the Magian interpreters of dreams, and when he heard from them the truth at each point he became afraid. And afterwards when this Mandanē was of an age to have a husband, he did not give her in marriage to any one of the Medes who were his peers, because he feared the vision; but he gave her to a Persian named Cambyses, whom he found to be of good descent and of a quiet disposition, counting him to be in station much below a Mede of middle rank.

108. And when Mandanē was married to Cambyses, in the first year Astyages saw another vision. It seemed to him that from the womb of this daughter a vine grew, and this vine overspread the whole of Asia. Having seen this vision and delivered it to the interpreters of dreams, he sent for

---

*The Philistine goddess Atargatis.

†Here and in 1.184 Herodotus refers to accounts that do not exist in any extant texts of his *Histories*.

‡Astyages became king in 594 B.C.

his daughter, being then with child, to come from the land of the Persians. And when she had come he kept watch over her, desiring to destroy whatever was born; for the Magian interpreters of dreams signified to him that the offspring of his daughter should be king in his place.

Astyages then desiring to guard against this, when Cyrus was born, called Harpagos, a man who was kin and whom he trusted above all the other Medes, the manager of all his affairs. To him he said: "Neglect not by any means, Harpagos, the matter which I command you to do, and beware lest you put me at risk and choosing the advantage of others instead, bring yourself afterwards to destruction. Take the child which Mandanē bore, and carry it to your house and slay it; and afterwards bury it however you yourself choose." To this he made answer: "King, never yet at any past time did you discern in me an offence against you, and I keep watch over myself also with a view to the time that comes after, that I may not wrong you. If it is indeed your pleasure that this be done, my service at least must be properly rendered."

109. Thus he replied, and when the child had been delivered to him adorned as for death, Harpagos went weeping to his house. And he related to his wife all Astyages' words. And she said to him: "Now, therefore, what do you intend to do?" and he replied: "Not according as Astyages enjoined: for not even if he becomes more deranged and more mad than he now is, will I agree to his will or serve him in such a murder as this. I will not slay the child for many reasons; first because he is akin to me, and then because Astyages is old and without male issue, and if after he is dead the power shall come to this his daughter, whose son he is now desiring to slay through me, does not the greatest of dangers then await me? To secure me, this child must die; but one of the servants of Astyages must be the slayer of it, and not one of mine."

110. Thus he spoke, and at once sent a messenger to a herdsman of Astyages who he knew fed his herds on the pastures most suitable for his purpose, in fact on the mountains most haunted by wild beasts. The name of this man was Mitradates, and he was married to a fellow-slave; and the name of the woman to whom he was married was Kyno in the tongue of the Hellenes and in the Median tongue Spaco, for what the Hellenes call *kyna* (bitch) the Medes call *spaca*. On the skirts of the mountains this herdsman had his cattle-pastures, from Agbatana towards the North and towards the Euxine Sea. For here in the direction of the Saspeirians the Median land is very mountainous and lofty and thickly covered with forests; but the rest of the land of Media is all level plain. So when this herdsman came, being summoned urgently, Harpagos said: "Astyages bids you take this child and place it on the most desolate part of the mountains, so that it may perish as quickly as possible. And he bade me say to you that if you do not kill it, but in any way preserve it from death, he will kill you with the nastiest torture. I have been appointed to oversee that the child is laid out."

111. Having heard this and having taken up the child, the herdsman went back by the way he came, and arrived at his dwelling. And his wife also, as it seems, having been every day on the point of bearing a child, by a providential chance gave birth just at that time, when the herdsman was gone to the city. And both were in anxiety, each for the other, the man having fear about the child-bearing of his wife, and the woman wondering why Harpagos had sent to summon her husband, not having done so often before. So as soon as he returned and stood before her, the woman seeing him again beyond her hopes was the first to speak, and asked him for what purpose Harpagos had sent for him so urgently. And he said: "Wife, when I came to the city I saw and heard that which I ought not have seen, and which I wish had never chanced to those whom we serve. For the house of Harpagos was all full of mourning, and I being astonished thereat went in. As soon as I entered I saw laid out to view an infant child gasping for breath and screaming, which was adorned with gold ornaments and embroidered clothing. When Harpagos saw me he bade me at once take up the child and carry it away and lay it on that part of the mountains which is most haunted by wild beasts, saying that it was Astyages who laid this task upon me, and making many threats, if I should fail to do this. And I took it up and bore it away, supposing that it was the child of some one of the servants of the house, for never could I have supposed whence it really was. I marvelled to see it adorned with gold and raiment, and I marvelled also because mourning was made for it openly in the house of Harpagos. And straightway as we went by the road, I learnt the whole matter from the servant who went with me out of the city and placed in my hands the babe, namely that it was in truth the son of Mandanē the daughter of Astyages, and of Cambyses the son of Cyrus, and that Astyages ordered the killing. And now here it is."

112. And as he said this the herdsman uncovered it and showed it to her. And she, seeing that the child was large and of fair form, wept and clung to the knees of her husband, beseeching him by no means to lay it forth. But he said that he could not do otherwise than so, for watchers would lurk everywhere sent by Harpagos to see that this was done, and he would perish by a dreadful death if he should fail to do this. And as she could not after all persuade her husband, the wife next said: "Since then I am unable to persuade you not to expose it, do this which I say, if indeed it needs to be seen laid out for burial. I also have borne a child, but I have borne it dead. Take this and expose it, and let us rear the child of the daughter of Astyages as if it were our own. Thus you will not be found out doing a wrong to those whom we serve, nor shall we have taken ill counsel for ourselves; for the dead child will obtain a royal burial and the surviving one will not lose his life."

113. To the herdsman it seemed that, the situation standing thus, his wife spoke well, and immediately he did so. The child which he was bearing to put to death, this he delivered to his wife, and his own, which was dead, he took and placed in the chest in which he had been bearing the other; and having adorned it with all the adornment of the other child, he bore it to the most desolate part of the mountains and placed it there. And when the third day came after the child had been laid out, the herdsman

went to the city, leaving one of his under-herdsmen to watch there, and when he came to the house of Harpagos he said that he was ready to display the dead body of the child; and Harpagos sent the most trusted of his spearmen, and through them he saw and buried the herdsman's child. This body then had burial, but him who was afterwards called Cyrus the wife of the herdsman had received and was bringing him up, giving him no doubt some other name, not Cyrus.

114. And when the boy was ten years old, this event happened to him and made him known. He was playing in the village in which were stalls for these oxen, with other boys of his age in the road. And the boys in their play chose as their king this one who was called the son of the herdsman. He set some of them to build palaces and others to be spearmen of his guard, and one of them no doubt he appointed to be the eye of the king, and to one he gave the office of bearing the messages,* appointing work for each one. Now one of these boys who was playing with the rest, the son of Artembares a man of repute among the Medes, did not do that which Cyrus appointed him to do; therefore Cyrus bade the other boys seize him hand and foot, and when they obeyed his command he dealt with the boy very roughly, scourging him. But he, so soon as he was let go, being made much more angry because he considered that he had been treated abusively, went down to the city and complained to his father of the treatment which he had met with from Cyrus, calling him not Cyrus, for this was not yet his name, but the son of the herdsman of Astyages. And Artembares in the anger of the moment went at once to Astyages, taking the boy with him; and he declared that he had suffered shocking things and said: "King, by your slave, the son of a herdsman, we have been thus insulted and injured," showing him the shoulders of his son.

115. And Astyages having heard and seen this, wished to punish the boy to avenge the honour of Artembares, and sent for both the herdsman and his son. And when both were present, Astyages looked at Cyrus and said: "Did you dare, being the son of so mean a father as this, to insult outrageously the son of this man who is first in my favour?" And he replied: "Master, I did so to him with right. For the boys of the village, of whom he was one, in their play set me up as king over them, for I appeared to them most fitted for this place. Now the other boys did what was commanded them, but this one disobeyed and paid no regard, until at last he received the due punishment. If therefore for this I am worthy to suffer any penalty, here I stand before you."

116. While the boy spoke, there came upon Astyages a sense of recognition of him, and the lineaments of his face seemed to him to resemble his own, and his answer appeared to be somewhat over free for his station, while the time of the laying forth seemed to agree with the age of the boy. Being struck with amazement by these things, for a time he was speechless. He finally recovered himself with difficulty. He said, desiring

---

*At 1.120 and 3.84 we find other references to this Persian chamberlain's office.

to dismiss Artembares, in order that he might get the herdsman by himself alone and examine him: "Artembares, I will so order these things that you and your son shall not find fault;" and so he dismissed Artembares. The servants upon the command of Astyages led Cyrus within. And when the herdsman was left alone with the king, Astyages being alone with him asked whence he had received the boy, and who it was who had delivered the boy to him. And the herdsman said that he was his own son, and that the mother was living with him still as his wife. But Astyages said that he was not well advised in desiring to be tortured, and as he said this he signaled to the spearmen of his guard to seize him. So he, as he was being led away to the torture, then declared the true story; and beginning from the beginning he went through the whole, telling the truth about it, and finally ended with entreaties, asking that he would grant him pardon.

117. So when the herdsman had made known the truth, Astyages now was unconcerned about him, but with Harpagos he was very greatly displeased and bade his spearmen summon him. And when Harpagos came, Astyages asked him: "By what death, Harpagos, did you destroy the child whom I delivered to you, born of my daughter?" Harpagos, seeing that the herdsman was in the king's palace, turned not to any false way of speech, lest he should be convicted and found out, but said: "King, so soon as I received the child, I thought about how I should do according to your wish, and how without offence to your command I might not be guilty of murder against your daughter and against yourself. I did therefore thus:—I called this herdsman and delivered the child to him, saying first that you were he who ordered him to slay it—and in this at least I did not lie, for you did so command. I delivered it to this man commanding him to place it upon a desolate mountain, and to stay by it and watch it until it should die, threatening him with all kinds of punishment if he should fail to accomplish this. And when he had done that which was ordered and the child was dead, I sent the most trusted of my eunuchs and through them I saw and buried the child. Thus, O king, it happened, and the child met this unnatural death.

118. So Harpagos declared the truth, and Astyages concealed the anger which he kept against him for that outcome. First he related the matter over again to Harpagos as the herdsman confessed it, and afterwards, when it had been thus repeated by him. He ended by saying that the child was alive and that the outcome pleased him. "I was greatly troubled by what was done to this child, and I thought it hardly trivial that I had fallen out with my daughter. Therefore consider that this is a happy change of fortune, and first send your son to be with the boy who is newly come, and then, seeing that I intend to make a sacrifice of thanksgiving for the preservation of the boy to those gods to whom that honour belongs, come yourself to dine with me."

119. When Harpagos heard this, he did reverence and thought it a great matter that his offence had turned out for his profit and moreover that he had been invited to dinner for the wonderful good fortune. He went to his house, and having entered it he at once sent forth his son, for he had only one son of about thirteen years old, bidding him go to the palace of Astyages and do whatever the king should command. He himself being overjoyed told his wife what had befallen him.

Astyages, when the son of Harpagos arrived, cut his throat and divided him limb from limb, and having roasted some pieces of the flesh and boiled others he caused them to be dressed for eating and kept them ready. And when the time arrived for dinner and the others guests were present and also Harpagos, then before the other guests and before Astyages himself were placed tables covered with flesh of sheep; but before Harpagos was placed the flesh of his own son, all but the head and the hands and the feet, and these were laid aside covered up in a basket.

Then when it seemed that Harpagos had eaten enough food, Astyages asked him whether he had been pleased with the banquet; and when Harpagos said that he had been very greatly pleased, appointed servants brought to him the head of his son covered up, together with the hands and the feet; and standing near they bade Harpagos uncover and take of them that which he desired.

When Harpagos obeyed and uncovered, he saw the remains of his son; and seeing them he did not fall apart but contained himself. Astyages asked him whether he perceived of what animal he had been eating the flesh. He said that he perceived, and that whatsoever the king might do was pleasing to him. After answering and having taken up the parts of the flesh which still remained he went to his house; and after that, I suppose, he intended to gather all the parts together and bury them.

120. On Harpagos Astyages laid this penalty; and about Cyrus he took thought, and summoned the same men of the Magians who had given judgment about his dream in the manner which has been said. Astyages asked them how they had given judgment about his vision; and they spoke as before, saying that the child must have become king if he had lived on and had not died before. He made answer to them thus: "The child is alive and not dead. While he was dwelling in the country, the boys of the village appointed him king; and he performed completely all those things which they do who are really kings; for he exercised rule, appointing spearmen of the guard and doorkeepers and bearers of messages and all else. Now therefore, to what does it seem to you that these things tend?" The Magians said: "If the child is still alive and became king without any arrangement, be confident concerning him and have good courage, for he shall not be ruler again the second time; since some even of our oracles have had but small results,* and that at least which has to do with dreams comes often in the end to a feeble accomplishment."

Astyages responded: "I myself also, Magians, am most disposed to believe that you are right, namely that since the boy was named king the dream has had its fulfilment and that this boy is no longer a source of

*Note Herodotus' sly critique of the idea that prophecy cannot be proved false.

danger to me. Nevertheless counsel me, having well considered what is likely to be most safe both for my house and for you." The Magians said: "To us also, King, it is crucial that your rule should stand firm; for in the other case it is transferred to strangers, coming round to this boy who is a Persian, and we Medes are made slaves and become insignificant in the eyes of the Persians, seeing that we are of different race. But while you are established as our king, one of our own nation, we both have our share of rule and receive great honours from you. Thus then we must by all means look out for you and your rule. And now, if we saw in this anything to cause fear, we would declare all to you beforehand. Since the dream has had its issue in a trifling matter, both we ourselves are of good cheer and we exhort you to be so likewise. Send this boy away from your eyes to the Persians and to his parents."

121. When he heard this Astyages rejoiced, and calling Cyrus spoke to him: "My son, I did you wrong by reason of a vision in a dream which has not come to pass, but you are yet alive by your own destiny; now therefore go in peace to the land of the Persians, and I will send men to conduct you. When you arrive, you shall find a father and a mother different from Mitradates the herdsman and his wife."

122. Thus Astyages sent Cyrus away; and when he had returned and come to the house of Cambyses, his parents received him; and after that, when they learnt who he was, they welcomed him with joy, for they had supposed without doubt that their son had perished right after his birth; and they inquired how he had survived. And he told them, saying that before this he had not known but had been utterly misinformed; on the way, however, he had learnt all his own fortunes. He had supposed without doubt that he was the son of the herdsman of Astyages, but since his journey from the city began he had learnt the whole story from those who conducted him. And he said that he had been brought up by the wife of the herdsman, and continued to praise her throughout, so that Kyno was the chief person in his tale. And his parents took up this name from him, and in order that their son might be thought by the Persians to have been preserved in some supernatural manner, they spread a report that Cyrus when he was exposed had been reared by a bitch.[*] From that source has come this report.

123. Then as Cyrus grew to be a man, the most courageous and the best beloved of all those of his age, Harpagos sought to become his friend and sent him gifts, because he desired to take vengeance on Astyages. For he saw not how from himself, who was in a private station, punishment should come upon Astyages; but when he saw Cyrus growing up, he endeavoured to make him an ally, finding a likeness between the misfortunes of Cyrus and his own. And even before that time he had effected something; for Astyages being harsh towards the Medes, Harpagos communicated severally with the chief men of the Medes, and persuaded them that

*See 1.110 for the origin of this rationalizing account.

they must make Cyrus their leader and cause Astyages to cease from being king. When he had effected this and all was ready, then Harpagos wishing to make known his design to Cyrus, who lived among the Persians, could do it in no other way, seeing that the roads were watched, but devised this scheme:—he made ready a hare, and having cut open its belly but without pulling off any of the fur, he put into it, just as it was, a piece of paper, having written upon it his proposals. Then he sewed up again the belly of the hare, and giving nets as if he were a hunter to that one of his servants whom he trusted most, he sent him away to the land of the Persians, enjoining him by word of mouth to give the hare to Cyrus, and to tell him at the same time to cut it up with his own hands and let no one else be present when he did so.

124. Cyrus having received from him the hare, cut it open; and having found within it the paper he read it over. And the writing said: "Son of Cambyses, over you the gods keep guard, for otherwise you would never have come to so much good fortune. Therefore take vengeance on Astyages your murderer, for so far as his will is concerned you are dead, but by the care of the gods and of me you are still alive. I think that you have long ago learnt this from first to last, both how it happened, and also what I have suffered from Astyages, because I did not kill you but gave you to the herdsman. If therefore you will be guided by me, you shall be ruler of all that land which now Astyages rules. Persuade the Persians to revolt, and march an army against the Medes. Whether I shall be appointed leader of the army against you, or any other of the Medes who are in repute, you have what you desire; for these will be the first to attempt to destroy Astyages, revolting from him and coming over to your side. Consider then that here at least all is ready, and therefore do this and do it with speed."

125. Cyrus having heard this began to consider how he might most efficiently persuade the Persians to revolt, and on consideration he found that this was the most convenient way:—He wrote first on a paper that which he desired to write, and he made an assembly of the Persians. Then he unfolded the paper and reading from it said that Astyages appointed him commander of the Persians; "and now, Persians," he continued, "I command you to come to me each one with a reaping-hook." Cyrus then proclaimed this command. (Now there are of the Persians many tribes, and some of them Cyrus gathered together and persuaded to revolt from the Medes, namely these, upon which all the other Persians depend, the Pasargadai, the Maraphians and the Maspians, and of these the Pasargadai are the most noble, of whom also the Achaimenidai are a clan, whence are sprung the Perseïd kings. But other Persian tribes there are, as follows:— the Panthaliaians, the Derusiaians and the Germanians, these are all tillers of the soil; and the rest are nomad tribes, namely the Daoi, Mardians, Dropicans and Sagartians.)

126. Now there was a certain region of the Persian land which was overgrown with thorns, extending some two to two and a quarter miles in each direction; and when all had come as commanded, Cyrus ordered them to clear this region for cultivation within one day. When the Persians had achieved the task proposed, then he bade them come to him on the next day bathed and clean. Meanwhile Cyrus, having gathered together in one place all the flocks of goats and sheep and the herds of cattle belonging to his father, slaughtered them and prepared with them to entertain the host of the Persians, and moreover with wine and other provisions of the most agreeable kind. So when the Persians came on the next day, he had them recline in a meadow and feasted them. And when they had finished dinner, Cyrus asked them whether that which they had on the former day or that which they had now seemed to them preferable. They said that the difference between them was great, for the former day had for them nothing but unpleasantness, and the present day nothing but good. Taking up this response Cyrus proceeded to lay bare his whole design: "Men of the Persians, this is your choice. If you do as I say, you have these and ten thousand other good things, with no servile labour; but if you don't do as I say, you have endless labours like that of yesterday. Now therefore do as I say and make yourselves free; for I seem to have been born by providential fortune to take these matters in hand; and I expect that you are not worse men than the Medes, either in other matters or in war. Since that is the situation, revolt now from Astyages."

127. So the Persians having obtained a leader willingly attempted to set themselves free, since they had already for a long time resented being ruled by the Medes. When Astyages heard that Cyrus was acting thus, he sent a messenger and summoned him. Cyrus bade the messenger report to Astyages that he would be with him sooner than he would himself desire. So Astyages hearing this armed all the Medes, and in his infatuation he appointed Harpagos to command the army, forgetting what he had done to him. Then when the Medes had marched out and began to fight with the Persians, some continued the battle, namely those who had no share in the plot, while others went over to the Persians; but the greater number were wilfully slack and fled.

128. So the Median army had been shamefully dispersed, but as soon as Astyages heard of it he said, threatening Cyrus: "But not even so shall Cyrus at least escape punishment." First he impaled the Magian interpreters of dreams who had persuaded him to let Cyrus go, and then he armed those of the Medes, youths and old men, who had been left behind in the city. These he led out and having engaged battle with the Persians he was worsted, and Astyages himself was taken alive, and he lost also those Medes whom he had led forth.

129. Then when Astyages was a prisoner, Harpagos came and stood near him and rejoiced over him and insulted him; and besides other things he said to pain his heart, he asked him especially how it pleased him to be a slave instead of a king, making reference to [the retribution for] that dinner at which Astyages had feasted him with the flesh of his own son.* He

---

*Balancing rights and wrongs is thematic in the *Histories,* see, for example, 8.104–106.

looking at him asked him in return whether he claimed the work of Cyrus
as his own deed. Harpagos said that since he had written the letter, the
deed was justly his. Then Astyages declared him to be at the same time
the most maladroit and the most unjust of men; the most maladroit
because, when it was in his power to become king (as it was, if the current
affair was really brought about by him), he had conferred the chief power
on another, and the most unjust, because on account of that dinner he had
reduced the Medes to slavery. For if he must needs confer the kingdom on
some other and not keep it himself, it was more just to give this good thing
to a Mede rather than a Persian; whereas now the Medes, who were guiltless of this, had become slaves instead of masters, and the Persians who
formerly were slaves of the Medes had now become their masters.*

130. Astyages then, having been king for five-and-thirty years, was thus
dethroned; and the Medes stooped under the yoke of the Persians because
of his cruelty, after they had ruled Asia above the river Halys for one hundred and twenty-eight years, except while the Scythians ruled. Afterwards
however they regretted that they had done this, and they revolted from
Dareios, and they were subdued again, being conquered in a battle. At this
time then, in the reign of Astyages, the Persians with Cyrus rose up against
the Medes and from that time forth were rulers of Asia. Cyrus did no
further harm to Astyages, but kept him with himself until he died. Thus
born and bred Cyrus became king; and after this he subdued Crœsus, who
was the first to begin the quarrel, as I have before said; and having subdued him he became ruler of all Asia.

131. These are the customs, so far as I know, which the Persians
practise:†—Images and temples and altars they do not consider it lawful to
erect, nay they even charge with folly those who do these things; and this,
as it seems to me, because they do not account the gods to be in the likeness of men, as do the Hellenes. But they perform sacrifices to Zeus going
up to the most lofty of the mountains, and the whole circle of the heavens
they call Zeus. They sacrifice to the Sun and the Moon and the Earth, to
Fire and to Water and to the Winds. These are the only gods to whom they
have sacrificed ever from the first; but they have learnt also to sacrifice to
Aphroditē Urania, having learnt it both from the Assyrians and the Arabians; and the Assyrians call Aphroditē Mylitta, the Arabians Alitta, and
the Persians Mitra. **132.** Now this is the manner of sacrifice for the gods established among the Persians:—they make no altars neither do they kindle fire; and when they mean to sacrifice they use no libation nor music of
the pipe nor chaplets nor barley-meal for sprinkling;‡ but when a man

*Cyrus became king in 559 B.C.
†Anthropology follows history, as in the organization of the Lydian section or
history, which Herodotus calls a *logos;* compare 1.93–94.
‡In contrast to the Hellenes; for example, fillets of wool were tied around the
heads of Hellenic priests.

wishes to sacrifice to any one of the gods, he leads the animal for sacrifice to an unpolluted place and calls upon the god, having his *tiara,* a Persian hat, wreathed round generally with myrtle. For himself alone separately the man who sacrifices may not request good things in his prayer, but he prays that it may be well with all the Persians and with the king; for he himself also is included of course in the whole body of Persians. And when he has cut up the victim into pieces and boiled the flesh, he spreads a layer of the freshest grass and especially clover, upon which he places immediately all the pieces of flesh; and when he has placed them in order, a Magian man stands by them and chants over them a theogony (for such they say that their incantation is), seeing that without a Magian it is not lawful for them to make sacrifices. Then after waiting a short time the sacrificer carries away the flesh and uses it for whatever he pleases.

133. And of all days they honour most that on which they were born. They think it right on this day to set out a feast more liberal than on other days; and in this feast the wealthier of them set upon the table an ox or a horse or a camel or an ass, roasted whole in an oven, and the poor among them set out small animals in the same way. They have few courses, but many served up after as dessert, and these not in a single course. The Persians say that the Hellenes leave dinner hungry, because after dinner they have nothing worth mentioning served up as dessert, whereas if any good dessert were served up they would not stop eating so soon. They very much enjoy wine-drinking, and it is not permitted to a man to vomit or to make water in presence of another. Thus do they taboo these things. They are wont to deliberate when drinking hard about the most important of their affairs, and whatever conclusion has pleased them, this on the next day, when they are sober, the master of the house where they happen to deliberate lays before them for discussion. If it pleases them when they are sober also, they adopt it, but if it does not please them, they let it go. Whatever they have had the first deliberation on when they are sober, they consider again when they are drinking.

134. When they meet one another in the roads, you may discern whether those who meet are of equal rank by this etiquette;—for instead of greeting by words they kiss one another on the mouth; but if one of them is a little inferior, they kiss one another on the cheeks, and if one is of much less noble rank than the other, he falls down before him and prostrates himself. And they honour most after themselves those nations which dwell nearest to them, and next those which dwell next nearest, and so they go on giving honour in proportion to distance; and they hold least in honour those who dwell furthest off from themselves, esteeming themselves to be by far the best of all the human race in every point, and thinking that others possess merit according to the proportion which is here stated, and that those who dwell furthest from themselves are the worst. And under the supremacy of the Medes the various nations used also to govern one another according to the same rule as the Persians observe in giving respect, the Medes governing the whole and in particular those who dwelt nearest to themselves, and these having rule over those who bordered upon them, and those again over the nations that were next to them. Each nation went forward thus ever from government by themselves to government through others.

135. The Persians more than any other men admit foreign usages; for they both wear the Median dress judging it to be more comely than their own, and also for fighting they wear the Egyptian corslet. Moreover they adopt all kinds of luxuries when they hear of them, and in particular they have learnt from the Hellenes to have sex with boys. Everyone marries several lawful wives, and they get also a much larger number of concubines. **136.** It is established as a sign of manly excellence next after excellence in fight, to be able to show many sons; and to those who have most the king sends gifts every year because they consider big numbers to be a source of strength. And they educate their children, beginning at five years old and going on till twenty, in three things only, in riding, in shooting, and in speaking the truth. Before the boy is five years old he does not come into the presence of his father, but lives with the women; and it is so done for this reason, that if the child should die while he is being brought up, he may not cause any grief to his father.

137. I commend this custom of theirs, and also the one next to be mentioned, namely that neither the king himself shall put any to death for one cause alone, nor any of the other Persians for one cause alone shall do hurt that is irremediable to any of his own servants; but if after reckoning he find that the wrongs done are more in number and greater than the services rendered,[*] then only he gives vent to his anger. Moreover they say that no one ever killed his own father or mother, but whatever deeds have been done which seemed to be of this nature, if examined must necessarily, they say, be found to be due either to changelings or to children of adulterous birth; for, say they, it is not reasonable to suppose that the true parent would be killed by his own son.

138. Whatever things it is not lawful for them to do, these it is not lawful for them even to speak of. The most disgraceful thing in their estimation is to tell a lie, and next to this to owe money, this last for many other reasons, but especially because it is necessary, they say, for him who owes money, also sometimes to tell lies. If one of the men of the city has leprosy or whiteness of skin, he does not come into a city nor mingle with the other Persians; and they say that he has these diseases because he has offended in some way against the Sun. If a stranger is taken by these diseases, in many regions they drive him out of the country altogether, and also white doves, alleging against them the same cause. And into a river they neither piss nor spit, neither do they wash their hands in it, nor allow any other to do these things, but they reverence rivers very greatly.

139. This moreover also has happened to them, which the Persians have themselves failed to notice but not I:—their names,[†] which are formed to

---

[*]This Persian calculus will save Sandokes at 7.194.

[†]Herodotus' remarks are incorrect and even inconsistent; see 6.98. Persian names for males end in a sibilant in Greek, but not all do so in Persian.

correspond with their bodily shapes or their magnificence of station, all
end with the same letter, which the Dorians call *san* and the Ionians *sigma;*
with this you will find, if you examine the matter, that all the Persian
names end, not some but all alike.

140. So much I am able to say for certain from my own knowledge
about them. What follows is reported about their dead as a secret mystery
and not with clearness, namely that the body of a Persian man is not
buried until it has been torn by a bird or a dog.[*] (The Magians I know for
a certainty have this practise, for they do it openly.) However that may be,
the Persians cover the body with wax and then bury it in the earth. Now the
Magians are distinguished in many ways from other men, as also from the
priests in Egypt. These last esteem it a matter of purity to kill no living
creature except the animals which they sacrifice; but the Magians kill with
their own hands all creatures except dogs and men, and they even make
this a great end to aim at, killing both ants and serpents and all other
creeping and flying things. About this custom then let it be as it was established from the first; and I return now to the former narrative.[†]

141. The Ionians and Aiolians, so soon as the Lydians had been subdued by the Persians, sent messengers to Cyrus at Sardis, desiring to be his
subjects on the same terms as they had with Crœsus. And when he heard
that which they proposed to him, he spoke to them a fable, saying that a
certain player on the pipe saw fishes in the sea and played on his pipe, supposing that they would come out to land; but being mistaken in his expectation, he took a casting-net and enclosed a great multitude of the fishes
and drew them forth from the water. When he saw them leaping about, he
said to the fishes: "Stop dancing now please, since you would not come out
and dance before when I piped." Cyrus spoke this fable to the Ionians and
Aiolians because the Ionians had refused to comply before, when Cyrus
himself by a messenger requested them to revolt from Crœsus, while now
when the conquest had been made they were ready to submit to Cyrus.
Thus he said to them in anger, and the Ionians, when they heard this answer brought back to their cities, put walls round about them, and gathered together to the Panionion, all except the men of Miletos, for with
these alone Cyrus had sworn an agreement on the same terms as the Lydian had granted. The rest of the Ionians resolved by common consent to
send messengers to Sparta, to ask the Spartans to help the Ionians.

142. These Ionians to whom belongs the Panionion had the fortune to
build their cities in the most favourable position for climate and seasons of
any men whom we know. Neither the regions above Ionia nor those below,
neither those towards the East nor those towards the West, produce the
same results as Ionia itself, the regions in the one direction being oppressed

---

[*]The ritual removal of flesh and organs from the bones, or excarnation, keeps
impurities of rotting bodies from nature's unmixed elements.
[†]At 1.95, Herodotus commenced the story of the rise of Persia.

by cold and moisture, and those in the other by heat and drought. And these do not use all the same speech, but have four different dialects. First of their cities on the side of the South lies Miletos, and next to it Myus and Prienē. These are settlements made in Caria, and speak the same language with one another; and the following are in Lydia:—Ephesos, Colophon, Lebedos, Teos, Clazomenai, Phocaia. These cities resemble not at all those mentioned before in the speech which they use, but they agree one with another. There remain besides three Ionian cities, of which two are established in the islands of Samos and Chios, and one is built upon the mainland, namely Erythrai. Now the men of Chios and of Erythrai use the same form of language, but the Samians have one for themselves alone. Thus four separate forms of language have arisen.

143. Of these Ionians then those of Miletos were sheltered from the danger, since they had sworn an agreement; and those of them who lived in islands had no cause of fear, for the Phenicians were not yet subjects of the Persians and the Persians themselves were not sea-men. Now these [Ionians on and near the mainland] were parted off from the other Ionians for no other reason than this:—The whole Hellenic nation was at that time weak, but of all its races the Ionian was much the weakest and of least account. Except Athens, indeed, it had no considerable city. Now the other Ionians, and among them the Athenians, avoided the name, not wishing to be called Ionians, nay even now I perceive that the greater number of them are ashamed of the name. But these twelve cities not only prided themselves on the name but established a temple of their own, to which they gave the name of Panionion, and they made resolution not to grant a share in it to any other Ionians (nor indeed did any ask to share it except those of Smyrna).

144. Just the Dorians of that district which is now called the Five Cities, but was formerly called the Six Cities, take care not to admit any of the neighbouring Dorians to the temple of Triopion, and even exclude from sharing in it those of their own body who commit any offence as regards the temple. For example, in the games of the Triopian Apollo they used to set bronze tripods as prizes for the victors, and the rule was that those who received them should not carry them out of the temple but dedicate them then and there to the god. There was a man then of Halicarnassos, whose name was Agasicles, who being a victor disregarded this rule, and carried away the tripod to his own house and hung it up there upon a nail. On this ground the other five cities, Lindos, Ialysos and Cameiros, Cos and Cnidos, excluded the sixth city Halicarnassos from sharing in the temple.

145. Upon these they laid this penalty but as for the Ionians, I think that they made of themselves twelve cities and would not receive any more into their body, because when they dwelt in Peloponnesus there were twelve divisions of them, just as now there are twelve divisions of the Achaians who drove the Ionians out. First, (beginning from the side of Sikyon) comes Pellenē, then Aigeira and Aigai, in which last is the river Crathis with a perpetual flow (whence the river of the same name in Italy received its name), and Bura and Helikē, to which the Ionians fled for refuge when they were worsted by the Achaians in fight, and Aigion and Rhypes and Patreis and Phareis and Olenos, where is the great river Peiros, and Dymē and Tritaieis, of which the last alone has an inland position. These form now twelve divisions of the Achaians, and in former times they were divisions of the Ionians.

146. For this reason then the Ionians also made for themselves twelve cities. At any rate to say that these amount to any more Ionians than the other Ionians, or have at all a nobler descent, is mere folly,[*] considering that a large part of them are Abantians from Eubœa, who have no share even in the name of Ionia, and Minyai of Orchomenos have been mingled with them, and Cadmeians and Dryopians and Phokians who seceded from their native State and Molossians and Pelasgians of Arcadia and Dorians of Epidauros and many other races have been mingled with them. Those of them who set out for their settlements from the City Hall of Athens and who esteem themselves the most noble by descent of the Ionians, these, I say, brought no women with them to their settlement, but took Carian women, whose parents they killed. On account of this slaughter these women laid down for themselves a rule, imposing oaths on one another, and handed it on to their daughters, that they should never eat with their husbands, nor should a wife call her own husband by name, because the Ionians had slain their fathers and husbands and children and then having done this took them to wife. This happened at Miletos.

147. Moreover some of them set Lykian kings over them, descendants of Glaucos and Hippolochos, while others were ruled by Cauconians of Pylos, descendants of Codros the son of Melanthos, and others again by princes of these two races combined. Since however these hold on to the name more than the other Ionians, let them be called, if they will, the Ionians of truly pure descent. In fact all are Ionians who have their descent from Athens and who keep the feast of Apaturia; and this all keep except the men of Ephesos and Colophon. These alone of all the Ionians do not keep the Apaturia, and that on the ground of some murder committed.

148. Now the Panionion is a sacred place on the north side of Mycalē, set apart by common agreement of the Ionians for Poseidon of Helikē; and this Mycalē is a promontory of the mainland running out Westwards towards Samos, where the Ionians gathering together from their cities used to hold a festival which they called the Panionia. (And not only the feasts of the Ionians but also those of all the Hellenes equally are subject to this rule, that their names all end in the same letter, just like the names of the Persians.) These then are the Ionian cities.

149. Those of Aiolia are as follows:—Kymē, which is called Phriconis, Larisai, Neon-teichos, Temnos, Killa, Notion, Aigiroēssa, Pitanē, Aigaiai, Myrina, Gryneia; these are the ancient cities of the Aiolians, eleven in number, since one, Smyrna, was severed from them by the Ionians. These

---

[*]Herodotus here argues against a previous writer, a geographer perhaps like Hecataios; compare 2.143 and 6.137.

cities, that is those on the mainland, used also to number twelve. And these Aiolians had the fortune to settle in a land which is more fertile than that of the Ionians but less favoured in climate.

150. Now the Aiolians lost Smyrna in the following manner:—certain men of Colophon, who had been worsted in factional strife and had been driven from their native city, were received there for refuge. After this the Colophonian exiles watched for a time when the men of Smyrna were celebrating a festival to Dionysos outside the walls, and then they closed the gates against them and got possession of the city. After this, when the whole body of Aiolians came to the rescue, they made an agreement that the Ionians should give up the movable goods, and that on this condition the Aiolians should abandon Smyrna. When the men of Smyrna had done this, the remaining eleven cities divided them amongst themselves and made them their own citizens. **151.** These then are the Aiolian cities upon the mainland, with the exception of those situated on Mount Ida, for these are separate from the rest. And of those which are in the islands, there are five in Lesbos, for the sixth which was situated in Lesbos, namely Arisba, was enslaved by the men of Methymna, though its citizens were of the same race as they; and in Tenedos there is one city, and another in what are called the "Hundred Isles." Now the Lesbians and the men of Tenedos, like those Ionians who dwelt in the islands, had no cause for fear; but the remaining cities came to a common agreement to follow the Ionian leadership.

152. Now when the messengers from the Ionians and Aiolians came to Sparta (for this business was carried out with speed), they chose before all others to speak for them the Phocaian, whose name was Pythermos. He then put upon him a purple cloak, in order that as many as possible of the Spartans might hear of it and come together, and having been introduced before the assembly he spoke at length,* asking the Spartans to help them. The Lacedemonians however would not listen to him, but resolved on the contrary not to help the Ionians. So they departed, and the Lacedemonians, having dismissed the messengers of the Ionians, sent men notwithstanding in a ship of fifty oars, to find out, as I imagine, about the affairs of Cyrus and about Ionia. These came to Phocaia and sent to Sardis the man of most repute among them, whose name was Lacrines, to report to Cyrus the message of the Lacedemonians, bidding him damage no city of Hellas, since they would not permit it.

153. When the herald had spoken thus, Cyrus is said to have asked those of the Hellenes whom he had with him, what men the Lacedemonians were and how many in number, that they made this proclamation to him; and hearing their answer he said to the Spartan herald: "Never yet did I fear men such as these, who have a place appointed in the midst of their city where they gather together and deceive one another by false oaths. If I continue in good health, not the misfortunes of the Ionians will

---

*Always a mistake with the laconic Spartans; compare 3.46 and 9.91.

be for them a subject of talk, but rather their own." These words Cyrus threw out scornfully with reference to the Hellenes in general, because they have markets and practise buying and selling there; for the Persians themselves are not wont to use markets nor have they any market-place at all. After this he entrusted Sardis to Tabalos a Persian, and the gold both of Crœsus and of the other Lydians he gave to Pactyas a Lydian to take charge of, and himself marched away to Agbatana, taking with him Crœsus and for the present not concerning himself with the Ionians. For Babylon stood in his way still, as also the Bactrian nation and the Sacans and the Egyptians; and against these he meant to make expeditions himself, while sending some other commander against the Ionians.

154. But when Cyrus had marched away from Sardis, Pactyas caused the Lydians to revolt from Tabalos and from Cyrus. This man went down to the sea, and having in his possession all the gold that there had been in Sardis, he hired for himself mercenaries and persuaded the men of the sea-coast to join his expedition. So he marched on Sardis and besieged Tabalos, having shut him up in the citadel. **155.** Hearing this on his way, Cyrus said to Crœsus as follows: "Crœsus, what end shall I find of these affairs? The Lydians will not cease as it seems, from giving trouble to me and from having it themselves. I imagine that it might be best to sell them all as slaves; for as it is, I see that things stand as if one should slay the father and then spare his sons. Just so I took prisoner and am carrying you away, who were much more than the father of the Lydians, while to the Lydians themselves I delivered up their city; and can I feel surprise after this that they have revolted from me?"

Thus he said what was in his mind, but Crœsus answered, fearing lest he should destroy Sardis: "King, you have spoken reasonably; but do not altogether give vent to your wrath, nor destroy an ancient city which is guiltless both of the former things and also of those which have come to pass now. The former things I did, and I bear the consequences wiped upon my head; and as for what is now being done, since the wrongdoer is Pactyas to whom you entrusted Sardis, let him pay the penalty. But the Lydians please pardon, and lay upon them commands as follows, in order that they may not revolt nor be a cause of danger to you:—forbid them to possess weapons of war, but bid them on the other hand put on tunics under their outer garments and loafers on their feet, and proclaim to them that they train their sons to play the lyre and the harp and to be retail-dealers. Soon you shall see, King, that they have become women instead of men, so that there will be no fear that they will revolt."

156. Crœsus suggested to him this, perceiving that this was better for the Lydians than to be reduced to slavery and sold; for he knew that if he did not offer a sufficient reason, he would not persuade Cyrus to change his mind, and he feared lest at some future time, if they should escape the present danger, the Lydians might revolt from the Persians and be destroyed. And Cyrus was pleased with the suggestion made and slackened his wrath, saying that he agreed with his advice. Then he called Mazares a Mede, and charged him to proclaim to the Lydians that which Crœsus suggested, and moreover to sell into slavery all the rest who had joined with the Lydians in the expedition to Sardis, and finally by all means to bring Pactyas himself alive to Cyrus.

157. Having given this charge upon the road, he continued his march to the native land of the Persians; but Pactyas hearing that an army was approaching to fight against him was struck with fear and fled at once to Kymē. Then Mazares the Mede marched upon Sardis with a certain portion of the army of Cyrus, and as he did not find Pactyas or his followers any longer at Sardis, he first compelled the Lydians to perform the commands of Cyrus, and by his commands the Lydians changed the whole manner of their life. After this Mazares proceeded to send messengers to Kymē bidding them give up Pactyas. The men of Kymē resolved to refer to the god at Branchidai the question of what counsel they should follow. For there was there an Oracle long since established, which all the Ionians and Aiolians were wont to consult; and this place is in the territory of Miletos above the port of Panormos.

158. So the men of Kymē sent messengers to the priests, the Branchidai, to inquire of the god, and they asked what course they should take about Pactyas so as to please the gods. When they thus inquired, the answer was given them that they should deliver Pactyas to the Persians. The men of Kymē, having heard this answer, were disposed to give him up. Then when the mass of the people were thus disposed, Aristodicos the son of Heracleides, a man of repute among the citizens, stopped the men of Kymē from doing so, distrusting the answer and thinking that those sent to inquire were not speaking the truth. At last other messengers were sent to the Oracle to ask a second time about Pactyas, and of them Aristodicos was one.

159. When these came to Branchidai, Aristodicos apart from the rest consulted the Oracle, asking: "Lord, a suppliant for protection came to us, Pactyas the Lydian, fleeing a violent death at the hands of the Persians; and they demand him from us, bidding the men of Kymē give him up. But we, though we fear the power of the Persians, yet have not dared up to this time to deliver the suppliant to them, until your counsel shall be clearly manifested to us, saying which policy we ought to follow." He thus inquired, but the god again declared to them the same answer, bidding them deliver up Pactyas to the Persians.

Upon this Aristodicos with a deliberate purpose did as follows:—he went all round the temple utterly destroying the nests of the sparrows and of all the other kinds of birds which had been hatched on the temple. While he was doing this, it is said that a voice came from the inner shrine directed to Aristodicos: "Thou most impious of men, why dost thou dare to do this? Dost thou from my temple ravage the suppliants for my protection?"

And Aristodicos, it is said, entirely unfazed replied to this: "Lord, do you thus come to the assistance of your suppliants, and yet bid the men of Kymē deliver up theirs?" and the god answered him again thus: "Yea, I bid you do so, that you may perish the more quickly for your impiety; so that you may not at any future time come to the Oracle to ask about delivering up suppliants."

160. When the men of Kymē heard this reported, not wishing either to be destroyed by delivering him up or to be besieged by keeping him with them, they sent him away to Mytilenē. Those of Mytilenē however, when Mazares sent messages to them, were preparing to deliver up Pactyas for a price, but what the price was I cannot say for certain, since the bargain was never completed; for the men of Kymē, when they learnt that this was being done by the Mytilenians, sent a vessel to Lesbos and conveyed away Pactyas to Chios. After this he was dragged forcibly from the temple of Athenē Poliuchos by the Chians and delivered up. The Chians delivered him up receiving Atarneus in return, (now this Atarneus is a region of Mysia opposite Lesbos). So the Persians having received Pactyas kept him under guard, meaning to produce him before Cyrus. And a long time elapsed during which none of the Chians either used barley-meal grown in this region of Atarneus, for pouring out in sacrifice to any god, or baked cakes for offering of the grain which grew there, but all the produce of this land was excluded from every kind of sacred service.

161. The men of Chios then had delivered up Pactyas; and after this Mazares made expedition against those who had joined in besieging Tabalos: and first he reduced to slavery those of Prienē, then he overran the whole plain of the Maiander providing spoil for his army, and Magnesia in the same manner. Right after this he fell sick and died. **162.** After he was dead, Harpagos came down to take his place in command, being also a Mede by race, (this was the man whom the king of the Medes Astyages feasted with the taboo banquet, and who helped to give the kingdom to Cyrus). This man, being appointed commander then by Cyrus, came to Ionia and proceeded to take the cities by building mounds against them. When he had enclosed any people within their walls, then he threw up mounds against the walls and took their city by storm; and the first city of Ionia upon which he made an attempt was Phocaia.[*]

163. Now these Phocaians were the first of the Hellenes who made long voyages, and these are they who opened up the Adriatic and Tyrsenia and Iberia and Tartessos. They made voyages not in round ships, but in vessels of fifty oars. These came to Tartessos and became friends with the king of the Tartessians whose name was Arganthonios: he was ruler of the Tartessians for eighty years and lived in all one hundred and twenty. The Phocaians became so exceedingly friendly with this man, that first he bade them leave Ionia and dwell wherever they desired in his own land; and as he did not prevail upon the Phocaians to do this, afterwards, hearing from them how the power of the Mede was increasing, he gave them money to build a wall round about their city. He did this without sparing expense, for the circuit of the wall is some miles in extent, and it is built all of large stones closely fitted together.[†]

---

[*]This Assyrian tactic has left archaeological traces elsewhere; this assault occurred c.540 B.C.

[†]No ruins survive of this pioneering city, so the circuit's length is unknown.

164. That is how the wall of the Phocaians was made. Harpagos having marched his army against them began to besiege them, at the same time holding forth to them proposals and saying that it was enough to satisfy him if the Phocaians were willing to throw down one battlement of their wall and consecrate in submission one single house. But the Phocaians, incensed at the thought of subjection, said that they wished to deliberate about the matter for one day and after that they would give their answer; and they asked him to withdraw his army from the wall while they were deliberating. Harpagos said that he knew very well what they meant to do, nevertheless he was willing to allow them to deliberate. So in the time that followed, when Harpagos had withdrawn his army from the wall, the Phocaians drew down their fifty-oared galleys to the sea, put into them their children and women and all their movable goods, and besides them the images out of the temples and the other votive offerings except such as were made of bronze or stone or consisted of paintings. All the rest they put into the ships, and having embarked themselves they sailed towards Chios; and the Persians obtained possession of Phocaia, the city being deserted of the inhabitants.

165. But as for the Phocaians, since the men of Chios would not sell them at their request the islands called Oinussai, from the fear lest these islands might be made a seat of trade and their island might be shut out, therefore they set out for Kyrnos (or Corsica) because in Corsica twenty years before this they had established a city named Alalia, in accordance with an oracle. (Now Arganthonios by that time was dead.) And when they were setting out for Corsica they first sailed in to Phocaia and slaughtered the Persian garrison, to whose charge Harpagos had delivered the city; then after they had achieved this they made solemn imprecations on any one of them who should be left behind from their voyage, and moreover they sank a mass of iron in the sea and swore that not until that mass should appear again on the surface would they return to Phocaia. However as they were setting forth to Corsica, more than half of the citizens were seized with yearning and regret for their city and for their native land, and they proved false to their oath and sailed back to Phocaia. But those of them who kept the oath still, weighed anchor from the islands of Oinussai and sailed.

166. When these came to Corsica, for five years they dwelt together with those who had come thither before, and they founded temples there. Then, since they plundered the property of all their neighbours, the Tyrsenians and Carthaginians made an expedition against them by agreement with one another, each with sixty ships. And the Phocaians also manned their vessels, sixty in number, and came to meet the enemy in that which is called the Sardinian sea. When they encountered one another in the sea-fight the Phocaians won a kind of Cadmean victory,* for forty of their ships were

---

*We say "Pyrrhic" for an unaffordable victory, but Pyrrhus, the king of Epirus in northwestern Greece, lived more than a century later than Herodotus; Pyrrhus battled the Romans in southern Italy but lost more resources and men than he gained with each victory.

destroyed and the remaining twenty were disabled, having had their prows bent aside. So they sailed in to Alalia and took up their children and their women and their other possessions as much as their ships proved capable of carrying, and then they left Corsica behind them and sailed to Rhegion.

167. But as for the crews of the ships that were destroyed, the Carthaginians and Tyrsenians obtained much the greater number of them, and these they brought to land and killed by stoning. After this the men of Agylla found that everything which passed by the spot where the Phocaians were laid after being stoned, became either distorted, or crippled, or paralysed, both small cattle and beasts of burden and human creatures. Consequently, the men of Agylla sent to Delphi desiring to purge themselves of the offence; and the Pythian prophetess bade them do that which the men of Agylla still continue to perform, that is to say, they make great sacrifices in honour of the dead, and hold at the place a contest of athletics and horse-racing. These then of the Phocaians suffered such a fate; but those of them who took refuge at Rhegion started from thence and took possession of that city in the land of Oinotria which now is called Hyelē.* This they founded having learnt from a man of Poseidonia that the Pythian prophetess by her answer meant them to found a temple to Kyrnos, who was a hero, and not to found a settlement in the island called Kyrnos, Corsica.

168. That's what happened to Phocaia in Ionia, and nearly the same thing also was done by the men of Teos. As soon as Harpagos took their wall with a mound, they embarked in their ships and sailed at once for Thrace; and there they founded the city of Abdera, which before them Timesios of Clazomenai founded† and had no profit therefrom, but was driven out by the Thracians; and now he is honoured as a hero by the Teïans in Abdera.

169. These alone of all the Ionians left their native cities because they would not endure subjection. The other Ionians except the Milesians did indeed contend in arms with Harpagos like those who left their homes, and proved themselves brave men, fighting each for his own native city; but when they were defeated and captured they remained all in their own place and performed that which was laid upon them. The Milesians, as I said before, had made a sworn agreement with Cyrus himself and kept still. Thus for the second time Ionia had been reduced to subjection. And when Harpagos had conquered the Ionians on the mainland, then the Ionians who dwelt in the islands, struck with fear by these things, gave themselves up to Cyrus.

170. When the Ionians had been badly handled but were continuing still to hold their gatherings as before at the Panionion, Bias a man of Prienē set forth to the Ionians, as I am informed, a most profitable counsel, by following which they might have been the most prosperous of all the Hellenes. He urged that the Ionians should set forth in one common expedition and

---

*Elea is famous as the center of the southern Italian pre-Socratic philosophers.
†About 635 B.C.

sail to Sardinia, and after that found a single city for all the Ionians. Thus they would escape subjection and would be prosperous, inhabiting the largest of all islands and being rulers over others; whereas, if they remained in Ionia, he did not perceive, he said, that freedom would any longer exist for them. This was the counsel given by Bias of Prienē after the Ionians had been ruined; but a good counsel too was given before the ruin of Ionia by Thales a man of Miletos, who was by descent of Phenician race. He advised the Ionians to have one single seat of government, and that this should be at Teos (for Teos, he said, was in the centre of Ionia), and that the other cities should be inhabited as before, but accounted just as if they were demes. These men set forth to them counsels of the kind which I have said.

171. Harpagos, after subduing Ionia, proceeded to march against the Carians and Caunians and Lykians, taking also Ionians and Aiolians to help him. Of these the Carians came to the mainland from the islands; for being long ago subjects of Minos and being called Leleges, they used to dwell in the islands, paying no tribute, so far back as I am able to arrive by hearsay, but whenever Minos required it, they used to supply his ships with seamen. Since Minos subdued much land and was fortunate in his fighting, the Carian nation was of all nations by much the most famous at that time together with him. And they produced three inventions which the Hellenes came to use. The Carians were those who first set the fashion of fastening crests on helmets, and of making the devices which are put upon shields, and these also were the first who made handles for their shields, whereas up to that time all who used shields carried them without handles and with leathern straps to guide them, having them hung about their necks and their left shoulders. Then after the lapse of a long time the Dorians and Ionians drove the Carians out of the islands, and so they came to the mainland.

With respect to the Carians the Cretans relate that it happened like that; the Carians themselves however do not agree with this account, but suppose that they are dwellers on the mainland from the beginning, and that they went always by the same name which they have now. They point as evidence of this to an ancient temple of Carian Zeus at Mylasa, in which the Mysians and Lydians share as being brother races of the Carians, for they say that Lydos and Mysos were brothers of Car; these share in it, but those who being of another race have come to speak the same language as the Carians have no share in it.

172. It seems to me however that the Caunians are dwellers there from the beginning, though they say themselves that they came from Crete: but they have been assimilated to the Carian race in language, or else the Carians to the Caunian race, I cannot with certainty determine which. They have customs however in which they differ very much from all other men as well as from the Carians; for example the fairest thing in their estimation is to meet together in numbers for drinking, according to equality of age or friendship, both men, women, and children; and again when they had founded temples for foreign deities, afterwards they changed their purpose and resolved to worship only their own native gods, and the whole body of Caunian young men put on their armour and made pursuit as far as the borders of the Calyndians, beating the air with their spears; and they said that they were casting the foreign gods out of the land. Such are the customs which these have.

173. The Lykians however have sprung originally from Crete (for in old time the whole of Crete was possessed by Barbarians). When the sons of Europa, Sarpedon and Minos, came to be at variance in Crete about the kingdom, Minos having got the better in the strife of parties drove out both Sarpedon himself and those of his party. Those expelled came to the land of Milyas in Asia, for the land which now the Lykians inhabit was anciently called Milyas, and the Milyans were then called Solymoi. Now while Sarpedon reigned over them, they were called by the name which they had when they came thither, and by which the Lykians are even now called by the neighbouring tribes, namely Termilai; but when from Athens Lycos the son of Pandion came to the land of the Termilai and to Sarpedon, he too having been driven out by his brother namely Aigeus, then by the name taken from Lycos they were called after a time Lykians. The customs which these have are partly Cretan and partly Carian; but one custom they have which is peculiar to them, and in which they agree with no other people, that is they call themselves by their mothers and not by their fathers; and if one asks his neighbour who he is, he will state his parentage on the mother's side and enumerate his mother's female ascendants. If a woman who is a citizen marry a slave, the children are accounted to be of gentle birth; but if a man who is a citizen, though he were the first man among them, have a slave for wife or concubine, the children are without civil rights.

174. Now the Carians were reduced to subjection by Harpagos without any brilliant deed displayed either by the Carians themselves or by those of the Hellenes who dwell in this land. Of these last there are besides others the men of Cnidos, settlers from Lacedemon, whose land runs out into the sea, being in fact the region which is called Triopion, beginning from the peninsula of Bybassos. Since all the land of Cnidos except a small part is washed by the sea (for the part of it which looks towards the North is bounded by the Gulf of Keramos, and that which looks to the South by the sea off Symē and Rhodes), therefore the men of Cnidos began to dig through this small part, which is about three thousand feet across, while Harpagos was subduing Ionia, desiring to make their land an island: and within the isthmus all was theirs, for where the territory of Cnidos ends in the direction of the mainland, here is the isthmus which they were digging across. And while the Cnidians were working at it with a great number of men, it was perceived that the men who worked suffered injury much more than might have been expected and in a more supernatural manner, both in other parts of their bodies and especially in their eyes, when the rock was being broken up; so they sent men to ask the Oracle at Delphi what the cause of the difficulty was. And the Pythian prophetess, as the men of Cnidos themselves report, gave them this reply in trimeter verse:—

"Fence not the place with towers, nor dig the isthmus through;
    Zeus would have made your land an island, had he willed."

When the Pythian prophetess had given this oracle, the men of Cnidos not only ceased from their digging but delivered themselves to Harpagos without resistance, when he came against them with his army.

175. There were also the Pedasians, who dwelt in the inland country above Halicarnassos; and among these, whenever anything hurtful is about to happen either to themselves or to their neighbours, the priestess of Athenē has a great beard: this befell them three times. These of all about Caria were the only men who held out for any time against Harpagos, and they gave him trouble more than any other people, having fortified a mountain called Lidē.

176. After a time the Pedasians were conquered; and the Lykians, when Harpagos marched his army into the plain of Xanthos, came out against him and fought, few against many, and displayed proofs of valour; but being defeated and confined within their city, they gathered together into the citadel their wives and their children, their property and their servants, and after that they set fire to this citadel, so that it was all in flames, and having done so and sworn terrible oaths with one another, they went out suddenly against the enemy and were slain in fight, all the men of Xanthos. The greater number of the Xanthians who now claim to be Lykians have come in from abroad, except only eighty households; but these eighty households happened at that time to be away from their native place, and so they escaped destruction. Thus Harpagos obtained possession of Xanthos, and nearly in the same way he got possession of Caunos, for the men of Caunos imitated in most respects the behaviour of the Lykians.

177. So Harpagos was conquering the coast regions of Asia; and Cyrus himself meanwhile was doing the same in the upper parts of it, subduing every nation and passing over none. Now most of these actions I shall pass over, but the undertakings which gave him trouble more than the rest and which are the most worthy of note, these I shall mention.

178. Cyrus, so soon as he had made subject to himself all other parts of the mainland, proceeded to attack the Assyrians. Now Assyria has doubtless many other great cities, but the most famous and the strongest, and the place where the seat of their monarchy had been established after Nineveh was destroyed, was Babylon.—It lies in a great plain, and in size it is such that each face measures nearly fourteen miles, the shape of the whole being square; thus the circuit of the city amounts in all to fifty-five miles. Such is the size of the city of Babylon, and it had magnificence greater than all other cities of which we have knowledge.* First there runs round it a trench deep and broad and full of water; then a wall 81 feet in thickness and 325 feet in height. Now the royal cubit is larger by three fingers than the

---

*Herodotus' numbers are much too large. Did he in fact visit this magnificent capital?

common cubit.* **179.** I must also tell in addition for what purpose the earth was used, which was taken out of the trench, and how they made the wall. As they dug the trench they made the earth which was carried out of the excavation into bricks, and having moulded enough bricks they baked them in kilns; and then afterwards, using hot asphalt for mortar and inserting reed mats at every thirty courses of brickwork, they built up first the edges of the trench [as a moat] and then the wall itself in the same manner. At the top of the wall along the edges they built chambers of one story facing one another; and between the rows of chambers they left space to drive a four-horse chariot. In the circuit of the wall there are set a hundred gates made of bronze throughout, and the gate-posts and lintels likewise. Now there is another city distant from Babylon a space of eight days' journey, of which the name is Is;† and there is a river there of no great size, and the name of the river is also Is, and it sends its stream into the river Euphrates. This river Is throws up together with its water lumps of asphalt in great abundance, and thence was brought the asphalt for the wall of Babylon.

180. Babylon then was walled in this manner; and there are two divisions of the city; for a river whose name is Euphrates parts it in the middle. This flows from the land of the Armenians and is large and deep and swift, and it flows out into the Erythraian sea. The wall then on each side has angles carried down to the river, and from this point the return walls stretch along each bank of the stream in the form of a rampart of baked bricks. The city itself is full of houses of three and four stories, and the roads by which it is cut up run in straight lines, including the cross roads which lead to the river; and opposite to each road there were set gates in the rampart which ran along the river, as many in number as the lanes, and these also were of bronze and led like the lanes to the river itself. **181.** This wall then which I have mentioned is as it were a cuirass for the town, and another wall runs round within it, not much weaker for defence‡ than the first but enclosing a smaller space. And in each division of the city was a building in the midst, in the one the king's palace of great extent and strongly fortified round, and in the other the temple of Zeus Belos§ with bronze gates, and this exists still up to my time and measures 1200 feet or 400 yards square each way, being of a square shape: and in the midst of the temple precinct is built a solid tower measuring 606 feet both in length and in breadth, and on this tower another tower has been erected, and another again upon this, and so on up to the number of eight towers. An ascent to these has been built running outside round about all the towers; and when one reaches about the middle of the ascent one finds a stopping-place and

---

*Herodotus' measurements, given in cubits, are translated here. (A royal cubit was approximately 19½ inches.)
†Now called Hit; still a source of bitumen and other petroleum products.
‡Or this wall is "not as thick."
§Belos is the Hellenized "Ba'al" ("the Lord"), worshiped later as Marduk.

seats to rest upon, on which those who ascend sit down and rest: and on the top of the last tower there is a large sanctuary, and in this cell a large couch is laid, well covered, and by it is placed a golden table. No image is there set up nor does any human being spend the night there except only one woman of the natives of the place, whomsoever the god shall choose from all the women, as say the Chaldeans who are the priests of this god.

182. These same men say also, but I do not believe them, that the god himself comes often to the cell and rests upon the couch, as happens likewise in the Egyptian Thebes according to the report of the Egyptians, for there also a woman sleeps in the temple of the Theban Zeus (and both these women are said to abstain from sexual intercourse with men), and as happens also with the prophetess of the god in Patara of Lykia, whenever there is one, for there is not always an Oracle there. Whenever there is one, then she is shut up during the nights in the temple within the cell. **183.** There is moreover in the temple at Babylon another cell below, wherein is a great image of Zeus sitting, made of gold, and by it is placed a large table of gold, and his footstool and seat are of gold also; and, as the Chaldeans reported, the weight of the gold of which these things are made is twenty-three tons. Outside this cell is an altar of gold; and there is also another altar of great size, where full-grown animals are sacrificed, whereas on the golden altar it is not lawful to sacrifice any but young sucklings only: and also on the larger altar the Chaldeans offer twenty-eight and one-half tons of frankincense every year at the time when they celebrate the feast in honour of this god. There was moreover in these precincts still remaining at the time of Cyrus, a statue 17.5 feet high, of solid gold. This I did not myself see, but that which is related by the Chaldeans I relate. Against this statue Dareios the son of Hystaspes formed a design, but he did not venture to take it. However Xerxes the son of Dareios took it, who also killed the priest when he forbade him to move the statue. This temple, then, is thus adorned with magnificence, and there are also many private votive-offerings.

184. Of this Babylon, besides many other rulers, of whom I shall make mention in the Assyrian history,* who improved the walls and temples, there were two women. Of these, the one who ruled first, named Semiramis, who lived five generations before the other, produced banks of earth in the plain which are a sight worth seeing; and before this the river used to flood like a sea over the whole plain.

185. The queen who lived after her time, named Nitocris,† was wiser than she who had reigned before. In the first place she left behind her monuments which I shall tell of; then secondly, seeing that the monarchy of the Medes was great and not apt to remain still, but that besides other

---

*A section not known to have been written; compare 1.106.

†Nitocris, queen c.600 B.C., is otherwise unknown in the copious records. King Nebuchadnezzar may lurk behind this name, in Persian and feminine form.

cities even Nineveh had been captured by it, she made provision against it in so far as she was able. First, as regards the river Euphrates which flows through the midst of their city, whereas before this it flowed straight, she by digging channels above made it so winding that it actually comes three times in its course to one of the villages in Assyria. The name of the village to which the Euphrates comes is Ardericca; and at this day those who travel from this Sea of ours to Babylon, in their voyage down the river Euphrates arrive three times at this same village and on three separate days. She also piled up a mound along each bank of the river, which is worthy to cause wonder for its size and height. At a great distance above Babylon, she dug a basin for a lake, which she caused to extend along at a very small distance from the river, excavating it everywhere to such depth as to reach water, and making the extent such that the circuit of it measured 48 miles. She used up the earth which was dug out of this excavation by piling it in mounds along the banks of the river. When this had been dug by her she brought stones and set them all round it as a facing wall. Both these things she did, that is she made the river to have a winding course, and she made the place which was dug out all into a swamp, in order that the river might run more slowly, having its force broken by going round many bends, and that the voyages might be winding to Babylon, and after the voyages there might succeed a long circuit of the pool. These works she carried out in that part where the entrance-passes to the country were, and the shortest way to it from Media, so that the Medes might not have dealings with her kingdom and learn of her affairs.*

186. These defences she cast round her city from excavation. She made the following addition which was dependent upon them:—The city was in two divisions, and the river occupied the space between; and in the time of the former rulers, when any one wished to pass over from the one division to the other, he had to pass over in a boat, and that, as I imagine, was troublesome. She however made provision also for this; for when she was digging the basin for the lake she left this other monument of herself derived from the same work, that is, she caused stones to be cut of very great length, and when the stones were prepared for her and the place had been dug out, she turned aside the whole stream of the river into the place which she had been digging; and while this was being filled with water, the ancient bed of the river dried up in the meantime. She both built up with baked bricks after the same fashion as the wall the edges of the river, where it flows through the city, and the places of descent leading from the small gateways to the river; and also about the middle of the city, as I judge, with the stones which she had caused to be dug out she proceeded to build a bridge, binding together the stones with iron and lead. Upon the top she laid across squared timbers, to remain there while it was daytime, over which the people of Babylon made the passage; but at night they used to take away these timbers so that they might not go backwards and

---

*Herodotus seems to confuse water-control mechanisms with military strategy.

forwards by night and steal from one another. When the place dug out had been made into a lake full of water by the river, and at the same time the bridge had been completed, then she conducted the Euphrates back into its ancient channel from the lake, and so the place dug out for a swamp was thought to have served a good purpose, and a bridge was provided for the men of the city.

187. This same queen also contrived a snare of the following kind:— Over that gate of the city through which the greatest number of people passed she set up for herself a tomb above the very gate itself. And on the tomb she engraved writing which said: "If any of the kings of Babylon who come after me shall be in want of wealth, let him open my tomb and take as much as he desires; but let him not open it for any other cause, if he be not in want; for that will not be the better way." This tomb was undisturbed until the kingdom came to Dareios; but to Dareios it seemed that it was a monstrous thing not to make any use of this gate, and also, when there was money lying there, not to take it, considering that the inscription itself invited him to do so. Now he would not make any use of this gate because the corpse would have been above his head as he drove through. He then, I say, opened the tomb and found not indeed money but the corpse, with writing which said: "If you had not been insatiable for wealth and basely covetous, you would not have opened the resting-places of the dead."

188. This queen then is reported to have been someone like that. The son of this woman, bearing the same name as his father, Labynetos,[*] was the ruler over the Assyrians against whom Cyrus was marching. Now the great king makes his marches not only well furnished from home with provisions for his table and with cattle, but also taking with him water from the river Choaspes, which flows by Susa, of which alone and of no other river the king drinks. A very great number of waggons, four-wheeled and drawn by mules, carry a supply of this water of the Choaspes boiled, in silver vessels, and go with him wherever he may march at any time. **189.** Now when Cyrus on his way towards Babylon arrived at the river Gyndes,—of which river the springs are in the mountains of the Matienians, and it flows through the Dardanians and runs into another river, the Tigris, which flowing by the city of Opis runs out into the Erythraian Sea,—when Cyrus was endeavouring to cross this river Gyndes, which is a navigable stream, then one of his sacred white horses in high spirit went into the river and endeavoured to cross, but the stream swept it under water and carried it off. And Cyrus was greatly angered against the river for having done thus insolently, and he threatened to make it so feeble that for the future even women would cross it easily without wetting the knee. So after this threat he postponed his march against Babylon and divided his army into two parts; and having divided it he stretched lines and marked out straight channels, one hundred and eighty on each bank of the Gyndes, directed

---

*See 1.74 also for this ruler, the Assyrian Nabunita, who ruled c.556 B.C.

every way. After he disposed his army along them he commanded them to dig. Since a great multitude was working, the work was completed indeed, but they spent the whole summer season at this spot working.

190. When Cyrus had taken vengeance on the river Gyndes by dividing it into three hundred and sixty channels, and when the next spring was just beginning, then he continued his advance upon Babylon. The men of Babylon had marched forth out of their city and were awaiting him. So when in his advance he came near the city, the Babylonians joined battle with him, and having been worsted in the fight they were shut up within their city. But knowing well even before this that Cyrus was not apt to remain still, and seeing him lay hands on every nation equally, they had brought in provisions beforehand for very many years. So while these ignored the siege, Cyrus was at a loss about what to do, for much time went by and his affairs made no progress.*

191. Therefore, whether it was some other man who suggested to him at a loss what to do, or whether he himself perceived what he ought to do, he did as follows:—The main body of his army he posted at the place where the river runs into the city, and then again behind the city he set others, where the river issues forth from the city; and he proclaimed to his army that so soon as they should see that the stream had become passable, they should enter by this way into the city. Having thus set them in their places and in this manner exhorted them he marched away himself with that part of his army which was not fit for fighting. When he came to the lake, Cyrus also did what the queen of the Babylonians had done as regards the river and the lake. That is to say, he conducted the river by a channel into the lake, which was at that time a swamp, and so made the former course of the river passable by the sinking of the stream. When this had been done, the Persians who had been posted for this very purpose entered by the bed of the river Euphrates into Babylon, the stream having sunk so far that it reached about to the middle of a man's thigh. Now if the Babylonians had had knowledge of it beforehand or had perceived Cyrus' tactic, they would have allowed the Persians to enter the city and then massacred them miserably. For if they had closed all the gates that led to the river and mounted themselves upon the ramparts built along the banks of the stream, they would have caught them as it were in a fish-trap. As it was, the Persians came upon them unexpectedly; and owing to the size of the city (so it is said by those who dwell there) after those about the extremities of the city had suffered capture, those Babylonians who dwelt in the middle did not know that they had been captured; but as they chanced to be holding a festival, they went on dancing and rejoicing during this time until they learnt the whole truth. Babylon then had thus been taken for the first time.

192. I shall show how great the resources of the Babylonians are, by many other proofs and among them by this:—For the support of the great

*Babylon was taken in 538 B.C.

king and his army, apart from the regular tribute the whole land of which he
is ruler has been distributed into portions. Now whereas twelve months go
to make up the year, for four of these he has his support from the territory
of Babylon, and for the remaining eight months from the whole of the rest
of Asia; thus the Assyrian land is in regard to resources one-third of all
Asia. The government, or satrapy as it is called by the Persians, of this territory is by far the best of all the governments. When Tritantaichmes son of
Artabazos had this province from the king, there came in to him every day
an *artab* full of silver coin (now the *artab* is a Persian measure and holds
more than the *medimnos* of Attica by three Attic *choinikes*);* and of horses
he had in this province as his private property, apart from the horses for
use in war, eight hundred stallions and sixteen thousand mares, for each of
these stallions served twenty mares. Moreover such a vast number of Indian hounds were kept that four large villages in the plain, being free from
other contributions, had been appointed to feed the hounds.

193. Such was the wealth which belonged to the ruler of Babylon. Now
the land of the Assyrians has but little rain; and this little gives nourish-
ment to the root of the grain, but the crop is ripened and the ear comes on
by the help of irrigation, not as in Egypt by the coming up of the river itself over the fields, but the crop is watered by hand or with swing-buckets.
For the whole Babylonian territory like the Egyptian is cut up into channels, and the largest of the channels is navigable for ships and runs south-
easterly in winter from the Euphrates to another river, namely the Tigris,
along the bank of which lay the city of Nineveh. This territory is of all that
we know the best by far for producing grain. It does not even attempt to
bear trees, either fig or vine or olive, but for producing grain it is so good
that it returns as much as two-hundred-fold for the average, and when it
bears at its best it produces three-hundred-fold. The leaves of the wheat
and barley there grow to be full four fingers broad; and from millet and
sesame seed how large a tree grows, I know myself but shall not record,
being well aware that even what has already been said relating to the
crops produced has been seriously incredible for those who have not visited the Babylonian land. They use no olive oil, but only that which they
make of sesame seed; and they have date-palms growing over all the plain,
most of them fruit-bearing, of which they make food, wine, and honey;
and to these they attend in the same manner as to fig-trees. In particular
they take the fruit of those palms which the Hellenes call male-palms,
and tie them upon the date-bearing palms, so that their gall-fly may enter
into the date and ripen it and that the fruit of the palm may not fall off.
The male-palm produces gall-flies in its fruit just as the wild-fig does.

194. But the greatest marvel of all the things in the land after the city itself, to my mind is this which I am about to tell: Their boats, those I mean
which go down the river to Babylon, are round and all of leather: for they
make ribs for them of willow which they cut in the land of the Armenians

*The dry measure here would be nearly 12 gallons.

who dwell above the Assyrians, and round these they stretch hides which serve as a covering outside by way of hull, not making broad the stern nor gathering in the prow to a point, but making the boats round like a shield. They stow the whole boat with straw and let it be carried down the stream full of cargo; and for the most part these boats bring down casks of palm-wood filled with wine.

The boat is kept straight by two steering-oars and two men standing upright, and the man inside pulls his oar while the man outside pushes. These vessels are made both very large and also smaller, the largest of them having a burden of as much as five thousand talents or 170 tons weight; and in each one there is a live ass, and in those of larger size several. So when they have arrived at Babylon in their voyage and have disposed of their cargo, they sell by auction the ribs of the boat and all the straw, but they pack the hides upon their asses and drive them off to Armenia, since it is not possible by any means to sail up the stream of the river, owing to the swiftness of the current. For this reason they make their boats not of timber but of hides. Then when they have come back to the land of the Armenians, driving their asses with them, they make other boats in the same manner. **195.** Such are their boats; and the following is the manner of dress which they use, namely a linen tunic reaching to the feet, and over this they put on another of wool, and then a white mantle thrown round, while they have shoes of a native fashion rather like Bœotian slippers. They wear their hair long and bind their heads with caps and they anoint their whole body with perfumes. Each man has a seal and a staff carved by hand, and on each staff is carved either an apple or a rose or a lily or an eagle or some other device, for their custom is to have a staff with a device upon it.

196. Such is the outfitting of their bodies. The customs which are established among them are as follows, the cleverest in our opinion being this, which I am informed that the Enetoi in Illyria also have. In every village once in each year they did this:—When the maidens grew to the age for marriage, they gathered these all together and brought them in a body to one place, and a crowd of men stood round. The crier caused each one severally to stand up, and proceeded to sell them, first the most comely of all, and afterwards, when she had been sold and had fetched a large sum of money, he would put up another who was the most comely after her. They were sold for marriage. Now all the wealthy men of the Babylonians who were ready to marry vied with one another in bidding for the most beautiful maidens; those however of the common sort who were ready to marry did not require a fine form, but they would accept money together with less comely maidens. For when the crier had made an end of selling the most comely of the maidens, then he would cause to stand up that one who was least shapely, or any one of them who might be crippled in any way, and he would make proclamation of her, asking who was willing for least gold to have her in marriage, until she was assigned to him who was willing to accept least. The gold came in from the sale of the comely maidens, and so those of beautiful form provided dowries for those which were unshapely or

crippled; but to give in marriage one's own daughter to whomsoever each
man would, was not allowed, nor to carry off the maiden after buying her
without a surety; for it was necessary for the man to provide sureties that he
would marry her, before he took her away; and if they did not agree well together, the law was laid down that he should pay back the money. They allowed any one who wished it to come from another village and buy. This
then was their most honourable custom; it does not however still exist at the
present time, but they have found out of late another way, [in order that the
men may not ill-treat them or take them to another city.]* Since the time of
conquest they were oppressed and ruined, and each one of the common
people when he lacks life's necessities prostitutes his female children.

197. Next in cleverness to that, is this other custom which was established among them:—they bear out the sick into the market-place; for
they make no use of physicians. So people come up to the sick man and
give advice about his disease, if any one himself ever suffered anything
like that which the sick man has, or saw any other who had suffered it; and
coming near they advise and recommend those means by which they have
themselves got rid of a like disease or seen some other get rid of it. To pass
by the sick man in silence is not permitted to them, nor to leave before one
has asked what disease he has.

198. They bury their dead in honey, and their modes of lamentation are
similar to those used in Egypt. And whenever a Babylonian man has intercourse with his wife, he sits and purifies himself by incense, and his wife
does the same on the other side, and when it is morning they wash themselves, both of them, for they will touch no vessel until they have washed
themselves. (The Arabians do likewise in this matter.)

199. Now the most shameful of the customs of the Babylonians is as
follows:—Every woman of the country must sit down in the precincts of
Aphroditē once in her life and have sex with a man who is a stranger.
Many women who do not deign to mingle with the rest, because they are
made arrogant by wealth, drive to the temple with pairs of horses in covered carriages, and so take their place, and a large number of attendants
follow after them. But the greater number do thus:—in the sacred enclosure of Aphroditē sit great numbers of women with a wreath of cord about
their heads; some come and others go; and there are straight aisles going
between the women in every direction, through which the strangers pass
by and make their choice. Here when a woman takes her seat she does not
depart again to her house until one of the strangers has thrown a silver
coin into her lap and has had sex with her outside the temple, and after
throwing it he must say these words only: "I call upon the goddess Mylitta
in your behalf." Mylitta is the Assyrians' name for Aphroditē. The silver
coin may be of any value; whatever it is she will not refuse it, for that is not
lawful for her, seeing that this coin is made sacred by the act. She follows
the man who has first thrown, and does not reject any. After that she

*The bracketed clause seems out of place or interpolated.

departs to her house, having discharged her duty to the goddess, nor will you be able thenceforth to give any gift so great as to seduce her. So then as many as possess beauty and stature are speedily released, but those who are ugly remain there much time, not being able to fulfil the law; for some of them remain even as much as three or four years. In some parts of Cyprus too there is a custom similar to this.

200. These customs then are established among the Babylonians. There are three tribes which eat nothing but fish. When they have caught them and dried them in the sun they do thus,—they throw them into brine, and then pound them with pestles and strain them through muslin; and they have them for food either kneaded into a soft cake, or baked like bread, according to their liking.

201. When this nation also had been subdued by Cyrus, he desired to bring the Massagetai into subjection to himself. This nation is reputed to be both great and warlike, and to dwell towards the East and the sunrise, beyond the river Araxes and over against the Issedonians. Some say that this nation is of Scythian race. **202.** Now the Araxes is said by some to be larger and by others to be smaller than the Ister.* They say that there are many islands in it about equal in size to Lesbos, and in them people dwell who feed in the summer upon roots of all kinds which they dig up; and certain fruits from trees, which have been discovered by them for food, they store up, it is said, in the season when they are ripe and feed upon them in the winter. Moreover it is said that other trees have been discovered by them which yield fruit of such a kind that when they have assembled together in companies in the same place and lighted a fire, they sit round in a circle and throw some of it into the fire, and they smell the fruit which is thrown on, as it burns, and are intoxicated by the scent as the Hellenes are with wine, and when more of the fruit is thrown on they become more intoxicated, until at last they rise up to dance and begin to sing. This is said to be their life-style. The river Araxes flows from the land of the Matienians, whence flows the Gyndes which Cyrus divided into the three hundred and sixty channels, and it discharges itself by forty branches, of which all except one end in swamps and shallow pools; and among them they say that men dwell who feed on fish eaten raw, and who use as clothing the skins of seals. One remaining branch of the Araxes flows with unimpeded course into the Caspian Sea.

203. Now the Caspian Sea is on its own, not having connection with the other Sea. All that Sea which the Hellenes navigate, and the Sea beyond the Pillars, which is called Atlantis, and the Erythraian Sea are in fact all one, but the Caspian is separate and lies apart. In length it is a voyage of fifteen days if one uses oars [as well as sails],† and in breadth, where it is

*The Greek name for the Danube.
†On a basis of 30 miles per day (see 2.11), the figures are low, since the Caspian's true measure is 750 by 280 miles.

broadest, a voyage of eight days. On the side towards the West of this Sea the Caucasus runs along by it, which is of all mountain-ranges both the greatest in extent and the loftiest. The Caucasus has many various races of men dwelling in it, living for the most part on the wild produce of the forests; and among them there are said to be trees which produce leaves of such a kind that by pounding them and mixing water with them they paint figures upon their garments, and the figures do not wash out, but grow old with the woollen stuff as if they had been woven into it at the first. Men say that the sexual intercourse of these people is unrestricted like that of cattle.

204. On the West then of this Sea called Caspian the Caucasus is the boundary, while towards the East and the rising sun a plain succeeds limitless in extent to the view. The Massagetai occupy a large part of this great plain, against whom Cyrus had become eager to march; for there were many strong reasons which incited and urged him onwards,—first the manner of his birth, that is to say the opinion held of him that he was more than a mere mortal man, and next the success which he had met with in his wars, for wherever Cyrus directed his march, it was impossible for that nation to escape.

205. Now the ruler of the Massagetai was a woman, who was queen after the death of her husband, and her name was Tomyris. To her Cyrus sent and wooed her, pretending that he desired to have her for his wife. Tomyris, understanding that he was wooing not herself but rather the kingdom of the Massagetai,* rejected his approaches. Cyrus after this, as he made no progress by craft, marched to the Araxes and campaigned openly against the Massagetai, forming bridges of boats over the river for his army to cross, and building towers upon the vessels which gave them safe passage across the river.

206. While he was engaged in this labour, Tomyris sent a herald and said: "King of the Medes, cease pursuing the work which you are now pressing forward; for you can not tell whether these things will end to your advantage. Cease and be king over your own people, and allow us to rule those whom we rule. Since however I know that you won't like this advice, but choose anything rather than to keep quiet, therefore if you are very anxious to make trial of the Massagetai in fight, come now, leave that labour of yoking together the banks of the river, and cross over into our land, when we have first withdrawn three days' journey from the river. Or if you desire rather to receive us into your land, do this same thing yourself."

Having heard this Cyrus called together the first men among the Persians, and having gathered these together he laid the matter before them for discussion, asking their advice as to what he should do. Their opinions all agreed, bidding him receive Tomyris and her army into his country. **207.** But Crœsus the Lydian, being present and finding fault with this opinion, declared an opinion to the contrary, saying: "King, I told you in former

---

*Herodotus explores Realpolitik in many incidents; see also 4.167, 7.5, etc.

time also, that since Zeus had surrendered me to you, I would avert according to my power whatever disaster I might see coming near your house. My sufferings, which have been bitter, have provided lessons in wisdom to me. If you think that you are immortal and that you command an army which is also immortal, it will be pointless for me to declare my judgment; but if you have realized that you are a mortal man yourself and command others who are so likewise, then learn this first, that for the affairs of men there is a revolving wheel, and that this in its revolution never permits the same persons always to have good fortune. I therefore now judge the matter laid before us contrary to that of these men. If we shall consent to receive the enemy in our land, this danger faces you:—if you are worsted you will lose in addition all your realm, for it is evident that if the Massagetai are victors they will not turn back and fly, but will march upon the provinces of your realm; and on the other hand if you shall be the victor, you will not be victor so fully as if you should overcome the Massagetai after crossing over into their land and should pursue them when they fled. For balancing that other scenario I mentioned before, I will set the same again here, and say that you, when you have conquered, will march straight against the realm of Tomyris. Moreover, it is a disgrace and not to be endured that Cyrus the son of Cambyses should yield to a woman and so withdraw from her land. Now therefore I believe that we should cross over and go forward from the crossing as far as they go in their retreat, and try to overcome them by doing as follows:—The Massagetai, as I am informed, are without experience of Persian good things, and have never enjoyed any great luxuries. Cut up therefore cattle without stint and prepare the meat and set out for these men a banquet in our camp. Moreover provide without stint bowls of unmixed wine and provisions of every kind; and having so done, leave behind the most worthless part of your army and let the rest begin to retreat from the camp towards the river. If I am not mistaken, they when they see a quantity of good things will fall to the feast, and after that it remains for us to display great deeds."

208. These were the conflicting opinions; and Cyrus, abandoning the former opinion and choosing that of Crœsus, gave notice to Tomyris to retire, as he was intending to cross over to her.* She then proceeded to retire, as she had at first engaged to do, but Cyrus delivered Crœsus into the hands of his son Cambyses, to whom he meant to give the kingdom, and gave him charge earnestly to honour him and to treat him well, if the crossing over to attack the Massagetai should not succeed. Having thus charged him and sent these to the land of the Persians, he and his army crossed over the river.

209. And when he had passed over the Araxes, night having come on he saw a vision in his sleep in the land of the Massagetai, as follows:—it seemed to Cyrus that he saw the eldest of the sons of Hystaspes having wings upon his shoulders, and that with the one of these he overshadowed

---

*Expedition against the Massagetai c.530 b.c.

Asia and with the other Europe. Now of Hystaspes the son of Arsames, who was a man of the Achaimenid clan, the eldest son was Dareios, who was then, I suppose, a youth of about twenty years, and he had been left behind in the land of the Persians, for he was not yet old enough to go out to the wars. When Cyrus awoke he mulled over the vision. Since the vision seemed to him to be of great import, he called Hystaspes, and having taken him aside he said: "Hystaspes, your son has been found plotting against me and against my throne: and how I know this for certain I will declare:—The gods care about me and show me beforehand all the future events that threaten me. So in the night that is past while sleeping I saw the eldest of your sons having upon his shoulders wings, and with the one of these he overshadowed Asia and with the other Europe. To judge by this vision then, no interpretation can avoid the conclusion that he is plotting against me. Therefore go by the quickest way back to Persia and take care that, when I return thither after having subdued these regions, you produce your son before me to be examined."

210. Cyrus said thus supposing that Dareios was plotting against him; but in fact the divine powers were showing him beforehand that he was destined to find his end there and that his kingdom was coming around to Dareios. Hystaspes replied: "King, may it never happen that any man of Persian race plot against you, and if there be any, may he perish as quickly as may be. You made the Persians free instead of slaves, and the rulers of all nations instead of being ruled by others. And if any vision announces to you that my son is planning rebellion against you, I hand him over to you to do with him what you wish."

211. Hystaspes then, having answered and having crossed over the Araxes, headed for the Persian land to keep watch over his son Dareios for Cyrus. Cyrus meanwhile went forward and marched one day from the Araxes according to the suggestion of Crœsus. After this when Cyrus and the sound part of the army of the Persians had marched back to the Araxes, and those unfit for fighting had been left behind, then one-third of the army of the Massagetai attacked and proceeded to kill, not without resistance, those whom the army of Cyrus had left behind. Seeing the feast that was set forth, when they had overcome their enemies they lay down and feasted, and being satiated with food and wine they went to sleep. Then the Persians came upon them and slew many of them, and took alive many more even than they slew, and among these the son of the queen Tomyris, who was leading the army of the Massagetai; and his name was Spargapises.

212. She then, when she heard that which had come to pass concerning the army and also the things concerning her son, sent a herald to Cyrus and said: "Cyrus, insatiable of blood, do not celebrate too much what has come to pass, namely because with that fruit of the vine, with which you fill yourselves and become so mad that as the wine descends into your bodies, wicked words float up upon its stream,—because setting a snare, I say, with such a drug as this you overcame my son, and not by valour in fight. Now therefore hear this my word, giving you good advice:—Restore to me my son and depart from this land without penalty, triumphant over a third

part of the army of the Massagetai. If you shall not do so, I swear to you by the Sun, who is lord of the Massagetai, that surely I will give you your fill of blood, blood-thirsty as you are."

213. These words were reported to him, but Cyrus disregarded them; and the son of the queen Tomyris, Spargapises, when he sobered up and he realized his plight, entreated Cyrus that he might be loosed from his chains and gained his request. So soon as his hands were free, he put himself to death. **214.** He then ended his life in this manner; but Tomyris, as Cyrus did not listen to her, gathered together all her power and joined battle with Cyrus. This battle I judge to have been the fiercest of all the battles fought by Barbarians, and I am informed that it happened thus:—first, it is said, they stood apart and shot at one another, and afterwards when their arrows were all shot away, they fell upon one another and engaged in close combat with their spears and daggers; and so they continued their fight with one another for a long time, and neither side would flee; but at last the Massagetai got the better in the fight. The greater part of the Persian army was destroyed there upon the spot, and Cyrus himself died there, after he had reigned twenty-nine years. Then Tomyris filled a skin with human blood and had search made among the Persian dead for the corpse of Cyrus. When she found it, she let his head down into the skin and doing outrage to the corpse she said this over it: "Though I yet live and have overcome you in fight, nevertheless you have destroyed me by taking my son with craft. I nevertheless according to my threat will give you your fill of blood." There are many tales told about the end of the life of Cyrus, but this one is to my mind the most worthy of belief.

215. The Massagetai dress similarly to the Scythians, and they have a manner of life which is also like theirs; and they have horsemen and also men who do not ride on horses, and moreover there are both archers and spearmen, and their custom it is to carry battle-axes.* For everything they use either gold or bronze. They use bronze for all spear-points or arrowheads or battle-axes, but for head-dresses and girdles and shoulder-belts they employ gold as ornament. They likewise put breast-plates of bronze about their horses' chests, but on their bridles and bits and cheek-pieces they employ gold. Iron however and silver they use not at all, for they do not have them in their land, but gold and bronze in abundance. **216.** These are the customs which they follow:—Each marries a wife, but they have their wives in common; for that practice which the Hellenes say that the Scythians have, is not in fact done by the Scythians but by the Massagetai, that is to say, whenever a man of the Massagetai may desire a woman he hangs up his quiver in front of her waggon and has sex with her freely. They have no precise limit of age laid down for their life, but when a man grows very old, his nearest of kin come together and slaughter him ceremoniously and cattle also with him; and then after that they boil the flesh and banquet upon it. This is considered by them the

---

*The *sagaris* is a hacking-edged weapon; compare 7.64.

happiest lot; but him who has ended his life by disease they do not eat, but cover him up in the earth, counting it a misfortune that he did not obtain ceremonious slaughter. They sow no crops but live on cattle and on fish, which they get in abundance from the river Araxes; moreover they are drinkers of milk. Of gods they reverence the Sun alone, and to him they sacrifice horses. The rule behind the ceremonious sacrifice is this:—to the swiftest of the gods they assign the swiftest of all mortal things.

BOOK II

EGYPT: GEOGRAPHY, CUSTOMS, HISTORY, TALES

1. AFTER CYRUS DIED, CAMBYSES succeeded to the royal power.* He was the son of Cyrus and of Cassandanē the daughter of Pharnaspes, for whose death, which came about before his own, Cyrus had made great mourning himself and also had proclaimed to all his subjects that they should mourn her. Cambyses, the son of this woman and of Cyrus, regarded the Ionians and Aiolians as slaves inherited from his father; and he proceeded to march an army against Egypt, taking with him as helpers not only the other nations which he ruled, but also the Hellenes over whom he had power.

2. Now the Egyptians, before Psammetichos† became king over them, supposed that they were the first of all men; but since Psammetichos having become king desired to know which nation was oldest, they believe that the Phrygians came into being before themselves, but they themselves before all other men. Now Psammetichos, when he was not able by inquiry to determine how to discover who had first come into being, contrived this experiment:—Taking two new-born children at random he gave them to a shepherd to bring up in his pastures, with this education:—no man should utter any word in their presence, and they should be placed by themselves in a hut where none might come, and at the proper time he should bring to them she-goats, and when he had satisfied them with milk do whatever else they needed. These things Psammetichos did and gave him this charge wishing to hear what word the children would speak first after they had ceased from senseless whimperings. And so it came to pass; for after two years had gone by, during which the shepherd did as ordered, at length, when he opened the door and entered, both the children fell before him in entreaty and uttered the word *bekos,* stretching forth their hands. At first when he heard this the shepherd kept silence; but since this word was often repeated, as he visited them constantly and attended to them, at last he declared the matter to his master, and at his command he brought in the children. Then Psammetichos having himself also heard it, began to inquire what nation of men named anything *bekos,* and he found that the Phrygians had this name for bread. Guided by an indication such as this, the

---

*Cambyses ruled from 529 to 522 B.C.; Herodotus' sources misrepresented his religious policies.
†Psammetichos became king c.670 B.C.

79

Egyptians conceded that the Phrygians were a more ancient people than themselves.

3. That so it happened I heard from the priests of that Hephaistos at Memphis; but the Hellenes relate, besides many other idle tales, that Psammetichos cut out the tongues of certain women and then made the children live with these women.

They related so much about the rearing of the children. I heard also other things at Memphis when I discussed stories with the priests of Hephaistos.* Moreover I visited both Thebes and Heliopolis because I wished to know whether the priests at these places would agree in their accounts with those at Memphis; for the men of Heliopolis are said to be the most learned in records of the Egyptians. Those of their narrations which I heard with regard to the gods I am not eager to relate in full, but I shall touch upon them only, because I consider that all men are equally informed and equally ignorant of these matters. Whatever I may record, I shall record only because I am compelled by the course of the story.

4. But as to those matters which concern men, the priests agreed with one another in saying that the Egyptians were the first of all men on earth to find out the course of the year, having divided the course of the seasons into twelve parts to make up the whole; and this they said they found out from the stars. They reckon more wisely than the Hellenes, as it seems to me, inasmuch as the Hellenes throw in an intercalated month every other year, to make the seasons right, whereas the Egyptians, reckoning the twelve months at thirty days each, bring in also every year five days beyond the number, and thus the circle of their seasons is completed and comes round to the same point whence it set out.

They said moreover that the Egyptians were the first who brought into use appellations for the twelve gods and the Hellenes took up the use from them; and that they were the first who assigned altars and images and temples to the gods, and who engraved figures on stones; and with regard to the greater number of these things they showed me evidence that they had happened so. They said also that the first *man* who became king of Egypt was Min, and that in his time all Egypt except the district of Thebes was a swamp, and none of the regions were then above water which now lie below the lake of Moiris, a voyage now of seven days up the river from the sea.
5. I thought that they were right about the land;† for it is manifest in truth even to a person who has not heard it beforehand but has only seen, at least if he has some understanding, that the Egypt to which the Hellenes come in ships is a land which has been won by the Egyptians as an addition. It is a gift of the river. Moreover the regions which lie above this lake also for a distance of three days' sail, about which they did not say anything of this kind, are nevertheless another instance of the same thing since the nature of the land of Egypt is such that when you are still approaching it in

*Herodotus here Hellenizes Ptah.
†Chapters 5–34 describe the unparalleled land and water supply of Egypt.

a ship and are distant a day's run from the land, if you let down a sounding-line you will bring up mud and will find yourself in 66 feet. This then so far shows that there is a silting forward of the land. **6.** Then secondly, as to Egypt itself, the extent of it along the sea is sixty *schoines* or 400 miles,* according to our definition of Egypt as extending from the Gulf of Plinthinē to the Serbonian lake, along which stretches Mount Casion. The sixty *schoines* are reckoned from this lake then. Men who are poor in land have their country measured by *orguiai*, while those who are less poor by *stades*, those who have much land by parasangs, and those who have land in very great abundance by *schoines*: now the parasang is equal to thirty *stades*, and each *schoine*, which is an Egyptian measure, is equal to sixty *stades*. So there would be an extent of three thousand six hundred *stades* for the coast-land of Egypt.† **7.** From thence and as far as Heliopolis inland Egypt is broad, and the land is all flat and without springs of water and formed of mud. The road as one goes inland from the sea to Heliopolis is about the same in length as that which leads from the altar of the twelve gods at Athens to Pisa and the temple of Olympian Zeus. Reckoning up you would find the difference very small by which these roads fall short of equality in length, not more indeed than 1¾ miles; for the road from Athens to Pisa of 172 miles lacks 1¾ miles, while the road to Heliopolis from the sea reaches that number completely.

8. From Heliopolis however, as you go up, Egypt is narrow; for on the one side a mountain-range belonging to Arabia stretches along by the side of it, going in a direction from the North towards the midday and the South, tending up-country without a break to the Erythraian Sea, in which range are the stone-quarries used for the pyramids at Memphis. On this side then the mountain ends where I have said, and then doubles back; and where it is widest, as I was informed, it is a journey of two months‡ across from East to West; and the borders of it towards the East are said to produce frankincense. Such then is the nature of this mountain-range; and on the side of Egypt towards Libya another range extends, rocky and enveloped in sand. Here are the pyramids, and it runs in the same direction as those parts of the Arabian mountains which go towards the midday. So then, I say, from Heliopolis the land no longer is wide by Egyptian standards, and for about four days' sail up the river Egypt properly so called is narrow. The space between the mountain-ranges which have been mentioned is plain-land, but where it is narrowest it did not seem to me to exceed 23 miles from the Arabian mountains to those which are called the Libyan.§ After this again Egypt is broad. **9.** Such is the nature of this land:

----

*This figure is about one-third too large; a better estimate is 300 miles.
†100 orguiai = 1 stade (about 606 feet; the Greek for "stades" is *stadia*, from which "stadium" is derived); 30 stades = 1 parasang; 2 parasangs (a Persian measure) = 1 schoenus = 6.9 miles; by the reckoning here the coast of Egypt measures 413 miles.
‡A puzzling and gross exaggeration.
§This figure is nearly double a correct one (there were no maps or pedometers).

and from Heliopolis to Thebes is a voyage up the river of nine days, and the distance of the journey is 558 miles, the number of *schoines* being eighty-one. If these measures of Egypt be put together, the result follows:— I have already before this shown that the distance along the sea amounts to 413 miles, and I will now declare the distance inland from the sea to Thebes, namely 702.5 miles. The distance from Thebes to the city called Elephantinē is 206.5 miles.

10. Of this land then, concerning which I have spoken, it seemed to me just as the priests said, that the greater part had been won as an addition by the Egyptians. It was evident to me that the space between the aforesaid mountain-ranges, which lie above the city of Memphis, once was a gulf of the sea, like the regions about Ilion and Teuthrania and Ephesos and the plain of the Maiander, if it be permitted to compare small things with great; and small these are in comparison, for of the rivers which heaped up the soil in those regions none is worthy to be compared in volume with a single one of the mouths of the Nile, which has five mouths. Moreover there are other rivers also, not in size at all equal to the Nile, which have performed great feats; of which I can mention the names of several, and especially the Acheloös, which flowing through Acarnania and issuing out into the sea has already made half of the Echinades islands into mainland.

11. Now there is in the land of Arabia, not far from Egypt, a gulf of the sea running in from that which is called the Erythraian Sea, very long and narrow, as I will tell. With respect to the length of the voyage along it, one who set out from the innermost point to sail out through it into the open sea, would spend forty days upon the voyage, using oars [as well as sails]. Where the gulf is broadest it is half a day's sail across: and there is in it an ebb and flow of tide every day. Just such another gulf I suppose that Egypt was, and that the one ran in towards Ethiopia from the Northern Sea, and the other, the Arabian, of which I am about to speak, tended from the South towards Syria, the gulfs boring in so as almost to meet at their extreme points, and passing by one another with but a small space left between. If then the stream of the Nile should turn aside into this Arabian gulf, what would hinder that gulf from being filled up with silt as the river continued to flow, at all events within a period of twenty thousand years? Indeed for my part I am of opinion that it would be filled up even within ten thousand years. How, then, in all the time that has elapsed before I was born should a gulf not be filled up even of much greater size than this by a river so great and so active?

12. As regards Egypt then, I both believe those who say that these things are so, and for myself also I believe strongly that they are so; because I have observed that Egypt runs out into the sea further than the adjoining land, and that shells are found upon the mountains of it, and an efflorescence of salt forms upon the surface, so that even the pyramids are being eaten away by it, and moreover that of all the mountains of Egypt, the range which lies above Memphis is the only one which has sand. I further notice that Egypt resembles neither the land of Arabia, which borders upon it, nor Libya, nor yet Syria (for they are Syrians who dwell in the parts of Arabia lying along the sea), but that it has soil which is black and easily breaks up, seeing that it is in truth mud and silt brought down from Ethiopia by the river. The soil of Libya, we know however, is reddish in colour and rather sandy, while that of Arabia and Syria is somewhat clayey and rocky. **13.** The priests also gave me a strong proof concerning this land. In the reign of king Moiris, whenever the river reached a height of at least 12 feet it watered Egypt below Memphis; and not yet nine hundred years had gone by since the death of Moiris, when I heard these things from the priests. Now however, unless the river rises to 24 feet, or 22.5 feet at the least, it does not go over the land. I think too that those Egyptians who dwell below the lake of Moiris and especially in that region which is called the Delta, if that land continues to grow in height according to this proportion and to increase similarly in extent, will suffer for all remaining time, from the Nile not overflowing their land, that same thing which they themselves said that the Hellenes would at some time suffer. Hearing that the whole land of the Hellenes has rain and is not watered by rivers as theirs is, they said that the Hellenes would at some time be disappointed of a great hope and would suffer the ills of famine. This saying means that if the god shall not send them rain, but shall allow drought to prevail for a long time, the Hellenes will be destroyed by hunger; for they have in fact no supply of water to save them except from Zeus alone.

14. This has been rightly said by the Egyptians with reference to the Hellenes. Now let me tell how the Egyptians themselves fare. If, in accordance with what I before said, their land below Memphis (for this is that which is increasing) shall continue to increase in height according to the same proportion as in past time, assuredly those Egyptians who dwell here will suffer famine, if their land shall not have rain nor the river be able to go over their fields. It is certain however that now they gather in fruit from the earth with less labour than any other men and also with less than the other Egyptians; for they have no labour in breaking up furrows with a plough nor in hoeing nor in any other of those labours which other men have about a crop; but when the river has come up of itself and watered their fields and after watering has left them again, then each man sows his own field and turns into it swine, and when he has trodden the seed into the ground by means of the swine, after that he waits for the harvest; and when he has threshed the grain by means of the swine, then he gathers it in.

15. If we desire to follow the opinions of the Ionians as regards Egypt, who say that the Delta alone is Egypt, reckoning its sea-coast to be from the watch-tower called Perseus to the fish-curing houses of Pelusion, a distance of forty *schoines,* and counting it to extend inland as far as the city of Kercasoros, where the Nile divides and runs to Pelusion and Canobos, while they assign the rest of Egypt partly to Libya and partly to Arabia,— if, I say, we should follow this account, we should thereby declare that in former times the Egyptians had no land to live in. As we have seen, their

Delta at any rate is alluvial, and has appeared (so to speak) lately, as the Egyptians themselves say and as I think. If then at the first there was no land for them to live in, why did they waste their labour to prove that they had come into being before all other men? They needed not to have made trial of the children to see what language they would first utter. However I disagree that the Egyptians came into being at the same time as that which is called by the Ionians the Delta, and I believe that they existed always ever since the human race came into being, and that as their land advanced forwards, many of them were left in their first abodes and many came down gradually to the lower parts. At least it is certain that in old times [the district of] Thebes had the name of Egypt, and of this the circumference measures 702 miles.

16. If then we judge aright of these matters, the opinion of the Ionians about Egypt is not sound: but if the judgment of the Ionians is right, I declare that neither the Hellenes nor the Ionians themselves know how to reckon since they say that the whole earth is made up of three divisions, Europe, Asia, and Libya because they ought to count in addition to these the Delta of Egypt, since it belongs neither to Asia nor to Libya; for at least it cannot be the river Nile by this reckoning which divides Asia from Libya [or Africa], but the Nile is cleft at the point of this Delta so as to flow round it, and the result is that this land would come between Asia and Libya.*

17. We dismiss then the opinion of the Ionians, and express a judgment of our own on this matter also, that Egypt is all that land which is inhabited by Egyptians, just as Kilikia is that which is inhabited by Kilikians and Assyria that which is inhabited by Assyrians, and we know of no boundary properly speaking between Asia and Libya except the borders of Egypt. If however we shall adopt the opinion commonly held by the Hellenes, we shall suppose that the whole of Egypt, beginning from the Cataract and the city of Elephantinē, is divided into two parts and that it thus partakes of both the names, since one side will thus belong to Libya and the other to Asia; for the Nile from the Cataract onwards flows to the sea cutting Egypt in two; and as far as the city of Kercasoros the Nile flows in one single stream, but from this city onwards it is parted into three ways; and one, which is called the Pelusian mouth, turns towards the East; the second of the ways goes towards the West, and this is called the Canobic mouth; but that way which is straight runs thus— when the river in its course downwards comes to the point of the Delta, then it cuts the Delta through the middle and so issues out to the sea. In this we have a portion of the water of the river which is not the smallest nor the least famous, and it is called the Sebennytic mouth. There are also two other mouths which part off from the Sebennytic and go to the sea, and these are called, one the Saïtic, the other the Mendesian mouth. The

---

*Herodotus argues with previous and contemporary geographers and logographers about Egypt's place in the configuration of continents.

Bolbitinitic and Bucolic mouths, on the other hand, are not natural but made by digging.

18. Moreover also the answer given by the Oracle of Ammon supports my opinion that Egypt is as big as I declare it to be in my account. I only heard this answer after I had formed my own opinion about Egypt. For those of the city of Marea and of Apis, dwelling in the parts of Egypt which border on Libya, believing that they were Libyans and not Egyptians, and also being burdened by the rules of religious observance, because they desired not to be debarred from the use of cows' flesh, sent to Ammon denying that they had anything in common with the Egyptians, for they dwelt outside the Delta and agreed with them in nothing; and they said they wished that it might be lawful for them to eat everything without distinction. The god however did not permit them to do so, but said that that land was Egypt which the Nile came over and watered, and that those were Egyptians who dwelling below the city of Elephantinē drank of that river. Thus the Oracle answered about this. **19.** The Nile, when it is in flood, goes over not only the Delta but also the land called Libyan and that called Arabian sometimes as much as two days' journey on each side, and at times even more than this or sometime less.

Neither from the priests nor yet from any other man was I able to obtain any knowledge about the nature of the river. I was desirous especially to learn from them why the Nile comes down increasing in volume from the summer solstice onwards for a hundred days, and then, when it has reached this number of days, turns and goes back, failing in its stream, so that through the whole winter season it continues to be low, until the summer solstice returns. I was able to receive account of none of these things from the Egyptians, when I inquired of them what power the Nile has whereby its nature is opposite to that of all other rivers. And I made inquiry, desiring to know both this and also why, unlike all other rivers, it does not give rise to any breezes blowing from it.

20. However some of the Hellenes who desired to gain distinction for cleverness have given three different accounts of this water: two of these I do not think it worth while even to speak of except only to indicate their nature; of which the one says that the Etesian Winds are the cause that makes the river rise, by preventing the Nile from flowing out into the sea. But often the Etesian Winds fail and yet the Nile does the same work as usual; and moreover, if these were the cause, all the other rivers also which flow in a direction opposed to the Etesian Winds ought to have been affected in the same way as the Nile, and even more, in as much as they are smaller and present to them a feebler flow of stream. There are many of these rivers in Syria and many also in Libya, and they are affected in no such manner as the Nile.

21. The second way shows more ignorance than that which has been mentioned, and it is more marvellous to tell; for it says that the river produces these effects because it flows from the Ocean, and that the Ocean flows round the whole earth.

22. The third of the ways is much the most attractive, but nevertheless it is the most mistaken of all. Indeed this way has no more truth in it than the rest, alleging as it does that the Nile flows from melting snow; whereas it flows out of Libya through the midst of the Ethiopians,* and so comes out into Egypt. How then should it flow from snow, when it flows from the hottest parts to those which are cooler? And indeed most of the facts are such as to convince a man (one at least capable of reasoning about such matters), that it is not at all likely that it flows from snow. The first and greatest evidence is afforded by the winds, which blow hot from these regions; the second is that the land is rainless always and without frost, whereas after snow has fallen rain must necessarily come within five days, so that if it snowed in those parts rain would fall there; the third evidence is afforded by the people dwelling there, who are of a black colour by reason of the burning heat. Moreover kites and swallows remain there through the year and do not leave the land; and cranes flying from the cold weather which comes on in the region of Scythia come regularly to these parts for wintering. If then it snowed ever so little in that land through which the Nile flows and in which it has its rise, none of these things would take place, as necessity compels us to admit. **23.** As for him who talked about the Ocean, he carried his tale into the region of the unknown, and so he cannot be refuted. I for my part know of no river Ocean existing, but I think that Homer or one of the poets before him invented the name and introduced it into his verse.

24. If however after faulting the opinions proposed, I am bound to declare my own about the matters which are in doubt, I will offer my thought on the reason why the Nile increases in the summer. In the winter season the Sun, being driven away from his former path through the heaven by the stormy winds, comes to the upper parts of Libya. If one sets forth the matter in the shortest way, all has now been said; for whatever region this god approaches most and stands directly above, this it may reasonably be supposed is most in want of water, and its native streams of rivers are dried up most.

25. At greater length, thus it is:—the Sun passing in his course by the upper parts of Libya, since at all times the air in those parts is clear and the country is warm, although there are cold winds, in passing through it the Sun does just as he was wont to do in the summer, when going through the midst of the heaven. That is he draws to himself the water, and having drawn it he drives it away to the upper parts of the country, and the winds take it up and scattering it abroad melt it into rain; so it is natural that the winds which blow from this region, namely the South and Southwest Winds, should be much the most rainy of all the winds.

I think however that the Sun does not send away all the water of the

---

*Ethiopia was the Greek name for eastern Africa south of Egypt. This third view was argued by the sophist Anaxagoras; the pre-Socratic philosopher Thales presented the first and the logographer Hecataios the second; Anaxagoras was closest to the facts, but Herodotus' issues and method are sound.

Nile of each year, but that he also lets some remain behind with himself. Then when the winter becomes milder, the Sun returns back again to the midst of the heaven, and from that time onwards he draws equally from all rivers; but in the meanwhile they flow in large volume, since water of rain mingles with them in great quantity, because their country receives rain then and is filled with torrent streams. In summer however they are weak, since not only the showers of rain fail then, but also they are drawn by the Sun. The Nile however, alone of all rivers, not having rain and being drawn by the Sun, naturally flows during this time of winter in much less than its proper volume, that is much less than in summer; for then it is drawn equally with all the other waters, but in winter it bears the burden alone. Thus I suppose the Sun to be the cause of these things.

26. He also is the cause in my opinion that the air in these parts is dry, since he makes it so by scorching up his path through the heavens. Thus summer prevails always in the upper parts of Libya. If however the station of the seasons had been changed, and where now in the heaven are placed the North Wind and winter, there was the station of the South Wind and of the midday, and where now is placed the South Wind, there was the North, if this had been so, the Sun being driven from the midst of the heaven by the winter and the North Wind would go to the upper parts of Europe, just as now he comes to the upper parts of Libya, and passing in his course throughout the whole of Europe I suppose that he would do to the Ister what he now works upon the Nile. **27.** As to the breeze, why none blows from the river, my opinion is that from very hot places it is not natural that anything should blow, and that a breeze usually blows from something cold.

28. Let these matters then be as they are and as they were at the first. Not one of the Egyptians or of the Libyans or of the Hellenes, who spoke with me, professed to know anything about the sources of the Nile, except the scribe of the sacred treasury of Athenē at the city of Saïs in Egypt. To me however this man seemed not to be speaking seriously when he said that he had certain knowledge of it; and he said as follows, namely that there were two mountains of which the tops ran up to a sharp point, situated between the city of Syenē, which is in the district of Thebes, and Elephantinē, and the names of the mountains were Crophi and Mophi. From the middle between these mountains flowed (he said) the sources of the Nile, which were fathomless in depth, and half of the water flowed to Egypt and towards the North Wind, the other half to Ethiopia and the South Wind. As for the fathomless depth of the source, he said that Psammetichos king of Egypt experimented on this matter; for he had a rope twisted of many thousand fathoms and let it down in this place, and it reached no bottom. By this the scribe (if this which he told was really as he said) gave me to understand that there were certain strong eddies there and a backward flow, and that since the water dashed against the mountains, therefore the sounding-line could not come to any bottom when it was let down.

29. From no other person was I able to learn anything about this matter; but for the rest I learnt so much as here follows by the most diligent inquiry; for I went myself as an eye-witness as far as the city of Elephantinē and from that point onwards I gathered knowledge by report. From the city of Elephantinē as one goes up the river there is country which slopes steeply; so that here one must attach ropes to the vessel on both sides, as one fastens an ox, and so make one's way onward; and if the rope break, the vessel is gone at once, carried away by the violence of the stream. Through this country it is a voyage of about four days in length, and in this part the Nile is winding like the river Maiander, and the distance amounts to twelve *schoines* [or 79 miles], which one must traverse in this manner. Then you will come to a level plain, in which the Nile flows round an island named Tachompso. (Now in the regions above Elephantinē there dwell Ethiopians, who also occupy half of the island, and Egyptians the other half.) Adjoining this island there is a great lake, round which dwell Ethiopian nomad tribes; and when you have sailed through this you will come to the stream of the Nile again, which flows into this lake. After this you will disembark and make a journey by land of forty days; for in the Nile sharp rocks stand forth out of the water, and there are many reefs, which a vessel cannot pass. Then after having passed through this country in the forty days, you will embark again in another vessel and sail for twelve days; and after this you will come to a great city called Meroē. This city is said to be the mother-city of all the other Ethiopians: and they who dwell in it reverence of the gods Zeus and Dionysos alone, and these they greatly honour; and they have an Oracle of Zeus established, and make warlike marches whensoever this god commands them by prophesy and to whatsoever place he commands.

30. Sailing from this city you will come to the "Deserters" in another period of time equal to that in which you came from Elephantinē to the mother-city of the Ethiopians. Now the name of these "Deserters" is *Asmach,* and this word signifies, when translated into the tongue of the Hellenes, "those who stand on the left hand of the king." These were two hundred and forty thousand Egyptians of the warrior class, who revolted and went over to these Ethiopians for the following reason:—In the reign of Psammetichos garrisons were set, one towards the Ethiopians at the city of Elephantinē, another towards the Arabians and Assyrians at Daphnai of Pelusion, and another towards Libya at Marea. (Even in my own time the garrisons of the Persians too are ordered in the same manner as these were in the reign of Psammetichos, for both at Elephantinē and at Daphnai the Persians have outposts.) The Egyptians then had served as outpost-guards for three years and no one relieved them from their guard; accordingly they took counsel together, and adopting a common plan they all in a body revolted from Psammetichos and set out for Ethiopia. Hearing this Psammetichos set forth in pursuit, and when he came up with them he pleaded with them much and endeavoured to persuade them not to desert the gods of their country and their children and wives. It is said that one of them pointed to his prick and said that wherever this was, there would they have both children and wives. When these came to Ethiopia they gave themselves over to the king of the Ethiopians; and he rewarded them as follows:—there were certain of the Ethiopians who had come to dispute him; and he invited them to drive these out and dwell in their land. So since these men settled in the land of the Ethiopians, the Ethiopians have come to be of milder manners, from having learnt Egyptian customs.

31. The Nile then, besides that part of its course which is in Egypt, is known as far as a four months' journey by river and land: for that is the number of months which one reckons in going from Elephantinē to these "Deserters." The river runs from the West and the setting of the sun. But what comes after that point no one can clearly say; for this land is desert by reason of the burning heat.

32. However I heard from men of Kyrenē, who told me that they had been to the Oracle of Ammon, and had spoken with Etearchos king of the Ammonians. They conversed about the Nile and how no one knew the sources of it; and Etearchos said that once there came to him men of the Nasamonians (this is a Libyan race which dwells in the Syrtis, and also in the land to the East of the Syrtis reaching to no great distance), and when the Nasamonians came and were asked by him whether they were able to tell him anything more than he knew about the desert parts of Libya, they said that there had been among them certain sons of chief men, who were of unruly disposition; and these when they grew up to be men had devised various other extravagant things and also they had told off by lot five of themselves to go to see the desert parts of Libya and to try whether they could discover more than those who had previously explored furthest. In those parts of Libya which are by the Northern Sea, beginning from Egypt and going as far as the headland of Soloeis, which is the extreme point of Libya, Libyans (and of them many races) extend along the whole coast, except so much as the Hellenes and Phenicians hold; but in the upper [or inland] parts, which lie above the sea-coast and above those people whose land comes down to the sea, Libya is full of wild beasts; and in the parts above the land of wild beasts it is full of sand, terribly waterless and utterly desert. These young men then (said they), being sent out by their companions well furnished with supplies of water and provisions, went first through the inhabited country, and after they had passed through this they came to the country of wild beasts, and after this they passed through the desert, making their journey towards the West; and having passed through a great tract of sand in many days, they saw at last trees growing in a level place; and having come up to them, they were beginning to pluck the fruit which was upon the trees. As they began to pluck it, there came upon them small men, of less stature than men of the common size, and these seized them and carried them away; and neither could the Nasamonians understand anything of their speech nor could those who were carrying them off understand anything of Nasamonian speech. They led them (so it was said) through very great swamps, and after passing through these they came to a city in which all the men were like those who carried them off in size and black in colour of skin; and by the city ran a great river, which ran from the West towards the sunrising, and in it were seen crocodiles.*

33. Of the account given by Etearchos the Ammonian let so much suffice as is here said, except that, as the men of Kyrenē told me, he alleged that the Nasamonians returned safe home, and that the people to whom they had come were all wizards. Now this river which ran by the city, Etearchos conjectured to be the Nile, and moreover reason compels us to think so; for the Nile flows from Libya and cuts Libya in the middle, and as I conjecture, judging what is not known by that which is evident to view, it starts at a distance from its mouth equal to that of the Ister. The river Ister begins from the Keltoi and the city of Pyrenē and so runs that it divides Europe in the middle (now the Keltoi are outside the Pillars of Heracles and border upon the Kynesians, who dwell furthest towards the sunset of all those who dwell in Europe). The Ister ends, having its course through the whole of Europe, by flowing into the Euxine Sea at the place where the Milesians have their settlement of Istria.

34. Now the Ister, since it flows through land which is inhabited, is known by the reports of many; but of the sources of the Nile no one can give an account, for the part of Libya through which it flows is uninhabited and desert. About its course however, so much as it was possible to learn by the most diligent inquiry, the story has been told. It runs out into Egypt. Now Egypt lies nearly opposite to the mountain districts of Kilikia; and from thence to Sinopē, which lies upon the Euxine Sea, is a journey in the same straight line of five days for a man travelling light. Sinopē lies opposite to the place where the Ister runs out into the sea: thus I think that the Nile passes through the whole of Libya and is of equal measure with the Ister. Of the Nile then let so much suffice as has been said.

35. I shall however make my report of Egypt at length, because it has wonders more in number than any other land, and works too it has to show as much as any land, which are great beyond expression. That is why then more shall be said concerning it.†

The Egyptians in agreement with their climate, which is unlike any other, and with the river, which shows a nature different from all other rivers, established for themselves manners and customs opposite to other men in almost all matters. Among them the women frequent the market and carry on trade, while the men remain at home and weave; and whereas others weave pushing the woof upwards, the Egyptians push it downwards. The men carry their burdens upon their heads and the women upon their shoulders. The women piss standing up and the men crouching down. They ease themselves in their houses and they eat outside in the streets, alleging as reason for this that it is right to do secretly the things that are unseemly though necessary, but those which are not unseemly, in public. No

---

*The explorers would trek 1,000 miles to reach the pygmies of the Niger.
†Chapters 35 to 98 describe Egyptian customs.

woman is a priest either of male or female divinity, but men of all, both male and female. To support their parents the sons are in no way compelled, if they do not desire to do so, but the daughters are forced to do so, be they ever so unwilling.

36. The priests of the gods in other lands wear long hair, but in Egypt they shave their heads. Among other men the custom is that in mourning those whom the matter concerns most nearly have their hair cut short, but the Egyptians, when deaths occur, let their hair grow long, both that on the head and that on the chin, having before been close shaven. Other men have their daily living separated from beasts, but the Egyptians have theirs together with beasts. Other men live on wheat and on barley, but to any one of the Egyptians who makes his living on these it is a great reproach; they make their bread of rice-wheat which some call spelt. They knead dough with their feet and clay with their hands, with which also they gather up dung. Whereas other men, except such as have learnt otherwise from the Egyptians, have their members as nature made them, the Egyptians practise circumcision. The men wear two garments, each and the women but one. Others make fast the rings and ropes of the sails outside the ship, the Egyptians do this inside. Finally in the writing of characters and reckoning with pebbles, while the Hellenes carry the hand from the left to the right, the Egyptians do this from the right to the left; and doing so they say that they do it themselves rightwise and the Hellenes leftwise. They use two kinds of characters for writing, of which the one kind is called sacred and the other common.

37. They are religious excessively beyond all other men, and with regard to this they have customs:—they drink from cups of bronze and rinse them out every day, and not some only do this but all. They wear garments of linen always newly washed. They make a special point of practicing circumcision: they circumcise themselves for the sake of cleanliness, preferring to be clean rather than comely. The priests shave themselves all over their body every other day, so that no lice or any other foul thing may come to be upon them when they minister to the gods; and the priests wear garments of linen only and sandals of papyrus, and they may not take any other garment or other sandals; these wash themselves in cold water twice in the day and twice again in the night; and other religious services they perform (one may almost say) of infinite number. They enjoy also many good things, for they do not consume or spend anything of their own substance, but there is sacred bread baked for them and they have each great quantity of flesh of oxen and geese coming to them each day, and also wine from grapes is given to them; but it is not permitted to them to taste of fish. Beans moreover the Egyptians do not at all sow in their land, and those which grow they neither eat raw nor boil for food; nay the priests do not endure even to look upon them, thinking this to be an unclean kind of legume. There is not one priest only for each of the gods but many, and of them one is chiefpriest, and whenever a priest dies his son is appointed to his place.

38. The male oxen they consider to belong to Epaphos, and on account of him they test them in the following manner:—If the priest sees one single black hair upon the beast he counts it not clean for sacrifice; and one of the priests who is appointed for the purpose makes investigation of these matters, both when the beast is standing upright and when it is lying on its back, drawing out its tongue moreover, to see if it is clean in respect of the appointed signs, which I shall mention in another part of the history.* He looks also at the hairs of the tail to see if it has them growing in the natural manner. If it be clean in respect of all these things, he marks it with a piece of papyrus, rolling this round the horns, and then when he has plastered sealing-earth over it he sets upon it the seal of his signet-ring, and after that they take the animal away. But for one who sacrifices a beast not sealed the appointed penalty is death.

39. In this way then the beast is tested; and this is their appointed manner of sacrifice:—they lead the sealed beast to the altar where they happen to be sacrificing, and then kindle a fire. Having poured libations of wine over the altar so that it runs down upon the victim and having called upon the god, they cut its throat, and having cut its throat they sever the head from the body. The body then of the beast they flay, but upon the head they make many imprecations first, and then they who have a market and Hellenes sojourning among them for trade, these carry it to the market-place and sell it, while they who have no Hellenes among them cast it away into the river. The form of imprecation which they utter upon the heads, requires praying that if any evil be about to befall either themselves who are offering sacrifice or the land of Egypt in general, it may come rather upon this head.† Now as regards the heads of the beasts which are sacrificed and the pouring over them of the wine, all the Egyptians have the same customs equally for all their sacrifices; and by reason of this custom none of the Egyptians eat of the head either of this or of any other kind of animal. **40.** Their manner of disembowelling the victims and of burning them is appointed among them differently for different sacrifices; I shall speak however of the sacrifices to that goddess whom they regard as the greatest of all, and for whom they celebrate the greatest feast. —When they have flayed the bullock and made imprecation, they take out the whole of its lower entrails but leave in the body the upper entrails and the fat; and they sever from it the legs and the end of the loin and the shoulders and the neck. Afterwards they fill the rest of the body of the animal with pure loaves and honey and raisins and figs and frankincense and myrrh and every other kind of spices, and they offer it, pouring over it great abundance of oil. They make their sacrifice after fasting, and while the offerings are being burnt, they all beat themselves, and when they have finished beating themselves they feast on that which they left unburnt of the sacrifice.

41. The clean male oxen, both full-grown animals and calves, are sacrificed by all the Egyptians; the females however they may not sacrifice,

<hr>

*In 3.28 we hear details; Apis is the reborn Osiris.
†Scapegoat rituals are widely known; compare the Bible, Leviticus 16:21.

since these are sacred to Isis; for the figure of Isis is in the form of a woman with cow's horns, just as the Hellenes present Io in pictures, and all the Egyptians without distinction reverence cows far more than any other kind of cattle; for which reason neither man nor woman of Egyptian race would kiss a man who is a Hellene on the mouth, nor will they use a knife or roasting-spits or a caldron belonging to a Hellene, nor taste of the flesh even of a clean animal if it has been cut with the knife of a Hellene. And the cattle of this kind which die they bury in the following manner:—the females they cast into the river, but the males they bury, each people in the suburb of their town, with one of the horns, or sometimes both, protruding to mark the place; and when the bodies have rotted away and the appointed time comes on, then to each city comes a boat from that which is called the island of Prosopitis (this is in the Delta, and the extent of its circuit is nine *schoines*). In this island of Prosopitis is situated, besides many other cities, that one from which the boats come to take up the bones of the oxen, and the name of the city is Atarbechis, and in it there is set up a holy temple of Aphroditē.* From this city many go abroad in various directions, some to one city and others to another, and when they have dug up the bones of the oxen they carry them off, and coming together they bury them in one single place. In the same manner as they bury the oxen they bury also their other cattle when they die; for about them also they have the same law laid down, and these also they abstain from killing.

42. Now all who have a temple set up to the Theban Zeus or who are of the district of Thebes sacrifice goats and abstain from sheep. Not all the Egyptians equally reverence the same gods, except only Isis and Osiris (who they say is Dionysos), these they all reverence alike. They who have a temple of Mendes or belong to the Mendesian district, these abstain from goats and sacrifice sheep. Now the men of Thebes and those who after their example abstain from sheep, say that this custom was established among them for this cause:—Heracles (they say) had an earnest desire to see Zeus, and Zeus did not desire to be seen of him; and at last when Heracles was urgent in entreaty Zeus contrived this device, that is to say, he flayed a ram and held in front of him the head of the ram which he had cut off, and he put over him the fleece and then showed himself to him. Hence the Egyptians make the image of Zeus with the face of a ram; and the Ammonians do so also after their example, being settlers both from the Egyptians and from the Ethiopians, and using a language which is a medley of both tongues. In my opinion it is from this god that the Ammonians took the name which they have, for the Egyptians call Zeus *Amun*. The Thebans then do not sacrifice rams but hold them sacred for this reason; on one day however in the year, on the feast of Zeus, they cut up in the same manner and flay one single ram and cover with its skin the image of Zeus, and then they bring up to it another image of Heracles. This done,

---

*Herodotus uses a Greek divine name for Egyptian Hathor, as he does for Isis, although Isis is above (and elsewhere) interpreted as Demeter.

all who are in the temple beat themselves for the ram, and then they bury
it in a sacred tomb.

43. About Heracles I heard the account given that he was of the number of the twelve gods; but of the other Heracles whom the Hellenes know
I was not able to hear in any part of Egypt: and moreover to prove that the
Egyptians did not take the name of Heracles from the Hellenes, but rather
the Hellenes from the Egyptians,—that is to say those of the Hellenes who
gave the name Heracles to the son of Amphitryon,—of that, I say, besides
many other items of evidence there is chiefly this, namely that the parents
of this Heracles, Amphitryon and Alcmenē, were both of Egypt by descent, and also that the Egyptians say that they do not know the names either of Poseidon or of the Dioscuroi, nor have these been accepted by
them as gods among the other gods. If they had received from the Hellenes the name of any divinity, they would naturally have preserved the
memory of these most of all, assuming that in those times as now some of
the Hellenes made voyages and were seafaring folk, as I suppose and as
my judgment compels me to think; so that the Egyptians would have
learnt the names of these gods even more than that of Heracles. In fact
however Heracles is a very ancient Egyptian god; and (as they say themselves) it is seventeen thousand years to the beginning of the reign of
Amasis from the time when the twelve gods, of whom they count that
Heracles one, were begotten of the eight gods.

44. I moreover, desiring to know something certain of these matters so
far as might be, made a voyage also to Tyre of Phenicia, hearing that in
that place there was a holy temple of Heracles;* and I saw that it was richly
furnished with many votive offerings besides, and especially there were
in it two pillars, the one of pure gold and the other of an emerald stone of
such size as to shine by night. Having spoken with the priests of the god,
I asked them how long time it was since their temple had been set up. I
found these also to be at variance with the Hellenes, for they said that at
the same time when Tyre was founded, the temple of the god also had
been set up, and that it was a period of two thousand three hundred years
since their people began to dwell at Tyre. I saw also at Tyre another temple
of Heracles, with the surname Thasian; and I came to Thasos also and
there I found a temple of Heracles set up by the Phenicians, who had
sailed out to seek for Europa and had colonised Thasos; and these things
happened full five generations of men before Heracles the son of Amphitryon was born in Hellas. So then my inquiries show clearly that Heracles is
an ancient god, and those of the Hellenes seem to me to act most rightly
who have two temples of Heracles set up, and who sacrifice to the one as
an immortal god and with the title Olympian, and make offerings of the
dead to the other as a hero.

45. Besides many other stories which the Hellenes tell without due
consideration, this tale is especially foolish which they tell about Heracles.

---

*That is, the Semitic Melqart, a sun god like Ba'al.

When he came to Egypt, the Egyptians put on him wreaths and led him forth in procession to sacrifice him to Zeus; and he for some time kept quiet, but when they were beginning the sacrifice of him at the altar, he trusted to his might and slew them all. I think that the Hellenes when they tell this tale are altogether without knowledge of the nature and customs of the Egyptians; for how should they for whom it is not lawful to sacrifice even beasts, except swine and the males of oxen and calves (such of them as are clean) and geese, how should these sacrifice human beings? Besides this, how is it in nature possible that Heracles, being one person only and moreover a man (as they assert), should slay many myriads? Having said this much may we meet kindness from both the gods and the heroes for our speech.

46. Now the reason why those of the Egyptians whom I have mentioned do not sacrifice goats, female or male, is this:—the Mendesians count Pan to be one of the eight gods (now these eight gods they say came into being before the twelve gods), and the painters and image-makers represent in painting and in sculpture the figure of Pan, just as the Hellenes do, with goat's face and legs, not supposing him to be really like this but to resemble the other gods; why they represent him in this form I prefer not to say. The Mendesians then reverence all goats and the males more than the females (and the goatherds too have greater honour than other herdsmen), but of the goats one especially is reverenced, and when he dies there is great mourning in all the Mendesian district. Both the goat and Pan are called in the Egyptian tongue *Mendes*. Moreover in my lifetime there happened in that district this marvel, that is to say a he-goat had intercourse with a woman publicly, and this was so done that all men saw it.

47. The pig is accounted by the Egyptians an abominable animal; and first, if any of them in passing by touch a pig, he goes into the river and dips himself immediately in the water together with his garments; and then too swineherds, though they be native Egyptians, unlike all others do not enter any of the temples in Egypt, nor is anyone willing to give his daughter in marriage to one of them or to take a wife from among them; but the swineherds both give in marriage to one another and take from one another. Now to the other gods the Egyptians do not think it right to sacrifice swine; but to the Moon and to Dionysos alone at the same time and on the same full-moon they sacrifice swine, and then eat their flesh. When they abominate swine at all their other feasts, the reason why they sacrifice them at this, has a story told by the Egyptians; and this story I know, but it is not a seemly one for me to tell.

Now the sacrifice of the swine to the Moon is performed as follows:—when the priest has slain the victim, he puts together the end of the tail and the spleen and the caul, and covers them up with the whole of the fat of the animal which is about the paunch, and then he offers them with fire; and the rest of the flesh they eat on that day of full moon upon which they have held the sacrifice, but on any day after this they will not taste of it. The poor however among them by reason of the scantiness of their means shape pigs of dough and having baked them they offer these as a sacrifice.

48. Then for Dionysos on the eve of the festival each one kills a pig by cutting its throat before his own doors, and after that he gives the pig to the swineherd who sold it to him, to carry away again; and the rest of the feast of Dionysos is celebrated by the Egyptians in the same way as by the Hellenes in almost all things except choral dances, but instead of the *phallos* they have invented another contrivance, namely figures of about a cubit in height worked by strings, which women carry about the villages, with the penis made to move up and down and not much less in size than the rest of the body. A flute goes before and they follow singing the praises of Dionysos. As to the reason why the figure has this member larger than is natural and moves it, though it moves no other part of the body, about this there is a sacred story told.

49. Now I think that Melampus the son of Amytheon was not ignorant of these rites of sacrifice, but was acquainted with them. Melampus first set forth to the Hellenes the name of Dionysos and the manner of sacrifice and the procession of the *phallos*. Strictly speaking indeed, he when he made it known did not reveal the whole, but those wise men who came after him made it known more at large. Melampus then taught of the *phallos* which is carried in procession for Dionysos, and from him the Hellenes learnt to do what they do. I say then that Melampus being a man of ability contrived for himself an art of divination, and having learnt from Egypt he taught the Hellenes many things, and among them those that concern Dionysos, making changes in some few points of them. I shall not say that that which is done in worship of the god in Egypt came accidentally to be the same with that which is done among the Hellenes, for then these rites would have been in character with the Hellenic worship and not lately brought in; nor certainly shall I say that the Egyptians took from the Hellenes either this or any other customary observance. I think it most probable that Melampus learnt the matters concerning Dionysos from Cadmos the Tyrian and from those who came with him from Phenicia to the land which we now call Bœotia.

50. Moreover the naming of almost all the gods has come to Hellas from Egypt: for that it has come from the Barbarians I find by inquiry is true, and I believe that most probably it has come from Egypt, because, except in the case of Poseidon and the Dioscuroi (as I have said before), and also of Hera and Hestia and Themis and the Charites and Nereïds, the Egyptians have practically always had the names of all the other gods in their country. What I say here is that which the Egyptians say themselves. The gods whose names they profess that they do not know, these I think received their naming from the Pelasgians, except Poseidon; but about this god the Hellenes learnt from the Libyans, for no people except the Libyans have had the name of Poseidon from the first and have paid honour to this god always. Nor have the Egyptians any custom of worshipping heroes.

51. These observances then, and others besides these which I shall mention, the Hellenes have adopted from the Egyptians; but to make, as they do, the images of Hermes with the *phallos* they have learnt not from the

Egyptians but from the Pelasgians, the custom having been taken over by the Athenians first of all the Hellenes and from these by the rest; for just at the time when the Athenians were beginning to rank among the Hellenes, the Pelasgians became dwellers with them in their land, and from this very cause it was that they began to be counted as Hellenes. Whosoever has been initiated in the mysteries of the Cabeiroi, which the Samothrakians perform having received them from the Pelasgians, that man knows the meaning of my speech; for these very Pelasgians who became dwellers with the Athenians used to dwell before that time in Samothrakē, and from them the Samothrakians received their mysteries. So then the Athenians were the first of the Hellenes who made the images of Hermes with the *phallos,* having learnt from the Pelasgians; and the Pelasgians told a sacred story about it, which is set forth in the mysteries in Samothrakē.

52. Now the Pelasgians formerly used to make all their sacrifices calling upon the gods in prayer, as I know from that which I heard at Dodona, but they gave no title or name to any of them, for they had not yet heard any, but they called them gods (θεούς) from some such notion as this, that they had set (θέντες) in order all things and so had the distribution of everything. After much time had elapsed, they learnt from Egypt the names of the gods, all except Dionysos, for his name they learnt long afterwards; and after a time the Pelasgians consulted the Oracle at Dodona about the names, for this prophetic seat is accounted to be the most ancient of the Oracles among the Hellenes, and at that time it was the only one. So when the Pelasgians asked the Oracle at Dodona whether they should adopt the names which had come from the Barbarians, the Oracle in reply told them to use the names. From this time they sacrificed using the names of the gods, and from the Pelasgians the Hellenes afterwards received them. **53.** Whence the several gods had their birth, or whether they all were from the beginning, and of what form they are, the Hellenes did not learn till yesterday, as it were, or the day before, since Hesiod and Homer I suppose were four hundred years before my time and not more, and they made a theogony for the Hellenes and gave the titles to the gods and distributed to them honours and arts, and set forth their forms. Any poets who are said to have been before these men were really in my opinion after them. The first views belong to the priestesses of Dodona, and the latter ideas regarding Hesiod and Homer are mine.*

54. The Egyptians tell the following tale about the Oracles both that among the Hellenes and that in Libya. The priests of the Theban Zeus told me that two women in the service of the temple had been carried away from Thebes by Phenicians, and that they had heard that one of them had been sold to go into Libya and the other to the Hellenes; and these women,

---

*Herodotus' chronology boldly dates much later than his contemporaries would the chief epic poets and boldly credits them with essential concepts of Greek theology. The dates for the poets are far too early still, based on evidence and arguments now available.

they said, first founded the prophetic seats among the nations which have been named. When I inquired whence they knew so perfectly of this tale, they said in reply that a great search had been made by the priests after these women, and that they had not been able to find them, but they had heard afterwards this tale about them. **55.** This I heard from the priests at Thebes, and what follows is said by the prophetesses of Dodona. They say that two black doves flew from Thebes in Egypt, and one came to Libya and the other to their land. And this latter settled upon an oak-tree and spoke with human voice, saying that it was necessary that a prophetic seat of Zeus should be established in that place; and they supposed that that was divine revelation for them, and made one accordingly. The dove which went away to the Libyans, they say, commanded the Libyans make an Oracle of Ammon; and this also belongs to Zeus. The priestesses of Dodona told me these things, of whom the eldest was named Promeneia, the next after her Timaretē, and the youngest Nicandra; and the other people of Dodona who were engaged about the temple gave accounts agreeing with theirs.

56. I however have an opinion about the matter as follows:—If the Phenicians did in truth carry away the consecrated women and sold one of them into Libya and the other into Hellas, I suppose that in the country now called Hellas, which was formerly called Pelasgia, this woman was sold into the land of the Thesprotians; and then being a slave there she set up a sanctuary of Zeus under a real oak-tree. Indeed it was natural that being an attendant of the sanctuary of Zeus at Thebes, she should there, in the place to which she had come, have a memory of him; and after this, when she got understanding of the Hellenic tongue, she established an Oracle, and she reported, I suppose, that her sister had been sold in Libya by the same Phenicians by whom she herself had been sold. **57.** Moreover, I think that the women were called doves by the people of Dodona for the reason that they were Barbarians and because it seemed to them that they uttered voice like birds; but after a time (they say) the dove spoke with human voice, that is when the woman began to speak so that they could understand; but so long as she spoke a Barbarian tongue she seemed to them to be uttering voice like a bird. If it had been really a dove, how could it speak with human voice? And in saying that the dove was black, they indicate that the woman was Egyptian. The ways of delivering oracles too at Thebes in Egypt and at Dodona closely resemble one another, as it happens, and also the method of divination by victims has come from Egypt.

58. Moreover, the Egyptians were the first of men who made solemn assemblies and processions and approaches with offerings to the temples, and from them the Hellenes have learnt them, and my evidence for this is that the Egyptian celebrations of these have been held from a very ancient time, whereas the Hellenic were introduced lately. **59.** The Egyptians hold their solemn assemblies not once a year but often, especially and with the greatest zeal and devotion at the city of Bubastis for Artemis, and next at Busiris for Isis; for in this last-named city there is a very great temple of Isis, and this city stands in the middle of the Delta of Egypt. (Isis is in the tongue of the Hellenes Demeter.) Thirdly, they have a solemn assembly at the city of Saïs for Athenē, fourthly at Heliopolis for the Sun (Helios), fifthly at the city of Buto in honour of Leto, and sixthly at the city of Papremis for Ares.

60. Now, when they are coming to the city of Bubastis they do as follows:—men and women sail together, and a great multitude of each sex in every boat; and some of the women have rattles and rattle with them, while some of the men play the flute during the whole time of the voyage, and the rest, both women and men, sing and clap their hands; and when as they sail they come opposite to any city on the way they bring the boat to land, and some of the women continue to do as I have said, others cry aloud and jeer at the women in that city, some dance, and some stand up and pull up their skirts. This they do by every city along the river-bank; and when they come to Bubastis they hold festival celebrating great sacrifices, and more wine is consumed upon that festival than during the rest of the year. To this place (so say the natives) men and women come together to the number of 700,000,* excluding children. **61.** Thus it is done here; and how they celebrate the festival in honour of Isis at the city of Busiris has been told by me before. As I said, they beat themselves after the sacrifice, all of them both men and women, very many myriads of people. For whom they beat themselves it is not lawful for me to say. The Carians dwelling in Egypt do this even more than the Egyptians themselves, inasmuch as they cut their foreheads also with knives; and by this it is manifested that they are strangers and not Egyptians.

62. At the times when they gather together at the city of Saïs for their sacrifices, on a certain night they all kindle many lamps in the open air round about the houses; now the lamps are saucers full of salt and oil mixed, and the wick floats by itself on the surface, and this burns during the whole night; and to the festival is given the name *Lychnocaia* (the lighting of lamps). Moreover those of the Egyptians who have not come to this solemn assembly observe the night of the festival and themselves also light lamps all of them, and thus not in Saïs alone are they lighted, but over all Egypt. The reason why light and honour are allotted to this night has a sacred story told.

63. To Heliopolis and Buto they go year by year and do sacrifice only. But at Papremis they do sacrifice and worship as elsewhere, and besides that, when the sun begins to go down, while some priests are occupied with the image of the god. The greater number of them stand in the entrance of the temple with wooden clubs, and more than a thousand other men intending to perform a vow, also have clubs of wood, and stand in a body opposite. The image, which is in a small shrine of wood covered with gold, they take to another sacred building the day before. The few then who have been left about the image, draw a four wheeled cart, which bears

---

*The number is unreasonably large but suggests devotion and Egypt's huge population.

the shrine and the image that is within the shrine, and the other priests
standing in the gateway try to prevent it from entering, and the men under
a vow come to the assistance of the god and strike them, while the others
defend themselves. Then a hard fight with clubs ensues, and they break
one another's heads, and I believe that many even die of the wounds they
receive; the Egyptians however told me that no one died. This solemn assembly the people of the place say that they established for the following
reason:—the mother of Ares, they say, used to dwell in this temple, and
Ares, having been brought up away from her, when he grew up came
thither desiring to visit his mother, and the attendants of his mother's temple, not having seen him before, did not permit him to pass in, but kept
him away; and he brought men to help him from another city and handled
roughly the attendants of the temple, and entered to visit his mother.
Hence, they say, this club-battling has become the custom in honour of
Ares during his festival.*

64. The Egyptians were the first who made it a religious custom not to
lie with women in temples, nor to enter into temples after going away from
women without first bathing. Almost all other men except the Egyptians
and the Hellenes lie with women in temples and enter into a temple after
going away from women without bathing, since they hold that there is no
difference in this respect between men and beasts. They say that they see
beasts and the various kinds of birds coupling together both in the temples
and in the sacred enclosures of the gods; if then this were not pleasing to
the god, the beasts would not do so.

65. Thus they justify that which they do, although I dislike it. But the
Egyptians are exceedingly careful in their observances, both in other ritual
matters and also in these:—Egypt, though it borders upon Libya, does not
abound in wild animals, but such as they have are one and all accounted by
them sacred, some of them living with men and others not. But if I should
explain why the sacred animals have been thus dedicated, I would discuss
matters pertaining to the gods, which I most desire to avoid. What I have
actually said touching slightly upon them, I said because I was constrained
by necessity.

About these animals there is a custom of this kind:—Both Egyptian
men and women have been appointed to provide the food for each kind of
beast separately, and their office is transferred from father to son. City-
dwellers perform vows to them in this way. When they make a vow to the
god to whom the animal belongs, they shave the head of their children, either the whole or the half or the third part of it, and then set the hair in
the balance against silver, and whatever it weighs, this the man gives to the
person who provides for the animals, and she cuts up fish of equal value
and gives it for food to the animals. Thus food for their support has been
appointed: and if any one willingly kill any of these animals, the penalty
is death, and if against his will, such penalty as the priests may appoint.

---

*Set is the name of the local god, here Hellenized as Ares.

Whoever shall kill an ibis or a hawk, whether it be with his will or against his will, must die.

66. Many animals live with men, and there would be many more but for the accidents which befall the cats. For when the females have produced young they are no longer in the habit of going to the males, and these seeking to mount them are not able. To this end then they contrive as follows,— they either take away by force or remove secretly the young from the females and kill them (but after killing they do not eat them), and the females being deprived of their young and desiring more, therefore come to the males, for the creature is fond of its young. Moreover when a fire occurs, the cats seem to behave in a marvelous manner. While the Egyptians stand at intervals and look after the cats, not taking any care to extinguish the fire, the cats slipping through or leaping over the men, jump into the fire. When this happens, great mourning comes upon the Egyptians. And in whatever houses a cat has died by a natural death, all those who dwell in this house shave their eyebrows only, but those in whose houses a dog has died shave their whole body and their head. **67.** The cats when they are dead are carried away to sacred buildings in the city of Bubastis, where after being embalmed they are buried; but the dogs they bury in their own cities in sacred tombs; and the ichneumons are buried just as the dogs. The shrew-mice however and the hawks they carry away to the city of Buto, and the ibises to Hermopolis;* the bears (which are not commonly seen) and the wolves, not much larger in size than foxes, they bury on the spot where they are found lying.

68. The nature of the crocodile is as follows:—during the four most wintry months this creature eats nothing. She has four feet and is an animal belonging to the land and the water both; for she produces and hatches eggs on the land, and the most part of the day she remains upon dry land, but the whole of the night in the river, for the water in truth is warmer than the unclouded open air and the dew. Of all the mortal creatures of which we have knowledge this grows to the greatest bulk from the smallest beginning; for the eggs which she produces are not much larger than those of geese and the newly-hatched young one is in proportion to the egg, but as he grows he becomes as much as $25\frac{1}{2}$ feet long and sometimes yet larger.† He has eyes like those of a pig and teeth large and tusky, in proportion to the size of his body; but unlike all other beasts he grows no tongue, neither does he move his lower jaw, but brings the upper jaw towards the lower, being in this too unlike all other beasts. He has moreover strong claws and a scaly hide upon his back which cannot be pierced; and he is blind in the water, but in the air he is of very keen sight. Since he lives in the water he keeps his mouth all full with leeches; and whereas all other

---

*Thoth is the Egyptian Hermes; many Ibis mummies were found at Hermopolis.
†Nile crocodiles reach 15 feet in length, but longer ones exist elsewhere in Africa. Herodotus' zoology focuses on the unexpected. Herodotus here borrows from his predecessor in Egypt, Hecataios; see 2.143.

birds and beasts fly from him, the trochilus is a creature which is at peace with him, seeing that from her he receives benefit; for the crocodile having come out of the water to the land and then having opened his mouth (this he is wont to do generally towards the West Wind), the trochilus upon that enters into his mouth and swallows down the leeches, and he being benefited is pleased and does no harm to the trochilus.

69. Now for some of the Egyptians the crocodiles are sacred animals, and for others not so, but they treat them on the contrary as enemies. Those however who dwell about Thebes and about the lake of Moiris hold them to be most sacred, and each of these two peoples keeps one crocodile selected from the whole number, which has been trained to tameness, and they put hanging ornaments of glass and gold into the ears of these and anklets round the front feet, and they give them food appointed and victims of sacrifices and treat them as well as possible while they live, and after they are dead they bury them in sacred tombs, embalming them.

Those who dwell about the city of Elephantine even eat them, not holding them to be sacred. They are called not crocodiles but *champsai,* and the Ionians gave them the name of crocodile, comparing their form to that of the crocodiles (lizards) which appear in their country in the stone walls. **70.** There are many ways to catch them and of various kinds. I shall write down the one that to me seems the most worthy of being told. A man puts the back of a pig upon a hook as bait, and lets it go into the middle of the river, while he himself upon the bank of the river has a young live pig, which he beats; and the crocodile hearing its cries makes for the direction of the sound, and when he finds the pig's back he swallows it down. Then they pull, and when he is drawn out to land, first of all the hunter immediately plasters up his eyes with mud, and having done so he very easily gets the mastery of him, but if he does not do so he meets trouble.

71. The river-horse [or hippopotamus] is sacred in the district of Papremis, but for the other Egyptians he is not sacred. He has this appearance: he is four-footed, cloven-hoofed like an ox, flat-nosed, with a mane like a horse and showing teeth like tusks, with a tail and voice like a horse, and in size as large as the largest ox; and his hide is so exceedingly thick that when it has been dried shafts of javelins are made of it. **72.** There are moreover otters in the river, which they consider to be sacred; and of fish also they esteem that one called the *lepidotos* to be sacred, and also the eel. These they say are sacred to the Nile, and among birds the fox-goose.

73. There is also another sacred bird called the phœnix which I did not myself see except in painting, for in truth he comes to them very rarely, at intervals, as the people of Heliopolis say, of five hundred years; and these say that he comes regularly when his father dies; and if he be like the painting, this is his size and nature: some of his feathers are of gold colour and others red, and in outline and size he is as nearly as possible like an eagle. This bird they say (but I cannot believe the story) contrives as follows:—setting forth from Arabia he conveys his father, they say, to the temple of the Sun (Helios) plastered up in myrrh, and buries him in the temple of the Sun; and he conveys him thus:—he forms first an egg of myrrh as large as he is able to carry, and then he makes trial of carrying it, and when he has made trial sufficiently, then he hollows out the egg and places his father within it and plasters over with other myrrh that part of the egg where he hollowed it out to put his father in, and when his father is laid in it, it proves (they say) to be of the same weight as it was; and after he has plastered it up, he conveys the whole to Egypt to the temple of the Sun. Thus they say that this bird behaves.

74. There are also about Thebes sacred serpents, not at all harmful to men, which are small in size and have two horns growing from the top of the head. These they bury when they die in the temple of Zeus, for to this god they say that they are sacred. **75.** There is a region moreover in Arabia, situated somewhere near the city of Buto, to which place I went to inquire about the winged serpents. There I saw bones of serpents and spines in quantity so great that it is impossible to report the number, and there were heaps of spines, some heaps large and others less large and others smaller still than these, and these heaps were many in number. This region in which the spines are scattered resembles an entrance from a narrow mountain pass to a great plain, which plain adjoins the plain of Egypt; and the story goes that at the beginning of spring winged serpents from Arabia fly towards Egypt, and the birds called ibises meet them at the entrance to this country and do not suffer the serpents to pass but kill them. On account of this deed it is (say the Arabians) that the ibis has come to be greatly honoured by the Egyptians, and the Egyptians also agree that it is for this reason that they honour these birds. **76.** The outward form of the ibis is this:—it is a deep black all over, and has legs like those of a crane and a very curved beak, and in size it is about equal to a rail or corncrake. This is the appearance of the black kind which fight with the serpents, but those which most crowd round men's feet (for there are two kinds of ibises) have the head bare and also the whole of the throat, and it is white in feathering except the head and neck and the extremities of the wings and the rump (all these parts are a deep black), while in legs and in the form of the head it resembles the other. As for the serpent its form is like that of the watersnake; and it has wings not feathered but most nearly resembling the wings of the bat. Let this suffice concerning sacred animals.

77. Of the Egyptians themselves, those who dwell in the part of Egypt which is sown for crops[*] practise memory more than any other men and are the most learned in historical questions by far of all those whom I have tested. Their manner of life is this:—For three successive days in each month they purge, hunting after health with emetics and douches, and they think that all the diseases which exist are produced in men by the food on which they live. The Egyptians are from other causes also the most healthy of all men next after the Libyans (in my opinion on account

---

[*]At 2.92 we hear of the marsh-dwelling Egyptians.

of the seasons, because the seasons do not change, for by the changes of things generally, and especially of the seasons, diseases are most apt to be produced in men). [Their diet follows:—] they eat bread, making loaves of millet, which they call *kyllestis,* and they use habitually a wine made out of barley, for vines they have not in their land.* They dry some of their fish in the sun and then eat them without cooking, others they eat cured in brine. Of birds they eat quails and ducks and small birds without cooking, after first curing them; and everything else which they have belonging to the class of birds or fishes, except such as have been set apart by them as sacred, they eat roasted or boiled. **78.** In the entertainments of the rich among them, when they have finished eating, a man bears round a wooden figure of a corpse in a coffin, made as like the reality as may be both by painting and carving, and measuring at most about 1.5 or 3 feet. He shows it to each of those who are drinking together, saying: "When you look at this, drink and be merry, for you shall be such as this when you are dead." Thus they do at their drinking parties.

79. The customs which they practise are derived from their fathers and they do not acquire others in addition; but besides other customary things among them which are worthy of mention, they have one song, that of Linos, the same who is sung of both in Phenicia and in Cyprus and elsewhere, having however a different name in the various nations. This song agrees exactly with that which the Hellenes sing calling on the name of Linos, so that besides many other things which concern Egypt, I wonder especially about this, namely whence they got the song of Linos. It is evident however that they have sung this song from time immemorial, and in the Egyptian tongue Linos is called Manerōs. The Egyptians told me that he was the only son of him who first became king of Egypt, and that he died before his time and was honoured with these lamentations by the Egyptians, and that this was their first and only song.

80. In another respect the Egyptians are in agreement with some of the Hellenes, namely with the Lacedemonians, but not with the rest, that is to say, the younger of them when they meet the elder give way and move out of the path, and when their elders approach they rise from their seat. In this which follows however they are not in agreement with any of the Hellenes,—instead of addressing one another in the roads they do reverence, lowering their hand down to their knee. **81.** They wear tunics of linen about their legs with fringes, which they call *calasiris;* above these they have garments of white wool thrown over. Woollen garments however are not taken into the temples, nor are they buried with them, for this is not permitted by religion. In these points they are in agreement with the observances called Orphic and Bacchic (which are really Egyptian), and also with those of the Pythagoreans, for one who takes part in these mysteries is also forbidden by religious rule to be buried in woollen garments. There is about this a sacred story told.

---

*The Egyptians' beer-drinking was not admired or imitated widely by the Greeks.

82. Besides these things the Egyptians have found out also to what god each month and each day belongs, and what fortunes a man will meet with who is born on any particular day, and how he will die, and what kind of a man he will be. The Hellenes who occupied themselves with poesy took up these inventions. Portents too have been discovered by them more than by all other men; for when a portent has happened, they observe and write down the event which comes of it, and if ever afterwards anything resembling this happens, they believe that the outcome will be similar.

83. Their divination is ordered thus:—the art is assigned not to any man but to certain of the gods, for there are in their land Oracles of Heracles, of Apollo, of Athenē, of Artemis, of Ares, and of Zeus, and moreover that which they hold most in honour of all, namely the Oracle of Leto in the city of Buto. The manner of divination however is not established among them according to the same fashion everywhere, but is different in different places.

84. The art of medicine among them is distributed thus:—each physician is a physician of one disease and of no more; and the whole country is full of physicians, for some profess themselves to be physicians of the eyes, others of the head, others of the teeth, others of the affections of the stomach, and others of the more obscure ailments.

85. Their fashions of mourning and of burial are these:—Whenever any household has lost a man of repute, all the women of that house at once plaster over their heads or even their faces with mud. Then leaving the corpse within the house they go themselves to and fro about the city and beat themselves, with their garments bound with a belt and their breasts exposed, and with them go all the women who are related to the dead man. On the other side the men beat themselves, they too having their garments bound with a belt. When they have done this, they then convey the body to the embalming. **86.** In this occupation certain persons employ themselves regularly and inherit this as a craft. These, whenever a corpse is conveyed to them, show to those who brought it wooden models of corpses made like reality by painting. The best way of embalming they say is that of him whose name I think it impiety to mention in such a matter.* The second which they show is less good than this and also less expensive; and the third is the least expensive of all. Having told them about this, they ask how they desire the corpse of their friend to be prepared. Then they after they have agreed for a certain price depart out of the way, and the others being left behind in the buildings embalm according to the best of these ways thus:—First with a crooked iron tool they draw out the brain through the nostrils, extracting it partly thus and partly by pouring in drugs; and after this with a sharp stone knife from Ethiopia they make a cut along the side and take out the whole contents of the belly, and when they have cleared out the cavity and cleansed it with palm-wine they cleanse it again with spices pounded up. Next they fill the belly with pure

---

*Herodotus alludes to a likeness of divine Osiris.

myrrh pounded up and with cassia and other spices except frankincense, and sew it together again. Having so done they mummify it covered in natron for seventy days. A longer time than this is not permitted for mummification. After the seventy days are past, they wash the corpse and roll its whole body up in fine linen cut into bands, smearing these beneath with acacia gum, which the Egyptians use generally instead of glue. Then the kinsfolk receive it from them and have a wooden casket shaped like a man, and in this they enclose the corpse, and having shut it up within, they store it then in a sepulchral chamber, setting it to stand upright against the wall.

87. Thus they treat the corpses which are prepared in the most costly way; but for those who desire the middle price avoiding great cost they prepare the corpse as follows:—having filled their syringes with the oil which is got from cedar-wood, with this they immediately fill the belly of the corpse, and this they do without having either cut it open or taken out the bowels, but they inject the oil by the anus, and having stopped the drench from returning back they keep it then the appointed number of days for embalming, and on the last of the days they let the cedar oil come out from the belly. It has such power that it brings out with it the bowels and interior organs of the body dissolved; and the natron dissolves the flesh, so that there is left of the corpse only the skin and the bones. When they have done this they give back the corpse at once in that condition without working upon it any more.

88. The third kind of embalming, by which are prepared the bodies of those who have less means, is as follows:—they cleanse out the belly with a purge and then keep the body for embalming during the seventy days, and at once after that they give it back to the bringers to carry away. **89.** The wives of men of rank when they die are not given at once to be embalmed, nor such women as are very beautiful or more famous than others, but on the third or fourth day after their death (and not before) they are delivered to the embalmers. They do this so that the embalmers may not sexually abuse their women, for they say that one of them was taken once doing so to the corpse of a woman lately dead, and his fellow-craftsman gave information.

90. Whenever any one, either of the Egyptians themselves or of strangers, is found to have been carried off by a crocodile or brought to his death by the river itself, the people of any city by which he may have been cast up on land must embalm him and lay him out in the fairest way they can and bury him in a sacred burial-place, nor may any of his relations or friends besides touch him, but the priests of the Nile themselves handle the corpse and bury it as that of one something more than man.

91. Hellenic usages they will by no means follow, and to speak generally they follow those of no other men whatever. This rule is observed by most of the Egyptians; but there is a large city named Chemmis in the Theban district near Neapolis, and in this city there is a temple of Perseus the son of Danaē which is of a square shape, and round it grow date-palms: the gateway of the temple is built of stone and of very great size,

and at the entrance of it stand two great statues of stone. Within this enclosure is a shrine and in it stands an image of Perseus. These people of
Chemmis say that Perseus often appears in their land and often within the
temple, and that a sandal which has been worn by him is found sometimes,
being three feet in length, and whenever this appears all Egypt prospers.
This they say, and they do honour to Perseus after Hellenic fashion thus:
they hold an athletic contest, which includes the whole range of games,
and they offer in prizes cattle and cloaks and skins. I inquired why to them
alone Perseus was wont to appear, and wherefore they were separated
from all the other Egyptians in that they held an athletic contest. They said
that Perseus had been born in their city, for Danaos and Lynkeus were
men of Chemmis and had sailed to Hellas, and from them they traced descent and came down to Perseus. They told me that he had come to Egypt
for the reason which the Hellenes also say, namely to bring from Libya the
Gorgon's head, and had then visited them also and recognised all his kinsfolk, and they said that he had well learnt the name of Chemmis before he
came to Egypt, since he had heard it from his mother, and that they celebrated an athletic contest for him by his own command.

92. All these are customs practised by the Egyptians who dwell above
the marshes. Those who are settled in the marsh-land have the same customs for the most part as the other Egyptians, both in other matters and
also in that they live each with one wife only, as do the Hellenes; but for
economy in respect of food they have invented these things besides:—
when the river has become full and the plains have been flooded, there
grow in the water great numbers of lilies, which the Egyptians call *lotos;*
these they cut with a sickle and dry in the sun, and then they pound that
which grows in the middle of the lotos and which is like the head of a
poppy, and they make of it loaves baked with fire. The root also of this lotos is edible and has a rather sweet taste. It is round in shape and about the
size of an apple. There are other lilies too, in flower resembling roses,
which also grow in the river, and from them the fruit is produced in a separate pod springing from the root by the side of the plant itself, and very
nearly resembles a wasp's comb. Edible seeds grow in great numbers of
the size of an olive-stone, and they are eaten either fresh or dried.

Besides this they pull up from the fens the papyrus which grows every
year, and the upper parts of it they cut off and turn to other uses, but that
which is left below for about eighteen inches in length they eat or sell: and
those who desire to have the papyrus at its very best bake it in an oven
heated red-hot, and then eat it. Some too of these people live on fish
alone, which they dry in the sun after having caught them and taken out
the entrails, and then when they are dry, they use them for food.

93. Fish which swim in shoals are not much produced in the rivers, but
are bred in the lakes, and they behave as follows:—When there comes
upon them the desire to breed, they swim out in shoals towards the sea;
and the males lead the way shedding forth their milt as they go, while the
females, coming after and swallowing it up, from it become impregnated.
When they have become full of young in the sea they swim up back again,

each shoal to its own haunts. The same fish however no longer lead the way as before, but the lead comes now to the females, and they leading the way in shoals do just as the males did, that is to say they shed forth their eggs by a few grains at a time, and the males coming after swallow them up. Now these grains are fish, and from the grains which survive and are not swallowed, the fish grow which afterwards are bred up. Now those of the fish which are caught as they swim out towards the sea are found to be rubbed on the left side of the head, but those which are caught as they swim up again are rubbed on the right side. This happens to them because as they swim down to the sea they keep close to the land on the left side of the river, and again as they swim up they keep to the same side, approaching and touching the bank as much as they can, for fear doubtless of straying from their course by reason of the stream. When the Nile begins to swell, the hollow places of the land and the depressions by the side of the river first begin to fill, as the water soaks through from the river, and so soon as they become full of water, at once they are all filled with little fishes; and whence these are in all likelihood produced, I think that I perceive. In the preceding year, when the Nile goes down, the fish first lay eggs in the mud and then retire with the last of the retreating waters; and when the time comes round again, and the water once more comes over the land, from these eggs are produced right away the fishes of which I speak. That is the fish account.

94. And for anointing those of the Egyptians who dwell in the fens use oil from the castor plant's fruit which oil the Egyptians call *kiki,* and they do it this way:—they sow along the banks of the rivers and pools these plants, which in a wild form grow of themselves in the land of the Hellenes; these are sown in Egypt and produce berries in great quantity but of an evil smell; and when they have gathered these, some cut them up and press the oil from them, others again roast them first and then boil them down and collect that which runs away from them. The oil is fat and not less suitable for burning than olive-oil, but it gives forth a disagreeable smell.

95. Against the gnats, which are very abundant, they have contrived as follows:—those who dwell above the fen-land are helped by the towers, to which they ascend when they go to rest; for the gnats by reason of the winds are not able to fly up high. Those who dwell in the fen-land have contrived another way instead of the towers, and this it is:—every man of them has got a casting net, with which by day he catches fish, but in the night he uses it for this purpose, that is to say he puts the casting-net round about the bed in which he sleeps, and then creeps in under it and goes to sleep. The gnats, if he sleeps rolled up in a garment or a linen sheet, bite through these, but through the net they do not even attempt to bite.

96. Their boats with which they carry cargoes are made of the thorny acacia, of which the form is very like that of the Kyrenian lotos, and gum exudes from it. From this tree they cut pieces of wood about three feet long and arrange them like bricks, fastening the boat together by running a great number of long bolts through the three-foot pieces; and when they have thus fastened the boat together, they lay crosspieces over the top, using no ribs for the sides; and within they caulk the seams with papyrus. They make one steering-oar for it, which is passed through the bottom of the boat; and they have a mast of acacia and sails of papyrus. These boats cannot sail up the river unless there be a very fresh wind blowing, but are towed from the shore: down-stream however they travel as follows:—they have a door-shaped crate made of tamarisk wood and reed mats sewn together, and also a stone of about 114 pounds weight bored with a hole; and of these the boatman lets the crate float on in front of the boat, fastened with a rope, and the stone drag behind by another rope. The crate then, as the force of the stream presses upon it, goes on swiftly and draws on the *baris* (for so these boats are called), while the stone dragging after it behind and sunk deep in the water keeps its course straight. These boats they have in great numbers and some of them carry many thousands of talents' burden.*

97. When the Nile comes over the land, the cities alone are seen rising above the water, resembling more nearly than anything else the islands in the Egean sea; for the rest of Egypt becomes a sea and the cities alone rise above water. Accordingly, whenever this happens, they ferry about not now on the channels of the river but over the midst of the plain. For example, as one sails up from Naucratis to Memphis the passage is then close by the pyramids, whereas the usual passage is not the same even here, but goes by the point of the Delta and the city of Kercasoros; while if you sail over the plain to Naucratis from the sea and from Canobos, you will go by Anthylla and the city called after Archander. **98.** Of these Anthylla is a city of note and is especially assigned to the wife of him who reigns over Egypt, to supply her with sandals, (this is the case since the time when Egypt came to be under the Persians). The other city seems to me to have its name from Archander the son-in-law of Danaos, who was the son of Phthios, the son of Achaios; for it is called the City of Archander. There might indeed be another Archander, but in any case the name is not Egyptian.

99. Hitherto my own observation and judgment and inquiry vouch for that which I have said; but from this point onwards I tell the Egyptian stories that I heard, and also some things I have myself seen.†

Of Min,‡ who first became king of Egypt, the priests said that he banked off the site of Memphis from the river. The whole stream of the river used to flow along by the sandy mountain-range on the side of Libya, but Min

---

*One talent weighs about 57.3 pounds or approximately 1/40 ton.
†Chapters 99–182 offer a history of Egypt, divided at 147 between the Egyptians' own accounts and those in which evidence from other nations confirms or disputes Egyptian stories. Herodotus distinguishes his autopsy and historical research from received reports (recall his cautionary comments at 2.123 and 7.152 whenever you choke on a story).
‡Menes reigned c.3400 B.C.; the stories are largely popular legends.

formed by embankments that bend of the river which lies to the South about 11.5 miles above Memphis, and thus he dried up the old stream and conducted the river so that it flowed in the middle between the mountains. Even now this bend of the Nile is kept by the Persians under very careful watch, that it may flow in its channel and the bank is repaired every year; for if the river should break through and overflow in this direction, Memphis risks being overwhelmed by flood. When this Min, who first became king, had made into dry land the part which was dammed off, he founded in it that city which is now called Memphis; for Memphis too is in the narrow part of Egypt [above the Delta]; and outside the city he dug round it on the North and West a lake communicating with the river, for the side towards the East is barred by the Nile itself. Then secondly he established in the city the temple of Hephaistos a great work and most worthy of mention.

100. After this man the priests enumerated to me from a papyrus roll the names of other kings, three hundred and thirty in number; and in all these generations of men eighteen were Ethiopians, one was a woman, a native Egyptian, and the rest were men and of Egyptian race. The name of the woman who reigned was the same as that of the Babylonian queen Nitocris. They said that desiring to take vengeance for her brother, whom the Egyptians had slain when he was their king and then had given his kingdom to her, she destroyed by trickery many Egyptians. For she caused to be constructed a very large chamber under ground, and making as though she would inaugurate it but in her mind devising other things, she invited those Egyptians whom she knew to be guiltiest of the murder, and gave a great banquet. Then while they were feasting, she let in the river upon them by a large secret conduit. They told no more than this of her, except that, when this had been accomplished, she threw herself into a room full of embers to escape vengeance.

101. As for the other kings, they could tell me of no great works which had been produced by them, and they said that they had no renown except the last of them, Moiris. He (they said) produced as a memorial of himself the gateway of the temple of Hephaistos* which is turned towards the North, and dug a lake, about which I shall state afterwards how long a circuit it has, and in it built pyramids of the size which I shall mention when I speak of the lake itself.† He, they said, produced these works, but of the rest no king produced any.

102. Therefore passing these by I shall recall the king who came after these, whose name was Sesostris. He (the priests said) first of all set out with ships of war from the Arabian gulf and subdued those who dwelt by the shores of the Erythraian Sea, until as he sailed he came to a sea which could be navigated no further by reason of shoals: then secondly, after he had returned to Egypt, according to the report of the priests, he took a great army and marched over the continent, subduing every nation which

---

*This is the Egyptian god Ptah; compare 3.37.
†See 2.149.

stood in his way. Those he found valiant and fighting desperately for their freedom, in their lands he set up pillars which told by inscriptions his own name and the name of his country, and how he had subdued them by his power; but as to those of whose cities he obtained possession without fighting or with ease, on their pillars he inscribed similar words as he did for the courageous, and in addition he drew upon them the genitals of a woman, desiring to signify by this that the people were cowards.

103. Doing such he traversed the continent, until at last he passed over to Europe from Asia and subdued the Scythians and also the Thracians. These, I am of opinion, were the furthest people to which the Egyptian army came, for in their country the pillars are found to have been set up, but in the land beyond they are no longer found. From this point he turned and began to go back; and when he came to the river Phasis, what happened then I cannot say for certain, whether king Sesostris himself divided off a certain portion of his army and left the men there as settlers in the land, or whether some of his soldiers were wearied by his distant marches and remained by the river Phasis. **104.** For the people of Colchis are evidently Egyptian, as I perceived myself before I heard it from others. So when I had come to consider the matter I asked them both; and the Colchians had remembrance of the Egyptians more than the Egyptians of the Colchians; but the Egyptians said they believed that the Colchians were a portion of the army of Sesostris. That this was so I conjectured myself not only because they are dark-skinned and have curly hair (this of itself amounts to nothing, for there are other races which are so), but more because the Colchians, Egyptians, and Ethiopians alone of all the races of men have practised circumcision of the genitals from the first. The Phenicians and the Syrians in Palestine* confess themselves that they have learnt it from the Egyptians, and the Syrians about the river Thermodon and the river Parthenios, and the Macronians, who are their neighbours, say that they have learnt it lately from the Colchians. These are the only races of men who practise circumcision, and these evidently practise it in the same manner as the Egyptians. Of the Egyptians themselves however and the Ethiopians, I am not able to say which learnt from the other, for undoubtedly it is a most ancient custom; but that the other nations learnt it by intercourse with the Egyptians, this among others is to me a strong proof, namely that those of the Phenicians who have intercourse with Hellas cease to follow the example of the Egyptians in this matter, and do not circumcise their children.

105. Now let me tell another thing about the Colchians to show how they resemble the Egyptians:—they alone work flax in the same fashion as the Egyptians, and the two nations are like one another in their whole manner of living and also in their language. The linen of Colchis is called by the Hellenes Sardonic, whereas that from Egypt is called Egyptian.

---

*Herodotus includes the Jews, presumably, but not the Philistines, who did not follow this ritual.

106. The pillars which Sesostris king of Egypt set up in the various countries are for the most part no longer extant; but in Syrian Palestine I myself saw them with the inscription upon them which I have mentioned and the emblem. Moreover in Ionia there are two figures of this man carved upon rocks, one on the road by which one goes from the land of Ephesos to Phocaia, and the other on the road from Sardis to Smyrna. In each place there is a figure of a man cut in the rock, of nearly seven feet in height, holding in his right hand a spear and in his left a bow and arrows, and the other equipment which he has is similar to this, for it is both Egyptian and Ethiopian. From the one shoulder to the other across the breast runs an inscription carved in sacred Egyptian characters, saying "This land with my shoulders I won for myself." But who he is and from whence, he does not declare in these places, though in other places he has. Some of those who have seen these carvings conjecture that the figure is that of Memnon, but herein they are very far from the truth.

107. As this Egyptian Sesostris was returning and bringing back many men of the nations whose lands he had subdued, when he came (said the priests) to Daphnai in the district of Pelusion on his journey home, his brother to whom Sesostris had entrusted the charge of Egypt invited him and his sons to a feast; and then he piled the house round with brushwood and set it on fire: and Sesostris when he discovered this immediately took counsel with his wife, for he was bringing with him (they said) his wife also; and she counselled him to lay out upon the pyre two of his sons, who were six in number, and so to make a bridge over the burning mass, and that they passing over their bodies should thus escape. This, they said, Sesostris did, and two of his sons were burnt to death in this manner, but the rest got away safe with their father.

108. Then Sesostris, having returned to Egypt and having taken vengeance on his brother, employed the multitude which he had brought in of those whose lands he had subdued, as follows:—these men drew the stones which in the reign of this king were brought to the temple of Hephaistos, being of very great size; and also these were compelled to dig all the channels which now are in Egypt; and thus (having no such purpose) they caused Egypt, which before was all fit for riding and driving, to be no longer fit thenceforth. From that time Egypt, though it is plain land, has become entirely unfit for riding and driving, and the cause has been these channels, which are many and run in all directions. But the reason why the king cut up the land was this, namely because those of the Egyptians who had their cities not on the river but in the middle of the country, being in want of water when the river went down from them, found their drink brackish drawing it from wells. **109.** For this reason Egypt was cut up. They said that this king distributed the land to all the Egyptians, giving an equal square portion to each man, and from this he made his revenue, having appointed them to pay a certain rent every year. If the river should take away anything from any man's portion, he would come to the king and declare that which had happened, and the king used to send men to examine and to find out by measurement how much less the piece of land had become, in order that for the future the man might pay less, in proportion to the rent appointed. I think that thus the art of geometry was found out and afterwards came into Hellas also. For as touching the sun-dial and the gnomon and the twelve divisions of the day, they were learnt by the Hellenes from the Babylonians. **110.** He moreover alone of all the Egyptian kings ruled Ethiopia; and he left as memorials of himself in front of the temple of Hephaistos two stone statues of forty-five feet each, representing himself and his wife, and others of thirty feet each representing his four sons. Long afterwards the priest of Hephaistos refused to permit Dareios the Persian to set up a statue of himself in front of them, saying that deeds had not been done by him equal to those which were done by Sesostris the Egyptian; for Sesostris had subdued other nations besides, not fewer than he, and also the Scythians; but Dareios had not been able to conquer the Scythians. Wherefore it was not just that he should set up a statue in front of those which Sesostris had dedicated, if he did not surpass him in his deeds. They say Dareios conceded the point.

111. Now after Sesostris' death, his son Pheros, they told me, received in succession the kingdom, and he made no warlike expedition, and moreover he chanced to become blind through the following accident:—when the river had come down in flood rising to a height of twenty-seven feet, higher than ever before that time, and had gone over the fields, a wind fell upon it and the river became agitated by waves. This king (they say) moved by presumptuous folly took a spear and cast it into the midst of the eddies of the stream; and immediately upon this he suffered a disease of the eyes and became blind.[*] For ten years then he was blind, and in the eleventh year there came to him an oracle from the city of Buto saying that the time of his punishment had expired, and that he should see again if he washed his eyes with the water of a woman who had engaged in sex with her own husband only and no other men. First he made trial of his own wife, and then, as he continued blind, he went on to try all the women in turn; and when he had at last regained his sight he gathered together all the women whose urine he had tried, excepting her by whom he had regained his sight, to one city which now is named Erythrabolos, and having gathered them he burnt them all alive and the city itself; but her by whom he had regained his sight, he took her for his wife. Then after he had escaped the malady of his eyes he dedicated offerings at each one of the temples which were of renown, and especially (to mention only that which is most noteworthy) he dedicated at the temple of the Sun works which are worth seeing, namely two obelisks of stone, each of a single block, measuring in length 150 feet and in breadth twelve feet.

112. After him, they said, there succeeded to the throne a man of Memphis, whose name in the tongue of the Hellenes was Proteus; now a sacred enclosure at Memphis honours him, very fair and well ordered, lying

---

[*]Recall this hubristic act when you read 7.35.

on that side of the temple of Hephaistos which faces North. Round about this enclosure dwell Phenicians of Tyre, and this whole region is called the Tyrians' Quarter. Within the enclosure of Proteus there is a temple called the temple of the "foreign Aphroditē," which temple I conjecture to be one of Helen the daughter of Tyndareus, not only because I have heard the tale how Helen dwelt with Proteus, but also especially because it is called by the name of the "foreign Aphroditē," for none of the other temples of Aphroditē have the additional word "foreign" with the name.

113. And the priests told me, when I inquired, that the things concerning Helen happened thus:—Alexander abducted Helen and was sailing away from Sparta to his own land, and when he had come to the Egean Sea contrary winds drove him from his course to the Sea of Egypt; and after that, since the blasts did not cease to blow, he came to Egypt itself and to that mouth of the Nile now named the Canobic and to Taricheiai. There was upon the shore, as still there is now, a temple of Heracles, in which if any man's slave take refuge and have the sacred marks set upon him, giving himself over to the god, one cannot lay hands upon him; and this custom has continued still unchanged from the beginning down to my own time. Accordingly the attendants of Alexander, having heard of the custom which existed about the temple, ran away from him, and sitting down as suppliants of the god, accused Alexander, because they desired to do him hurt, telling the whole tale about Helen and about the wrong done to Menelaos; and this accusation they made not only to the priests but also to the coastal guard of this river-mouth, whose name was Thonis.

114. Thonis then having heard their tale sent at once a message to Proteus at Memphis, saying: "There has come a stranger, a Teucrian by race, who has done in Hellas an unholy deed; for he has deceived the wife of his own host, and is come hither bringing with him this woman herself and very much wealth, having been carried out of his way by winds to your land. Shall we then allow him to sail out unharmed, or shall we first take away from him what he brought?" In reply Proteus sent back a messenger who said: "Seize this man, whoever he may be, who has done impiety to his own host, and bring him into my presence, that I may know what he will find to say." **115.** Hearing this, Thonis seized Alexander and detained his ships, and after that he brought the man himself up to Memphis and with him Helen and the wealth he had, and also the suppliants. So when all had been conveyed thither, Proteus began to ask Alexander who he was and from whence he was voyaging; and he both recounted to him his descent and told him the name of his native land, and moreover related from which port he was sailing. After this Proteus asked him whence he had taken Helen; and when Alexander went astray in his evasive account and did not speak the truth, those who had become suppliants convicted him of falsehood, relating in full the whole tale of the wrong. At length Proteus declared this sentence, saying, "Did I not count it a matter of great moment not to kill any strangers who hitherto being driven from their course by winds have come to my land, I should have taken vengeance on you on behalf of the man of Hellas, seeing that you, most base of men, having received from him hospitality, responded to him with a most impious deed. For you entered the wife of your own host; and even this was not enough for you, but you stirred her up with desire and have gone off with her like a thief. Moreover not even this by itself was enough, but you are come hither with plunder taken from the house of your host. Now therefore depart, seeing that I still consider it vital not to kill strangers. This woman indeed and the wealth which you have I will not allow you to carry away, but I shall keep them safe for the Hellene who was your host, until he come himself and desire to bring them home; to you however and your fellow-voyagers I proclaim that you depart from your anchoring within three days and go from my land to some other; if not, you will be dealt with as enemies."

116. This the priests said was the manner of Helen's coming to Proteus; and I suppose that Homer also had heard this story, but since it was not so suitable to the composition of his epic poem as the other which he followed, he dismissed it finally, making it clear that he was acquainted with that story also. He purposely but inconsistently described the wanderings of Alexander in the Iliad (nor did he elsewhere retract the tale). When he brought Helen away he was carried out of his course, wandering to various lands, and that he came among other places to Sidon in Phenicia. The poet mentions this in the "Big Day for Diomedes," and the verses run thus:

"There she had robes many-coloured, the works of women of Sidon,
  Those whom her son himself the god-like of form Alexander
  Carried from Sidon, when the broad sea-path he sailed over
  Bringing back Helenē home, begotten of a noble father."

And in the Odyssey also he mentions it in these verses:[*]

"Such had the daughter of Zeus, such drugs of exquisite cunning,
  Good, while to her the wife of Thon, Polydamna, had given,
  Dwelling in Egypt, the land where the bountiful meadow produces
  Drugs more than all lands else, many good being mixed, many evil."

And thus too Menelaos says to Telemachos:

"Still the gods held me in Egypt, although desiring to come back
    hither,
  Held me from voyaging home, since I performed not due sacrifice."

In these lines he makes it clear that he knew of Alexander's wandering to Egypt, for Syria borders upon Egypt and the Phenicians, of whom Sidon is a city, dwell in Syria. **117.** By these lines and by this passage it is also not least and most clearly shown that the "Cyprian Epic" was not written by

---

*Herodotus quotes the *Iliad* 6.289 ff. and the *Odyssey* 4.227 ff. and 4.351 ff.

Homer but by some other man. For in this it is said that on the third day
after leaving Sparta Alexander reached Ilion bringing with him Helen,
having had a "gently-blowing wind and a smooth sea," whereas in the Iliad
it says that he wandered from his course when he brought her. Let us now
leave Homer and the "Cyprian" Epic.

118. But this much I will say. I asked the priests whether the Hellenes tell
but an idle tale about what happened around Ilion; and they answered
that they had their knowledge by inquiries from Menelaos himself. After
the rape of Helen there came indeed, they said, to the Teucrian [or Trojan]
land a large army of Hellenes to help Menelaos; and when the army had
come out of the ships to land and had pitched its camp there, they sent
messengers to Ilion, with whom went also Menelaos himself; and when
these entered within the wall they demanded back Helen and the wealth
which Alexander had stolen from Menelaos and had taken away; and
moreover they demanded satisfaction for the wrongs done. The Teucrians
told the same tale then and afterwards, both with oath and without oath,
namely that they had not Helen nor the wealth for which demand was
made, but that both were in Egypt; and that they could not justly be compelled to give satisfaction for that which Proteus the king of Egypt had.
The Hellenes however thought that they were being mocked by them and
besieged the city, until at last they took it; and when they had taken the
wall and did not find Helen, but heard the same tale as before, then they
believed the former tale and sent Menelaos himself to Proteus.

119. And Menelaos having come to Egypt and having sailed up to
Memphis, told the truth of these matters, not only found great entertainment, but also received Helen unhurt, and all his own wealth besides. Then
however, after he had been thus dealt with, Menelaos showed himself un-
grateful to the Egyptians; for when he set forth to sail away, contrary
winds detained him, and as this situation lasted long, he devised an impious deed. He took two children of natives and sacrificed them. After this,
when he was detected, he became abhorred, and being pursued he escaped and got away with his ships straight to Libya; but whither he went
after this, the Egyptians were not able to tell. Of these things they said that
they found out part by inquiries, and the rest, namely what happened in
their own land, they related from certain knowledge.

120. Thus the priests of the Egyptians told me; and I myself also agree
with the story which was told of Helen, adding this consideration, namely
that if Helen had been in Ilion she would have been given up to the Hellenes, whether Alexander consented or no; for Priam assuredly and the
others of his house were not so mad that they wanted to run the risk of
ruin for themselves and their children and their city, in order that Alexander might have Helen as his wife. Even supposing that at first they had
been so inclined, yet when many others of the Trojans besides were losing
their lives as often as they fought with the Hellenes, and always two or three
or even more of the sons of Priam himself were slain when a battle took
place (if one may trust the Epic poets at all),—when things were in a bad
way, I consider that even if Priam himself had had Helen as his wife, he

would have given her back to the Achaians, if at least by so doing he might be freed from the disaster which oppressed him. Nor was the kingdom passing to Alexander next, so that when Priam was old the government would be in his hands; but Hector, who was both older and more of a man than he, would certainly have received it after the death of Priam; and it was wrong for him to allow his brother to go on with his wrong-doing, considering that great evils were coming to pass on his account both to himself privately and to all the other Trojans. In truth however they lacked the power to give Helen back; and the Hellenes did not believe them, though they spoke the truth; because, in my opinion, the divine power was purposing to cause them utterly to perish, and so make it evident to men that for great wrongs great also are the penalties which come from the gods.[*] And this is my opinion concerning these matters.

121. After Proteus, they told me, Rhampsinitos succeeded to the kingdom, who left as a memorial of himself that gateway to the temple of Hephaistos which is turned towards the West, and in front of the gateway he set up two statues, in height thirty-eight feet, of which the one which stands on the North side is called by the Egyptians Summer and the one on the South side Winter; and to that one which they call Summer they do reverence and make offerings, while to the other which is called Winter they do the opposite of these things.

(*a*) This king, they said, got great wealth of silver, which none of the kings born after him could surpass or even come near to; and wishing to store his wealth in safety he had built a chamber of stone, one of the walls whereof standing near the outside of his palace. The builder of this, having designs on it, contrived this trick. He disposed one of the stones in such a manner that it could be taken out easily from the wall either by two men or even by one. So when the chamber was finished, the king stored his money in it, and after some time the builder, being near the end of his life, called his sons to him (for he had two) and he related how he had contrived the building of the treasury of the king, and all in forethought for them, that they might have abundant means of living. And when he had clearly set forth to them everything concerning the removal of the stone, he gave them the measurements, saying that if they paid heed to this matter they would be stewards of the king's treasury. So he ended his life, and his sons made no long delay in setting to work, but went to the palace by night. Having found the stone in the wall of the chamber they dealt with it easily and carried forth for themselves great wealth.

(*b*) And the king happening to open the chamber, he marvelled when he saw fewer vessels than the full amount, and he did not know on whom he should lay the blame, since the seals were unbroken and the chamber had been close shut; but when upon his opening the chamber a second and a third time the money was each time seen to be diminished, for the thieves

---

[*]*Tisis* (retribution) applies in all realms; compare 1.2, 4.205, 5.56, 7.10, 8.105–106, and 8.109.

did not slacken their plundering, he did as follows:—he ordered traps to be made and he set these round about the vessels in which the money was; and when the thieves had come as at former times and one of them had entered, then so soon as he came near to one of the vessels he was straightway caught in the trap. When he perceived his bad situation, straightway calling his brother he showed him the problem, and ordered him enter as quickly as possible and cut off his head, lest being seen and known he might cause the destruction of his brother also. And to the other it seemed that he spoke well, and he was persuaded and did so; and fitting the stone back into its place he went home bearing the head of his brother.

(*c*) Now when it day came, the king entered into the chamber and was very greatly amazed, seeing the body of the thief held in the trap without his head, and the chamber unbroken, with no way to come in or go out. At a loss he hung up the dead body of the thief upon the wall and set guards there, with charge if they saw any one weeping or wailing to seize him and bring him before the king. And when the dead body had been hung up, the mother was greatly grieved, and speaking with the son who survived she commanded him, in whatever way he could, to find a way to take down and bring home the body of his brother; and if he should neglect to do this, she convincingly threatened that she would inform the king that he had the money.

(*d*) So as the mother harshly nagged the surviving son, and he though saying many things to her did not persuade her, he contrived this trick:— Providing himself with asses he filled some skins with wine and laid them upon the asses, and after that he drove them along. After he came opposite those who were guarding the suspended corpse, he drew towards him two or three of the necks of the skins and loosened the cords with which they were tied. Then when the wine was running out, he began to smack his head and cry out loudly, as if he did not know to which ass he should turn first; and when the guards saw the wine flowing out in streams, they ran together to the road with drinking vessels in their hands and collected the wine that was poured out, counting it their gain; and he abused them all violently, making as if he were angry, but when the guards tried to appease him, after a time he feigned to be pacified and to abate his anger, and at length he drove his asses out of the road and began to set their loads right. Then more talk arose among them, and one or two of them made jests at him and brought him to laugh with them; and in the end he made them a present of one of the skins in addition to what they had. Upon that they lay down there without more ado, being minded to drink, and they took him into their company and invited him to remain with them and join them in their drinking. He (as the plan supposed) was persuaded and stayed. Then as they in their drinking bade him welcome in a friendly manner, he made a present to them also of another of the skins; and so at length having drunk liberally the guards became completely intoxicated; and being overcome by sleep they fell asleep on the spot where they had been drinking. He then, as night was far advanced, first took down the body of his brother, and then in mockery shaved the right cheeks of all the guards; and after that he put the dead body upon the asses and drove them away home, having accomplished his mother's orders.

(e) Upon this the king, when it was reported to him that the dead body of the thief had been stolen, displayed great anger; and desiring by all means to find out whoever devised these things, did this (so at least they said, but I do not believe the account),—he caused his own daughter to sit before a house, and enjoined her to have sex with all equally, and before having sex with any one to compel him to tell her what was the most cunning and what the most unholy deed which he had ever done in all his lifetime. Whosoever should relate the thief's achievements, him she must seize and not let him leave. Then when she was doing as her father ordered, the thief, hearing why she was doing this and having a desire to get the better of the king, did thus:—from the body of one lately dead he cut off the arm at the shoulder and went with it under his mantle. Having gone in to the daughter of the king, and being asked that which the others also were asked, he related that he had done the most unholy deed when he cut off the head of his brother, who had been caught in a trap in the king's treasure-chamber, and the most cunning deed when he made drunk the guards and took down the dead body of his brother hanging up. When she heard it she tried to take hold of him, but the thief held out to her in the darkness the arm of the corpse, which she grasped and held, thinking that she was holding the arm of the man himself; but the thief left it in her hands and departed, escaping through the door.

(f) Now when this also was reported to the king, he was at first amazed at the ready invention and daring of the fellow, and then afterwards he sent round to all the cities and made proclamation granting a free pardon to the thief, and also promising a great reward if he would come into his presence. The thief accordingly trusting to the proclamation came to the king, and Rhampsinitos greatly marvelled at him, and gave him his daughter for wife, counting him to be the most knowing of all men; for as the Egyptians were distinguished from all other men, so was he from the other Egyptians.

122. They said that later this king went down alive to that place which by the Hellenes is called Hades, and there played dice with Demeter, and in some throws he overcame her and in others he was overcome by her; and he came back again having as a gift from her a handkerchief of gold. They told me that because of the going down of Rhampsinitos the Egyptians after he came back celebrated a feast, which, I know of my own knowledge also, that they still observe even to my time; but whether it is for this cause that they keep the feast or for some other, I cannot say. However, the priests weave a robe completely on the very day of the feast, and immediately they bind up the eyes of one of them with a fillet, and having led him with the robe to the way to the temple of Demeter, they depart back again themselves. This priest, they say, with his eyes bound up is led by two wolves to the temple of Demeter, which is 2⅓ miles distant

from the city, and then afterwards the wolves lead him back again from the temple to the same spot.

123. Now as to the tales told by the Egyptians, any man may accept them if such things appear credible; as for me, it is to be understood throughout the whole of the history that I write what I hear reported by the people in each place. The Egyptians say that Demeter and Dionysos are rulers of the world below; and the Egyptians also first reported the doctrine that the soul of man is immortal, and that when the body dies, the soul enters into another creature which chances then to be coming to the birth, and when it has gone the round of all the creatures of land and sea and of the air, it enters again into a human body at birth; and that it makes this round in a period of three thousand years. This doctrine certain Hellenes adopted, some earlier and some later, as if it were of their own invention, and of these men I know the names but I abstain from recording them.*

124. Down to the time when Rhampsinitos was king, they told me there was in Egypt nothing but orderly rule, and Egypt prospered greatly; but after him Cheops became king over them and brought them every kind of evil. He shut up all the temples, and having first kept them from sacrifices there, he then ordered all the Egyptians work for him. So some were appointed to draw stones from the stone-quarries in the Arabian mountains to the Nile, and others he ordered to receive the stones after they had been carried over the river in boats, and to draw them to those which are called the Libyan mountains; and they worked by a hundred thousand men at a time, each group three months continually. This oppression lasted ten years while the causeway was made by which they drew the stones. This causeway is a work not much less, as it appears to me, than the pyramid. The length of it is $^6/_{10}$ of a mile and the breadth sixty feet and the height, where it is highest, forty-eight feet, and it is made of smoothed stone with figures carved upon it. For this, they said, the ten years were spent, and for the underground chambers on the heights upon which the pyramids stand, which he caused to be made as sepulchral chambers for himself in an island, having conducted to it a channel from the Nile.† For the making of the pyramid itself took a period of twenty years; and the pyramid is square, each side measuring eight hundred feet, and the height of it is the same. It is built of stone smoothed and fitted together in the most perfect manner, not one of the stones being less than thirty feet in length.

125. This pyramid was made after the manner of steps, which some call "rows" and others "bases:" and when they had first made it thus, they raised the remaining stones with machines made of short pieces of timber, raising them first from the ground to the first stage of the steps, and when

---

*Pythagoras and Empedocles, among others, preached metempsychosis; Herodotus' reticence remains variously explained.

†There is no such known channel (compare 2.127), but the measurements are reasonably correct.

the stone got up to this it was placed upon another machine standing on the first stage, and so from this it was drawn to the second upon another machine; for as many as were the courses of the steps, so many machines there were also, or perhaps they transferred one and the same machine, made so as easily to be carried, to each stage successively, in order that they might take up the stones; for let it be told in both ways, as it is reported. However that may be, the highest parts of it were finished first, and afterwards they proceeded to finish that which came next to them, and lastly they finished the parts of it near the ground and the lowest ranges.

On the pyramid it is declared in Egyptian writing how much was spent on radishes and onions and leeks for the workmen, and if I rightly remember that which the interpreter said in reading to me this inscription, a sum of one thousand six hundred talents of silver was spent;[*] and if this is so, how much besides is likely to have been expended upon the iron with which they worked, and upon bread and clothing for the workmen, seeing that they were building the works for the time which has been mentioned and were occupied for no small time besides, as I suppose, in the cutting and bringing of the stones and in working at the excavation under the ground?

126. Cheops[†] moreover came, they said, to such wickedness that being in want of money he caused his own daughter to sit before a house [as a prostitute], and ordered her to obtain from those who came a certain amount of money (how much it was they did not tell me). She not only obtained the sum appointed by her father, but also she formed a design for herself privately to leave behind a memorial, and she requested each man who came in to her for sex to give her one stone for her building. From these stones, they told me, the pyramid was built which stands in front of the great pyramid in the middle of the three, each side being one hundred and fifty feet in length.

127. This Cheops, the Egyptians said, reigned fifty years; and after he was dead his brother Chephren succeeded him. This king behaved like his brother, in all the rest and also he made a pyramid, not indeed attaining to the measurements of the former (this I know, having myself also measured it), and moreover there are no underground chambers beneath nor does a channel come from the Nile flowing to this one as to the other, in which the water coming through a conduit flows round an island within, where they say that Cheops himself is laid. For a basement he built the first course of Ethiopian stone of divers colours; and this pyramid he made forty feet lower than the other as regards size, building it close to the great pyramid. These stand both upon the same height, which is about a hundred feet high. And Chephren they said reigned fifty and six years.

128. Here then they reckon one hundred and six years, during which

---

[*]That is, 91,200 pounds, an incredible figure; there are no inscriptions on the pyramids.

[†]The Egyptian pyramid builders are Khufu (Cheops), Khafra (Chephren), and Menkaura (Mykerinos).

they say that there was nothing but evil for the Egyptians, and the temples were kept closed and not opened during that time. The Egyptians by reason of their hatred are not very willing to name these kings; nay, they even call the pyramids after the name of Philitis the shepherd, who at that time pastured flocks in those regions. **129.** After him, they said, Mykerinos became king over Egypt, who was the son of Cheops; and to him his father's deeds were displeasing, and he both opened the temples and gave liberty to the people, who were ground down to the extremity of evil, to return to their own business and to their sacrifices. He also decided their causes more justly than all the other kings. In regard to this then they commend this king beyond the other kings in Egypt before him; for he not only gave good decisions, but also when a man complained of the decision, he gave him recompense from his own goods and thus satisfied him. But while Mykerinos was acting mercifully to his subjects and practising this good conduct, calamities befell him. First his daughter died, the only child whom he had in his house. Grieved beyond measure by his loss, and desiring to bury his daughter in a manner surpassing others, he made a cow of wood, which he covered with gold, and then within it he buried this daughter who had died. **130.** This cow was not covered up in the ground, but it might be seen even down to my own time in the city of Saïs, placed within the royal palace in a chamber which was greatly adorned; and they offer incense of all kinds before it every day, and each night a lamp burns beside it all through the night. Near this cow in another chamber stand images of the concubines of Mykerinos, as the priests at Saïs told me; in fact colossal wooden statues stand there, about twenty at most, made with naked bodies; but who they are I cannot say, except to pass on what is reported.

131. Some however tell about this cow and the colossal statues the following tale: Mykerinos was enamoured of his own daughter and afterwards raped her; and upon this they say that the girl hanged herself for grief, and he buried her in this cow; and her mother cut off the hands of the maids who had betrayed the daughter to her father; wherefore now the images have suffered what the maids suffered in life. In thus saying they babble nonsense, as it seems to me, especially what they say about the hands of the statues; for as to this, we ourselves saw that their hands had dropped off from the passage of time, and they were to be seen still lying at their feet even in my time.* **132.** The cow is covered with a crimson robe, except only the head and the neck, which are seen overlaid with gold very thickly; and between the horns the disc of the sun is figured in gold. The cow is not standing up but kneeling, and in size it is equal to a large living cow. Every year it is carried forth from the chamber, when the Egyptians beat themselves for that god not to be named by me in this connection. At these times they also carry forth the cow to the daylight, for they say that she asked of her father Mykerinos, when she was dying, that she might look upon the sun once a year.

---

*A good example of archaeological criticism.

133. After the calamity of his daughter this other thing happened, they said, to this king:—An oracle came to him from the city of Buto, saying that he was destined to live but six years more, in the seventh year to end his life. He being indignant at it sent to the Oracle a reproach against the god, complaining in reply that whereas his father and uncle, who had shut up the temples and had not only not remembered the gods, but also had been destroyers of men, had lived for a long time, he himself, who worshipped the gods, was destined to end his life so soon. A second message came from the Oracle, which said that it was for this very cause that his life was coming to a swift close; for he had not done that which he ought to do. It was destined that Egypt should suffer evils for a hundred and fifty years, and the two kings who had arisen before him had perceived this, but he had not. Mykerinos having heard this, and considering that this sentence had been passed upon him beyond recall, procured many lamps and whenever night came on he lighted these and began to drink and take his pleasure, ceasing neither by day nor by night; and he went about to the marsh-country and to the woods and wherever he heard there were the best places for pleasure and enjoyment. This he devised (having a mind to prove that the Oracle spoke falsely) in order that he might have twelve years of life instead of six, the nights being turned into days.

134. This king also left behind him a pyramid, much smaller than that of his father, of a square shape and measuring on each side three hundred feet lacking twenty, built moreover of Ethiopian stone up to half the height. This pyramid some of the Hellenes say was built by the prostitute Rhodopis, not therein speaking rightly. I perceive that they who speak thus do not even know who Rhodopis was, for otherwise they would not have attributed to her the building of a pyramid like this, on which have been spent (so to speak) innumerable thousands of talents. Moreover they do not know that Rhodopis flourished in the reign of Amasis, and not in this king's reign; for Rhodopis lived very many years later than the kings who left behind these pyramids. By descent she was of Thrace, and she was a slave of Iadmon the son of Hephaistopolis a Samian, and a fellow-slave of Esop the maker of fables; for he too was once the slave of Iadmon, as this fact especially proved. When the people of Delphi repeatedly made proclamation in accordance with an oracle, to find some one who would take up the blood-money for the death of Esop, no one else appeared, but at length the grandson of Iadmon, called Iadmon also, took it up thus proving that Esop too was the slave of Iadmon.

135. Rhodopis came to Egypt brought by Xanthes the Samian, and having come thither to exercise her calling she was redeemed from slavery for a great sum by a man of Mytilenē, Charaxos son of Scamandronymos and brother of Sappho the lyric poet. Thus was Rhodopis set free, and she remained in Egypt and by her sexual charms won so much that she made great gain of money for one like Rhodopis, though not enough for the cost of such a pyramid as this. In truth there is no need to ascribe to her very great riches, considering that the tithe of her wealth may still be seen even to this time by any one who desires it. Rhodopis wished to leave behind her a memorial in Hellas, something to be made that had never been thought of or dedicated in a temple by any besides, and to dedicate this at Delphi as a memorial of herself. Accordingly with the tithe of her wealth she caused to be made spits of iron of size large enough to pierce a whole ox, and many in number, going as far as her tithe allowed her, and she sent them to Delphi. These are even at the present time lying there, heaped all together behind the altar which the Chians dedicated, and just opposite to the temple's chief room. Now at Naucratis, as it happens, the prostitutes are sexually alluring. This woman first, about whom the story is told, became so famous that all the Hellenes without exception came to know the name of Rhodopis, and then after her one whose name was Archidichē became a subject of song all over Hellas, though she was less gossiped about than the other. Charaxos, after redeeming Rhodopis returned back to Mytilenē, but Sappho in an ode violently abused him. Of Rhodopis then I say no more.

136. After Mykerinos the priests said Asychis became king of Egypt, and he made for Hephaistos the temple gateway to the East, by far the most beautiful and the largest of the gateways; for while they all have figures carved upon them and innumerable marvels of building besides, this has much more. In this king's reign they told me that, as the circulation of money was very slow, a law was made for the Egyptians that a man might have that money lent to him which he needed, by offering as security the dead body of his father; and there was added moreover to this law another, namely that he who lent the money should have a claim also to the whole of the sepulchral chamber belonging to him who received it, and that the man who offered that security should be subject to this penalty, if he refused to pay back the debt: neither the man himself should be allowed to have burial, when he died, either in that family burial-place or in any other, nor should he be allowed to bury any kinsmen whom he lost by death.

This king desiring to surpass the kings of Egypt who had arisen before him left as a memorial of himself a pyramid which he made of bricks, and on it there is an inscription carved in stone saying: "Despise not me in comparison with the pyramids of stone, seeing that I excel them as much as Zeus excels the other gods; for with a pole they struck into the lake, and whatever of the mud attached itself to the pole, this they gathered up and made bricks, and in such manner they finished me." Such were the deeds which this king performed.

137. After him* reigned a blind man of the city of Anysis, whose name was Anysis. In his reign the Ethiopians and Sabacōs the king of the Ethiopians marched upon Egypt with a great host of men; so this blind man departed, flying to the marsh-country, and the Ethiopian was king over Egypt for fifty years, during which he performed such deeds:—whenever any

---

*At this point Herodotus jumps from the pyramid pharaohs (third to sixth dynasties; c.2600) over the Ethiopian dynasty to c.700, the twenty-fifth dynasty.

Egyptian committed any transgression, he would never put him to death, but he gave sentence upon each man according to the greatness of the wrong-doing, appointing them to work at throwing up an embankment before that city whence each man came who committed wrong. Thus the cities were made higher still than before; for they were embanked first by those who dug the channels in the reign of Sesostris, and then secondly in the reign of the Ethiopian, and thus they were made very high. While other cities in Egypt also stood high, I think in the town at Bubastis especially the earth was piled up. In this city there is a temple most worthy of mention, for though there are other temples which are larger and built with more cost, none more than this is a pleasure to regard. Now Bubastis in the Hellenic tongue is Artemis.

138. Her temple is ordered thus:—Except the entrance it is completely surrounded by water; for channels come in from the Nile, not joining one another, but each extending as far as the entrance of the temple, one flowing round on the one side and the other on the other side, each a hundred feet broad and shaded over with trees; and the gateway has a height of 60 feet, and it is adorned with very noteworthy figures nine feet high. This temple is in the middle of the city and is looked down upon from all sides as one goes round, for since the city has been banked up to a height, while the temple has not been moved from the place where it was first built, it is possible to look down into it. Round it runs a stone wall with figures carved upon it, while within it there is a grove of very large trees planted round a large temple-house, within which is the image of the goddess. The breadth and length of the temple is 600 feet every way. Opposite the entrance there is a road paved with stone for about 1800 feet, which leads through the market-place towards the East, with a breadth of about four hundred feet; and on this side and on that grow trees of height reaching to heaven: and the road leads to the temple of Hermes.* This temple then is thus ordered.

139. Finally deliverance from the Ethiopian came about (they said) as follows:—he fled because he had seen in his sleep a vision, in which it seemed to him that a man came and stood by him and counselled him to gather together all the priests in Egypt and cut them asunder in the midst. Having seen this dream, he said that it seemed to him that the gods were foreshowing him as an advance notice, in order that he might do an impious deed, and so receive some evil either from the gods or from men. He would not however do so, but in truth (he said) the time had expired, during which it had been prophesied to him that he should rule Egypt before departing. For when he was in Ethiopia the Oracles which the Ethiopians consult had told him that it was fated for him to rule Egypt fifty years. Since then this time was now expiring, and the vision of the dream disturbed him, Sabacōs left Egypt of his own free will.

140. Then when the Ethiopian left Egypt, the blind man came back from the marsh-country and began to rule again, having lived there during

---

*That is, Egyptian Thoth.

fifty years upon an island which he had made by heaping up ashes and earth. Whenever any of the Egyptians visited him bringing food, as it was assigned without the knowledge of the Ethiopian, he bade them bring also some ashes for their tribute. This island none could find before Amyrtaios; that is, for more than seven hundred years the kings before Amyrtaios were not able to find it. Now the name of this island is Elbo, and its size is a little over a mile each way.

141. After him the priest of Hephaistos came to the throne, whose name was Sethōs. This man, they said, neglected and held in no regard the warrior class of the Egyptians, considering that he would have no need of them; and besides other slights upon them, he also took from them the acres of choice grain-land which had been given to them as a special gift in the reigns of the former kings, 9 acres to each man. After this, Sennacherib king of the Arabians and of the Assyrians marched a great host against Egypt.* Then the warriors of the Egyptians refused to come to the rescue, and the priest in his predicament entered the sanctuary of the temple and complained to the image of the god about the danger impending over him. As he was thus lamenting, sleep came upon him, and it seemed to him in his vision that the god came and stood by him and encouraged him, saying that he should suffer no evil if he went forth to meet the army of the Arabians; for he would himself send helpers. Trusting in these things seen in sleep, he took with him, they said, those of the Egyptians who were willing to follow him, and encamped in Pelusion, for by this way the invasion came. Not one of the warrior class followed him, but shop-keepers and artisans and men of the market. Then after they came, there swarmed by night upon their enemies mice of the fields, and ate up their quivers and their bows, and moreover the handles of their shields, so that on the next day they fled, and being defenceless great numbers fell. And at the present time this king stands in the temple of Hephaistos in stone, holding upon his hand a mouse, and by inscribed letters he says: "Let him who looks upon me reverence the gods."

142. So far in the history the Egyptians and the priests made the report, declaring that from the first king down to this priest of Hephaistos who reigned last, there had been three hundred and forty-one generations of men, and that in them there had been the same number of chief-priests and of kings.† But three hundred generations of men are equal to ten thousand years, for a hundred years is three generations of men; and in the one-and-forty generations which remain, those I mean which were added to the three hundred, there are one thousand three hundred and forty years. Thus in the period of eleven thousand three hundred and forty years they said that there had been born no god in human form; nor even before that time or afterwards among the remaining kings who arose in Egypt,

---

*The invasion of Sennacherib the Assyrian (with Arab guides) occurred c.700 B.C.
†In 2.142–146 Herodotus interrupts the narrative to consider chronology and emphasize Egyptian antiquity.

did they report that anything of the kind had come to pass. In this time they said that the sun had moved four times from his accustomed place of rising, and where he now sets he had twice had his rising, and in the place whence he now rises he had twice had his setting; and in the meantime nothing in Egypt had been changed from its usual state, neither that which comes from the earth nor that which comes to them from the river nor that which concerns diseases or deaths.

143. And formerly when Hecataios the travel-writer was in Thebes, and had traced his descent and connected his family with a god in the sixteenth generation before, the priests of Zeus did for him much the same as they did for me (though I had not provided my descent).[*] They led me into the sanctuary of the temple, a big one, and they counted up the number, showing colossal wooden statues in number the same as they said; for each chief-priest sets up in his lifetime an image of himself. The priests, counting and showing me these, declared to me that each one of them was a son succeeding his own father, and they went up through the series of images from the image of the one who had died last, until they had declared this of the whole number. And when Hecataios had traced his descent and connected his family with a god in the sixteenth generation, they traced a counter-descent, besides their numbering, rejecting the idea that a man had been born from a god. They traced their counter-descent thus, saying that each one of the statues had been *piromis* son of *piromis,* until they had declared this of the whole three hundred and forty-five statues. Neither with a god nor a hero did they connect their descent. (*Piromis* means in the tongue of Hellas "honourable and good man.") **144.** From their declaration then it followed, that the images were of men with form like this, and far removed from gods. But in the time before these men they said that gods were the rulers in Egypt, not mingling with men, and that one of these always had power at a time; and the last of them who was king over Egypt was Oros the son of Osiris, whom the Hellenes call Apollo. He ruled Egypt last, having deposed Typhon. Now Osiris in the tongue of Hellas is Dionysos.

145. Among the Hellenes Heracles and Dionysos and Pan are accounted the latest-born of the gods; but with the Egyptians Pan is a very ancient god, and he is one of those called the eight gods, while Heracles is of the second rank, who are called the twelve gods, and Dionysos is of the third rank, namely those born of the twelve gods. Now I have shown already how many years old Heracles is according to the Egyptians themselves, reckoning down to the reign of Amasis, and Pan is said to have existed for yet more years than these, and Dionysos for the smallest number of years as compared with the others; and even for this last they reckon, down to the reign of Amasis, fifteen thousand years. This the Egyptians say that they know for a certainty, since they always kept a reckoning and

---

[*]Herodotus acknowledges his use of a pioneer writer of geography and genealogy, and criticizes his naivete.

wrote down the years. Now the Dionysos who is said to have been born of
Semelē the daughter of Cadmos, was born about sixteen hundred years before my time, and Heracles who was the son of Alcmenē, about nine hundred years, and that Pan who was born of Penelopē, for of her and of
Hermes Pan is said by the Hellenes to have been born, came into being
later than the wars of Troy, about eight hundred years before my time.

146. Every man may adopt that one of these two accounts which he
shall find the more credible. I however have already declared my opinion
about them. For if these also, like Heracles the son of Amphitryon, had
appeared before all men's eyes and had lived their lives to old age in Hellas, I mean Dionysos the son of Semelē and Pan the son of Penelopē, then
one would have said that these also had been born mere men, having the
names of gods who had come into being long before. As it is, with regard
to Dionysos the Hellenes say that as soon as he was born Zeus sewed him
up in his thigh and carried him to Nysa, which is above Egypt in the land
of Ethiopia; and as to Pan, they cannot say whither he went after he was
born. Hence it has become clear to me that the Hellenes learnt the names
of these gods later than those of the other gods, and trace their descent
as if their birth occurred when they first learnt their names.

Thus far then the history is told by the Egyptians themselves; **147,** but I
will now recount what other nations also tell, and the Egyptians in agreement, about what happened in this land. I will add to this things that I have
myself seen.

Being set free after the reign of the priest of Hephaistos, the Egyptians,
since they could not live any time without a king, set up twelve kings, having divided all Egypt into twelve parts. These made intermarriages with
one another and reigned, making agreement that they would not put down
one another by force, nor seek advantage over one another, but would live
in perfect friendship. They made these agreements, guarding them very
strongly from violation, because an oracle had been given to them when
they began to exercise their rule, that he of them who should pour a libation with a bronze cup in the temple of Hephaistos, should be king of all
Egypt (for they used to assemble together in all the temples).

148. Moreover they resolved to join all together and leave a memorial
of themselves; and having so resolved they caused a labyrinth to be made,
situated a little above the lake of Moiris and nearly opposite to the City of
Crocodiles. This I saw myself, and I found it greater than words can say.
For if one should put together and reckon up all the buildings and all the
great works produced by Hellenes, they would prove to be inferior in
labour and expense to this labyrinth, though it is true that both the temple
at Ephesos and that at Samos are works worthy of note. The pyramids also
were greater than words can say, and each one of them is equal to many
works of the Hellenes, great as they may be; but the labyrinth surpasses
even the pyramids. It has twelve courts covered in, with gates facing one
another, six upon the North side and six upon the South, one after another,
and the same wall surrounds them all outside; and there are in it two kinds

of chambers, the one kind below the ground and the other above upon these, three thousand in number, of each kind fifteen hundred. The upper set of chambers we ourselves saw, going through them, and we tell of them having looked upon them with our own eyes. The chambers under ground we heard about only; for the Egyptians who had charge of them were not willing on any account to show them, saying that here were the sepulchres of the kings who had first built this labyrinth and of the sacred crocodiles. Accordingly we speak of the chambers below by what we received from hearsay, while those above we saw ourselves and found them to be works beyond the human. For the passages through the chambers, and the goings this way and that way through the courts, which were admirably adorned, afforded endless matter for marvel, as we went through from a court to the chambers beyond it, and from the chambers to colonnades, and from the colonnades to other rooms, and then from the chambers again to other courts. Over the whole of these is a roof made of stone like the walls; and the walls are covered with figures carved upon them, each court being surrounded with pillars of white stone fitted together most perfectly; and at the end of the labyrinth, by the corner of it, there is a pyramid of 240 feet, upon which large figures are carved, and into this there is an underground way.

149. Such is this labyrinth: but a cause for marvel even greater than this is afforded by the lake, which is called the lake of Moiris, along the side of which this labyrinth is built. The measure of its circuit is 413 miles (being sixty *schoines*), and this is the same number of furlongs as the extent of Egypt itself along the sea.[*] The lake extends lengthwise from North to South, and in depth at the deepest it is 300 feet. That this lake is artificial and formed by digging is self-evident, for about in the middle of the lake stand two pyramids, each rising above the water to a height of 300 feet, the part which is built below the water being of just the same height; and upon each is placed a colossal statue of stone sitting upon a chair. Thus the pyramids are 600 feet high; and these 600 feet equal a stade of six hundred feet, the *orguia* being measured as six feet or four cubits, the feet being four palms each, and the cubits six.[†] The water in the lake does not come from the place where it is, for the country there is very deficient in water, but it has been brought thither from the Nile by a canal. For six months the water flows into the lake, and for six months out into the Nile again; and whenever it flows out, then for the six months it brings into the royal treasury 57 lbs of silver a day from the fish which are caught, and almost twenty pounds when the water comes in.

150. The natives of the place moreover said that this lake had an outlet under ground to the Syrtis which is in Libya, turning towards the interior

---

[*]The Fayum lake basin was closer to 170 miles in circumference before reclamation; it was a natural depression 120 feet below sea level.

[†]A key passage for Herodotus' measurements, most of the ones in Egypt probably provided by casual guides who knew some Greek; see 2.154.

of the continent upon the Western side and running along by the mountain which is above Memphis. Now since I did not see anywhere existing
the earth dug out of this excavation (for that was a matter which drew my
attention), I asked those who dwelt nearest to the lake where the dug out
earth was. These told me where it had been carried away; and I readily believed them, for I knew by report that a similar thing had been done at
Nineveh, the city of the Assyrians. There certain thieves once contrived to
carry away the wealth of Sardanapallos son of Ninos, the king. The monies
were very great and were kept in treasure-houses under the earth. Accordingly they began from their own dwelling, and making estimate of
their direction they dug underground towards the king's palace; and the
earth which was brought out of the excavation they used to carry away,
when night came, to the river Tigris which flows by Nineveh, until at last
they accomplished their desire. Similarly, as I heard, the digging of the lake
in Egypt was effected, except that it was done not by night but in the day;
for as they dug the Egyptians carried to the Nile the earth which was dug
out; and the river, when it received it, would naturally bear it away and disperse it. Thus this lake is said to have been dug out.

151. Now the twelve kings continued to rule justly, but one day after
sacrifice in the temple of Hephaistos they were about to make libation, on
the last day of the feast, and the chief-priest, in bringing out for them the
golden cups with which they poured libations, miscounted and brought
eleven only for the twelve. Then that one* standing last in order, namely
Psammetichos, since he had no cup took off his helmet, which was bronze,
and having held it out he made libation. All the other kings were wont to
wear helmets and they happened to have them then. Now Psammetichos
held out his helmet with no treacherous meaning; but they taking note of
Psammetichos' act and of the oracle, namely how it had been declared to
them that whosoever of them should make libation with a bronze cup
should be sole king of Egypt, recollecting, I say, the saying of the Oracle,
they did not indeed determine to slay Psammetichos, since they found by
examination that he had not done it with any forethought, but they determined to strip him of almost all his power and to drive him away into the
marsh-country, and that from the marsh-country he should not hold any
dealings with the rest of Egypt.

152. This Psammetichos had formerly been a fugitive from the Ethiopian
Sabacōs who had killed his father Necōs. He had then been a fugitive
in Syria; and when the Ethiopian had departed in consequence of the vision of the dream, the Egyptians from the district of Saïs brought him
back to his own country. Then afterwards, when he was king, it was his fate
to be a fugitive a second time on account of the helmet, being driven by the
eleven kings into the marsh-country.

So then holding that he had been grievously wronged by them, he
thought how he might take vengeance on those who had driven him out.

---

*Psammetichos became king c.664 B.C. and ruled to c.610.

After he had sent to the Oracle of Leto in the city of Buto, where the Egyptians have their most truthful Oracle, to him came the reply that vengeance would come when men of bronze appeared from the sea. And he was strongly disposed not to believe that bronze men would come to help him; but after no long time had passed, certain Ionians and Carians who had sailed for plunder were compelled to come to shore in Egypt, and they having landed and being clad in bronze armour, one of the Egyptians, not having before seen men clad in bronze armour, came to the marsh-land and brought a report to Psammetichos that bronze men had come from the sea and were plundering the plain. Perceiving that the saying of the Oracle was coming to pass, he dealt in a friendly manner with the Ionians and Carians, and with large promises he persuaded them to join him. Then when he had persuaded them, with the help of those Egyptians who favoured his cause and of these foreign mercenaries he overthrew the kings.

153. Having thus got power over all Egypt, Psammetichos made for Hephaistos that gateway of the temple at Memphis which is turned towards the South; and he built a court for Apis, in which Apis is kept when he appears, opposite to the gateway of the temple, surrounded all with pillars and covered with figures; and instead of columns there stand to support the roof of the court colossal statues eighteen feet high. Now Apis is Epaphos in the tongue of the Hellenes.

154. To the Ionians and to the Carians who had helped him Psammetichos granted portions of land to dwell in, opposite to one another with the river Nile between, and these were called "Encampments."* These portions of land he gave them, and he paid them besides all that he had promised. Moreover he placed with them Egyptian boys to have them taught the Hellenic tongue; and from these, who learnt the language thoroughly, are descended the present class of interpreters in Egypt. Now the Ionians and Carians occupied these portions of land for a long time, towards the sea and a little below the city of Bubastis, on the Pelusian mouth of the Nile. These men king Amasis afterwards removed and established them at Memphis, making them into a guard for himself against the Egyptians. Once they were settled in Egypt, we who are Hellenes reliably know by intercourse with them all that happened in Egypt from king Psammetichos and afterwards; for these were the first men of foreign tongue who settled in Egypt. In the land from which they were removed there remained down to my time the sheds where their ships were drawn up and the ruins of their houses. Thus then Psammetichos obtained Egypt.

155. I have made mention often before this of the Oracle which is in Egypt, and now I will give an account that it deserves. This Oracle in Egypt is sacred to Leto, and it is established in a great city near that mouth of the Nile which is called Sebennytic, as one sails up from the sea; and the name of this city where the Oracle is found is Buto, as I said before. In this Buto there is a temple of Apollo and Artemis; and the shrine of Leto, in which

---

*These were mentioned in 2.112.

the Oracle is, is both great in itself and has a gateway sixty feet high. I will now tell what caused me most to marvel. There is in this sacred enclosure a shrine of Leto made of monolithic stone walls as regards both height and length, and each wall is equal in these two directions, being sixty feet; and for the covering in of the roof there lies another stone upon the top, the gable measuring six feet.

156. This shrine then of all the things that were to be seen by me in that sanctuary is the most marvellous, and among those which come next is the island called Chemmis. This is situated in a deep and broad lake by the side of the temple at Buto, and the Egyptians say that this island floats. I myself did not see it either floating about or moved, and I wonder at hearing of it, if it be indeed a floating island. In this island there is a great temple of Apollo, and three altars are set up within, and there are planted in the island many palm-trees and other trees, both bearing fruit and not. And the Egyptians, when they say that it is floating, add this story, namely that in this island, which formerly was not floating, Leto, one of the eight gods who first came into existence, dwelt in the city of Buto where she has this Oracle. She received Apollo from Isis as a charge and preserved him, concealing him in the island which is said now to be a floating island, at that time when Typhon came after him seeking everywhere and desiring to find the son of Osiris. Now they say that Apollo and Artemis are children of Dionysos and of Isis, and that Leto became their nurse and preserver; and in the Egyptian tongue Apollo is Oros, Demeter is Isis, and Artemis is Bubastis. From this story and from no other Æschylus the son of Euphorion plundered this which I shall say, wherein he differs from all the preceding poets. He represented Artemis as the daughter of Demeter. For this reason then, they say, it became a floating island.

157. Such is the story which they tell. Psammetichos was king over Egypt for four-and-fifty years, of which for thirty years save one he was sitting before Azotos, a great city of Syria, besieging it, until at last he took it. This Azotos held out for the longest time under a siege of all cities about which we know.

158. The son of Psammetichos was Necōs, and he became king of Egypt. This man was the first who attempted the channel leading to the Erythraian Sea, which Dareios the Persian afterwards completed. The length of this is a voyage of four days, and in breadth it was so dug that two triremes could go side by side driven by oars;* and the water is brought into it from the Nile. The channel is conducted a little above the city of Bubastis by Patumos the Arabian city, and runs into the Erythraian Sea. It is dug first along those parts of the plain of Egypt which lie towards Arabia, just above which run the mountains which extend opposite Memphis, where are the stone-quarries,—along the base of these mountains the channel is conducted from West to East for a great way; and after that it is directed

---

*Excavations reveal a breadth of 150 feet and a depth of 17 feet; see also Xerxes' Athos Canal, at 7.24.

towards a break in the hills and tends from these mountains towards the
noon-day and the South to the Arabian gulf. Now in the place where the
journey is least and shortest from the Northern to the Southern Sea (which
is also called Erythraian), that is from Mount Casion, which is the boundary between Egypt and Syria, the distance is exactly* 115 miles to the Arabian gulf; but the channel is much longer, since it is more winding; and in
the reign of Necōs 120,000 Egyptians perished there while digging it. Now
Necōs ceased in the midst of his digging, because the utterance of an Oracle impeded him, to the effect that he was working for the Barbarian. The
Egyptians call all men Barbarians who do not agree with them in speech.

159. Thus having ceased from the work of the channel, Necōs betook
himself to waging wars, and triremes were built by him, some for the
Northern Sea and others in the Arabian gulf for the Erythraian Sea; and
of these the sheds are still to be seen. These ships he used when he needed
them; and also on land Necōs engaged battle at Magdolos with the Syrians, and conquered them; and after this he took Cadytis, which is a great
city of Syria. He dedicated to Apollo the dress which he wore when he
made these conquests, sending it to Branchidai of the Milesians. After this,
having reigned in all sixteen years, he died, and handed on the kingdom to
his son Psammis.

160. While this Psammis was king of Egypt, ambassadors sent by the
Eleians came to him. They boasted that they ordered the contest at Olympia
in the most just and honourable manner possible and thought that not even
the Egyptians, the smartest of men, could find out anything besides. Now
when the Eleians came to Egypt and explained why they had come, then
this king called together those Egyptians who were reputed the smartest,
and when the Egyptians had come together they heard the Eleians tell of
all that fell to them to do in regard to the contest; and when they had related everything, they said that they had come to learn any improvements
which the Egyptians might discover besides, anything fairer. They then having consulted together asked the Eleians whether their own citizens took
part in the contest; and they said that it was permitted to any one who desired it, both their own people and the other Hellenes equally, to compete.
The Egyptians said that in so ordering the games they had fallen short of
full fairness. There was no way that they would not side with their own
fellow-citizen, if he was contending, and so act unfairly to the stranger. If
they really desired, as they said, to order the games fairly, and if this was the
cause for which they had come to Egypt, they told them to order the contest for strangers alone to contend in, and to permit no Eleian to contend.
Such suggestion the Egyptians made to the Eleians.

161. When Psammis had been king of Egypt for only six years and
had made an expedition to Ethiopia and immediately afterwards died,
Apries the son of Psammis succeeded him.† This man came to be the most

*Seventy miles as the crow flies, but the road measure would always be greater.
†Apries became king in 589 B.C.

prosperous of all the kings up to that time except only his forefather Psammetichos; and he reigned five-and-twenty years, during which he led an army against Sidon and fought a sea-fight with the king of Tyre. Since however he had to meet a bad end, it came from a cause that I shall relate at greater length in the Libyan history,* and at present but shortly. Apries having sent a great expedition against the Kyrenians, met with correspondingly great disaster; and the Egyptians considering him to blame for this revolted from him, supposing that Apries had with forethought sent them out to certain destruction, in order (as they said) that there might be a slaughter of them, and he might the more securely rule over the surviving Egyptians. Being furious at this, both these men who had returned from the expedition and also the friends of those who had perished revolted openly.

162. Hearing this Apries sent Amasis to them, to cause them to cease by persuasion; and when he had come and was seeking to restrain the Egyptians, as he was speaking and telling them to calm down, one of the Egyptians stood up behind him and put a helmet upon his head, saying as he did so that he put it on to crown him king. And to him this action was in some degree not unwelcome, as he proved by his behaviour; for as soon as the revolted Egyptians had set him up as king, he prepared to march against Apries. Apries hearing this sent to Amasis one of the Egyptians who was close to him, a man or reputation, whose name was Patarbemis, enjoining him to bring Amasis alive into his presence. When Patarbemis came and summoned Amasis, the latter, who happened to be sitting on horseback, lifted up his leg and farted, bidding him take that back to Apries. Nevertheless, they say, Patarbemis demanded that he should go to the king, seeing that the king had sent to summon him; and he answered him that he had for some time past been preparing to do so, and that Apries would have no occasion to find fault with him, for he would both come himself and bring others with him. Then Patarbemis both perceiving his intention from his words, and also seeing his preparations, departed in haste, desiring to make his activities known as quickly as possible to the king. When he came back to Apries not bringing Amasis, the king paid no heed to that which he said, but being moved by violent anger, he ordered his ears and his nose cut off. And the rest of the Egyptians who still remained on his side, when they saw the man of most repute among them thus suffering shameful outrage, waited no longer but joined the others in revolt, and turned themselves over to Amasis. **163.** Then Apries having heard this also, armed his foreign mercenaries and marched against the Egyptians. He had about him Carian and Ionian mercenaries to the number of thirty thousand; and his royal palace was in the city of Saïs, of great size and worthy to be seen. So Apries and his army were going against the Egyptians, and Amasis and those with him were going against the mercenaries; and both sides came to the city of Momemphis and were about to fight one another.

---

*At 4.159 Herodotus keeps his word.

164. Now there are seven classes of the Egyptians, and of these one class is called the priests, and another the warriors, while the others are the cowherds, swineherds, shopkeepers, interpreters, and boatmen. This is the number of the classes of the Egyptians, and their names are given them from their occupations. The warriors are called Calasirians and Hermotybians, and they are of the following districts—for all Egypt is divided into districts called "nomes". **165.** The districts of the Hermotybians are those of Busiris, Saïs, Chemmis, Papremis, the island called Prosopitis, and the half of Natho—of these districts are the Hermotybians, who when most numerous amounted to 160,000 men. Of these not one has learnt anything of handicraft, but they devote themselves to war entirely. **166.** The districts of the Calasirians are those of Thebes, Bubastis, Aphthis, Tanis, Mendes, Sebennytos, Athribis, Pharbaithos, Thmuïs Onuphis, Anytis, Myecphoris— this last is on an island opposite to the city of Bubastis. These are the districts of the Calasirians; and they, when most numerous, amounted to 250,000 men; nor is it lawful for these, any more than for the others, to practise any craft; but they practise for war only, handing down the tradition from father to son. **167.** Now whether the Hellenes have learnt this also from the Egyptians, I am not able to say for certain, since I see that the Thracians also and Scythians and Persians and Lydians and almost all the Barbarians esteem those of their citizens who learn the arts, and the descendants of them, as less honourable than the rest; while those who have got free from all practise of manual arts are accounted noble, and especially those who are devoted to war. In any case, the Hellenes have all learnt this, and especially the Lacedemonians; but the Corinthians least of all slight those who practise handicrafts.

168. The following privilege was specially granted to this class and to none others of the Egyptians except the priests, that is to say, each man had nine acres of land specially granted to him free from taxes. The *aroura* of land measures a hundred Egyptian cubits every way, and the Egyptian cubit is, as it happens, equal to that of Samos, about 18 inches. This, I say, was a special privilege granted to all, and they also rotated certain advantages and not the same men twice. A thousand of the Calasirians and a thousand of the Hermotybians acted as body-guard to the king each year; and these had besides their 9 acres an allowance given them each day of five pounds weight of bread to each man, and two pounds of beef, and two pints of wine. This was the allowance always given to those who were serving as the king's bodyguard.

169. So when Apries leading his foreign mercenaries, and Amasis* at the head of all the Egyptians, in their approach to one another had come to the city of Momemphis, they engaged in battle. Although the foreign troops fought well, yet being much inferior in number they were defeated. But Apries is said to have supposed that not even a god would be able to remove him from his rule, so firmly did he think that it was established. In

---

*Amasis became king in 570 b.c. and ruled until 529 b.c. as Ahmose.

that battle then, I say, he was worsted, and being taken alive was brought away to the city of Saïs, to that which had formerly been his own dwelling but thenceforth was the palace of Amasis. There for some time he was kept in the palace, and Amasis treated him well; but at last, since the Egyptians blamed him, saying that he acted not rightly in keeping alive him who was the greatest foe both to themselves and to him, therefore he delivered Apries over to the Egyptians. They strangled him, and after that buried him in the burial-place of his fathers in the temple of Athenē, close to the sanctuary, on the left hand as you enter. Now the men of Saïs buried all those of this district who had been kings, within the temple; for the tomb of Amasis also, though it is further from the sanctuary than that of Apries and his forefathers, yet this too is within the court of the temple, and it consists of a colonnade of stone of great size, with pillars carved to imitate date-palms, and otherwise sumptuously adorned; and within the colonnade are double doors, and inside the doors a sepulchral chamber. **170.** Also at Saïs there is the burial-place of him whom I account it not pious to name in this connection, which is in the temple of Athenē behind the house of the goddess, stretching along the whole wall of it; and in the sacred enclosure stand great obelisks of stone, and near them is a lake adorned with an edging of stone and fairly made in a circle, being in size, as it seemed to me, equal to that which is called the "Round Lake" in Delos. **171.** On this lake they perform by night the show of his sufferings, and this the Egyptians call Mysteries. I know more fully in detail how they take place, but "let my lips be sealed." I shall leave similarly unspoken all except what piety permits me to tell of the mystic rites of Demeter, which the Hellenes call *thesmophoria*. The daughters of Danaos brought this rite out of Egypt and taught it to the women of the Pelasgians; then afterwards when all the inhabitants of Peloponnese were driven out by the Dorians, the rite was lost, and only those who were left behind of the Peloponnesians and not driven out, the Arcadians, preserved it.

172. After Apries was overthrown, Amasis became king, being of the district of Saïs, and the name of the city whence he was is Siuph. Now at the first the Egyptians despised Amasis and held him in no great regard, because he had been a man of the people and was not of distinguished family; but afterwards Amasis won them over to himself by wisdom and not wilfulness. Among innumerable other goods which he had, there was a foot-basin of gold in which both Amasis himself and all his guests washed their feet. This he broke up, and of it he caused to be made the image of a god, and set it up in the city, where it was most convenient; and the Egyptians went continually to visit the image and did great reverence to it. Then Amasis, having learnt what the men of the city were doing, called together the Egyptians and made known to them that the image had been produced from the foot-basin, into which formerly the Egyptians used to vomit and piss, and in which they washed their feet, whereas now they did it great reverence; and just so, he continued, had he himself now fared, as the foot-basin; for though formerly he was a man of the people, yet now he was their king, and he urged them accordingly honour him and have deference for him.

173. In such manner he won the Egyptians to himself, so that they consented to be his absolute subjects. Thus he managed his affairs:—In the early morning, and until the filling of the market he did with a good will the business which was brought before him; but after this he passed the time in drinking and in jesting at his boon-companions, and was frivolous and playful. And his troubled friends admonished him in such words as these: "King, you do not rightly govern yourself in thus descending to behaviour so trifling; for you ought rather to have been sitting throughout the day stately upon a stately throne and administering business; and so the Egyptians would have been assured that they were ruled by a great man, and you would have a better reputation. As it is, you are acting far from royal." And he answered them: "They who have bows stretch them when they need to use them, and when they have finished using them they unstring them again. If they were stretched tight always they would break, so that the men could not use them when they needed them. So also is the state of man. If he should always be in earnest and not relax himself for sport some time, he would either go mad or be struck with apoplexy before he was aware. Knowing this well, I allot time to each of the two ways of living." Thus he replied to his friends.

174. It is said however that Amasis, even when he was in a private station, was a lover of drinking and of jesting, and not at all seriously disposed; and whenever his means of livelihood failed him through his drinking and luxurious living, he would go about and steal; and they from whom he stole would charge him with having their property, and when he denied it would bring him before the judgment of an Oracle, whenever there was one in their place; and many times he was convicted by the Oracles and many times he was absolved. When finally he became king he did as follows:—as many of the gods as had absolved him and pronounced him not to be a thief, to their temples he paid no regard, nor gave anything for the further adornment of them, nor even visited them to offer sacrifice, considering them to be worth nothing and to possess lying Oracles; but as many as had convicted him of being a thief, to these he paid very great regard, considering them to be truly gods, and to produce Oracles which did not lie.

175. First in Saïs he built and completed for Athenē a temple-gateway which is a great marvel, and he far surpassed herein all before, both in regard to height and greatness, so large are the stones and of such quality. Then he dedicated great colossal statues and man-headed sphinxes[*] very large, and for restoration he brought other stones of monstrous size. Some of these he caused to be brought from the stone-quarries which are opposite Memphis, others of very great size from the city of Elephantinē, distant a voyage of not less than twenty days from Saïs: and of them all I marvel most at this, namely a monolith chamber which he brought from the city of Elephantinē. They were three years in bringing this, and two thousand men were appointed to convey it, who all were of the class of

---

*Greek sphinxes are female.

boatmen. Of this house the length outside is thirty-two feet, the breadth is twenty-one feet, and the height twelve. These are the measures of the mono-lith house outside; but the length inside is twenty-eight feet, the breadth eighteen-feet, and the height 7½ feet. This lies by the side of the entrance to the temple; for within the temple they did not draw it, because, as it is said, while the house was being drawn along, the chief architect of it groaned aloud, seeing that much time had been spent and he was wearied by the work; and Amasis took it to heart and did not allow them to draw it further. Some say on the other hand that a man was killed by it, of those who were heaving it with levers, and that it was not drawn in for that reason. **176.** Amasis also dedicated in all the other temples in repute, works which are worth seeing for their size, and among them also at Memphis the colossal statue which lies on its back in front of the temple of Hephaistos, whose length is five-and-seventy feet. On the same base made of the same stone are set two colossal statues, each of twenty feet in length, one on this side and the other on that side of the large statue. There is also an-other stone statue of the same size in Saïs, lying in the same manner as that at Memphis. Moreover Amasis was he who built and finished for Isis her temple at Memphis, which is of great size and very worthy to be seen.

177. In the reign of Amasis it is said that Egypt became most prosper-ous, both in regard to that which comes to the land from the river and in regard to that which comes from the land to its inhabitants, and that at this time the inhabited towns in it numbered in all twenty thousand. Amasis too established the law that every year each one of the Egyptians should declare to the ruler of his district, from what source he got his livelihood, and if any man did not do this or did not make declaration of an honest way of living, he should be punished with death. Now Solon the Athenian received from Egypt this law and had it enacted for the Athenians, and they have continued to observe it, since it is an entirely admirable law.

178. Moreover Amasis became a lover of the Hellenes; and besides other proofs of friendship which he gave to several among them, he also granted the city of Naucratis[*] for those who came to Egypt to dwell; and to those who did not desire to stay, but who made voyages thither, he granted portions of land to set up altars and make sacred enclosures for their gods. Their greatest enclosure and that one which is most famous and most frequented is called the Hellenion, and this was established by the following cities in common:—of the Ionians Chios, Teos, Phocaia, Clazom-enai; of the Dorians Rhodes, Cnidos, Halicarnassos, Phaselis; and of the Aiolians Mytilenē alone. To these belongs this enclosure and these are the cities which appoint superintendents of the port; and all other cities which claim a share in it, are making a claim without any right. Besides this the Eginetans established on their own account a sacred enclosure dedicated to Zeus, the Samians one to Hera, and the Milesians one to Apollo.

---

*On the Canobic branch, 70 miles from the sea.

179. Now in old times Naucratis alone was an open trading-place, and no other place in Egypt. If any one came to any other of the Nile mouths, he was compelled to swear that he came not of his own will, and when he had thus sworn his innocence he had to sail with his ship to the Canobic mouth, or if it were not possible to sail by reason of contrary winds, then he had to carry his cargo round the head of the Delta in boats to Naucratis. So highly was Naucratis privileged. **180.** Moreover when the Amphictyons had let out the contract for building the temple which now exists at Delphi, agreeing to pay a sum of three hundred talents, (for the temple which formerly stood there had been burnt down of itself), it fell to the share of the people of Delphi to provide the fourth part of the payment; and accordingly the Delphians went about to various cities and collected contributions. And when they did this they got from Egypt as much as from any place, for Amasis gave them a thousand talents' weight of alum, while the Hellenes who dwelt in Egypt gave them [only] twenty pounds of silver.

181. Also with the people of Kyrenē* Amasis made an agreement for friendship and alliance; and he resolved too to marry a wife from there, either because he desired to have a wife of Hellenic race, or, apart from that, on account of friendship for the people of Kyrenē. In any case, he married, some say the daughter of Battos, others of Arkesilaos, and others of Critobulos, a man of repute among the citizens; and her name was Ladikē. Now whenever Amasis lay with her he found himself unable to have intercourse, but with his other wives he associated as usual. After this happened repeatedly, Amasis said to his wife named Ladikē: "Woman, you have given me drugs, and you shall surely perish more miserably than any other woman." Then Ladikē, when despite her denials Amasis was not at all appeased in his anger against her, made a vow in her soul to Aphroditē, that if Amasis on that night had intercourse with her (seeing that this was the remedy for her danger), she would send an image to be dedicated to her at Kyrenē. After the vow immediately Amasis had intercourse, and thenceforth whenever Amasis came in to her he had intercourse with her; and after this he became greatly attached to her. And Ladikē paid the vow that she had made to the goddess; for she had an image made and sent it to Kyrenē, and it was still preserved even to my own time, standing with its face turned away from the city of the Kyrenians. This Ladikē Cambyses, having conquered Egypt and heard from her who she was, sent back unharmed to Kyrenē.

182. Amasis also dedicated offerings in Hellas, first at Kyrenē an image of Athenē covered with gold and a painted statue-portrait of himself; then in the temple of Athenē at Lindos two images of stone and a corslet of linen worthy to be seen; and also at Samos two wooden figures of himself dedicated to Hera, which were standing even to my own time in the great temple, behind the doors. Now at Samos he dedicated offerings because of

---

*Important Greek colony in Libya, described at 4.156–165.

the guest-friendship between himself and Polycrates the son of Aiakes; at Lindos for no guest-friendship but because the temple of Athenē at Lindos is said to have been founded by the daughters of Danaos, who had touched land there when they were fleeing from the sons of Aigyptos. These offerings were dedicated by Amasis; and he was the first who conquered Cyprus and subdued it to tributary status.

BOOK III

PERSIAN CONQUEST OF EGYPT, SAMOS, KING DAREIOS OF PERSIA

1. AGAINST AMASIS THEN CAMBYSES the son of Cyrus was making his march,* taking with him other nations of which he was ruler, and Hellenes, both Ionians and Aiolians: and the cause of the expedition was as follows:—Cambyses sent an envoy to Egypt and asked Amasis to give him his daughter; and he made the request by counsel of an Egyptian, who brought this upon Amasis having a quarrel with him. When Cyrus sent to Amasis and asked him for a physician of the eyes, whosoever was best in Egypt, Amasis had selected him from all the physicians in Egypt and had torn him from his wife and children and sent him to Persia. The Egyptian urged Cambyses on, bidding him ask Amasis for his daughter, in order that he might either be grieved if he gave her, or if he refused to give her, might offend Cambyses. So Amasis, who was disturbed by the power of the Persians and afraid of it, knew neither how to give nor how to refuse: for he was well assured that Cambyses did not intend to have her as his wife but as a concubine. So he did as follows:—there was a daughter of Apries the former king, very tall and comely of form and the only person left of his house, and her name was Nitetis. This girl Amasis adorned with raiment and with gold, and sent her away to Persia as his own daughter: but after a time, when Cambyses saluted her calling her by the name of her father, the girl said to him: "O king, you do not perceive how you have been deceived by Amasis; for he adorned me with ornaments and sent me away giving me to you as his own daughter, whereas in truth I am the daughter of Apries against whom Amasis rose up with the Egyptians and murdered him, who was his lord and master." These words uttered and this occasion having arisen, led Cambyses the son of Cyrus against Egypt, moved to very great anger. **2.** Such is the report made by the Persians; but as for the Egyptians they claim Cambyses as one of themselves, saying that he was born of this very daughter of Apries; for they say that Cyrus was he who sent to Amasis for his daughter, and not Cambyses. In saying this however they say not rightly; nor can they have failed to observe (for the Egyptians fully as well as any other people are acquainted with the laws and customs of the Persians), first that it is not customary among them for a bastard to become king, when there is a son born of a true marriage, and secondly that Cambyses was the son of Cassandanē the daughter of Pharnaspes, a man of the Achaimenid family, and not the son

---

*Cambyses invaded Egypt c.525 B.C.; the narrative resumes from 2.1.

141

of the Egyptian woman: but they pervert the story, claiming to be kindred with the house of Cyrus.

3. The following story is also told, which for my part I do not believe, namely that one of the Persian women came in to the wives of Cyrus, and when she saw standing by the side of Cassandanē children comely of form and tall, she was loud in her praises of them, expressing great admiration; and Cassandanē, who was the wife of Cyrus, spoke as follows: "Nevertheless, though I am the mother of such children as these, Cyrus treats me with dishonour and holds in honour her whom he has brought in from Egypt." Thus she spoke, they say, being vexed by Nitetis, and upon that Cambyses the elder of her sons said: "For this cause, mother, when I am grown to be a man, I will make that which is above in Egypt to be below, and that which is below above."* This he is reported to have said when he was perhaps about ten years old, and the women were astonished by it: and he, they say, kept it ever in mind, and so at last when he had become a man and had obtained the royal power, he made the expedition against Egypt.

4. Another thing also contributed to this expedition, which was as follows:—There was among the foreign mercenaries† of Amasis a man who was by race of Halicarnassos, and his name was Phanes, one who was both capable in judgment and valiant in that which pertained to war. This Phanes, having (as we may suppose) some quarrel with Amasis, fled from Egypt in a ship, desiring to come to speech with Cambyses. As he was of no small repute among the mercenaries and was very closely acquainted with all the affairs of Egypt, Amasis pursued him and considered it a matter of some moment to capture him. He pursued him by sending after him the most trusted of his eunuchs with a trireme, who captured him in Lykia; but having captured him he did not bring him back to Egypt, since Phanes got the better of him by cunning; for he made his guards drunk and escaped to Persia. So when Cambyses had made his resolve to march upon Egypt, and was in difficulty about the march, as to how he should get safely through the waterless region, this man came to him and besides informing of the other matters of Amasis, he instructed him also as to the march, advising him to send to the king of the Arabians and ask that he would give him safe passage through this region.

5. Now by this way only is there a known entrance to Egypt. From Phenicia to the borders of the city of Cadytis belongs to the Syrians of Palestine, and from Cadytis, which is a city I suppose not much less than Sardis, from this city the trading stations on the sea-coast as far as the city of Ienysos belong to the king of Arabia, and then from Ienysos again the country belongs to the Syrians as far as the Serbonian lake, along the side of which Mount Casion extends towards the Sea. After that, from the Serbonian lake, in which the story goes that Typhon is concealed, from

---

*Polarity, we have seen, is a principal tool in Herodotean analysis.
†These have been mentioned already at 2.152 and 2.154.

this point onwards the land is Egypt. Now the region which lies between the city of Ienysos on the one hand and Mount Casion and the Serbonian lake on the other, which is as much as a three days' journey, is grievously destitute of water.

6. And one thing I shall tell of, which few of those who go in ships to Egypt have observed, and it is this:—into Egypt from all parts of Hellas and also from Phenicia are brought twice every year earthenware jars full of wine, and yet it may almost be said that you cannot see there one single empty wine-jar. In what manner then, it will be asked, are they used up? The head-man of each place must collect all the earthenware jars from his own town and convey them to Memphis, and those at Memphis must fill them with water and convey them to these same waterless regions of Syria: thus the jars which come regularly to Egypt and are emptied there, are carried to Syria to be added to that which has come before.

7. The Persians thus prepared this approach to Egypt, furnishing it with water in this manner, from the time when they first took possession of Egypt. Seeing that water was not yet provided, Cambyses, in accordance with what he was told by his Halicarnassian guest, sent envoys to the Arabian king and from him asked and obtained the safe passage, having given him pledges of friendship and received them in return.

8. Now the Arabians respect pledges of friendship as much as any men in all the world; and they give them in the following manner:—A man different from those who desire to give the pledges to one another, standing in the midst between the two, cuts with a sharp stone the inner parts of the hands, along by the thumbs, of those who are giving the pledges to one another, and then he takes a thread from the cloak of each one and smears with the blood seven stones laid in the midst between them; and as he does this he calls upon Dionysos and Urania. When the man has completed these ceremonies, he who has given the pledges commends to the care of his friends the stranger (or the fellow-tribesman, if he is giving the pledges to such), and the friends think it right that they also should have regard for the pledges given. Of gods they believe in Dionysos and Urania alone: moreover they say that the cutting of their hair is done after the same fashion as that of Dionysos himself; and they cut their hair in a circle round, shaving away the hair of the temples. Now they call Dionysos Orotalt and Urania they call Alilat.

9. So then when the Arabian king had given the pledge of friendship to the men who had come to him from Cambyses, he contrived as follows:— he took skins of camels and filled them with water and loaded them upon the backs of all the living camels that he had; and having so done he drove them to the waterless region and there awaited the army of Cambyses. This which has been related is the more credible of the accounts given, but the less credible must also be related, since it is a current account. There is a great river in Arabia called Corys, and this runs out into the Sea which is called Erythraian. From this river then it is said that the king of the Arabians, having got a conduit-pipe made by sewing together raw ox-hides and other skins, of such a length as to reach to the waterless region, allegedly

conducted the water through these, and had great cisterns dug in the waterless region, that they might receive the water and preserve it. Now it is
a journey of twelve days from the river to this waterless region; and moreover the story says that he conducted the water by three conduit-pipes to
three different parts of it.

10. Meanwhile Psammenitos the son of Amasis was encamped at the
Pelusian mouth of the Nile waiting for the coming of Cambyses: for
Cambyses did not find Amasis yet living when he marched upon Egypt, but
Amasis had died after having reigned forty and four years during which
no great misfortune had befallen him. When he had died and had been
embalmed he was buried in the burial-place in the temple, which he had
built for himself.* Now when Psammenitos son of Amasis was reigning as
king, there happened to the Egyptians a prodigy, the greatest that had ever
happened: for rain fell at Thebes in Egypt, where never before had rain
fallen nor afterwards down to my time, as the Thebans themselves say; for
in the upper parts of Egypt no rain falls at all: but at that time rain fell at
Thebes in a drizzling shower. **11.** Now when the Persians had marched
quite through the waterless region and were encamped near the Egyptians with design to engage battle, then the foreign mercenaries of the
Egyptian king, who were Hellenes and Carians, having a quarrel with
Phanes because he had brought against Egypt an army of foreign speech,
contrived against him as follows:—Phanes had children whom he had left
behind in Egypt: these they brought into their camp and into the sight of
their father, and they set up a mixing-bowl between the two camps, and
after that they brought up the children one by one and cut their throats
so that the blood ran into the bowl. Then when they had gone through the
whole number of the children, they brought and poured into the bowl
both wine and water, and not until the mercenaries had all drunk of the
blood, did they engage battle. Then after a battle had been fought with
great stubbornness, and very many had fallen of both the armies, the
Egyptians at length turned to flight.

12. I was witness moreover of a great marvel, being informed of it by
the natives of the place; for of the bones scattered about of those who fell
in this fight, each side separately, since the bones of the Persians were lying
apart on one side according as they were divided at first, and those of the
Egyptians on the other, the skulls of the Persians are so weak that if you
shall hit them only with a pebble you will make a hole in them, while those
of the Egyptians are so exceedingly strong that you would hardly break
them if you struck them with a large stone. The cause of it, they said, was
this, and I for my part readily believed them, namely that the Egyptians beginning from their early childhood shave their heads, and the bone is thick-
ened by exposure to the sun: and this is also the cause of their not becoming
bald-headed; for among the Egyptians you see fewer bald-headed men than
among any other race. This then is the reason why these have their skulls

---

*See 2.169 for royal burials.

strong; and the reason why the Persians have theirs weak is that they keep them delicately in the shade from the first by wearing *tiaras,* that is felt caps. I saw a similar thing to this at Papremis, in the case of those who were slain together with Achaimenes the son of Dareios, by Inarōs the Libyan.

13. The Egyptians when they turned to flight from the battle fled in disorder: and they being shut up in Memphis, Cambyses sent a ship of Mytilenē up the river bearing a Persian herald, to summon the Egyptians to make terms of surrender; but they, when they saw that the ship had entered into Memphis, pouring forth in a body from the "White Fortress" both destroyed the ship and also tore the men in it limb from limb, and so bore them into the fortress. After this the Egyptians being besieged, in course of time surrendered themselves; and the Libyans who dwell on the borders of Egypt, being struck with terror by that which had happened to Egypt, delivered themselves up without resistance, and they both laid on themselves a tribute and sent presents: likewise also those of Kyrenē and Barca, being struck with terror equally with the Libyans, acted in a similar manner: and Cambyses accepted graciously the gifts which came from the Libyans, but as for those which came from the men of Kyrenē, finding fault with them, as I suppose, because they were too small in amount (for the Kyrenians sent in fact five hundred pounds' weight of silver), he took the silver by handfuls and scattered it with his own hand among his soldiers.

14. On the tenth day after he received the surrender of the fortress of Memphis, Cambyses set the king of the Egyptians Psammenitos, who had been king for six months, to sit in the suburb of the city, to humble him,— him I say with other Egyptians he set there, and he proceeded to try his spirit as follows:—having arrayed his daughter in the clothing of a slave, he sent her forth with a pitcher to fetch water, and with her he sent also other maidens chosen from the daughters of the chief men, arrayed as was the daughter of the king: and as the maidens were passing by their fathers with cries and lamentation, the other men all began to cry out and answered their laments, seeing that their children had been evilly entreated, but Psammenitos when he saw it before his eyes and perceived it bent himself down to the earth. Then when the water-bearers had passed by, next Cambyses sent his son with two thousand Egyptians besides who were of the same age, with ropes bound round their necks and bits placed in their mouths; and these were being led away to execution to avenge the death of the Mytilenians who had been destroyed at Memphis with their ship. The Royal Judges[*] had decided that for each man ten of the noblest Egyptians should lose their lives in retaliation. He then, when he saw them passing out by him and perceived that his son was leading the way to die, did the same as he had done with respect to his daughter, while the other Egyptians who sat round him were lamenting and showing signs of grief.

---

*Chapter 31 offers more information on their views.

When these also had passed by, it chanced that a man of his table companions, advanced in years, who had been deprived of all his possessions and had nothing except such things as a beggar possesses, and was asking alms from the soldiers, passed by Psammenitos the son of Amasis and the Egyptians who were sitting in the suburb of the city. When Psammenitos saw him he uttered a great cry of lamentation, and he called his companion by name and beat himself upon the head.

Now there were, it seems, men set to watch him, who made known to Cambyses all that he did on the occasion of each going forth: and Cambyses marvelled at that which he did, and he sent a messenger and asked him thus: "Psammenitos, your master Cambyses asks you for what reason, when you saw your daughter evilly entreated and your son going to death, you did not cry aloud nor lament for them, whereas you did honour with these signs of grief the beggar who, as he hears from others, is not in any way related to you."

Thus he asked, and the other answered as follows: "O son of Cyrus, my own troubles were too great for me to lament them aloud, but the trouble of my companion was such as called for tears, seeing that he has been deprived of great wealth, and has come to beggary upon the threshold of old age." When this saying was reported by the messenger, it seemed to them that it was well spoken; and, as is reported by the Egyptians, Crœsus shed tears (for he also, as fortune would have it, had accompanied Cambyses to Egypt) and the Persians who were present shed tears also; and there entered some pity into Cambyses himself, and immediately he bade them save the life of the son of Psammenitos from among those who were being put to death, and also he bade them raise Psammenitos himself from his place in the suburb of the city and bring him into his own presence.

15. As for the son, those who went for him found that he was no longer alive, but had been cut down first of all, but Psammenitos himself they raised from his place and brought him into the presence of Cambyses, with whom he continued to live for the rest of his time without suffering any violence; and if he had known how to keep himself from meddling with mischief, he would have received Egypt to rule it, since the Persians are wont to honour the sons of kings, and even if the kings have revolted from them, they give back the power into the hands of their sons.

That it is their established rule to act so, one may judge by many instances, especially by the case of Thannyras the son of Inarōs,* who received back the power which his father had, and by that of Pausiris the son of Amyrtaios, for he too received back the power of his father: yet it is certain that no men ever up to this time did more evil to the Persians than Inarōs and Amyrtaios. As it was, however, Psammenitos devised evil and received the due reward: for he was found to be inciting the Egyptians to revolt; and when this became known to Cambyses, Psammenitos drank bull's blood and died at once.

---

*Inarōs was put to death in 455 B.C.

16. From Memphis Cambyses came to the city of Saïs with the purpose of doing that which in fact he did: for when he had entered the palace of Amasis, he gave command to bring the corpse of Amasis out of his burial-place; and when this had been accomplished, he gave command to scourge it and pluck out the hair and stab it, and to dishonour it in every possible way besides. When they had done this too until they were wearied out, for the corpse being embalmed held out against the violence and did not fall to pieces in any part, Cambyses gave command to consume it with fire, enjoining thereby a thing which was not permitted by religion, for the Persians hold fire to be a god.

To consume corpses with fire then is by no means according to the custom of either people, of the Persians for the reason which has been mentioned, since they say that it is not right to give the dead body of a man to a god; while the Egyptians have the belief established that fire is a living wild beast, and that it devours everything which it catches, and when it is satiated with the food it dies itself together with that which it devours: but it is by no means their custom to give the corpse of a man to wild beasts, for which reason they embalm it, that it may not be eaten by worms as it lies in the tomb.

Thus then Cambyses was enjoining them to do that which is taboo for either people. However, the Egyptians say that it was not Amasis who suffered this outrage, but another of the Egyptians who was of the same stature of body as Amasis; and that to him the Persians did outrage, thinking that they were doing it to Amasis: for they say that Amasis learnt from an Oracle that which was about to happen with regard to himself after his death; and accordingly, to avert the evil which threatened to come upon him, he buried the dead body of this man who was scourged within his own sepulchral chamber near the doors, and enjoined his son to lay his own body as much as possible in the inner recess of the chamber. These injunctions, said to have been given by Amasis, were not in my opinion really given at all, but I think that the Egyptians pretend so from pride and with no good ground.

17. After this Cambyses planned three expeditions, one against the Carthaginians, another against the Ammonians, and a third against the "Long-lived" Ethiopians, who dwell in that part of Libya* by the Southern Sea: he resolved to send his naval force against the Carthaginians, and a body chosen from his land-army against the Ammonians; and to the Ethiopians to send spies first, both to see whether the table of the Sun existed really, which is said to exist among these Ethiopians, and in addition to spy out all else, but pretending to be bearers of gifts for their king. **18.** Now the table of the Sun is said to be as follows:—there is a meadow in the suburb of their city full of meat boiled of all four-footed creatures; and in this, it is said, those of the citizens in authority place the flesh by night, managing the matter carefully, and by day any man who wishes comes

---

*Herodotus applies this name to what we call the continent of Africa.

there and feasts himself; and the natives (it is reported) say that the earth
of herself produces these things continually. **19.** Of such nature is the so-
called table of the Sun said to be. So when Cambyses had resolved to send
the spies, he sent for those men of the Ichthyophagoi* who understood the
Ethiopian tongue, to come from the city of Elephantinē: and while they
were going to fetch these men, he gave command to the fleet to sail against
Carthage: but the Phenicians refused, for they were bound not to do so by
solemn vows, and they would not be acting piously if they made expedition against their own sons: and as the Phenicians were not willing, the rest
were rendered unequal to the attempt. Thus then the Carthaginians escaped being enslaved by the Persians; for Cambyses did not think right to
apply force to compel the Phenicians, both because they had delivered
themselves over to the Persians of their own accord and because the
whole naval force was dependent upon the Phenicians. Now the men of
Cyprus also had delivered themselves over to the Persians, and were joining in the expedition against Egypt.

20. Then as soon as the Ichthyophagoi came to Cambyses from
Elephantinē, he sent them to the Ethiopians, telling them what they should
say and giving them gifts to bear with them, a purple garment, and a collar
of twisted gold with bracelets, and an alabaster box of perfumed ointment,
and a jar of palm-wine. Now these Ethiopians are said to be the tallest and
the most beautiful of all men; and besides other customs different from all
other men, it is said, with regard to the royal power,—whomsoever of the
men of their nation they judge to be the tallest and to have strength in
proportion to his stature, this man they appoint to reign over them.

21. So when the Ichthyophagoi had come to this people they presented
their gifts to the king who ruled them, and at the same time they said: "The
king of the Persians Cambyses, desiring to become a friend and guest to
you, sent us with command to parley, and he gives you for gifts these
things which he himself most delights to use." The Ethiopian however,
perceiving that they had come as spies, responded: "Neither did the king
of the Persians send you bearing gifts because he thought it a matter of
great moment to become my guest-friend, nor do you speak true things
(for you have come as spies of my kingdom), nor again is he a righteous
man; for if he had been righteous he would not have coveted a land other
than his own, nor would he be leading away into slavery men at whose
hands he has received no wrong. Now however give him this bow and speak
to him these words: The king of the Ethiopians gives this counsel to the
king of the Persians, that when the Persians draw their bows (of equal size
to mine) as easily as I do this, then he should march against the Long-lived
Ethiopians,† provided that he be superior to them in numbers; but until
that time he should feel gratitude to the gods that they do not put it into

---

*That is, "Fish-eaters"; they lived on the southern coast of the Red Sea.
†The accounts of the Ethiopians are partly mythical, partly tall tales of travelers,
partly a foil to Persian and Greek self-satisfaction.

the mind of the sons of the Ethiopians to acquire another land in addition
to their own."

22. Having thus said and having unbent the bow, he delivered it to
those who had come. Then he took the garment of purple and asked what
it was and how it had been made: and when the Ichthyophagoi had told
him the truth about the purple-fish and the dyeing of the tissue, he said
that the men were deceitful and deceitful also were their garments. Then
secondly he asked concerning the twisted gold of the collar and the
bracelets; and when the Ichthyophagoi were setting forth to him the manner in which it was fashioned, the king broke into a laugh and said, supposing them to be fetters, that they had stronger fetters than these in their
country. Thirdly he asked about the perfumed ointment, and when they
had told him of the manner of its making and of the anointing with it, he
said the same as he had before said about the garment. Then when he
came to the wine, and had learned about the manner of its making, being
exceedingly delighted with the taste of the drink he asked besides what
food the king ate, and what was the longest time that a Persian man lived.
They told him that he ate bread, explaining to him first the manner of
growing the wheat, and they said that eighty years was the longest term of
life appointed for a Persian man. In answer to this the Ethiopian said that
he did not wonder that they lived but a few years, when they fed upon
dung; for indeed they would not be able to live even so many years as this,
if they did not renew their vigour with the drink, indicating to the
Ichthyophagoi the wine; for in regard to this, he said, his people were
much behind the Persians.

23. Then when the Ichthyophagoi asked the king in return about the
length of days and the manner of life of his people, he answered that the
greater number of them reached the age of a hundred and twenty years,
and some surpassed even this; and their food was boiled flesh and their
drink was milk. And when the spies marvelled at the number of years, he
conducted them to a certain spring, in the water of which they washed and
became more sleek of skin, as if it were a spring of oil; and from it there
came a scent as it were of violets: and the water of this spring, said the
spies, was so exceedingly weak that it was not possible for anything to float
upon it, either wood or any of those things which are lighter than wood,
but they all went to the bottom. If this water which they have be really
such as it is said to be, it would doubtless be the cause why the people are
long-lived, as making use of it for all the purposes of life. Then when they
departed from this spring, he led them to a prison-house for men, and
there all were bound in fetters of gold. Now among these Ethiopians
bronze is the rarest and most precious of all things. Then when they had
seen the prison-house they saw also the so-called table of the Sun. **24.** They
saw last of all their receptacles of dead bodies, which are said to be made
of crystal in the following manner:—when they have dried the corpse,
whether it be after the Egyptian fashion or in some other way, they cover
it over completely with white plaster and then adorn it with painting, making the figure entirely like the living man. After this they put about it a

block of crystal hollowed out; for this they dig up in great quantity and it is very easy to work: and the dead body being in the middle of the block is visible through it, but produces no unpleasant smell nor any other effect which is unseemly, and it has all its parts visible like the dead body itself. For a year then the near relations of the man keep the block in their house, giving to the dead man the first share of everything and offering to him sacrifices: and after this period they carry it out and set it up round about the city.

25. After they had seen all, the spies departed; and when they reported these things, Cambyses was enraged and proceeded to march his army against the Ethiopians, not having ordered any provision of food nor considered with himself that he was intending to march an army to the furthest extremities of the earth.* Like one not in his right senses, when he heard the report of the Ichthyophagoi he began the march, ordering those of the Hellenes who were present to remain behind in Egypt, and taking with him his whole land force. When in the course of his march he had arrived at Thebes, he divided off about fifty thousand of his army, and these he enjoined to make slaves of the Ammonians and to put to fire the Oracle of Zeus, but he himself with the remainder of his army went on against the Ethiopians. But before the army had passed over the fifth part of the way, all their provisions came to an end completely; and then after the provisions the beasts of burden also were eaten up. Now if Cambyses when he perceived this had changed his plan and led his army back, he would have been a wise man in spite of his first mistake; as it was however, he paid no regard, but went forward without stopping. The soldiers accordingly, so long as they were able to get anything from the ground, prolonged their lives by eating grass; but when they came to the sand, some did a fearful deed. Out of each company of ten they selected by lot one of themselves and devoured him: and Cambyses, when he heard it, being alarmed by this eating of one another gave up the expedition against the Ethiopians and headed back again; and he arrived at Thebes having suffered loss of a great number of his army. Then from Thebes he came down to Memphis and allowed the Hellenes to sail home.

26. Thus fared the expedition against the Ethiopians: and those of the Persians who had been sent to march against the Ammonians set forth from Thebes and went on their way with guides. It is known that they arrived at the city of Oasis, inhabited by Samians said to be of the Aischrionian tribe, and seven days' journey from Thebes over sandy desert.† This place is called in the speech of the Hellenes the "Isle of the Blessed." It is said that the army reached this place, but from that point onwards, except the Ammonians themselves and those who have heard the account from

---

*A theme Herodotus treats generically at 3.106–108.

†The Oasis of Ammon at Siwah (2.32, 4.181) is north of the Great Oasis at Khargeh, west of Thebes, about seven days' journey from that city, as Herodotus writes; Herodotus' account is confused.

them, no man is able to say anything about them; for they neither reached
the Ammonians nor returned. This however is added to the story by the
Ammonians themselves:—they say that as the army was going from this
Oasis through the sandy desert to attack them, and had got to a point
about mid-way between them and the Oasis, while they were taking their
morning meal a violent South Wind blew upon them, and bearing with it
heaps of the desert sand it buried them. They disappeared and were seen
no more. Thus the Ammonians say.

27. When Cambyses arrived at Memphis, Apis appeared to the Egyptians, whom the Hellenes call Epaphos:* and when he had appeared, the
Egyptians began to wear their fairest garments and to have festivities.
Cambyses supposing that they were certainly acting so by way of rejoicing
because he had fared ill, called for the officers who had charge of Memphis; and when they had come into his presence, he asked them why when
he was at Memphis on the former occasion, the Egyptains were doing
nothing of this kind, but only now, when he came there after losing a large
part of his army. They said that a god had appeared to them, who was wont
to appear at intervals of long time, and that whenever he appeared, then
all the Egyptians rejoiced and kept festival. Hearing this Cambyses said
that they were lying, and as liars he condemned them to death. **28.** Having
put these to death, next he called the priests into his presence; and when
the priests answered him likewise, he said that it should not be without his
knowledge if a tame god had come to the Egyptians; and having so said he
bade the priests bring Apis away into his presence: so they went to bring
him. Now this Apis-Epaphos is a calf born of a cow who after this is not
permitted to conceive any other offspring; and the Egyptians say that a
flash of light comes down from heaven upon this cow, and of this she produces Apis. This calf which is called Apis is black and has the following
signs, namely a white square upon the forehead, and on the back the likeness of an eagle, and in the tail the hairs are double, and on the tongue
there is a mark like a beetle. **29.** When the priests had brought Apis, Cambyses being somewhat affected with madness drew his dagger, and aiming
at the belly of Apis, struck his thigh. Then he laughed and said to the
priests: "O you wretched creatures, are gods born such as this, with blood
and flesh, and sensible of the stroke of iron weapons? Worthy indeed of
Egyptians is such a god as this. You however at least shall not escape without punishment for making a mock of me."† Having thus spoken he ordered those whose duty it was to do such things, to scourge the priests
without mercy, and to put to death any one of the other Egyptians whom
they should find keeping the festival. Thus the festival of the Egyptians
had been brought to an end, and the priests were being chastised, and Apis
wounded by the stroke in his thigh lay dying in the temple.

---

*At 2.38 Herodotus described the holy bull.
†Violations of the sacred are symptomatic of Herodotean despots; the Persian
religion, however, was intensely spiritual and anti-idolatrous. Compare 1.131.

30. Him, when he had brought his life to an end by reason of the wound, the priests buried without the knowledge of Cambyses. Cambyses, as the Egyptians say, immediately after this evil deed became absolutely mad, not having been really in his right senses even before. The first of his evil deeds was that he put to death his brother Smerdis, who was of the same father and the same mother as himself. This brother he had sent away from Egypt to Persia in envy, because alone of all the Persians he had been able to draw the bow which the Ichthyophagoi brought from the Ethiopian king, to an extent of about two finger-breadths; while of the other Persians not one had proved able to do this. Then when Smerdis had gone away to Persia, Cambyses saw a vision in his sleep of this kind:—it seemed to him that a messenger came from Persia and reported that Smerdis sitting upon the royal throne had touched the heaven with his head. Fearing therefore with regard to this lest his brother might slay him and reign in his stead, he sent Prexaspes to Persia, the man whom of all the Persians he trusted most, with command to slay him. He accordingly went up to Susa and slew Smerdis. Some say that he took him out to the chase and so slew him, others that he brought him to the Erythraian Sea and drowned him.

31. This they say was the first beginning of the evil deeds of Cambyses; and next after this he put to death his sister, who had accompanied him to Egypt, to whom also he was married, she being his sister by both parents. Now he took her to wife in the following manner (for before this the Persians had not been wont at all to marry their sisters). Cambyses fell in love with one of his sisters, and desired to take her to wife; so since he had it in mind to do that which was not customary, he called the Royal Judges and asked them whether there existed any law which permitted him who desired it to marry his sister.

Now the Royal Judges are men chosen out from among the Persians, and hold their office until they die or until some injustice is found in them. These pronounce decisions for the Persians and are the expounders of the ordinances of their fathers, and all matters are referred to them. So when Cambyses asked them, they gave him an answer which was both upright and safe, saying that they found no law which permitted a brother to marry his sister, but apart from that they had found a law to the effect that the king of the Persians might do whatsoever he desired. Thus on the one hand they did not tamper with the law for fear of Cambyses, and at the same time, that they might not perish themselves in maintaining the law, they found another law beside that which was asked for, which supported him who wished to marry his sisters. So Cambyses took to wife her with whom he was in love, and soon he took another sister. Of these it was the younger whom he put to death, she having accompanied him to Egypt.

32. About her death, as about the death of Smerdis, two different stories are told. The Hellenes say that Cambyses had matched a lion's cub in fight with a dog's whelp, and this wife of his was also a spectator of it; and when the whelp was being overcome, another whelp, its brother, broke its chain and came to help it; and having become two instead of one, the whelps then got the better of the cub: and Cambyses was pleased at the sight, but she sitting by him began to weep; and Cambyses perceived it and asked wherefore she wept; and she said that she had wept when she saw that the whelp had come to the assistance of its brother, because she remembered Smerdis and perceived that there was no one who would come to his assistance. The Hellenes say that it was for this saying that she was killed by Cambyses: but the Egyptians say that as they were sitting round at table, the wife took a lettuce and pulled off the leaves all round, and then asked her husband whether the lettuce was fairer when thus plucked round or when covered with leaves, and he said "when covered with leaves." She then spoke thus: "Nevertheless you once produced the likeness of this lettuce, when you stripped bare the house of Cyrus." And he moved to anger leapt upon her, being with child, and she miscarried and died.

33. These were the acts of madness done by Cambyses towards his own family, whether the madness was produced really on account of Apis or from some other cause, as many ills seize upon men; for it is said moreover that Cambyses had from his birth a certain grievous malady, that which is called by some the "sacred" disease:[*] and it was certainly nothing strange that when the body was suffering grievously, the mind should not be sound either. **34.** The following also are acts of madness committed against other Persians:—To Prexaspes, the man whom he honoured most and who used to bear his messages[†] (his son also was cup-bearer to Cambyses, and this too was no small honour),—to him it is said that he spoke as follows: "Prexaspes, what kind of a man do the Persians esteem me to be, and what speech do they hold concerning me?" and he said: "Master, in all other respects you are greatly commended, but they say that you are excessively fond of wine." Thus he spoke concerning the Persians; and upon that Cambyses was roused to anger, and answered thus: "It appears that the Persians say I am given to wine, and that therefore I am irrational and not in my right mind; and their former speech then was not sincere." For before this time, it seems, when the Persians and Crœsus were sitting with him in council, Cambyses asked what kind of a man they thought he was as compared with his father Cyrus, and they answered that he was better than his father, for he not only possessed all that his father had possessed, but also in addition to this had acquired Egypt and the Sea. Thus the Persians spoke; but Crœsus, who was present and was not satisfied with their judgment, spoke thus to Cambyses: "To me, O son of Cyrus, you do not appear to be equal to your father, for not yet do you have a son such as he left behind him in you." Hearing this Cambyses was pleased, and commended the judgment of Crœsus. **35.** So calling to mind this, he said in anger to Prexaspes: "Learn then now for yourself whether the Persians speak truly, or whether when they say this they are

---

[*]Probably epilepsy; the essay "On the Sacred Disease"—in the Hippocratic collection but probably not by Hippocrates—examines what was known and thought about this peculiar affliction.

[†]Compare the chamberlain mentioned at 1.114.

themselves out of their senses: for if I, shooting at your son there standing before the entrance of the chamber, hit him in the very middle of the heart, the Persians will be proved to be speaking falsely, but if I miss, then you may say that the Persians are speaking the truth and that I am not in my right mind." He drew his bow and hit the boy; and when the boy had fallen down, it is said that he ordered them to cut open his body and examine the place where he was hit; and as the arrow was found to be sticking in the heart, he laughed and was delighted, and said to the father of the boy: "Prexaspes, it has now been made evident, as you see, that I am not mad, but that it is the Persians who are out of their senses; and now tell me, whom of all men did you ever see before this time hit the mark so well in shooting?" Then Prexaspes, seeing that the man was not in his right senses and fearing for himself, said: "Master, I think that not even God himself could have hit the mark so fairly." Thus he did at that time; at another time he condemned twelve of the Persians, men equal to the best, on a charge of no moment, and buried them alive with the head downwards.

36. When he was doing these things, Crœsus the Lydian judged it right to admonish him: "O king, do not indulge the heat of your youth and passion in all things, but restrain and hold yourself back: it is a good thing to be prudent, and forethought is wise. You however are putting to death men who are of your own people, condemning them on charges of no moment, and you are putting to death men's sons also. If you do many such things, beware lest the Persians revolt. As for me, your father Cyrus gave me charge, earnestly bidding me to admonish you, and suggest whatever I should find to be good." Thus he counselled him, manifesting goodwill towards him; but Cambyses answered: "Do *you* venture to counsel *me,* who excellently ruled your own country, and well counselled my father, bidding him pass over the river Araxes and go against the Massagetai, when they were willing to pass over into our land, and so utterly ruined yourself by ill government of your own land, and utterly ruined Cyrus, who followed your counsel. However you shall not escape punishment now, for know that before this I had very long been desiring to find some pretext against you." He took his bow meaning to shoot him, but Crœsus started up and ran out; since he could not shoot him, he gave orders to his attendants to take and slay him. The attendants however, knowing his moods, concealed Crœsus, with the intention that if Cambyses should change his mind and seek to have Crœsus again, they might produce him and receive gifts as the price of saving his life; but if he did not change his mind nor feel desire to have him back, then they might kill him. Not long afterwards Cambyses did in fact desire to have Crœsus again, and the attendants perceiving this reported to him that he was still alive. Cambyses said that he rejoiced with Crœsus that he was still alive, but that they who had preserved him should not get off free, but he would put them to death, and thus he did.

37. Many such acts of madness did he both to Persians and allies, remaining at Memphis and opening ancient tombs and examining the dead bodies. Likewise also he entered into the temple of Hephaistos and very much derided the image of the god.* The image of Hephaistos very nearly resembles the Phenician *Pataicoi,* which the Phenicians carry about on the prows of their triremes. For him who has not seen these, I will indicate its nature,—it is the likeness of a dwarfish man. He entered also into the temple of the Cabeiroi, into which it is not lawful for any one to enter except the priest only, and the images there he even set on fire, after much mockery of them. Now these also are like the images of Hephaistos, and it is said that they are the children of that god.

38. It is clear to me therefore by every kind of proof that Cambyses was completely mad; for otherwise he would not have attempted to deride religious rites and customary observances. For if one should propose to all men a choice, bidding them select the best customs from all the customs that there are, each race of men, after examining them all, would select those of their own people; thus all think that their own customs are by far the best: and so it is not likely that any but a madman would joke about such things. Now that all men thus think about their customs, we may judge by many proofs and especially by this which follows:—Dareios in the course of his reign summoned those of the Hellenes who were present in his land, and asked them for what price they would consent to eat up their fathers when they died; and they answered that for no price would they do so. After this Dareios summoned those Indians who are called Callatians, who eat their parents, and asked them in presence of the Hellenes, who understood what was said by an interpreter, for what payment they would consent to consume with fire the bodies of their fathers when they died; and they cried aloud and bade him not mention such words. These things are established by usage, and I think that Pindar spoke rightly in his verse, when he said that "of all things law is king."†

39. Now while Cambyses was marching upon Egypt, the Lacedemonians also had made an expedition against Samos and against Polycrates the son of Aiakes, who had risen against the government and obtained rule over Samos.‡ At first he had divided the State into three parts and had given a share to his brothers Pantagnotos and Syloson; but afterwards he put to death one of these, and the younger, namely Syloson, he drove out, and so obtained possession of the whole of Samos. Then, he made a guest-friendship with Amasis the king of Egypt, sending him gifts and receiving gifts in return. After this the power of Polycrates increased rapidly, and there was much fame of it not only in Ionia, but also over the rest of Hellas:

*A Hellenization of Ptah; compare 2.101.
†Pindar meant natural law, not cultural norm (*nomos*), if the passage is the same one Plato quotes in *Gorgias* 484b.
‡Polycrates became despot of Samos c.532 B.C. Herodotus knows a good deal of Samian history and topography. Aiakes is the subject of the inscription mentioned in the second note at 3.47.

for to whatever part he directed his forces, everything went fortunately for
him: and he had a hundred fifty-oared galleys and a thousand archers, and
he plundered from all, making no distinction of any; for it was his wont to
say that he would win more gratitude from his friend by giving back to
him that which he had taken, than by not taking at all. So he had conquered many of the islands and also many cities of the continent, and besides other things he gained the victory in a sea-fight over the Lesbians, as
they were coming to help the Milesians with all their forces, and conquered them. (These men dug the whole trench round the wall of the city
of Samos working in chains.)

40. Now Amasis, as may be supposed, did not fail to perceive that Polycrates was very fortunate, and it concerned him that much more good fortune yet continued to come to Polycrates. He wrote upon a paper these
words and sent them to Samos: "Amasis to Polycrates thus:—It is a pleasant thing indeed to hear that one who is a friend and guest is faring well;
yet to me your great good fortune is not pleasing, since I know that the Divinity is jealous; and I think that I desire, both for myself and for those
about whom I have care, that in some of our affairs we should be prosperous and in others should fail, and thus go through life alternately faring
well and ill, rather than that we should be prosperous in all things: for
never yet did I hear tell of any one who was prosperous in all things and
did not come to an utterly evil end at the last. Now therefore follow my
counsel and act as I shall say with respect to your prosperous fortunes.
Take thought and consider, and that which you find most valued, and for
the loss of which you will most be vexed in your soul, that take and cast
away in such a manner that it shall never again come to the sight of men;
and if in future from that time forward good fortune does not befall you in
alternation with calamities, apply remedies in the manner by me suggested."

41. Polycrates, reflecting that Amasis suggested to him good counsel,
sought to find which one of his treasures he would be most afflicted to
lose; and seeking he found this. He had a signet which he used to wear, en-
chased in gold and made of an emerald stone; and it was the work of
Theodoros the son of Telecles of Samos.* Seeing then that he thought it
good to cast this away, he did thus:—he manned a fifty-oared galley with
sailors and went on board himself; and then he bade them put out into the
deep sea. And when he had got to a distance from the island, he took off
the signet-ring, and in the sight of all he threw it into the sea. Then he
sailed home; and he mourned for his loss. **42.** But on the fifth or sixth day
after these things it happened to him that a fisherman having caught a large
and beautiful fish, thought it right that this should be given as a gift to Polycrates. He bore it therefore to the door of the palace and said that he desired
to come into the presence of Polycrates, and when he had obtained this he
gave him the fish, saying: "O king, having taken this fish I did not think fit to
bear it to the market, although I am one who lives by the labour of his

*See 1.51 for an account of this artisan's bowl.

hands; but it seemed to me that it was worthy of you and of your rule: therefore I bring it and present it to you." He then, being pleased at the words
spoken, answered thus: "You did exceedingly well, and double thanks are
due to you, for your words and also for your gift; and we invite you to come
to dinner." The fisherman then, thinking this a great thing, went away to his
house; and the servants as they were cutting up the fish found in its belly the
signet-ring of Polycrates. Then as soon as they had seen it and taken it up,
they bore it rejoicing to Polycrates, and giving him the signet-ring they told
him in what manner it had been found: and he perceiving that the matter
was of God, wrote upon paper all that he had done and all that had happened, and he despatched it to Egypt.

43. When Amasis had read the paper which had come from Polycrates,
perceived that it was impossible for man to rescue man from the event
which was to come to pass, and that Polycrates was destined not to end
well, being prosperous in all things, since he found again even what he cast
away. Therefore he sent an envoy to him in Samos and said that he broke
off the guest-friendship; and this he did lest when a fearful and great
mishap befell Polycrates, he might himself be grieved in his soul as for a
man who was his guest.

44. It was this Polycrates then, prosperous in all things, against whom
the Lacedemonians were making an expedition, being invited by those
Samians who afterwards settled at Kydonia in Crete, to come to their assistance.* Now Polycrates had sent an envoy to Cambyses the son of
Cyrus without the knowledge of the Samians, as he was gathering an army
to go against Egypt, and had asked him to send to him in Samos and to ask
for an armed force. Cambyses very readily sent to Samos to ask Polycrates
to send a naval force with him against Egypt. Polycrates selected of the citizens those whom he most suspected of desiring to rise against him and
sent them away in forty triremes, charging Cambyses not to send them
back.

45. Now some say that those of the Samians who were sent away by
Polycrates never reached Egypt, but when they arrived on their voyage at
Carpathos, they reckoned among themselves, and resolved not to sail on
any further: others say that they reached Egypt and being kept under
guard there, they made their escape. Then, as they were sailing in to
Samos, Polycrates encountered them with ships and battled with them;
and those who were returning home had the better and landed in the island; but having fought a land-battle in the island, they were worsted, and
so sailed to Lacedemon. Some however say that those from Egypt defeated Polycrates in the battle; but this in my opinion is not correct, for
there would have been no need for them to invite the assistance of the
Lacedemonians if they had been able by themselves to bring Polycrates to
terms. Moreover, it is not reasonable either, seeing that he had foreign
mercenaries and native archers very many in number, to suppose that he

*A "ring" phrase with chapter 39.

was worsted by the returning Samians, who were but few. Then Polycrates gathered together the children and wives of his subjects and confined them in the ship-sheds, keeping them ready so that, if his subjects deserted to the side of the returning exiles, he might burn them with the sheds.

46. When the Samians who had been driven out by Polycrates reached Sparta, they were introduced before the magistrates and spoke at length, being urgent in their request. The magistrates however at the first introduction replied that they had forgotten the things which had been spoken at the beginning, and did not understand those which were spoken at the end. After this they were introduced a second time, and bringing with them a bag they said nothing else but that the bag was in want of meal: to which the others replied that they had overdone it with the bag.* However, they resolved to help them. **47.** Then the Lacedemonians prepared a force and made expedition to Samos, in repayment of former services, as the Samians say, because the Samians had first helped them with ships against the Messenians; but the Lacedemonians say that they made the expedition not so much from desire to help the Samians at their request, as to take vengeance on their own behalf for the robbery of the mixing-bowl which they had been bearing as a gift to Crœsus,† and of the corslet which Amasis the king of Egypt had sent as a gift to them; for the Samians had carried off the corslet also in the year before they took the bowl; and it was of linen with many figures woven into it and embroidered with gold and with cotton; and each thread of this corslet is worthy of admiration, for although itself fine it has in it three hundred and sixty fibres, all plain to view. Amasis dedicated another like this as an offering to Athenē at Lindos.

48. The Corinthians also participated energetically in this expedition against Samos; for there had been an offence perpetrated against them also by the Samians a generation before‡ the time of this expedition and about the same time as the robbery of the bowl. Periander the son of Kypselos had despatched three hundred sons of the chief men of Corcyra to Alyattes at Sardis to be made eunuchs; and when the Corinthians who were conducting the boys had put in to Samos, the Samians, being informed of the story and for what purpose they were being conducted to Sardis, first instructed the boys to lay hold of the temple of Artemis, and then they refused to permit the Corinthians to drag the suppliants away from the temple. The Corinthians cut the boys off from supplies of food, the Samians made a festival, which they celebrate even to the present time in the same manner: for when night came on, as long as the boys were suppliants they arranged dances of

*The Spartans are Laconians, whence "laconic"; Herodotus is amused by their hostility to speech. Compare 9.91.

†See 1.70 for Samian piracy; also, an inscription at Samos commemorates their depredations.

‡Periander reigned from 625 to 585 B.C.; chronological problems arise here since Periander died long before the Samian offence. See 5.92 for a description of this tyrant.

maidens and youths, and in arranging the dances they made it a rule of the festival that sweet cakes of sesame and honey should be carried, in order that the Corcyrean boys might snatch them and so have support. This went on so long that at last the Corinthians who had charge of the boys departed. The Samians carried the boys back to Corcyra. **49.** Now, if after the death of Periander the Corinthians had been on friendly terms with the Corcyreans, they would not have joined in the expedition against Samos for the cause which has been mentioned; but as it is, they have quarreled with one another, [although kin,] since they first colonised the island. This then was the cause why the Corinthians had a grudge against the Samians.

50. Now Periander had chosen out the sons of the chief men of Corcyra and was sending them to Sardis to be made eunuchs, for revenge; since the Corcyreans had first begun the offence and had done to him a deed of reckless wrong. For after Periander had killed his wife Melissa, he experienced another misfortune as follows:—He had by Melissa two sons, the one of seventeen and the other of eighteen years. These sons their mother's father Procles, who was despot of Epidauros, sent for and kindly entertained, as was to be expected seeing that they were the sons of his own daughter. But when he was sending them back, he said in taking leave of them: "Do you know, boys, who it was that killed your mother?" Of this saying the elder of them took no account, but the younger, whose name was Lycophron, was grieved so greatly at hearing it, that when he reached Corinth again he would neither address his father, nor speak to him when his father would have conversed with him, nor give any reply when he asked questions, regarding him as the murderer of his mother. At length Periander enraged with his son drove him out of his house.

51. He asked of the elder son what his mother's father had said to them in his conversation. He then related how Procles had received them in a kindly manner, but of the saying which he had uttered when he parted from them he had no remembrance, since he had taken no note of it. So Periander said that he must have suggested to them something, and urged him further with questions; and he after that remembered, and told of this also. Then Periander taking note of it and not desiring to show any indulgence, sent a messenger to those with whom the son who had been driven forth was living at that time, and forbade them to receive him into their houses. Whenever having been driven away from one house he came to another, he was driven away also from this, since Periander threatened those who received him, and commanded them to exclude him; and so being driven away again he would go to another house, where persons lived who were his friends, and they perhaps received him because he was the son of Periander, notwithstanding that they feared.

52. At last Periander made a proclamation that whosoever should either receive him into their houses or converse with him should be bound to pay a fine to Apollo, stating the amount that it should be. Accordingly, by reason of this proclamation no one was willing either to converse with him or to receive him into their house; and moreover even he himself did not think fit to attempt it, since it had been forbidden, but he lay about in

the porticoes enduring exposure: and on the fourth day after this, Periander seeing him fallen into squalid misery and starvation felt pity for him;
and abating his anger he approached him and began to say: "Son, which of
these two is to be preferred, the fortune which you now experience and
possess, or to inherit the power and the wealth which I possess now, by being submissive to your father's will? You however, being my son and the
ruler of wealthy Corinth, chose nevertheless the life of a vagabond by re-
sisting and displaying anger against him with whom it behoved you least;
for if any misfortune happened in those matters, for which you have suspicion against me, this has happened to me first, and I share the misfortune
more than others, inasmuch as I did the deed myself. However, having
learnt by how much to be envied is better than to be pitied, and at the
same time what a grievous thing it is to be angry against your parents and
against those who are stronger than you, come back now to the house."
Periander with these words endeavoured to restrain him; but he answered
nothing else to his father, but said only that he ought to pay a fine to the
god for having spoken to him. Then Periander, perceiving that the malady
of his son was hopeless and could not be overcome, despatched a ship to
Corcyra, and so sent him away out of his sight, for he was ruler also of that
island; and having sent him away, Periander proceeded to make war
against his father-in-law Procles, esteeming him most to blame for the
condition in which he was; and he took Epidauros and took also Procles
himself and made him a prisoner.

53. When however, as time went on, Periander had passed his prime
and perceived that he was no longer able to overlook and manage the
government of the State, he sent to Corcyra and summoned Lycophron to
come back and take the supreme power; for in the elder of his sons he did
not see the required capacity, but perceived clearly that he was too dull.
Lycophron however did not deign even to give an answer to the bearer of
his message. Then Periander, clinging still in affection to the youth, sent to
him next his own daughter, the sister of Lycophron, supposing that he
would yield to her persuasion more than to that of others; and she arrived
there and spoke to him thus:

"Boy, do you desire that both the despotism should fall to others and
also the substance of your father, carried off as plunder, rather than return
and possess them? Come back home: cease to torment yourself. Pride is a
mischievous possession. Heal not evil with evil. Many prefer that which is
reasonable to that which is strictly just; and many ere now in seeking the
things of their mother have lost the things of their father. Despotism is an
insecure thing, and many desire it: moreover he is now an old man and
past his prime. Give not your good things unto others."

She thus said to him the most persuasive things, having been before instructed by her father: but he in answer said, that he would never come to
Corinth so long as he heard that his father was yet alive. When she had reported this, Periander the third time sent an envoy, and said that he desired himself to come to Corcyra, exhorting Lycophron at the same time to
come back to Corinth and to be his successor on the throne. The son having

agreed to return on these terms, Periander was preparing to sail to Corcyra and his son to Corinth; but the Corcyreans, having learnt all, put the young man to death, in order that Periander might not come to their land. For this cause Periander took vengeance on Corcyra.

54. The Lacedemonians then had come with a great armament and were besieging Samos; and having made an attack upon the wall, they occupied the tower which stands by the sea in the suburb of the city, but afterwards when Polycrates came up to the rescue with a large body they were driven away. Meanwhile by the upper tower upon the ridge of the mountain the foreign mercenaries and many of the Samians themselves had come out to fight, and these stood their ground against the Lacedemonians for a short time and then began to fly backwards; and the Lacedemonians followed and were slaying them.

55. Now if the Lacedemonians there present had all of them been equal on that day to Archias and Lycopas, Samos would have been captured; for Archias and Lycopas alone rushed within the wall together with the flying Samians, and being shut off from retreat were slain within the city. I myself moreover had converse in Pitanē (for to that deme he belonged) with the third in descent from this Archias, another Archias the son of Samios the son of Archias, who honoured the Samians of all strangers most; and not only so, but he said that his own father had been called Samios because *his* father Archias had died by a glorious death in Samos; and he said that he honoured Samians because his grandfather had been granted a public funeral by the Samians.

56. The Lacedemonians then, when they had been besieging Samos for forty days and made no progress, set forth to return to Peloponnesus. But according to the less credible account which has been put abroad of these matters Polycrates struck in lead a great quantity of a certain native coin, and having gilded the coins over, gave them to the Lacedemonians, and upon that they set forth to depart. This was the first expedition which the Lacedemonians (being Dorians) made into Asia.

57. Those of the Samians who had made the expedition against Polycrates themselves also sailed away, when the Lacedemonians were about to desert them, and came to Siphnos: for they needed money, and the people of Siphnos were then at their greatest height of prosperity and possessed wealth more than all the other islanders, since they had in their island mines of gold and of silver. There is a treasury[*] dedicated at Delphi with the tithe of the money which came in from these mines, and furnished in a manner equal to the wealthiest of these treasuries: and the people used to divide among themselves the money which came in from the mines every year. So when they were establishing the treasury, they consulted the Oracle as to whether their present prosperity was capable of remaining with them for a long time, and the Pythian prophetess gave them this reply:

---

[*]Type of small structure at the Panhellenic sanctuaries that advertised its builders' piety and achievements.

"But when with white shall be shining the hall of the city in Siphnos,
And when the market is white of brow, one wary is needed
Then, to beware of a battalion of wood and a red-coloured herald."

Now just at that time the market-place and city hall of the Siphnians had
been decorated with Parian marble.

58. This oracle they were not able to understand either then at first or
when the Samians had arrived: for as soon as the Samians had put in to
Siphnos they sent one of their ships to bear envoys to the city: now in old
times all ships were painted with red, and this was that which the Pythian
prophetess was declaring beforehand to the Siphnians, bidding them
guard against the "army of wood" and the "red-coloured herald." The
messengers accordingly came and asked the Siphnians to lend them ten
talents; and as they refused to lend to them, the Samians began to lay
waste their lands: so when they were informed of it, immediately the Siphnians came to the rescue, and having engaged battle with them were defeated, and many of them were cut off by the Samians and shut out of the
city; and the Samians after this imposed upon them a payment of a hundred talents.

59. Then from the men of Hermiōn they received by payment of money
the island of Hydrea, which is near the coast of Peloponnese, and they
gave it in charge to the Troizenians, but they themselves settled at Kydonia
which is in Crete, not sailing thither for that purpose but in order to drive
the Zakynthians out of the island. Here they remained and were prosperous for five years, so much so that they were the builders of the temples
which are now existing in Kydonia, and also of the house of Dictyna. In
the sixth year however the Eginetans together with the Cretans conquered them in a sea-fight and brought them to slavery; and they cut off
the prows of their ships, which were shaped like boars, and dedicated them
in the temple of Athenē in Egina. This the Eginetans did because they had
a grudge against the Samians; for the Samians had first made expedition
against Egina, when Amphicrates was king in Samos, and had done much
hurt to the Eginetans and suffered much hurt also from them. Such was
the cause of this event. **60.** About the Samians I have spoken at greater
length, because they have three works which are greater than any others
that have been made by Hellenes:* first a passage beginning from below
and open at both ends, dug through a mountain over 900 feet in height;
the length of the passage is four thousand two hundred and fifty feet† and
the height and breadth each eight feet, and throughout the whole of it another passage has been dug thirty feet in depth‡ and three feet in breadth,
through which the water is conducted and comes by the pipes to the city,

---

*Herodotus promised details of great works in the opening paragraph of book I
and implied such a concern at 1.93.
†Inaccurate: closer to 3,450 feet.
‡True only at the city end of the tunnel, to provide sufficient fall for the water.

brought from an abundant spring: and the designer of this work was a Megarian, Eupalinos the son of Naustrophos. The second is a mole in the sea about the harbour, going down to a depth of as much as 120 feet; and the length of the mole is more than 1,200 feet. The third work which they have executed is a temple larger than all the other temples of which we know. The first designer was Rhoicos the son of Philes, a native of Samos. For this reason I have spoken longer of the Samians.

61. Now while Cambyses the son of Cyrus was spending a long time in Egypt[*] and had lost his right mind, there rose up against him two brothers, Magians, of whom one had been left behind by Cambyses as caretaker of his household. This man, I say, rose up against him perceiving that the occurrence of the death of Smerdis was being kept secret, and few of the Persians were aware of it, while the greater number believed that he was still alive. Therefore he endeavoured to obtain the kingdom, and he formed this plan:—he had a brother (who, as I said, rose up with him against Cambyses), and this man in form very closely resembled Smerdis the son of Cyrus, whom Cambyses had slain, his own brother. He was like Smerdis, in form, and he had the same name, Smerdis. Having persuaded this man that he would manage everything for him, the Magian Patizeithes brought him and seated him upon the royal throne: and having so done he sent heralds about to the various provinces, and one to the army in Egypt, to proclaim to them that they must obey Smerdis the son of Cyrus for the future—instead of Cambyses.

62. So then the other heralds made this proclamation, and also the one who was appointed to go to Egypt. Finding Cambyses and his army at Agbatana in Syria, he stood in the midst and began to proclaim as commanded to him by the Magian. Hearing this from the herald, and supposing that the herald was speaking the truth and that he had himself been betrayed by Prexaspes, that is to say, that when Prexaspes was sent to kill Smerdis he had not done so, Cambyses looked upon Prexaspes and said: "Prexaspes, was it thus that you performed for me the thing which I ordered you to do" He said: "Master, the saying is not true that Smerdis your brother has risen up against you, nor that you will have any contention arising from him, either great or small: for I myself, having done as you commanded me to do, buried him with my own hands. If therefore the dead have risen again to life, then you may expect that Astyages also the Mede will rise up against you; but if it is as it was beforetime, there is no fear that any trouble shall spring up for you, at least from him. Now therefore I think it well that some should pursue after the herald and examine him, asking from whom he has come to proclaim to us that we are to obey Smerdis as king."

63. When Prexaspes had thus spoken, Cambyses was pleased with the advice, and accordingly the herald was pursued at once and returned.

---

[*]The revolt of the Magians and death of Cambyses occurred in 522 B.C.

Then when he had come back, Prexaspes asked him as follows: "Man, you say that you are come as a messenger from Smerdis the son of Cyrus: now therefore speak the truth and go away in peace. I ask you whether Smerdis himself appeared before your eyes and charged you to say this, or some one of those who serve him." He said: "Smerdis the son of Cyrus I have never yet seen, since the day that king Cambyses marched to Egypt: but the Magian whom Cambyses appointed to be guardian of his household, he, I say, gave me this charge, saying that Smerdis the son of Cyrus was he who laid the command upon me to speak these things to you." Thus he spoke to them, adding no falsehoods to the first, and Cambyses said: "Prexaspes, you have done that which was commanded like an honest man, and have escaped censure; but who of the Persians may this be who has risen up against me and usurped the name of Smerdis?" He said: "I think, O king, I understand what has come to pass: the Magians have risen against you, Patizeithes namely, whom you did leave as caretaker of your household, and his brother Smerdis."

64. Then Cambyses, when he heard the name of Smerdis, perceived at once the true meaning of this report and of the dream, for he thought in his sleep that some one had reported to him that Smerdis was sitting upon the royal throne and had touched the heaven with his head: and perceiving that he had slain his brother without need, he began to lament for Smerdis; and having lamented for him and sorrowed greatly for the whole mishap, he was leaping upon his horse, meaning as quickly as possible to march his army to Susa against the Magian; and as he leapt upon his horse, the cap of his scabbard fell off, and the sword being left bare struck his thigh. Having been wounded then in the same part where he had formerly struck Apis the god of the Egyptians, and believing that he had been struck with a mortal blow, Cambyses asked what was the name of that town, and they said "Agbatana." Now even before this he had been informed by the Oracle at the city of Buto that in Agbatana he should die: and he supposed that he should die in old age at Agbatana in Media, where was his chief seat of power; but the oracle, it appeared, meant in Agbatana of Syria. So when by questioning now he learnt the name of the town, being struck with fear both by the calamity caused by the Magian and at the same time by the wound, he came to his right mind, and understanding the oracle he said: "Here it is fated that Cambyses the son of Cyrus shall end his life."

65. So much only he said at that time; but about twenty days afterwards he sent for the most honourable of the Persians who were with him, and said to them as follows: "Persians, it has become necessary for me to make known to you the thing which I kept concealed beyond all other things. Being in Egypt I saw a vision in my sleep, which I would I had never seen, and it seemed to me that a messenger came from home and reported to me that Smerdis was sitting upon the royal throne and had touched the heaven with his head. Fearing then lest I should be deprived of my power by my brother, I acted quickly rather than wisely; for it seems that it is not possible for man to avert that which is destined to come to pass. I therefore,

fool that I was, sent away Prexaspes to Susa to kill Smerdis; and, after this
crime, I lived in security, never considering the danger that some other
man might at some time rise up against me, now that Smerdis had been
removed. Altogether missing the mark of that which was about to happen,
I have both made myself the murderer of my brother, when there was no
need, and I have been deprived none the less of the kingdom; for it was in
fact Smerdis the Magian of whom the divine power declared to me beforehand in the vision that he should rise up against me. So then, as I say,
this deed has been done by me, and you must imagine that you no longer
have Smerdis the son of Cyrus alive. But it is in truth the Magians who are
masters of your kingdom, he whom I left as guardian of my household and
his brother Smerdis. The man then who ought above all others to have
taken vengeance on my behalf for the dishonour which I have suffered
from the Magians, has ended his life by an unholy death received from the
hands of those who were his nearest of kin; and since he is no more, it becomes most needful for me, as the thing next best of those which remain,
to charge you, Persians, with that which dying I desire should be done for
me. This then I lay upon you, calling upon the gods of the royal house to
witness it,—upon you all and most of all upon those of the Achaimenidai
who are present here,—do not permit the return of the chief power to the
Medes, but that if they have acquired it by craft, by craft they be deprived
of it by you, or if they have conquered it by any kind of force, by force and
by a strong hand you recover it. And if you do this, may the earth bring
forth her produce and may your wives and your cattle be fruitful, while
you remain free for ever; but if you do not recover the power nor attempt
to recover it, I pray that curses the contrary of these blessings may come
upon you, and moreover that each man of the Persians may have an end to
his life like that which has come upon me." Then as soon as he had finished
speaking these things, Cambyses began to bewail and make lamentation
for all his fortunes.

66. And the Persians, when they saw that the king had begun to grieve,
both rent the garments which they wore and made lamentation without
stint. After this, when the bone had become diseased and the thigh had
mortified, Cambyses the son of Cyrus was carried off by the wound, having reigned in all seven years and five months, and being absolutely childless both of male and female offspring. The Persians meanwhile who were
present there were very little disposed to believe that the power was in the
hands of the Magians: on the contrary, they were surely convinced that
Cambyses had said that which he said about the death of Smerdis to deceive them, in order that all the Persians might be moved to war against
him. These then were surely convinced that Smerdis the son of Cyrus was
established to be king; for Prexaspes also very strongly denied that he had
slain Smerdis, since it was not safe, now that Cambyses was dead, for him
to say that he had destroyed with his own hand the son of Cyrus.

67. Thus when Cambyses had brought his life to an end, the Magian became king without disturbance, usurping the place of his namesake Smerdis
the son of Cyrus; and he reigned during the seven months which were

wanting yet to Cambyses for the completion of the eight years: and during them he performed acts of great benefit to all his subjects, so that after his death all those in Asia except the Persians themselves mourned for his loss: for the Magian sent messengers abroad to every nation over which he ruled, and proclaimed freedom from military service and from tribute for three years.

68. This proclamation he made as soon as he established himself upon the throne: but in the eighth month it was discovered who he was in the following manner:—Otanes the son of Pharnaspes, in birth and in wealth not inferior to any of the Persians, was the first who had had suspicion of the Magian, that he was not Smerdis the son of Cyrus but the person that he really was, drawing his inference from these facts, namely that he never went abroad out of the fortress, and that he did not summon into his presence any of the honourable men among the Persians. Having formed a suspicion of him, he proceeded to do as follows:—Cambyses had taken to wife his daughter, whose name was Phaidymē; and this same daughter the Magian at that time was keeping as his wife and living with her as with all the rest also of the wives of Cambyses. Otanes therefore sent a message to this daughter and asked her who the man was by whose side she slept, whether Smerdis the son of Cyrus or some other. She sent back word to him saying that she did not know, for she had never seen Smerdis the son of Cyrus, nor did she know otherwise who he was who lived with her. Otanes then sent a second time and said: "If you do not yourself know Smerdis the son of Cyrus, then ask Atossa who this man is, with whom both she and you live as wives; for assuredly it must be that she knows her own brother." **69.** To this the daughter sent back word: "I am not able either to come to speech with Atossa or to see any other of the women who live here with me; for as soon as this man, whosoever he may be, succeeded to the kingdom, he separated us and placed us in different apartments by ourselves." When Otanes heard this, the matter became more and more clear to him, and he sent another message in to her, which said: "Daughter, it is right for you, nobly born as you are, to undertake any risk which your father bids you. If in truth this is not Smerdis the son of Cyrus but the man whom I suppose, he ought not to escape with impunity either for taking you to his bed or for holding the dominion of Persians, but he must pay the penalty. Now therefore do as I shall say. When he sleeps by you and you perceive that he is sound asleep, feel his ears; and if it prove that he has ears, then believe that you are living with Smerdis the son of Cyrus, but if not, believe that it is with the Magian Smerdis." To this Phaidymē sent an answer saying that, if she should do so, she would run a great risk; for supposing he should chance not to have his ears, and she were detected feeling for them, she was well assured that he would put her to death; but nevertheless she would do this. So she undertook to do this for her father. This Magian Smerdis had had his ears cut off by Cyrus the son of Cambyses when he was king, for some grave offence. This Phaidymē then, the daughter of Otanes, proceeding to perform all that she had undertaken for her father, when her turn came to go to the Magian (for the wives of the Persians go in to them regularly each in her turn), came and lay down beside him. When the Magian was in deep sleep, she felt his ears; and perceiving not with difficulty but easily that her husband had no ears, so soon as it became day she sent and informed her father.

70. Then Otanes took to him Aspathines and Gobryas, who were leading men among the Persians and also his own most trusted friends, and related to them the whole matter: and they, as it then appeared, had suspicions also themselves that it was so; and when Otanes reported this to them, they readily accepted his proposals. They resolved that each one should associate with himself that man of the Persians whom he trusted most; so Otanes brought in Intaphrenes, Gobryas brought in Megabyzos, and Aspathines brought in Hydarnes. When they had thus become six, Dareios the son of Hystaspes arrived at Susa, having come from the land of Persia, where his father was governor. Accordingly when he came, the six men of the Persians resolved to associate Dareios also with themselves. **71.** These then having come together, being seven in number, gave pledges of faith to one another and deliberated together; and when it came to Dareios to declare his opinion, he spoke to them as follows: "I thought that I alone knew this, namely that it was the Magian who was reigning as king and that Smerdis the son of Cyrus had brought his life to an end; and for this very reason I am come with earnest purpose to contrive death for the Magian. Since however it has come to pass that you also know and not I alone, I think it well to act at once and not to put the matter off, for delay is a mistake." To this replied Otanes: "Son of Hystaspes, you are the scion of a noble stock,* and you are showing yourself, as it seems, in no way inferior to your father: do not however hasten this enterprise so much without consideration, but take it up more prudently; for we must first become more in numbers, and then undertake the matter." In answer to this Dareios said: "Men who are here present, if you shall follow the way suggested by Otanes, know that you will perish miserably; for some one will carry word to the Magian, getting gain thereby privately for himself. Your best way would have been to do this action upon your own risk alone; but since it seemed good to you to refer the matter to a greater number, and you communicated it to me, either let us do the deed to-day, or be you assured that if this present day shall pass by, no one else shall anticipate me as your accuser, but I will myself tell these things to the Magian."

72. To this Otanes, when he saw Dareios in violent haste, replied: "Since you compel us to hasten the matter and do not permit us to delay, come expound to us yourself in what manner we shall pass into the palace and lay hands upon them: for that there are guards set in various parts, you know probably yourself as well as we, if not from sight at least from hearsay; and in what manner shall we pass through these?" Dareios replied: "Otanes, there are many things that are not possible to set forth in speech, but only in deed; and other things there are which in speech can be set

---

*That is, an Achaimenid.

forth, but from them comes no famous deed. Know that the guards which
are set are not difficult to pass: for in the first place, we being what we are,
there is no one who will not let us go by, partly, as may be supposed, from
having respect for us, and partly also perhaps from fear; and secondly I
have myself a most specious pretext by means of which we may pass by;
for I shall say that I am just now come from the Persian land and desire to
declare to the king a certain message from my father: for where it is necessary that a lie be spoken, let it be spoken;[*] seeing that we all aim at the
same object, both they who lie and they who speak always the truth; those
lie whenever they are likely to gain anything by persuading with their lies,
and these tell the truth in order that they may draw to themselves gain by
the truth, and that things may be entrusted to them more readily. Thus,
while practising different ways, we aim all at the same thing. If however
they were not likely to make any gain by it, the truth-teller would lie and
the liar would speak the truth, with indifference. Whosoever then of the
door-keepers shall let us pass by of his own will, for him it shall be the better afterwards; but whosoever shall endeavour to oppose our passage, let
him then and there be marked as our enemy [and killed], and after that let
us push in and set about our work." **73.** Then said Gobryas: "Friends, at what
time will there be a fairer opportunity for us either to recover our rule, or,
if we are not able to get it again, to die? seeing that we being Persians on
the one hand lie under the rule of a Mede, a Magian, and that too a man
whose ears have been cut off. Moreover all those of you who stood by the
side of Cambyses when he was sick remember assuredly what he laid upon
the Persians as he was bringing his life to an end, if they should not attempt to win back the power; and this we did not accept then, but supposed that Cambyses had spoken in order to deceive us. Now therefore
I give my vote that we follow the opinion of Dareios, and that we do not
depart from this assembly to go anywhere else but straight to attack the
Magian." Thus spoke Gobryas, and they all approved of this proposal.

74. Now while these were thus taking counsel together, this was coming
to pass by coincidence:—The Magians taking counsel together had resolved to join Prexaspes with themselves as a friend, both because he had
suffered grievous wrong from Cambyses, who had killed his son by shooting him, and because he alone knew for a certainty of the death of Smerdis
the son of Cyrus, having killed him with his own hands, and finally because
Prexaspes enjoyed great repute among the Persians. They summoned him
and endeavoured to win him to be their friend, engaging him by pledge
and with oaths, that he would assuredly keep to himself and not reveal the
deception which had been practised by them upon the Persians, and promising to give him things innumerable in return. After Prexaspes had promised, the Magians, having persuaded him so far, proposed to him a second
thing, and said that they would call together all the Persians to come up to
the wall of the palace, and bade him climb a tower and address them,

---

*Dareios is more a Greek sophist than a Persian here; compare 1.138.

saying that they were living under the rule of Smerdis the son of Cyrus and no other. This they so enjoined because they supposed that he had the greatest credit among the Persians, and because he had frequently declared the opinion that Smerdis the son of Cyrus was still alive, and had denied that he had slain him.

75. When Prexaspes said that he was ready to do this also, the Magians called together the Persians and caused him to mount a tower and bade him address them. Then he chose to forget those things which they asked of him, and beginning with Achaimenes he traced the descent of Cyrus on the father's side, and then, when he reached Cyrus, he related at last what great benefits he had conferred upon the Persians; and having gone through this recital he proceeded to declare the truth, saying that formerly he kept it secret, since it was not safe for him to tell what he had done, but at the present time he was compelled to make it known. He proceeded to say how he had himself slain Smerdis the son of Cyrus, being compelled by Cambyses, and that the Magians were now ruling. Then he made imprecation of many evils on the Persians, if they did not recover the power and take vengeance upon the Magians, and upon that he threw himself down from the tower headfirst. Thus Prexaspes ended his life, having been always a man of repute.

76. Now the seven of the Persians, when they had resolved to lay hands upon the Magians and not to delay, made prayer to the gods and went, knowing nothing about Prexaspes: and as they were halfway there, they heard about Prexaspes. Upon that they left the road and again considered with themselves, Otanes and his supporters strongly urging that they should delay and not act when things were boiling over, while Dareios and those of his party urged that they should do that which had been resolved, and not delay. Then while they were contending, there appeared seven pairs of hawks pursuing two pairs of vultures, plucking out their feathers and tearing them. Seeing this the seven all approved the opinion of Dareios and thereupon they went to the king's palace, encouraged by the sight of the birds.

77. When they appeared at the gates, it happened nearly as Dareios supposed, for the guards, having respect for men who were chief among the Persians, and not suspecting anything of the kind in hand, allowed them to pass in under the guiding of heaven, and none asked them any question. Then when they had passed into the court, they met the eunuchs who transmitted messages to the king; and these inquired of them for what purpose they had come, and at the same time they threatened with punishment the keepers of the gates for having let them pass in, and tried to stop the seven when they attempted to go forward. Then they gave the word to one another and drawing their daggers stabbed these men there upon the spot, who tried to stop them, and themselves went running towards the men's chamber.

78. Now both the Magians happened to be there within, consulting about what Prexaspes had done. So when they saw that the eunuchs had been attacked and were crying aloud, they ran back, and perceiving the

situation they turned to self-defence: and one of them got down his bow
and arrows before he was attacked, while the other had recourse to his
spear. Then they engaged in combat. That one of them who had taken up
his bow and arrows found them of no use, since his enemies were close at
hand and pressed hard upon him, but the other defended himself with his
spear, and first he struck Aspathines in the thigh, and then Intaphrenes in
the eye; and Intaphrenes lost his eye by reason of the wound, but not
his life. These then were wounded by one of the Magians, but the other,
when his bow and arrows proved useless to him, fled into a bedchamber
which opened into the chamber of the men, intending to close the door;
and with him there rushed in two of the seven, Dareios and Gobryas. And
when Gobryas was locked in combat with the Magian, Dareios stood aside
and was at a loss what to do, because it was dark, and he was afraid lest he
should strike Gobryas. Then seeing him standing by idle, Gobryas asked
why he did not use his hands, and he said: "Because I am afraid I may
strike you." Gobryas answered: "Thrust with your sword even though it
stab through us both." So Dareios was persuaded, and he thrust with his
dagger and happened to hit the Magian. **79.** So when they had slain the
Magians and cut off their heads, they left behind those of their number
who were wounded, both because they were unable to go, and also in order that they might take charge of the fortress. The five others taking with
them the heads of the Magians ran with shouting and clashing of arms and
called upon the other Persians to join them, telling them what they had
done and showing the heads, and at the same time they proceeded to slay
every one of the Magians who crossed their path. So the Persians when
they heard of the seven's deed and of the deceit of the Magians, decided to
do the same, and drawing their daggers they killed the Magians wherever
they found one; so that if night had not come on and stopped them, they
would not have left a single Magian alive. This day the Persians celebrate
more than all others, and on it they keep a great festival which is called the
festival of the Slaughter of the Magians, on which no Magian is permitted
to appear abroad, but the Magians stay within their houses throughout
that day.

80. When the tumult had subsided and more than five days had elapsed,
those who had risen against the Magians began to take counsel about the
general state, and there were spoken speeches which some of the Hellenes
do not believe were really uttered, but spoken they were nevertheless.*
Otanes urged that they should resign the government into the hands of
the whole body of the Persians, and his words were as follows: "To me it
seems best that no single one of us should henceforth be ruler, for that is
neither pleasant nor profitable. You saw the insolent temper of Cambyses,
to what lengths it went, and you have had experience also of the insolence
of the Magian: and how should the rule of one alone be a well-ordered

---

*The controversy reappears at 6.43, which describes the Persians deposing Hel-
lenic tyrants.

thing, seeing that the monarch may do what he desires without rendering any account of his acts? Even the best of all men, if he were placed in this position, would change from his wonted disposition: for insolence is engendered in him by the good things which he possesses, and envy is implanted in man from the beginning; and having these two things, he has all vice: for he does many reckless wrongs, partly moved by insolence proceeding from abundance, and partly by envy. And yet a despot at least ought to have been free from envy, seeing that he has all manner of good things. He is however naturally in just the opposite temper towards his subjects; for he grudges to the nobles that they should survive and live, but delights in the basest of the citizens, and he is more ready than any other man to receive calumnies. Then of all things he is the most inconsistent; for if you express admiration of him moderately, he is offended that no very great court is paid to him, whereas if you pay court to him extravagantly, he is offended with you for being a flatterer. And most important of all is this:—he disturbs the customs handed down from our fathers, he is a ravisher of women, and he puts men to death without trial. On the other hand the rule of many has first a name attaching to it which is the fairest of all names, that is to say 'Equality';* next, the multitude does none of those things which the monarch does: offices of state are exercised by lot, and the magistrates are compelled to render account of their action: and finally all matters of deliberation are referred to the public assembly. I therefore propose that we let monarchy go and increase the power of the multitude; for in the many is contained everything."

81. After Otanes Megabyzos urged that they should entrust matters to the rule of a few, saying: "I agree with what Otanes said in opposition to a tyranny, but urging that we should make over the power to the multitude, he has missed the best counsel. Nothing is more senseless or insolent than a worthless crowd; and for men flying from the insolence of a despot to fall into that of unrestrained popular power is by no means to be endured. He, if he does anything, does it knowing what he does, but the people cannot even know; for how can that know which has neither been taught anything noble by others nor perceived anything of itself, but pushes on matters with violent impulse and without understanding, like a torrent stream? Let foes to the Persians adopt rule of the people; but let us choose a company of the best men, and to them attach the chief power. We shall ourselves be in the number of these, and it is likely that the resolutions taken by the best men will be the best."

82. After Megabyzos thirdly Dareios proceeded to declare his opinion: "To me it seems that in those things which Megabyzos said with regard to the multitude he spoke rightly, but in those which he said with regard to

---

*Isonomíe, "equal distribution of rights," a word that later describes plans for Samos and Miletos (3.142 and 5.37), resembles demokratíe, "some kind of democracy," a word used to describe some governments in Ionia and Athens (6.43 and 6.131).

the rule of a few, not rightly. Three things are set before us, and each is supposed to be best in its own kind, that is to say a good popular government, and the rule of a few, and thirdly the rule of one. I say that this last is by far superior to the others; for nothing better can be found than the rule of an individual of the best kind; seeing that using the best judgment he would be guardian of the multitude without reproach; and resolutions directed against enemies would so best be kept secret. In an oligarchy however it happens often that many, while practising virtue with regard to the commonwealth, have strong private enmities arising among themselves; for as each man desires to be himself the leader and to prevail in counsels, they develop feuds with one another, whence arise factions among them, and out of the factions comes murder, and from murder results the rule of one man; and thus it shows itself to be the best. Again, when the people rules, it is impossible that corruption should not arise, and when corruption thus arises in the commonwealth, corrupt men develop not enmities but strong ties of friendship: for they who are acting corruptly to the injury of the commonwealth put their heads together secretly. And this continues so until at last some one takes the leadership of the people and stops the course of such men. The man of whom I speak is admired by the people, and being so admired he suddenly appears as monarch. Thus he too furnishes herein an example to prove that the rule of one is best. Finally, to sum up all in a single word, whence arose the liberty which we possess, and who gave it to us? Was it a gift of the people or of an oligarchy or of a monarch?* I therefore propose that we, having been set free by one man, should preserve that form of rule, and in other respects also that we should not annul the customs of our fathers which are ordered well; for that is not the better way."

83. These three opinions then had been proposed, and the other four gave their assent to this last. So when Otanes, who was desirous to give equality to the Persians, found his opinion defeated, he spoke thus: "Partisans, one of us must become king, selected either by casting lots, or by entrusting the decision to the multitude of the Persians and taking him whom it shall choose, or by some other means. I therefore shall not be a competitor with you, for I do not desire either to rule or to be ruled; and on this condition I withdraw from my claim to rule, namely that I shall not be ruled by any of you, either I myself or my descendants at any future time." When he had said this, the six made agreement with him on those terms, and he withdrew from the assembly; and at the present time this house remains free alone of all the Persian houses, and submits to rule only so far as it wishes, not transgressing the laws of the Persians.

84. The rest however of the seven continued to deliberate how they should establish a king most justly. They also resolved that to Otanes and

---

*Reference to Cyrus, liberator of the Persians; compare their emancipation at 1.128–130, c.550 B.C.

his descendants in succession, if the kingdom should come to any other of the seven, there should be given as special gifts a Median dress every year and all those presents which are esteemed among the Persians to be the most valuable. They determined that these things should be given to him because he first suggested to them the matter and combined them together. These were special gifts for Otanes; and this they also determined for all in common, namely that any one of the seven who wished might pass in to the royal palaces without any to bear in a message, unless the king happened to be sleeping with his wife; and that it should not be lawful for the king to marry from any other family, but only from those who had made insurrection with him. About the kingdom they determined this, namely that the man whose horse should first neigh at sunrise in the suburb of the city when they were mounted upon their horses, he should have the kingdom.

85. Now Dareios had a clever groom, whose name was Oibares. To this man, when they had left their assembly, Dareios spoke: "Oibares, we have resolved to do about the kingdom thus, namely that the man whose horse first neighs at sunrise, when we are mounted upon our horses, he shall be king. Now therefore, if you have any cleverness, contrive that we may obtain this prize, and not any other man." Oibares replied thus: "If, my master, it depends in truth upon this whether you be king or no, have confidence so far as concerns this and keep a good heart, for none other shall be king before you; such charms have I at my command." Then Dareios said: "If then you have any such trick, it is time to devise it and not to put things off, for our trial is to-morrow." Oibares therefore hearing this did as follows:— when night was coming on he took one of the mares, namely that one which the horse of Dareios preferred, and this he led into the suburb of the city and tied her up: then he brought to her the horse of Dareios, and having for some time led him round her, making him go close by so as to touch the mare, at last he let the horse mount. 86. Now at dawn the six came to the place as they had agreed, riding upon their horses; and as they rode through the suburb of the city, when they came near the place where the mare had been tied up on the former night, the horse of Dareios ran up to the place and neighed. Just when the horse had done this, there came lightning and thunder from a clear sky; and these things consummated Dareios' claim, for they seemed to have come to pass by some design, and the others leapt down from their horses and did obeisance to Dareios.*

87. Some say that the contrivance of Oibares was this, but others say as follows (for the Persians tell the story in both ways), namely that he touched with his hands the parts of this mare and kept his hand hidden in his trousers; and when at sunrise they were about to let the horses go, this Oibares pulled out his hand and applied it to the nostrils of the horse of Dareios; and the horse, perceiving the smell, snorted and neighed.

---

*Dareios became king in 521 B.C.; the "signs" sent by Ormazd and Mithra, the Persian gods of light, resemble omens in *Odyssey* 20.

88. So Dareios the son of Hystaspes had been declared king; and in Asia all except the Arabians were his subjects, having been subdued by Cyrus and again afterwards by Cambyses. The Arabians however were never obedient to the Persians under conditions of subjection, but had become guest-friends when they let Cambyses pass to Egypt: for against the will of the Arabians the Persians would not be able to invade Egypt. Moreover Dareios made the most noble marriages possible in the estimation of the Persians; for he married two daughters of Cyrus, Atossa and Artystonē, of whom the one, Atossa, had before been the wife of Cambyses her brother and then afterwards of the Magian, while Artystonē was a virgin; and besides them he married the daughter of Smerdis the son of Cyrus, whose name was Parmys; and he also took to wife the daughter of Otanes, her who had discovered the Magian; and all things became filled with his power. And first he had made a carving in stone, and set it up; and on it there was the figure of a man on horseback, and he wrote upon it: "Dareios son of Hystaspes by the excellence of his horse," mentioning the name of it, "and of his horse-keeper Oibares obtained the kingdom of the Persians."

89. He established twenty provinces, which the Persians themselves call *satrapies;*[*] and having established the provinces and set over them rulers, he appointed tribute to come to him from them according to races, joining also to the chief races those who dwelt on their borders, or passing beyond the immediate neighbours and assigning to various races those which lay more distant. He divided the provinces and the yearly payment of tribute as follows. Those of them who brought in silver were commanded to pay by the standard of the Babylonian talent, but those who brought in gold paid by the Euboïc talent. The Babylonian talent is equal to eight-and-seventy Euboïc pounds.[†] For in the reign of Cyrus, and again of Cambyses, nothing was fixed about tribute, but they used to bring gifts: and on account of this appointing of tribute and other things like this, the Persians say that Dareios was a shopkeeper, Cambyses a master, and Cyrus a father; the one because he dealt with all his affairs like a shopkeeper, the second because he was harsh and had little regard for any one, and the other because he was gentle and contrived for them all things good.

90. From the Ionians and the Magnesians who dwell in Asia and the Aiolians, Carians, Lykians, Milyans and Pamphylians (for one single sum was appointed by him as tribute for all these) there came in four hundred talents of silver. This was appointed by him to be the first division. From the Mysians and Lydians and Lasonians and Cabalians and Hytennians there came in five hundred talents: this is the second division. From the Hellespontians who dwell on the right as one sails in and the Phrygians and

---

[*]Dareios organized 20 satrapies c.522 B.C.; Herodotus describes the tribute each paid to Dareios.

[†]The Babylonian talent was one-third heavier, about 67 pounds.

the Thracians who dwell in Asia and the Paphlagonians and Mariandynoi and Cappadocian Syrians the tribute was three hundred and sixty talents: this is the third division. From the Kilikians, besides three hundred and sixty white horses, one for every day in the year, there came also five hundred talents of silver; of these one hundred and forty talents were spent upon the horsemen which served as a guard to the Kilikian land, and the remaining three hundred and sixty came in year by year to Dareios: this is the fourth division.

91. From that division which begins with the city of Posideion, founded by Amphilochos the son of Amphiaraos on the borders of the Kilikians and the Cappadocian Syrians, and extends as far as Egypt, not including the territory of the Arabians (for this was free from payment), the amount was three hundred and fifty talents; and in this division are the whole of Phenicia and Syria which is called Palestine and Cyprus: this is the fifth division. From Egypt and the Libyans bordering on Egypt, and from Kyrenē and Barca, for these were so ordered as to belong to the Egyptian division, there came in seven hundred talents, without reckoning the money produced by the lake of Moiris, that is to say from the fish;[*] without reckoning this, I say, or the grain which was contributed in addition by measure, there came in seven hundred talents; for as regards the grain, they contribute by measure one hundred and twenty thousand bushels for the use of those Persians who are established in the "White Fortress" at Memphis, and for their foreign mercenaries: this is the sixth division. The Sattagydai and Gandarians and Dadicans and Aparytai, joined together, brought in one hundred and seventy talents: this is the seventh division. From Susa and the rest of the land of the Kissians there came in three hundred: this is the eighth division.

92. From Babylon and from the rest of Assyria there came in to him a thousand talents of silver and five hundred boys for eunuchs: this is the ninth division. From Agbatana and from the rest of Media and the Paricanians and Orthocorybantians, four hundred and fifty talents: this is the tenth division. The Caspians and Pausicans and Pantimathoi and Dareitai, contributing together, brought in two hundred talents: this is the eleventh division. From the Bactrians as far as the Aigloi the tribute was three hundred and sixty talents: this is the twelfth division.

93. From Pactyïkē and the Armenians and the people bordering upon them as far as the Euxine, four hundred talents: this is the thirteenth division. From the Sagartians and Sarangians and Thamanaians and Utians and Mycans and those who dwell in the islands of the Erythraian Sea, where the king settles those who are called the "Removed," from all these together a tribute was produced of six hundred talents: this is the fourteenth division. The Sacans and the Caspians brought in two hundred and fifty talents: this is the fifteenth division. The Parthians and Chorasmians and Sogdians and Areians three hundred talents: this is the sixteenth

---

*The lake and its tax are described at 2.149.

division. **94.** The Paricanians and Ethiopians in Asia brought in four hundred talents: this is the seventeenth division. To the Matienians and Saspeirians and Alarodians was appointed a tribute of two hundred talents: this is the eighteenth division. To the Moschoi and Tibarenians and Macronians and Mossynoicoi and Mares three hundred talents were ordered: this is the nineteenth division. Of the Indians the number is far greater than that of any other race of whom we know; and they brought in a tribute larger than all the rest, that is to say three hundred and sixty talents of gold-dust: this is the twentieth division.

95. Now if we compare Babylonian with Euboïc talents, the silver is found to amount to nine thousand eight hundred and eighty talents; and if we reckon the gold at thirteen times the value of silver, weight for weight, the gold-dust is found to amount to four thousand six hundred and eighty Euboïc talents. These being all added together, the total which was collected as yearly tribute for Dareios amounts to fourteen thousand five hundred and sixty Euboïc talents: the sums which are less I do not mention.

96. This was the tribute which came in to Dareios from Asia and from a small part of Libya: but as time went on, other tribute came in also from the [Aegean Greek] islands and from those who dwell in Europe as far as Thessaly. This tribute the king stores up in his treasury in the following manner:—he melts it down and pours it into jars of earthenware, and when he has filled the jars he takes off the earthenware jar from the metal; and when he wants money he cuts off so much as he needs on each occasion.

97. These were the provinces and the assessments of tribute. The Persian land alone has not been mentioned by me as paying a contribution, for the Persians have their land to dwell in free from payment. The following moreover had no tribute fixed for them to pay, but brought gifts, namely the Ethiopians who border upon Egypt, whom Cambyses subdued as he marched against the Long-lived Ethiopians, those who dwell about Nysa, which is called "sacred," and who celebrate the festivals in honour of Dionysos: these Ethiopians and those who dwell near them have the same kind of seed as the Callantian Indians, and they have underground dwellings. These both together brought every other year, and continue to bring even to my own time, two quart measures of unmelted gold and two hundred blocks of ebony and five Ethiopian boys and twenty large elephant tusks. The Colchians also brought gifts, and with them those who border upon them extending as far as the range of Caucasus (for the Persian rule extends as far as these mountains, but those who dwell in the parts beyond Caucasus toward the North regard the Persians no longer). These continued to bring the gifts which they had fixed for themselves every four years even down to my own time, that is to say, a hundred boys and a hundred maidens. Finally, the Arabians brought a thousand talents of frankincense every year. Such were the gifts brought to the king apart from the tribute.

98. Now this great quantity of gold, out of which the Indians bring in to the king the gold-dust which has been mentioned, is obtained as I shall tell:—That part of the Indian land which is towards the rising sun is sand;

for of all the peoples in Asia of which we know or about which any certain report is given, the Indians dwell furthest away towards the East and the sunrising; seeing that the country to the East of the Indians is desert on account of the sand. Now there are many tribes of Indians, and they do not agree with one another in language; and some of them are pastoral and others not so, and some dwell in the swamps of the [Indus] river and feed upon raw fish, which they catch by fishing from boats made of cane; and each boat is made of one joint of cane. These Indians of which I speak wear clothing made of rushes: they gather and cut the rushes from the river and then weave them together into a kind of mat and put it on like a corslet.

99. Others of the Indians, dwelling to the East of these, are pastoral and eat raw flesh: these are called Padaians, and they practise the following customs:—whenever any of their tribe falls ill, whether it be a woman or a man, if a man then the men who are his nearest associates put him to death, saying that he is wasting away with the disease and his flesh is being spoilt for them. Meanwhile he denies stoutly and says that he is not ill, but they do not agree with him; and after they have killed him they feast upon his flesh: but if it be a woman who falls ill, the women who are her greatest intimates act in the same manner as the men. For in fact even if a man has come to old age they slay him and feast upon him; but very few of them come to be reckoned as old, for they kill every one who falls into sickness, before he reaches old age. **100.** Other Indians have another manner of life:—they neither kill any living thing nor do they sow any crops nor is it their custom to possess houses; but they feed on herbs, and they have a grain of the size of millet, in a sheath, which grows of itself from the ground; this they gather and boil with the sheath, and make it their food: and whenever any of them falls into sickness, he goes to the desert country and lies there, and none of them pay any attention either to one who is dead or to one who is sick.* **101.** The sexual intercourse of all these Indians of whom I have spoken is open like that of cattle, and they have all one colour of skin, resembling that of the Ethiopians: moreover the semen which they emit is not white like that of other races, but black like their skin; and the Ethiopians also are similar in this respect. These tribes of Indians dwell further off than the Persian power extends, and towards the South, and they never became subjects of Dareios.

102. Others however of the Indians are on the borders of the city of Caspatyros and the country of Pactyïkē, dwelling towards the North of the other Indians; and they have a manner of living nearly the same as that of the Bactrians: these are the most warlike of the Indians, and these are they who make expeditions for the gold. For in the parts where they live it is desert on account of the sand; and in this desert and sandy tract are produced ants, which are in size smaller than dogs but larger than foxes, for

*The Hellenic anthropologist notes two extremes of diet: cannibalism and vegetarianism.

some of them are kept at the residence of the king of Persia, which were caught here. These ants then make their dwelling under ground and carry up the sand just in the same manner as the ants found in the land of the Hellenes, which they themselves also very much resemble in form; and the sand which is brought up contains gold. To obtain this sand the Indians make expeditions into the desert, each one having yoked together three camels, placing a female in the middle and a male like a trace-horse to draw by each side. On this female he mounts himself, having arranged carefully that she shall be taken to be yoked from young ones, the more lately born the better. For their female camels are not inferior to horses in speed, and moreover they are much more capable of bearing weights. **103.** As to the form of the camel, I do not here describe it, since the Hellenes for whom I write are already acquainted with it, but I shall tell that which is not commonly known about it:—the camel has in the hind legs four thighs and four knees, and its organs of generation are between the hind legs, turned towards the tail.*

104. The Indians, I say, ride out to get the gold in the manner and with the kind of yoking which I have described, making calculation so that they may be engaged in carrying it off at the time when the greatest heat prevails; for the heat causes the ants to disappear underground. Now among these nations the sun is hottest in the morning hours, not at midday as with others, but from sunrise to the time of closing the market: and during this time it produces much greater heat than at midday in Hellas, so that it is said that then they drench themselves with water. Midday however has about equal degree of heat with the Indians as with other men, while after midday their sun becomes like the morning sun with other men, and after this, as it goes further away, it produces still greater coolness, until at last at sunset it makes the air very cool indeed. **105.** When the Indians have come to the place with bags, they fill them with the sand and ride away back as quickly as they can, for immediately the ants, perceiving, as the Persians allege, by the smell, begin to pursue them. This animal, they say, is superior to every other creature in swiftness, so that unless the Indians got a start in their course, while the ants were gathering together, not one of them would escape. So then the male camels, for they are inferior in speed of running to the females, if they drag behind are even let loose from the side of the female, one after the other; the females however, remembering the young which they left behind, do not show any slackness in their course. Thus the Indians get most of the gold, as the Persians say; there is however other gold also in their land obtained by digging, but in smaller quantities.

106. It seems indeed that the extremities of the inhabited world had allotted to them by nature the fairest things, just as it was the lot of Hellas to have its seasons far more fairly tempered than other lands: for first, India is the most distant of inhabited lands towards the East, as I have said, and in this land not only the animals, birds as well as four-footed beasts, are

---

*This last claim is true; the prior is false, although based on observation.

much larger than in other places (except the horses, which are surpassed by those of Media called Nesaian), but also there is gold in abundance there, some got by digging, some brought down by rivers, and some carried off as I explained just now: and there also the trees which grow wild produce wool which surpasses in beauty and excellence that from sheep, and the Indians wear clothing obtained from these trees.[*]

107. Then again Arabia is the furthest of inhabited lands in the direction of the midday, and in it alone of all lands grow frankincense and myrrh and cassia and cinnamon and gum-mastic. All these except myrrh are got with difficulty by the Arabians. Frankincense they collect by burning the storax, which is brought thence to the Hellenes by the Phenicians; by producing smoke they take it; for these trees which produce frankincense are guarded by winged serpents, small in size and of various colours, which watch in great numbers about each tree. The same kind of birds attempt to invade Egypt. They cannot be driven away from the trees by anything except the smoke of storax. **108.** The Arabians say also that all the world would have been filled with these serpents, if that did not happen which I knew happened with regard to vipers. It seems that the Divine Providence, as indeed is to be expected, seeing that it is wise, has made all those animals prolific which are of cowardly spirit and good for food, in order that they may not be all eaten up and their race fail, whereas it has made those which are bold and noxious have small progeny. For example, because the hare is hunted by every beast and bird as well as by man, it is very prolific. It is the only beast which becomes pregnant again before the former young are born, and has in its womb some of its young covered with fur and others bare; and while one is just being shaped in the uterus, another is being conceived. The lioness, however, which is the strongest and most courageous of creatures, produces one cub once only in her life; for when she produces young she casts out her womb together with her young; and the cause of it is this:—when the cub being within the mother begins to move about, then having claws by far sharper than those of any other beast he tears the womb, and as he grows larger he proceeds much further in his scratching. At last the time of birth approaches and there is now nothing at all left of it in a sound condition. **109.** Just so also, if vipers and the winged serpents of the Arabians were produced in the ordinary course of their nature, man would not be able to live upon the earth; but as it is, when they couple with one another and the male is in the act of generation, as he lets go the seed, the female seizes hold of his neck, and fastening on to it does not relax her hold till she has eaten it through. The male then dies, but the female pays the penalty of retribution for the male:—the young while they are still in the womb take vengeance for their father by eating through their mother, and having eaten through her belly they thus escape for themselves. Other serpents however, which are not hurtful to man, produce eggs and hatch from them a very large number of offspring.

---

[*]Herodotus means cotton, which grows on a shrub; compare 7.65 on Indian dress.

Now vipers are distributed over all the earth; but the others, which are winged, are found in great numbers together only in Arabia: therefore they appear to be numerous.

110. This frankincense then is obtained thus by the Arabians; and cassia is obtained as follows:—they bind up in cows'-hide and other kinds of skins all their body and their face except only the eyes, and then go to get the cassia. This grows in a pool not very deep, and round the pool and in it lodge, it seems, winged beasts nearly resembling bats, and they squeak horribly and are courageous in fight. These they must keep off from their eyes, and so cut the cassia.

111. Cinnamon* they collect in a yet more marvellous manner than this; for where it grows and what land produces it they are not able to tell, except only that some say (and it is a probable account) that it grows in those regions where Dionysos was brought up; and they say that large birds carry those dried sticks (which we have learnt from the Phenicians to call cinnamon) to nests which are made of clay and stuck on to precipitous sides of mountains, which man can find no means of scaling. Then the Arabians practise the following contrivance:—they divide up the limbs of the oxen and asses that die and of their other beasts of burden, into pieces as large as convenient, and convey them to these places, and when they have laid them down not far from the nests, they withdraw to a distance from them: and the birds fly down and carry the limbs of the beasts of burden off to their nests. These nests are not able to bear them, but break down and fall to the "earth; and the men come up to them and collect the cinnamon. Thus cinnamon comes from this nation to the other countries of the world.

112. Gum-mastic however, which the Arabians call *ladanon,* comes in a still more extraordinary manner; for though it is the most sweet-scented of all things, it comes in the most evil-scented thing, since it is found in the beards of he-goats, produced there like resin from wood: this is of use for the making of many perfumes, and the Arabians use it more than anything else as incense. **113.** Let what we have said suffice with regard to spices; and from the land of Arabia there blows a scent of them most marvellously sweet. They have also two kinds of sheep which are worthy of admiration and are not found in any other land. One kind has the tail long, not less than four and one-half feet; and if one should allow them to drag these after them, they would have sores from their tails being worn away against the ground; but as it is, every one of the shepherds knows enough of carpentering to make little cars, which they tie under the tails, fastening the tail of each animal to a separate little car. The other kind of sheep has the tail broad, even as much as a foot and a half in breadth.

114. As one passes toward the South West, the Ethiopian land is that which extends furthest of all inhabited lands towards the sunset. This produces both gold in abundance and huge elephants and trees of all kinds

---

*Cassia and cinnamon are both aromatic tree barks.

growing wild and ebony, and men who are the tallest, the most beautiful and the most long-lived.

115. These are the extremities in Asia and in Libya; but as to the extremities of Europe towards the West, I am not able to speak with certainty: for neither do I accept the tale that there is a river called in Barbarian tongue Eridanos,* flowing into the sea which lies towards the North, whence it is said that amber comes; nor do I know of the real existence of "Tin islands"† from which tin comes to us: for first the very name Eridanos itself declares that it is Hellenic and that it does not belong to a Barbarian speech, but was invented by some poet; and secondly I am not able to hear from any one who has been an eye-witness, though I took pains to discover this, that there is a sea on the other side of Europe. However that may be, tin and amber certainly come to us from the extremity of Europe.

116. Then again towards the North of Europe, there is evidently a quantity of gold by far larger than in any other land: as to how it is got, here again I am not able to say for certain, but it is said to be carried off from the griffins by Arimaspians, a one-eyed race of men.‡ But I do not believe this tale either, that nature produces one-eyed men which in all other respects are like other men. However, it would seem that the extremities which bound the rest of the world on every side and enclose it in the midst, possess the things which by us are thought to be the most beautiful and rare.

117. Now there is a plain in Asia bounded by mountains on all sides, and through the mountains there are five clefts. This plain belonged once to the Chorasmians, and it lies on the borders of the Chorasmians themselves, the Hyrcanians, Parthians, Sarangians, and Thamanaians; but from the time that the Persians began to rule, it belongs to the king. From this enclosing mountain of which I speak there flows a great river, and its name is Akes. This formerly watered the lands of these nations which have been mentioned, being divided into five streams and conducted through a separate cleft in the mountains to each separate nation; but from the time that they have come to be under the Persians, they have suffered as follows:— the king built up the clefts in the mountains and set gates at each cleft; and so, since the water has been shut off from its outlet, the plain within the mountains is made into a sea, because the river runs into it and has no way out in any direction. Those therefore who in former times had used the water, not being able now to make use of it are in great trouble: for during the winter they have rain from heaven, as also other men have, but in the summer they desire to use the water when they sow millet and sesame seed. So then, the water not being granted to them, they come to the Persians both themselves and their wives, and standing at the gates of the king's court they cry and howl. The king orders that for those who need it most, the gates which lead to their land shall be opened; and when their land has

---

*This could be the Rhine or the Rhone or the Po.
†Perhaps the British isles where tin was long obtained.
‡The Arimaspians are mentioned again at 4.13.

become satiated with drinking in the water, these gates are closed, and he orders the gates to be opened for others, that is to say those most needing it of the rest who remain: and, as I have heard, he exacts large sums of money for opening them, besides the regular tribute.*

118. Intaphrenes of the seven men who had risen against the Magian, was put to death immediately after their insurrection for an outrage which I shall relate. He desired to enter into the king's palace and confer with the king; for the law was in fact so, that those who had risen up against the Magian were permitted to go in to the king's presence without any one to announce them, unless the king happened to be lying with his wife. Accordingly Intaphrenes did not deem it necessary that any one should announce his coming; but as one of the seven, he desired to enter. The gate-keeper however and the bearer of messages endeavoured to prevent him, saying that the king was lying with his wife. Intaphrenes believing that they were not speaking the truth, drew his Persian sword and cut off their ears and their noses, and stringing these upon his horse's bridle he tied them round their necks and so let them go.

119. Upon this they showed themselves to the king and told the cause for which they had suffered this; and Dareios, fearing that the six might have done this by common design, sent for each one separately and made trial of his inclinations, as to whether he approved. When he was fully assured that Intaphrenes had not done this in combination with them, he took both Intaphrenes himself and his sons and all his kinsmen, being much disposed to believe that he was plotting insurrection against him with the help of his relations; and he put them in bonds as for execution. Then the wife of Intaphrenes, coming constantly to the doors of the king's court, wept and grieved; and doing this continually she moved Dareios to pity her. Accordingly he sent a messenger and said to her: "Woman, king Dareios grants to you to save from death one of your kinsmen who are lying in bonds, whomsoever you desire." She then, having considered with herself, answered thus: "If in truth the king grants me the life of one, I choose of them all my brother." Dareios being informed of this, and marvelling at her speech, sent and addressed her thus: "Woman, the king asks you what was in your mind, that you left your husband and your children to die, and chose your brother to survive, seeing that he is surely less near in blood than your children, and less dear than your husband." She answered: "O king, I might, if heaven willed, have another husband and other children, if I should lose these; but another brother I could by no means have, seeing that my father and my mother are no longer alive. This was in my mind when I said those words." To Dareios then it seemed that the woman had spoken well, and he let go not only him for whose life she asked, but also the eldest of her sons, because he was pleased with her: but all the others he slew. One therefore of the seven had perished immediately.

---

*Herodotus reveals limited knowledge of hydrology, but canalization and irrigation were prerogatives of the despots of "'hydraulic civilizations."

120. Now about the time of Cambyses' sickness it had come to pass as follows:—There was one Oroites, a Persian, who had been appointed by Cyrus to be governor of the province of Sardis. This man had set his desire upon an unholy thing; for though from Polycrates the Samian he had neither suffered anything nor heard any offensive word nor even seen him before that time, he desired to take him and put him to death, as most report:—while Oroites and another Persian whose name was Mitrobates, ruler of the province of Daskyleion, were sitting at the door of the king's court, they came from words to strife with one another; and as they debated their several claims to excellence, Mitrobates taunting Oroites said: "Do *you* count yourself a man, who never yet has won for the king the island of Samos, which lies close to your province, when it is so exceedingly easy of conquest that one of the natives of it rose up against the government with fifteen men-at-arms and got possession of the island, and is now despot of it?" Some say that because he heard this and was stung by the reproach, he formed the desire, not so much to take vengeance on him who had said this, as to bring Polycrates to destruction at all costs, since by reason of him he was ill spoken of. **121.** The lesser number however of those who tell the tale say that Oroites sent a herald to Samos to ask for something or other, but what it was is not mentioned; and Polycrates happened to be lying down in the men's banquet hall of his palace, and Anacreon also of Teos was present with him. Somehow, whether it was by intention and because he made no account of the business of Oroites, or whether some chance occurred to bring it about, it happened that the envoy of Oroites came into his presence and spoke with him, and Polycrates, who chanced to be turned away towards the wall, neither turned round at all nor made any answer.

122. The cause then of the death of Polycrates is reported in these two different ways, and we may believe whichever of them we please. Oroites however, having his residence at that Magnesia upon the river Maiander, sent Myrsos the son of Gyges, a Lydian, to Samos bearing a message, since he had perceived the designs of Polycrates. For Polycrates was the first of the Hellenes of whom we have any knowledge, who set his mind upon having command of the sea, excepting Minos the Cnossian and any other who may have had command of the sea before his time. Of the allegedly mortal race Polycrates was the first;[*] and he had great expectation of becoming ruler of Ionia and of the islands. Oroites accordingly, having perceived that he had this design, sent a message to him: "Oroites to Polycrates says this: I hear that you have plans to get great power, and that you have not wealth according to your high thoughts. Now therefore if you do as I shall say, you will do well for yourself on the one hand, and also save me from destruction: for king Cambyses is planning death for me, and this is reported to me so that I cannot doubt it. Carry away out of danger both myself and with me my wealth; and of this keep a part

---

*Herodotus here distinguishes the age of heroes from the historical epoch.

for yourself and a part let me keep, and then so far as wealth may bring it about, you shall rule all Hellas. And if you do not believe that which I say about the money, send some one, whosoever happens to be most trusted and to him I will show it."

123. Polycrates having heard this rejoiced, and was disposed to agree; and as he had a great desire, it seems, for wealth, he first sent Maiandrios the son of Maiandrios, a native of Samos who was his secretary, to see it: this man was the same who not long after these events dedicated all the ornaments of the men's banqueting-hall in the palace of Polycrates, ornaments well worth seeing, as an offering to the temple of Hera. Oroites accordingly, having heard that the person sent to examine might be expected soon to come, did as follows. He filled eight chests with stones except a small depth at the very top of each, and laid gold above upon the stones; then he tied up the chests and kept them in readiness. So Maiandrios came and looked at them and brought back word to Polycrates. **124.** He upon that prepared to set out, although the diviners and also his friends strongly dissuaded him from it, and in spite moreover of a vision which his daughter had seen in sleep—it seemed to her that her father was raised up on high and was bathed by Zeus and anointed by the Sun. Having seen this vision, she endeavoured to dissuade Polycrates from leaving his land to go to Oroites, and besides that, as he was going to his fifty-oared galley she accompanied his departure with prophetic words. He threatened her that if he should return safe, she should remain unmarried for long; but she prayed that this might come to pass, for she desired rather, she said, to be unmarried for long than to be an orphan, having lost her father.

125. Polycrates however neglected every counsel and set sail to go to Oroites, taking with him, besides many others of his friends, Demokedes also the son of Calliphon, a man of Croton, who was a physician and practised his art better than any other man of his time. Then when he arrived at Magnesia, Polycrates was miserably put to death in a manner unworthy both of himself and of his high ambition.* Except those who became despots of the Syracusans, not one besides of the Hellenic despots is worthy to be compared with Polycrates in magnificence. And when he had killed him in a manner not fit to be told, Oroites impaled his body; and of those who accompanied him, he released the Samians, bidding them be grateful to him that they were free men; but all those of his company who were either aliens or servants, he held in the estimation of slaves and kept them. Polycrates then being hung up accomplished wholly the vision of his daughter, for he was bathed by Zeus whenever it rained, and anointed by the Sun, giving forth sweat from his body.

126. To this end then came the great prosperity of Polycrates, as Amasis the king of Egypt had foretold. Not long afterwards retribution overtook Oroites in his turn for the murder of Polycrates. For after the death of

---

*Polycrates died c.522 B.C.

Cambyses and the reign of the Magians Oroites remained at Sardis and did no service to the Persians, when they had been deprived of their empire by the Medes. Moreover during this time of disturbance he slew Mitrobates the governor in Daskyleion, who had brought up against him the matter of Polycrates as a reproach; and he slew also Cranaspes the son of Mitrobates, both men of repute among the Persians. Besides other deeds of arrogance, once when a bearer of messages had come from Dareios, not being pleased with the message he slew him as he was returning, having set men to ambush him by the way; and having slain him he made away with the bodies both of the man and horse. **127.** Dareios accordingly, when he had come to the throne, was desirous of taking vengeance upon Oroites for all his wrongdoings and especially for the murder of Mitrobates and his son. However he did not think it good to act openly and to send an army against him, since his own affairs were still in a disturbed state and he had only lately come to the throne, while he heard that the strength of Oroites was great, seeing that he had a bodyguard of a thousand Persian spearmen and was in possession of the satrapies of Phrygia and Lydia and Ionia. Therefore Dareios contrived as follows:—having called together those of the Persians who were of most repute, he said to them: "Persians, which of you all will undertake to perform this matter for me with cleverness, and not by force or with tumult? for where cleverness is needed, there is no need of force. Which of you, I say, will either bring Oroites alive to me or slay him? for he never yet did any service to the Persians, and on the other hand he has done to them great evil. First he destroyed two of us, Mitrobates and his son; then he slays the men who go to summon him, sent by me, displaying arrogance not to be endured. Before therefore he shall accomplish any other evil against the Persians, we must check his course by death."

128. Thus Dareios asked, and thirty men undertook the matter, each one separately desiring to do it himself; and Dareios stopped their contention and bade them cast lots. Bagaios the son of Artontes obtained the lot from among them all. Bagaios accordingly did thus:—he wrote many papers dealing with various matters and on them set the seal of Dareios, and with them he went to Sardis. When he arrived there and came into the presence of Oroites, he took the covers off the papers one after another and gave them to the Royal Secretary to read; for all the governors of provinces have Royal Secretaries. Now Bagaios thus gave the papers in order to make trial of the spearmen of the guard, whether they would accept the motion to desert Oroites; and seeing that they paid great reverence to the papers and still more to the words which were recited from them, he gave another paper in which were contained these words: "Persians, king Dareios forbids you to serve as guards to Oroites:" and they hearing this lowered to him the points of their spears. Then Bagaios, seeing that in this they were obedient to the paper, took courage upon that and gave the last of the papers to the secretary; and in it was written: "King Dareios commands the Persians who are in Sardis to slay Oroites." So the spearmen of the guard, when they heard this, drew their swords and slew him then and there. Thus did retribution for the murder of Polycrates the Samian overtake Oroites.

129. When the wealth of Oroites had come or had been carried up to Susa, it happened soon after that king Dareios while engaged in hunting wild beasts twisted his foot in leaping off his horse, and it was twisted, as it seems, rather violently, for the ball of his ankle-joint was put out of the socket. Now he had been accustomed before to keep about him those of the Egyptians who were accounted the first in the art of medicine, and he made use of their assistance then. These by wrenching and forcing the foot made the evil continually greater. For seven days then and seven nights Dareios was sleepless owing to the pain which he suffered; and at last on the eighth day, when he was in a wretched state, some one who had heard talk before while yet at Sardis of the skill of Demokedes of Croton, reported this to Dareios; and he bade them bring him straightaway into his presence. So having found him somewhere unnoticed among the slaves of Oroites, they brought him forth dragging fetters after him and clothed in rags.

130. When he had been placed in the midst of them, Dareios asked him whether he understood the art; but he would not admit it, fearing lest, if he declared himself to be what he was, he might lose for ever the hope of returning to Hellas. Dareios saw that he understood that art but was practising another, evasion, and he commanded those who had brought him to produce scourges and pricks. Accordingly upon that he spoke out, saying that he did not understand it precisely, but that he had kept company with a physician and had some poor knowledge of the art. Then after this, when Dareios had committed the case to him, by using Hellenic drugs and applying mild remedies after the former violent means, he caused him to get sleep, and in a short time made him perfectly well, though he had never hoped to be sound of foot again. Upon this Dareios presented him with two pairs of golden fetters; and Demokedes asked him whether it was by design that he had given to him a double share of his suffering, because he had made him well. Being pleased by this saying, Dareios sent him to visit his wives, and the eunuchs in bringing him in said to the women that this was he who had restored to the king his life. Then each one of them plunged a cup into the gold-chest and presented Demokedes with so abundant a gift that his servant, whose name was Skiton, following and gathering up the "Daric" coins which fell from the cups, collected for himself a very large sum of gold.

131. This Demokedes came from Croton, and became the associate of Polycrates in this way:—at Croton he lived in strife with his father, who was of a harsh temper, and when he could no longer endure him, he departed and came to Egina. Being established there he surpassed in the first year all the other physicians, although he was without equipment and had none of the instruments which are used in the art. In the next year the Eginetan State engaged him for a payment of one talent, in the third year he was engaged by the Athenians for one and two-thirds talents, and in the fourth by Polycrates for two talents. Thus he arrived in Samos; and it was by reason of this man more than anything else that the physicians of Croton got their reputation. This event happened at the time when the physicians of Crotōn began to be spoken of as the first in Hellas, while the Kyrenians were reputed to have the second place. [About this same time also the Argives had the reputation of being the first musicians in Hellas.]*

132. Then Demokedes having healed king Dareios had a very great house in Susa, and had been made a table-companion of the king; and except for the opportunity of returning to the land of the Hellenes, he had everything. And first as regards the Egyptian physicians who tried to heal the king before him, when they were about to be impaled because they had been proved inferior to a physician who was a Hellene, he asked their lives of the king and rescued them from death. Secondly, he rescued an Eleian prophet, who had accompanied Polycrates and had remained unnoticed among the slaves. In short Demokedes was very favoured by the king.

133. Soon after this another thing came to pass:—Atossa the daughter of Cyrus and wife of Dareios had a tumour upon her breast, which afterwards burst and then was spreading further. While it was not large, she concealed it and said nothing to anybody, because she was ashamed; but afterwards when she was in evil case, she sent for Demokedes and showed it to him. He said that he would make her well, and caused her to swear that she would surely do for him in return that which he should ask of her; and he would ask, he said, none of such things as are shameful. **134.** So when after this by his treatment he had made her well, then Atossa instructed by Demokedes uttered to Dareios in his bedchamber some such words as these: "O king, though you have such great power, you sit still, and do not win in addition any nation or power for the Persians: and yet it is reasonable that a man who is both young and master of much wealth should be seen to perform some great deed, in order that the Persians may know surely that he is a man by whom they are ruled. It is expedient indeed in two ways that you should do so, both in order that the Persians may know that their ruler is a man, and in order that they may be worn down by war and not have leisure to plot against you. For now you might display some great deed, while you are still young; seeing that as the body grows strong the spirit also grows strong with it, but as it grows old the spirit grows old also with it, and is blunted for every kind of action." Thus she spoke according to instructions received, and he answered thus: "Woman, you have said all the things which I myself have in my mind to do; for I have made the plan to yoke together a bridge from this continent to the other and to make expedition against the Scythians, and these designs will be by way of being fulfilled within a little time." Then Atossa said: "Look now,—forbear to go first against the Scythians, for these will be in your power whenever you desire: but, I pray you, make an expedition against Hellas; for I am desirous to have Lacedemonian women and Argive and Athenian and Corinthian, for attendants, because I hear of them by report: and you have the man who of all men is most fitted to show you all things

---

*Probably a copyist's addition.

which relate to Hellas and to be your guide, that man, I mean, who healed
your foot." Dareios answered: "Woman, since it seems good to you that we
should first make trial of Hellas, I think it better to send first to them men
of the Persians together with him of whom you speak, to make investigation, that when these have learnt and seen, they may report each several
thing to us; and then I shall go to attack them with full knowledge of all."

135. Thus he said, and he proceeded to do as he spoke. As soon as day
dawned, he summoned fifteen Persians, men of repute, and bade them
pass through the coasts of Hellas in company with Demokedes, and take
care not to let Demokedes escape from them, but bring him back at all
costs. Having thus commanded them, next he summoned Demokedes
himself and asked him to act as a guide for the whole of Hellas and show
it to the Persians, and then return back. He bade him take all his movable
goods and carry them as gifts to his father and his brothers, saying that
he would give him in their place many times as much; and besides this, he
said, he would contribute to the gifts a merchant ship filled with all manner of goods, which should sail with him. Dareios, as it seems to me, promised him these things with no crafty design; but Demokedes was afraid
that Dareios was making trial of him, and did not make haste to accept all
that was offered, but said that he would leave his own things where they
were, so that he might have them when he came back; he said however
that he accepted the merchant ship which Dareios promised him for the
presents to his brothers. Dareios then, having thus given command to him
also, sent them away to the sea.

136. So these, when they had gone to Phenicia and in Phenicia to the
city of Sidon, immediately manned two triremes, and besides them they
also filled a large ship of burden with all manner of goods. Then when they
had made all things ready they set sail for Hellas, and touching at various
places they saw the coast regions of it and wrote down a description, until
at last, when they had seen the greater number of the famous places,
they came to Taras in southern Italy. There as a kindness to Demokedes
Aristophilides the king of the Tarentines unfastened and removed the
steering-oars of the Median ships, and also confined the Persians in prison,
because, as he alleged, they came as spies. While they were being thus
dealt with, Demokedes went away and reached Crotōn; and when he had
now reached his own native place, Aristophilides set the Persians free and
gave back to them those parts of their ships which he had taken away.
137. The Persians then sailing and pursuing Demokedes reached Crotōn,
and finding him in the market-place they laid hands upon him; and some
of the men of Crotōn fearing the Persian power were willing to give him up,
but others took hold of him and struck with their staves at the Persians, who
pleaded in these words: "Men of Crotōn, take care what you are about:
you are rescuing a man who was a slave of king Dareios and who ran away
from him. How, think you, will king Dareios be content to receive such arrogant insult; and how shall this which you do be well for you, if you take
him away from us? Against what city, think you, shall we make expedition
sooner than against this, and what city before this shall we endeavour to

reduce to slavery?" Thus saying they did not however persuade the men of
Crotōn, but having had Demokedes rescued from them and the ship of
burden which they were bringing with them taken away, they set sail to go
back to Asia, and did not endeavour to visit any more parts of Hellas or to
find out about them, being now deprived of their guide. Thus much however Demokedes gave them as a charge when they were putting forth to
sea, bidding them say to Dareios that Demokedes was betrothed to the
daughter of Milon, for the wrestler Milon had a great name at the king's
court; and I suppose that Demokedes was urgent for this marriage, spending much money to further it, in order that Dareios might see that he was
held in honour also in his own country.

138. The Persians however, after they had put out from Crotōn, were
shipwrecked in Iapygia; and as they were remaining there as slaves, Gillos
a Tarentine exile rescued them and brought them back to king Dareios. In
return for this Dareios offered to give him whatever he should desire; and
Gillos chose that he might have the power of returning to Taras, narrating
first the story of his misfortune. In order that he might not disturb all Hellas,
as would be the case if on his account a great armament should sail to invade Italy, he said it was enough for him that the men of Cnidos should be
those who brought him back, without any others; because he supposed
that by these, who were friends with the Tarentines, his return from exile
would most easily be effected. Dareios accordingly having promised proceeded to perform; for he sent a messenger to Cnidos and bade them
bring back Gillos to Taras: and the men of Cnidos obeyed Dareios, but
nevertheless they did not persuade the Tarentines, and they were not
strong enough to apply force. These were the first Persians who came from
Asia to Hellas, and for the reason which has been mentioned these were
sent as spies.

139. After this king Dareios took Samos before all other cities, whether
of Hellenes or Barbarians, and for a cause:—When Cambyses the son of
Cyrus was marching upon Egypt, many Hellenes arrived in Egypt, some,
as might be expected, joining in the campaign to make profit, and some
also coming to see the land itself; and among these was Syloson the son of
Aiakes and brother of Polycrates, an exile from Samos. To this Syloson a
fortunate chance occurred, of this sort:—he had taken and put upon him a
flame-coloured mantle, and was hawking it about the market-place in
Memphis; and Dareios, who was then one of the spearmen of Cambyses
and not yet held in any great estimation, seeing him had a desire for the
mantle, and going up to him offered to buy it. Then Syloson, seeing that
Dareios very greatly desired the mantle, by some divine inspiration said:
"I will not sell this for any sum, but I will give it you for nothing, if, as it appears, it must be yours at all costs." To this Dareios agreed and received
from him the garment.

140. Now Syloson supposed without any doubt that he had altogether
lost this by easy simplicity; but when in course of time Cambyses was
dead, and the seven Persians had risen up against the Magian, and of the
seven Dareios had obtained the kingdom, Syloson heard that the kingdom

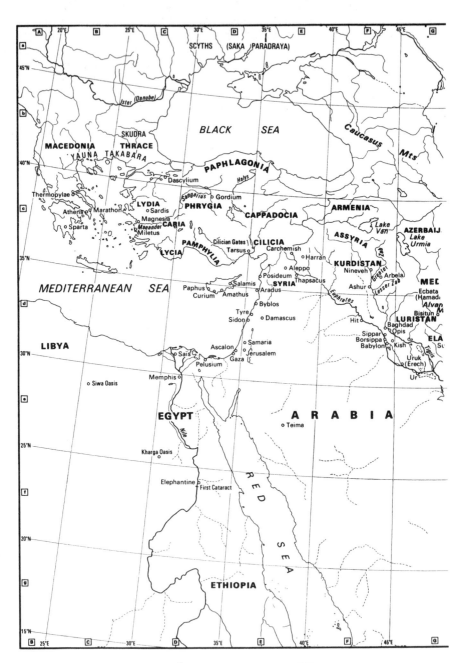

MAP 1. THE ACHAIMENID EMPIRE.

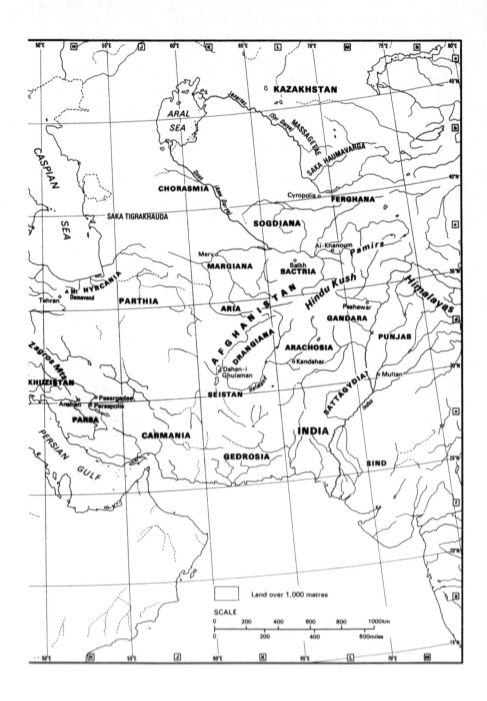

had come about to that man to whom once in Egypt he had given the garment at his request: accordingly he went up to Susa and sat down at the
great entrance of the king's palace, and said that he was a benefactor of
Dareios. The keeper of the door hearing this reported it to the king; and he
marvelled at it and said to him: "Who then of the Hellenes is my benefactor, to whom I am bound by gratitude? seeing that it is now but a short
time that I possess the kingdom, and as yet scarcely one of them has come
up to our court; and I may almost say that I have no debt owing to a Hellene. Nevertheless bring him in before me, that I may know what he means
when he says these things." Then the keeper of the door brought Syloson
before him, and when he had been set in the midst, the interpreters asked
him who he was and what he had done, that he called himself a benefactor
of the king. Syloson accordingly told all that had happened about the mantle, and how he was the man who had given it; to which Dareios made this
answer: "Most noble of men, you are he who when as yet I had no power
gave me a gift, small it may be, but nevertheless the kindness is counted
with me to be as great as if I should now receive some great thing from
some one. Therefore I will give you in return gold and silver in abundance,
that you may not ever repent that you rendered a service to Dareios the
son of Hystaspes." To this Syloson replied: "To me, O king, give neither
gold nor silver, but recover and give to me my fatherland Samos, which
now that my brother Polycrates has been slain by Oroites is possessed by
our slave. This give to me without bloodshed or selling into slavery."
141. Dareios having heard this prepared to send an expedition with
Otanes as commander of it, who had been one of the seven, charging him
to accomplish for Syloson all that which he had requested. Otanes then
went down to the sea-coast and was preparing the expedition.

142. Now Maiandrios the son of Maiandrios was holding the rule over
Samos, having received the government as a trust from Polycrates; and he,
though desiring to show himself the most righteous of men, did not succeed in so doing: for when the death of Polycrates was reported to him, he
did as follows:—first he founded an altar to Zeus the Liberator and
marked out a sacred enclosure round it, namely that which exists still in
the suburb of the city. After he had done this he gathered together an assembly of all the citizens and spoke: "To me, as you know as well as I, has
been entrusted the sceptre of Polycrates and all his power; and now it is
open to me to be your ruler. What, however, I would fault my neighbour
for doing, I will myself refrain from. As I did not approve of Polycrates
acting as master of men who were not inferior to himself, so neither do I
approve of any other who does such things. Now Polycrates for his part
fulfilled his own appointed destiny, and I now give the power into the
hands of the people, and proclaim to you equality.* These privileges however I think it right to have assigned to me, namely that from the wealth of
Polycrates six talents should be taken out and given to me as a special gift;

---

*The concept favored by Otanes at 3.80.

and in addition to this I choose for myself and for my descendants in succession the priesthood of Zeus the Liberator, to whom I myself founded a temple, while I bestow liberty upon you." He made these offers to the Samians; but one of them rose up and said: "Nay, but unworthy too are you to be our ruler, seeing that you are of mean birth and a pestilent fellow besides. Rather take care that you give an account of the money which you had to deal with." **143.** Thus said one man of repute among the citizens, whose name was Telesarchos; and Maiandrios perceiving that if he resigned the power, some other would be set up as despot instead of himself, did not keep to his purpose of resigning it; but having retired to the fortress he sent for each man separately, pretending that he was going to give an account of the money, and so seized and fettered them. These then had been put in bonds; but Maiandrios after this was overtaken by sickness, and his brother, whose name was Lycaretos, expecting that he would die, put all the prisoners to death, in order that he might himself more easily get possession of the power over Samos. All this happened because, as it appears, they did not choose to be free.

144. So when the Persians arrived at Samos bringing Syloson home from exile, no one raised a hand against them, and moreover the party of Maiandrios and Maiandrios himself said that they were ready to retire out of the island under a truce. Otanes therefore having agreed on these terms and having made a treaty, the most honourable of the Persians had seats placed for them in front of the fortress and were sitting there. **145.** Now the despot Maiandrios had a brother who was somewhat mad, and his name was Charilaos. This man for some offence which he had committed had been confined in an underground dungeon. Having heard what was being done and having put his head through the bars, when he saw the Persians peacefully sitting there he began to cry out and asked to speak with Maiandrios. So Maiandrios hearing his voice bade them loose him and bring him into his presence; and as soon as he was brought he began to abuse and revile him, trying to persuade him to attack the Persians, and saying thus: "Basest of men, did you put me in bonds and judge me worthy of the dungeon under ground, your own brother who did no wrong worthy of bonds, and when you see the Persians casting you forth from the land and making you homeless, do you not dare to take any revenge, though they are so exceedingly easy to be overcome? Nay, but if in truth you are afraid of them, give me your mercenaries and I will take vengeance on them for their coming here; and I am willing to let you go out of the island."

146. Thus spoke Charilaos, and Maiandrios accepted that which he said, not, as I think, because he had reached such a height of folly as to suppose that his own power would overcome that of the king, but rather because he grudged Syloson that he should receive from him the State without trouble, and with no injury inflicted upon it. Therefore he desired to provoke the Persians to anger and make the Samian power as feeble as possible before he gave it up to him, being well assured that the Persians, when they had suffered evil, would be likely to be bitter against the Samians as well as against those who did the wrong, and knowing also that he had a safe way of escape from the island whenever he desired: for he had had a secret passage made under ground, leading from the fortress to the sea. Maiandrios then himself sailed out from Samos; but Charilaos armed all the mercenaries, and opening wide the gates sent them out upon the Persians, who were not expecting any such thing, but supposed that all had been arranged: and the mercenaries falling upon them began to slay those of the Persians who had seats carried for them and were of most account. The rest of the Persian force came to the rescue, and the mercenaries were hard pressed and forced to retire to the fortress.

147. Then Otanes the Persian commander, seeing that the Persians had suffered greatly, purposely forgot the commands which Dareios gave him when he sent him forth, not to kill any one of the Samians nor to sell any into slavery, but to restore the island to Syloson free from all suffering of calamity. He gave the word to his army to slay every one whom they should take, man or boy, without distinction. So while some of the army were besieging the fortress, others were slaying every one who came their way, in sanctuary or out of sanctuary equally.

148. Meanwhile Maiandrios had escaped from Samos and was sailing to Lacedemon. After arriving, he caused to be brought up to the city the things which he had taken with him when he departed. Then he did as follows:—first, he would set out his cups of silver and of gold, and then while the servants were cleaning them, he would be engaged in conversation with Cleomenes the son of Anaxandrides, then king of Sparta, and would bring him on to his house; and when Cleomenes saw the cups he marvelled and was astonished at them, and Maiandrios would bid him take away with him as many as he pleased. Maiandrios said this twice or three times, but Cleomenes herein showed himself the most upright of men; for he not only did not think fit to take that which was offered, but perceiving that Maiandrios would make presents to others of the citizens, and so obtain assistance for himself, he went to the Ephors and said that it was better for Sparta that the stranger of Samos should depart from Peloponnesus, lest he might persuade either himself or some other man of the Spartans to act basely. They accordingly accepted his counsel, and expelled Maiandrios by proclamation. **149.** As to Samos, the Persians, after rounding up and sweeping the population off it,[*] delivered it to Syloson stripped of men. Afterwards however the commander Otanes even joined in settling people there, moved by a vision of a dream and by a disease which seized him in the genital organs.

150. After this naval force had gone against Samos, the Babylonians revolted, being exceedingly well prepared; for during all the time of the reign of the Magian and of the insurrection of the seven, during all this time and the attendant confusion they were preparing themselves for the siege of their city. Somehow they were not observed to be doing this. Then when

---

*Ionia suffers this depopulation by dragnet again at 6.31.

they made open revolt, they did as follows:—after setting apart their mothers first, each man set apart also for himself one woman, whomsoever he wished of his own household, and all the remainder they gathered together and killed by suffocation. Each man set apart the one who has been mentioned to serve as a maker of bread, and they suffocated the rest in order that they might not consume their provisions. **151.** Dareios being informed of this and having gathered together all his power, organized an expedition against them, and when he had marched his army up to Babylon he began to besiege them; but they cared nothing about the siege, for the Babylonians used to go up to the battlements of the wall and show contempt of Dareios and of his army by dancing gestures and mocking words; and one of them uttered this saying: "Why, O Persians, do you remain sitting here, and not depart? For then only shall you capture us, when mules shall bring forth young." This was said by one of the Babylonians, not supposing that a mule would ever bring forth young.

152. So when a year and seven months had now passed by, Dareios began to be vexed and his whole army with him, not being able to conquer the Babylonians. And yet Dareios had used against them every kind of device and every possible means, but not even so could he conquer them. He had even attempted the ruse by which Cyrus conquered them;[*] but the Babylonians kept careful guard and he was not able to conquer them. **153.** Then in the twentieth month Zopyros the son of that Megabyzos who had been of the seven men who slew the Magian witnessed a prodigy,—one of the mules which served as bearers of provisions for him produced young: and when this was reported to him, and Zopyros had himself seen the foal, because he did not believe the report, he charged those who had seen it not to tell any one, and he considered with himself what to do. And having regard to the ominous words spoken by the Babylonian, who had said at first that when mules should produce young, then the wall would be taken, it seemed to Zopyros that Babylon could be taken. He thought that both the man had spoken and his mule had produced young by divine dispensation.

154. Since then it seemed to him that it was now fated that Babylon should be captured, he went to Dareios and inquired of him whether he thought it a matter of very great moment to conquer Babylon; and hearing in answer that he thought it of great consequence, he considered again how he might be the man to take it and how the work might be his own: for among the Persians benefits are honoured and deemed worthy of a high degree of promotion. He considered accordingly that he was not able to conquer it by any means other than if he should mutilate himself and desert to their side. So, counting himself little, he maltreated his own body in a manner which could not be cured; for he cut off his nose and his ears, and shaved his hair round in an unseemly way, and scourged himself, and so entered the presence of Dareios.

---

*Reference to river diversion c.538 B.C., described at 1.191; Dareios' siege began soon after his accession, c.521 B.C.

155. And Dareios was distraught when he saw the man of most repute with him thus maltreated; and leaping up from his seat he cried aloud and asked him who was the person who had mutilated him, and for what deed. He replied: "That man does not exist, except you, who has so great power as to bring me into this condition; and not any stranger, O king, has done this, but I myself to myself, accounting it a very grievous thing that the Assyrians should mock the Persians." He replied: "You most reckless of men, you set the fairest name to the foulest deed when you said that on account of those who are besieged you did bring yourself into a condition which cannot be cured. How, O senseless one, will the enemy surrender to us more quickly, because you have mutilated yourself? Surely you were out of your mind in thus destroying yourself." And he said, "If I had communicated to you that which I was about to do, you would not have permitted me to do it; but as it was, I did it on my own account. Now therefore, unless something is wanting on your part, we shall conquer Babylon: for I shall go straightway as a deserter to the wall; and I shall say to them that I suffered this treatment at your hands: and I think that when I have convinced them that this is so, I shall obtain the command of a part of their forces. On the tenth day after I shall enter within the wall take of those troops who are dispensible and set a thousand by the gate of the city which is called the gate of Semiramis; and after this again on the seventeenth day set, please, two thousand by the gate which is called the gate of the Ninevites; and after this seventh day let twenty days elapse, and then lead other four thousand and place them by the gate called the gate of the Chaldeans: and let neither the former men nor these have any weapons to defend them except daggers, but this weapon let them have. Then after the twentieth day at once bid the rest of the army make an attack on the wall all round, and set the Persians, please, by those gates which are called the gate of Belos and the gate of Kissia. As I think, when I have displayed great deeds, the Babylonians will entrust to me, besides their other things, also the keys which draw the bolts of the gates. After that it shall be up to me and the Persians to do what has to be done."

156. Having given these instructions he proceeded to the gate of the city, turning to look behind him as he went, as if he were in truth a deserter; and those who were set over that part of the wall, seeing him from the towers ran down, and slightly opening one wing of the gate asked who he was, and for what purpose he had come. And he addressed them and said that he was Zopyros, and that he came as a deserter to them. The gate-keepers accordingly when they heard this led him to the public assembly of the Babylonians; and being introduced before it he began to lament his fortunes, saying that he had suffered at the hands of Dareios that which he had in fact suffered at his own, and that he had suffered this because he had counselled the king to withdraw his army, since in truth there seemed to be no means of taking the town: "And now," he went on to say, "I am come for very great good to you, O Babylonians, but for very great evil to Dareios and his army, and to the Persians, for he shall surely not escape with impunity for having thus maltreated me; and I know all the courses of his counsels."

157. Thus he spoke, and the Babylonians, when they saw the man of most reputation among the Persians deprived of nose and ears and smeared over with blood from scourging, supposing assuredly that he was speaking the truth and had come to help, were ready to put in his power that for which he asked them, and he asked them that he might command a certain force. When he had obtained this from them, he did that which he had agreed with Dareios that he would do; for he led out on the tenth day the army of the Babylonians, and having surrounded the thousand men whom he had enjoined Dareios first to set there, he slew them. The Babylonians accordingly, perceiving that the deeds which he displayed were in accordance with his words, were extremely delighted and were ready to serve him in all things. After the lapse of the days which had been agreed upon, he again chose men of the Babylonians and led them out and slew the two thousand men of the troops of Dareios. Seeing this deed also, all the Babylonians had the name of Zopyros upon their tongues and were loud in his praise. He then again, after the lapse of the days which had been agreed upon, led them out to the place appointed, and surrounded the four thousand and slew them. When this also had been done, Zopyros was everything among the Babylonians, and he was appointed both commander of their army and guardian of their walls.

158. But when Dareios made an attack according to the agreement on every side of the wall, then Zopyros discovered all his craft: for while the Babylonians, having gone up on the wall, were defending themselves against the attacks of the army of Dareios, Zopyros opened the gates called the gates of Kissia and of Belos, and let the Persians pass within the wall. And of the Babylonians those who saw that which was done fled to the temple of Zeus Belos, but those who did not see remained each in his own appointed place, until at last they also learnt that they had been betrayed.

159. Thus was Babylon conquered for the second time: and Dareios when he had overcome the Babylonians, first took away the wall from round their city and pulled down all the gates; for when Cyrus took Babylon before this, he did neither of these things. Secondly Dareios impaled the leading men to the number of about three thousand, but to the rest of the Babylonians he gave back their city to dwell in. To provide that the Babylonians should have wives, in order that their race might be propagated, Dareios did as follows (for their own wives, as has been declared at the beginning, the Babylonians had suffocated, anticipating their need of food):—he ordered the nations who dwelt round to bring women to Babylon, fixing a certain number for each nation, so that the sum total of fifty thousand women was brought together, and from these women the present Babylonians are descended.

160. As for Zopyros, in the judgment of Dareios no one of the Persians surpassed him in good service, either of those who came after or of those who had gone before, excepting Cyrus alone; for to Cyrus no man of the Persians ever yet ventured to compare himself. Dareios is said to have declared often that he would rather that Zopyros were free from the injury than that he should have twenty Babylons added to his possession in addition to that one which he had. Moreover he gave him great honours; for not only did he give him every year those things which by the Persians are accounted the most honourable, but also he granted him Babylon to rule free from tribute, so long as he should live; and he added many other gifts. The son of this Zopyros was Megabyzos, who was made commander in Egypt against the Athenians and their allies; and the son of this Megabyzos was Zopyros, who went over to Athens as a deserter from the Persians.*

---

*Around 440 B.C.; perhaps Zopyros was Herodotus' source for many Persian narratives.

BOOK IV

SCYTHIA AND DAREIOS' FAILURE, NORTH AFRICA

1. AFTER BABYLON HAD BEEN taken, the march of Dareios himself* against the Scythians took place: for now that Asia was flourishing in respect of population, and large sums were being gathered as revenue, Dareios formed the desire to take vengeance upon the Scythians, because they had first invaded the Median land and had overcome in fight those who opposed them; and thus they had been the beginners of wrong. The Scythians in truth, as I have before said, had ruled over Upper [or Eastern] Asia for eight-and-twenty years;† for they had invaded Asia in their pursuit of the Kimmerians, and they had deposed the Medes from their rule, who had rule over Asia before the Scythians came. Now when the Scythians had been absent from their own land for eight-and-twenty years, they were returning to it when they were met by a task not less severe than that which they had had with the Medes, since they found a large army opposing them. For the wives of the Scythians, because their husbands were absent for a long time, had associated with the slaves.

2. Now the Scythians put out the eyes of all their slaves because of the milk which they drink. They get the milk thus:—they take blow-pipes of bone just like flutes, and these they insert in the vagina of the mare and blow with their mouths, and others milk while they blow: and they say that they do this because the veins of the mare are thus filled, being blown out, and so the udder is let down. When they have drawn the milk they pour it into wooden vessels hollowed out, and they set the blind slaves in order around the vessels and agitate the milk. Then that which comes to the top they skim off, considering it the more valuable part, whereas they esteem that which settles down to be less good. For this reason‡ the Scythians put out the eyes of all whom they catch; for they are not tillers of the soil but nomads. **3.** From their slaves and from their wives had been born and bred up a generation of young men, who having learnt the manner of their birth set themselves to oppose the Scythians as they were returning from the Medes. And first they cut off their land by digging a broad trench extending from the Tauric mountains to the Maiotian lake, at the point where this is broadest; then afterwards when the Scythians attempted to invade the land, they took up a position against

---

*The Scythian expedition occurred c.515 B.C.
†At 1.106 Herodotus describes the rise and fall of this Scythian empire.
‡The lack of logic suggests that something has dropped out of the manuscripts.

them and fought; and as they fought many times, and the Scythians were not able to get any advantage in the fighting, one of them said: "What a thing is this that we are doing, Scythians! We are fighting against our own slaves, and we are not only becoming fewer in number ourselves by being slain in battle, but also we are killing them, and so we shall have fewer to rule over in future. Now therefore I suggest that we leave spears and bows and that each one take his horse-whip and go up close to them: for so long as they saw us with arms in our hands, they thought themselves equal to us and of equal birth; but when they shall see that we have whips instead of arms, they will perceive that they are our slaves, and having acknowledged this they will not await our onset." **4.** The Scythians proceeded to follow his advice and the others being panic-stricken by their actions forgot their fighting and fled. Thus the Scythians had ruled over Asia; and in such manner, when they were driven out again by the Medes, they had returned to their own land. For this Dareios wished to have vengeance, and was gathering an army against them.

5. Now the Scythians say* that their nation is the youngest of all nations, and that this is how that came to pass:—The first man who ever existed in this region, which then was desert, was one Targitaos: and of this Targitaos they say, though I do not believe it for my part, the parents were Zeus and the daughter of the river Borysthenes. Targitaos, they report, was produced from some such origin as this, and of him were begotten three sons, Lipoxaïs and Arpoxaïs and the youngest Colaxaïs. In the reign of these there came down from heaven certain things wrought of gold, a plough, a yoke, a battle-axe, and a cup, and fell in the Scythian land. First the eldest saw and came near them, desiring to take them, but the gold blazed with fire when he approached it: then when he had gone away from it, the second approached, and again it did the same thing. These then the gold repelled by blazing with fire; but when the third and youngest came up to it, the flame was quenched, and he carried them to his own house. The elder brothers then, acknowledging the significance of this thing, delivered the whole of the kingly power to the youngest.

6. From Lipoxaïs, they say, are descended those Scythians who are called the race of the Auchatai; from the middle brother Arpoxaïs those who are called Catiaroi and Traspians, and from the youngest of them the "Royal" tribe, who are called Paralatai: and the whole together are called, they say, Scolotoi, after the name of their king; but the Hellenes gave them the name of Scythians. **7.** Thus the Scythians say they were produced; and from the time of their origin, that is to say from the first king Targitaos, to the passing over of Dareios against them, they say is a period of a thousand years and no more. Now this sacred gold is guarded by the kings with the utmost care, and they visit it every year with solemn sacrifices of

*The Scythian account or *logos* balances in many ways the Egyptian *logos* (and the following African *logos*); in other ways, the Scythians anticipate the Greeks.

propitiation: moreover if any one goes to sleep while watching in the open
air over this gold during the festival, the Scythians say that he does not live
out the year; and there is given him for this so much land as he shall ride
round himself on his horse in one day. Now as the land was large, Colaxaïs,
they say, established three kingdoms for his sons; and of these he made
one larger than the rest, and in this the gold is kept. But as to the upper
parts which lie on the North side of those who dwell above this land, they
say one can neither see nor pass through any further by reason of feathers
which are poured down; for both the earth and the air are full of feathers,
and this shuts off the view.*

8. Thus say the Scythians about themselves and about the region above
them; but the Hellenes who dwell about the Pontus say as follows:—
Heracles driving the cattle of Geryon came to this land, then desert, which
the Scythians now inhabit; and Geryon, says the tale, dwelt away from the
region of the Pontus, living in the island called by the Hellenes Erytheia,
near Gadeira which is outside the Pillars of Heracles by the Ocean.—As
to the Ocean, they say indeed that it flows round the whole earth beginning from the place of the sun-rising, but they do not prove this by facts.—
Thence Heracles came to the land now called Scythia; and as a storm came
upon him together with icy cold, he drew over him his lion's skin and went
to sleep. Meanwhile the mares harnessed in his chariot disappeared by a
miraculous chance, as they were feeding. **9.** Then when Heracles woke he
sought for them; and having gone over the whole land, at last he came to
the region which is called Hylaia; and there he found in a cave a kind of
twofold creature formed by the union of a maiden and a serpent, whose
upper parts from the buttocks upwards were those of a woman, but her
lower parts were those of a snake. Having seen her and marvelled at her,
he asked her then whether she had seen any mares straying anywhere; and
she said that she had them herself and would not give them up until he lay
with her; and Heracles lay with her on condition of receiving them. She
then tried to put off the giving back of the mares, desiring to have Heracles with her as long as possible, while he on the other hand desired to get
the mares and depart. At last she gave them back and said: "These mares
when they came hither I saved for you, and you rewarded me for saving
them; for I have by you three sons. Tell me then, what must I do with these
when they shall be grown to manhood, whether shall I settle them here,
for over this land I have power alone, or send them away to you?" She
thus asked of him, and he, they say, replied: "When you see that the boys
are grown to men, do this and you shall do right:—whichever of them you
see able to stretch this bow as I do now, and to be girded up with this belt,
him cause to be the settler of this land; but whosoever of them fails in the
deeds which I enjoin, send him forth out of the land. If you do thus, you
will both have delight yourself and perform that which has been ordered."
10. Upon this he drew one of his bows (for up to that time Heracles, they

---

*Herodotus interprets this statement at 4.31.

say, carried two) and showed her the belt, and then he delivered to her both the bow and the belt, which had at the end of its clasp a golden cup; and then he departed. She then, when her sons had been born and had grown to be men, gave them names first, calling one of them Agathyrsos and the next Gelonos and the youngest Skythes; then bearing in mind the charge given to her, she did as commanded. And two of her sons, Agathyrsos and Gelonos, not having proved themselves able to attain to the task set before them, departed from the land, being cast out by her who bore them; but Skythes the youngest of them performed the task and remained in the land. From Skythes the son of Heracles were descended, they say, the succeeding kings of the Scythians (Skythians): and they say moreover that it is by reason of the cup that the Scythians still even to this day wear cups attached to their girdles: and this habit alone his mother contrived for Skythes. Such is the story told by the Hellenes who dwell about the Pontus.

11. There is however also another story, and to this I am most inclined myself. It is to the effect that the nomad Scythians dwelling in Asia, being hard pressed in war by the Massagetai, left their abode and crossing the river Araxes came towards the Kimmerian land (for the land which now is occupied by the Scythians is said to have been in former times the land of the Kimmerians); and the Kimmerians, when the Scythians were coming against them, took counsel together, seeing that a great host was coming to fight against them; and it proved that their opinions were divided, both opinions being vehemently maintained, but the better being that of their kings. The opinion of the people was that it was necessary to depart and that they ought not to run the risk of fighting against so many, but that of the kings was to fight for their land with those who came against them. Since neither the people were willing by any means to agree to the counsel of the kings nor the kings to that of the people, the people planned to depart without fighting and to deliver up the land to the invaders, while the kings resolved to die and to be laid in their own land, and not to flee with the mass of the people, considering the many goods which they had enjoyed, and the many evils which it might be supposed would come upon them, if they fled from their native land. Having resolved upon this, they parted into two bodies, and making their numbers equal they fought with one another. When these had all been killed by one another's hands, then the Kimmerians buried them by the bank of the river Tyras (where their burial-place is still to be seen), and having buried them, then they made their way out from the land, and the Scythians when they came upon it found the land deserted of its inhabitants. **12.** And there are at the present time in the land of Scythia Kimmerian walls, and a Kimmerian ferry; and there is also a region which is called Kimmeria, and the so-called Kimmerian Bosphorus. It is known moreover that the Kimmerians, in their flight to Asia from the Scythians, also made a settlement on that peninsula on which now stands the Hellenic city of Sinopē; and it is known too that the Scythians pursued them and invaded the land of Media, having missed their way; for while the Kimmerians kept ever along by the sea in their flight, the Scythians pursued them keeping Caucasus on their right hand, until at last they invaded Media, directing their course inland. This then which has been told is another story, and it is common both to Hellenes and Barbarians.

13. Aristeas however the son of Caÿstrobios, a man of Proconnesos, said in the verses which he composed, that he came to the land of the Issedonians being possessed by Phœbus, and that beyond the Issedonians dwelt Arimaspians, a one-eyed race, and beyond these the gold-guarding griffins, and beyond them the Hyperboreans extending as far as the sea: and all these except the Hyperboreans, beginning with the Arimaspians, were continually making war on their neighbours, and the Issedonians were gradually driven out of their country by the Arimaspians and the Scythians by the Issedonians, and so the Kimmerians, who dwelt on the Southern Sea, being pressed by the Scythians left their land. Thus neither does he agree in regard to this land with the report of the Scythians.

14. As to Aristeas who composed this, I have said already whence he was; and I will tell also the tale which I heard told about him in Proconnesos and Kyzicos. They say that Aristeas, who was in birth inferior to none of the citizens, entered into a fuller's shop in Proconnesos and there died; and the fuller closed his workshop and went away to report the matter to those who were related to the dead man. And when the news had now been spread abroad about the city that Aristeas was dead, a man of Kyzicos who had come from the town of Artakē entered into controversy with those who said so, and declared that he had met him going towards Kyzicos and had spoken with him: and while he was vehement in dispute, those who were related to the dead man came to the fuller's shop with the things proper in order to take up the corpse for burial; and when the house was opened, Aristeas was not found there either dead or alive. In the seventh year after this he appeared at Proconnesos and composed those verses which are now called by the Hellenes the *Arimaspeia,* and having composed them he disappeared the second time.*

15. So much is told by these cities. What follows I know happened to the people of Metapontion in southern Italy two hundred and forty years after the second disappearance of Aristeas, as I found by putting together the evidence at Proconnesos and Metapontion. The people of Metapontion say that Aristeas himself appeared in their land and bade them set up an altar of Apollo and place by its side a statue bearing the name of Aristeas of Proconnesos; for he told them that to their land alone of all the Hellenic Italiotes Apollo had come. He, who now was Aristeas, was then a raven when he accompanied the god. Having said this he disappeared; and the Metapontines say that they sent to Delphi and asked the god what the

---

*Aristeas' narratives include elements of Asiatic shamanism like bilocation (the ability to be in two places at one time) and metamorphosis.

apparition of the man meant. The Pythian prophetess bade them obey the command, and told them that if they obeyed, it would be the better for them. They therefore performed the commands; and there stands a statue now bearing the name of Aristeas close to the altar dedicated to Apollo, and round it stand laurel trees. The altar is set up in the market-place. Let this suffice for Aristeas.

16. Now of the land about which this history has been begun, no one knows dependably what lies beyond it. I cannot learn of any one who alleges that he knows as an eye-witness; and even Aristeas, the man I mentioned just now, did not allege, although he was composing mere verse, that he went further than the Issedonians. Beyond them he spoke by hearsay, and reported that it was the Issedonians who said these things. So far however as we were able to arrive at something dependable by hearsay, carrying inquiries as far as possible, all this shall be told.

17. Beginning with the trading station of the Borysthenites,*—for of the parts along the sea this is the central point of all Scythia,—the first regions are occupied by the Callipidai, who are Hellenic Scythians; and above these is another race, who are called Alazonians. These last and the Callipidai in all other respects have the same customs as the Scythians, but they both sow wheat and use it as food, and also onions, leeks, lentils and millet. Above the Alazonians dwell Scythians who till the ground, and these sow their wheat not for food but to sell. Beyond them dwell the Neuroi; and beyond the Neuroi towards the North is a region without inhabitants, so far as we know. **18.** These races are along the river Hypanis to the West of the Borysthenes; but after crossing the Borysthenes,† first from the sea-coast is Hylaia, and beyond this as one goes up the river dwell agricultural Scythians, whom the Hellenes who live upon the river Hypanis call Borysthenites, calling themselves at the same time citizens of Olbia. These agricultural Scythians occupy the region which extends Eastwards for a distance of three days' journey,‡ reaching to a river which is called Panticapes, and Northwards for a distance of eleven days' sail up the Borysthenes. Then immediately beyond these begin the empty lands and extends for a great distance; and on the other side of the empty lands dwell the Androphagoi,§ a race apart by themselves and having no connection with the Scythians. To the North then begins a region which is really uninhabited and has no race of men in it, so far as we know. **19.** The region which lies to the East of these agricultural Scythians, after one has crossed the river Panticapes, is occupied by nomad Scythians, who neither sow anything nor plough the earth; and this whole region is bare of trees except Hylaia. These nomads

*The Milesian colony of Olbia, founded c.647 B.C.
†The modern Dnieper; the Hypanis is probably the Bug.
‡About 70 miles.
§"The Man-Eaters."

occupy a country which extends to the river Gerros, a distance of fourteen* days' journey Eastwards. **20.** Then on the other side of the Gerros
we have those parts which are called the "Royal" lands and those Scythians who are the bravest and most numerous and who consider the other
Scythians their slaves. These reach Southwards to the Tauric land, and
Eastwards to the trench which those who were begotten of the blind
slaves dug, and to the trading station which is called Cremnoi upon the
Maiotian lake; and some parts of their country reach to the river Tanaïs.
Beyond the Royal Scythians towards the North dwell the Melanchlainoi,
of a different race and not Scythian. The region beyond the Melanchlainoi
is marshy and not inhabited, so far as we know.

21. After one has crossed the river Tanaïs† the country is no longer
Scythia, but the first of the divisions belongs to the Sauromatai, who beginning at the corner of the Maiotian lake occupy land extending towards
the North Wind fifteen days' journey, and wholly bare of trees both cultivated and wild. Above these, holding the next division of land, dwell the
Budinoi, who occupy a land wholly overgrown with forest consisting of all
kinds of trees. **22.** Then beyond the Budinoi towards the North, first there
is desert for seven days' journey; and after the desert turning aside somewhat more towards the East Wind we come to land occupied by the Thyssagetai, a numerous people and of separate race from the others. These
live by hunting; and bordering upon them in these same regions are men
called Iyrcai, who also live by hunting, which they practise in the following
manner:—the hunter climbs up a tree and lies in wait there for his game
(now trees are abundant in all this country), and each has a horse at hand,
which has been taught to lie down upon its belly in order that it may make
itself low, and also a dog: and when he sees the wild animal from the tree,
he first shoots his arrow and then mounts upon his horse and pursues it,
and the dog seizes hold of it. Above these in a direction towards the East
dwell other Scythians, who have revolted from the Royal Scythians and so
have come to this region.

23. As far as the country of these Scythians the whole land which has
been described is level plain and has a deep soil; but after this point it is
stony and rugged. Then when one has passed through a great extent of this
rugged country, there dwell in the skirts of lofty mountains men who are
said to be all bald-headed from their birth, male and female equally, and
who have flat noses and large chins and speak a language of their own, using the Scythian manner of dress, and living on the produce of trees. The
tree on the fruit of which they live is called the Pontic tree, and it is about
the size of a fig-tree: this bears a fruit the size of a bean, containing a stone.
When the fruit has ripened, they strain it through cloths and there flows
from it a thick black juice, and this juice which flows from it is called

*"Four" fits the facts better, and some editors emend.
†The modern Don.

*as-chy.** This they either lick up or drink mixed with milk, and from its lees, that is the solid part, they make cakes and use them for food; for they have not many cattle, since the pastures there are by no means good. Each man has his dwelling under a tree, in winter covering the tree all round with close white felt-cloth, and in summer without it. These are injured by no men, for they are said to be sacred, and they possess no weapon of war. These decide the disputes arising among their neighbours; and besides this, whatsoever fugitive takes refuge with them is injured by no one and they are called Argippaians.

24. Now as far as these bald-headed men there is abundantly clear information about the land and about the nations on this side of them; for not only do certain of the Scythians go to them, from whom it is not difficult to get information, but also some of the Hellenes who are at the trading-station of the Borysthenes and the other trading-places of the Pontic coast. The Scythians who go to them transact their business through seven interpreters and in seven different languages. **25.** So far as these, I say, the land is known; but concerning the region to the North of the bald-headed men no one can speak with certainty, for lofty and impassable mountains divide it off, and no one passes over them. However these bald-headed men say (though I do not believe it) that the mountains are inhabited by men with goats' feet; and that after one has passed beyond these, others are found who sleep through six months of the year. This I do not admit at all as true. However, the country to the East of the bald-headed men is known with certainty, being inhabited by the Issedonians, but that which lies North beyond both the bald-headed men and the Issedonians is unknown, except so far as we know it from the accounts given by these nations just mentioned.

26. The Issedonians are said to have these customs:—when a man's father is dead, all the relations bring cattle to the house, and then having slain them and cut up the flesh, they cut up also the dead body of the father of their entertainer, and mixing all the flesh together they set forth a banquet. His skull however they strip of the flesh and clean it out and then gild it over, and after that they deal with it as a sacred relic and perform for the dead man great sacrifices every year. This each son does for his father, just as the Hellenes keep the day of memorial for the dead. In other respects however this race too is said to live righteously, and their women have equal rights with the men. **27.** These then also are known; but as to the region beyond them, it is the Issedonians who report there one-eyed men and gold-guarding griffins. Scythians report this having received it from them, and from the Scythians we, that is the rest of mankind, have got our belief. We call them in Scythian language Arimaspians, for the Scythians call the number one *arima* and the eye *spu*.

28. This whole land is so exceedingly severe in climate, that for eight

---

*The wild-cherry; Herodotus describes physical characteristics, language, and customs, but not (here) religion.

months of the year there is frost so hard as to be intolerable; and during these if you pour out water you will not be able to make mud, but only if you kindle a fire can you make it. The sea also is frozen and the whole of the Kimmerian Bosphorus, so that the Scythians who are settled within the trench* make expeditions and drive their waggons over into the country of the Sindians. Thus it continues to be winter for eight months, and even for the remaining four it is cold in those parts. This winter is distinguished in its character from all the winters in other parts of the world; for there is no rain to speak of at the usual season for rain, whereas in summer it rains continually; and thunder does not come at the time when it comes in other countries, but is very frequent in the summer; and if thunder comes in winter, it is marvelled at as a prodigy. Just so, if an earthquake happens, whether in summer or in winter, it is accounted a prodigy in Scythia. Horses are able to endure this winter, but neither mules nor asses can endure it at all, whereas in other countries horses if they stand in frost lose their limbs by mortification, while asses and mules endure it. **29.** I think also that it is for this reason that the hornless breed of oxen in that country have no horns growing; and there is a verse of Homer in the *Odyssey*† supporting my opinion, which runs thus:—

"Also the Libyan land, where the sheep very quickly grow hornèd,"

for it is rightly said that in hot regions the horns come quickly, whereas in extreme cold the animals either have no horns growing at all, or hardly any.

30. In that land then this results from the cold; but (since my history proceeded from the first seeking occasions for additions) I feel wonder that in the whole land of Elis mules cannot be bred, though that region is not cold, nor is there any other evident cause. The Eleians themselves say that in consequence of some curse mules are not begotten in their land; but when the time approaches for the mares to conceive, they drive them out into the neighbouring lands and there in the land of their neighbours they allow to them the he-asses until the mares are pregnant, and then they drive them back.

31. As to the feathers, the Scythians say that the air is full of them, and that they render them unable either to see or to pass through the further parts of the continent, but I think this:—in the parts beyond this land it snows continually, though less in summer than in winter, as might be supposed. Now whosoever has seen close at hand snow falling thickly, knows what I mean without further explanation, for the snow is like feathers. On account of this wintry weather, the Northern parts of this continent are uninhabitable. I think therefore that by the feathers the Scythians and those who dwell near them mean to suggest the snow. This then goes to the furthest reaches of the accounts given.

---

*See 4.3 and 4.20; the Tauris is the modern Crimea.
†*Odyssey* 4.85, where Menelaos reminisces about his African odyssey.

32. About a Hyperborean* people the Scythians report nothing, nor do any others who dwell in this region, unless indeed it be the Issedonians. In my opinion neither do these report anything; for if they did the Scythians also would report it, as they do about the one-eyed people. Hesiod however has spoken of Hyperboreans, and so also has Homer in the poem of the "Epigonoi," or "Successors," at least if Homer was really the composer of that Epic. **33.** But much more about them is reported by the people of Delos than by any others. For these say that sacred offerings bound up in wheat straw are carried from the land of the Hyperboreans and come to the Scythians, and then from the Scythians the neighbouring nations in succession receive them and convey them Westwards, finally as far as the Adriatic: thence they are sent forward towards the South, and the people of Dodona receive them first of all the Hellenes, and from these they come down to the Malian gulf and are passed over to Eubœa, where city sends them on to city till they come to Carystos. After this Andros is left out, for the Carystians are those who bring them to Tenos, and the Tenians to Delos. Thus they say that these sacred offerings come to Delos; but at first, they say, the Hyperboreans sent two maidens bearing the sacred offerings, whose names, say the Delians, were Hyperochē and Laodikē, and with them for their protection the Hyperboreans sent five men of their nation to attend them, those namely who are now called *Perphereës* and have great honours paid to them in Delos. Since however the Hyperboreans found that those who were sent away did not return back, they were troubled to think that it would always befall them to send and not to receive back; and so they bore the offerings to the borders of their land bound up in wheat straw, and laid a charge upon their neighbours, bidding them send these forward from themselves to another nation. These things then, they say, come to Delos being thus sent forward; and I know of my own knowledge of similar offerings, namely that the women of Thrace and Paionia, when they sacrifice to Artemis "the Queen," do not make their offerings without wheat straw.
34. These I know do this; and for those maidens from the Hyperboreans, who died in Delos, both the girls and the boys of the Delians cut off their hair: the former before marriage cut off a lock and having wound it round a spindle lay it upon the tomb (now the tomb is on the left hand as one goes into the temple of Artemis, and over it grows an olive-tree), and all the boys of the Delians wind some of their hair about a green shoot of some tree, and they also place it upon the tomb. **35.** The maidens have this honour paid them by the dwellers in Delos. The same people say that Argē and Opis also, being maidens, came to Delos, passing from the Hyperboreans by the same nations which have been mentioned, even before Hyperochē and Laodikē. These last, they say, came bearing for Eileithuia the tribute which they had laid upon themselves for the speedy birth of Artemis and Apollo, but Argē and Opis came with the divinities them-

---

*"Ultra-Northerners" are noble savages in Greek myth.

selves, and other honours have been assigned to them by the people of Delos. The women, they say, collect for them, naming them by their names in the hymn which Olen a man of Lykia composed in their honour; and both the natives of the other islands and the Ionians have learnt from them to sing hymns naming Opis and Argē and collecting. This Olen came from Lykia and composed also the other ancient hymns which are sung in Delos. Moreover they say that when the thighs of the victim are consumed upon the altar, the ashes of them are cast upon the grave of Opis and Argē. Now their grave is behind the temple of Artemis, turned towards the East, close to the banqueting hall of the Keïans.

36. Let this suffice for the Hyperboreans. The tale of Abaris, who is reported to have been a Hyperborean, I do not tell, how he carried the arrow about over all the earth, eating no food. If however there are any Hyperboreans, it follows that there are also Hypernotians; and I laugh when I see that, though many before this have drawn maps of the Earth, yet no one has set the matter forth in an intelligent way; seeing that they draw Ocean flowing round the Earth, which is circular exactly as if drawn with compasses, and they make Asia equal in size to Europe. In a few words I shall declare the size of each division and of what nature it is as regards outline.

37. The Persians inhabit Asia extending to the Southern Sea, which is called the Erythraian; and above these towards the North dwell the Medes, and above the Medes the Saspeirians, and above the Saspeirians the Colchians, extending to the Northern Sea,[*] into which the river Phasis runs. These four nations inhabit from sea to sea. **38.** From them Westwards two peninsulas stretch out from Asia into the sea, and these I will describe. The first peninsula on the one of its sides, that is the Northern, stretches along beginning from the Phasis and extending to the sea, going along the Pontus and the Hellespont as far as Sigeion in the land of Troy; and on the Southern side the same peninsula stretches from the Myriandrian gulf, which lies near Phenicia, in the direction of the sea as far as the headland Triopion; and in this peninsula dwell thirty races of men.[†] **39.** This then is one of the peninsulas, and the other beginning from the land of the Persians stretches along to the Erythraian Sea, including Persia and next after it Assyria, and Arabia after Assyria: and this ends, or rather is commonly supposed to end, at the Arabian gulf, into which Dareios conducted a channel from the Nile. Now in the line stretching to Phenicia from the land of the Persians the country is broad and the space abundant, but after Phenicia this peninsula goes by the shore of our Sea along Palestine, Syria, and Egypt, where it ends; and in it there are three nations only. **40.** These are the parts of Asia which tend towards the West from the Persian land; but as to those which lie beyond the Persians and Medes and Saspeirians and Colchians towards the East

---

and the sunrising, on one side the Erythraian Sea runs along by them, and
on the North both the Caspian Sea and the river Araxes, which flows towards the rising sun: and Asia is inhabited as far as the Indian land; but
from this onwards towards the East it becomes uninhabited, nor can any
one say what manner of land it is.

41. Such and so large is Asia: and Libya is included in the second peninsula; for after Egypt Libya succeeds at once. Now about Egypt this peninsula is narrow, for from our Sea to the Erythraian Sea extend 100,000
fathoms, which would amount to 115 miles; but after this narrow part, the
portion of the peninsula which is called Libya* is extremely broad.

42. I wonder then at those who have parted off and divided the world
into Libya, Asia, and Europe, since the difference between these is not
small; for in length Europe extends along by both, while in breadth it
is clear to me that it is beyond comparison larger, for Libya furnishes
proofs about itself that it is surrounded by sea, except so much of it as borders upon Asia; and this fact was shown by Necōs king of the Egyptians
first about whom we know. He when he had ceased digging the channel[†]
which goes through from the Nile to the Arabian gulf, sent Phenicians
with ships, bidding them sail and come back through the Pillars of Heracles to the Northern Sea and so to Egypt. The Phenicians therefore set
forth from the Erythraian Sea and sailed through the Southern Sea; and
when autumn came, they would put to shore and sow the land, wherever in
Libya they might happen to be as they sailed, and then they waited for the
harvest: and having reaped the grain they would sail on, so that after two
years had elapsed, in the third year they turned through the Pillars of Heracles and arrived again in Egypt. And they reported a thing which I cannot
believe, but another man may, namely that in sailing round Libya[‡] they
had the sun on their right hand.

43. Thus did this country first become known, and after this the
Carthaginians make report of it; for as to Sataspes the son of Teaspis
the Achaimenid, he did not sail round Libya, though he was sent for this
very purpose, but was struck with fear by the length of the voyage and the
uninhabited land, and so returned and did not accomplish the task which
his mother laid upon him. For this man had raped a daughter of Zopyros
the son of Megabyzos, a virgin; and then when he was about to be impaled by order of king Xerxes for this offence, the mother of Sataspes,
who was a sister of Dareios, entreated for his life, saying that she would
herself lay upon him a greater penalty than Xerxes. He should be compelled (she said) to sail round Libya, until in sailing round it he came to
the Arabian gulf. So then Xerxes having agreed upon these terms, Sataspes went to Egypt, and obtaining a ship and sailors from the Egyptians,

---

*The Greek name for the continent that we call Africa.
†See 2.158 for the tale.
‡Sailing west at the Cape of Good Hope; Herodotus rejects the story but supplies
good evidence for its truth, describing the sun's position south of the Equator.

he sailed to the Pillars of Heracles; and having sailed through them and turned the point of Libya which is called the promontory of Soloeis, he sailed on towards the South. Then after he had passed over much sea in many months, as there was needed ever more and more voyaging, he turned about and sailed back again to Egypt. Returning to king Xerxes, he reported that at the furthest point which he reached he was sailing by dwarfish people,* who used clothing made from the palm-tree, and who, whenever they came to land with their ship, left their towns and fled away to the mountains: and they, he said, did no injury when they entered into the towns, but took food from them only. And the cause, he said, why he had not completely sailed round Libya was that the ship could not advance any further but stuck fast.† Xerxes however did not believe that he was speaking the truth, and since he had not performed the appointed task, he impaled him, inflicting upon him the penalty pronounced before. A eunuch belonging to this Sataspes ran away to Samos as soon as he heard that his master was dead, carrying with him large sums of money; and of this a man of Samos took possession, whose name I know, but I purposely pass it over without mention.‡

44. The greater part of Asia was explored by Dareios, who desiring to know of the river Indus, which is the second most prolific river for producing crocodiles of all rivers,—to know, I say, of this river where it runs into the sea, he sent with ships others whom he trusted to speak the truth, and Skylax also, a man of Caryanda. These starting from the city of Caspatyros and the land of Pactyïkē, sailed down the river towards the East and the sunrise to the sea; and then sailing over the sea Westwards they came in the thirtieth month to that place from whence the king of the Egyptians had sent out the Phenicians of whom I spoke before, to sail round Libya. After these had made their voyage round the coast, Dareios both subdued the Indians and his troops sailed this sea. Thus Asia also, excepting the parts of it which are towards the rising sun, has been found to be similar to Libya in size and sea boundaries.

45. As to Europe however, it is clearly not known by any, either as regards the parts which are towards the rising sun or those towards the North, whether it be surrounded by sea: but in length it is known to stretch along by both the other divisions. And I cannot conceive why to the Earth, which is one, three different names are given derived from women, and why there were set as boundaries to divide it the river Nile of Egypt and the Phasis in Colchis (or as some say the Maiotian river Tanaïs and the Kimmerian ferry). Nor can I learn who made the boundaries, or for what reason they gave the names. Libya indeed is said by most of the Hellenes to have its name from Libya a woman of the country, and Asia from the wife of Prometheus: but

---

*The pygmies are also mentioned at 2.32.
†Probably an accurate reference to the trade winds.
‡Such deliberate omissions (compare 1.51) reflect the celebratory purpose of the *Histories*.

this last name is claimed by the Lydians, who say that Asia has been called after Asias the son of Cotys the son of Manes, and not from Asia the wife of Prometheus; and from him too they say the Asian tribe in Sardis has its name. As to Europe however, it is neither known by any man whether it is surrounded by sea, nor does it appear whence it got this name or who gave it, unless we shall say that the land received its name from Europa the Tyrian; and if so, it would appear that before this it was nameless like the rest. She however evidently belongs to Asia and did not come to this land which is now called by the Hellenes Europe, but only from Phenicia to Crete, and from Crete to Lykia. Let this suffice now for these matters; for we will adopt commonly accepted names.

46. Now the region of the Euxine upon which Dareios was preparing to march has, apart from the Scythian race, the most ignorant nations. We can neither put forward any nation of those who dwell within the region of Pontus as eminent in cleverness, nor do we know of any man of learning having arisen there, apart from the Scythian nation and Anacharsis.* By the Scythian race one most important problem has been solved most cleverly of men of whom we know; but in other respects I am not impressed with them. That most important discovery is such that none can escape again who has come to attack them, and if they do not desire to be found, it is not possible to catch them. They who have neither cities founded nor walls built, but carry their houses with them and are mounted archers, living not by the plough but by cattle, and whose dwellings are upon cars, these assuredly are invincible and impossible to approach. **47.** This they have found out, seeing that their land is suitable to it and at the same time the rivers are their allies: for first this land is plain land and is grassy and well watered, and then rivers flow through it not much fewer than the canals in Egypt. I will name the noteworthy and those navigable from the sea, Ister with five mouths, and after this Tyras, Hypanis, Borysthenes, Panticapes, Hypakyris, Gerros and Tanaïs. These flow thus.

48. The Ister,† which is the greatest of all the rivers which we know,‡ flows always with equal volume in summer and winter alike. It is the Westernmost of all the Scythian rivers, and it has become the greatest because other rivers flow into it. And these five make it great flowing through the Scythian land, namely that which the Scythians call Porata and the Hellenes Pyretos, and besides this, Tiarantos and Araros and Naparis and Ordessos. The first-mentioned of these is a great river lying towards the East, and there it joins waters with the Ister, the second Tiarantos is more to the West and smaller, and the Araros and Naparis and Ordessos flow into the Ister going between these two. **49.** These are the native Scythian rivers which join to swell its stream, while from the Agathyrsians flows the Maris and joins the Ister, and from the summits of Haimos flow three other great

---

*Herodotus rejects Greek theories of the "noble savages."
†The Danube.
‡At least 20 rivers are now known to be longer than the Danube.

rivers towards the North and fall into it, namely Atlas and Auras and Tibisis. Through Thrace and the Thracian Crobyzians flow the rivers Athrys and Noēs and Artanes, running into the Ister; and from the Paionians and Mount Rhodopē the river Kios, cutting through Mount Haimos in the midst, runs into it also. From the Illyrians the river Angros flows Northwards and runs out into the Triballian plain and into the river Brongos, and the Brongos flows into the Ister; thus the Ister receives both these, being great rivers. From the region which is North of the Ombricans, the river Carpis and another river, the Alpis, flow also towards the North into it; for the Ister flows in fact through the whole of Europe, beginning in the land of the Keltoi, who after the Kynesians dwell furthest towards the sunset of all Europeans; and thus flowing through all Europe it falls into the sea by the side of Scythia.

50. So then these named rivers and many others join their waters together make Ister the greatest of rivers; since if we compare the single streams, the Nile is superior in volume of water; for into this no river or spring flows, to contribute to its volume. And the Ister flows at an equal level always both in summer and in winter for some such cause as this, as I suppose. In winter it is of the natural size, or becomes only a little larger than its nature, seeing that this land receives very little rain in winter, but constantly has snow; whereas in summer the snow which fell in the winter, in quantity abundant, melts and runs from all parts into the Ister. This snow running into the river helps to swell its volume, and with it also many and violent showers of rain, for it rains during the summer. Thus the waters which mingle with the Ister are more copious in summer than they are in winter by about as much as the water which the Sun draws to himself in summer exceeds that which he draws in winter; and by the setting of these things against one another there is produced a balance; so that the river seems in fact to be of equal volume always.

51. Second after the Ister comes the Tyras,* which starts from the North and begins its course from a large lake which is the boundary between the land of the Scythians and that of the Neuroi. At its mouth are settled those Hellenes who are called Tyritai.

52. The third river is the Hypanis,† which starts from Scythia and flows from a great lake round which feed white wild horses; and this lake is rightly called "Mother of Hypanis." From this then the river Hypanis takes its rise and for a distance of five days' sail it flows shallow and with sweet water still; but from this point on towards the sea for four days' sail it is very bitter, for there flows into it the water of a bitter spring, which is so exceedingly bitter that, small as it is, it changes the water of the Hypanis by mingling with it, though few are equal in greatness to that river. This spring is on the border between the lands of the agricultural Scythians and of the Alazonians, and the name of the spring and of the place from which it

---

*The Dniester.
†The Bug; Herodotus describes the three rivers in a west, north, east order.

flows is in Scythian Exampaios, and in the Hellenic tongue Hierai Hodoi or "Sacred Ways." Now the Tyras and the Hypanis approach one another in their windings in the land of the Alazonians, but after this each turns off and widens the space between them as they flow.

53. Fourth is the river Borysthenes, which is both the largest of these after the Ister, and also in our opinion the most serviceable not only of Scythian but also of all the world's rivers besides, excepting only the Nile of Egypt, for to this no river compares. The Borysthenes provides both pastures which are the fairest and the richest for cattle, and fish which are better by far and more numerous than those of any other river, and also it is the sweetest water to drink and flows with clear stream, though others beside it are turbid, and along its banks crops are produced better than elsewhere, while in parts where it is not sown, grass grows deeper. Moreover at its mouth salt forms in abundance, and it produces also huge fish without spines, sturgeon which they call *antacaioi,* to be used for salting, and many other things worthy of wonder. Now as far up as the Gerrians, a voyage of forty days, the Borysthenes is known to flow from the North; but above this none can tell through what nations it flows. It certainly runs through uninhabited territory to the land of the agricultural Scythians; for these Scythians dwell along its banks for a distance of ten days' sail. Of this river alone and of the Nile I cannot tell where the sources are, nor, I think, can any of the Hellenes. When the Borysthenes comes near the sea in its course, the Hypanis mingles with it, running out into the same marsh. The space between these two rivers, which is as it were a beak of land, is called the point of Hippoles, and in it is placed a temple of Kybele the Mother, and opposite the temple upon the river Hypanis are settled the Borsythenites.

54. This is known about these rivers; and after these comes a fifth river besides, called Panticapes. This also flows both from the North and from a lake, and in the space between this river and the Borysthenes dwell the agricultural Scythians: it runs out into the region of Hylaia, and having passed by this it mingles with the Borysthenes. **55.** Sixth comes the river Hypakyris, which starts from a lake, and flowing through the midst of the nomad Scythians runs out into the sea by the city of Carkinitis, skirting on its right bank the region of Hylaia and the so-called racecourse of Achilles.* **56.** Seventh is the Gerros, which parts off from the Borysthenes near that part of the country where the Borysthenes ceases to be known,—it parts off, I say, in this region and has the same name which this region itself has, namely Gerros; and as it flows to the sea it borders the country of the nomad and that of the Royal Scythians, and runs out into the Hypakyris. **57.** The eighth is the river Tanaïs or Don, which starts in its flow at first from a large lake, and runs out into a still larger lake called Maiotis, which is the boundary between the Royal Scythians and the Sauromatai. Into this Tanaïs falls another river, whose name is Hyrgis.

---

*An 80-mile beach parallel to the shore.

58. Such are the notable rivers with which the Scythians are provided. For cattle the grass which comes up in the land of Scythia is the most productive of bile of any grass which we know; and that this is so you may judge when you open the bodies of the cattle.

59. Thus they have abundant supply of the most important resources; their other customs are as follows. The gods whom they propitiate by worship are these only:—Hestia most of all, then Zeus and the Earth, supposing that Earth is the wife of Zeus, and after these Apollo, and Aphroditē Urania, and Heracles, and Ares. Of these all the Scythians have the worship established, and the so-called Royal Scythians sacrifice also to Poseidon. Now Hestia is called in Scythian* Tabiti, and Zeus, being most rightly named in my opinion, is called Papaios, and Earth Api, and Apollo Oitosyros, and Aphroditē Urania is called Argimpasa, and Poseidon Thagimasidas. It is not their custom however to make images, altars or temples to any except Ares, but for him it is their custom.

60. They have all the same manner of sacrifice established for all their religious rites equally, and it is thus performed:—the victim itself stands with its fore-feet tied, and the sacrificing priest stands behind the victim, and by pulling the end of the cord he throws the beast down; and as the victim falls, he calls upon the god to whom he is sacrificing, and then at once throws a noose round its neck, and putting a small stick into it he turns it round and so strangles the animal, without either lighting a fire or making any first offering from the victim or pouring any libation over it.†
When he has strangled it and flayed off the skin, he proceeds to boil it.
61. Now as the land of Scythia is exceedingly ill wooded, they contrive thus to boil the flesh:—having flayed the victims, they strip the flesh off the bones and then put it into caldrons, if they happen to have any, of native make, which very much resemble Lesbian mixing-bowls except that they are much larger,—into these they put the flesh and boil it by lighting under it the bones of the victim. If however they have no caldron, they put all the flesh into the stomachs of the victims and adding water they light the bones under them; and these blaze up beautifully, and the stomachs easily hold the flesh when it has been stripped off the bones. Thus an ox is made to boil itself, and the other kinds of victims each boil themselves also. When the flesh is boiled, the sacrificer takes a first offering of the flesh and of the vital organs and casts it in front of him. They sacrifice various kinds of cattle, but especially horses.

62. To the other gods they sacrifice thus and these kinds of beasts, but to Ares as follows:—In each district of the several tribal territories they have a temple of Ares set up in this way:—bundles of brushwood are heaped up for about 1,800 feet square, but less in height; and on the top a level square is made, and three of the sides rise sheer but by the remaining one side the pile may be ascended. Every year they pile on a hundred and

---

*Herodotus assumes an equivalency and provides the Greek "translation."
†Herodotus contrasts, as usual, native to Greek customs.

fifty waggon-loads of brushwood, for it is constantly settling down by reason of winter weather. Upon this pile of which I speak each people has
an ancient scimitar set up, and this offering represents Ares. To this scimitar they bring yearly offerings of cattle and of horses; and they have
the following sacrifice in addition, beyond what they make to the other
gods. They sacrifice one man in every hundred of all the enemies whom
they take captive in war, not as they sacrifice cattle, but in a different manner. They first pour wine over their heads, and after that they cut the
throats of the men, so that the blood runs into a bowl; and then they carry
this up to the top of the pile of brushwood and pour the blood over the
sword. Meanwhile below by the side of the temple they are doing thus:—
they cut off all the right arms of the slaughtered men with the hands and
throw them up into the air, and then when they have finished offering the
other victims, they go away; and the arm lies wheresoever it has chanced to
fall, and the corpse apart from it.* **63.** Such are the sacrifices which are established among them; but of swine these make no use, nor indeed are
they wont to keep them at all in their land.

64. That which relates to war is thus ordered with them:—When a
Scythian has slain his first man, he drinks some of his blood: and of all
those whom he slays in the battle he bears the heads to the king; for if he
has brought a head he shares in the spoil which they have taken, but otherwise not. And he takes off the skin of the head by cutting it round about
the ears and then taking hold of the scalp and shaking it off; afterwards
he scrapes off the flesh with the rib of an ox, and works the skin about
with his hands; and when he has thus kneaded it, he keeps it as a napkin
to wipe the hands upon, and hangs it from the bridle of the horse on
which he himself rides, and takes pride in it; for the man who has the
greatest number of skins to wipe the hands upon is judged to be the
bravest. Many also make cloaks to wear of the skins stripped off, sewing
them together like shepherds' coats of skins. Many take the skin together
with the finger-nails off the right hands of their enemies when they are
dead, and make them into covers for their quivers: now human skin it
seems is both thick and glossy in appearance, more brilliantly white than
almost any other skin. Many also take the skins off the whole bodies of
men and stretch them on pieces of wood and carry them about on their
horses.

65. Such are their established customs about these things; and to the
skulls themselves, not of all but of their greatest enemies, they do thus:—
the man saws off all below the eyebrows and clears out the inside; and if
he is a poor man he only stretches ox-hide round it and then makes use of
it; but if he be rich, besides stretching the ox-hide he gilds it over within,
and makes use of it as a drinking-cup. They do this also if any of their own
family have been at variance with them and the man gets the better of his
adversary in trial before the king. When strangers come to him whom he

---

*Magical practice believed to render helpless the spirit of the dead foe.

highly esteems, he sets these skulls before them, and adds the comment that people of his own family had made war against him, and that he had got the better of them; and this they hold to be a proof of manly virtue.

66. Once every year each ruler of a district mixes in his own district a bowl of wine, from which those Scythians drink who have slain enemies; but those who have not done this do not taste of this wine, but sit apart dishonoured; and this is the greatest of all disgraces among them. Those of them who have slain a very great number of men, drink with two cups together at the same time.

67. There are many diviners among the Scythians, and they divine with a number of willow rods in the following manner:—they bring large bundles of rods, and having laid them on the ground they unroll them, and setting each rod by itself apart they prophesy; and while speaking thus, they roll the rods together again, and after that they place them together on each other a second time in one bundle. This manner of divination they have from their fathers. The Enareës or "man-women"* say that Aphroditē gave them the gift of divination, and they divine accordingly with the bark of the linden-tree. Having divided the linden-bark into three strips, the man twists them together in his fingers and untwists them again, and as he does this he utters the oracle.

68. When the king of the Scythians is sick, he sends for three of the diviners who are most in repute, who divine in the manner which has been said. These say for the most part something like this, namely that so and so has sworn falsely by the hearth of the king, and they name one of the citizens, whosoever it may happen to be. The prevailing custom of the Scythians is to swear by the hearth of the king when they desire to swear the most solemn oath. He then who they say has sworn falsely, is brought in at once held fast on both sides; and when he has come the diviners charge him with this, that he is shown by their divination to have sworn falsely by the hearth of the king, and that for this reason the king is suffering pain. He denies and says that he did not swear falsely, and complains indignantly. When he denies it, the king sends for other diviners twice as many in number, and if these also by looking into their divination pronounce him guilty of having sworn falsely, at once they cut off the man's head, and the diviners who came first part his goods among them by lot; but if the diviners who came in afterwards acquit him, other diviners come in, and again others after them. If then the greater number acquit the man, the sentence is that the first diviners shall themselves be put to death.

69. They put them to death in this way:—first they fill a waggon with brushwood and yoke oxen to it; then having bound the feet of the diviners and tied their hands behind them and stopped their mouths with gags, they fasten them down in the middle of the brushwood, and having set fire to it they scare the oxen and let them go: and often the oxen are burnt to

---

death together with the diviners, and often they escape after being scorched, when the pole to which they are fastened has been burnt: and they burn diviners thus for other causes also, calling them false prophets. Now when the king puts any to death, he does not leave alive their sons either, but he puts to death all the males, not doing any hurt to the females.

70. In the following manner the Scythians make oaths to whomsoever they make them:—they pour wine into a great earthenware cup and mingle with it blood of those who are taking the oath to one another, either making a prick with an awl or cutting with a dagger a little way into their body, and then they dip into the cup a scimitar and arrows and a battle-axe and a javelin. Afterwards, they invoke many curses on the breaker of the oath, and afterwards they drink it off, both the oath-takers and the most honourable of their company.

71. The burial-place of the kings is in the land of the Gerrians, the place up to which the Borysthenes is navigable.* In this place, when their king has died, they make a large square excavation in the earth. After this is ready, they take up the corpse, once the body has been covered over with wax and the belly ripped open and cleansed, filled with cut up galingale and spices and parsley-seed and anise, and then sewn together again. Then they convey it in a waggon to another nation. Those who receive the corpse do the same as the Royal Scythians, that is they cut off a part of their ear and shave their hair round about and cut themselves all over the arms and tear their forehead and nose and pass arrows through their left hand. Thence they convey in the waggon the corpse of the king to another of the nations over whom they rule; and they to whom the corpse came before accompany them. When they have gone round to all conveying the corpse, then they are in the land of the Gerrians, who have their settlements furthest away of all the nations over whom they rule, and they have reached the spot where the burial-place is.

After that, having placed the corpse in the tomb upon a bed of leaves, they stick spears along this side and that of the corpse and stretch pieces of wood over them, and then they cover the place with matting. Then they strangle and bury in the remaining space of the tomb one of the king's mistresses, his cup-bearer, his cook, his horse-keeper, his attendant, and his bearer of messages, and also horses, and a first portion of all things else, and cups of gold; for silver they do not use at all, nor yet bronze in burial. They all join together to pile up a great mound, vying with one another and zealously endeavouring to make it as large as possible.

72. Afterwards, when the year comes round again, they do as follows:— they take the most capable of the remaining servants,—and these are native Scythians, for those serve him whom the king himself commands to do so, and his servants are not bought for money,—of these attendants then they strangle fifty and also fifty of the finest horses; and when they

---

*The tumuli of southern Russia have yielded splendid gold objects and many other artifacts that confirm Herodotus' veracity and accuracy.

have taken out their bowels and cleansed the belly, they fill it with chaff and sew it together again. Then they set the half of a wheel upon two stakes with the hollow side upwards, and the other half of the wheel upon other two stakes, and in this manner they fix a number of these; and after this they run thick stakes through the length of the horses as far as the necks, and they mount them upon the wheels; and the front pieces of wheel support the shoulders of the horses, while those behind bear up their bellies, going by the side of the thighs; and both front and hind legs hang in the air. On the horses they put bridles and bits, and stretch the bridles tight in front of them and then tie them to pegs in the ground. The fifty young men who have been strangled are mounted each one upon his horse, with a straight stake run through each body along by the spine up to the neck; and a part of this stake projects below, which they fasten in a socket made in the other stake that runs through the horse. Having set such horsemen in a circle round the tomb, they then ride away.

73. Thus they bury their kings; but as for the other Scythians, when they die their nearest relations carry them round laid in waggons to their friends in succession; and of them each one when he receives the body entertains those who accompany it, and before the corpse they serve up of all things about the same quantity as before the others. Private persons are carried about for forty days, and then they are buried: and after burying them the Scythians cleanse themselves in the following way:—they soap their heads and wash them well, and then, for their body, they set up three stakes leaning towards one another and about them they stretch woollen felt coverings, and when they have closed them as much as possible they throw stones heated red-hot into a basin placed in the middle of the stakes and the felt coverings. **74.** Now they have hemp growing in their land, which is very like flax except in thickness and in height, for in these respects the hemp is much superior.* This grows both of itself and with cultivation; and of it the Thracians even make garments, which are very like those made of flaxen thread, so that he who was not specially conversant with it would not be able to decide whether the garments were of flax or of hemp; and he who had not before seen stuff woven of hemp would suppose that the garment was made of flax.

75. The Scythians then take the seed of this hemp and creep under the felt coverings, and then they throw the seed upon the stones which have been heated red-hot: and it burns like incense and produces a vapour so thick that no vapour-bath in Hellas would surpass it: and the Scythians being delighted with the vapour-bath howl like wolves. This is to them instead of washing, for in fact they do not wash their bodies at all in water. Their women however pound with a rough stone the wood of the cypress and cedar and frankincense tree, pouring in water with it, and then with this pounded stuff, which is thick, they plaster all their body and also their

---

*The Greek word *cannabis* provides English with "canvas"; marijuana is indeed an intoxicant.

face; and not only does a sweet smell attach to them by reason of this, but also when they take off the plaster on the next day, their skin is clean and shining.

76. This nation also is very averse to adopting strange customs,* rejecting even those of other tribes among themselves and especially those of the Hellenes, as the history of Anacharsis and also afterwards of Skyles proved. Anacharsis, when he was returning to the abodes of the Scythians, after having visited many lands and displayed in them much wisdom, as he sailed through the Hellespont he put in to Kyzicos: and since he found the people of Kyzicos celebrating a festival very magnificently in honour of the Mother of the gods, Anacharsis vowed to the Mother that if he should return safe and sound to his own land, he would both sacrifice to her with the same rites as he saw the men of Kyzicos do, and also hold a night festival. So when he returned to Scythia he went down into the region called Hylaia (this is along the racecourse of Achilles and is quite full, as it happens, of trees of all kinds), and proceeded to perform all the ceremonies of the festival in honour of the goddess, with a kettledrum and with images hung about himself. And one of the Scythians perceived him doing this and declared it to Saulios the king; and the king came himself also, and when he saw Anacharsis doing this, he shot him with an arrow and killed him.† Accordingly at the present time if one asks about Anacharsis, the Scythians say that they do not know him, and for this reason, because he left his own country, went to Hellas and adopted foreign customs. And as I heard from Tymnes a steward‡ of Ariapeithes, he was the uncle on the father's side of Idanthyrsos king of the Scythians, and the son of Gnuros, the son of Lycos, the son of Spargapeithes. If then Anarcharsis was of this house, let him know that he died by the hand of his brother, for Idanthyrsos was the son of Saulios, and Saulios killed Anacharsis.

77. However I have heard also another story, told by the Peloponnesians, that Anacharsis was sent out by the king of the Scythians, and became a disciple of Hellas; and that when he returned back he said to his dispatcher, that the Hellenes, except the Lacedemonians, had no leisure for important things; but these alone knew how to converse sensibly. This story however has been invented without any ground by the Hellenes themselves; and certainly the man was slain as related above.

78. That is what happened to this man by reason of foreign customs and contact with Hellenes; very many years afterwards Skyles the son of Ariapeithes suffered nearly the same fate. For Ariapeithes the king of the

---

*Like the xenophobic Egyptians (for example, 2.91) but not like the Hellenes, who adopt and adapt useful practices—see, for example, 1.94, 1.171, 2.48–52, 2.109, 4.180–189, and 5.58.

†About 550 B.C.

‡Perhaps a Carian agent of the king at Olbia; see 5.37. A notable example of a named source; compare 3.55 and 9.16.

Scythians with other sons had Skyles born to him. He was born of a woman who was of Istria, and certainly not a native of Scythia; and this mother taught him the language and letters of Hellas. Afterwards in course of time Ariapeithes was brought to his end by treachery at the hands of Spargapeithes the king of the Agathyrsians, and Skyles succeeded to the kingdom; and he took not only that kingdom but also the wife of his father, whose name was Opoia. This Opoia was a native Scythian and from her was born Oricos to Ariapeithes. Now when Skyles was king of the Scythians, he was by no means satisfied with the Scythian manner of life, but was much more inclined towards Hellenic ways because of his training, and he used to do as follows:—When he came with the Scythians in arms to the city of the Borysthenites (now these Borysthenites say that they are Milesians), he would leave his band in the suburbs of the city and go himself within the walls and close the gates. After that he would lay aside his Scythian equipment and take Hellenic garments, and wearing them he would go about the market-place with no guards or any other man accompanying him (and they watched the gates meanwhile, that none of the Scythians might see him wearing this dress). In other respects too he adopted Hellenic manners of life, and he worshipped the gods according to the customs of the Hellenes. Then having stayed a month or more than that, he would put on the Scythian dress and depart. This he did many times, and he both built for himself a house in Borysthenes and also took a woman of the place as his wife.

79. Since however it was fated that evil should happen to him, it came about by an occasion of this kind:—he formed a desire to be initiated in the orgiastic rites of Bacchus-Dionysos, and as he was just about to receive initiation, a very great portent occurred. He had in the city of the Borysthenites a compound with a house of great size and built with large expense, which I just mentioned, and round it were placed sphinxes and griffins of white stone: on this house the god caused a bolt to fall; and the house was altogether burnt down, but Skyles none the less for this completed his initiation. Now the Scythians make the rites of Bacchus a reproach against the Hellenes, for they say that it is not fitting to invent a god like this, who impels men to frenzy. So when Skyles had been initiated in the rites of Bacchus, one of the Borysthenites hurried off to the Scythians and said: "Whereas you laugh at us, O Scythians, because we perform the rite of Bacchus and because the god seizes us, now this divinity has seized also your king; and he is both joining in the rite of Bacchus and maddened by the influence of the god. And if you disbelieve me, follow and I will show you." The chief men of the Scythians followed him, and the Borysthenite led them secretly into the town and set them upon a tower. So when Skyles passed by with the company of revellers, and the Scythians saw him joining in the rite of Bacchus, they were exceedingly grieved at it, and they went out and declared to the whole band that which they had seen.

80. After this when Skyles was riding out again to his own abode, the Scythians took his brother Octamasades for their leader, who was a son of the daughter of Teres, and rebelled against Skyles. When he perceived what was being done to him and the reason, he fled for refuge to Thrace; and Octamasades being informed of this, proceeded to march upon Thrace. So when he had arrived at the river Ister, the Thracians met him; and as they were about to engage battle, Sitalkes sent a messenger to Octamasades and said: "Why must we make trial of one another in fight? You are my sister's son and you have in your power my brother. Give him back to me, and I will deliver to you your brother Skyles: and let us not either of us set our armies in peril, either you or I." Thus Sitalkes proposed to him by a herald; for there was with Octamasades a brother of Sitalkes, who had gone into exile for fear of him. And Octamasades agreed to this, and by giving up his own mother's brother to Sitalkes he received his brother Skyles in exchange: and Sitalkes when he received his brother led him away as a prisoner, but Octamasades cut off the head of Skyles there upon the spot. Thus do the Scythians carefully guard their own customary observances, and such are the penalties which they inflict upon those who acquire foreign customs beside their own.

81. How many the Scythians are I was not able to ascertain precisely, but I heard various reports of the number. Reports say both that they are very many in number and also that they are few, at least true Scythians. Thus far however they gave me evidence to see:—there is between the river Borysthenes and the Hypanis a place called Exampaios, which I mentioned somewhat before this, saying that there was in it a spring of bitter water, from which the water flows and makes the river Hypanis unfit to drink. In this place there is set a bronze bowl, in size at least six times as large as the mixing-bowl at the entrance of the Pontus, which Pausanias the son of Cleombrotos dedicated. For him who has never seen that, I will make the matter clear by saying that the bowl in Scythia holds easily six hundred amphors,* and the thickness of this Scythian bowl is six fingers. This then the natives of the place told me had been made of arrow-heads. Their king, they said, whose name was Ariantas, wishing to know how many the Scythians were, ordered all the Scythians to bring one arrow-head, each from his own arrow, and whosoever should not bring one, he threatened with death. So a great multitude of arrow-heads was brought, and he resolved to make of them a memorial and to leave it behind him. From these then, they said, he made this bronze bowl and dedicated it in this place Exampaios.

82. This is what I heard about the number of the Scythians. Now this land has no marvellous things except that it has rivers which are by far larger and more numerous than those of any other land. One thing however shall be mentioned and which is worthy of wonder even besides the rivers and the greatness of the plain. They point out a footprint of Heracles in the rock by the bank of the river Tyras, which in shape is like the mark of a man's foot but in size is three feet long. This then is Scythia; and I will go back now to the history which I was about to tell at first.

---

*Approximately 5,300 gallons.

83. While Dareios was preparing to go against the Scythians and was sending messengers to appoint to some the furnishing of a land-army, to others that of ships, and to others the bridging over of the Thracian Bosphorus, Artabanos, the son of Hystaspes and brother of Dareios, urged him not to make the march against the Scythians, telling him how difficult the Scythians were to deal with. Since however he did not persuade him, though he gave him good counsel, he ceased to urge; and Dareios, when all his preparations had been made, began to march his army forth from Susa. **84.** Then one of the Persians, Oiobazos, made request to Dareios that as he had three sons and all were serving in the expedition, one might be left behind for him: and Dareios said that as he was a friend and made a reasonable request, he would leave behind all the sons. So Oiobazos was greatly rejoiced, supposing that his sons had been freed from service, but Dareios commanded those who were in charge of such things to put to death all the sons of Oiobazos.

85. These then were left, having been slain on the spot. Dareios meanwhile set forth from Susa and arrived at the place on the Bosphorus where the bridge of ships had been made, in the territory of Calchedon; and there he embarked in a ship and sailed to the so-called Kyanean rocks, which the Hellenes say formerly moved backwards and forwards; and taking his seat at the temple he gazed upon the Pontus, a sight well worth seeing. Of all seas indeed it is the most marvellous in its nature. The length of it is 1,275 miles, and the breadth, where it is broadest, 378 miles: and of this great Sea the mouth is but 0.5 mile broad, and the length of the mouth, that is of the neck of water which is called Bosphorus, where, as I said, the bridge of ships had been made, is not less than 13.8 miles.* This Bosphorus extends to the Propontis; and the Propontis, being in breadth 57.4 miles and in length 161 miles, has its outlet into the Hellespont, which is but 0.8 mile broad at the narrowest place, though it is 46 miles in length:† and the Hellespont runs out into that open sea which is called the Egean.

86. These measurements I have made as follows:—a ship completes on an average in a long day a distance of eighty miles, and in a night sixty-eight miles. Now we know that to the river Phasis from the mouth of the Sea (for it is here that the Pontus is longest) is a voyage of nine days and eight nights, which amounts to one thousand two hundred, seventy-five miles or eleven thousand one hundred stades. Then from the land of the Sindians to Themiskyra on the river Thermodon (for here is the broadest part of the Pontus) it is a voyage of three days and two nights, which amounts to 375 miles or three thousand three hundred stades. This Pontus then and also the Bosphorus and the Hellespont have been measured by me, and that is what they are. This Pontus also has a lake which has its outlet into it, which lake is not much less in size than the Pontus itself. It is called Maiotis and "Mother of the Pontus."

---

*Herodotus overestimates the length grossly.
†Here Herodotus underestimates the length. See 2.6 for ancient units of measure.

87. Dareios then having gazed upon the Pontus sailed back to the bridge, of which Mandrocles a Samian had been chief constructor; and having gazed upon the Bosphorus also, he set up two squared pillars by it of white stone with characters cut upon them, on the one Assyrian and on the other Hellenic, being the names of all the nations which he was leading with him. He was leading with him all over whom he was ruler. The whole number of them without the naval force was reckoned to be seven hundred thousand* including cavalry, and six hundred ships had been gathered. These pillars the Byzantians conveyed to their city afterwards, and used them for the altar of Artemis Orthosia, excepting one stone, which was left standing by the side of the temple of Dionysos in Byzantion, covered over with Assyrian characters. Now the place on the Bosphorus where Dareios made his bridge is, as I conclude, midway between Byzantion and the temple at the mouth of the Pontus.

88. After this Dareios, pleased with the floating bridge, rewarded the chief constructor, Mandrocles the Samian, with gifts tenfold; and as an offering from these Mandrocles had a painting made of figures to present the whole scene of the bridge over the Bosphorus and king Dareios sitting in a prominent seat and his army crossing over; this he caused to be painted and dedicated it as an offering in the [Samian] temple of Hera, with the following inscription:

"Bosphorus having bridged over, the straits fish-abounding, to Hera
    Mandrocleës dedicates this, of his work to record;
  A crown on himself he set, and he brought to the Samians glory,
  And for Dareios performed everything after his mind."

89. This memorial was made for him who constructed the bridge. Dareios, after he had rewarded Mandrocles with gifts, passed over into Europe, having first commanded the Ionians to sail into the Pontus as far as the river Ister, and when they arrived at the Ister, there to wait for him, making a bridge meanwhile over the river; for the chief of his naval force were the Ionians, the Aiolians and the Hellespontians. So the fleet sailed through between the Kyanean rocks and made straight for the Ister; and then they sailed up the river a two days' voyage from the sea and proceeded to make a bridge across the neck of the river, where the mouths of the Ister divide. Dareios meanwhile, having crossed the Bosphorus on the floating bridge, was advancing through Thrace, and when he came to the sources of the river Tearos he encamped for three days.

90. Now the Tearos is said by those who dwell near it to be the best of all rivers, both in other respects which tend to healing and especially for curing diseases of the skin both in men and in horses: and its springs are thirty-eight in number, flowing all from the same rock, of which some are

---

*The figure is larger than possible.

cold and others warm. The way to them is of equal length from the city of Heraion near Perinthos and from Apollonia upon the Euxine Sea, that is to say two days' journey by each road. This Tearos runs into the river Contadesdos and the Contadesdos into the Agrianes and the Agrianes into the Hebros, which flows into the sea by the city of Ainos. **91.** Dareios then, having come to this river and having encamped there, was pleased with the river and set up a pillar there also, with an inscription as follows : "The head-springs of the river Tearos give the best and fairest water of all rivers; and to them came leading an army against the Scythians the best and fairest of all men, Dareios the son of Hystaspes, of the Persians and of all the Continent king." These words were written there.

92. Dareios then set out and came to another river whose name is Artescos, which flows through the land of the Odrysians and where he did as follows:—he appointed a place for his army and bade every man as he passed by it place one stone. When the army had performed this, then he marched away his army leaving behind great mounds of these stones.

93. But before he came to the Ister he conquered first the Getai, who believe in immortality: for the Thracians who occupy Salmydessos and are settled above the cities of Apollonia and Mesambria, called the Kyrmianai and the Nipsaioi, delivered themselves over to Dareios without fighting; but the Getai, who are the bravest and the most upright in their dealings of all the Thracians, having become obstinate were quickly subdued. **94.** And their belief in immortality holds that they do not die, but that he who is killed goes to Salmoxis, a divinity,* whom some of them call Gebeleizis; and at intervals of four years they send one of themselves, whomsoever the lot may select, as a messenger to Salmoxis, charging him with such requests as they have on each occasion. They send him thus:— certain of them who are appointed for this have three javelins, and others meanwhile take hold on both sides of him who is being sent to Salmoxis, both by his hands and his feet, and first they swing him up, then throw him into the air so as to fall upon the spear-points: and if when he is pierced through he is killed, they think that the god is favourable to them; but if he is not killed, they find fault with the messenger himself, calling him a worthless man, and then having found fault with him they send another: and they give him the charge beforehand, while he is yet alive. These same Thracians also shoot arrows up towards the sky when thunder and lightning come, and use threats to the god, not believing that there exists any other god except their own.

95. This Salmoxis I hear from the Hellenes who dwell about the Hellespont and the Pontus, was a man, and he became a slave in Samos, and was in fact a slave of Pythagoras the son of Mnesarchos.† Then having become free he gained great wealth, and afterwards returned to his own land. Since

---

*The divine prototype of the Asiatic shaman.

†Native of Samos, born c.580 B.C.; he emigrated to Croton in southern Italy, where he founded an alternative-style community.

the Thracians are both primitive and rather simple-minded, this Salmoxis, being acquainted with the Ionian way of living and with manners more complex than the Thracians were used to see, and since he had associated with Hellenes (and not only that but with Pythagoras, not the least able philosopher of the Hellenes), he prepared a banqueting-hall, where he received and feasted the chief men of the tribe and instructed them meanwhile that neither he himself nor his guests nor their descendants in succession after them would die. They would come to a place where they would live for ever and have all things good. While he was doing and saying these things, he was making for himself meanwhile a chamber under the ground; and when his chamber was finished, he disappeared from among the Thracians and went down into the underground chamber, where he continued to live for three years. They grieved for his loss and mourned for him as dead. Then in the fourth year he appeared to the Thracians, and in this way the things which Salmoxis said became credible to them. **96.** Thus they say that he did. As to this matter and the chamber under ground, I neither disbelieve it nor do I very strongly believe, but I think that this Salmoxis lived many years before Pythagoras. However, whether there ever lived a man Salmoxis, or whether he is simply a native deity of the Getai, farewell to him now.

These Thracians having such manners, were subdued by the Persians and accompanied the rest of the army. **97.** When Dareios and with him the land-army arrived at the Ister, then after all had passed over, Dareios commanded the Ionians to break up the floating bridge and to accompany him by land, as well as the rest of the troops in the ships. When the Ionians were just about to break it up and to do his commands, Coës the son of Erxander, who was commander of the Mytilenians, said thus to Dareios, having first inquired whether he was disposed to listen to an opinion from one who desired to declare it: "O king, seeing that you are about to march upon a land where no cultivated ground will be seen nor any inhabited town, let this bridge remain where it is, leaving to guard it those same men who constructed it. Then, if we find the Scythians and fare as we desire, we have a way of return; and also even if we shall not be able to find them, at least our way of return is secured. That we should be worsted by the Scythians in fight I never feared yet, but rather that we might not be able to find them, and might suffer some disaster in wandering about. Perhaps some one will say that in speaking thus I am speaking for my own advantage, in order that I may remain behind; but in truth I am bringing forward, O king, the opinion which I found best for you, and I myself will accompany you and will not be left behind." With this opinion Dareios was very greatly pleased and made answer to him in these words: "Friend from Lesbos, when I have returned safe to my house, be sure to appear before me, in order that I may requite you with good deeds for good counsel." **98.** After having tied sixty knots in a thong, he called the despots of the Ionians to speak with him and said: "Men of Ionia, know that I have given up the opinion which I formerly declared with regard to the bridge. Keep this thong and do as I shall say:—so soon as you shall have seen me go forward against the Scythians, from that time begin, and untie a knot on each day: and if within this time I am not here, and you find that the days marked by the knots have passed by, then sail away to your own lands. Till then, since our resolve has thus been changed, guard the floating bridge, showing all diligence to keep it safe and to guard it. And thus acting, you will please me greatly." Thus said Dareios and hastened on his march forwards.

99. Now in front of Scythia in the direction towards the Mediterranean sea lies Thrace; and where a bay is formed in this land, there begins Scythia, into which the Ister flows out, the mouth of the river being turned towards the South-East. I am about to describe the coast land of the true Scythia beginning at the Ister, with regard to measurement. At once from the Ister begins this original land of Scythia, and it lies towards the midday and the South Wind, extending as far as the city called Carkinitis. After this the part which lies on the coast of the same sea still, a country which is mountainous and runs out in the direction of the Pontus, is occupied by the Tauric race, as far as the peninsula which is called the "Rugged Chersonese";* and this extends to the sea which lies towards the East: for two sides of the Scythian boundaries lie along by the sea, one by the sea on the South, and the other by that on the East, just as it is with Attica: and in truth the Tauroi occupy a part of Scythia which has much resemblance to Attica;† it is as if in Attica another race and not the Athenians occupied the cape of Sunion, supposing it to project more at the point into the sea, that region namely which is cut off by a line from Thoricos to the town of Anaphlystos. Such I say, to compare small things such as this with great, is the form of the Tauric land. For him however who has not sailed along this part of the coast of Attica I will make it clear by another comparison:—it is as if in Iapygia another race and not the Iapygians had cut off for themselves and were holding that extremity of the land which is bounded by a line beginning at the harbour of Brentesion and running to Taras. And in mentioning these two similar cases I am suggesting many other things also to which the Tauric land has resemblance.

100. After the Tauric land immediately come Scythians again, occupying the parts above the Tauroi and the coasts of the Eastern sea, that is to say the parts to the West of the Kimmerian Bosphorus and of the Maiotian lake,‡ as far as the river Tanaïs, which runs into the corner of this lake. Starting right from the Ister, in the upper parts which tend inland, Scythia is bounded by the Agathyrsians first, then by the Neuroi, afterwards by the Androphagoi, and lastly by the Melanchlainoi. **101.** Scythia then being

---

*That is, the contemporary Crimea.
†The analogy is incorrect for both Attica and Calabria; the comparisons suggest the expected locales of Herodotus' audiences.
‡The Sea of Azov is connected to the Black Sea by this other strait.

looked upon as a four-sided figure with two of its sides bordered by the sea, has its border lines equal to one another in each direction, that which tends inland and that which runs along by the sea: for from the Ister to the Borysthenes is ten days' journey, and from the Borysthenes to the Maiotian lake ten days' more; and the distance inland to the Melanchlainoi, who are settled above the Scythians, is a journey of twenty days. Now I have reckoned the day's journey at twenty-three miles. By this reckoning the [longitudinal] cross lines of Scythia would be four hundred sixty miles in length, and the perpendiculars which tend inland would be the same number of miles. Such is the size of this land.

102. The Scythians meanwhile realizing that they were not able to repel the army of Dareios alone by a pitched battle, proceeded to send messengers to those who dwelt near them: and already the kings of these nations had come together and were taking counsel with one another, since so great an army was marching towards them. Now those who had come together were the kings of the Tauroi, Agathyrsians, Neuroi, Androphagoi, Melanchlainoi, Gelonians, Budinoi and Sauromatai.

103. Of these the Tauroi have the following customs:—they sacrifice to the "Maiden" both shipwrecked persons and also those Hellenes whom they can capture by putting out to sea against them. Their manner of sacrifice is this:—when they have made the first offering from the victim they strike his head with a club. Some say that they push the body down from the top of the cliff (for it is upon a cliff that the temple is placed) and set the head up on a stake; but others, while agreeing as to the head, say nevertheless that the body is not pushed down from the top of the cliff, but buried in the earth. This divinity to whom they sacrifice, the Tauroi themselves say is Iphigeneia the daughter of Agamemnon. Whatsoever enemies they have conquered they treat in this fashion:— each man cuts off a head and bears it away to his house; then he impales it on a long stake and sets it up above his house raised to a great height, generally above the chimney; and they say that these are suspended above as guards to preserve the whole house. This people has its living by plunder and war.

104. The Agathyrsians are the most luxurious of men and wear gold ornaments for the most part: also they have promiscuous intercourse with their women, in order that they may be brethren to one another and being all nearly related may not feel envy or malice one against another. In their other customs they have come to resemble the Thracians.

105. The Neuroi practise the Scythian customs. One generation before the expedition of Dareios they were forced to quit their land altogether by reason of serpents. Their land produced serpents in vast numbers, and they fell upon them in still larger numbers from the desert country above their borders; until at last being hard pressed they left their own land and settled among the Budinoi. These men it would seem are wizards; the Scythians and the Hellenes who are settled in the Scythian land say about them that once in every year each of the Neuroi becomes a wolf for a few days and then returns again to his original form. For my part I do not believe them when they say this, but they say it nevertheless, and swear it moreover.

106. The Androphagoi have the most savage manners of all human beings, and they neither acknowledge any rule of right nor observe any customary law. They are nomads and wear clothing like that of the Scythians, but have a language of their own; and alone of all these nations they are man-eaters.

107. The Melanchlainoi wear all of them black clothing, whence also they have their name; and they practise the customs of the Scythians.

108. The Budinoi are a great and numerous race, and are all very blue-eyed and fair of skin. In their land is built a city of wood, the name of which is Gelonos, and each side of the wall is 3.4 miles in length and lofty at the same time, all being of wood; and the houses are of wood also and the temples; for there are in it temples of Hellenic gods furnished after Hellenic fashion with sacred images and altars and rooms, all of wood; and they keep festivals every other year to Dionysos and celebrate the rites of Bacchus: for the Gelonians are originally Hellenes, and they moved from the trading stations on the coast and settled among the Budinoi; and they use partly the Scythian language and partly the Hellenic. The Budinoi however do not use the same language as the Gelonians, nor is their manner of living the same.

109. The Budinoi are natives of the soil and a nomad people, and alone of the nations in these parts feed on fir-cones; but the Gelonians are tillers of the ground and feed on grain and have gardens, and resemble them not at all either in appearance or in complexion of skin. However by the Hellenes the Budinoi also are called Gelonians, but incorrectly. Their land is all thickly overgrown with forests of all kinds of trees, and in the thickest forest there is a large and deep lake, and round it marshy ground and reeds. Otters are caught in this and beavers and certain other wild animals with square-shaped faces. The fur of these is sewn as a fringe round their coats of skin, and they use the testicles for curing diseases of the womb.

110. About the Sauromatai the following tale is told:—When the Hellenes had fought with the Amazons,—now the Amazons are called by the Scythians *Oiorpata,* which name means in the Hellenic tongue "slayers of men," for "man" they call *oior,* and *pata* means "to slay,"—as the story goes, the Hellenes, having conquered them in the battle at the Thermodon, were sailing away and conveying with them in three ships as many Amazons as they were able to take prisoners. These in the open sea set upon the men and cast them out of the ships; but they knew nothing about ships, nor how to use rudders or sails or oars, and after they had cast out the men they were driven about by wave and wind and came to that part of the Maiotian lake where Cremnoi stands; now Cremnoi is in the land of the free or "Royal" Scythians. There the Amazons disembarked from their ships and made their way into the country, and having met first with a feeding troop of horses they seized them, and mounted upon these they plundered the property of the Scythians.

111. The Scythians meanwhile were not able to understand the matter, for they did not know either their speech or their dress or the race to which they belonged, but were in wonder as to whence they had come and thought that they were men, of an age corresponding to their appearance. Finally they fought a battle against them, and after the battle the Scythians got possession of the bodies of the dead, and thus they discovered that they were women. They decided therefore by no means to go on trying to kill them, but to send against them the youngest men from among themselves, making conjecture of the number so as to send just as many men as there were women. These were told to encamp near them, and do whatsoever they should do; if however the women should come after them, they were not to fight but to retire before them, and when the women stopped, they were to approach near and encamp. This plan was adopted by the Scythians because they desired to have children born from them. **112.** The young men accordingly were sent out following orders. When the Amazons perceived that they had not come to do them any harm, they let them alone; and the two camps approached nearer to one another every day. The young men, like the Amazons, had nothing except their arms and their horses, and got their living, as the Amazons did, by hunting and by taking booty.

113. Now the Amazons at midday used to scatter abroad either one by one or by two together, dispersing to a distance from one another to relieve themselves; and the Scythians also having perceived this did the same thing. One of the Scythians came near to one of those Amazons who were apart by themselves, and she did not repulse him but allowed him to lie with her. She could not speak to him, for they did not understand one another's speech, but she made signs to him with her hand to come on the following day to the same place and to bring another with him, signifying to him that there should be two of them, and that she would bring another with her. The young man therefore, when he returned, reported this to the others; and on the next day he came himself to the place and also brought another, and he found the Amazon awaiting him with another in her company. Then hearing this the rest of the young men also in their turn tamed for themselves the remainder of the Amazons; **114,** and after this they joined their camps and lived together, each man having for his wife her with whom he had had dealings at first; and the men were not able to learn the speech of the women, but the women came to comprehend that of the men. So when they understood one another, the men spoke to the Amazons as follows: "We have parents and we have possessions; now therefore let us no longer lead a life of this kind, but let us go away to the main body of our people and dwell with them; and we will have you for wives and no others." They however spoke thus in reply: "We should not be able to live with your women, for we and they have not the same customs. We shoot with bows and hurl javelins and ride horses, but the works of women we never learnt; whereas your women do none of these things which we said, but stay in the waggons and work at the works of women, neither going out to the chase nor anywhere else. We therefore should not be able to live in agreement with them: but if you desire to keep us for your wives and to be thought honest men, go to your parents and obtain from them your share of the goods, and then let us go and dwell by ourselves."

115. The young men agreed and did this; and when they had obtained the share of goods which belonged to them and had returned back to the Amazons, the women spoke as follows: "We are possessed by fear and trembling to think that we must dwell in this place, having not only separated you from your fathers, but also done great damage to your land. Since then you think it right to have us as your wives, do this together with us,—come and let us remove from this land and pass over the river Tanaïs and dwell there." **116.** The young men agreed to this also, and they crossed over the Tanaïs and made their way towards the rising sun for three days' journey from the Tanaïs, and also towards the North Wind for three days' journey from the Maiotian lake. Having arrived at the place where they are now settled, they took up their abode from thenceforward the women of the Sauromatai practise their ancient way of living, going out regularly on horseback to the chase both in company with the men and apart from them, and going regularly to war, and wearing the same dress as the men. **117.** And the Sauromatai make use of the Scythian tongue, speaking it barbarously however from the first, since the Amazons did not learn it thoroughly. As regards marriages their rule is this, that no maiden is married until she has slain a man of their enemies; and some of them even grow old and die before they are married, because they are not able to fulfil the requirement of the law.

118. To the kings of these nations then, which have been mentioned in order, the messengers of the Scythians came, finding them gathered together, and spoke declaring to them how the Persian king, after having subdued all things on the other continent, had laid a bridge over the neck of the Bosphorus and had crossed over to that continent, and having crossed over and subdued the Thracians, was making a bridge over the river Ister, desiring to bring under his power all these regions also. "Therefore," they said, "by no means stand aloof and allow us to be destroyed, but let us become all of one mind and oppose him who is coming against us. If you shall not do so, we on our part shall either be forced by necessity to leave our land, or we shall stay in it and make a treaty with the invader; for what else can we do if you are not willing to help us? and for you after this it will be in no respect easier; for the Persian has come not at all less against you than against us, nor will it content him to subdue us and abstain from you. And of the truth of that which we say we will mention strong evidence: if the Persian had been making his expedition against us alone, because he desired to take vengeance for the former servitude, he ought to have abstained from all the rest and to have come at once to invade our land, and he would thus have made it clear to all that he was marching to fight against the Scythians and not against the rest. In fact however, ever since he crossed over to this continent, he has compelled all who came in his way to submit to him, and he holds under him now not only the other Thracians but also the Getai, who are our nearest neighbours."

119. When the Scythians proposed this, the kings who had come from the various nations took counsel together, and their opinions were divided. The kings of the Gelonians, of the Budinoi and of the Sauromatai agreed and accepted the proposal that they should help the Scythians, but those of the Agathyrsians, Neuroi, Androphagoi, Melanchlainoi and Tauroi answered the Scythians as follows: "If you had not been the first to do wrong to the Persians and to begin war, then we should have surely thought that you were speaking justly in asking for those things for which you now ask, and we should have yielded to your request and shared your fortunes. As it is however, you on the one hand made invasion without us into their land, and ruled the Persians so long as God permitted you; and they in their turn, since the same God stirs them up, are repaying you with the like. As for us however, neither at that time did we do any wrong to these men nor now shall we attempt to do wrong to them unprovoked: if however the Persians shall come against our land also, and do wrong first to us, we also shall refuse to submit. Until we shall see this, we shall remain by ourselves, for we are of opinion that the Persians have come not against us, but against those who were the authors of the wrong."

120. When the Scythians heard this answer reported, they planned not to fight a pitched battle openly, since these did not join them as allies, but to retire before the Persians and to drive away their cattle before them, choking up with earth the wells and the springs of water by which they passed and destroying the grass from the ground, having parted themselves for this into two bodies; and they resolved that the Sauromatai should be added to one of their divisions, namely that over which Scopasis was king, and that these should move on, if the Persian turned in that direction, straight towards the river Tanaïs, retreating before him by the shore of the Maiotian lake; and when the Persian marched back again, they should come after and pursue him. This was one division of their kingdom, appointed to go by the way which has been said; and the other two of the kingdoms, the large one over which Idanthyrsos was king, and the third of which Taxakis was king, were to join together in one, with the Gelonians and the Budinoi added to them, and they also were to retire before the Persians one day's march in front of them, going on out of their way and doing as planned. First they were to move on straight for the countries which had refused to give their alliance, in order that they might involve these also in the war, and though these had not voluntarily undertaken the war with the Persians, they were to involve them in it nevertheless against their will. After that they were to return to their own land and attack the enemy, if it should seem good to them in council to do so.

121. Having formed this plan the Scythians went to meet the army of

Dareios, sending off the best of their horsemen before them as scouts; but all the waggons in which their children and their women lived they sent on, and with them all their cattle (leaving only so much as was sufficient to supply them with food), and charged them that they should proceed continually towards the North. These, I say, were sent off to safety. **122.** When the scouts who went in front of the Scythians discovered the Persians distant about three days' march from the Ister, then the Scythians having discovered them continued to pitch their camp one day's march in front, destroying utterly that which grew from the ground. When the Persians saw that the horsemen of the Scythians had made their appearance, they came after them following in their track, while the Scythians continually moved on. After this, since they had directed their march towards the first of the divisions, the Persians continued to pursue towards the East and the river Tanaïs; and when the Scythians crossed over the river Tanaïs, the Persians crossed over after them and continued still to pursue, until they had passed quite through the land of the Sauromatai and had come to that of the Budinoi.

123. Now so long as the Persians were passing through Scythia and the land of the Sauromatai, they had nothing to destroy, seeing that the land was bare, but when they invaded the land of the Budinoi, then they fell in with the wooden wall, which had been deserted by the Budinoi and left wholly unoccupied, and this they destroyed by fire. Having done so they continued to follow on further in the track of the enemy, until they had passed through the whole of this land and had arrived at the empty land. This "empty" region is occupied by no men, and it lies above the land of the Budinoi, extending for a seven days' journey; and above this desert dwell the Thyssagetai, and four large rivers flow from them through the land of the Maiotians and run into that which is called the Maiotian lake, their names being as follows,—Lycos, Oaros, Tanaïs, Syrgis. **124.** When therefore Dareios came to the "empty" region, he ceased from his course and halted his army upon the river Oaros. He began to build eight large fortifications at equal distances from one another, that is to say about seven miles, of which the ruins still existed down to my time; and while he was occupied in this, the Scythians whom he was pursuing came round by the upper parts and returned back to Scythia. Accordingly, since these had altogether disappeared and were no longer seen by the Persians at all, Dareios left those fortifications half finished, and turning back himself began to go towards the West, supposing that these were the whole body of the Scythians and that they were flying towards the West.

125. And marching his army as quickly as possible, when he came to Scythia he met with the two divisions of the Scythians together, and having fallen in with these he continued to pursue them, while they retired out of his way one day's journey in advance. Dareios did not cease to come after them, while the Scythians according to the plan which they had made continued to retire before him towards the land of those who had refused to give their alliance, and first towards that of the Melanchlainoi; and when Scythians and Persians both together had invaded and disturbed these, the

Scythians led the way to the country of the Androphagoi; and when these also had been disturbed, they proceeded to the land of the Neuroi; and while these too were being disturbed, the Scythians went on retiring before the enemy to the Agathyrsians.

The Agathyrsians however, seeing that their next neighbours also were flying from the Scythians and had been disturbed, sent a herald before the Scythians invaded their land and proclaimed to the Scythians not to set foot upon their confines, warning them that if they should attempt to invade the country, they would first have to fight with them. The Agathyrsians then having given this warning came out in arms to their borders, meaning to drive off those who were coming upon them; but the Melanchlainoi and Androphagoi and Neuroi, when the Persians and Scythians together invaded their land, did not betake themselves to brave defence but forgot their former threat and fled in confusion ever further towards the North to the uninhabited region. The Scythians however, when the Agathyrsians had warned them off, did not attempt any more to come to these, but led the Persians from the country of the Neuroi back to their own land.

126. Now as this went on for a long time and did not cease, Dareios sent a horseman to Idanthyrsos king of the Scythians and said: "Most wondrous man, why do you fly for ever, when you might do one of these two things?—if you think yourself able to make opposition to my power, stand still and cease from wandering abroad, and fight; but if you acknowledge yourself too weak, cease then in that case also from your course, and come to speech with your master, bringing to him gifts of earth and of water."

127. The king of the Scythians Idanthyrsos answered thus: "My case, O Persian, stands thus:—Never yet did I fly because I was afraid, either before this time from any other man, or now from you; nor have I done anything different now from that which I used to do in time of peace: and as to the cause why I do not fight with you at once, this also I will declare. We have neither cities nor land sown with crops, about which we should fear lest they be captured or laid waste, and so join battle more speedily with you; but if it be necessary by all means to come to this speedily, know that we have sepulchres in which our fathers are buried; therefore come now, find out these and attempt to destroy them, and you shall know then whether we shall fight with you for the sepulchres or whether we shall not fight. Before that however, unless the motion comes upon us, we shall not join battle with you. About fighting let this suffice; but as to masters, I acknowledge none over me but Zeus my ancestor and Hestia the queen of the Scythians. To you then in place of gifts of earth and water I shall send such things as you deserve to get; and in return for your saying that you are my master, for that I say, you will weep." This is the proverbial "saying of the Scythians."

128. The herald then had departed to report back to Dareios; and the kings of the Scythians, hearing of subjection to a master, were filled with wrath. They sent the division appointed to join the Sauromatai, that division which Scopasis commanded, bidding them speak to the Ionians, those who were guarding the bridge of the Ister. Meanwhile the remainder resolved not to lead the Persians wandering about any more, but to attack them constantly as they were getting provisions. Therefore they observed the soldiers of Dareios as they got provisions, and did as planned. The cavalry of the Scythians always routed that of the enemy, but the Persian horsemen as they fled fell back upon the men on foot, and these would come up to their assistance; and meanwhile the Scythians when they had driven away the cavalry turned back, fearing the men on foot. Also by night the Scythians used to make similar attacks.

129. The strange thing which most helped the Persians and hindered the Scythians in their attacks upon the camp of Dareios, I will mention, namely the voice of the asses and the appearance of the mules. Scythia produces neither ass nor mule, as I declared before, nor is there in all the Scythian country either ass or mule on account of the cold. The asses accordingly by riotously braying used to throw into confusion the cavalry of the Scythians; and often, as they were in the middle of riding against the Persians, when the horses heard the voice of the asses they turned back in confusion and were possessed with wonder, pricking up their ears, because they had never heard such a voice nor seen such a creature before. **130.** So far then the Persians had the advantage for a small part of the war. But the Scythians, whenever they saw that the Persians were disquieted, then in order that they might remain a longer time in Scythia and in remaining might suffer want of everything, would leave some of their own cattle behind with the herdsmen, while they themselves rode out of the way to another place, and the Persians would come upon the cattle and take them, and they were elated at what they had done.

131. As this happened often, at length Dareios began to feel his lack of supplies. The kings of the Scythians perceiving this sent a herald bearing as gifts to Dareios a bird and a mouse and a frog and five arrows. The Persians asked the bearer of the gifts the meaning of the gifts; but he said that nothing more had been commanded to him but to give them and get away as speedily as possible; and he bade the Persians find out for themselves, if they had wisdom, what the gifts meant to express. **132.** Having heard this the Persians set to thinking. The opinion of Dareios* was that the Scythians were giving to him both themselves and also earth and water, making his conjecture by this, namely that a mouse is produced in the earth and feeds on the same produce of the earth as man, and a frog in the water, while a bird has great resemblance to a horse; and moreover that in giving the arrows they were delivering up their own might in battle. The opinion of Gobryas, one of the seven men who killed the Magian, disputed Dareios' interpretation, for he conjectured that the gifts expressed this: "Unless you become birds and fly up to the heaven, O Persians, or become mice and sink down under the earth, or

*Herodotus, here and elsewhere, mocks interpretations of oracles and riddles (a kind of rebus here) that merely reflect the interpreter's wishes.

become frogs and leap into the lakes, you shall not return back home, but shall be smitten by these arrows."

133. While the Persians were making conjecture of the gifts, the single division of the Scythians, appointed at first to keep guard along the Maiotian lake and then to go to the Ister and speak with the Ionians, arrived at the bridge and spoke as follows: "Ionians, we have come bringing you freedom, if at least you are willing to listen to us; for we are informed that Dareios gave you command to guard the bridge for sixty days only, and then, if he had not arrived within that time, to leave for your own land. Now therefore, if you do as we say, you will be without blame from his part and without blame also from ours: stay the appointed days and then after that leave." They then, when the Ionians had agreed to do this, hastened back again by the quickest way. **134.** Meanwhile, after the coming of the gifts to Dareios, the Scythians who were left had arrayed themselves against the Persians with both foot and horse, meaning to engage battle. Now when the Scythians had been placed in battle-array, a hare darted through them into the space between the two armies, and each company of them, as they saw the hare, began to run after it. When the Scythians were thus thrown into disorder and were raising loud cries, Dareios asked what was this clamour arising from the enemy. Hearing that they were running after the hare, he said to his advisors: "These men have very slight regard for us, and I perceive now that Gobryas spoke rightly about the Scythian gifts. Since now I myself too think as he did, we need good counsel, in order that our retreat may be safe." To this replied Gobryas: "O king, even by report I was almost assured of the impossibility of dealing with these men; and when I came, I learnt it still more thoroughly, since I saw them mocking us. Now therefore my opinion is, that as soon as night comes on, we kindle the camp-fires as we do at other times, and deceive those of our men who are weakest to endure hardships, and tie up all the asses and get away, before either the Scythians make for the Ister to destroy the bridge or something be resolved by the Ionians which may ruin us."

135. Thus Gobryas advised; and after this, when night came on, Dareios acted on this opinion. Those of his men weakened by fatigue and whose loss was of least account, these he left behind in the camp, and also the tied-up asses. He left behind the asses and the weaker men of his army— the asses in order that they might make a noise which should be heard, and the men really because of their weakness, but on a pretence stated openly that he was about to attack the Scythians with the effective part of the army, and that they meanwhile were to defend the camp. Having thus instructed those who were left behind, and having kindled camp-fires, Dareios hastened by the quickest way towards the Ister. The asses, having no longer about them the usual throng, for that reason very much more whinnied loudly. The Scythians, hearing the asses, supposed surely that the Persians were remaining in their former place.

136. But when it was day, those who were left behind perceived that they had been betrayed by Dareios, and they held out their hands in submission to the Scythians, telling them what their case was; and the Scythians, when they heard this, joined together as quickly as possible, that is to say the two combined divisions of the Scythians and the single division, and also the Sauromatai, Budinoi, and Gelonians, and began to pursue the Persians, making straight for the Ister. Since the Persian army mostly consisted of men on foot, and was not acquainted with the roads (the roads not being marked with tracks), while the Scythian army consisted of horsemen and was acquainted with the shortest cuts upon the way, they missed one another and the Scythians arrived at the bridge much before the Persians. Then having learnt that the Persians had not yet arrived, they said to the Ionians who were in the ships: "Ionians, the days of your number are past, and you do wrong in that you yet remain waiting: but as you stayed before from fear, so now break up the passage as quickly as you may, and depart free and unhurt, feeling gratitude both to the gods and to the Scythians. We will so convince him who was formerly your master, that he shall never again march with an army upon any nation."

137. Upon this the Ionians held a council; and Miltiades the Athenian, who was commander and despot of the men of the Chersonese in Hellespont, opined that they should follow the advice of the Scythians and set Ionia free. Histiaios the Milesian was of the opinion opposite to this; for he said that at the present time it was by Dareios that each ruled as despot over a city; and if the power of Dareios should be destroyed, neither he himself could rule over the Milesians, nor could any other of them rule over any city; for each of the cities would choose to have popular rather than despotic rule. When Histiaios declared his opinion thus, at once all turned to this opinion, whereas at the first they were adopting that of Miltiades. **138.** Now these were voting on the two opinions, men of consequence in the eyes of the king,—first the despots of the Hellespontians, Daphnis of Abydos, Hippoclos of Lampsacos, Herophantos of Parion, Metrodoros of Proconnesos, Aristagoras of Kyzicos, and Ariston of Byzantion; and from Ionia, Strattis of Chios, Aiakes of Samos, Laodamas of Phocaia, and Histiaios of Miletos, whose opinion had been proposed in opposition to that of Miltiades; and the only important Aiolian present was Aristagoras of Kymē. **139.** When these adopted the opinion of Histiaios, they resolved to follow it with deeds and words, namely to break up that part of the bridge which was on the side towards the Scythians, for a distance equal to the range of an arrow, both in order that they might be thought to be doing something, though in fact doing nothing, and for fear that the Scythians might make an attempt using force to cross the Ister by the bridge. In breaking up that part of the bridge towards Scythia they resolved to say that they would do all that the Scythians desired. This they added to the opinion proposed, and then Histiaios coming forth on their behalf answered the Scythians as follows: "Scythians, you come bringing good news, and your haste is timely; and you on your part give us good guidance, while we on ours render to you suitable service. For, as you see, we are breaking up the passage, and we shall show all zeal in our desire to be free. While we are breaking up the bridge, you should be seeking those of whom you speak, and when you have found them, take vengeance on them on behalf of us as well as of yourselves in such manner as they deserve."

140. The Scythians then, believing again that the Ionians were speaking the truth, turned back to search for the Persians, but they missed altogether their line of march through the land. Of this the Scythians themselves were the cause, since they had destroyed the pastures for horses in that region and had choked up with earth the springs of water; for if they had not done this, it would have been possible for them easily, if they wished, to discover the Persians. As it was, by those things wherein they thought they had taken their measures best, they failed of success. The Scythians then were passing through those regions of their own land where there was grass for the horses and springs of water, and were seeking for the enemy there, thinking that they too were taking a course in their retreat through such country as this; while the Persians in fact marched keeping carefully to the track which they had made before, and so they found the passage of the river, though only with difficulty. Since they arrived by night and found the bridge broken up, they were overcome by fear, lest the Ionians should have deserted them.

141. Now there was with Dareios an Egyptian who had a voice louder than that of any other man on earth, and this man Dareios ordered to take his stand upon the bank of the Ister and to call Histiaios of Miletos. He accordingly proceeded to do so; and Histiaios, hearing the first hail, produced all the ships to carry the army over and also put together the bridge.

142. Thus the Persians escaped, and the Scythians in their search missed the Persians the second time also. Their judgment of the Ionians is that on the one hand, if they be regarded as free men, they are the most worthless and cowardly of all men, but on the other hand, if regarded as slaves, they are the most attached to their master and the least disposed to run away of all slaves. This reproach is cast against the Ionians by the Scythians.

143. Dareios then marching through Thrace arrived at Sestos in the Chersonese; and from that place, he himself returned in his ships to Asia, but to command his army in Europe he left Megabazos a Persian, whom Dareios once honoured by uttering among Persians this saying:—Dareios was beginning to eat pomegranates, and at once when he opened the first, Artabanos his brother asked him of what he would desire to have as many as there were seeds in the pomegranate. Dareios said that he would desire to have men like Megabazos as many as those seeds in number, rather than to have Hellas subject to him. In Persia, he honoured him thus in word, and at this time he left him in command with eighty thousand of his army.

144. This Megabazos uttered one saying whereby he left an imperishable memory with the peoples of Hellespont. Once at Byzantion he heard that the men of Calchedon had settled in that region seventeen years before the Byzantians, and having heard it he said that those of Calchedon at that time chanced to be blind; for assuredly they would not have chosen the worse place, when they might have settled in the better, if they had not been blind. This Megabazos was left in command among the Hellespontians, and he proceeded to subdue all who did not join the Medes.

145. While he then was doing thus, a great expedition was launched against Libya, on an occasion which I shall relate after first relating this.—The children's children of those who voyaged in the Argo, having been driven forth by those Pelasgians who carried away at Braurōn the women of the Athenians,*—having been driven forth I say by these from Lemnos, had departed and sailed to Lacedemon, and sitting down on Mount Taÿgetos they kindled a fire. The Lacedemonians seeing this sent a messenger to inquire who they were and whence; and they answered saying that they were Minyai and children of the heroes who sailed in the Argo, for these, they said, had put in to Lemnos and propagated the race of which they sprang. The Lacedemonians having heard the story of the descent of the Minyai, sent a second time and asked for what purpose they had come into the country and lit a blaze. They said that they had been cast out by the Pelasgians, and were come now to the land of their fathers.† It was most just that this should happen; and they said that their request was to be permitted to dwell with these, having a share of their privileges and a portion of the land. And the Lacedemonians were content to receive the Minyai upon the terms which they themselves desired, the chief impulse being the sons of Tyndareus were voyagers in the Argo. So they gave the Minyai a share of land and distributed them in the tribes; and they immediately made marriages, and gave in marriage to others the women whom they brought with them from Lemnos.

146. However, when no very long time had passed, the Minyai soon became arrogant, asking for a share of the royal power and also doing other impious things. Therefore the Lacedemonians resolved to put them to death; and having seized them they cast them into a prison. Now the Lacedemonians execute by night all those whom they put to death, and no man by day. When therefore they were just about to kill them, the wives of the Minyai, native Spartans and daughters of the first citizens of Sparta, entreated to be allowed to enter the prison and converse—each with her own husband. They let them pass in, not supposing that any trick would be practised by them. They however, when they had entered, delivered to their husbands all the garments which they were wearing, and themselves received those of their husbands. The Minyai having put on the women's clothes went forth out of prison as women, and having escaped they went again to Taÿgetos and sat down there.

147. Now at this same time Theras the son of Autesion, the son of Tisamenos, the son of Thersander, the son of Polyneikes, was preparing to set forth from Lacedemon to found a settlement. This Theras, born of the race of Cadmos, was mother's brother to the sons of Aristodemos, Eurysthenes and Procles; and while these sons were yet children, Theras as their guardian held the royal power in Sparta. When however his nephews were

---

*Forward reference to the outrage recounted at 6.137–138.

†They were descended from Castor and Polydeuces, sons of King Tyndareus; compare 5.75.

grown and had taken up the power, then Theras, being grieved that he should be ruled by others after he had tasted rule himself, said that he would not remain in Lacedemon, but would sail away to his kinsmen. Now there were in the island which now is called Thera, but formerly was called Callista, descendants of Membliaros the son of Poikiles, a Phenician. Cadmos the son of Agenor in his search for Europa put in to land at the island which is now called Thera; and, whether it was that the country pleased him when he had put to land, or for some other reason, he left in this island, besides other Phenicians, Membliaros also, of his own kinsmen. These occupied the island called Callista for eight generations of men, before Theras came from Lacedemon.

148. Theras was preparing to set forth to these, taking with him people from the tribes, and intending to settle together with those who have been mentioned, not with any design to drive them out, but claiming them strongly as kinsfolk. And when the Minyai escaped from the prison went and sat down on Taÿgetos, Theras entreated the Lacedemonians, as they were proposing to put them to death, not to slaughter them. He engaged to take them out of the land. The Lacedemonians having agreed to this proposal, he sailed away with three thirty-oared galleys to the descendants of Membliaros, not taking with him all the Minyai, but a few only. The greater number of them turned towards the land of the Paroreatai and Caucones, and having driven these out of their country, they parted themselves into six divisions and founded in their territory the following towns,—Lepreon, Makistos, Phrixai, Pyrgos, Epion, Nudion. The Eleians sacked the greater number of these within my own lifetime. The island meanwhile got its name of Thera after Theras who led the settlement. **149.** And since his son said that he would not sail with him, therefore he said that he would leave him behind as a sheep among wolves; and in accordance with that saying this young man got the name of Oiolycos [or "Sheepwolf"], and it chanced that this name prevailed over his former name. From Oiolycos was begotten Aigeus, after whom are called the Aigeidai, a powerful clan in Sparta. The men of this tribe, since their children did not live to grow up, established by the suggestion of an oracle a temple to the Avenging Deities [or Erinyes] of Laïos and Œdipus, and after this the same thing was continued in Thera by the descendants of these men.

150. Up to this point of the story the Lacedemonians agree with the men of Thera; but from here the Therans alone report the following. Grinnos the son of Aisanios, a descendant of the Theras who has been mentioned, and king of the island of Thera, came to Delphi bringing the offering of a hecatomb from his State; and accompanying him, besides others came also Battos the son of Polymnestos, who was by descent of the family of Euphemos of the Minyan race. Now when Grinnos the king of the Theraians was consulting the Oracle about other matters, the Pythian prophetess gave answer bidding him found a city in Libya; and he made reply saying: "Lord Apollo, I am by this time somewhat old and heavy to stir, but bid some one of these younger ones do this." As he said this he pointed towards Battos. Afterwards when he had come away they were confused about the Oracle, neither having any knowledge of Libya, where on earth it was, nor daring to send out a colony into the unknown. **151.** Then for seven years there was no rain in Thera, and in these years all the trees in their island were withered up excepting one. The Theraians consulted the Oracle, and the Pythian prophetess alleged this matter of colonising Libya to be the cause. As then they had no remedy for their evil, they sent messengers to Crete, to find out whether any of the Cretans or of the aliens resident in Crete had ever come to Libya. These as they wandered round about the country came also to the city of Itanos, and there they met a fisher for purple named Corobios, who said that he had been carried away by winds and had come to Libya, to the island of Platea. This man they persuaded by payment and took him to Thera, and from Thera there set sail men to explore, at first only a few. Corobios guided them to this same island of Platea, and they left Corobios there, with provisions for a certain number of months, and sailed themselves as quickly as possible to report about the island to the men of Thera.

152. Since however these stayed away longer than the time appointed, Corobios found himself destitute; and after this a ship of Samos, of which the master was Colaios, while sailing to Egypt was carried out of its course and came to this island of Platea; and the Samians hearing the whole story from Corobios left him provisions for a year. They themselves then sailed on, endeavouring to reach Egypt but carried away continually by the East Wind; and as the wind did not cease to blow, they passed through the Pillars of Heracles and came to Tartessos by divine providence.* Now this trading-place was at that time untapped by any, so that when these returned home they made profit from their cargo greater than any other Hellenes of whom we have certain knowledge, with the exception at least of Sostratos the son of Laodamas the Eginetan, for with him no man can contend. And the Samians set apart six talents,† the tenth part of their gains, and had a bronze vessel made like an Argolic mixing-bowl and round it heads of griffins projecting in a row; and this they dedicated as an offering in the temple of Hera, setting as supports under it three colossal statues of bronze ten and a half feet in height, resting upon their knees. By reason first of this act a great friendship was formed by those of Kyrenē and Thera with the Samians. **153.** The Theraians meanwhile, when they arrived at Thera after having left Corobios in the island, reported that they had colonised an island on the coast of Libya. The men of Thera resolved to send one of every two brothers selected by lot and men besides taken from all the regions of the island, which are seven in number; and further that Battos should be both their leader and their king. Then they sent forth two fifty-oared galleys to Platea.

---

*Region on the Atlantic coast of southern Spain beyond the Straits of Gibraltar; compare 1.163 for Phocaian landings.
†About 350 pounds of silver.

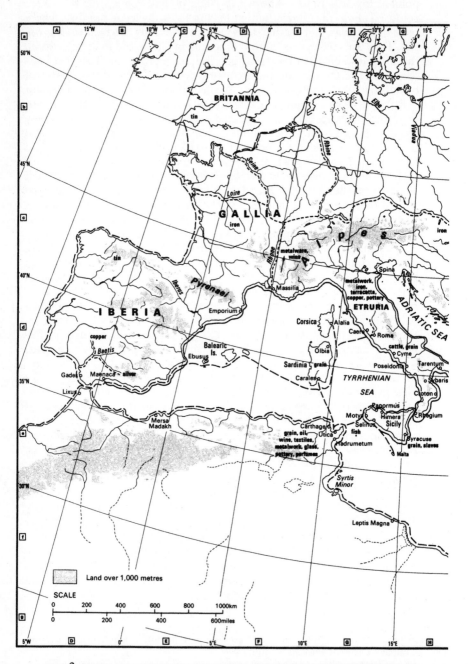

MAP 2. GREEK AND PHOENICIAN TRADE IN THE PERIOD OF THE PERSIAN WARS.

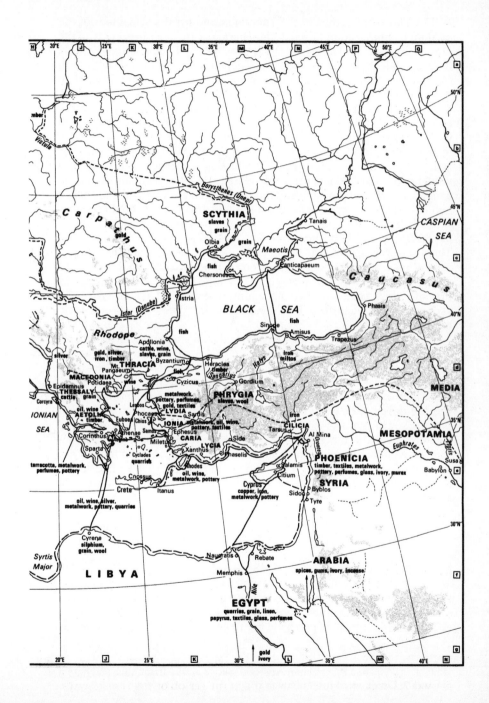

154. This is the report of the Theraians; and for the remainder of the account from this point onwards the Theraians are in agreement with the men of Kyrenē. In what concerns Battos the Kyrenians tell an entirely different tale from those of Thera. Their account is this:—There is in Crete a city called Oäxos in which one Etearchos became king, who when he had a daughter, whose mother was dead, named Phronimē, took to wife another woman notwithstanding. She having come into the house afterwards, thought fit to be a stepmother to Phronimē in deed as well as name, giving her evil treatment and devising everything possible to hurt her. Finally she charges her with promiscuity and persuades her husband that that is the truth. He then being convinced by his wife, devised an unholy deed against his daughter. In Oäxos was one Themison, a merchant of Thera, whom Etearchos took as a guest-friend and caused him to swear that he would serve him in whatsoever he should require. When he had caused him to swear this, he brought and delivered to him his daughter and bade him take her away and cast her into the sea. Themison was so angry at the deceit practised in the oath that he dissolved his guest-friendship. He received the girl and sailed away, and when he got out into the open sea, to free himself from blame as regards the oath which Etearchos had made him swear, he tied her with ropes on each side and let her down into the sea, and then drew her up and came to Thera.

155. After that, Polymnestos, a respected man among the Theraians, received Phronimē from him and kept her as his concubine. Afterwards a son was born to him from her with a speech impediment and a lisp. Both Theraians and Kyrenians say that he was given the name Battos, but I think that some other name was then given.* He was named Battos instead of this after he came to Libya, taking for himself this surname from the oracle which was given to him at Delphi and from the rank which he had obtained; for the Libyans call a king *battos*. I think the Pythian prophetess in her prophesying called him so, using the Libyan tongue, because she knew that he would be a king in Libya. For when he had grown to be a man, he came to Delphi to inquire about his voice; and when he asked, the prophetess thus answered him:

"For a voice thou camest, O Battos, but thee lord Phœbus Apollo
   Sendeth as settler forth to the Libyan land sheep-abounding,"

just as if she should say in Greek, "For a voice thou camest, O *king*." He answered: "Lord Apollo, I came to you to inquire concerning my voice, but you answer me other things which are not possible, bidding me go as a settler to Libya; but with what power, or with what force of men should I go?" Yet he did not at all persuade her to give him any other reply; and as

---

*Pindar, in *Pythian* 5.87, calls him Aristotle. Battos is an African title, and here a pun on the Greek word for "stammerer."

she was prophesying to him again the same things as before, Battos departed while she was yet speaking, and went away to Thera.

156. After this there came evil fortune both to himself and to the other men of Thera; and the Theraians, not understanding that which befell them, sent to Delphi to inquire about the evils which they were suffering. The Pythian prophetess gave them reply that if they joined with Battos in founding Kyrenē in Libya, they would fare the better. After this the Theraians sent Battos with two fifty-oared galleys; and these sailed to Libya, and then came away back to Thera, for they did not know what else to do. But the Theraians pelted them with missiles when they endeavoured to land, and would not allow them to put to shore, but bade them sail back again. They accordingly being compelled sailed back, and they made a settlement in an island lying near the coast of Libya, called, as was said before, Platea. This island is said to be of the same size as the now existing city of Kyrenē.

157. In this they continued to dwell two years; but as they had no prosperity, they left one of their number behind and all the rest sailed away to Delphi, and having come to the Oracle they consulted it, saying that they were dwelling in Libya and that, though they were dwelling there, they fared no better. The Pythian prophetess answered them thus:

"Better than I if thou knowest the Libyan land sheep-abounding,
  Not having been there than I who have been, at thy wisdom I
    wonder."

Battos and his companions sailed back again; for in fact the god would not let them off from the task of settlement till they had come to Libya itself. After having arrived at the island and taken up him whom they had left, they settled in Libya itself at a spot opposite the island, called Aziris, which is enclosed by most fair woods on both sides and a river flows by it on one side. **158.** In this spot they dwelt for six years; and in the seventh year the Libyans persuaded them to leave it, making request and saying that they would conduct them to a better region. So the Libyans led them from that place making them start towards evening-time; and in order that the Hellenes might not see the fairest of all the regions as they passed through it, they led them past this region called Irasa by night, having calculated the time of daylight. Then having conducted them to the so-called spring of Apollo, they said, "Hellenes, here is a fit place to dwell, for here the heaven is pierced with holes."*

159. Now during the lifetime of the first settler Battos, who reigned forty years, and of his son Arkesilaos, who reigned sixteen years, the Kyrenians continued to dwell there with the same number as when they first set forth to the colony; but in the time of the third king, called Battos the Prosperous, the Pythian prophetess gave an oracle wherein she urged the Hellenes

---

*Kyrenē, founded c.630 B.C., has fertile land because of rainfall on the highlands; compare 4.185.

in general to sail and join the Kyrenians in colonising Libya. For the Kyrenians invited them, promising a division of land. The oracle which she uttered was:

"Who to the land much desirèd, to Libya, too late cometh,
    After the land be divided, I say he shall some day repent it."

Then great numbers were gathered at Kyrenē, and the Libyans who dwelt round had much land cut off from their possessions. Therefore they with their king whose name was Adicran, as they were not only deprived of their country but also were treated very insolently by the Kyrenians, sent to Egypt and delivered themselves to Apries king of Egypt. He gathered a great army of Egyptians, sent it against Kyrenē. The men of Kyrenē marched out to the region of Irasa and to the spring Thestē, and there joined battle with the Egyptians and defeated them in the battle. Since the Egyptians had not before made trial of Hellenes in fight and therefore despised them, they were slaughtered and few of them returned back to Egypt. In consequence of this and because they laid the blame upon Apries, the Egyptians revolted from him.*

160. This Battos had a son called Arkesilaos, who first when he became king quarrelled with his own brothers, until they finally departed to another region of Libya, and making the venture their own founded that city which was then and now called Barca. When they founded this, they induced the Libyans to revolt from the Kyrenians. After this, Arkesilaos made an expedition against those Libyans who had received them and who had also revolted from Kyrenē, and the Libyans fearing him departed and fled towards the Eastern tribes of Libyans. Arkesilaos followed after them as they fled, until he arrived in his pursuit at Leucōn in Libya, and there the Libyans resolved to attack him. Accordingly they engaged in battle and defeated the Kyrenians so utterly that seven thousand Kyrenian hoplites fell there. After this disaster Arkesilaos, being sick and having swallowed a potion, was strangled by his brother Haliarchos, and Haliarchos was killed treacherously by the wife of Arkesilaos, whose name was Eryxo.

161. Then Battos the son of Arkesilaos succeeded to the kingdom, who was lame, not sound in his feet. The Kyrenians with a view to the misfortune which had befallen them sent men to Delphi to ask what form of rule they should adopt, in order to live best; and the Pythian prophetess bade them take to themselves a reformer of their State from Mantineia of the Arcadians. The men of Kyrenē accordingly made request, and those of Mantineia gave them their most highly esteemed citizen, whose name was Demonax. This man therefore having come to Kyrenē and having ascertained things exactly, in the first place caused them to have three tribes, distributing them thus:—one division he made of the Theraians and their dependants, another of the Peloponnesians and Cretans, and a third of all

---

*This revolt occurred in 570 B.C.; the battle was mentioned at 2.161.

the Cycladic islanders. Then secondly for the king Battos he set apart domains of land and priesthoods, but all the other powers which the kings used to possess, he assigned as of public right to the people.

162. During the reign of this Battos things continued this way, but in the reign of his son Arkesilaos a great disturbance about the offices of the State arose. Arkesilaos son of Battos the Lame and of Pheretimē said that he would not accept what the Mantineian Demonax had arranged, but asked for the restoration of the royal rights of his forefathers. Stirring up strife he was worsted and went into exile to Samos,* and his mother to Salamis in Cyprus. Now at that time the ruler of Salamis was Euelthon, the same who dedicated as an offering the censer at Delphi, a work well worth seeing, which is placed in the treasury of the Corinthians. Having come to him, Pheretimē asked him for an army to restore herself and her son to Kyrenē. Euelthon however was ready to give her anything else rather than that; and she when she received each gift he gave her said that this too was a fair gift, but fairer still would be that other gift of an army for which she was asking. As she kept saying this to every thing given, at last Euelthon sent out to her a present of a golden spindle and distaff, with wool also upon it: and when Pheretimē uttered again the same saying about this present, Euelthon said that such things as this were given as gifts to women and not an army.

163. Arkesilaos meanwhile, in Samos, was gathering every one together by a promise of dividing land; and while a great host was being collected, Arkesilaos set out to Delphi to inquire of the Oracle about returning from exile: and the Pythian prophetess gave him this answer: "For four named Battos and four named Arkesilaos, eight generations of men, Loxias grants to you to be kings of Kyrenē, but beyond this he counsels you not even to attempt it. You however must keep quiet when you come back to your land; and if you find the furnace full of jars, heat not the jars fiercely, but let them go with a fair wind: if however you heat the furnace fiercely, enter not into the place flowed round by water; for if you do you shall die, both you and the bull which is fairer than all the rest."

164. Thus the Pythian prophetess answered Arkesilaos; and he, having allied with him those in Samos, made his return to Kyrenē; and when he had got possession of the power, he did not remember the saying of the Oracle but endeavoured to exact penalties from his opponents who had driven him out. Of these some escaped from the country altogether, but some Arkesilaos got into his power and sent them away to Cyprus to be put to death. These were driven out of their course to Cnidos, and the men of Cnidos rescued them and sent them away to Thera. Some others however of the Kyrenians fled to a great tower belonging to Aglomachos a private citizen, and Arkesilaos burnt them by piling up brushwood round. Then after he had finished them off he perceived that the Oracle meant

---

*Arkesilaos fled to Samos c.530 B.C.

this, in that the Pythian prophetess forbade him, if he found the jars in the furnace, to heat them fiercely; and he voluntarily kept away from the city of the Kyrenians, fearing the death which had been prophesied by the Oracle and supposing that Kyrenē was flowed round by water. Now he had to wife a kinswoman of his own, the daughter of the king of Barca whose name was Alazeir. He came to him, but men of Barca together with certain of the exiles from Kyrenē, perceiving him shopping in the market-place, killed him, and also besides him his father-in-law Alazeir. Arkesilaos accordingly, having missed the meaning of the oracle, whether with his will or against his will, fulfilled his own destiny.

165. His mother Pheretimē meanwhile, so long as Arkesilaos having worked evil for himself dwelt at Barca, herself held the royal power of her son at Kyrenē, both exercising his other rights and also sitting in council. When she heard that her son had been slain in Barca, she departed and fled to Egypt; for she had on her side services done for Cambyses the son of Cyrus by Arkesilaos, since this was the Arkesilaos who had given over Kyrenē to Cambyses and had laid a tribute upon himself. Pheretimē then having come to Egypt sat down as a suppliant of Aryandes, bidding him help her, and alleging as a reason that it was on account of his inclination to the side of the Medes that her son had been slain. **166.** Now this Aryandes had been appointed ruler of the province of Egypt by Cambyses; and after the time of these events he lost his life because he competed with Dareios. For having heard and seen that Dareios desired to leave behind him as a memorial of himself a thing done by no other king, he imitated him, until at last he received his reward. Whereas Dareios refined gold and made it as pure as possible, and of this caused coins to be struck, Aryandes, being ruler of Egypt, did the same thing with silver; and even now the purest silver is that which is called Aryandic. Dareios then having learnt that he was doing this put him to death, bringing against him another charge of attempting rebellion.

167. Now this Aryandes had compassion on Pheretimē and gave her all the troops that were in Egypt, both the land and the sea forces, appointing Amasis a Maraphian to command the land-army and Badres, of the race of the Pasargadai, to command the fleet. But before he sent away the army, Aryandes despatched a herald to Barca and asked who it was who had killed Arkesilaos; and the men of Barca all took it upon themselves, for they said they suffered formerly many great evils at his hands. Having heard this, Aryandes at last sent away the army together with Pheretimē. This charge then was the pretext alleged; but in fact the army was being sent out (as I believe) for the purpose of subduing Libya, since there are many Libyan nations of various kinds, and but few of them were subject to the king, while the greater number paid no regard to Dareios.

168. Now the Libyans dwell in Africa as follows:—Beginning from Egypt, first of the Libyans are settled the Adyrmachidai, who generally share the same customs as the Egyptians, but wear clothing similar to that of the other Libyans. Their women wear a bronze bangle upon each leg, and they have long hair on their heads, and when they catch their lice, each one bites her own in retaliation and then throws them away. These are the only people of the Libyans who do this; and they alone display to the king their maidens when they are about to be married, and whosoever of them proves to be pleasing to the king is deflowered by him. These Adyrmachidai extend along the coast from Egypt as far as the port which is called Plynos. **169.** Next after these come the Giligamai, occupying the country towards the West as far the island of Aphrodisias. In the space within this limit lies off the coast the island of Platea, where the Kyrenians made their settlement; and on the coast of the mainland there is Port Menelaos, and Aziris, where the Kyrenians used to dwell. From this point begins the *silphion** and it extends along the coast from the island of Platea as far as the entrance of the Syrtis. This nation practises customs nearly resembling those of the rest. **170.** Next to the Giligamai on the West are the Asbystai: these dwell inland from Kyrenē, and the Asbystai do not reach down to the sea, for the region along the sea is occupied by the Kyrenians. These most of all the Libyans are drivers of four-horse chariots, and their customs generally endeavour to imitate the Kyrenians. **171.** Next after the Asbystai on the West come the Auschisai: these dwell inland from Barca and reach down to the sea by Euesperides: and in the middle of the country of the Auschisai dwell the Bacales, a small tribe, who reach down to the sea by the city of Taucheira in the territory of Barca: these practise the same customs as those inland from Kyrenē.

172. Next after these Auschisai towards the West come the Nasamonians, a numerous race, who in the summer leave their flocks behind by the sea and go up to the region of Augila to gather the fruit of the date-palms, which grow in great numbers and very large and are all fruit-bearing.[†] These hunt the wingless locusts, and they dry them in the sun and then pound them up, and after that they sprinkle them upon milk and drink them. Their custom is for each man to have many wives, and they share their sexual intercourse with them in nearly the same manner as the Massagetai,[‡] that is they set up a staff in front of the door and so have intercourse. When a Nasamonian man marries his first wife, the custom is for the bride on the first night to go through the whole number of the feast-guests having intercourse with them, and each man when he has lain with her gives a gift, whatsoever he has brought with him from his house. The forms of oath and of divination which they use are as follows:—they swear by the men among themselves who are reported to have been the most righteous and brave, laying hands upon their tombs; and they divine by visiting the sepulchral mounds of their ancestors and lying down to sleep upon them after having prayed; and whatsoever thing the man sees in his

---

*This plant, probably asaphoetida, figures on the coins of Kyrene and Barca; it had medicinal uses.

†See 2.32–33 for this exploration of the Sahara and beyond.

‡Reference to the polygamy of the Europeans, described at 1.216.

dream, this he accepts. They practise also the exchange of pledges in the following manner: one gives the other to drink from his hand, and drinks himself from the hand of the other; and if they have no liquid, they take of the dust from the ground and lick it.

173. Adjoining the Nasamonians is the country of the Psylloi. These have perished utterly in the following manner:—The South Wind blowing upon them dried up all their cisterns of water, and their land was waterless, lying all within the Syrtis. They then having taken a resolve by common consent, marched in arms against the South Wind (I report what the Libyans say), and when they had arrived at the sandy tract, the South Wind blew and buried them in the sand. These then having utterly perished, the Nasamonians from that time forward possess their land.

174. Above these towards the South in the region of wild beasts dwell the Garamantians, who fly from every man and avoid the company of all; they neither possess any weapon of war, nor know how to defend themselves against enemies. **175.** These dwell above the Nasamonians; and next to the Nasamonians along the sea coast towards the West come the Macai, who shave their hair so as to leave tufts, letting the middle of their hair grow long, but round this on all sides shaving it close to the skin; and for fighting they carry shields made of ostrich skins. Through their land the river Kinyps runs out into the sea, flowing from a hill called the "Hill of the Charites." This Hill of the Charites is overgrown thickly with wood, while the rest of Libya which has been spoken of before is bare of trees; and the distance from the sea to this hill is twenty-three miles. **176.** Next to these Macai are the Gindanes, whose women wear a number of anklets made of the skins of animals, for a reason like this, as it is said:—for every man who has sex with her she binds on an anklet, and the woman who has most is esteemed the best, since she has been loved by the greatest number of men. **177.** In a peninsula which stands out into the sea from the land of these Gindanes dwell the Lotophagoi, who live by eating the fruit of the *lotos* only. Now the fruit of the lotos is in size like that of the mastich-tree, and in sweetness it resembles that of the date-palm. The Lotophagoi even make for themselves wine from this fruit.

178. Next after the Lotophagoi along the sea-coast are the Machlyans, who also make use of the lotos, but less than those above mentioned. These extend to a great river named the river Triton, and this runs out into a great lake called Tritonis, in which there is an island named Phla. About this island they say an oracle was given to the Lacedemonians that they should make a settlement in it. **179.** The following story moreover is also told, namely that Jason, when the Argo had been completed by him under Mount Pelion, put into it a hecatomb and with it also a tripod of bronze, and sailed round Peloponnese, desiring to come to Delphi. When he got near Malea, a North Wind seized his ship and carried it off to Libya, and before he caught sight of land he had come into the shoals of the lake Tritonis. Then as he was at a loss how he should bring his ship forth, the story goes that Triton appeared to him and bade Jason give him the tripod, saying that he would show them the right course and let them go away without hurt. Jason consented to it, then Triton showed them the passage out between the shoals and set the tripod in his own temple, after having first uttered a prophecy over the tripod and having declared to Jason and his company the whole matter: whensoever one of the descendants of those who sailed with him in the Argo should carry away this tripod, then it was determined by fate that a hundred cities of Hellenes should be established about lake Tritonis. Having heard this the native Libyans concealed the tripod.

180. Next to these Machlyans are the Auseans. These and the Machlyans dwell round lake Tritonis, and the river Triton is the boundary between them. While the Machlyans grow their hair long at the back of the head, the Auseans do so in front. At a yearly festival of Athenē their maidens take their stand in two parties and fight against one another with stones and staves, and they say that in doing so they are fulfilling the rites handed down by their fathers for the divinity who was sprung from that land, whom we call Athenē. Those of the maidens who die of the wounds received they call "false-maidens." But before they let them begin the fight they do this:—all join together and equip the maiden who is judged to be fairest on each occasion, with a Corinthian helmet and with full Hellenic armour, and then causing her to enter a chariot they conduct her round about the lake. Now I cannot tell with what they equipped the maidens in old time, before the Hellenes were settled near them; but I suppose that they used to be equipped with Egyptian armour, for I affirm that from Egypt both the shield and the helmet have come to the Hellenes. They say moreover that Athenē is the daughter of Poseidon and of lake Tritonis, and that she had some cause of complaint against her father and therefore gave herself to Zeus, and Zeus made her his own daughter. Such is the story which these tell; and they have their intercourse with women in common, not marrying but having intercourse like cattle. When the child of any woman has grown big, he is brought before a meeting of the men held within three months of that time, and whomsoever of the men the child resembles, his son he is accounted to be.

181. Thus then have been mentioned those nomad Libyans who live along the sea-coast: and above these inland is the region of Libya which has wild beasts; and above the wild-beast region there stretches a raised belt of sand, extending from Thebes of the Egyptians to the Pillars of Heracles. In this belt at intervals of about ten days' journey there are fragments of salt in great lumps forming hills, and at the top of each hill there shoots up from the middle of the salt a spring of water cold and sweet; and about the spring dwell men, at the furthest limit towards the desert, and beyond the wild-beast region. First, at a distance of ten days' journey from Thebes, are the Ammonians, whose temple is derived from that of the Theban Zeus, for the image of Zeus in Thebes also, as I have said before,* has the head of a ram. These, as it chances, have also other water

---

*See 2.42 for ram stories.

of a spring, which in the early morning is warm; at the time in mid-morning when the market fills, cooler; when midday comes, it is quite cold, and then they water their gardens; but as the day declines, it abates from its coldness, until at last, when the sun sets, the water is warm; and it continues to increase in heat still more until it reaches midnight, when it boils and throws up bubbles; and when midnight passes, it becomes cooler gradually till dawn of day. This spring is called the fountain of the Sun.

182. After the Ammonians, as you go on along the belt of sand, at an interval again of ten days' journey there is a hill of salt like that of the Ammonians, and a spring of water, with men dwelling about it; and the name of this place is Augila. To this the Nasamonians come year by year to gather the fruit of the date-palms. **183.** From Augila at a distance again of ten days' journey there is another hill of salt and spring of water and a great number of fruit-bearing date-palms, as there are also in the other places: and men dwell here who are called the Garamantians, a very great nation, who bring in earth to lay over the salt and then sow crops. From this point is the shortest way to the Lotophagoi, for from these it is a journey of thirty days to the country of the Garamantians.* Among them also are produced the cattle which feed backwards; and they feed backwards for this reason, because they have their horns bent down forwards, and therefore they walk backwards as they feed; for forwards they cannot go, because the horns run into the ground in front of them; but in nothing else do they differ from other cattle except in this and in the thickness and firmness to the touch of their hide. These Garamantians of whom I speak hunt the "Cave-dwelling" Ethiopians with their four-horse chariots, for the Cave-dwelling Ethiopians are the swiftest of foot of all men about whom we hear report. The Cave-dwellers feed upon serpents and lizards and such creeping things, and they use a language which resembles no other, for in it they squeak just like bats.

184. From the Garamantians at a distance again of ten days' journey there is another hill of salt and spring of water, and men dwell round it called Atarantians, who alone of all men about whom we know are nameless; for while all taken together have the name Atarantians, each separate man of them has no name given to him.† These curse the Sun when he is at his hottest, and moreover revile him with all foul terms, because he oppresses them by his burning heat, both themselves and their land. After this at a distance again of ten days' journey there is another hill of salt and spring of water, and men dwell round it. Near this salt hill is a mountain named Atlas, which is small in circuit and rounded on every side; and so exceedingly lofty is it said to be, that it is not possible to see its summits, for clouds never leave them either in the summer or in the winter.‡ This

---

*The plateau is closest to the sea near Tripoli in modern Libya.
†Perhaps a misunderstood reflection of an African belief in name-magic and a taboo in sharing knowledge of the name.
‡The Atlas range is more than 500 miles long.

the natives say is the pillar of heaven. After this mountain these men got their name, for they are called Atlantians; they are said neither to eat anything that has life nor to have any dreams.

185. As far as these Atlantians I am able to mention in order the names of those who are settled in the belt of sand; but for the parts beyond these I can do so no more. However, the belt extends as far as the Pillars of Heracles and also in the parts outside them: and there is a mine of salt in it at a distance of ten days' journey from the Atlantians, and men dwelling there; and these all have their houses built of the lumps of salt, since these parts of Libya which we have now reached are without rain; for if it rained, the walls being made of salt would not be able to last: and the salt is dug up there both white and purple in colour. Beyond the sand-belt, in the parts which are in the direction of the South and towards the interior of Libya, the country is uninhabited, without water and without wild beasts, rainless and treeless, and there is no trace of moisture in it.

186. I have said that from Egypt as far as lake Tritonis Libyans dwell who are nomads, eating flesh and drinking milk; and these do not taste at all of the flesh of cows, for the same reason as the Egyptians also abstain from it, nor do they keep swine. Moreover the women of the Kyrenians too think it not right to eat cows' flesh, because of the Egyptian Isis, and they even keep fasts and celebrate festivals for her; and the women of Barca, in addition to abstaining from cows' flesh, do not taste of swine either. **187.** But in the region to the West of lake Tritonis the Libyans cease to be nomads, and they do not practise the same customs, nor do to their children anything like the nomads do. The nomad Libyans, whether all of them I cannot say for certain, but many of them, do as follows:—when their children are four years old, they burn with a greasy piece of sheep's wool the veins in the crowns of their heads, and some of them burn the veins of the temples, so that for all their lives to come the cold humour may not run down from their heads and do them hurt. For this reason (they say) they are so healthy; for the Libyans are in truth the most healthy of all races concerning which we have knowledge, whether for this reason or not I cannot say for certain, but the most healthy they certainly are. If, when they burn the children, a convulsion comes on, they have found out a remedy for this; for they pour upon them he-goat urine and so save them. I report what the Libyans themselves say.

188. The following manner of sacrifice the nomads have:—they cut off a part of the animal's ear as a first offering and throw it over the house, and having done this they twist its neck. They sacrifice only to the Sun and the Moon; that is to say, all the Libyans sacrifice to these, but those who dwell round the lake Tritonis sacrifice most of all to Athenē, and next to Triton and Poseidon.

189. It would appear also that the Hellenes made the dress and the *aigis* of the images of Athenē after the model of the Libyan women; for except that the dress of the Libyan women is of leather, and the tassels which hang from their *aigis* are not formed of serpents but of leather thongs, in all other respects Athenē is dressed like them. Moreover the name too declares that the dress of the figures of Pallas has come from Libya, for the Libyan women wear over their other garments bare goat-skins (*aigeas*) with tasselled fringes and coloured over with red madder, and from the name of these goat-skins the Hellenes formed the name *aigis*. I think also that in these regions first arose the practise of cultic crying aloud during the performance of sacred rites, for the Libyan women do this and do it very well. The Hellenes have learnt from the Libyans also the yoking together of four horses. **190.** The nomads bury those who die in just the same manner as the Hellenes, except only the Nasamonians. These bury bodies in a sitting posture, taking care at the moment when the man expires to place him sitting and not to let him die lying down on his back. They have dwellings composed of the stems of asphodel entwined with rushes, and so made that they can be carried about. Such are the customs followed by these tribes.

191. On the West of the river Triton next after the Auseans come Libyans who are tillers of the soil, and whose custom it is to possess fixed habitations; and they are called Maxyans. They grow their hair long on the right side of their heads and cut it short upon the left, and smear their bodies over with red ochre. These say that they belong to the men who came from Troy.*

This country and the rest of Libya which is towards the West is both much more frequented by wild beasts and much more thickly wooded than the country of the nomads. Whereas the part of Libya which is situated towards the East, where the nomads dwell, is low-lying and sandy up to the river Triton, that which succeeds it towards the West, the country of those who till the soil, is exceedingly mountainous and thickly-wooded and full of wild beasts. In the land of these are found both the monstrous serpent and the lion and the elephant, and bears and venomous snakes and horned asses, besides the dog-headed men, and the headless men with their eyes set in their breasts (at least so say the Libyans about them), and the wild men and wild women, and a great multitude of other beasts which are not fabulous like these.†

192. In the land of the nomads however there exist none of these, but other animals as follows:—white-rump antelopes, gazelles, buffaloes, asses, not the horned kind but others which go without water (for in fact these never drink), antelopes [?] whose horns are made into the sides of the Phenician lyre (this animal is in size about equal to an ox), small foxes, hyenas, porcupines, wild rams, wolves, jackals, panthers, boryes, land-crocodiles about four and a half feet in length and very much resembling lizards, ostriches, and small snakes, each with one horn.‡ These wild animals exist in

---

*The absence of any description of the North African Carthaginians, possessors of a powerful empire, is remarkable. Perhaps Herodotus had a Carthaginian source; see 4.195 and 4.197.

†One indication of the limits of Herodotus' credulity.

‡Several species in this list cannot be identified. Later historians (like Ctesias) and naturalists were more inclined to believe in nonexistent creatures. Most of the species of fauna mentioned here have been confirmed by zoologists.

this country, as well as those which exist elsewhere, except the stag and the wild boar; but Libya has no stags nor wild boars at all. Also there are in this country three kinds of mice, one is called the "two-legged" mouse, another the *zegeris* (a name which is Libyan and signifies in the Hellenic tongue a "hill"), and a third the "prickly" mouse or sea-urchin. There are also weasels produced in the *silphion,* which are very like those of Tartessos. Such are the wild animals which the land of the Libyans possesses, so far as we were able to research by inquiries extended as far as possible.

193. Next to the Maxyan Libyans are the Zauekes, whose women drive their chariots for them to war. **194.** Next to these are the Gyzantes, among whom honey is made in great quantity by bees, but in much greater quantity still it is said to be made by men, who work at it as a trade. However that may be, these all smear themselves over with red ochre and eat monkeys, which are produced in very great numbers upon their mountains. **195.** Opposite these, as the Carthaginians say, there lies an island called Kyrauis, twenty-three miles in length but narrow, to which one may walk over from the mainland; and it is full of olives and vines. In it they say there is a pool, from which the native girls with birds' feathers smeared over with pitch bring up gold-dust out of the mud. Whether this is really so I do not know, but I write what is reported. It might all be true, for even in Zakynthos I saw myself pitch brought up out of a pool of water. There are several pools, and the largest of them measures seventy feet in diameter and is six feet in depth. Into this they plunge a pole with a myrtle-branch bound to it, and then with the branch of myrtle they bring up pitch, which has the smell of asphalt, but in other respects it is superior to the pitch of Pieria. This they pour into a pit dug near the pool; and when they have collected a large quantity, then they pour it into the jars from the pit: and whatever thing falls into the pool goes under ground and reappears in the sea, which is a half-mile distant from the pool. Thus then the report about the island off the coast of Libya is also probably enough true.

196. The Carthaginians say also this, namely that there is a place in Libya and men dwelling there, outside the Pillars of Heracles, to whom when they have come and have taken the merchandise forth from their ships, they set it in order along the beach and embark again in their ships, and after that they send up smoke; and the natives of the country seeing the smoke come to the sea, and then they lay down some gold equivalent for the merchandise and retire from the merchandise.* The Carthaginians upon that disembark and examine it, and if the gold is in their opinion sufficient for the value of the merchandise, they take it up and go their way; but if not, they embark again in their ships and sit there; and the others approach and straightway add more gold to the former, until they satisfy them. They say that neither party wrongs the other; for neither do the Carthaginians lay hands on the gold until it is made equal to the value of

---

*Instances of such voiceless barter and trade in Gambia were confirmed by early modern travelers, such as Portuguese merchant adventurers.

their merchandise, nor do the others lay hands on the merchandise until the Carthaginians have taken the gold.

197. These are the Libyan tribes whom we are able to name; and of these the greater number neither now pay any regard to the king of the Medes nor did they then. Thus much also I have to say about this land, namely that it is occupied by four races and no more, so far as we know; and of these races two are natives of the soil and the other two not so; for the Libyans and the Ethiopians are natives, the one race dwelling in the Northern parts of Libya and the other in the Southern,* while the Phenicians† and the Hellenes are immigrants.

198. I think moreover that in goodness of soil Libya has no special excellence compared with Asia or Europe, except only the region of Kinyps, for the same name is given to the land as to the river. This region is equal to the best of lands in bringing forth grain, the fruit of Demeter, nor does it at all resemble the rest of Libya; for it has black soil and is watered by springs, and neither has it fear of drought nor is it hurt by drinking too abundantly of rain; for rain it does in this part of Libya. Of the produce of the crops the same measures hold good here as for the Babylonian land. And that is good land also which the Euesperites occupy, for when it bears best it produces a hundred-fold, but the land in the region of Kinyps produces sometimes as much as three-hundred-fold.

199. Moreover the land of Kyrenē, which is the highest land of the part of Libya which is occupied by nomads, has within its confines three seasons of harvest, at which we may marvel. The parts by the sea-coasts first have their fruits ripe for reaping and for gathering the vintage; and when these have been gathered in, the parts which lie above the sea-side places, those situated in the middle, which they call the hills, are ripe for the gathering in; and as soon as this middle crop has been gathered in, that in the highest part of the land comes to perfection and is ripe; so that by the time the first crop has been eaten and drunk up, the last is just coming in. Thus the harvest for the Kyrenians lasts eight months. Let this information suffice for these things.

200. Now when the Persian helpers of Pheretimē, having been sent from Egypt by Aryandes, had arrived at Barca, they laid siege to the city, proposing to the inhabitants that they should give up those who were guilty of the murder of Arkesilaos.‡ Since all their people had taken a share in the guilt, they did not accept the proposals. Then they besieged Barca for nine months, both digging underground passages which led to the wall and making vigorous attacks upon it. Now the passages dug were discovered by a worker of bronze with a shield covered over with bronze, who had thought of this plan:—carrying it round within the wall he applied it to the ground in the city, and whereas the other places to which he

---

*That is, the Berbers and the Negroes.
†That is, Semitic settlers of Carthage c.900 B.C.
‡The expedition against Barca occurred c.516 B.C. The narrative returns to where we left it at 4.167.

applied it were noiseless, at those places where digging was going on the bronze of the shield gave a sound; and the men of Barca would make a countermine there and slay the Persians who were digging mines. This then was discovered as I have said, and the attacks were repulsed by the men of Barca. **201.** Then as they were suffering hardship for a long time and many were falling on both sides, and especially on that of the Persians, Amasis the commander of the land-army contrived as follows:—perceiving that the Barcaians were not to be conquered by force but might be conquered by guile, he dug by night a broad trench and over it he laid timber of no great strength, and brought earth and laid it above on the top of the timber, making it level with the rest of the ground. At daybreak he invited the men of Barca to a parley; and they gladly consented, and at last they agreed to make a treaty. The treaty was on these terms, the oaths being taken over the hidden trench, namely that so long as this earth should continue to be as it was, so long the oath should remain firm, and that the men of Barca should promise to pay tribute of due amount to the king, and the Persians should do no further mischief to the men of Barca. After the oath the men of Barca trusting to these engagements both went forth themselves from their city and let any enemy who desired pass within their wall, having opened all the gates; but the Persians first broke down the concealed bridge and then began to run inside the city wall. And they broke down the bridge to keep their oaths, since they had sworn to the men of Barca that the oath should remain firm continually for so long as the earth should remain as it then was, but after that they had broken it down, the oath no longer remained firm. **202.** Now the most guilty of the Barcaians, when they were delivered to her by the Persians, Pheretimē impaled in a ring round about the wall; and she cut off the breasts of their wives and adorned the wall round with these also in order. The rest of the men of Barca she bade the Persians carry off as spoil, except so many of them as were of the house of Battos and not sharers in the guilt of the murder; and to these Pheretimē gave charge of the city.

203. So the Persians having made slaves of the rest of the Barcaians departed to go back. When they appeared at the gates of the city of Kyrenē, the Kyrenians let them go through their town in order to avoid neglect of some oracle. Then as the army was going through, Badres the commander of the fleet urged that they should capture the city, but Amasis the commander of the land-army would not consent to it; for he said that they had been sent against no other city of the Hellenes except Barca. When however they had passed through and were encamping on the hill of Zeus Lycaios, they repented of not having taken possession of Kyrenē; and they endeavoured again to pass into it, but the men of Kyrenē would not allow them. Although no one fought against them, suddenly upon the Persians, there fell a sudden panic, and they ran away for about seven miles and then encamped. A messenger came from Aryandes summoning them back; so the Persians asked the Kyrenians to give them provisions for their march and obtained their request; and having received these, they departed to go to Egypt. After this the Libyans met and harried them, and killed for the sake of their clothes and equipment those of them who were ever left back or straggled behind, until at last they came to Egypt.

204. This army of the Persians reached Euesperides, and this was their furthest point in Libya. The Barcaians whom they had reduced to slavery they removed again from Egypt and brought them to the king; and king Dareios gave them a village in the land of Bactria in which to settle. To this village they gave the name of Barca, and it still continued to be inhabited by them even down to my own time, in the land of Bactria.

205. Pheretimē however did not happily end her life any more than they. As soon as she had returned from Libya to Egypt after having avenged herself on the Barcaians, she died an evil death, having suddenly started to boil over with worms while yet alive. As it seems, too severe punishments inflicted by men prove irritating to the gods. Such and so great was the punishment inflicted by Pheretimē the wife of Battos on the men of Barca.

BOOK V

THE IONIANS REVOLT,
THE ATHENIANS ASSIST

1. IN THE MEANTIME THE Persians who had been left behind in Europe by Dareios, of whom Megabazos* was the commander, had subdued the people of Perinthos first of the Hellespontians, since they refused to be subject to Dareios. These had in former times also been hardly dealt with by the Paionians: for the Paionians from the Strymon had been commanded by an oracle of their god to march against the Perinthians; and if the Perinthians, when encamped opposite to them, should shout aloud and call to them by their name, they were to attack them; but if they should not shout to them, they were not to attack them: and thus the Paionians proceeded to do. Now when the Perinthians were encamped opposite to them in the suburb of their city, a challenge was made and a single combat took place in three different forms; for they matched a man against a man, and a horse against a horse, and a dog against a dog. Then, as the Perinthians were getting the better in two of the three, in their exultation they raised a shout of *paiōn*,† and the Paionians conjectured that this was the very thing which was spoken of in the oracle, and said doubtless to one another, "Now surely the oracle is being accomplished for us, now it is time for us to act." So the Paionians attacked the Perinthians when they had raised the shout of paiōn, and they had much the better in the fight, and left but few of them alive. **2.** Thus it happened to them in former times with the Paionians; and at this time, although the Perinthians proved themselves brave men in defence of their freedom, the Persians and Megabazos got the better of them by numbers. Then after Perinthos had been conquered, Megabazos marched his army throughout the length of Thracia, forcing every city and every race of those who dwell there to submit to the king, for so it had been commanded him by Dareios, to subdue Thracia.

3. Now the Thracian race is the most numerous, except the Indians, in all the world: and if it should come to be all ruled over by one man, or to agree together in one, it would be irresistible in fight and the strongest by far of all nations, in my opinion. Since however this is impossible for them and cannot ever come to pass among them, they are in fact weak

---

*Megabazos was in Thrace c.514–512 B.C.
†As *Paiōn* was the Greek name of and appeal to Apollo, this is one of many oracular puns.

for that reason. They have many names, belonging to their various tribes in different places; but they all follow customs which are nearly the same in all respects, except the Getai and Trausians and those who dwell above the Crestonians. **4.** Of these the practices of the Getai, who believe themselves to be immortal, have been spoken of by me already:* and the Trausians perform everything else in the same manner as the other Thracians, but in regard to those who are born and die among them they do as follows:— when a child has been born, the nearest of kin sit round it and make lamentation for all the evils of which he must fulfil the measure, now that he is born, enumerating the whole number of human ills; but when a man is dead, they cover him up in the earth with sport and rejoicing, saying at the same time from what great evils he has escaped and is now in perfect bliss. **5.** Those who dwell above the Crestonians do as follows:—each man has many wives, and when any man of them is dead, a great competition takes place among his wives, with much exertion on the part of their friends, about the question which of them was loved most by their husband; and she who is preferred by the decision and so honoured, is first praised by both men and women, then her throat is cut over the tomb by her nearest of kin, and afterwards she is buried together with her husband; and the others are exceedingly grieved at it, for this is counted as the greatest reproach to them. **6.** Of the other Thracians the custom is to sell their children to be carried away out the country; and over their maidens they do not keep watch, but allow them to have commerce with whatever men they please, but over their wives they keep very great watch; and they buy their wives for great sums of money from their parents. To be pricked with figures† is accounted a mark of noble rank, and not to be so marked is a sign of low birth. Not to work is counted most honourable, and to be a worker of the soil is above all things dishonourable: to live on war and plunder is the most honourable thing. **7.** These are their most remarkable customs; and of the gods they worship only Ares and Dionysos and Artemis.‡ Their kings however, apart from the rest of the people, worship Hermes more than all gods, and swear by him alone; and they say that they are descended from Hermes. **8.** The manner of burial for the rich among them is this:—for three days they expose the corpse to view, and they slay all kinds of victims and feast, having first made lamentation. Then they perform the burial rites, either consuming the body with fire or covering it up in the earth without burning; and afterwards when they have heaped

---

*That is, at 4.93–94; the Getai, who dwelled above Mount Haemos, shared the Hellenic pessimism about life.

†Suttee, juvenile promiscuity, marriage by purchase, and tattooing, sometimes with totems, are widespread (if non-Greek) practices.

‡Herodotus often explains barbarian gods by citing Hellenic gods with one or more similar attributes. The actual identification is usually incorrect, but Ares and Dionysos have real Thracian analogues.

up a mound they celebrate games with every kind of contest, in which reasonably the greatest prizes are assigned for single combat. This is the manner of burial among the Thracians.

9. Of the region lying further on towards the North of this country no one can declare accurately who the men are who dwell in it; but the parts which lie immediately beyond the Ister* are known to be uninhabited and vast in extent. The only men of whom I can hear who dwell beyond the Ister are those who are said to be called Sigynnai, and who use the Median fashion of dress. Their horses, it is said, have shaggy hair all over their bodies, as much as five fingers long; and these are small and flat-nosed and too weak to carry men, but when yoked in chariots they are very high-spirited; therefore the natives of the country drive chariots. The boundaries of this people extend, it is said, to the parts near the Enetoi, who live on the Adriatic;† and people say that they are colonists from the Medes. In what way however these have come to be colonists from the Medes I am not able for my part to conceive, but everything is possible in the long course of ages. However that may be, the Ligurians who dwell in the region inland above Massalia call traders *sigynnai*, and the men of Cyprus give the same name to spears. **10.** Now the Thracians say that the other side of the Ister is occupied by bees, and that by reason of them it is not possible to pass through and proceed further: but to me it seems that when they so speak, they say that which is not probable; for these creatures are known to be intolerant of cold, and to me it seems that the regions which go up towards the pole are uninhabitable by reason of the cold climate. These then are the tales reported about this country; and however that may be, Megabazos was then making the coast-regions of it subject to the Persians.

11. Meanwhile Dareios, so soon as he had crossed over the Hellespont and come to Sardis, called to mind the service rendered to him by Histiaios the Milesian and also the advice of the Mytilenian Coës,‡ and having sent for them to come to Sardis he offered them a choice of rewards. Histiaios then, being despot of Miletos, did not make request for any government in addition to that, but he asked for the district of Myrkinos which belonged to the Edonians, desiring there to found a city. Histiaios chose this for himself; but Coës, not being a despot but a man of the people, asked to be made despot of Mytilenē. **12.** After the desires of both had been fulfilled, they betook themselves to that which they had chosen: and at this same time it chanced that Dareios saw a certain thing which made him desire to command Megabazos to conquer the Paionians and remove them forcibly from Europe into Asia: and the thing was this:—There were certain Paionians named Pigres and Mantyas, who when Dareios had crossed over into Asia, came to Sardis, because they desired themselves to have

---

*The Danube, compared to the Nile at 2.33–34 and described at 4.47–49.
†Reference to the later "Venetians."
‡See 4.137–139, 4.141, 4.97; 5.11, and 5.37–38.

rule over the Paionians, and with them they brought their sister, who was tall and comely. Then having watched for a time when Dareios took his seat publicly in the suburb of the Lydian city, they dressed up their sister in the best way they could, and sent her to fetch water, having a water-jar upon her head and leading a horse after her by a bridle round her arm, and at the same time spinning flax. Now when the woman passed out of the city by him, Dareios paid attention to the matter, for that which was done by the woman was not of Persian nor yet of Lydian fashion, nor indeed after the manner of any people of Asia. He sent therefore some of his spearmen, bidding them watch what the woman would do with the horse. They accordingly followed after her; and she having arrived at the river watered the horse, and having watered him and filled her jar with the water, she passed along by the same way, bearing the water upon her head, leading the horse after her by a bridle round her arm, and at the same time turning the spindle.

13. Then Dareios, marvelling both at that which he heard from those who went to observe and also at that which he saw himself, bade them bring her into his presence: and when she was brought, her brothers also came, who had been watching these things at no great distance off. So then when Dareios asked of what country she was, the young men said that they were Paionians and that she was their sister; and he replied: "Who then are these Paionians, and where upon the earth do they dwell?" and he asked them also what they desired, that they had come to Sardis. They declared to him that they had come to give themselves up to him, and that Paionia was a country situated upon the river Strymon, and that the Strymon was not far from the Hellespont, and finally that they were colonists from the Teucrians of Troy. All these things they told him; and he asked whether all the women of that land were as industrious as their sister; and they very readily replied to this also, saying that it was so, for it was with a view to that very thing that they had been doing this. **14.** Then Dareios wrote a letter to Megabazos, whom he had left to command his army in Thrace, bidding him remove the Paionians from their place of habitation and bring them to the king, both themselves and their children and their wives. Then immediately a horseman set forth to ride in haste bearing the message to the Hellespont, and having passed over to the other side he gave the paper to Megabazos. So he having read it and having obtained guides from Thrace, set forth to march upon Paionia: **15,** and the Paionians, being informed that the Persians were coming against them, gathered all their powers together and marched out in the direction of the sea, supposing that the Persians when they invaded them would make their attack on that side. The Paionians then were prepared, as I say, to drive off the army of Megabazos when it came against them; but the Persians hearing that the Paionians had gathered their powers and were guarding the entrance which lay towards the sea, directed their course with guides along the upper road; and passing unperceived by the Paionians they fell upon their cities, which were left without men, and finding them without defenders they easily took possession of them. The

Paionians when they heard that their cities were in the hands of the enemy, at once dispersed, each tribe to its own place of abode, and proceeded to deliver themselves up to the Persians. Thus then it happened that these tribes of the Paionians, namely the Siropaionians, the Paioplians and all up to the lake Prasias, were removed from their place of habitation and brought to Asia. **16.** But those who dwell about mount Pangaion, and about the Doberians and Agrianians and Odomantians, and about the lake Prasias itself, were not conquered at all by Megabazos. He tried however to remove even those who lived in the lake and who had their dwellings in the following manner:—a platform fastened together and resting upon lofty piles stood in the middle of the water of the lake, with a narrow approach to it from the mainland by a single bridge. The piles which supported the platform were no doubt originally set there by all the members of the community working together, but since that time they continue to set them by observance of this rule, that is to say, every man who marries brings from the mountain called Orbelos three piles for each wife and sets them as supports; and each man takes to himself many wives. And they have their dwelling thus, that is each man has possession of a hut upon the platform in which he lives and of a trap-door leading through the platform down to the lake: and their infant children they tie with a rope by the foot, for fear that they should roll into the water. To their horses and beasts of burden they give fish for fodder; and of fish there is so great quantity that if a man open the trap-door and let down an empty basket by a cord into the lake, after waiting quite a short time he draws it up again full of fish. Of the fish there are two kinds, and they call them *paprax* and *tilon*.

17. So then those of the Paionians who had been conquered were being brought to Asia: and Megabazos meanwhile, after he had conquered the Paionians, sent as envoys to Macedonia seven Persians, who after himself were the men of most repute in the army. These were being sent to Amyntas to demand of him earth and water for Dareios the king. Now from lake Prasias there is a very short way into Macedonia; for first, quite close to the lake, there is the mine from which after this time there came in regularly a talent of silver every day to Alexander; and after the mine, when you have passed over the mountain called Dysoron, you are in Macedonia.

18. These Persians then, who had been sent to Amyntas, having arrived came into the presence of Amyntas and proceeded to demand earth and water for king Dareios. This he was willing to give, and also he invited them to be his guests; and he prepared a magnificent dinner and received the Persians with friendly hospitality. Then when dinner was over, the Persians while drinking pledges to one another* said thus: "Macedonian guest-friend, it is the custom among us Persians, when we set forth a great dinner, then to bring in also our concubines and lawful wives to sit beside us.

---

*Compare 3.38 for variety in customs.

Do you then, since you did readily receive us and do now entertain us magnificently as your guests, and since you are willing to give to king Dareios earth and water, consent to follow our custom." To this Amyntas replied: "Persians, among us the custom is not so, but that men should be separate from women. Since however you being our masters make this request in addition, this also shall be given you."

Having so said Amyntas proceeded to send for the women; and when they came being summoned, they sat down in order opposite to the Persians. Then the Persians, seeing women of comely form, spoke to Amyntas and said that this which had been done was by no means well devised; for it was better that the women should not come at all, than that they should come and should not seat themselves by their side, but sit opposite and be a pain to their eyes. So Amyntas being compelled bade them sit by the side of the Persians; and when the women obeyed, immediately the Persians, being much intoxicated, began to touch their breasts, and some no doubt also tried to kiss them. **19.** Amyntas seeing this kept quiet, notwithstanding that he felt anger, because he excessively feared the Persians; but Alexander the son of Amyntas, who was present and saw this, being young and without experience of calamity was not able to endure any longer; but being impatient of it he said to Amyntas: "My father, grant that which your age demands, and go away to rest, nor persevere longer in the drinking; but I will remain here and give to our guests all that is convenient." On this Amyntas, understanding that Alexander was intending to do some violence, said: "My son, I think that I understand your words, as the heat of anger moves you, namely that you desire to send me away and then do some deed of violence: therefore I ask of you not to do violence to these men, that it may not be our ruin, but endure to see that which is being done: as to my departure however, in that I will do as you say."

20. When Amyntas after having made of him this request had departed, Alexander said to the Persians: "With these women you have perfect freedom, guests, to have sex with all, if you so desire, or with as many of them as you will. About this matter you shall be they who give the word; but now, since already the hour is approaching for you to go to bed and I see that you have well drunk, let these women go away, if so it is pleasing to you, to bathe themselves; and when they have bathed, then receive them back into your company." Having so said, since the Persians readily agreed, he dismissed the women, when they had gone out, to the women's chambers.

Alexander himself equipped men equal in number to the women and smooth-faced, in the dress of the women, and giving them daggers he led them into the banqueting-room; and as he led them in, he said thus to the Persians: "Persians, it seems to me that you have been entertained with a feast to which nothing was wanting; for other things, as many as we had, and moreover such as we were able to find out and furnish, are all supplied to you, and there is this especially besides, which is the chief thing of all, that is, we give you freely in addition our mothers and our sisters, in order that you may perceive fully that you are honoured by us with that treatment which you deserve, and also in order that you may report to the king who sent you that a man of Hellas, ruler under him of the Macedonians, entertained you well at board and bed." Having thus said Alexander caused a Macedonian man in the guise of a woman to sit by each Persian, and they, when the Persians attempted to lay hands on them, slew them. **21.** So these perished by this fate, both they themselves and their company of servants; for there came with them carriages and servants and all the usual pomp of equipage, and this was all made away with at the same time as they. Afterwards in no long time a great search was made by the Persians for these men, and Alexander stopped them with cunning by giving large sums of money and his own sister, whose name was Gygaia;—by giving, I say, these things to Bubares a Persian, commander of those who were searching for the men who had been killed, Alexander stopped their search.

22. Thus the death of these Persians was kept concealed. And that these descendants of Perdiccas are Hellenes, as they themselves say, I happen to know myself, and not only so, but I will prove in the succeeding history that they are Hellenes.* Moreover the Hellanodicai, who manage the games at Olympia, decided that they were so: for when Alexander wished to contend in the games and had descended for this purpose into the arena, the Hellenes who were to run against him tried to exclude him, saying that the contest was not for Barbarians to contend in but for Hellenes: since however Alexander proved that he was of Argos, he was judged to be a Hellene, and when he entered the contest of the footrace his lot came out with that of the first pair.

23. Thus then it happened with regard to these things: and at the same time Megabazos had arrived at the Hellespont bringing with him the Paionians; and thence after passing over the strait he came to Sardis. Then, since Histiaios the Milesian was already engaged in fortifying with a wall the place which he had asked and obtained from Dareios as a reward for keeping safe the bridge of boats (this place is called Myrkinos, lying along the bank of the river Strymon), Megabazos, having perceived what Histiaios was doing, as soon as he came to Sardis bringing the Paionians, said thus to Dareios: "O king, what a thing is this that you have done, granting permission to a Hellene who is skilful and cunning, to found a city in Thracia in a place where there is forest for shipbuilding in abundance and great quantity of wood for oars and mines of silver and great numbers both of Hellenes and Barbarians living round, who when they have obtained a leader will do that which he shall command them both by day and by night. Therefore stop this man from doing so, that you be not involved in a domestic war: and stop him by sending for him in a courteous manner; but when you have got him into your hands, then cause that he shall never again return to the land of the Hellenes."

---

*See 8.137.

24. Thus saying Megabazos easily persuaded Dareios, who thought that he was a true prophet of that which was likely to come to pass: and upon that Dareios sent a messenger to Myrkinos and said as follows: "Histiaios, king Dareios says these things:—By taking thought I find that there is no one more sincerely well disposed than you are to me and to my power; and this I know having learnt by deeds not words. Now therefore, since I have it in my mind to accomplish great matters, come hither to me by all means, that I may communicate them to you." Histiaios therefore, trusting to these sayings and at the same time accounting it a great thing to become a counsellor of the king, came to Sardis; and when he had come Dareios spoke to him as follows: "Histiaios, I sent for you for this reason, namely because when I had returned from the Scythians and you were gone away out of the sight of my eyes, never did I desire to see anything again within so short a time as I desired then both to see you and that you should come to speech with me; since I perceived that the most valuable of all possessions is a friend who is a man of understanding and also sincerely well-disposed, both which qualities I know exist in you, and I am able to bear witness of them in regard to my affairs. Now therefore (for you did well in that you came hither) this is what I propose to you:— leave Miletos alone and also your newly-founded city in Thracia, and coming with me to Susa, have whatsoever things I have, eating at my table and being my counsellor."

25. Thus said Dareios, and having appointed Artaphrenes his own brother and the son of his father to be governor of Sardis, he marched away to Susa taking with him Histiaios, after he had first named Otanes to be commander of those who dwelt along the sea coasts. This man's father Sisamnes, who had been made one of the Royal Judges, king Cambyses slew, because he had judged a cause unjustly for money, and flayed off all his skin: then after he had torn away the skin he cut leathern thongs out of it and stretched them across the seat where Sisamnes had been wont to sit to give judgment; and having stretched them in the seat, Cambyses appointed the son of that Sisamnes whom he had slain and flayed, to be judge instead of his father, enjoining him to remember in what seat he was sitting to give judgment. **26.** This Otanes then, who was made to sit in that seat, had now become the successor of Megabazos in the command: and he conquered the Byzantians and Calchedonians, and he conquered Antandros in the land of Troas, and Lamponion; and having received ships from the Lesbians he conquered Lemnos and Imbros, which were both at that time still inhabited by Pelasgians. **27.** Of these the Lemnians fought well, and defending themselves for a long time were at length brought to ruin; and over those of them who survived the Persians set as governor Lycaretos the brother of that Maiandrios who had been king of Samos. This Lycaretos ruled in Lemnos till his death. And the cause of it was this:—he continued to reduce all to slavery and subdue them, accusing some of desertion to the Scythians and others of doing damage to the army of Dareios as it was coming back from Scythia.

28. Otanes then effected so much when he was made commander: and after this for a short time there was an abatement of evils; and then again evils began a second time to fall upon the Ionians, arising from Naxos and Miletos. For Naxos was superior to all the other islands in wealth, and Miletos at the same time had just then come to the very height of its prosperity and was the ornament of Ionia; but before these events for two generations of men it had been afflicted most violently by faction, until the Parians reformed it; for these the Milesians chose of all the Hellenes to be reformers of their State. **29.** Now the Parians thus reconciled their factions:—the best men of them came to Miletos, and seeing that the Milesians were in a grievously ruined state, they said that they desired to go over their land: and while doing this and passing through the whole territory of Miletos, whenever they saw in the desolation of the land any field that was well cultivated, they wrote down the name of the owner of that field. Then when they had passed through the whole land and had found but few of such men, as soon as they returned to the city they called a general gathering and appointed these men to manage the State, whose fields they had found well cultivated; for they said that they thought these men would take care of the public affairs as they had taken care of their own: and the rest of the Milesians, who before had been divided by factions, they commanded to be obedient to these men.

30. The Parians then had thus reformed the Milesians; but at the time of which I speak evils began to come to Ionia from these States,* Miletos and Naxos, in the following manner:—From Naxos certain men of the wealthier class were driven into exile by the people, and having gone into exile they arrived at Miletos. Now of Miletos it happened that Aristagoras son of Molpagoras was ruler in charge, being both a son-in-law and also a cousin of Histiaios the son of Lysagoras, whom Dareios was keeping at Susa: for Histiaios was despot of Miletos, and it happened that he was at Susa at this time when the Naxians came, who had been in former times guest-friends of Histiaios. So when the Naxians arrived, they made request of Aristagoras, to see if perchance he would supply them with a force, and so they might return from exile to their own land: and he, thinking that if by his means they should return to their own State, he would be ruler of Naxos, but at the same time making a pretext of the guest-friendship of Histiaios, made proposal to them thus: "I am not able to engage that I can supply you with sufficient force to bring you back from exile against the will of those Naxians who have control of the State; for I hear that the Naxians have an army which is eight thousand shields strong and many ships of war: but I will use every endeavour to devise a means; and my plan is this:—it chances that Artaphrenes is my friend: now Artaphrenes, you must know, is a son of Hystaspes and brother of Dareios the king; and he is ruler of all the people of the sea-coasts in Asia, with a great army and many ships. This man then I think will do whatsoever we shall request of him." Hearing this the

---

*The expedition to Naxos took place c.501 B.C.

Naxians gave over the matter to Aristagoras to manage as best he could, and they bade him promise gifts and the expenses of the expedition, saying that they would pay them; for they had full expectation that when they should appear at Naxos, the Naxians would do all their bidding, and likewise also the other islanders. For of these islands, that is the Cyclades, not one was as yet subject to Dareios.

31. Aristagoras accordingly having arrived at Sardis, said to Artaphrenes that Naxos was an island not indeed large in size, but fair nevertheless and of fertile soil, as well as near to Ionia, and that there was in it much wealth and many slaves: "Do you therefore send an expedition against this land, and restore to it those who are now exiles from it: and if you shall do this, first I have ready for you large sums of money apart from the expenses incurred for the expedition (which it is fair that we who conduct it should supply), and next you will gain for the king not only Naxos itself but also the islands which are dependent upon it, Paros and Andros and the others which are called Cyclades; and setting out from these you will easily attack Eubœa, an island which is large and wealthy, as large indeed as Cyprus, and very easy to conquer. To subdue all these a hundred ships are sufficient." He made answer in these words: "You have been a reporter of good things to the house of the king; and in all these things you advise well, except as to the number of the ships: for instead of one hundred there shall be prepared for you two hundred by the beginning of the spring. And it is right that the king himself also should join in approving this matter." **32.** So Aristagoras hearing this went back to Miletos greatly rejoiced; and Artaphrenes meanwhile, when he had sent to Susa and communicated that which was said by Aristagoras, and Dareios himself also had joined in approving it, made ready two hundred triremes and a very great multitude both of Persians and their allies, and appointed to be commander of these Megabates a Persian, one of the Achaimenidai and a cousin to himself and to Dareios, to whose daughter afterwards Pausanias the son of Cleombrotos the Lacedemonian (at least if the story be true) betrothed himself, having formed a desire to become despot of Hellas. Having appointed Megabates, I say, to be commander, Artaphrenes sent away the armament to Aristagoras.

33. So when Megabates had taken up from Miletos Aristagoras and the Ionian force together with the Naxians, he sailed with the pretence of going to the Hellespont; but when he came to Chios, he directed his ships to Caucasa, in order that he might from thence pass them over to Naxos with a North Wind. Then, since it was not fated that the Naxians should be destroyed by this expedition, there happened an event which I shall narrate. As Megabates was going round to visit the guards set in the several ships, it chanced that in a ship of Myndos there was no one on guard; and he being very angry bade his spearmen find out the commander of the ship, whose name was Skylax, and bind him in an oar-hole of his ship in such a manner that his head should be outside and his body within. When Skylax was thus bound, some one reported to Aristagoras that Megabates had bound his guest-friend of Myndos and was doing to him shameful outrage.

He accordingly came and asked the Persian for his release, and as he did not obtain anything of that which he requested, he went himself and let him loose. Being informed of this Megabates was exceedingly angry and broke out in rage against Aristagoras; and he replied: "What have you to do with these matters? Did not Artaphrenes send you to obey me, and to sail whithersoever I should order? Why meddle with things which concern you not?" Thus said Aristagoras; and the other being enraged at this, when night came on sent men in a ship to Naxos to declare to the Naxians all the danger that threatened them.

34. For the Naxians were not at all expecting that this expedition would be against them: but when they were informed of it, immediately they brought within the wall the property which was in the fields, and provided for themselves food and drink as for a siege, and strengthened their wall. These then were making preparations as for war to come upon them; and the others meanwhile having passed their ships over from Chios to Naxos, found them well defended when they made their attack, and besieged them for four months. Then when the money which the Persians had brought with them had all been consumed by them, and not only that, but Aristagoras himself had spent much in addition, and the siege demanded ever more and more, they built walls for the Naxian exiles and departed to the mainland again with ill success.

35. So Aristagoras was not able to fulfil his promise to Artaphrenes; and at the same time he was hard pressed by the demand made to him for the expenses of the expedition, and had fears because of the ill success of the armament and because he had become an enemy of Megabates; and he supposed that he would be deprived of his rule over Miletos. Having all these various fears he began to make plans of revolt: for it happened also that just at this time the man who had been marked upon the head had come from Histiaios who was at Susa, signifying that Aristagoras should revolt from the king. For Histiaios, desiring to signify to Aristagoras that he should revolt, was not able to do it safely in any other way, because the roads were guarded, but shaved off the hair of the most faithful of his slaves, and having marked his head by pricking it, waited till the hair had grown again; and as soon as it was grown, he sent him away to Miletos, giving him no other charge but this, namely that when he should have arrived at Miletos he should bid Aristagoras shave his hair and look at his head: and the marks, as I have said before, signified revolt. This thing Histiaios was doing, because he was greatly vexed by being detained at Susa. He had great hopes then that if a revolt occurred he would be let go to the sea-coast; but if no change of government was made at Miletos he had no expectation of ever returning thither again.

36. Accordingly Histiaios with this intention was sending the messenger; and it chanced that all these things happened to Aristagoras together at the same time.* He took counsel therefore with his partisans, declaring

*The Ionic revolt occurred in 500 B.C.

to them both his own opinion and the message from Histiaios; and while all the rest expressed an opinion to the same effect, urging him namely to make revolt, Hecataios the historian urged first that they should not undertake war with the king of the Persians, enumerating all the nations over whom Dareios was ruler, and his power: and when he did not succeed in persuading him, he counselled next that they should manage to make themselves masters of the sea. Now this, he continued, could not come to pass in any other way, so far as he could see, for he knew that the force of the Milesians was weak, but if the treasures should be taken which were in the temple at Branchidai, which Crœsus the Lydian dedicated as offerings, he had great hopes that they might become masters of the sea; and by this means they would not only themselves have wealth at their disposal, but the enemy would not be able to carry the things off as plunder. Now these treasures were of great value, as I have shown in the first part of the history.* This opinion did not prevail; but nevertheless it was resolved to make revolt, and that one of them should sail to Myus, to the force which had returned from Naxos and was then there, and endeavour to seize the commanders who sailed in the ships.

37. So Iatragoras was sent for this purpose and seized by craft Oliatos the son of Ibanollis of Mylasa, and Histiaios the son of Tymnes of Termera, and Coës the son of Erxander, to whom Dareios had given Mytilenē as a gift, and Aristagoras the son of Heracleides of Kymē, and many others; and then Aristagoras openly made revolt and devised all that he could to the hurt of Dareios. And first he pretended to resign the despotic power and give to Miletos equality,† in order that the Milesians might be willing to revolt with him: then afterwards he proceeded to do this same thing in the rest of Ionia also; and some of the despots he drove out, but those whom he had taken from the ships which had sailed with him to Naxos, these he surrendered, because he desired to do a pleasure to their cities, delivering them over severally to that city from which each one came.

38. Now the men of Mytilenē, so soon as they received Coës into their hands, brought him out and stoned him to death; but the men of Kymē let their despot go, and so also most of the others let them go. Thus then the despots were deposed in the various cities; and Aristagoras the Milesian, after having deposed the despots, bade each people appoint commanders in their several cities, and then himself set forth as an envoy to Lacedemon; for in truth it was necessary that he should find out some powerful alliance.

39. Now at Sparta Anaxandrides the son of Leon was no longer surviving as king, but had brought his life to an end; and Cleomenes the son of Anaxandrides was holding the royal power, not having obtained it by merit but by right of birth. For Anaxandrides had to wife his own sister's daughter and she was by him much beloved, but no children were born to

---

*See 1.92.
†*Isonomiē,* for which see 3.80.

him by her. This being so, the Ephors summoned him before them and said: "If you do not for yourself take thought in time, yet we cannot suffer this to happen, that the race of Eurysthenes should become extinct. Do you therefore put away from you the wife whom you now have, since, as you know, she bears you no children, and marry another: and in doing so you will please the Spartans." He made answer saying that he would do neither of these two things, and that they did not give him honourable counsel, in that they advised him to send away the wife whom he had, though she had done him no wrong, and to take to his house another; and in short he would not follow their advice.

40. Upon this the Ephors and the Senators deliberated together and proposed to Anaxandrides as follows: "Since then we perceive that you are firmly attached to the wife whom you now have, consent to do this, and set not yourself against it, lest the Spartans take some counsel about you other than might be wished. We do not ask you to put away the wife whom you have; but do you give to her all that you give now and at the same time take to your house another wife in addition to this one, to bear you children." When they spoke to him after this manner, Anaxandrides consented, and from this time forth he kept two separate households, having two wives, a thing which was not by any means after the Spartan fashion. **41.** Then when no long time had elapsed, the wife who had come in afterwards bore this Cleomenes of whom we spoke; and just when she was bringing to the light an heir to the kingdom of the Spartans, the former wife, who had during the time before been childless, then by some means conceived, chancing to do so just at that time: and though she was in truth with child, the kinsfolk of the wife who had come in afterwards, when they heard of it cried out against her and said that she was making a vain boast, and that she meant to pass off another child as her own. Since then they made a great show of indignation, as the time was fast drawing near, the Ephors being incredulous sat round and watched the woman during the birth of her child: and she bore Dorieus and then straightway conceived Leonidas and after him at once Cleombrotos,—nay, some even say that Cleombrotos and Leonidas were twins. The wife however who had born Cleomenes and had come in after the first wife, being the daughter of Prinetades the son of Demarmenos, did not bear a child again.

42. Now Cleomenes, it is said, was not quite in his right senses but on the verge of madness, while Dorieus was of all his equals in age the first, and felt assured that he would obtain the kingdom by merit. Seeing then that he had this opinion, when Anaxandrides died and the Lacedemonians following the usual custom established the eldest, namely Cleomenes, upon the throne, Dorieus being indignant and not thinking it fit that he should be a subject of Cleomenes, asked the Spartans to give him a company of followers and led them out to found a colony, without either inquiring of the Oracle at Delphi to what land he should go to make a settlement, or doing any of the things which are usually done; but being vexed he sailed away with his ships to Libya, and the Theraians were his guides thither. Then having come to Kinyps in Africa he made a settlement in the fairest spot of all Libya, along the banks of the river; but afterwards in the third year he was driven out from thence by the Macai and the other Libyans and the Carthaginians, and returned to Peloponnesus. **43.** Then Antichares a man of Eleon gave him counsel out of the oracles of Laïos to make a settlement at Heracleia in Sicily, saying that the whole land of Eryx belonged to the Heracleidai, since Heracles himself had won it: and hearing this he went immediately to Delphi to inquire immediately of the Oracle whether he would be able to conquer the land to which he was setting forth; and the Pythian prophetess replied to him that he would conquer it. Dorieus therefore took with him the armament which he conducted before to Libya, and voyaged along the coast of southwest Italy. **44.** Now at this time,* the men of Sybaris say that they and their king Telys were about to make an expedition against Crotōn, and the men of Crotōn being exceedingly alarmed asked Dorieus to help them and obtained their request. So Dorieus joined them in an expedition against Sybaris and helped them to conquer Sybaris. This is what the men of Sybaris say of the doings of Dorieus and his followers; but those of Crotōn say that no stranger helped them in the war against the Sybarites except Callias alone, a diviner of Elis and one of the descendants of Iamos, and he in the following manner:—he ran away, they say, from Telys the despot of the Sybarites, when the sacrifices did not prove favourable, as he was sacrificing for the expedition against Crotōn, and so he came to them.

45. Such, I say, are the tales which these tell, and they produce as evidence of them the following facts:—the Sybarites point to a sacred enclosure and temple by the side of the dried-up bed of the Crathis, which they say that Dorieus, after he had joined in the capture of the city, set up to Athenē surnamed "of the Crathis"; and besides they consider the death of Dorieus himself to be very strong evidence, thinking that he perished because he acted contrary to the oracle which was given to him; for if he had not done anything by the way but had continued to do that for which he was sent, he would have conquered the land of Eryx and having conquered it would have become possessor of it, and he and his army would not have perished. On the other hand the men of Crotōn declare that many things were granted in the territory of Crotōn as special gifts to Callias the Eleian, of which the descendants of Callias were still in possession down to my time, and that nothing was granted to Dorieus or the descendants of Dorieus: but if Dorieus had in fact helped them in the war with Sybaris, many times as much, they say, would have been given to him as to Callias. These then are the evidences which the two sides produce, and we may assent to whichever of them we think credible. **46.** Now there sailed with Dorieus others also of the Spartans, to be joint-founders with him of the colony, namely Thessalos and Paraibates and Keleas and Euryleon; and these when they had reached Sicily with all their armament, were slain, being defeated in battle by the Phenicians and the men of Egesta;

---

*Sybaris was destroyed in 510 B.C.

and Euryleon only of the joint-founders survived this disaster. This man then having collected the survivors of the expedition, took possession of Minoa the colony of Selinus, and he helped to free the men of Selinus from their despot Peithagoras. Afterwards, when he had deposed him, he laid hands himself upon the despotism in Selinus and became sole ruler there, though but for a short time; for the men of Selinus rose in revolt against him and slew him, notwithstanding that he had fled for refuge to the altar of Zeus Agoraios.*

47. There had accompanied Dorieus also and died with him Philip the son of Butakides, a man of Crotōn, who having betrothed himself to the daughter of Telys the Sybarite, became an exile from Crotōn; and then being disappointed of this marriage he sailed away to Kyrenē, whence he set forth and accompanied Dorieus with a trireme of his own, himself supplying the expenses of the crew. Now this man had been a victor at the Olympic games, and he was the most beautiful of the Hellenes who lived in his time; and on account of his beauty he obtained from the men of Egesta that which none else ever obtained from them, for they established a hero-temple over his tomb, and they propitiate him still with sacrifices.

48. In this manner Dorieus ended his life: but if he had endured to be a subject of Cleomenes and had remained in Sparta, he would have been king of Lacedemon; for Cleomenes reigned no very long time,† and died leaving no son to succeed him but a daughter only, whose name was Gorgo.

49. However, Aristagoras the despot of Miletos arrived at Sparta‡ while Cleomenes was reigning: and accordingly with him he came to speech, having, as the Lacedemonians say, a tablet of bronze, on which was engraved a map of the whole Earth, with all the sea and all the rivers. And when he came to speech with Cleomenes he said to him as follows: "Marvel not, Cleomenes, at my earnestness in coming hither, for the case is this.—That the sons of the Ionians should be slaves instead of free is a reproach and a grief most of all indeed to ourselves, but of all others most to you, inasmuch as you are the leaders of Hellas. Now therefore I entreat you by the gods of Hellas to rescue from slavery the Ionians, who are your own kinsmen: and you may easily achieve this, for the Barbarians are not valiant in fight, whereas you have attained to the highest point of valour in that which relates to war: and their fighting is of this fashion, namely with bows and arrows and a short spear, and they go into battles wearing trousers and with caps§ on their heads. Thus they are easily conquered. Then again they who occupy that continent have good things in such quantity as not all the other nations of the world together possess; first gold, then silver and bronze and embroidered garments and beasts of burden and slaves; all which you might have for yourselves, if you so desired. And the nations

---

*"Zeus of the Market-Place."
†Herodotus is wrong here, since Cleomenes reigned c.521–489 B.C.
‡Aristagoras was at Sparta in 500 B.C.
§See the warrior catalog at 7.64.

moreover dwell in such order one after the other as I shall declare:—the Ionians here; and next to them the Lydians, who not only dwell in a fertile land, but are also exceedingly rich in gold and silver,"—and as he said this he pointed to the map of the Earth, which he carried with him engraved upon the tablet,—"and here next to the Lydians," continued Aristagoras, "are the Eastern Phrygians, who have both the greatest number of sheep and cattle of any people that I know, and also the most abundant crops. Next to the Phrygians are the Cappadokians, whom we call Syrians; and bordering upon them are the Kilikians, coming down [he pointed] to this sea, in which lies the island of Cyprus here; and these pay five hundred talents to the king for their yearly tribute. Next to these Kilikians are the Armenians, whom you may see here, and these also have great numbers of sheep and cattle. Next to the Armenians are the Matienians occupying this country here; and next to them is the land of Kissia here, in which land by the banks of this river Choaspes is situated that city of Susa where the great king has his residence, and where the money is laid up in treasuries.

"After you have taken this city you may then with good courage enter into a contest with Zeus in the matter of wealth. Nay, but can it be that you feel yourselves bound to take upon you the risk of battles against Messenians and Arcadians and Argives, who are equally matched against you, for the sake of land which is not much in extent nor very fertile, and for confines which are but small, though these peoples have neither gold nor silver at all, for the sake of which desire incites one to fight and to die,— can this be, I say, and will you choose some other way now, when it is possible for you easily to have the rule over all Asia?" Aristagoras spoke thus, and Cleomenes answered him saying: "Guest-friend from Miletos, I defer my answer to you till the day after to-morrow."

50. Thus far then they advanced at that time; and when the appointed day arrived for the answer, and they had come to the place agreed upon, Cleomenes asked Aristagoras how many days' journey it was from the sea of the Ionians to the residence of the king. Now Aristagoras, who in other respects acted cleverly and imposed upon him well, in this point made a mistake: for whereas he ought not to have told him the truth, at least if he desired to bring the Spartans out to Asia, he said in fact that it was a journey up from the sea of three months: and the other cutting short the rest of the account which Aristagoras had begun to give of the way, said: "Guest-friend from Miletos, get you away from Sparta before the sun has set; for you speak a word which sounds not well in the ears of the Lacedemonians, desiring to take them a journey of three months away from the sea."

51. Cleomenes having so said went away to his house: but Aristagoras took the suppliant's branch and went to the house of Cleomenes; and having entered as a suppliant, he bade Cleomenes send away the child and listen to him; for the daughter of Cleomenes was standing by him, whose name was Gorgo, and this as it chanced was his only child, being of the age now of eight or nine years. Cleomenes however bade him say that which he desired to say, and not to stop on account of the child. Then Aristagoras proceeded to promise him money, beginning with ten talents, if he would accomplish for him that for which he was asking; and when Cleomenes refused, Aristagoras went on increasing the sums of money offered, until at last he had promised fifty talents, and at that moment the child cried out: "Father, the stranger will do you hurt,* if you do not leave him and go." Cleomenes then, pleased by the counsel of the child, departed into another room, and Aristagoras went away from Sparta altogether, and had no opportunity of explaining any further about the way up from the sea to the residence of the king.

52. As regards this road the truth is as follows.—Everywhere there are royal stations and excellent resting-places, and the whole road runs through country which is inhabited and safe. Through Lydia and Phrygia there extend twenty stages, amounting to ninety-four and a half parasangs or 330 miles; and after Phrygia succeeds the river Halys, at which there is a narrow pass which one must needs pass through in order to cross the river, and a strong guard-post is established there. Then after crossing over into Cappadokia it is twenty-eight stages, being a hundred and four parasangs or 364 miles, by this way to the borders of Kilikia; and on the borders of the Kilikians you will pass through two passes and go by two guard-posts: then after passing through these it is three stages, amounting to fifteen and a half parasangs or fifty-four miles, to journey through Kilikia; and the boundary of Kilikia and Armenia is a navigable river called Euphrates. In Armenia the number of stages with resting-places is fifteen, and of parasangs fifty-six and a half or 197 miles, and there is a guard-post on the way: then from Armenia, when one enters the land of Matienē, there are thirty-four stages, amounting to a hundred and thirty-seven parasangs or 479 miles; and through this land flow four navigable rivers, which cannot be crossed but by ferries, first the Tigris, then a second and third called both by the same name, Zabatos, though they are not the same river nor do they flow from the same region (for the first-mentioned of them flows from the Armenian land and the other from that of the Matienians), and the fourth of the rivers is called Gyndes, the same which once Cyrus divided into three hundred and sixty channels.† Passing thence into the Kissian land, there are eleven stages, forty-two and a half parasangs or 149 miles, to the river Choaspes, which is also a navigable stream; and upon this is built the city of Susa. The number of these stages amounts in all to one hundred and eleven.

53. This is the number of stages with resting-places, as one goes up from Sardis to Susa: and if the royal road has been rightly measured as regards parasangs, and if the parasang is equal to thirty stades, (as undoubtedly it is), the number of stades from Sardis to that which is called the palace of Memnon is thirteen thousand five hundred, the number of parasangs being

---

*Gorgo misread Aristagoras' vehement gestures, and Cleomenes accepted this as an omen; compare 9.102.

†See 1.189.

four hundred and fifty or 1,550 miles. So if one travels a hundred and fifty stades or seventeen and one quarter miles each day, just ninety days are spent on the journey. **54.** Thus the Milesian Aristagoras, when he told Cleomenes the Lacedemonian that the journey up from the sea to the residence of the king was one of three months, spoke correctly: but if any one demands a more exact statement yet than this, I will give him that also: for we ought to reckon in addition to this the length of the road from Ephesos to Sardis; and I say accordingly that the whole number of stades from the sea of Hellas to Susa (for by that name the city of Memnon is known) is fourteen thousand and forty or 1,611 miles; for the number of stades from Ephesos to Sardis is five hundred and forty or sixty-two miles: thus the three months' journey is lengthened by three days added.

55. Aristagoras then being driven out of Sparta proceeded to Athens; which had been set free from the rule of despots in the way which I shall tell.—When Hipparchos the son of Peisistratos and brother of the despot Hippias, after seeing a vision of a dream which signified it to him plainly, had been slain by Aristogeiton and Harmodios, who were originally by descent Gephyraians, the Athenians continued for four years after this to be despotically governed no less than formerly,—nay, even more. **56.** Now the vision of a dream which Hipparchos had was this:— in the night before the Panathenaia it seemed to Hipparchos that a man came and stood by him, tall and of fair form, and riddling spoke to him these verses:

> "With enduring soul as a lion endure unendurable evil:
>   No one of men who doth wrong shall escape from the judgment
>   appointed."

These verses, as soon as it was day, he publicly communicated to the interpreters of dreams; but afterwards he put away thought of the vision and began to take part in that procession during which he lost his life.*

57. Now the Gephyraians, of whom were those who murdered Hipparchos, according to their own account were originally descended from Eretria; but as I find by carrying inquiries back, they were Phenicians of those who came with Cadmos to the land which is now called Bœotia, and they dwelt in the district of Tanagra, which they had had allotted to them in that land. Then after the Cadmeians had first been driven out by the Argives, these Gephyraians next were driven out by the Bœotians and turned then towards Athens: and the Athenians received them on certain fixed conditions to be citizens of their State, laying down rules that they should be excluded from a number of things not worth mentioning here. **58.** Now these Phenicians who came with Cadmos, of whom were the Gephyraians, brought in among the Hellenes many arts when they settled in this land of Bœotia, and especially letters, which did not exist, as it

---

*Hipparchos was assassinated in 514 B.C.

appears to me, among the Hellenes before this time;* and at first they brought in those which are used by the Phenician race generally, but afterwards, as time went on, they changed with their speech the form of the letters also. During this time the Ionians were the race of Hellenes who dwelt near them in most of the places where they were; and these, having received letters by instruction of the Phenicians, changed their form slightly and so made use of them, and in doing so they declared them to be called "phenicians," as was just, seeing that the Phenicians had introduced them into Hellas. Also the Ionians from ancient time call paper "skins," because formerly, paper being scarce, they used skins of goats and sheep; nay, even in my own time many of the Barbarians write on such skins. **59.** I myself too once saw Cadmeian characters in the temple of Ismenian Apollo at Thebes of the Bœotians, engraved on certain tripods, and in most respects resembling the Ionic letters: one of these tripods has the inscription,

"Me Amphitryon offered from land Teleboian returning:"

this inscription would be of an age contemporary with Laïos the son of Labdacos, the son of Polydoros, the son of Cadmos. **60.** Another tripod says thus in hexameter rhythm:

"Me did Scaios offer to thee, far-darting Apollo,
    Victor in contest of boxing, a gift most fair in thine honour:"

now Scaios would be the son of Hippocoön (at least if it were really he who offered it, and not another with the same name as the son of Hippocoön), being of an age contemporary with Œdipus the son of Laïos: **61.** and the third tripod, also in hexameter rhythm, says:

"Me Laodamas offered to thee, fair-aiming Apollo,
    He, of his wealth, being king, as a gift most fair in thine honour:"

now it was in the reign of this very Laodamas the son of Eteocles that the Cadmeians were driven out by the Argives and turned to go to the Enchelians; and the Gephyraians being then left behind were afterwards forced by the Bœotians to retire to Athens. Moreover they have temples established in Athens, in which the other Athenians have no part, and besides others which are different from the rest, there is especially a temple of Demeter Achaia and a celebration of her mysteries.

62. I have told now of the vision of a dream seen by Hipparchos, and also whence the Gephyraians were descended, of which race were the murderers of Hipparchos; and in addition to this I must resume and continue

*Early Greek inscriptions often read right to left and Herodotus' speculation about the Semitic origin of alphabetic writing is correct.

the story which I was about to tell at first, how the Athenians were freed from despots. When Hippias was despot and was dealing harshly with the Athenians because of the death of Hipparchos, the Alcmaionidai, who were of Athenian race and were fugitives from the sons of Peisistratos, as they did not succeed in their attempt made together with the other Athenian exiles to return by force, but met with great disaster when they attempted to return and set Athens free, after they had fortified Leipsydrion which is above Paionia in northern Attica,—these Alcmaionidai after that, still devising every means against the sons of Peisistratos, accepted the contract to build and complete the temple at Delphi, that namely which now exists but then did not as yet: and being wealthy and men of repute already from ancient time, they completed the temple in a manner more beautiful than the plan required, and especially in this respect, that having agreed to make the temple of tufa or common limestone, they built the front parts of it of Parian marble. **63.** So then, as the Athenians say, these men being settled at Delphi persuaded the Pythian prophetess by gifts of money, that whenever men of the Spartans should come to inquire of the Oracle, either privately or publicly sent, she should propose to them to set Athens free. The Lacedemonians therefore, since the same utterance was delivered to them on all occasions, sent Anchimolios the son of Aster, who was of repute among their citizens, with an army to drive out the sons of Peisistratos from Athens, although these were very closely connected with them by guest-friendship; for they held that the concerns of the god should be preferred to those of men: and this force they sent by sea in ships. He therefore, having put in to shore at Phaleron, disembarked his army; but the sons of Peisistratos being informed of this beforehand called in to their aid an auxiliary force from Thessaly, for they had made an alliance with the Thessalians; and the Thessalians at their request sent by public resolution a body of a thousand horse and also their king Kineas, a man of Conion.

So having obtained these as allies, the sons of Peisistratos contrived as follows:—they cut down the trees in the plain of Phaleron and made this district fit for horsemen to ride over, and after that they sent the cavalry to attack the enemy's camp, who falling upon it slew (besides many others of the Lacedemonians) Anchimolios himself also: and the survivors of them they shut up in their ships. Such was the issue of the first expedition from Lacedemon: and the burial-place of Anchimolios is at Alopecai in Attica, near the temple of Heracles which is at Kynosarges. **64.** After this the Lacedemonians equipped a larger expedition and sent it forth against Athens; and they appointed to be commander of the army their king Cleomenes the son of Anaxandrides, and sent it this time not by sea but by land. With these, when they had invaded the land of Attica, first the Thessalian horse engaged battle; and in no long time they were routed and there fell of them more than forty men; so the survivors departed without more ado and went straight back to Thessaly. Then Cleomenes came to the city together with those of the Athenians who desired to be free, and began to besiege the despots shut up in the Pelasgian wall. **65.** And the

Lacedemonians would never have captured the sons of Peisistratos at all; for they on their side had no design to make a long blockade, and the others were well provided with food and drink; so that they would have gone away back to Sparta after besieging them for a few days only: but as it was, a thing happened just at this time which was unfortunate for those, and at the same time of assistance to these; for the children of the sons of Peisistratos were captured, while being secretly removed out of the country: and when this happened, all their matters were thereby cast into confusion, and they surrendered receiving back their children on the terms which the Athenians desired, namely that they should depart out of Attica within five days.* After this they departed out of the country and went to Sigeion on the Scamander, after their family had ruled over the Athenians for six-and-thirty years. These also were originally Pylians and sons of Neleus, descended from the same ancestors as the family of Codros and Melanthos, who had formerly become kings of Athens being settlers from abroad. Hence too Hippocrates had given to his son the name of Peisistratos as a memorial, calling him after Peisistratos the son of Nestor.†

Thus the Athenians were freed from despots; and the things worthy to be narrated which they did or suffered after they were liberated, up to the time when Ionia revolted from Dareios and Aristagoras the Milesian came to Athens and asked them to help him, these I will set forth first before I proceed further.‡

66. Athens, which even before that time was great, then, after having been freed from despots, became gradually yet greater; and in it two men exercised power, namely Cleisthenes a descendant of Alcmaion, the same who is reported to have bribed the Pythian prophetess, and Isagoras the son of Tisander, of a family which was highly reputed, but his original descent I am not able to declare; his kinsmen however offer sacrifices to the Carian Zeus. These men came to party strife for power; and when Cleisthenes was being worsted in the struggle, he made common cause with the people. After this he caused the Athenians to be in ten tribes, who were formerly in four; and he changed the names by which they were formerly called after the sons of Ion, namely Geleon, Aigicoreus, Argades, and Hoples, and invented for them names taken from other heroes, all native Athenians except Ajax, whom he added as a neighbour and ally, although he was no Athenian.§

67. Now in these things it seems to me that this Cleisthenes was imitating his mother's father Cleisthenes the despot of Sikyon:‖ for Cleisthenes when he went to war with Argos first caused to cease in Sikyon the

---

*Hippias was expelled in 510 B.C.

†Legendary rulers of the western Greek seaport Pylos, active in both the *Iliad* and the *Odyssey*.

‡The narrative "resumes" at 5.97.

§Abbreviated account of the form of government later called "democracy."

‖Cleisthenes was despot of Sikyon c.600–570 B.C.

contests of rhapsodists, which were concerned with the poems of Homer, because Argives and Argos are celebrated in them almost everywhere; then secondly, since there was (as still there is) in the market-place itself of the Sikyonians a hero-temple of Adrastos the son of Talaos, Cleisthenes had a desire to cast him forth out of the land, because he was an Argive. So having come to Delphi he consulted the Oracle as to whether he should cast out Adrastos; and the Pythian prophetess answered him saying that Adrastos was king of the Sikyonians, whereas he was a stoner* of them. So since the god did not permit him to do this, he went away home and considered means by which Adrastos should be brought to depart of his own accord: and when he thought that he had discovered them, he sent to Thebes in Bœotia and said that he desired to introduce into his city Melanippos the son of Astacos, and the Thebans gave him leave. So Cleisthenes introduced Melanippos into his city, and appointed for him a sacred enclosure within the precincts of the Council-Chamber itself, and established him there in the strongest position. Now Cleisthenes introduced Melanippos (for I must relate this also) because he was the greatest enemy of Adrastos, seeing that he had killed both his brother Mekisteus and his son-in-law Tydeus: and when he had appointed the sacred enclosure for him, he took away the sacrifices and festivals of Adrastos and gave them to Melanippos. Now the Sikyonians were accustomed to honour Adrastos with very great honours; for this land was formerly the land of Polybos, and Adrastos was daughter's son to Polybos, and Polybos dying without sons gave his kingdom to Adrastos: the Sikyonians then not only gave other honours to Adrastos, but also with reference to his sufferings they specially honoured him with tragic choruses, not paying the honour to Dionysos but to Adrastos. Cleisthenes however gave back the choruses to Dionysos, and the other rites besides this he gave to Melanippos. **68.** Thus he had done to Adrastos; and he also changed the names of the Dorian tribes, in order that the Sikyonians might not have the same tribes as the Argives; in which matter he showed great contempt of the Sikyonians, for the names he gave were taken from the names of a pig and an ass by changing only the endings, except in the case of his own tribe, to which he gave a name from his own rule. These last then were called Archelaoi or 'Rulers', while of the rest those of one tribe were called Hyatai or 'Swine-ites', of another Oneatai or Ass-ites', and of the remaining tribe Choireatai or 'Pig-ites'. These names of tribes were used by the men of Sikyon not only in the reign of Cleisthenes, but also beyond that for sixty years after his death; then however they considered the matter and changed them into Hylleis, Pamphyloi, and Dymanatai, adding to these a fourth, to which they gave the name Aigialeis after Aigialeus the son of Adrastos.

69. Thus had the Cleisthenes of Sikyon done: and the Athenian Cleisthenes, who was his daughter's son and was called after him, despising, as

---

*A pun is probably buried in the Greek.

I suppose, the Ionians, as he the Dorians, imitated his namesake Cleisthenes in order that the Athenians might not have the same tribes as the Ionians: for when at the time of which we speak he added to his own party the whole body of the common people of the Athenians, which in former time he had despised, he changed the names of the tribes and made them more in number than they had been; he made in fact ten rulers of tribes instead of four, and by tens also he distributed the demes in the tribes; and having added the common people to his party he was much superior to his opponents. **70.** Then Isagoras, as he was being worsted in his turn, contrived a plan in opposition to him, that is to say, he called in Cleomenes the Lacedemonian to help him, who had been a guest-friend to himself since the siege of the sons of Peisistratos; moreover Cleomenes was accused of being intimate with the wife of Isagoras. First then Cleomenes sent a herald to Athens demanding the expulsion of Cleisthenes and with him many others of the Athenians, calling them the men who were under the curse: this message he sent by instruction of Isagoras, for the Alcmaionidai and their party were accused of the murder to which reference was thus made, while he and his friends had no part in it. **71.** Now the men of the Athenians who were "under the curse" got this name as follows:—there was one Kylon among the Athenians, a man who had gained the victory at the Olympic games: this man behaved with arrogance, wishing to make himself despot;* and having formed for himself an association of the men of his own age, he endeavoured to seize the Acropolis: but not being able to get possession of it, he sat down as a suppliant before the image of the goddess.† These men were taken from their place as suppliants by the presidents of the naucraries,‡ who then administered affairs at Athens, on the condition that they should be liable to any penalty short of death; and the Alcmaionidai are accused of having put them to death. This had occurred before the time of Peisistratos.

72. Now when Cleomenes sent demanding the expulsion of Cleisthenes and of those under the curse, Cleisthenes himself retired secretly; but after that nevertheless Cleomenes appeared in Athens with no very large force, and having arrived he proceeded to expel as accursed seven hundred Athenian families, of which Isagoras had suggested to him the names. Having done this he next endeavoured to dissolve the Senate, and he put the offices of the State into the hands of three hundred, who were the partisans of Isagoras. The Senate however making opposition and not being willing to submit, Cleomenes with Isagoras and his partisans seized the

---

*This rising of Kylon occurred c.620 B.C.

†Athenē Polias, the "City-Protector," who dwells on the Athenian Acropolis and was later housed in the temple there, called the Erechtheion.

‡Fornara 22 provides further information on this board. (References to "Fornara" are to document numbers in Charles Fornara's *Archaic Times to the End of the Peloponnesian War;* see "For Further Reading.")

Acropolis. Then the rest of the Athenians joined together by common consent and besieged them for two days; and on the third day so many of them as were Lacedemonians departed out of the country under a truce. Thus was accomplished for Cleomenes the ominous saying which was uttered to him: for when he had ascended the Acropolis with the design of taking possession of it, he was going to the sanctuary of the goddess, as to address her in prayer; but the priestess stood up from her seat before he had passed through the door, and said, "Lacedemonian stranger, go back and enter not into the temple, for it is not lawful for Dorians to pass in hither." He said: "Woman, I am not a Dorian, but an Achaian." So then, paying no attention to the ominous speech, he made his attempt and then was expelled again with the Lacedemonians; but the rest of the men the Athenians laid in bonds to be put to death, and among them Timesitheos the Delphian, with regard to whom I might mention very great deeds of strength and courage which he performed. **73.** These then having been thus laid in bonds were put to death; and the Athenians after this sent for Cleisthenes to return, and also for the seven hundred families which had been driven out by Cleomenes: and then they sent envoys to Sardis, desiring to make an alliance with the Persians; for they were well assured that the Lacedemonians and Cleomenes had been utterly made their foes. So when these envoys had arrived at Sardis and were saying that which they had been commanded to say, Artaphrenes the son of Hystaspes, the governor of Sardis, asked what men these were who requested to be allies of the Persians, and where upon the earth they dwelt; and having heard this from the envoys, he summed up his answer to them thus, saying that if the Athenians were willing to give earth and water to Dareios, he was willing to make alliance with them, but if not, he bade them begone: and the envoys taking the matter upon themselves said that they were willing to do so, because they desired to make the alliance.

74. These, when they returned to their own land, were highly censured: and Cleomenes meanwhile, conceiving that he had been outrageously dealt with by the Athenians both with words and with deeds, was gathering together an army from the whole of the Peloponnese, not declaring the purpose for which he was gathering it, but desiring to take vengeance on the people of the Athenians and intending to make Isagoras despot; for he too had come out of the Acropolis together with Cleomenes. Cleomenes then with a large army entered Eleusis,* while at the same time the Bœotians by agreement with him captured Oinoë; and Hysiai, the demes which lay upon the extreme borders of Attica, and the Chalkidians on the other side invaded and began to ravage various districts of Attica. The Athenians then, though attacked on more sides than one, thought that they would remember and repel the Bœotians and Chalkidians afterwards, and arrayed themselves against the Peloponnesians who were in Eleusis. **75.** Then as the armies were just about to join battle, the Corinthians first, considering with themselves

---

*This invasion took place c.508 B.C.

that they were not acting rightly, changed their minds and departed; and after that Demaratos the son of Ariston did the same, who was king of the Spartans as well as Cleomenes, though he had joined with him in leading the army out from Lacedemon and had not been before this at variance with Cleomenes. In consequence of this dissension a law was laid down at Sparta that it should not be permitted, when an army went out, that both the kings should go with it, for up to this time both used to go with it, and that as one of the kings was set free from service, so one of the sons of Tyndareus* also should be left behind; for before this time both of these too were called upon by them for help and went with the armies. **76.** At this time then in Eleusis the rest of the allies, seeing that the kings of the Lacedemonians did not agree and also that the Corinthians had deserted their place in the ranks, themselves too departed and got away quickly. And this was the fourth time that the Dorians had come to Attica, twice having invaded it to make war against it, and twice to help the mass of the Athenian people,— first when they at the same time colonised Megara (this expedition may rightly be designated as taking place when Codros was king of the Athenians), for the second and third times when they came making expedition from Sparta to drive out the sons of Peisistratos, and fourthly on this occasion, when Cleomenes at the head of the Peloponnesians invaded Eleusis: thus the Dorians invaded Athens then for the fourth time.

77. This army then having been ingloriously broken up, the Athenians after that, desiring to avenge themselves, made expedition first against the Chalkidians; and the Bœotians came to the Euripos to help the Chalkidians. The Athenians therefore, seeing those who had come to help, resolved first to attack the Bœotians before the Chalkidians. Accordingly they engaged battle with the Bœotians and had much the better of them, and after having slain very many they took seven hundred of them captive. On this very same day the Athenians passed over into Eubœa and engaged battle with the Chalkidians as well; and having conquered these also, they left four thousand holders of allotments in the land belonging to the "Breeders of Horses": now the wealthier of the Chalkidians were called the Breeders of Horses. And as many of them as they took captive, they kept in confinement together with the Bœotians who had been captured, bound with fetters; and then after a time they let them go, having fixed their ransom at two pounds of silver apiece: but their fetters, in which they had been bound, they hung up on the Acropolis; and these were still existing even to my time hanging on walls which had been scorched with fire by the Mede,† and just opposite the sanctuary which lies towards the West. The tenth part of the ransom also they dedicated for an offering, and made of it a four-horse chariot of bronze, which stands on the left hand as you first enter the Propylaia in the Acropolis, and on it is the following inscription:‡

---

*See 4.145.
†See 8.53.
‡This inscription has been recovered; see Fornara 42.

"Matched in the deeds of war with the tribes of Bœotia and Chalkis
    The sons of Athens prevailed, conquered and tamed them in fight:
In chains of iron and darkness they quenched their insolent spirit;
    And to Athenē present these, of their ransom a tithe."

78. The Athenians accordingly increased in power; and it is evident, not by one instance only but in every way, that Equality is an excellent thing, since the Athenians while they were ruled by despots were not better in war than any of those who dwelt about them, whereas after they had got rid of despots they became far the first. This proves that when they were kept down they were wilfully slack, because they were working for a master, whereas when they had been set free each one was eager to achieve something for himself.

79. These then were faring thus: and the Thebans after this sent to the god, desiring to be avenged on the Athenians; the Pythian prophetess however said that vengeance was not possible for them by their own strength alone, but bade them report the matter to the "many-voiced" and ask help of those who were "nearest" to them. So when those who were sent to consult the Oracle returned, they made a general assembly and reported the oracle; and when the Thebans heard them say that they were to ask help of those who were nearest to them, they said: "Surely those who dwell nearest to us are the men of Tanagra and Coroneia and Thespiai; and these always fight zealously on our side and endure the war with us to the end: what need is there that we ask of these? Rather perhaps that is not the meaning of the oracle." **80.** While they commented upon it thus, at length one perceived, and spoke as follows: "I seem to myself to understand that which the oracle means to tell us. Asopos is said to have had two daughters born to him, Thebē and Egina; and as these are sisters, I think that the god gave us for answer that we should ask the men of Egina to become our helpers." Then as there seemed to be no opinion expressed which was better than this, they sent immediately and asked the men of Egina to help them, calling upon them in accordance with the oracle; and they, when these made request, said that they sent with them the sons of Aiacos to help them. **81.** After that the Thebans, having made an attempt with the alliance of the sons of Aiacos and having been roughly handled by the Athenians, sent again and gave them back the sons of Aiacos and asked them for men. So the Eginetans, exalted by great prosperity and calling to mind an ancient grudge against the Athenians, then on the request of the Thebans commenced a war against the Athenians without notice: for while the Athenians were intent on the Bœotians, they sailed against them to Attica with ships of war, and they devastated Phaleron and also many demes in the remainder of the coast region, and so doing they deeply stirred the resentment of the Athenians.

82. Now the grudge which was due beforehand from the Eginetans to the Athenians came about from a beginning which was as follows:—The land of the Epidaurians yielded to its inhabitants no fruit; and accordingly with reference to this calamity the Epidaurians went to inquire at Delphi, and the Pythian prophetess bade them set up images of Damia and Auxesia, and said that when they had set up these, they would meet with better fortune. The Epidaurians then asked further whether they should make the images of bronze or of stone; and the prophetess bade them not use either of these, but make them of the wood of a cultivated olive-tree. The Epidaurians therefore asked the Athenians to allow them to cut for themselves an olive-tree, since they thought that their olives were the most sacred; nay some say that at that time there were no olives in any part of the earth except at Athens. The Athenians said that they would allow them on condition that they should every year bring due offerings to Athenē Polias, "the City-Protector," and to Erechtheus. The Epidaurians then, having agreed to these terms, obtained that which they asked, and they made images out of these olive-trees and set them up: and their land bore fruit and they continued to fulfil towards the Athenians that which they had agreed to do. **83.** Now during this time and also before this the Eginetans were subject to the Epidaurians, and besides other things they were wont to pass over to Epidauros to have their disputes with one another settled by law: but after this time they built for themselves ships and made revolt from the Epidaurians, moved thereto by wilfulness. So as they were at variance with them, they continued to inflict damage on them, since in fact they had command of the sea, and especially they stole away from them these images of Damia and Auxesia, and they brought them and set them up in the inland part of their country at a place called Oia, which is about 2.3 miles distant from their city. Having set them up in this spot they worshipped them with sacrifices and choruses of women accompanied with scurrilous jesting, ten men being appointed for each of the deities to provide the choruses: and the choruses spoke evil of no man, but only of the women of the place. Now the Epidaurians also had the same rites; and they have also rites which may not be divulged. **84.** These images then having been stolen, the Epidaurians no longer continued to fulfil towards the Athenians that which they had agreed. The Athenians accordingly sent and expressed displeasure to the Epidaurians; and they declared saying that they were doing no wrong; for during the time when they had the images in their country they continued to fulfil that which they had agreed upon, but since they had been deprived of them, it was not just that they should make the offerings any more; and they bade them demand these from the men of Egina, who had the images. So the Athenians sent to Egina and demanded the images back; but the Eginetans said that they had nothing to do with the Athenians.

85. The Athenians then report that in one single trireme were despatched those of their citizens who were sent by the State after this demand; who having come to Egina, attempted to tear up from off their pedestals the images, (alleging that they were made of wood which belonged to the Athenians), in order to carry them back with them: but not being able to get hold of them in this manner (say the Athenians) they threw ropes round them and were pulling them, when suddenly, as they pulled, thunder came on and an earthquake at the same time with the thunder; and the crew of the trireme who were pulling were made mad by these, and being brought to this condition they killed one another as if they were enemies, until at last but one of the whole number was left; and he returned alone to Phaleron. **86.** Thus the Athenians report that it came to pass: but the Eginetans say that it was not with a single ship that the Athenians came; for a single ship, and even a few more than one, they could have easily repelled, even if they had not happened to have ships of their own: but they say that the Athenians sailed upon their country with a large fleet of ships, and they gave way before them and did not fight a sea-battle. They cannot however declare with certainty whether they gave way thus because they admitted that they were not strong enough to fight the battle by sea, or because they intended to do something of the kind which they actually did. The Athenians then, they say, as no one met them in fight, landed from their ships and made for the images; but not being able to tear them up from their pedestals, at last they threw ropes round them and began to pull, until the images, as they were being pulled, did both the same thing (and here they report something which I cannot believe, but some other man may), for they say that the images fell upon their knees to them and that they continue to be in that position ever since this time. The Athenians, they say, were doing thus; and meanwhile they themselves (say the Eginetans), being informed that the Athenians were about to make an expedition against them, got the Argives to help them; and just when the Athenians had disembarked upon the Eginetan land, the Argives had come to their rescue, and not having been perceived when they passed over from Epidauros to the island, they fell upon the Athenians before these had heard anything of the matter, cutting them off secretly from the way to their ships; and at this moment it was that the thunder and the earthquake came upon them.

87. This is the report which is given by the Argives and Eginetans both, and it is admitted by the Athenians also that but one alone of them survived and came back to Attica: only the Argives say that this one remained alive from destruction wrought by them upon the army of Athens, while the Athenians say that the divine power was the destroyer. However, even this one man did not remain alive, but perished, they say, in the following manner:—when he returned to Athens he reported the calamity which had happened; and the wives of the men who had gone on the expedition to Egina, hearing it and being very indignant that he alone of all had survived, came round this man and proceeded to stab him with the brooches of their mantles, each one of them asking of him where her husband was. Thus he was slain; and to the Athenians it seemed that the deed of the women was a much more terrible thing even than the calamity which had happened; and not knowing, it is said, how they should punish the women in any other way, they changed their fashion of dress to that of Ionia,—for before this the women of the Athenians wore Dorian dress, very like that of Corinth,—they changed it therefore to the linen tunic, in order that they might not have use for brooches. **88.** In truth however this fashion of dress is not Ionian originally but Carian, for the old Hellenic fashion of dress for women was universally the same as that which we now call Dorian. Moreover it is said that with reference to these events the Argives and Eginetans made it a custom among themselves in both countries to have the brooches made half as large again as the size which was then established in use, and that their women should offer Damia and Auxesia brooches especially in the temple of these goddesses, and also that they should carry neither pottery of Athens nor anything else of Athenian make to the temple, but that it should be the custom for the future to drink there from pitchers made in the lands themselves.

89. The women of the Argives and Eginetans from this time onwards because of the quarrel with the Athenians continued to wear brooches larger than before, and still do so even to my time; and the origin of the enmity of the Athenians towards the Eginetans came in the manner which has been said. So at this time, when the Thebans invited them, the Eginetans readily came to the assistance of the Bœotians, calling to mind what occurred about the images. The Eginetans then were laying waste, as I have said, the coast regions of Attica; and when the Athenians were resolved to make an expedition against the Eginetans, an oracle came to them from Delphi bidding them stay for thirty years reckoned from the time of the wrong done by the Eginetans, and in the one-and-thirtieth year to appoint a sacred enclosure for Aiacos and then to begin the war against the Eginetans, and they would succeed as they desired; but if they should make an expedition against them at once, they would suffer in the meantime very much evil and also inflict very much, but at last they would subdue them. When the Athenians heard the report of this, they appointed a sacred enclosure for Aiacos, namely that which is now established close to the market-place, but they could not endure to hear that they must stay for thirty years, when they had suffered injuries from the Eginetans.

90. While however they were preparing to take vengeance, a matter arose from the Lacedemonians which proved a hindrance to them: for the Lacedemonians, having learnt that which had been contrived by the Alcmaionidai with respect to the Pythian prophetess, and that which had been contrived by the Pythian prophetess against themselves and the sons of Peisistratos, were doubly grieved, not only because they had driven out into exile men who were their guest-friends, but also because after they had done this no gratitude was shown to them by the Athenians. Moreover in addition to this, they were urged on by the oracles which said that many injuries would be suffered by them from the Athenians; of which oracles they had not been aware before, but they had come to know them then, since Cleomenes had brought them to Sparta. In fact Cleomenes had obtained from the Acropolis of the Athenians those oracles which the sons of Peisistratos possessed before and had left in the temple when they were driven out; and Cleomenes recovered them after they had been left behind. **91.** At this time then, when the Lacedemonians had recovered the oracles and when they saw that the Athenians were increasing in power and were not at all willing to submit to them, observing that the Athenian race now that it was free was becoming a match for their own, whereas when held down by despots it was weak and ready to be ruled,—perceiving, I say, all these things, they sent for Hippias the son of Peisistratos to come from Sigeion on the Hellespont, whither the family of Peisistratos go for refuge; and when Hippias had come upon the summons, the Spartans sent also for envoys to come from their other allies and spoke to them as follows:

"Allies, we are conscious within ourselves that we have not acted rightly; for incited by counterfeit oracles we drove out into exile men who were very closely united with us as guest-friends and who undertook the task of rendering Athens submissive to us, and then after having done this we delivered over the State to a thankless populace, which so soon as it had raised its head, having been freed by our means drove out us and our king with wanton outrage; and now exalted with a good opinion of itself it is increasing in power, so that the neighbours of these men first of all, that is the Bœotians and Chalkidians, have already learnt, and perhaps some others also will afterwards learn, that they committed an error. As however we erred in doing those things of which we have spoken, we will try now to take vengeance on them, going thither together with you; since it was for this very purpose that we sent for Hippias, whom you see here, and for you also, to come from your cities, in order that with common counsel and a common force we might conduct him to Athens and render back to him that which we formerly took away."

92. Thus they spoke; but the majority of the allies did not approve of their words. The rest however kept silence, but the Corinthian Socles spoke as follows: (*a*) "Surely now the heaven shall be below the earth, and the earth raised up on high above the heaven, and men shall have their dwelling in the sea, and fishes shall have that habitation which men had before,* seeing that you, Lacedemonians, are doing away with free governments and are preparing to bring back despotisms again into our cities, than which there is no more unjust or more murderous thing among men. For if in truth this seems to you to be good, namely that the cities should be ruled by despots, you yourselves first set up a despot in your own State, and then endeavour to establish them also for others: but as it is, you are acting unfairly towards your allies, seeing that you have had no experience of despots yourselves and provide with the greatest care at Sparta that this may never come to pass. If however you had had experience of it, as we have had, you would be able to contribute juster opinions of it than at present. (*b*) For the established order of the Corinthian State was this:—the government was an oligarchy, and the oligarchs, who were called Bacchiadai,† had control over the State and made marriages among themselves. Now one of these men, named Amphion, had a daughter born to him who was lame, and her name was Labda. This daughter, since none of the Bacchiadai wished to marry her, was taken to

---

*Socles employs the rhetorical trope of *adynata* ("impossibilities"); compare 1.164–167, the Phocaean oath.
†The oligarchy of the Bacchiadai ruled from 745 to 655 B.C.

wife by Aëtion the son of Echecrates, who was of the deme of Petra, but by
original descent a Lapith and of the race of Caineus. Neither from this wife
nor from another were children born to him, therefore he set out to Delphi
to inquire about offspring; and as he entered, immediately the prophetess
addressed him in these lines:

> " 'Much to be honoured art thou, yet none doth render thee honour.
> Labda conceives, and a rolling rock [Petra] she will bear, which
>   shall ruin
> Down on the heads of the kings, and with chastisement visit
>   Corinthos.'

This answer given to Aëtion was by some means reported to the Bacchiadai, to whom the oracle which had come to Corinth before this was not
intelligible, an oracle which had reference to the same thing as that of
Aëtion and said thus:

> " 'An eagle conceives in the rocks and shall bear a ravening lion,
> Strong and fierce to devour, who the knees of many shall loosen.
> Ponder this well in your minds, I bid you, Corinthians, whose
>   dwelling
> Lies about fair Peirenē's spring and in craggy Corinthos.'

(c) This oracle, I say, having come before to the Bacchiadai was obscure;
but afterwards when they heard that which had come to Aëtion, immediately they understood the former also, that it was in accord with that of
Aëtion; and understanding this one also they kept quiet, desiring to destroy
the offspring which should be born to Aëtion. Then, so soon as his wife
bore a child, they sent ten of their own number to the deme in which Aëtion
had his dwelling, to slay the child; and when these had come to Petra and
had passed into the court of Aëtion's house, they asked for the child; and
Labda, not knowing anything of the purpose for which they had come,
and supposing them to be asking for the child on account of friendly feeling towards its father, brought it and placed it in the hands of one of them.
Now they, it seems, had resolved by the way that the first of them who received the child should dash it upon the ground. However, when Labda
brought and gave it, it happened by divine providence that the child
smiled* at the man who had received it; and when he perceived this, a feeling of compassion prevented him from killing it, and having this compassion he delivered it to the next man, and he to the third. Thus it passed
through the hands of all the ten, delivered from one to another, since none
of them could bring himself to destroy its life. So they gave the child back
to its mother and went out; and then standing by the doors they abused and
found fault with one another, laying blame especially on the one who had

*Almost all smiles and laughs in Herodotus lead to catastrophe.

first received the child, because he had not done according to that which had been resolved; until at last after some time they determined again to enter and all to take a share in the murder. (*d*) From the offspring of Aëtion however it was destined that evils should spring up for Corinth: for Labda was listening to all this as she stood close by the door, and fearing lest they should change their mind and take the child a second time and kill it, she carried it and concealed it in the place which seemed to her the least likely to be discovered, that is to say a *Kypselos* or grain-chest, feeling sure that if they should return and come to a search, they were likely to examine everything: and this in fact happened. So when they had come, and searching had failed to find it, they thought it best to return and say to those who had sent them that they had done all that which they had been charged by them to do. (*e*) They then having departed said this; and after this the son of Aëtion grew, and because he had escaped this danger, the name of Kypselos was given him as a surname derived from the grain-chest. Then when Kypselos had grown to manhood and was seeking divination, a two-edged answer was given him at Delphi, placing trust in which he made an attempt upon Corinth and obtained possession of it. Now the answer was as follows:

> " 'Happy is this man's lot of a truth, who enters my dwelling,
> Offspring of Aëtion, he shall rule in famous Corinth,
> Kypselos, he and his sons, but his children's children no longer.'

Such was the oracle: and Kypselos when he became despot was a man of this character,—many of the Corinthians he drove into exile, many he deprived of their wealth, and very many more of their lives.[*] (*f*) And when he had reigned for thirty years and had brought his life to a prosperous end, his son Periander became his successor in the despotism.[†] Now Periander at first was milder than his father; but after he had had dealings through messengers with Thrasybulos the despot of Miletos, he became far more murderous even than Kypselos. For he sent a messenger to Thrasybulos and asked what settlement of affairs was the safest for him to make, in order that he might best govern his State: and Thrasybulos led forth the messenger who had come from Periander out of the city, and entered into a field of growing grain; and as he passed through the crop of grain, while inquiring and asking questions repeatedly of the messenger about the occasion of his coming from Corinth, he kept cutting off the heads of those ears of grain which he saw higher than the rest; and as he cut off their heads he cast them away, until he had destroyed in this manner the finest and richest part of the crop. So having passed through the place and having suggested no word of counsel, he dismissed the messenger. When the messenger returned to Corinth, Periander was anxious to hear the counsel which had been given; but he said that Thrasybulos had

---

*Kypselos was despot from 655 to 625 B.C.
†Periander reigned 625–585 B.C.

given him no counsel, and added that he wondered at the deed of Perian-der in sending him to such a man, for the man was out of his senses and a waster of his own goods,—relating at the same time that which he had seen Thrasybulos do. (*g*) So Periander, understanding that which had been done and perceiving that Thrasybulos counselled him to put to death those who were eminent among his subjects, began then to display all manner of evil treatment to the citizens of the State; for whatsoever Kypselos had left undone in killing and driving into exile, this Periander completed. And in one day he stripped all the wives of the Corinthians of their clothing on account of his own wife Melissa. For when he had sent messengers to the Thesprotians on the river Acheron to ask the Oracle of the dead about a deposit made with him by a guest-friend, Melissa appeared and said she would not tell in what place the deposit was laid, for she was cold and had no clothes, since those which he had buried with her were of no use to her, not having been burnt; and this, she said, would be an evi-dence to him that she was speaking the truth, namely that when the oven was cold, Periander had put his loaves into it. When the report of this was brought back to Periander, the token made him believe, because he had had sex with Melissa after she was dead; and straightway after receiving the message he caused proclamation to be made that all the wives of the Corinthians should come out to the temple of Hera. They accordingly went as to a festival in their fairest adornment; and he having set the spearmen of his guard in ambush, stripped them all alike, both the free women and their attendants; and having gathered together all their clothes in a place dug out, he set fire to them, praying at the same time to Melissa. Then after he had done this and had sent a second time, the apparition of Melissa told him in what spot he had laid the deposit entrusted to him by his guest-friend.

"Such a thing, you must know, Lacedemonians, is despotism, and such are its deeds: and we Corinthians marvelled much at first when we saw that you were sending for Hippias, and now we marvel even more because you say these things; and we adjure you, calling upon the gods of Hellas, not to establish despotisms in the cities. If however you will not cease from your design, but endeavour to restore Hippias contrary to that which is just, know that the Corinthians at least do not give their consent to that which you do."

93. Socles being the envoy of Corinth thus spoke, and Hippias made an-swer to him, calling to witness the same gods as he, that assuredly the Corinthians would more than all others regret the loss of the sons of Peisis-tratos, when the appointed days should have come for them to be troubled by the Athenians.* Thus Hippias made answer, being acquainted with the oracles more exactly than any other man: but the rest of the allies, who for a time had restrained themselves and kept silence, when they heard Socles speak freely, gave utterance every one of them to that which they felt, and

---

*Forward reference to the Peloponnesian War (431–404 B.C.) during which these words were "published."

adopted the opinion of the Corinthian envoy, adjuring the Lacedemonians
not to do any violence to a city of Hellas.

94. Thus was this brought to an end: and Hippias being dismissed from
thence had Anthemus offered to him by Amyntas king of the Macedonians and Iolcos by the Thessalians. He however accepted neither of these,
but retired again to Sigeion; which city Peisistratos had taken by force of
arms from the Mytilenians, and having got possession of it had appointed
his own natural son Hegesistratos, born of an Argive woman, to be despot
of it: he however did not without a struggle keep possession of that which
he received from Peisistratos; for the Mytilenians and Athenians carried
on war for a long time, having their strongholds respectively at Achilleion
and at Sigeion, the one side demanding that the place be restored to them,
and the Athenians on the other hand not admitting this demand, but proving by argument that the Aiolians had no better claim to the territory of
Ilion than they and the rest of the Hellenes, as many as joined with Menelaos
in exacting vengeance for the rape of Helen. **95.** Now while these carried
on the war, besides many other things of various kinds which occurred in
the battles, once when a fight took place and the Athenians were conquering, Alcaios the poet, taking to flight, escaped indeed himself, but the
Athenians retained possession of his arms and hung them up on the walls
of the temple of Athenē which is at Sigeion. About this matter Alcaios
composed a song and sent it to Mytilenē, reporting therein his misadven-
ture to one Melanippos, who was his friend. Finally Periander the son of
Kypselos made peace between the Athenians and the Mytilenians, for to
him they referred the matter as arbitrator; and he made peace between
them on the condition that each should continue to occupy that territory
which they then possessed. **96.** Sigeion then in this manner had come under the rule of the Athenians. And when Hippias had returned to Asia
from Lacedemon, he set everything in motion, stirring up enmity between
the Athenians and Artaphrenes, and using every means to secure that
Athens should come under the rule of himself and of Dareios. Hippias, I
say, was thus engaged; and the Athenians meanwhile hearing of these
things sent envoys to Sardis, and endeavoured to prevent the Persians
from following the suggestions of the exiled Athenians. Artaphrenes however commanded them, if they desired to be preserved from ruin, to receive Hippias back again. This proposal the Athenians were not by any
means disposed to accept when it was reported; and as they did not accept
this, it became at once a commonly received opinion among them that
they were enemies of the Persians.

97. While they had these thoughts and had been set at enmity with the
Persians, at this very time Aristagoras the Milesian, ordered away from
Sparta by Cleomenes the Lacedemonian, arrived at Athens; for this was
the city which had most power of all the rest besides Sparta. And
Aristagoras came forward before the assembly of the people and said the
same things as he had said at Sparta about the wealth which there was in
Asia, and about the Persian manner of making war, how they used neither
shield nor spear and were easy to overcome. Thus I say he said, and also he

added this, namely that the Milesians were colonists from the Athenians, and that it was reasonable that the Athenians should rescue them, since they had such great power; and there was nothing which he did not promise, being very urgent in his request, until at last he persuaded them: for it would seem that it is easier to deceive many than one, seeing that, though he did not prove able to deceive Cleomenes the Lacedemonian by himself, yet he did this to thirty thousand Athenians.* The Athenians then, I say, being persuaded, voted a resolution to despatch twenty ships to help the Ionians, and appointed to command them Melanthios one of their citizens, who was in all things highly reputed. These ships proved to be the beginning of evils for the Hellenes and the Barbarians.

98. Aristagoras however sailed on before and came to Miletos; and then having devised a plan from which no advantage was likely to come for the Ionians (nor indeed was he doing what he did with a view to that, but in order to vex king Dareios), he sent a man to Phrygia to the Paionians who had been taken captive by Megabazos from the river Strymon, and who were dwelling in a district and village of Phrygia apart by themselves; and when the messenger came to the Paionians he spoke these words: "Paionians, Aristagoras the despot of Miletos sent me to offer to you salvation, if you shall be willing to do as he says; for now all Ionia has revolted from the king, and you have an opportunity of coming safe to your own land: to reach the sea shall be your concern, and after this it shall be thenceforth ours." The Paionians hearing this received it as a most welcome proposal, and taking with them their children and their women they began a flight to the sea; some of them however were struck with fear and remained in the place where they were. Having come to the coast the Paionians crossed over thence to Chios, and when they were already in Chios there arrived in their track a large body of Persian horsemen pursuing the Paionians. These, as they did not overtake them, sent over to Chios to bid the Paionians return back: the Paionians however did not accept their proposal, but the men of Chios conveyed them from Chios to Lesbos, and the Lesbians brought them to Doriscos, and thence they proceeded by land and came to Paionia.

99. Aristagoras meanwhile, when the Athenians had arrived with twenty ships, bringing with them also five triremes of the Eretrians, who joined the expedition not for the sake of the Athenians but of the Milesians themselves, to repay them a debt which they owed (for the Milesians in former times had borne with the Eretrians the burden of all that war which they had with the Chalkidians at the time when the Chalkidians on their side were helped by the Samians against the Eretrians and Milesians),†—when these, I say, had arrived and the other allies were on the spot, Aristagoras proceeded to make a march upon Sardis. On this march

---

*Statement that militates against the view that Herodotus was pro-Athenian or pro-democratic.

†See Fornara 7 for the extremely limited evidence for this Lelantine war.

he did not go himself, but remained at Miletos and appointed others to be in command of the Milesians, namely his brother Charopinos and of the other citizens one Hermophantos. **100.** With this force then the Ionians came to Ephesos, and leaving their ships at Coresos in the land of Ephesos, went up themselves in a large body, taking Ephesians to guide them in their march. So they marched along by the river Caÿster, and then when they arrived after crossing the range of Tmolos, they took Sardis without any resistance, all except the citadel, but the citadel Artaphrenes himself saved from capture, having with him a considerable force of men. **101.** From plundering the city after they had taken it they were prevented by this:— the houses in Sardis were mostly built of reeds, and even those of them which were of brick had their roofs thatched with reeds: of these houses one was set on fire by a soldier, and immediately the fire going on from house to house began to spread over the whole town.[*] So then as the town was on fire, the Lydians and all the Persians who were in the city being cut off from escape, since the fire was prevailing in the extremities round about them, and not having any way out of the town, flowed together to the market-place and to the river Pactolos, which brings down gold-dust for them from Tmolos, flowing through the middle of their market-place, and then runs out into the river Hermos, and this into the sea;—to this Pactolos, I say, and to the market-place the Lydians and Persians gathered themselves together, and were compelled to defend themselves. The Ionians then, seeing some of the enemy standing on their defence and others in great numbers coming on to the attack, were struck with fear and retired to the mountain called Tmolos, and after that at nightfall departed to go to their ships.

102. Sardis then was destroyed by fire, and in it also the temple of the native goddess Kybebē; which the Persians alleged afterwards as a reason for setting on fire in return the temples in the land of the Hellenes. However at the time of which I speak the Persians who occupied districts within the river Halys, informed beforehand of this movement, were gathering together and coming to the help of the Lydians; and, as it chanced, they found when they came that the Ionians no longer were in Sardis; but they followed closely in their track and came up with them at Ephesos: and the Ionians stood indeed against them in array, but when they joined battle they had very much the worse; and besides other persons of note whom the Persians slaughtered, there fell also Eualkides commander of the Eretrians, a man who had won wreaths in contests of the games and who was much celebrated by Simonides of Keos:[†] and those of them who survived the battle dispersed to their various cities.

103. Thus then they fought at that time; and after the battle the Athenians left the Ionians altogether, and when Aristagoras was urgent in calling

---

[*]Sardis was burned in 499 B.C.

[†]The name "Good Strength" is ominous; the reference to the celebratory poetry implies the nature of archaic and early classical fame.

upon them by messengers for assistance, they said that they would not help them: the Ionians however, though deprived of the alliance of the Athenians, none the less continued to prepare for the war with the king, so great had been the offences already committed by them against Dareios. They sailed moreover to the Hellespont and brought under their power Byzantion and all the other cities which are in those parts; and then having sailed forth out of the Hellespont, they gained in addition the most part of Caria to be in alliance with them: for even Caunos, which before was not willing to be their ally, then, after they had burnt Sardis, was added to them also. **104.** The Cyprians too, excepting those of Amathus, were added voluntarily to their alliance; for these also had revolted from the Medes in the following manner:—there was one Onesilos, younger brother of Gorgos king of Salamis, and son of Chersis, the son of Siromos, the son of Euelthon. This man in former times too had been wont often to advise Gorgos to make revolt from the king, and at this time, when he heard that the Ionians had revolted, he pressed him very hard and endeavoured to urge him to it. Since however he could not persuade Gorgos, Onesilos watched for a time when he had gone forth out of the city of Salamis, and then together with the men of his own faction he shut him out of the gates. Gorgos accordingly being robbed of the city went for refuge to the Medes, and Onesilos was ruler of Salamis and endeavoured to persuade all the men of Cyprus to join him in revolt. The others then he persuaded; but since those of Amathus were not willing to do as he desired, he sat down before their city and besieged it.

105. Onesilos then was besieging Amathus; and meanwhile, when it was reported to king Dareios that Sardis had been captured and burnt by the Athenians and the Ionians together, and that the leader of the league for bringing about these things was the Milesian Aristagoras, it is said that at first being informed of this he made no account of the Ionians, because he knew that they at all events would not escape unpunished for their revolt, but he inquired who the Athenians were; and when he had been informed, he asked for his bow, and having received it and placed an arrow upon the string, he discharged it upwards towards heaven, and as he shot into the air he said: "Zeus, grant me to take vengeance upon the Athenians!" Having so said he charged one of his attendants, that when dinner was set before the king he should say always three times: "Master, remember the Athenians." **106.** When he had given this charge, he called into his presence Histiaios the Milesian, whom Dareios had now been keeping with him for a long time, and said: "I am informed, Histiaios, that your deputy, to whom you did depute the government of Miletos, has made rebellion against me; for he brought in men against me from the other continent and persuaded the Ionians also,—who shall pay the penalty to me for that which they did,—these, I say, he persuaded to go together with them, and thus he robbed me of Sardis. Now therefore how think you that this is well? and how without your counsels was anything of this kind done? Take heed lest you afterwards find reason to blame yourself for this." Histiaios replied: "O king, what manner of speech is this that you have uttered,

saying that I counselled a matter from which it was likely that any vexa-
tion would grow for you, either great or small? What have I to seek for in
addition to that which I have, that I should do these things; and of what am
I in want? for I have everything that you have, and I am thought worthy by
you to hear all your counsels. Nay, but if my deputy is indeed acting in any
such manner as you have said, be assured that he has done it merely on his
own account. I however, for my part, do not even admit the report to be
true, that the Milesians and my deputy are acting in any rebellious fashion
against your power: but if it prove that they are indeed doing anything of
that kind, and if that which you have heard, O king, be the truth, learn then
what a thing you did in removing me away from the sea-coast; for it seems
that the Ionians, when I had gone out of the sight of their eyes, did that
which they had long had a desire to do; whereas if I had been in Ionia, not
a city would have made the least movement. Now therefore as quickly as
possible let me set forth to go to Ionia, that I may order all these matters
for you as they were before, and deliver into your hands this deputy of
Miletos who contrived these things: and when I have done this after your
mind, I swear by the gods of the royal house that I will not put off from me
the tunic which I wear when I go down to Ionia, until I have made Sardinia
tributary to you, which is the largest of all islands." **107.** Thus saying Histiaios endeavoured to deceive the king, and Dareios was persuaded and let
him go, charging him, when he should have accomplished that which he
had promised, to return to him again at Susa.

108. In the meantime, while the news about Sardis was going up to the
king, and while Dareios, after doing that which he did with the bow, came
to speech with Histiaios, and Histiaios having been let go by Dareios was
making his journey to the sea-coast,—during all that time the events were
happening which here follow.—As Onesilos of Salamis was besieging
those of Amathus, it was reported to him that Artybios a Persian, bringing
with him in ships a large Persian army, was to be expected shortly to arrive
in Cyprus. Being informed of this, Onesilos sent heralds to different places
in Ionia to summon the Ionians to his assistance; and they took counsel together and came without delay with a large force. Now the Ionians arrived
in Cyprus just at the time when the Persians having crossed over in ships
from Kilikia were proceeding by land to attack Salamis, while the Phenicians with the ships were sailing round the headland which is called the
"Keys of Cyprus." **109.** This being the case, the despots of Cyprus called together the commanders of the Ionians and said: "Ionians, we of Cyprus
give you a choice which enemy you will rather fight with, the Persians or
the Phenicians: for if you will rather array yourselves on land and make
trial of the Persians in fight, it is time now for you to disembark from your
ships and array yourselves on the land, and for us to embark in your ships
to contend against the Phenicians; but if on the other hand you will rather
make trial of the Phenicians,—whichever of these two you shall choose,
you must endeavour that, so far as it rests with you, both Ionia and Cyprus
shall be free." To this the Ionians replied: "We were sent out by the common authority of the Ionians to guard the sea, and not to deliver our ships

to the Cyprians and ourselves fight with the Persians on land. We therefore will endeavour to do good service in that place to which we were appointed; and you must call to mind all the evils which you suffered from the Medes, when you were in slavery to them, and prove yourselves good men." **110.** The Ionians made answer in these words; and afterwards, when the Persians had come to the plain of Salamis, the kings of the Cyprians set in order their array, choosing the best part of the troops of Salamis and of Soloi to be arrayed against the Persians and setting the other Cyprians against the rest of the enemy's troops; and against Artybios, the commander of the Persians, Onesilos took up his place in the array by his own free choice.

111. Now Artybios was riding a horse which had been trained to rear up against a hoplite. Onesilos accordingly being informed of this, and having a shield-bearer, by race of Caria, who was of very good repute as a soldier and full of courage besides, said to this man: "I am informed that the horse of Artybios rears upright and works both with his feet and his mouth against any whom he is brought to attack. Do you therefore consider the matter, and tell me now which of the two you will rather watch for and strike, the horse or Artybios himself." To this his attendant replied: "O king, I am ready to do both or either of these two things, and in every case to do that which you shall appoint for me; but I will declare to you the way in which I think it will be most suitable for your condition. I say that it is right for one who is king and commander to fight with a king and commander; for if you shall slay the commander of the enemy, it turns to great glory for you; and again, if he shall slay you, which heaven forbid, even death when it is at the hands of a worthy foe is but half to be lamented: but for us who are under your command it is suitable to fight with the others who are under his command and with his horse: and of the tricks of the horse have you no fear at all, for I engage to you that after this at least he shall never stand against any man more." Thus he spoke; and shortly afterwards the opposed forces joined battle both on land and with their ships. **112.** On that day the Ionians for their part greatly distinguished themselves and overcame the Phenicians, and of them the Samians were best:[*] and meanwhile on land, when the armies met, they came to close quarters and fought; and as regards the two commanders, what happened was this:—when Artybios came to fight with Onesilos sitting upon his horse, Onesilos, as he had concerted with his shield-bearer, struck at Artybios himself, when he came to fight with him; and when the horse put its hoofs against the shield of Onesilos, then the Carian struck with a sickle and smote off the horse's feet. **113.** So Artybios the commander of the Persians fell there on the spot together with his horse: and while the others also were fighting, Stesenor the despot of Curion deserted them, having with him a large force of men,—now these Curians are said to be settlers from

---

[*]Herodotus seems to have pro-Samian sources and probably spent considerable time there; compare 3. 60.

Argos,—and when the Curians had deserted, immediately also the war-chariots of the men of Salamis proceeded to do the same as the Curians. When these things took place, the Persians had the advantage over the Cyprians; and after their army had been put to rout, many others fell and among them Onesilos the son of Chersis, he who brought about the revolt of the Cyprians, and also the king of the Solians, Aristokypros the son of Philokypros,—that Philokypros whom Solon the Athenian, when he came to Cyprus, commended in verse above all other despots. **114.** So the men of Amathus cut off the head of Onesilos, because he had besieged them; and having brought it to Amathus they hung it over the gate of the city: and as the head hung there, when it had now become hollow, a swarm of bees entered into it and filled it with honeycomb. This having so come to pass, the Amathusians consulted an Oracle about the head, and they received an answer bidding them take it down and bury it and sacrifice to Onesilos every year as a hero; and if they did this, it would go better with them. **115.** The Amathusians accordingly continued to do so even to my own time. But the Ionians who had fought the sea-fight in Cyprus, when they perceived that the fortunes of Onesilos were ruined and that the cities of the Cyprians were besieged, except Salamis, and that this city had been delivered over by the Salaminians to Gorgos the former king,—as soon as they perceived this, the Ionians sailed away back to Ionia. Now of the cities in Cyprus Soloi held out for the longest time under the siege; and the Persians took it in the fifth month by undermining the wall round.

116. The Cyprians then, after they had made themselves free for one year, had again been reduced to slavery afresh: and meanwhile Daurises, who was married to a daughter of Dareios, and Hymaies and Otanes, who were also Persian commanders and were married also to daughters of Dareios, after they had pursued those Ionians who had made the expedition to Sardis and defeating them in battle had driven them by force to their ships,—after this distributed the cities amongst themselves and proceeded to sack them. **117.** Daurises directed his march to the cities on the Hellespont, and he took Dardanos and Abydos and Percotē and Lampsacos and Paisos, of these he took on each day one; and as he was marching from Paisos against the city of Parion, the report came that the Carians had made common cause with the Ionians and were in revolt from the Persians. He turned back therefore from the Hellespont and marched his army upon Caria. **118.** And, as it chanced, a report of this was brought to the Carians before Daurises arrived; and the Carians being informed of it gathered together at the place which is called the "White Pillars" and at the river Marsyas, which flows from the region of Idrias and runs out into the Maiander. When the Carians had been gathered together there, among many other counsels which were given, the best, as it seems to me, was that of Pixodaros the son of Mausolos, a man of Kindyē, who was married to the daughter of the king of the Kilikians, Syennesis. The opinion of this man was to the effect that the Carians should cross over the Maiander and engage battle with the Persians having the river at their backs, in order that the Carians, not being able to fly backwards and being compelled to remain where they were, might prove themselves even better men in fight than they naturally would.* This opinion did not prevail; but they resolved that the Persians rather than themselves should have the Maiander at their backs, evidently—I suppose—in order that if there should be a flight of the Persians and they should be worsted in the battle, they might never return home, but might fall into the river. **119.** After this, when the Persians had come and had crossed the Maiander, the Carians engaged with the Persians on the river Marsyas and fought a battle which was obstinately contested and lasted long; but at length they were worsted by superior numbers: and of the Persians there fell as many as two thousand, but of the Carians ten thousand. Then those of them who escaped were shut up in Labraunda within the sanctuary of Zeus Stratios, which is a large sacred grove of plane-trees; now the Carians are the only men we know who offer sacrifices to Zeus Stratios. These men then, being shut up there, were taking counsel together about their safety, whether they would fare better if they delivered themselves over to the Persians or if they left Asia altogether. **120.** And while they were thus taking counsel, there came to their aid the Milesians and their allies. Then the Carians dismissed the plans which they were before considering and prepared to renew the war again from the beginning: and when the Persians came to attack them, they engaged with them and fought a battle, and they were worsted yet more completely than before; and while many were slain of all the parties, the Milesians suffered most. **121.** Then afterwards the Carians repaired this loss and retrieved their defeat; for being informed that the Persians had set forth to march upon their cities, they laid an ambush on the road which is by Pedasos, and the Persians falling into it by night were destroyed both they and their commanders, namely Daurises and Amorges and Sisimakes; and with them died also Myrsos the son of Gyges. Of this ambush the leader was Heracleides the son of Ibanollis, a man of Mylasa.

122. These then of the Persians were thus destroyed; and meanwhile Hymaies, who was another of those who pursued after the Ionians that had made the expedition to Sardis, directed his march to the Propontis and took Kios in Mysia; and having conquered this city, when he was informed that Daurises had left the Hellespont and was marching towards Caria, he left the Propontis and led his army to the Hellespont: and he conquered all the Aiolians who occupy the district of Ilion, and also the Gergithes, who were left behind as a remnant of the ancient Teucrians. While conquering these tribes Hymaies himself ended his life by sickness in the land of Troas. **123.** He thus brought his life to an end; and Artaphrenes the governor of the province of Sardis was appointed with Otanes the third of the commanders to make the expedition against Ionia and that part of Aiolia which bordered upon it. Of Ionia these took the city of Clazomenai, and of the Aiolians Kymē.

---

*Compare Croesus' advice to Cyrus at 1.207.

124. While the cities were thus being taken, Aristagoras the Milesian, being, as he proved in this instance, not of very distinguished courage, since after having disturbed Ionia and made preparation of great matters he counselled running away when he saw these things,* (moreover it had become clear to him that it was impossible to overcome king Dareios),— he, I say, having regard to these things, called together those of his own party and took counsel with them, saying that it was better that there should be a refuge prepared for them, in case that they should after all be driven out from Miletos, and proposing the question whether he should lead them thence to Sardinia, to form a colony there, or to Myrkinos in the land of the Edonians, which Histiaios had been fortifying, having received it as a gift from Dareios. This was the question proposed by Aristagoras. **125.** Now the opinion of Hecataios the son of Hegesander the historian† was that he should not take a colony to either of these places, but build a wall of defence for himself in the island of Leros and keep still, if he should be forced to leave Miletos; and afterwards with this for his starting point he would be able to return to Miletos. 126. This was the counsel of Hecataios; but Aristagoras was most inclined to go forth to Myrkinos. He therefore entrusted the government of Miletos to Pythagoras, a man of repute among the citizens, and he himself sailed away to Thrace, taking with him every one who desired to go; and he took possession of the region for which he had set out. But starting from this to make war, he perished by the hands of the Thracians, that is both Aristagoras himself and his army, when he was encamped about a certain city and the Thracians desired to go out from it under a truce.

---

*Aristagoras fled in 497 B.C.
†See also 2.143, 5.36, 5.125, and 6.137.

BOOK VI

THE IONIAN DEFEAT, SPARTA AND ATHENS, THE MARATHON CAMPAIGN

1. ARISTAGORAS ACCORDINGLY, AFTER HAVING caused Ionia to revolt, thus brought his life to an end; and meanwhile Histiaios the despot of Miletos, having been let go by Dareios had arrived at Sardis: and when he came from Susa, Artaphrenes the governor of Sardis asked him for what reason he supposed the Ionians had revolted; and he said that he could not tell, and moreover he expressed wonder at that which had happened, pretending that he knew nothing of the state of affairs. Then Artaphrenes seeing that he was using dissimulation said, having knowledge of the truth about the revolt: "Thus it is with you, Histiaios, about these matters,—this shoe was stitched by you, and put on by Aristagoras." **2.** Thus said Artaphrenes with reference to the revolt; and Histiaios fearing Artaphrenes because he understood the matter, ran away the next night at nightfall and went to the sea-coast, having deceived king Dareios, seeing that he had engaged to subdue Sardinia the largest of islands, and instead of that he was endeavouring to take upon himself the leadership of the Ionians in the war against Dareios. Then having crossed over to Chios he was put in bonds by the Chians, being accused by them of working for a change of their State by suggestion of Dareios. When however the Chians learnt the whole story and heard that he was an enemy to the king, they released him. **3.** Then Histiaios, being asked by the Ionians for what reason he had so urgently charged Aristagoras to revolt from the king and had wrought so great evil for the Ionians, did not by any means declare to them that which had been in truth the cause, but reported to them that king Dareios had resolved to remove the Phenicians from their land and to settle them in Ionia, and the Ionians in Phenicia; and for this reason, he said, he had given the charge. Thus he attempted to alarm the Ionians, although the king had never resolved to do so at all.

4. After this Histiaios acting through a messenger, namely Hermippos a man of Atarneus, sent papers to the Persians who were at Sardis, implying that he had already talked matters over with them about a revolt: and Hermippos did not deliver them to those to whom he was sent, but bore the papers and put them into the hands of Artaphrenes. He then, perceiving all that was being done, bade Hermippos bear the papers sent by Histiaios and deliver them to those to whom he was sent to bear them, and to deliver to him the replies sent back by the Persians to Histiaios. These things having been discovered, Artaphrenes upon that put to death many of the Persians.

5. As regards Sardis therefore there was confusion of the design; and when Histiaios had been disappointed of this hope, the Chians attempted to restore him to Miletos at the request of Histiaios himself. The Milesians however, who had been rejoiced before to be rid of Aristagoras, were by no means eager to receive another despot into their land, seeing that they had tasted of liberty: and in fact Histiaios, attempting to return to Miletos by force and under cover of night, was wounded in the thigh by one of the Milesians. He then, being repulsed from his own city, returned to Chios; and thence, as he could not persuade the Chians to give him ships, he crossed over to Mytilenē and endeavoured to persuade the Lesbians to give him ships. So they manned eight triremes and sailed with Histiaios to Byzantion, and stationing themselves there they captured the ships which sailed out of the Pontus, excepting where the crews of them said that they were ready to do the bidding of Histiaios.

6. While Histiaios and the men of Mytilenē were acting thus, a large army both of sea and land forces was threatening to attack Miletos itself; for the commanders of the Persians had joined together to form one single army and were marching upon Miletos, considering the other towns of less account. Of their naval force the most zealous were the Phenicians, and with them also served the Cyprians, who had just been subdued, and the Kilikians and Egyptians. **7.** These, I say, were advancing upon Miletos and the rest of Ionia; and meanwhile the Ionians being informed of this were sending deputies chosen from themselves to the Panionion.* When these had arrived at that place and took counsel together, they resolved not to gather a land-army to oppose the Persians, but that the Milesians should defend their walls by themselves, and that the Ionians should man their fleet, leaving out not one of their ships, and having done so should assemble as soon as possible at Ladē, to fight a sea-battle in defence of Miletos. Now Ladē is a small island lying opposite the city of the Milesians. **8.** Then the Ionians manned their ships and came thither, and with them also those Aiolians who inhabit Lesbos; and they were drawn up in order thus:—the extremity of the line towards the East was held by the Milesians themselves, who furnished eighty ships; next to them were the Prienians with twelve ships and the men of Myus with three; next to those of Myus were the Teians with seventeen ships, and after the Teians the Chians with a hundred; after these were stationed the men of Erythrai and of Phocaia, the former furnishing eight ships and the latter three; next to the Phocaians were the Lesbians with seventy ships, and last, holding the extremity of the line towards the West, were stationed the Samians with sixty ships. Of all these the total number proved to be three hundred and fifty-three triremes. **9.** These were the ships of the Ionians; and of the Barbarians the number of ships was six hundred. When these too were come to the Milesian coast and their whole land-army was also there, then the commanders of the Persians, being informed of the number of the Ionian ships, were struck with fear lest they should be unable to overcome them,

---

*See 1.148 on this ethnic council and center.

and thus on the one hand should not be able to conquer Miletos from not having command of the sea, and at the same time should run a risk of being punished by Dareios. Reflecting upon these things they gathered together the despots of the Ionians who were exiles with the Medes, having been deposed from their governments by Aristagoras the Milesian, and who chanced to be then joining in the expedition against Miletos,—of these men they called together those who were present and spoke to them as follows: "Ionians, now let each one of you show himself a benefactor of the king's house, that is to say, let each one of you endeavour to detach his own countrymen from the body of the alliance: and make your proposals promising at the same time that they shall suffer nothing unpleasant on account of the revolt, and neither their temples nor their private houses shall be burnt, nor shall they have any worse treatment than they had before this; but if they will not do so, but will by all means enter into a contest with us, threaten them and tell them this, which in truth shall happen to them, namely that if they are worsted in the fight they shall be reduced to slavery, and we shall make their sons eunuchs, and their maidens we shall remove to Bactra, and deliver their land to others." **10.** They thus spoke; and the despots of the Ionians sent each one by night to his own people announcing to them this. The Ionians however, that is those to whom these messages came, continued obstinate and would not accept the thought of treason to their cause; and each people thought that to them alone the Persians were sending this message.

11. This happened as soon as the Persians came to Miletos; and after this the Ionians being gathered together at Ladē held meetings; and others no doubt also made speeches to them, but especially the Phocaian commander Dionysios, who said as follows: "Seeing that our affairs are set upon the razor's edge, Ionians, whether we shall be free or slaves, and slaves too to be dealt with as runaways, now therefore if you shall be willing to take upon yourselves hardships, you will have labour for the time being, but you will be able to overcome the enemy and be free; whereas if you continue to be self-indulgent and without discipline, I have no hope for you that you will not pay the penalty to the king for your revolt. Nay, but do as I say, and deliver yourselves over to me; and I engage, if the gods grant equal conditions, that either the enemy will not fight with us, or that fighting he shall be greatly discomfited." **12.** Hearing this the Ionians delivered themselves to Dionysios; and he used to bring the ships out every day in single file, that he might practise the rowers by making the ships break through one another's line,* and that he might get the fighting-men in the ships under arms; and then for the rest of the day he would keep the ships at anchor; and thus he gave the Ionians work to do during the whole day. For seven days then they submitted and did that which he commanded; but on the day after these the Ionians, being unaccustomed to such toils and being exhausted with hard work and hot sun, spoke to one another thus: "Against which of the deities

---

*Compare 8.9, where Herodotus describes the tactic at Artemision.

have we offended, that we thus fill up the measure of evil? for surely we have gone mad and wandered out of our right mind, in that we have delivered ourselves over to a Phocaian, an impostor, who furnishes but three ships: and he has taken us into his hands and maltreats us with evil dealing from which we can never recover; and many of us in fact have fallen into sicknesses, and many others, it may be expected, will suffer the same thing shortly; and for us it is better to endure anything else in the world rather than these ills, and to undergo the slavery which will come upon us, whatever that shall be, rather than to be oppressed by that which we have now. Come, let us not obey him after this any more." So they said, and immediately after this every one refused to obey him, and they pitched their tents in the island like an army, and kept in the shade, and would not go on board their ships or practise any exercises.

13. Perceiving what was being done by the Ionians, the commanders of the Samians then at length accepted from Aiakes the son of Syloson those proposals which Aiakes sent before at the bidding of the Persians, asking them to leave the alliance of the Ionians; the Samians, I say, accepted these proposals, perceiving that there was great want of discipline on the part of the Ionians, while at the same time it was clear to them that it was impossible to overcome the power of the king; and they well knew also that even if they should overcome the present naval force of Dareios, another would be upon them five times as large. Having found an occasion for self-excuse then, so soon as they saw that the Ionians refused to be serviceable, they counted it gain for themselves to save their temples and their private property. Now Aiakes, from whom the Samians accepted the proposals, was the son of Syloson, the son of Aiakes, and being despot of Samos he had been deprived of his rule by Aristagoras the Milesian, like the other despots of Ionia. 14. So when the Phenicians sailed to the attack, the Ionians also put out their ships from shore against them, sailing in single file:* and when they came near and engaged battle with one another, as regards what followed I am not able exactly to record which of the Ionians showed themselves cowards or good men in this sea-fight, for they throw blame upon one another. The Samians however, it is said, according to their agreement with Aiakes put up their sails then and set forth from their place in the line to sail back to Samos, excepting only eleven ships: of these the captains stayed in their places and took part in the sea-fight, refusing to obey the commanders of their division; and the public authority of the Samians granted them on account of this to have their names written up on a pillar with their fathers' names also, as having proved themselves good men; and this pillar exists still in the market-place.† Then the Lesbians also, when they saw that those next them in order were taking to flight, did the same things as the Samians had done, and so also most of the Ionians did the very same thing. 15. Of those which remained in their

---

*The battle of Ladē and the capture of Miletos probably occurred in 494 B.C.
†Note again Herodotus' interest in monuments commemorating great deeds.

places in the sea-fight the Chians suffered very severely, since they displayed brilliant deeds of valour and refused to play the coward. These furnished, as was before said, a hundred ships and in each of them forty picked men of their citizens served as fighting-men or marines; and when they saw the greater number of their allies deserting them, they did not think fit to behave like the cowards among them, but left alone with a few only of their allies they continued the fight and kept breaking through the enemy's line; until at last, after they had conquered many ships of the enemy, they lost the greater number of their own. **16.** The Chians then with the remainder of their ships fled away to their own land; but those of the Chians whose ships were disabled by the damage which they had received, being pursued fled for refuge to Mycalē; and their ships they ran ashore there and left them behind, while the men proceeded over the mainland on foot: and when the Chians had entered the Ephesian territory on their way, then since they came into it by night and at a time when a festival of Thesmophoria was being celebrated by the women of the place, the Ephesians, not having heard beforehand how it was with the Chians and seeing that an armed body had entered their land, supposed certainly that they were robbers and had a design upon the women; so they came out to the rescue in a body and slew the Chians.

17. Such was the fortune which befell these men: but Dionysios the Phocaian, when he perceived that the cause of the Ionians was ruined, after having taken three ships of the enemy sailed away, not to Phocaia any more, for he knew well that it would be reduced to slavery together with the rest of Ionia, but he sailed immediately straight to Phenicia; and having there sunk merchant ships and taken a great quantity of goods, he sailed thence to Sicily. Then with that for his starting-point he became a freebooter, not plundering any Hellenes, but Carthaginians and Tyrsenians only.

18. The Persians then, being conquerors of the Ionians in the sea-fight, besieged Miletos by land and sea, undermining the walls and bringing against it all manner of engines; and they took it completely in the sixth year from the revolt of Aristagoras, and reduced the people to slavery; so that the disaster agreed with the oracle which had been uttered with reference to Miletos. **19.** For when the Argives were inquiring at Delphi about the safety of their city, there was given to them an oracle which applied to both, that is to say, part of it had reference to the Argives themselves, while that which was added afterwards referred to the Milesians. The part of it which had reference to the Argives I will record when I reach that place in the history,* but that which the Oracle uttered with reference to the Milesians, who were not there present, is as follows:

> "And at that time, O Miletos, of evil deeds the contriver,
>   Thou shalt be made for many a glorious gift and a banquet:

---

*See 6.77 on the Argives' struggle with Cleomenes.

Then shall thy wives be compelled to wash the feet of the long-haired,
And in Didyma then my shrine shall be tended by others."

At the time of which I speak these things came upon the Milesians, since
most of the men were killed by the Persians, who are long-haired, and the
women and children were dealt with as slaves; and the temple at Didyma,
with the sacred building and the sanctuary of the Oracle, was first plundered and then burnt. Of the things in this temple I have made mention
frequently in other parts of the history.* **20.** After this the Milesians who
had been taken prisoner were conducted to Susa; and king Dareios did to
them no other evil, but settled them upon the Sea called Erythraian, in the
city of Ampē, by which the Tigris flows when it runs out into the sea. Of
the Milesian land the Persians themselves kept the surroundings of the
city and the plain, but the heights they gave to the Carians of Pedasa for a
possession.

21. When the Milesians suffered this treatment from the Persians, the
men of Sybaris, who were dwelling in Laos and Skidros, being deprived of
their own city, did not repay like with like: for when Sybaris was taken by
the men of Crotōn, the Milesians all from youth upwards shaved their
heads and put on great mourning: for these cities were more than all others of which we know bound together by ties of friendship. Not like the
Sybarites were the Athenians; for these made it clear that they were
grieved at the capture of Miletos, both in many other ways and also by
this, that when Phrynichos had composed a drama called the "Capture of
Miletos" and had put it on the stage, the body of spectators fell to weeping, and the Athenians moreover fined the poet a thousand drachmas on
the ground that he had reminded them of their own calamities; and they
ordered also that no one in future should represent this drama.

22. Miletos then had been stripped bare of its former inhabitants: but
of the Samians they who had substance were by no means satisfied with
that which had been concerted by the commanders of their fleet with the
Medes; and taking counsel immediately after the sea-fight it seemed good
to them, before their despot Aiakes arrived in the country, to sail away and
make a colony, and not to stay behind and be slaves of the Medes and of
Aiakes: for just at this time the people of Zanclē in Sicily were sending
messengers to Ionia and inviting the Ionians to come to the "Fair Strand,"
desiring there to found a city of Ionians. Now this which is called the Fair
Strand is in the land of the Sikelians and on that side of Sicily which lies
towards Tyrsenia. So when these gave the invitation, the Samians alone of
all the Ionians set forth, having with them those of the Milesians who had
escaped: and in the course of this matter it happened as follows:—**23.** The
Samians as they made their way towards Sicily reached Locroi Epizephyrioi,
and at the same time the people of Zanclē, both themselves and their king,
whose name was Skythes, were encamped about a city of the Sikelians,

---

*Compare 1.92 and 5.36.

desiring to conquer it. Perceiving these things, Anaxilaos the despot of Rhegion, being then at variance with those of Zanclē, communicated with the Samians and persuaded them that they ought to leave the Fair Strand alone, to which they were sailing, and take possession of Zanclē instead, since it was left now without men to defend it. The Samians accordingly did as he said and took possession of Zanclē; and upon this the men of Zanclē, being informed that their city was possessed by an enemy, set out to rescue it, and invited Hippocrates the despot of Gela to help them, for he was their ally. When however Hippocrates also with his army had come up to their rescue, first he put Skythes the ruler of the Zanclaians in fetters, on the ground that he had been the cause of the city being lost, and together with him his brother Pythogenes, and sent them away to the town of Inycos; then he betrayed the cause of the remaining Zanclaians by coming to terms with the Samians and exchanging oaths with them; and in return for this it had been promised by the Samians that Hippocrates should receive as his share the half of all the movable goods in the city and of the slaves, and the whole of the property in the fields round. So the greater number of the Zanclaians he put in bonds and kept himself as slaves, but the chief men of them, three hundred in number, he gave to the Samians to put to death; which however the Samians did not do. **24.** Now Skythes the ruler of the Zanclaians escaped from Inycos to Himera, and thence he came to Asia and went up to the court of Dareios: and Dareios accounted him the most righteous of all the men who had come up to him from Hellas; for he obtained leave of the king and went away to Sicily, and again came back from Sicily to the king; and at last he brought his life to an end among the Persians in old age and possessing great wealth. The Samians then, having got rid of the rule of the Medes, had gained for themselves without labour the fair city of Zanclē.

25. After the sea-battle which was fought for Miletos, the Phenicians by command of the Persians restored to Samos Aiakes the son of Syloson, since he had been to them of much service and had done for them great things; and the Samians alone of all who revolted from Dareios, because of the desertion of their ships which were in the sea-fight, had neither their city nor their temples burnt. Then after the capture of Miletos the Persians immediately got possession of Caria, some of the cities having submitted to their power voluntarily, while others of them they brought over by force.

26. Thus it came to pass as regards these matters: and meanwhile Histiaios the Milesian, who was at Byzantion and was seizing the merchant vessels of the Ionians as they sailed forth out of the Pontus, received the report of that which had happened about Miletos. He entrusted the matters which had to do with the Hellespont to Bisaltes the son of Apollophanes, a man of Abydos, while he himself with the Lesbians sailed to Chios; and when a body of the Chians who were on guard did not allow him to approach, he fought with them at that spot in the Chian land which is called the "Hollows." Histiaios then not only slew many of these, but also, taking Polichnē of the Chians as his base, he conquered with the help of the Lesbians the remainder of the Chians as well, since they had suffered great loss by the sea-fight. **27.** And heaven is wont perhaps to give signs beforehand whenever great evils are about to happen to a city or a race of men; for to the Chians also before these events remarkable signs had come. In the first place when they had sent to Delphi a chorus of a hundred youths, two only returned home, the remaining ninety-eight of them having been seized by a plague and carried off; and then secondly in their city about the same time, that is shortly before the sea-fight, as some children were being taught their letters in school the roof fell in upon them, so that of a hundred and twenty children only one escaped. These signs God showed to them beforehand; and after this the sea-fight came upon them and brought their State down upon its knees; and then after the sea-fight came Histiaios also with the Lesbians; and as the Chians had suffered great loss, he without difficulty effected the conquest of them.

28. Thence Histiaios made an expedition against Thasos, taking with him a large force of Ionians and Aiolians; and while he was encamped about the town of Thasos, a report came to him that the Phenicians were sailing up from Miletos to conquer the rest of Ionia. Being informed of this he left Thasos unconquered and himself hastened to Lesbos, taking with him his whole army. Then, as his army was in want of food, he crossed over from Lesbos to reap the corn in Atarneus and also that in the plain of the Caïcos, which belonged to the Mysians. In these parts there chanced to be a Persian named Harpagos commanding a considerable force; and this man fought a battle with him after he had landed, and he took Histiaios himself prisoner and destroyed the greater part of his army. **29.** And Histiaios was taken prisoner in the following manner:—As the Hellenes were fighting with the Persians at Malenē in the district of Atarneus, after they had been engaged in close combat for a long time, the cavalry at length charged and fell upon the Hellenes; and the cavalry in fact decided the battle. So when the Hellenes had been turned to flight, Histiaios trusting that he would not be put to death by the king on account of his present fault, conceived such a desire to live that when he was being caught in his flight by a Persian and was about to be run through by him in the moment of his capture, he spoke in Persian and made himself known, saying that he was Histiaios the Milesian. **30.** If then upon being taken prisoner he had been brought to king Dareios, he would not, as I think, have suffered any harm, but Dareios would have forgiven the crime with which he was charged; as it was however, for this very reason and in order that he might not escape from punishment and again become powerful with the king, Artaphrenes the governor of Sardis and Harpagos who had captured him, when he had reached Sardis on his way to the king, put him to death there and then, and his body they impaled, but embalmed his head and brought it up to Dareios at Susa. Dareios having been informed of this, found fault with those who had done so, because they had not brought him up into his presence alive; and he bade wash the head of Histiaios and bestow upon it proper care, and then bury it, as that of one who had been greatly a benefactor both of the king himself and of the Persians.

31. Thus it happened about Histiaios; and meanwhile the Persian fleet, after wintering near Miletos, when it put to sea again in the following year conquered without difficulty the islands lying near the mainland, Chios, Lesbos and Tenedos; and whenever they took one of the islands, the Barbarians, as each was conquered, swept the inhabitants off it; and this they do in the following manner:—they extend themselves from the sea on the North to the sea on the South, each man having hold of the hand of the next, and then they pass through the whole island hunting the people out of it. They took also the Ionian cities on the mainland in the same manner, except that they did not sweep off the inhabitants thus, for it was not possible. **32.** Then the commanders of the Persians proved not false to the threats with which they had threatened the Ionians when these were encamped opposite to them: for in fact when they had conquered the cities, they chose out the most comely of the boys and castrated them, making eunuchs of them, and the fairest of the maidens they carried off by force to the king; and not only this, but they also burnt the cities together with the temples. Thus for the third time had the Ionians been reduced to slavery, first by the Lydians and then twice in succession by the Persians.

33. Departing from Ionia the fleet proceeded to conquer all the places of the Hellespont on the left as one sails in, for those on the right had been subdued already by the Persians themselves, approaching them by land. Now the cities of the Hellespont in Europe are these:—first comes the Chersonese, in which there are many cities, then Perinthos, the strongholds of the Thracian border, Selymbria, and Byzantion. The people of Byzantion and those of Calchedon opposite did not even wait for the coming of the Phenician ships, but had left their own land first and departed, going within the Euxine; and there they settled in the city of Mesambria. So the Phenicians, having burnt these places which have been mentioned, directed their course next to Proconnesos and Artakē; and when they had delivered these also to the flames, they sailed back to the Chersonese to destroy the remaining cities which they had not sacked when they touched there before: but against Kyzicos they did not sail at all; for the men of Kyzicos even before the time when the Phenicians sailed in had submitted to the king of their own accord, and had made terms with Oibares the son of Megabazos, the Persian governor at Daskyleion.*

34. In the Chersonese then the Phenicians made themselves masters of all the other cities except the city of Cardia. Of these cities up to that time Miltiades the son of Kimon, the son of Stesagoras, had been despot, Miltiades the son of Kypselos having obtained this government in the manner which here follows:—The inhabitants of this Chersonese were Dolonkian Thracians; and these Dolonkians, being hard pressed in war by the Apsinthians, sent their kings to Delphi to consult the Oracle about the war. And the Pythian prophetess answered them that they must bring into their land as founder of a settlement the man who should first offer them

---

*See 3.120, where c.522 Daskyleion was already the satrapal capital for the province of the Hellespont.

hospitality as they returned from the temple. The Dolonkians then passed
along the Sacred Road through the land of the Phokians and of the Bœotians, and as no man invited them, they turned aside and came to Athens.
35. Now at that time in Athens the government was held by Peisistratos,
but Miltiades also the son of Kypselos had some power, who belonged to a
family which kept four-horse chariot teams, and who was descended originally from Aiacos and Egina, though in more recent times his family was
Athenian, Philaios the son of Ajax having been the first of his house who
became an Athenian. This Miltiades was sitting in the entrance of his own
dwelling, and seeing the Dolonkians going by with dress which was not of
the native Athenian fashion and with spears, he shouted to them; and
when they approached, he offered them lodging and hospitality. They then
having accepted and having been entertained by him, proceeded to declare all the utterance of the Oracle; and having declared it they asked him
to do as the god had said: and Miltiades when he heard it was at once disposed to agree, because he was vexed by the rule of Peisistratos and desired to get out of the way. He set out therefore immediately to Delphi to
inquire of the Oracle whether he should do that which the Dolonkians
asked of him: **36,** and as the Pythian prophetess also bade him do so, Miltiades the son of Kypselos, who had before this been victor at Olympia
with a four-horse chariot, now taking with him of the Athenians everyone
who desired to share in the expedition, sailed with the Dolonkians and
took possession of the land: and they who had invited him to come to
them made him despot over them. First then he made a wall across the
isthmus of the Chersonese from the city of Cardia to Pactyē, in order that
the Apsinthians might not be able to invade the land and do them damage.
Now the number of stades across the isthmus at this place is six-and-thirty
(or four miles), and from this isthmus the Chersonese within is altogether
four hundred and twenty stades (or just under fifty miles) in length.
37. Having made a wall then across the neck of the Chersonese and having
in this manner repelled the Apsinthians, Miltiades made war upon the
people of Lampsacos first of all others; and the people of Lampsacos laid
an ambush and took him prisoner. Now Miltiades had come to be a friend
of Crœsus the Lydian; and Crœsus accordingly, being informed of this
event, sent and commanded the people of Lampsacos to let Miltiades go;
otherwise he threatened to destroy them utterly like a pine-tree. Then
when the people of Lampsacos were perplexed in their counsels as to
what that saying should mean with which Crœsus had threatened them,
namely that he would destroy them utterly like a pine-tree, at length one
of the elder men with difficulty perceived the truth, and said that a pine
alone of all trees when it has been cut down does not put forth any further
growth but perishes, being utterly destroyed. The people of Lampsacos
therefore fearing Crœsus loosed Miltiades and let him go. **38.** He then escaped by means of Crœsus; but afterwards he brought his life to an end
leaving no son to succeed him, but passing over his rule and his possessions to his nephew Stesagoras, who was the son of Kimon, his brother on
the mother's side: and the people of the Chersonese still offer sacrifices to

him after his death as it is usual to do to a founder, and hold in his honour a contest of horse-races and athletic exercises, in which none of the men of Lampsacos are allowed to contend. After this there was war with those of Lampsacos; and it happened to Stesagoras also that he died without leaving a son, having been struck on the head with an axe in the City Hall by a man who pretended to be a deserter, but who proved himself to be in fact an enemy and a rather hot one moreover.

39. Then after Stesagoras also had ended his life in this manner, Miltiades son of Kimon and brother of that Stesagoras who was dead, was sent in a trireme to the Chersonese to take possession of the government by the sons of Peisistratos, who had dealt well with him at Athens also, pretending that they had had no share in the death of his father Kimon, of which in another part of the history I will set forth how it came to pass.* Now Miltiades, when he came to the Chersonese, kept himself within his house, paying honours in all appearance to the memory of his brother Stesagoras; and the chief men of the inhabitants of the Chersonese in every place, being informed of this, gathered themselves together from all the cities and came in a body to condole with him, and when they had come they were laid in bonds by him. Miltiades then was in possession of the Chersonese, supporting a body of five hundred mercenary troops; and he married the daughter of Oloros the king of the Thracians, who was named Hegesipylē.

40. Now this Miltiades son of Kimon had at the time of which we speak but lately returned to the Chersonese; and after he had returned, there befell him other misfortunes worse than those which had befallen him already; for two years before this he had been a fugitive out of the land from the Scythians, since the nomad Scythians provoked by king Dareios had joined all in a body and marched as far as this Chersonese, and Miltiades had not awaited their attack but had become a fugitive from the Chersonese, until at last the Scythians departed and the Dolonkians brought him back again. These things had happened two years before the calamities which now oppressed him: **41,** and now,† being informed that the Phenicians were at Tenedos, he filled five triremes with the property which he had at hand and sailed away for Athens. And having set out from the city of Cardia he was sailing through the gulf of Melas; and as he passed along by the shore of the Chersonese, the Phenicians fell in with his ships, and while Miltiades himself with four of his ships escaped to Imbros, the fifth of his ships was captured in the pursuit by the Phenicians. Of this ship it chanced that Metiochos the eldest of the sons of Miltiades was in command, not born of the daughter of Oloros the Thracian, but of another woman. Him the Phenicians captured together with his ship; and being informed about him, that he was the son of Miltiades, they brought him up to the king, supposing that they would lay up for themselves a great

---

*See 6.103.
†493 B.C.

obligation; because it was Miltiades who had declared as his opinion to the
Ionians that they should do as the Scythians said, at that time when the
Scythians requested them to break up the bridge of boats and sail away to
their own land. Dareios however, when the Phenicians brought up to him
Metiochos the son of Miltiades, did Metiochos no harm but on the con-
trary very much good; for he gave him a house and possessions and a Per-
sian wife, by whom he had children born who have been ranked as
Persians. Miltiades meanwhile came from Imbros to Athens.

42. This year the Persians did nothing more which tended to strife with
the Ionians, but these things which were very much to their advantage.—
Artaphrenes the governor of Sardis sent for envoys from all the cities and
compelled the Ionians to make agreements among themselves, so that they
might give satisfaction for wrongs and not plunder one another's land.
This he compelled them to do, and also he measured their territories by
parasangs,—that is the name which the Persians give to the length of thirty
stades [or 3.4 miles],—he measured, I say, by these, and appointed a certain
amount of tribute for each people, which continues still unaltered from that
time even to my own days, as it was appointed by Artaphrenes; and the
tribute was appointed to be nearly of the same amount for each as it had
been before. **43.** These were things which tended to peace for the Ionians;
but at the beginning of the spring, the other commanders having all been
removed by the king, Mardonios the son of Gobryas came down to the
sea,* bringing with him a very large land-army and a very large naval force,
being a young man and lately married to Artozostra daughter of king
Dareios. When Mardonios leading this army came to Kilikia, he embarked
on board a ship himself and proceeded together with the other ships, while
other leaders led the land-army to the Hellespont. Mardonios however
sailing along the coast of Asia came to Ionia: and here I shall relate a thing
which will be a great marvel to those of the Hellenes who do not believe
that to the seven men of the Persians Otanes declared as his opinion that
the Persians ought to have popular rule;† for Mardonios deposed all the
despots of the Ionians and established popular governments in the cities.
Having so done he hastened on to the Hellespont; and when there was collected a vast number of ships and a large land-army, they crossed over the
Hellespont in the ships and began to make their way through Europe, and
their way was directed against Eretria and Athens. **44.** These, I say, furnished them the pretence for the expedition, but they had it in their minds
to subdue as many as they could of the Hellenic cities; and in the first place
they subdued with their ships the Thasians, who did not even raise a hand
to defend themselves: then with the land-army they gained the Macedonians to be their servants in addition to those whom they had already;
for all the nations on the East of the Macedonians had become subject to
them already before this. Crossing over then from Thasos to the opposite

*The expedition of Mardonios took place in 492 B.C.
†See 3.80, where Herodotus reports a theoretical debate about different regimes.

coast, they proceeded on their way near the land as far as Acanthos, and
then starting from Acanthos they attempted to get round Mount Athōs;
but as they sailed round, there fell upon them a violent North Wind, against
which they could do nothing, and handled them very roughly, casting away
very many of their ships on Mount Athōs. It is said indeed that the number
of the ships destroyed was about three hundred, and more than twenty
thousand men; for as this sea which is about Athōs is very full of sea mon-
sters, some were seized by these and so perished, while others were dashed
against the rocks; and some of them did not know how to swim and perished for that cause, others again by reason of cold. **45.** Thus fared the fleet;
and meanwhile Mardonios and the land-army while encamping in Macedonia were attacked in the night by the Brygian Thracians, and many of
them were slain by the Brygians and Mardonios himself was wounded.
However not even these escaped being enslaved by the Persians, for Mardonios did not depart from that region until he had made them subject. But
when he had subdued these, he proceeded to lead his army back, since he
had suffered great loss with his land-army in fighting against the Brygians
and with his fleet in going round Athōs. So this expedition departed back to
Asia having gained no honour by its contests.

46. In the next year after this [491 B.C.] Dareios first sent a messenger to
the men of Thasos, who had been accused by their neighbours of planning
revolt, and bade them take away the wall round their town and bring their
ships to Abdera. The Thasians in fact, as they had been besieged by Histiaios the Milesian and at the same time had large revenues coming in, were
using their money in building ships of war and in surrounding their city
with a stronger wall. Now the revenues came to them from the mainland
and from the mines: from the gold-mines in Scaptē Hylē there came in
generally eighty talents a year, and from those in Thasos itself a smaller
amount than this but so much that in general the Thasians, without taxes
upon the produce of their soil, had a revenue from the mainland and from
the mines amounting yearly to two hundred talents, and when the amount
was highest, to three hundred. **47.** I myself saw these mines, and by much
the most marvellous of them were those which the Phenicians discovered,
who made the first settlement in this island in company with Thasos; and
the island had the name which it now has from this Thasos the Phenician.
These Phenician mines are in that part of Thasos which is between the
places called Ainyra and Koinyra and opposite Samothrakē, where there
is a great mountain which has been all turned up in the search for metal.
Thus it is with this matter: and the Thasians on the command of the king
both razed their walls and brought all their ships to Abdera.

48. After this Dareios began to make trial of the Hellenes, what they
meant to do, whether to make war with him or to deliver themselves up.
He sent abroad heralds therefore, and appointed them to go some to one
place and others to another throughout Hellas, bidding them demand
earth and water for the king. These, I say, he sent to Hellas; and meanwhile
he was sending abroad other heralds to his own tributary cities which lay
upon the sea-coast, and he bade them have ships of war built and also

vessels to carry horses. **49.** They then were engaged in preparing these things; and meanwhile when the heralds had come to Hellas, many of those who dwelt upon the mainland gave that for which the Persian made demand, and all those who dwelt in the islands did so, to whomsoever they came to make their demand. The islanders, I say, gave earth and water to Dareios, and among them also those of Egina and when these had so done, the Athenians immediately denounced them, supposing that the Eginetans had given with hostile purpose against themselves, in order to make an expedition against them in combination with the Persians; and also they were glad to get hold of an occasion against them. Accordingly they went backward and forwards to Sparta and accused the Eginetans of that which they had done, as having proved themselves traitors to Hellas. **50.** In consequence of this accusation Cleomenes the son of Anaxandrides, king of the Spartans, crossed over to Egina meaning to seize those of the Eginetans who were the most guilty; but as he was attempting to seize them, certain of the Eginetans opposed him, and among them especially Crios the son of Polycritos, who said that he should not with impunity carry off a single Eginetan, for he was doing this (said he) without authority from the Spartan State, having been persuaded to it by the Athenians with money; otherwise he would have come and seized them in company with the other king: and this he said by reason of a message received from Demaratos. Cleomenes then as he departed from Egina, asked Crios [or "Ram"] what was his name, and he told him the truth; and Cleomenes said to him: "Surely now, O Ram, you must cover over your horns with bronze for you will shortly have a great trouble to contend with."

51. Meanwhile Demaratos the son of Ariston was staying behind in Sparta and bringing charges against Cleomenes, he also being king of the Spartans but of the inferior house; which however is inferior in no other way (for it is descended from the same ancestor), but the house of Eurysthenes has always been honoured more, apparently because he was the elder brother. **52.** For the Lacedemonians, who herein agree with none of the poets, say that Aristodemos the son of Aristomachos, the son of Cleodaios, the son of Hyllos, being their king, led them himself (and not the sons of Aristodemos) to this land which they now possess. Then after no long time the wife of Aristodemos, whose name was Argeia,—she was the daughter, they say, of Autesion, the son of Tisamenos, the son of Thersander, the son of Polyneikes,—she, it is said, brought forth twins; and Aristodemos lived but to see his children and then ended his life by sickness. So the Lacedemonians of that time resolved according to established custom to make the elder of the children their king; but they did not know which of them they should take, because they were like one another and of equal size; and when they were not able to make out, or even before this, they inquired of their mother; and she said that even she herself did not know them one from the other. She said this, although she knew in truth very well, because she desired that by some means both might be made kings. The Lacedemonians then were in a strait; and being in a strait they sent to Delphi to inquire what they should do in the matter. And the Pythian prophetess bade them regard both the children as their kings, but honour most the first in age. The prophetess, they say, thus gave answer to them; and when the Lacedemonians were at a loss none the less how to find out the elder of them, a Messenian whose name was Panites made a suggestion to them: this Panites, I say, suggested to the Lacedemonians that they should watch the mother and see which of the children she washed and fed before the other; and if she was seen to do this always in the same order, then they would have all that they were seeking and desiring to find out, but if she too was uncertain and did it in a different order at different times, it would be plain to them that even she had no more knowledge than any other, and they must turn to some other way. Then the Spartans following the suggestion of the Messenian watched the mother of the sons of Aristodemos and found that she gave honour thus to the first-born both in feeding and in washing; for she did not know with what design she was being watched. They took therefore the child which was honoured by its mother and brought it up as the first-born at public expense, and to it was given the name of Eurysthenes, while the other was called Procles. These, when they had grown up, both themselves were at variance, they say, with one another, though they were brothers, throughout the whole time of their lives, and their descendants also continued after the same manner.

53. This is the report given by the Lacedemonians alone of all the Hellenes; but this which follows I write in accordance with that which is reported by the Hellenes generally,—I mean that the names of these kings of the Dorians are rightly enumerated by the Hellenes up to Perseus the son of Danaē (leaving the god out of account), and proved to be of Hellenic race; for even from that time they were reckoned as Hellenes. I said "up to Perseus" and did not take the descent from a yet higher point, because there is no name mentioned of a mortal father for Perseus, as Amphitryon is for Heracles.* Therefore with reason, as is evident, I have said "rightly up to Perseus"; but if one enumerates their ancestors in succession going back from Danaē the daughter of Acrisios, the rulers of the Dorians will prove to be Egyptians by direct descent. **54.** Thus I have traced the descent according to the account given by the Hellenes; but as the story is reported which the Persians tell, Perseus himself was an Assyrian and became a Hellene, whereas the ancestors of Perseus were not Hellenes; and as for the ancestors of Acrisios, who (according to this account) belonged not to Perseus in any way by kinship, they say that these were, as the Hellenes report, Egyptians. **55.** Let it suffice to have said so much about these matters; and as to the question how and by what exploits being Egyptians they received the sceptres of royalty over the Dorians, we will omit these things, since others have told about them; but the things with which other narrators have not dealt, of these I will make mention.†

---

*Herodotus separates the realm of human history from that of the mythical.
†The sentence offers precious but unsatisfactory evidence about earlier prose writers.

56. These are the royal rights which have been given by the Spartans to their kings, namely, two priesthoods, of Zeus Lakedaimon and Zeus Uranios; and the right of making war against whatsoever land they please, and that no man of the Spartans shall hinder this right, or if he do, he shall be subject to the curse; and that when they go on expeditions the kings shall go out first and return last; that a hundred picked men shall be their guard upon expeditions; and that they shall use in their goings forth to war as many cattle as they desire, and take both the hides and the backs of all that are sacrificed. **57.** These are their privileges in war; and in peace moreover things have been assigned to them as follows:—if any sacrifice is performed at the public charge, it is the privilege of the kings to sit down to the feast before all others, and that the attendants shall begin with them first, and serve to each of them a portion of everything double of that which is given to the other guests, and that they shall have the first pouring of libations and the hides of the animals slain in sacrifice; that on every new moon and seventh day of the month there shall be delivered at the public charge to each one of these a full-grown victim in the temple of Apollo, and a measure of barley-groats and a Laconian "quarter" of wine; and that at all the games they shall have seats of honour specially set apart for them: moreover it is their privilege to appoint as protectors of strangers whomsoever they will of the citizens, and to choose each two "Pythians:" now the Pythians are men sent to consult the god at Delphi, and they eat with the kings at the public charge. And if the kings do not come to the dinner, it is the rule that there shall be sent out for them to their houses two quarts of barley-groats for each one and half a pint of wine; but if they are present, double shares of everything shall be given them, and moreover they shall be honoured in this same manner when they have been invited to dinner by private persons. The kings also, it is ordained, shall have charge of the oracles which are given, but the Pythians also shall have knowledge of them. It is the rule moreover that the kings alone give decision on the following cases only, that is to say, about the maiden who inherits her father's property, namely who ought to have her, if her father have not betrothed her to any one, and about public ways; also if any man desires to adopt a son, he must do it in presence of the kings: and it is ordained that they shall sit in council with the Senators, who are in number eight-and-twenty, and if they do not come, those of the Senators who are most closely related to them shall have the privileges of the kings and give two votes besides their own, making three in all.[*]

58. These rights have been assigned to the kings for their lifetime by the Spartan State; and after they are dead these which follow:—horsemen go round and announce that which has happened throughout the whole of the Laconian land, and in the city women go about and strike upon a copper kettle. Whenever this happens so, two free persons of each household

---

[*]Herodotus may not here imply that each king had two votes, but Thucydides (1.20) criticizes someone who maintained this.

must go into mourning, a man and a woman, and for those who fail to do this great penalties are appointed. Now the custom of the Lacedemonians about the death of their kings is the same as that of the Barbarians who dwell in Asia, for most of the Barbarians practise the same custom as regards the death of their kings. Whensoever a king of the Lacedemonians is dead, then from the whole territory of Lacedemon, not reckoning the Spartans, a certain fixed number of the *perioikoi* or "dwellers round" are compelled to go to the funeral ceremony: and when there have been gathered together of these and of the Helots and of the Spartans themselves many thousands in the same place, with their women intermingled, they beat their foreheads with a good will and make lamentation without stint, saying that this one who has died last of their kings was the best of all: and whenever any of their kings has been killed in war, they prepare an image to represent him, laid upon a couch with fair coverings, and carry it out to be buried. Then after they have buried him, no assembly is held among them for ten days, nor is there any meeting for choice of magistrates, but they have mourning during these days.

59. In another respect too these resemble the Persians; that is to say, when the king is dead and another is appointed king, this king who is newly coming in sets free any man of the Spartans who was a debtor to the king or to the State; while among the Persians the king who comes to the throne remits to all the cities the arrears of tribute which are due. **60.** In the following point also the Lacedemonians resemble the Egyptians; that is to say, their heralds and fluteplayers and cooks inherit the crafts of their fathers, and a fluteplayer is the son of a fluteplayer, a cook of a cook, and a herald of a herald; other men do not lay hands upon the office because they have loud and clear voices, and so shut them out of it, but they practise their craft by inheritance from their fathers.

61. Thus are these things done: and at this time of which we speak,* while Cleomenes was in Egina doing deeds which were for the common service of Hellas, Demaratos brought charges against him, not so much because he cared for the Eginetans as because he felt envy and jealousy of him. Then Cleomenes, after he returned from Egina, planned to depose Demaratos from being king, making an attempt upon him on account of this matter which follows:—Ariston being king in Sparta and having married two wives, yet had no children born to him; and since he did not acknowledge that he was himself the cause of this, he married a third wife; and he married her thus:—he had a friend, a man of the Spartans, to whom of all the citizens Ariston was most inclined; and it chanced that this man had a wife who was of all the women in Sparta the fairest by far, and one too who had become the fairest from having been the foulest. For as she was mean in her aspect, her nurse, considering that she was the daughter of wealthy persons and was of uncomely aspect, and seeing moreover that her parents were troubled by it,—perceiving I say these things, her nurse

---

*Resuming the narrative from 6.51.

devised as follows:—every day she bore her to the temple of Helen, which is in the place called Therapnē, lying above the temple of Phœbus; and whenever the nurse bore her thither, she placed her before the image and prayed the goddess to deliver the child from her unshapeliness. And once as the nurse was going away out of the temple, it is said that a woman appeared to her, and having appeared asked her what she was bearing in her arms; and she told her that she was bearing a child; upon which the other bade her show the child to her, but she refused, for it had been forbidden to her by the parents to show it to any one: but the woman continued to urge her by all means to show it to her. So then perceiving that the woman earnestly desired to see it, the nurse at last showed the child. Then the woman stroking the head of the child said that she should be the fairest of all the women in Sparta; and from that day her aspect was changed. Afterwards when she came to the age for marriage, she was married to Agetos the son of Alkeides, this friend of Ariston of whom we spoke.

62. Now Ariston it seems was ever stung by desire for this woman, and accordingly he contrived as follows:—he made an engagement himself with his comrade, whose wife this woman was, that he would give him as a gift one thing of his own possessions, whatsoever he should choose, and he bade his comrade make return to him in similar fashion. He therefore, fearing nothing for his wife, because he saw that Ariston also had a wife, agreed to this; and on these terms they imposed oaths on one another. After this Ariston on his part gave that which Agetos had chosen from the treasures of Ariston, whatever the thing was; and he himself, seeking to obtain from him the like return, endeavoured then to take away the wife of his comrade from him: and he said that he consented to give anything else except this one thing only, but at length being compelled by the oath and by the treacherous deception, he allowed her to be taken away from him. 63. Thus had Ariston brought into his house the third wife, having dismissed the second: and this wife, not having fulfilled the ten months but in a shorter period of time, bore him that Demaratos of whom we were speaking; and one of his servants reported to him as he was sitting in council with the Ephors, that a son had been born to him. He then, knowing the time when he took to him his wife, and reckoning the months upon his fingers, said, denying with an oath, "The child would not be mine." This the Ephors heard, but they thought it a matter of no importance at the moment; and the child grew up and Ariston repented of that which he had said, for he thought Demaratos was certainly his own son; and he gave him the name "Demaratos" for this reason, namely because before these things took place the Spartan people [dēmos] all in a body had made a vow [arē] praying that a son might be born to Ariston, as one who was pre-eminent in renown over all the kings who had ever arisen in Sparta. 64. For this reason the name Demaratos was given to him. And as time went on Ariston died, and Demaratos obtained the kingdom: but it was fated apparently that these things should become known and should cause Demaratos to be deposed from the kingdom; and therefore Demaratos came to be at variance greatly with Cleomenes both at the former time when he withdrew his army from

Eleusis, and also now especially, when Cleomenes had crossed over to take those of the Eginetans who had gone over to the Medes.

65. Cleomenes then, being anxious to take vengeance on him, concerted matters with Leotychides the son of Menares, the son of Agis, who was of the same house as Demaratos, under condition that if he should set him up as king instead of Demaratos, he would go with him against the Eginetans. Now Leotychides had become a bitter foe to Demaratos on account of this matter which follows:—Leotychides had betrothed himself to Percalos the daughter of Chilon son of Demarmenos; and Demaratos plotted against him and deprived Leotychides of his marriage, carrying off Percalos himself beforehand, and getting her for his wife. Thus had arisen the enmity of Leotychides against Demaratos; and now by the instigation of Cleomenes Leotychides was deposed against Demaratos, saying that he was not rightfully reigning over the Spartans, not being the son of Ariston: and after this deposition he prosecuted a suit against him, recalling the old saying which Ariston uttered at the time when his servant reported to him that a son was born to him, and he reckoning up the months denied with an oath, saying that it was not his. Taking his stand upon this utterance, Leotychides proceeded to prove that Demaratos was not born of Ariston nor was rightfully reigning over Sparta; and he produced as witnesses those Ephors who chanced then to have been sitting with Ariston in council and to have heard him say this. **66.** At last, as there was contention about those matters, the Spartans resolved to ask the Oracle at Delphi whether Demaratos was the son of Ariston. The question then having been referred by the arrangement of Cleomenes to the Pythian prophetess, thereupon Cleomenes gained over to his side Cobon the son of Aristophantos, who had most power among the Delphians, and Cobon persuaded Perialla the prophetess of the Oracle to say that which Cleomenes desired to have said. Thus the Pythian prophetess, when those who were sent to consult the god asked her their question, gave decision that Demaratos was not the son of Ariston. Afterwards however these things became known, and both Cobon went into exile from Delphi and Perialla the prophetess of the Oracle was removed from her office.

67. With regard to the deposing of Demaratos from the kingdom it happened thus:[*] but Demaratos became an exile from Sparta to the Medes on account of a reproach which here follows:—After he had been deposed from the kingdom Demaratos was holding a public office to which he had been elected. Now it was the time of the Gymnopaidiai; and as Demaratos was a spectator of them, Leotychides, who had now become king himself instead of Demaratos, sent his attendant and asked Demaratos in mockery and insult what kind of a thing it was to be a magistrate after having been king; and he vexed at the question made answer and said that he himself had now had experience of both, but Leotychides not; this question however, he said, would be the beginning either of countless evil or countless good fortune for the Lacedemonians. Having

---

*Demaratos was deposed in 491 B.C.

thus said, he veiled his head and went forth out of the theatre to his own house; and immediately he made preparations and sacrificed an ox to Zeus, and after having sacrificed he called his mother. **68.** Then when his mother had come, he put into her hands some of the inner parts of the victim, and besought her, saying as follows: "Mother, I beseech you, appealing to the other gods and above all to this Zeus the guardian of the household, to tell me the truth, who is really and truly my father. For Leotychides spoke in his contention with me, saying that you did come to Ariston with child by your former husband; and others besides, reporting that which is doubtless an idle tale, say that you had sex with one of the servants, namely the keeper of the asses, and that I am his son. I therefore entreat you by the gods to tell me the truth; for if you have done any of these things which are reported, you have not done them alone, but with many other women; and the report is commonly believed in Sparta that there was not in Ariston seed which should beget children; for if so, then his former wives also would have borne children."

69. Thus he spoke, and she made answer as follows: "My son, since you do beseech me with entreaties to speak the truth, the whole truth shall be told to you. When Ariston had brought me into his house, on the third night there came to me an apparition in the likeness of Ariston, and having lain with me it put upon me the garlands which it had on; and the apparition straightway departed, and after this Ariston came; and when he saw me with garlands, he asked who it was who had given me them; and I said that he had given them, but he did not admit it: and I began to take oath of it, saying that he did not well to deny it, for he had come (I said) a short time before and had lain with me and given me the garlands. Then Ariston, seeing that I made oath of it, perceived that the matter was of the gods; and first the garlands were found to be from the hero-temple which stands by the outer door of the house, which they call the temple of Astrabacos, and secondly the diviners gave answer that it was this same hero. Thus, my son, you have all, as much as you desire to learn; for either you are begotten of this hero and the hero Astrabacos is your father, or Ariston is your father, for on that night I conceived you: but as to that wherein your foes most take hold of you, saying that Ariston himself, when your birth was announced to him, in the hearing of many declared that you were not his son, because the time, the ten months namely, had not yet been fulfilled, in ignorance of such matters he cast forth that saying; for women bring forth children both at the ninth month and also at the seventh, and not all after they have completed ten months; and I bore you, my son, at the seventh month: and Ariston himself also perceived after no long time that he had uttered this saying in folly. Do not then accept any other reports about your begetting, for you have heard in all the full truth; but to Leotychides himself and to those who report these things may their wives bear children by keepers of asses!" **70.** Thus she spoke; and he, having learnt that which he desired to learn, took supplies for travelling and set forth to go to Elis, pretending that he was going to Delphi to consult the Oracle: but the Lacedemonians, suspecting that he was attempting to escape, pursued him; and it

chanced that before they came Demaratos had passed over to Zakynthos
from Elis; and the Lacedemonians crossing over after him laid hands upon
his person and carried away his attendants from him. Afterwards however,
since those of Zakynthos refused to give him up, he passed over from
thence to Asia, to the presence of king Dareios; and Dareios both received
him with great honour as a guest, and also gave him land and cities. Thus
Demaratos had come to Asia, and such was the fortune which he had had,
having been distinguished in the estimation of the Lacedemonians in many
other ways both by deeds and by counsels, and especially having gained for
them an Olympic victory with the four-horse chariot, being the only one
who achieved this of all the kings who ever arose in Sparta.

71. Demaratos being deposed, Leotychides the son of Menares succeeded to the kingdom; and he had born to him a son Zeuxidemos, whom
some of the Spartans called Kyniscos. This Zeuxidemos did not become
king of Sparta, for he died before Leotychides, leaving a son Archidemos:
and Leotychides having lost Zeuxidemos married a second wife Eury-
damē, the sister of Menios and daughter of Diactorides, by whom he had
no male issue, but a daughter Lampito, whom Archidemos the son of
Zeuxidemos took in marriage, she being given to him by Leotychides.
72. Leotychides however did not himself live to old age in Sparta, but paid
a retribution for Demaratos as follows:—he went as commander of the
Lacedemonians to invade Thessaly,* and when he might have reduced all
to subjection, he accepted gifts of money amounting to a large sum; and
being taken in the act there in the camp, as he was sitting upon a glove full
of money, he was brought to trial and banished from Sparta, and his house
was razed to the ground. So he went into exile to Tegea and ended his life
there. **73.** These things happened later; but at this time, when Cleomenes
had brought to a successful issue the affair which concerned Demaratos,
immediately he took with him Leotychides and went against the Eginetans, being very greatly enraged with them because of their insults towards
him. So the Eginetans on their part, since both the kings had come against
them, thought fit no longer to resist; and the Spartans selected ten men
who were the most considerable among the Eginetans both by wealth and
by birth, and took them away as prisoners, and among others also Crios
the son of Polycritos and Casambos the son of Aristocrates, who had the
greatest power among them; and having taken these away to the land of
Attica, they deposited them as a charge with the Athenians, who were the
bitterest enemies of the Eginetans.

74. After this Cleomenes, since it had become known that he had devised evil against Demaratos, was seized by fear of the Spartans and retired
to Thessaly. Thence he came to Arcadia, and began to make revolutionary
mischief and to combine the Arcadians against Sparta; and besides other
oaths with which he caused them to swear that they would assuredly follow
him whithersoever he should lead them, he was very desirous also to bring

*This expedition to Thessaly took place c.478 B.C.

the chiefs of the Arcadians to the city of Nonacris and cause them to swear by the water of Styx; for near this city it is said by the Arcadians that there is the water of Styx, and there is in fact something of this kind: a small stream of water is seen to trickle down from a rock into a hollow ravine, and round the ravine runs a wall of rough stones. Now Nonacris, where it happens that this spring is situated, is a city of Arcadia near Pheneos. **75.** The Lacedemonians, hearing that Cleomenes was acting thus, were afraid, and proceeded to bring him back to Sparta to rule on the same terms as before: but when he had come back, immediately a disease of madness seized him (who had been even before this somewhat insane). For example, whenever he met any of the Spartans, he dashed his staff against the man's face. And as he continued to do this and had gone quite out of his senses, his kinsmen bound him in stocks. Then being so bound, and seeing his warder left alone by the rest, he asked him for a knife; and the warder not being at first willing to give it, he threatened him with that which he would do to him afterwards when he had been freed if he did not; until at last the warder fearing the threats, for he was one of the Helots, gave him a knife. Then Cleomenes, when he had received the steel, began to maltreat himself from the legs upwards: for he went on cutting his flesh lengthways from the legs to the thighs and from the thighs to the loins and flanks, until at last he came to the belly; and cutting this into strips he died in that manner. And this happened, as most of the Hellenes report,* because he persuaded the Pythian prophetess to advise that which was done about Demaratos; but as the Athenians alone report, it was because when he invaded Eleusis he laid waste the sacred enclosure of the goddesses, Demēter and Korē; and according to the report of the Argives, because from their sanctuary dedicated to Argos he caused to come down those of the Argives who had fled for refuge from the battle and slew them, and also set fire to the grove itself, holding it in no regard. **76.** For when Cleomenes was consulting the Oracle at Delphi, the answer was given him that he should conquer Argos; so he led the Spartans† and came to the river Erasinos, which is said to flow from the Stymphalian lake; for this lake, they say, running out into a viewless chasm, appears again above ground in the land of Argos; and from thence onwards this water is called by the Argives Erasinos: having come, I say, to this river, Cleomenes did sacrifice to it; and since the sacrifices were not at all favourable for him to cross over, he said that he admired the Erasinos for not betraying the men of its country, but the Argives should not even so escape. After this he retired back from thence and led his army down to Thyrea; and having done sacrifice to the Sea by slaying a bull, he brought them in ships to the land of Tiryns and Nauplia. **77.** Being informed of this, the Argives came to the rescue towards the sea; and when they had got near Tiryns and were at the place which is called Sepeia, they encamped opposite to the Lacedemonians leaving no very

---

*A good example of the conscientious preservation of diverse explanations.
†This war with Argos occurred c.495 B.C.

wide space between the armies. There the Argives were not afraid of the open fighting, but only lest they should be conquered by craft; for to this they thought referred the oracle which the Pythian prophetess gave in common to these and to the Milesians, saying as follows:

> "But when the female at length shall conquer the male in the battle,
> Conquer and drive him forth, and glory shall gain among Argives,
> Then many wives of the Argives shall tear both cheeks in their
>   mourning;
> So that a man shall say some time, of the men that come after,
> 'Quelled by the spear it perished, the three-coiled terrible serpent.' "

The conjunction of all these things caused fear to the Argives, and with a view to this they resolved to make use of the enemy's herald; and having so resolved they proceeded to do as follows:—whenever the Spartan herald proclaimed anything to the Lacedemonians, the Argives also did that same thing.

78. So Cleomenes, perceiving that the Argives were doing whatever the herald of the Lacedemonians proclaimed, passed the word to the Lacedemonians that when the herald should proclaim that they were to get breakfast, then they should take up their arms and go to attack the Argives. This was carried out even so by the Lacedemonians; for as the Argives were getting breakfast according to the herald's proclamation, they attacked them; and many of them they slew, but many more yet took refuge in the sacred grove of Argos, and upon these they kept watch, sitting round about the place. Then Cleomenes did this:—**79.** He had with him deserters, and getting information by inquiring of these, he sent a herald and summoned forth those of the Argives who were shut up in the sanctuary, mentioning each by name; and he summoned them forth saying that he had received their ransom. Now among the Peloponnesians ransom is two pounds weight of silver appointed to be paid for each prisoner. So Cleomenes summoned forth about fifty of the Argives one by one and slew them; and it chanced that the rest who were in the enclosure did not perceive that this was being done; for since the grove was thick, those within did not see how it fared with those who were without, at least until one of them climbed up a tree and saw from above. Accordingly they then no longer came forth when they were called. **80.** So Cleomenes thereupon ordered all the Helots to pile up brushwood round the sacred grove; and they obeying, he set fire to the grove. And when it was now burning, he asked one of the deserters to what god the grove was sacred, and the man replied that it was sacred to Argos. When he heard that, he groaned aloud and said, "Apollo who utters oracles, surely you have greatly deceived me, saying that I should conquer Argos: I conjecture that the oracle has had its fulfilment for me already."

81. After this Cleomenes sent away the greater part of his army to go back to Sparta, but he himself took a thousand of the best men and went to the temple of Hera to sacrifice: and when he wished to sacrifice upon the altar, the priest forbade him, saying that it was not permitted by religious rule for a stranger to sacrifice in that place. Cleomenes however bade the Helots take away the priest from the altar and scourge him, and he himself offered the sacrifice. Having so done he returned back to Sparta; **82,** and after his return his opponents brought him up before the Ephors, saying that he had received gifts and therefore had not conquered Argos, when he might easily have conquered it. He said to them,—but whether he was speaking falsely or whether truly I am not able with certainty to say,—however that may be, he spoke and said that when he had conquered the sanctuary of Argos, it seemed to him that the oracle of the god had had its fulfilment for him; therefore he did not think it right to make an attempt on the city, at least until he should have had recourse to sacrifice, and should have learnt whether the deity [Hera] permitted him or whether she stood opposed to him: and as he was sacrificing for augury in the temple of Hera, a flame of fire blazed forth from the breasts of the image; and thus he knew the certainty of the matter, namely that he would not conquer Argos: for if fire had blazed forth from the head of the image, he would have been conqueror of the city from top to bottom, but since it blazed from the breasts, everything had been accomplished for him which the god desired should come to pass. Thus speaking he seemed to the Spartans to speak credibly and reasonably, and he easily escaped his pursuers.

83. Argos however was so bereft of men that their slaves took possession of all the State, ruling and managing it until the sons of those who had perished grew to be men. Then these, endeavouring to gain Argos back to themselves, cast them out; and the slaves being driven forth gained possession of Tiryns by fighting. Now for a time these two parties had friendly relations with one another; but afterwards there came to the slaves a prophet named Cleander, by race a Phigalian from Arcadia: this man persuaded the slaves to attack their masters; and in consequence of this there was war between them for a long time, until at last with difficulty the Argives overcame them.

84. The Argives then say that this was the reason why Cleomenes went mad and had an evil end: but the Spartans themselves say that Cleomenes was not driven mad by any divine power, but that he had become a drinker of unmixed wine from having associated with Scythians, and that he went mad in consequence of this: for the nomad Scythians, they say, when Dareios had made invasion of their land, desired eagerly after this to take vengeance upon him; and they sent to Sparta and tried to make an alliance, and to arrange that while the Scythians themselves attempted an invasion of Media by the way of the river Phasis, the Spartans should set forth from Ephesos and go up inland, and then that they should meet in one place: and they say that Cleomenes when the Scythians had come for this purpose, associated with them largely, and that thus associating more than was fit, he learnt from them the practise of drinking wine unmixed with water; and for this cause (as the Spartans think) he went mad. Thenceforth, as they say themselves, when they desire to drink stronger wine, they say "Fill up in Scythian fashion." Thus the Spartans report about Cleomenes; but to me it seems that this was a retribution which Cleomenes paid for Demaratos.

85. Now when the Eginetans heard that Cleomenes had met his end, they sent messengers to Sparta to denounce Leotychides for the matter of the hostages which were being kept at Athens: and the Lacedemonians caused a court to assemble and judged that the Eginetans had been dealt with outrageously by Leotychides; and they condemned him to be taken to Egina and delivered up in place of the men who were being kept at Athens. Then when the Eginetans were about to take Leotychides, Theasides the son of Leoprepes, a man of repute in Sparta, said to them: "What are you proposing to do, men of Egina? Do you mean to take away the king of the Spartans, thus delivered up to you by his fellow-citizens? If the Spartans now being in anger have decided so, beware lest at some future time, if you do this, they bring an evil upon your land which may destroy it." Hearing this the Eginetans abstained from taking him; but they came to an agreement that Leotychides should accompany them to Athens and restore the men to the Eginetans.

86. When however Leotychides came to Athens and asked for the deposit back, the Athenians, not being willing to give up the hostages, produced pretexts for refusing, and alleged that two kings had deposited them and they did not think it right to give them back to the one without the other: so since the Athenians said that they would not give them back, Leotychides spoke to them as follows:

(*a*) "Athenians, do whichever thing you yourselves desire; for you know that if you give them up, you do that which religion commands, and if you refuse to give them up, you do the opposite of this: but I desire to tell you what kind of a thing came to pass once in Sparta about a deposit. We Spartans report that there was in Lacedemon about two generations before my time one Glaucos the son of Epikydes. This man we say attained the highest merit in all things besides, and especially he was well reported of by all who at that time dwelt in Lacedemon for his uprightness: and we relate that after a time it happened to him thus:—a man of Miletos came to Sparta and desired to have speech with him, alleging the reasons which follow: 'I am a Milesian,' he said, 'and I am come hither desiring to have benefit from your uprightness, Glaucos; for as there was much report of your uprightness throughout all the rest of Hellas and also in Ionia, I considered with myself that Ionia is ever in danger, whereas Peloponnesus is safely established, and also that we never see wealth continue in the possession of the same persons long;—reflecting, I say, on these things and taking counsel with myself, I resolved to turn into money the half of all my possessions, and to place it with you, being well assured that if it were placed with you I should have it safe. Do you therefore, I pray you, receive the money, and take and keep these tallies; and whosoever shall ask for the money back having the tokens answering to these, to him restore it.'

(*b*) The stranger who had come from Miletos said so much; and Glaucos accepted the deposit on the terms proposed. Then after a long time had gone by, there came to Sparta the sons of him who had deposited the money with Glaucos; and they came to speech with Glaucos, and producing the tokens asked for the money to be given back: but he repulsed them answering them again thus: 'I do not remember the matter, nor does my mind bring back to me any knowledge of those things whereof you speak; but I desire to recollect and do all that is just; for if I received it, I desire to restore it honestly; and if on the other hand I did not receive it at all, I will act towards you in accordance with the customs of the Hellenes: therefore I defer the settling of this matter with you for three months from now.' (c) The Milesians accordingly went away grieved, for they supposed that they had been robbed of the money; but Glaucos set forth to Delphi to consult the Oracle: and when he inquired of the Oracle whether he should rob them of the money by an oath, the Pythian prophetess rebuked him with these lines:

"'Glaucos, thou, Epikydes' son, yea, this for the moment,
    This, to conquer their word by an oath and to rob, is more gainful.
    Swear, since the lot of death waits also for him who swears truly.
    But know thou that Oath hath a son, one nameless and handless and
        footless,
    Yet without feet he pursues, without hands he seizes, and wholly
    He shall destroy the race and the house of the man who offendeth.
    But for the man who swears truly his race is the better hereafter.'

Having heard this Glaucos entreated that the god would pardon him for that which he had said, but the prophetess said that to make trial of the god and to do the deed were things equivalent. (d) Glaucos then, having sent for the Milesians, gave back to them the money: but the reason for which, Athenians, I set forth to relate to you this story, shall now be told. At the present time there is no descendant of Glaucos existing, nor any hearth which is esteemed to be that of Glaucos, but he has been utterly destroyed and rooted up out of Sparta. Thus it is good not even to entertain a thought about a deposit other than that of restoring it, when they who made it ask for it again."

87. When Leotychides had thus spoken, since not even so were the Athenians willing to listen to him, he departed back; and the Eginetans, before paying the penalty for their former wrongs wherein they did outrage to the Athenians to please the Thebans,* acted as follows:—complaining of the conduct of the Athenians and thinking that they were being wronged, they made preparations to avenge themselves upon the Athenians; and since the Athenians were celebrating a four-yearly festival at Sunion, they lay in wait for the sacred ship which was sent to it and took it, the vessel being full of men who were the first among the Athenians; and having taken it they laid the men in bonds. **88.** The Athenians after they had suffered this wrong from the Eginetans no longer delayed to contrive all things possible

---

*See 5.80–81, where the Eginetans conducted a sneak attack.

to their hurt. And there was in Egina a man of repute, one Nicodromos the son of Cnoithos: this man had cause of complaint against the Eginetans for having before this driven him forth out of the island; and hearing now that the Athenians had resolved to do mischief to the Eginetans, he agreed with the Athenians to deliver up Egina to them, telling them on what day he would make his attempt and by what day it would be necessary for them to come to his assistance. **89.** After this Nicodromos, according as he had agreed with the Athenians, seized that which is called the old city, but the Athenians did not come to his support at the proper time; for, as it chanced, they had not ships sufficient to fight with the Eginetans; so while they were asking the Corinthians to lend them ships, during this time their cause went to ruin. The Corinthians however, being at this time exceedingly friendly with them, gave the Athenians twenty ships at their request; and these they gave by selling them at five drachmas apiece, for by the law it was not permitted to give them as a free gift. Having taken these ships of which I speak and also their own, the Athenians with seventy ships manned in all sailed to Egina, and they were later by one day than the time agreed. **90.** Nicodromos meanwhile, as the Athenians did not come to his support at the proper time, embarked in a ship and escaped from Egina, and with him also went others of the Eginetans; and the Athenians gave them Sunion to dwell in, starting from whence these men continued to plunder the Eginetans who were in the island. **91.** This happened afterwards: but at the time of which we speak the well-to-do class among the Eginetans prevailed over the men of the people, who had risen against them in combination with Nicodromos, and then having got them into their power they were bringing their prisoners forth to execution. From this there came upon them a curse which they were not able to expiate by sacrifice, though they devised against it all they could; but they were driven forth from the island before the goddess became propitious to them.* For they had taken as prisoners seven hundred of the men of the people and were bringing them forth to execution, when one of them escaped from his bonds and fled for refuge to the entrance of the temple of Demeter the Giver of Laws, and he took hold of the latch of the door and clung to it; and when they found that they could not drag him from it by pulling him away, they cut off his hands and so carried him off, and those hands remained clinging to the latch of the door.

92. Thus did the Eginetans to one another: and when the Athenians came, they fought against them with seventy ships, and being worsted in the sea-fight they called to their assistance the same whom they had summoned before, namely the Argives. These would no longer come to their help, having cause of complaint because ships of Egina compelled by Cleomenes had put in to the land of Argos and their crews had landed with the Lacedemonians; with whom also had landed men from ships of Sikyon in this same invasion: and as a penalty for this there was laid upon them by the Argives a fine of a thousand talents, five hundred for each

---

*The Eginetans were driven out of their island in 431 B.C.

State. The Sikyonians accordingly, acknowledging that they had committed a wrong, had made an agreement to pay a hundred talents and be free
from the penalty; the Eginetans however did not acknowledge their wrong,
but were more stubborn. For this reason then, when they made request,
none of the Argives now came to their help at the charge of the State, but
volunteers came to the number of a thousand; and their leader was a commander named Eurybates, a man who had practised the pentathlon with its
five contests. Of these men the greater number never returned back, but
were slain by the Athenians in Egina; and the commander himself, Eurybates, fighting, as if in practice, in single combat killed in this manner three
men and was himself slain by the fourth, Sophanes namely of Dekeleia.
93. The Eginetans however engaged in contest with the Athenians in ships,
when these were in disorder, and defeated them; and they took of them
four ships together with their crews.

94. So the Athenians were at war with the Eginetans; and meanwhile
the Persian was carrying forward his design, since he was put in mind ever
by his servant to remember the Athenians, and also because the sons of
Peisistratos were near at hand and brought charges continually against the
Athenians, while at the same time Dareios himself wished to take hold of
this pretext and subdue those nations of Hellas which had not given him
earth and water. Mardonios then, since he had fared miserably in his expedition, he removed from his command; and appointing other generals to
command he despatched them against Eretria and Athens, namely Datis,
who was a Mede by race, and Artaphrenes the son of Artaphrenes, a
nephew of the king: and he sent them forth with the charge to reduce
Athens and Eretria to slavery and to bring the slaves back into his presence.* **95.** When these who had been appointed to command came in their
march from the king to the Aleïan plain in Kilikia, taking with them a
large and well-equipped land-army, then while they were encamping
there, the whole naval armament came up, which had been appointed for
the several nations to furnish; and there came to them also the ships for
carrying horses, which in the year before Dareios had ordered his tributar-
ies to make ready. In these they placed their horses, and having embarked
the land-army in the ships they sailed for Ionia with six hundred triremes.
After this they did not keep their ships coasting along the mainland towards the Hellespont and Thrace, but they started from Samos and made
their voyage by the Icarian Sea and between the islands; because, as I think,
they feared more than all else the voyage round Athōs, seeing that two
years before while making the passage by this way they had come to great
disaster. Moreover also Naxos required this itinerary, since it had not been
conquered at the former time. **96.** And when they had arrived at Naxos,
coming against it from the Icarian Sea (for it was against Naxos first that
the Persians intended to make expedition, remembering the former

---

*The expedition of Datis and Artaphrenes took place in 490 B.C.

events), the Naxians departed immediately fleeing to the mountains, and did not await their attack; but the Persians made slaves of those of them whom they caught and set fire to both the temples and the town. Then they put out to sea to attack the other islands.

97. Meanwhile, the Delians also had left Delos and fled away to Tenos; and when the armament was sailing in thither, Datis sailed on before and did not allow the ships to anchor at the island of Delos, but at Rhenaia on the other side of the channel; and he himself, having found out by inquiry where the men of Delos were, sent a herald and addressed them thus: "Holy men, why are you fled away and departed, having judged me unfairly? For even I of myself have wisdom at least so far, and moreover it has been thus commanded me by the king, not to harm at all that land in which the two divinities were born, neither the land itself nor the inhabitants of it. Now therefore return to your own possessions and dwell in your island." Thus he proclaimed by a herald to the Delians; and after this he piled up and burned upon the altar three hundred talents' weight of frankincense. **98.** Datis having done these things sailed away with his army to fight against Eretria first, taking with him both Ionians and Aiolians; and after he had put out to sea from thence, Delos was moved, not having been shaken (as the Delians reported to me) either before that time or since that down to my own time; and this no doubt the god manifested as a portent to men of the evils that were about to be; for in the time of Dareios the son of Hystaspes and Xerxes the son of Dareios and Artoxerxes the son of Xerxes, three generations following upon one another, there happened more evils to Hellas than during the twenty other generations which came before Dareios, some of the evils coming to it from the Persians, and others from the leaders themselves of Hellas warring together for supremacy. Thus it was not unreasonable that Delos should be moved, which was before unmoved. And in an oracle it was thus written about it:

"Delos too will I move, unmoved though it hath been aforetime."

Now in the Hellenic tongue the names which have been mentioned have this meaning—Dareios means "compeller," Xerxes "warrior," Artoxerxes "great warrior."* Thus then might the Hellenes rightly call these kings in their own tongue.

99. The Barbarians then, when they had departed from Delos, touched at the islands as they went, and from them received additional forces and took sons of the islanders as hostages: and when in sailing round about the islands they put in also to Carystos, seeing that the Carystians would neither give them hostages nor consent to join in an expedition against cities that were their neighbours, meaning Eretria and Athens, they began to

---

*These Herodotean translations are incorrect; better translations of the old Persian are: "Good-Upholder," "King-Hero," and "Possessing a Kingdom of Justice."

besiege them and to ravage their land; until at last the Carystians also came over to the will of the Persians. **100.** The Eretrians meanwhile being informed that the armament of the Persians was sailing to attack them, requested the Athenians to help them; and the Athenians did not refuse their support, but gave as helpers those four thousand to whom had been allotted the land of the wealthy Chalkidians. The Eretrians however, as it turned out, had no sound plan of action, for while they sent for the Athenians, they had in their minds two different designs: some of them, that is, proposed to leave the city and go to the heights of Eubœa; while others of them, expecting to win gain for themselves from the Persian, were preparing to surrender the place. Having got knowledge of how things were as regards both these plans, Aischines the son of Nothon, one of the leaders of the Eretrians, told the whole condition of their affairs to those of the Athenians who had come, and entreated them to depart and go to their own land, that they might not also perish. So the Athenians did according to this counsel given to them by Aischines. **101.** And while these passed over to Oropos and saved themselves, the Persians sailed on and brought their ships to land about Temenos and Choireai and Aigilea in the Eretrian territory; and having taken possession of these places, right away they began to disembark their horses and prepared to advance against the enemy. The Eretrians however did not intend to come forth against them and fight; but their endeavour was if possible to hold out by defending their walls, since the counsel prevailed not to leave the city. Then a violent assault was made upon the wall, and for six days there fell many on both sides; but on the seventh day Euphorbos the son of Alkimachos and Philagros the son of Kyneos, men of repute among the citizens, gave up the city to the Persians. These having entered the city plundered and set fire to the temples in retribution for the temples which were burned at Sardis,* and also reduced the people to slavery according to the commands of Dareios.

102. Having got Eretria into their power, they stayed a few days and then sailed for the land of Attica, pressing on hard and supposing that the Athenians would do the same as the Eretrians had done. And since Marathon was the most convenient place in Attica for horsemen to act and was also very near to Eretria, therefore Hippias the son of Peisistratos was guiding them thither. **103.** When the Athenians had information of this, they too went to Marathon to the rescue of their land; and they were led by ten generals, of whom the tenth was Miltiades, whose father Kimon son of Stesagoras had been compelled to go into exile from Athens because of Peisistratos the son of Hippocrates: and while he was in exile it was his fortune to win a victory at the Olympic games with a four-horse chariot, wherein, as it happened, he did the same thing as his half-brother Miltiades had done, who had the same mother as he. Then afterwards in the next succeeding Olympic games he gained a victory with the same mares and allowed Peisistratos to be proclaimed as victor; and having

---

*This theme of retribution refers to 5.101 but also recalls 1.1–5.

resigned to him the victory he returned to his own native land under an agreement for peace. Then after he had won with the same mares at another Olympic festival, it was his hap to be slain by the sons of Peisistratos, Peisistratos himself being no longer alive. These killed him near the City Hall, having set men to lie in wait for him by night; and the burial-place of Kimon is in the outskirts of the city, on the other side of the road which is called the way through Coilē, and just opposite him those mares are buried which won in three Olympic games. This same thing was done also by the mares belonging to Euagoras the Laconian, but besides these by none others. Now the elder of the sons of Kimon, Stesagoras, was at that time being brought up in the house of his father's brother Miltiades in the Chersonese, while the younger son was being brought up at Athens with Kimon himself, having been named Miltiades after Miltiades the settler of the Chersonese. **104.** This Miltiades then at the time of which we speak [490 B.C.] had come from the Chersonese and was a general of the Athenians, after escaping death in two forms; for not only did the Phenicians, who had pursued after him as far as Imbros, endeavour earnestly to take him and bring him up to the presence of the king, but also after this, when he had escaped from these and had come to his own native land and seemed to be in safety from that time forth, his opponents, who had laid wait for him there, brought him up before a court and prosecuted him for his despotism in the Chersonese. Having escaped these also, he had then been appointed a general of the Athenians, being elected by the people.

105. First of all, while they were still in the city, the generals sent off to Sparta a herald, namely Pheidippides, an Athenian all-day runner and a practised one. With this man, as Pheidippides himself said and as he made report to the Athenians, Pan chanced to meet by mount Parthenion, which is above Tegea; and calling aloud the name of Pheidippides, Pan bade him report to the Athenians and ask for what reason they had no care of him, though he was well disposed to the Athenians and had been serviceable to them on many occasions before that time, and would be so also yet again. Believing that this tale was true, the Athenians, when their affairs had been now prosperously settled, established under the Acropolis a temple of Pan; and in consequence of this message they propitiate him with sacrifice offered every year and with a torch-race. **106.** However at that time, the time namely when he said that Pan appeared to him, this Pheidippides sent by the generals reached Sparta on the day after he left the city of the Athenians; and when he had come to the magistrates he said: "Lacedemonians, the Athenians make request of you to come to their help and not to allow a city most anciently established among the Hellenes to fall into slavery to Barbarians; for even now Eretria has been enslaved and Hellas has become the weaker by a city of renown." He, as I say, reported to them that with which he had been charged, and it pleased them well to come to help the Athenians; but it was impossible for them to do so at once, since they did not desire to break their law; for it was the ninth day of the month, and on the ninth day they said they would not go forth, nor until the circle of the moon should be full.

107. These then were waiting for the full moon: and meanwhile Hippias the son of Peisistratos was guiding the Barbarians in to Marathon, after having seen on the night just past a vision in his sleep of this kind,—it seemed to Hippias that he lay with his own mother. He conjectured then from the dream that he should return to Athens and recover his rule, and then bring his life to an end in old age in his own land. From the dream, I say, he conjectured this; and after this, as he guided them in, first he disembarked the slaves from Eretria on the island belonging to the Styrians, called Aigleia; and then, as the ships came in to shore at Marathon, he moored them there, and after the Barbarians had come from their ships to land, he was engaged in disposing them in their places. While he was ordering these things, it came upon him to sneeze and cough more violently than was his wont. Then since he was advanced in years, most of his teeth were shaken thereby, and one of these teeth he cast forth by the violence of the cough: and the tooth having fallen from him upon the sand, he was very desirous to find it; since however the tooth was not to be found when he searched, he groaned aloud and said to those who were by him: "This land is not ours, nor shall we be able to make it subject to us; but so much part in it as belonged to me the tooth possesses."

108. Hippias then conjectured that his vision had been thus fulfilled: and meanwhile, after the Athenians had been drawn up in the sacred enclosure of Heracles, there joined them the Plataians coming to their help in a body: for the Plataians had given themselves to the Athenians, and the Athenians before this time undertook many toils on behalf of them; and this was the manner in which they gave themselves:*—Being oppressed by the Thebans, the Plataians at first desired to give themselves to Cleomenes the son of Anaxandrides and to the Lacedemonians, who chanced to come thither; but these did not accept them, and said to them as follows: "We dwell too far off, and such support as ours would be to you but cold comfort; for you might many times be reduced to slavery before any of us had information of it: but we counsel you rather to give yourselves to the Athenians, who are both neighbours and also not bad helpers." Thus the Lacedemonians counselled, not so much on account of their goodwill to the Plataians as because they desired that the Athenians should have trouble by being involved in conflict with the Bœotians.† The Lacedemonians, I say, thus counselled the men of Plataia; and they did not fail to follow their counsel, but when the Athenians were doing sacrifice to the twelve gods, they sat down as suppliants at the altar and so gave themselves. Then the Thebans having been informed of these things marched against the Plataians, and the Athenians came to their assistance: and as they were about to join battle, the Corinthians did not permit them to do so, but being by chance there, they reconciled their strife; and both parties having put the

---

*The Plataians gave themselves up to the Athenians in 519 B.C. (Thucydides 3.68).
†An example of Herodotus' unromantic appreciation of political realities; compare 4.167 and 6.133.

matter into their hands, they laid down boundaries for the land, with the condition that the Thebans should leave those of the Bœotians alone who did not desire to be reckoned with the other Bœotians. The Corinthians having given this decision departed; but as the Athenians were going back, the Bœotians attacked them, and having attacked them they were worsted in the fight. Upon that the Athenians passed beyond the boundaries which the Corinthians had set to be for the Plataians, and they made the river Asopos itself to be the boundary of the Thebans towards the land of Plataia and towards the district of Hysiai. The Plataians then had given themselves to the Athenians in the manner which has been said, and at this time they came to Marathon to bring them help.

109. Now the opinions of the generals of the Athenians were divided, and the one party urged that they should not fight a battle, seeing that they were few to fight with the army of the Medes, while the others, and among them Miltiades, advised that they should do so: and when they were divided and the worse opinion was likely to prevail, then, since he who had been chosen by lot* to be polemarch of the Athenians had a vote in addition to the ten (for in old times the Athenians gave the polemarch an equal vote with the generals) and at that time the polemarch was Callimachos of the deme of Aphidnai, to him came Miltiades and said as follows: "With you now it rests, Callimachos, either to bring Athens under slavery, or by making her free to leave behind you for all the time that men shall live a memorial such as not even Harmodios and Aristogeiton have left. For now the Athenians have come to a danger the greatest to which they have ever come since they were a people; and on the one hand, if they submit to the Medes, it is determined what they shall suffer, being delivered over to Hippias, while on the other hand, if this city shall gain the victory, it may become the first of the cities of Hellas. How this may happen and how it comes to you of all men to have the decision of these matters, I am now about to tell. Of us the generals, who are ten in number, the opinions are divided, the one party urging that we fight a battle and the others that we do not fight. Now if we do not, I expect that some great spirit of discord will fall upon the minds of the Athenians and so shake them that they shall go over to the Medes; but if we fight a battle before any unsoundness appear in any part of the Athenian people, then we are able to gain the victory in the fight, if the gods grant equal conditions. These things then all belong to you and depend upon you; for if you attach yourself to my opinion, you have both a fatherland which is free and a native city which shall be the first among the cities of Hellas; but if you choose the opinion of those who are earnest against fighting, you shall have the opposite of those good things of which I told you." **110.** Thus speaking Miltiades gained Callimachos to his side; and the opinion of the polemarch being added, it was thus determined to fight a battle. After this,

---

*It is unclear whether the "War Archon" in 490 B.C. was elected or selected by lot; Herodotus refers to the better-known method of his epoch, later by 70 years or so.

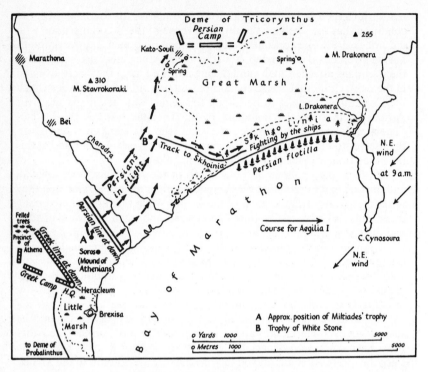

Map 3. THE BATTLE OF MARATHON.

those generals whose opinion was in favour of fighting, as the turn of each one of them to command for the day came round, gave over their command to Miltiades; and he, accepting it, would not however yet bring about a battle, until his own turn to command had come.

111. And when it came round to him,[*] then the Athenians were drawn up for battle in the order which here follows:—On the right wing the polemarch Callimachos was leader (for the custom of the Athenians then was this, that the polemarch should have the right wing); and he leading, next after him came the tribes in order as they were numbered one after another, and last were drawn up the Plataians occupying the left wing: for ever since this battle, when the Athenians offer sacrifices in the solemn assemblies which are made at the four-yearly festivals, the herald of the Athenians prays thus, "that good things may come to the Athenians and to the Plataians both." On this occasion however, when the Athenians were being drawn up at Marathon something of this kind was done:—their army being made equal in length of front to that of the Medes, came to be drawn up in

---

[*]The battle of Marathon was fought on or about September 12 in 490 B.C.

the middle with a depth of but few ranks, and here their army was weakest, while each wing was strengthened with numbers. **112.** And when they had been arranged in their places and the sacrifices proved favourable, then the Athenians were let go, and they set forth at a run to attack the Barbarians. Now the space between the armies was not less than eight stades [or 1,600 yards]: and the Persians seeing them advancing to the attack at a run, made preparations to receive them; and they charged the Athenians with madness which must be fatal, seeing that they were few and yet were pressing forwards at a run, having neither cavalry nor archers. Such was the thought of the Barbarians; but the Athenians when all in a body they had joined in combat with the Barbarians, fought in a memorable fashion: for they were the first of all the Hellenes about whom we know who went to attack the enemy at a run, and they were the first also who endured to face the Median garments and the men who wore them, whereas up to this time the very name of the Medes was to the Hellenes a terror to hear. **113.** Now while they fought in Marathon, much time passed by; and in the centre of the army, where the Persians themselves and the Sacans were drawn up, the Barbarians were winning,—here, I say, the Barbarians had broken the ranks of their opponents and were pursuing them inland, but on both wings the Athenians and the Plataians were winning the victory; and being victorious they left that part of the Barbarians which had been routed to fly without molestation, and bringing together the two wings they fought with those who had broken their centre, and the Athenians were victorious. So they followed after the Persians as they fled, slaughtering them, until they came to the sea; and then they called for fire and began to take hold of the ships. **114.** In this part of the work was slain the polemarch Callimachos after having proved himself a good man,* and also one of the generals, Stesilaos the son of Thrasylaos, was killed; and besides this Kynegeiros the son of Euphorion while taking hold there of the ornament at the stern of a ship had his hand cut off with an axe and fell; and many others also of the Athenians who were men of note were killed. **115.** Seven of the ships the Athenians got possession of in this manner, but with the rest the Barbarians pushed off from land, and after taking the captives from Eretria off the island where they had left them, they sailed round Sunion, purposing to arrive at the city before the Athenians. And an accusation became current among the Athenians to the effect that they formed this design by contrivance of the Alcmaionidai; for these, it was said, having concerted matters with the Persians, displayed to them a shield when they had now embarked in their ships.

116. These then, I say, were sailing round Sunion; and meanwhile the Athenians came to the rescue back to the city as speedily as they could, and they arrived there before the Barbarians came; and having arrived from the temple of Heracles at Marathon they encamped at another temple of Heracles, namely that which is in Kynosarges. The Barbarians however

---

*Fornara 49 and 50 preserve the polemarch's dedication and the Athenians' thank-offering.

came and lay with their ships in the sea which is off Phaleron, (for this was
then the seaport of the Athenians), they anchored their ships, I say, off this
place, and then proceeded to sail back to Asia.

117. In this fight at Marathon there were slain of the Barbarians about
six thousand four hundred men, and of the Athenians a hundred and
ninety and two. Such was the number which fell on both sides; and it happened also that a marvel occurred there:—an Athenian, Epizelos the son
of Cuphagoras, while fighting in the close combat and proving himself a
good man, was deprived of the sight of his eyes, neither having received a
blow in any part of his body nor having been hit with a missile, and for the
rest of his life from this time he continued to be blind: and I heard that he
used to tell a tale of this kind, namely that it seemed to him that a tall man
in full armour stood against him, whose beard overshadowed his whole
shield; and this apparition passed him by, but killed his comrade who
stood next to him. Thus, as I was informed, Epizelos told the tale.

118. Datis however, as he was going with his army to Asia, when he had
come to Myconos saw a vision in his sleep; and of what nature the vision
was it is not reported, but as soon as day dawned he caused a search to be
made of the ships, and finding in a Phenician ship an image of Apollo overlaid with gold, he inquired whence it had been carried off. Then having
been informed from what temple it came, he sailed in his own ship to Delos: and finding that the Delians had returned then to the island, he deposited the image in the temple and charged the men of Delos to convey it
back to Delion in the territory of the Thebans, which is situated by the sea-
coast just opposite Chalkis. Datis having given this charge sailed away: the
Delians however did not convey the statue back, but after an interval of
twenty years the Thebans themselves brought it to Delion by reason of an
oracle. **119.** Now as to those Eretrians who had been reduced to slavery,
Datis and Artaphrenes, when they reached Asia in their voyage, brought
them up to Susa; and king Dareios, though he had great anger against the
Eretrians before they were made captives, because the Eretians had done
wrong to him unprovoked, yet when he saw that they had been brought
up to him and were in his power, he did them no more evil, but established
them as settlers in the Kissian land upon one of his own domains, of which
the name is Ardericca: and this is distant two hundred and ten furlongs
from Susa and forty from the well which produces things of three different
kinds; for they draw from it asphalt, salt and oil, in the manner which here
follows:—the liquid is drawn with a swipe, to which there is fastened half a
skin instead of a bucket, and a man strikes this down into it and draws up,
and then pours it into a cistern, from which it runs through into another
vessel, taking three separate ways. The asphalt and the salt become solid at
once, and the oil which is called by the Persians *rhadinakē,* is black and
gives out a disagreeable smell. Here king Dareios established the Eretrians
as settlers; and even to my time they continued to occupy this land, keeping
still their former language. Thus it happened with regard to the Eretrians.

120. Of the Lacedemonians there came to Athens two thousand after the
full moon, making great haste to be in time, so that they arrived in Attica on

the third day after leaving Sparta: and though they had come too late for the battle, yet they desired to behold the Medes; and accordingly they went on to Marathon and looked at the bodies of the slain: then afterwards they departed home, commending the Athenians and the work which they had done.

121. Now it is a cause of wonder to me,* and I do not accept the report, that the Alcmaionidai could ever have displayed to the Persians a shield by a previous understanding, with the desire that the Athenians should be under the Barbarians and under Hippias; seeing that they are evidently proved to have been haters of despots as much or more than Callias the son of Phainippos and father of Hipponicos, while Callias for his part was the only man of all the Athenians who dared, when Peisistratos was driven out of Athens, to buy his goods offered for sale by the State, and in other ways also he contrived against him everything that was most hostile: [**122.**† Of this Callias it is fitting that every one should have remembrance for many reasons: first because of that which has been before said, namely that he was a man of excellence in freeing his country; and then also for that which he did at the Olympic games, wherein he gained a victory in the horse-race and was second in the chariot-race, and he had before this been a victor at the Pythian games, so that he was distinguished in the sight of all the Hellenes by the sums which he expended; and finally because he showed himself a man of such liberality towards his daughters, who were three in number; for when they came to be of ripe age for marriage, he gave them a most magnificent dowry and also indulged their inclinations; for whomsoever of all the Athenians each one of them desired to choose as a husband for herself, to that man he gave her.] **123,** and similarly the Alcmaionidai were haters of despots equally or more than he. Therefore this is a cause of wonder to me, and I do not admit the accusation that these displayed the shield; seeing that they were in exile from the despots during their whole time,‡ and that by their contrivance the sons of Peisistratos gave up their rule. Thus it follows that they were the men who set Athens free much more than Harmodios and Aristogeiton, as I judge: for these by slaying Hipparchos exasperated the rest of the family of Peisistratos, and did not at all cause the others to cease from their despotism; but the Alcmaionidai did evidently set Athens free, at least if these were in truth the men who persuaded the Pythian prophetess to signify to the Lacedemonians that they should set Athens free, as I have set forth before.§ **124.** It may be said however that

---

*A good example of historical argument in Herodotus, based on two antithetical attitudes toward an important family.

†Chapter 122 is probably the work of a later interpolator.

‡Fornara 23 provides disconfirming evidence, an archon list on which an Alcmaionid, Cleisthenes, appears as chief magistrate under the tyrants.

§A cross-reference to 5.90; see also Fornara 40, other ancient evidence of the Alcmaionid efforts.

they had some cause of complaint against the people of the Athenians, and therefore endeavoured to betray their native city. But on the contrary there were no men in greater repute than they, among the Athenians at least, nor who had been more highly honoured. Thus it is not reasonable to suppose that by them a shield should have been displayed for any such purpose. A shield was displayed however; that cannot be denied, for it was done: but as to who it was who displayed it, I am not able to say more than this.

125. Now the family of Alcmaionidai was distinguished in Athens in the earliest times also, and from the time of Alcmaion and of Megacles after him they became very greatly distinguished. For first Alcmaion the son of Megacles showed himself a helper of the Lydians from Sardis who came from Crœsus to the Oracle at Delphi, and assisted them with zeal; and Crœsus having heard from the Lydians who went to the Oracle that this man did him service, sent for him to Sardis; and when he came, he offered to give him a gift of as much gold as he could carry away at once upon his own person. With a view to this gift, its nature being such, Alcmaion made preparations and devised as follows:—he put on a large tunic leaving a deep fold in the tunic to hang down in front, and he drew on his feet the widest boots which he could find, and so went to the treasury to which they conducted him. Then he fell upon a heap of gold-dust, and first he packed in by the side of his legs so much of the gold as his boots would contain, and then he filled the whole fold of the tunic with the gold and sprinkled some of the gold-dust on the hair of his head and took some into his mouth, and having so done he came forth out of the treasury, with difficulty dragging along his boots and resembling anything in the world rather than a man; for his mouth was stuffed full, and every part of him was swelled out: and upon Crœsus came laughter when he saw him, and he not only gave him all that, but also presented him in addition with more not inferior in value to that. Thus this house became exceedingly wealthy, and thus the Alcmaion of whom I speak became a breeder of chariot-horses and won a victory at Olympia. **126.** Then in the next generation after this, Cleisthenes the despot of Sikyon exalted the family, so that it became of much more note among the Hellenes than it had been formerly. For Cleisthenes the son of Aristonymos, the son of Myron, the son of Andreas, had a daughter whose name was Agaristē; and as to her he formed the desire to find out the best man of all the Hellenes and to assign her to him in marriage. So when the Olympic games were being held and Cleisthenes was victor in them with a four-horse chariot, he caused a proclamation to be made, that whosoever of the Hellenes thought himself worthy to be the son-in-law of Cleisthenes should come on the sixtieth day, or before that if he would, to Sikyon; for Cleisthenes intended to conclude the marriage within a year, reckoning from the sixtieth day. Then all those of the Hellenes who had pride either in themselves or in their high descent,* came as wooers, and for them Cleisthenes had a running-course and a wrestling-place made and kept them expressly for their use.

---

*There follows an epic-style catalog of suitors.

127. From Italy came Smindyrides the son of Hippocrates of Sybaris, who of all men on earth reached the highest point of luxury (now Sybaris at this time was in the height of its prosperity), and Damasos of Siris, the son of that Amyris who was called the Wise; these came from Italy: from the Ionian gulf came Amphimnestos the son of Epistrophos of Epidamnos, this man from the Ionian gulf: from Aitolia came Males, the brother of that Titormos who surpassed all the Hellenes in strength and who fled from the presence of men to the furthest extremities of the Aitolian land: from Peloponnesus, Leokedes the son of Pheidon the despot of the Argives, that Pheidon who established for the Peloponnesians the measures which they use, and who went beyond all other Hellenes in wanton insolence, since he removed from their place the presidents of the games appointed by the Eleians and himself presided over the games at Olympia.* Amiantos the son of Lycurgos an Arcadian from Trapezus, and Laphanes an Azanian from the city of Paios, son of that Euphorion who (according to the story told in Arcadia) received the Dioscuroi as guests in his house and from thenceforth was wont to entertain all men who came, and Onomastos the son of Agaios of Elis; these, I say, came from Peloponnesus itself: from Athens came Megacles the son of that Alcmaion who went to Crœsus, and besides him Hippocleides the son of Tisander, one who surpassed the other Athenians in wealth and in comeliness of form: from Eretria, which at that time was flourishing, came Lysanias, he alone from Eubœa: from Thessalia came Diactorides of Crannon, one of the family of the Scopadai: and from the Molossians, Alcon.
128. So many in number did the wooers prove to be: and when these had come by the appointed day, Cleisthenes first inquired of their native countries and of the descent of each one, and then keeping them for a year he made trial continually both of their manly virtue and of their disposition, training and temper, associating both with each one separately and with the whole number together: and he made trial of them both by bringing out to bodily exercises those of them who were younger, and he especially tested them in the common feast or symposium: for during all the time that he kept them he did everything that could be done, and at the same time he entertained them magnificently. Now it chanced that those of the wooers pleased him most who had come from Athens, and of these Hippocleides the son of Tisander was rather preferred, both by reason of manly virtues and also because he was connected by descent with the family of Kypselos at Corinth.
129. Then when the appointed day came for the marriage banquet and for Cleisthenes himself to declare whom he selected from the whole number, Cleisthenes sacrificed a hundred oxen and feasted both the wooers themselves and all the people of Sikyon; and when the dinner was over, the wooers began to vie with one another both in music and in speeches for the entertainment of the company; and as the drinking went forward and Hippocleides was very much holding the attention of the others, he

---

*See Fornara 4 for other information on this important tyrant.

bade the flute-player play for him a dance-measure; and when the flute-player did so, he danced: and it so befell that he pleased himself in his dancing, but Cleisthenes looked on at the whole matter with suspicion. Then Hippocleides after a certain time bade one bring in a table; and when the table came in, first he danced upon it Laconian figures, and then also Attic, and thirdly he planted his head upon the table and gesticulated with his legs. Cleisthenes meanwhile, when he was dancing the first and the second time, though he abhorred the thought that Hippocleides should now become his son-in-law, because of his dancing and his shamelessness, yet restrained himself, not desiring to break out in anger against him; but when he saw that he thus gesticulated with his legs, he was no longer able to restrain himself, but said: "You have danced away your marriage, however good your dancing, son of Tisander!" and Hippocleides answered: "Hippocleides cares not!" **130,** and hence comes this saying. Then Cleisthenes caused silence to be made, and spoke to the company as follows: "Men who are wooers of my daughter, I commend you all, and if it were possible I would gratify you all, neither selecting one of you to be preferred, nor rejecting the remainder. Since of course it is not possible, as I am deliberating about one maiden only, to act so as to please all, therefore to those of you who are rejected from this marriage I give as a gift a talent of silver to each one for the worthy estimation you had of me, in that you desired to marry from my house, and for the time of absence from your homes; and to the son of Alcmaion, Megacles, I offer my daughter Agaristē in betrothal according to the customs of the Athenians." Thereupon Megacles said that he accepted the betrothal, and so the marriage was determined by Cleisthenes.

131. Thus it happened as regards the judgment of the wooers, and thus the Alcmaionidai got renown over all Hellas. And these having been married, there was born to them that Cleisthenes who established the tribes and the democracy for the Athenians, he being called after the Sikyonian Cleisthenes, his mother's father; this son, I say, was born to Megacles, and also Hippocrates: and of Hippocrates came another Megacles and another Agaristē, called after Agaristē the daughter of Cleisthenes, who having been married to Xanthippos the son of Ariphron and being with child, saw a vision in her sleep, and it seemed to her that she had brought forth a lion: then after a few days she bore to Xanthippos Pericles.*

132. After the defeat at Marathon, Miltiades, who even before was well reputed with the Athenians, came then to be in much higher estimation: and when he asked the Athenians for seventy ships and an army with supplies of money, not declaring to them against what land he was intending to make an expedition, but saying that he would enrich them greatly if they would go with him, for he would lead them to a land of such a kind that

---

*The sole reference in Herodotus to the dominant Athenian statesman of the mid-fifth century.

they would easily get from it gold in abundance,—thus saying he asked for the ships; and the Athenians, elated by these words, delivered them over to him.* **133.** Then Miltiades, when he had received the army, proceeded to sail to Paros with the pretence that the Parians had first attacked Athens by making expedition with triremes to Marathon in company with the Persian: this was the pretext which he put forward, but he had also a grudge against the Parians on account of Lysagoras the son of Tisias, who was by race of Paros, for having accused him to Hydarnes the Persian. So when Miltiades had arrived at the place to which he was sailing, he began to besiege the Parians with his army, first having shut them up within their wall; and sending in to them a herald he asked for a hundred talents, saying that if they refused to give them, his army should not return back until it had conquered them completely. The Parians however had no thought of giving any money to Miltiades, but contrived only how they might defend their city, devising various things besides and also this,—wherever at any time the wall proved to be open to attack, that point was raised when night came on to double its former height. **134.** So much of the story is reported by all the Hellenes, but as to what followed the Parians alone report, and they say that it happened thus:—When Miltiades was at a loss, it is said, there came a woman to speak with him, who had been taken prisoner, a Parian by race whose name was Timo, an under-priestess of the Earth goddesses Demeter & Persephone; she, they say, came into the presence of Miltiades and counselled him that if he considered it a matter of much moment to conquer Paros, he should do that which she should suggest to him; and upon that she told him her meaning. He accordingly passed through to the hill which is before the city and leapt over the fence of the temple of Demeter Giver of Laws, not being able to open the door; and then having leapt over he went towards the sanctuary with the design of doing something within, whether it were that he meant to lay hands on some of the things which should not be touched, or whatever else he intended to do; and when he had reached the door, immediately a shuddering fear came over him and he set off to go back the same way as he came, and as he leapt down from the wall of rough stones his thigh was dislocated, or, as others say, he struck his knee against the wall. **135.** Miltiades accordingly, being in a wretched case, set forth to sail homewards, neither bringing wealth to the Athenians nor having added to them the possession of Paros, but having besieged the city for six-and-twenty days and laid waste the island: and the Parians being informed that Timo the under-priestess of the goddesses had acted as a guide to Miltiades, desired to take vengeance upon her for this, and they sent messengers to Delphi to consult the god, so soon as they had leisure from the siege; and these messengers they sent to ask whether they should put to death the under-priestess of the goddesses, who had been a guide to their enemies for the capture of her native city and had revealed to Miltiades the mysteries

---

*The expedition to Paros took place in 489 B.C.

which might not be uttered to a male person. The Pythian prophetess however forbade them, saying that Timo was not the true author of these things, but since it was destined that Miltiades should end his life not well, she had appeared to guide him to his evil fate. **136.** Thus the Pythian prophetess replied to the Parians: and the Athenians, when Miltiades had returned back from Paros, began to talk of him, and among the rest especially Xanthippos the son of Ariphron, who brought Miltiades up before the people claiming the penalty of death and prosecuted him for his deception of the Athenians: and Miltiades did not himself make his own defence, although he was present, for he was unable to do so because his thigh was mortifying; but he lay in public view upon a bed, while his friends made a defence for him, making mention much both of the battle which had been fought at Marathon and of the conquest of Lemnos, namely how he had conquered Lemnos and taken vengeance on the Pelasgians, and had delivered it over to the Athenians: and the people came over to his part as regards the acquittal from the penalty of death, but they imposed a fine of fifty talents for the wrong committed: and after this Miltiades died, his thigh having gangrened and mortified, and the fifty talents were paid by his son Kimon.

137. Now Miltiades son of Kimon had thus taken possession of Lemnos:—After the Pelasgians had been cast out of Attica by the Athenians, whether justly or unjustly,—for about this I cannot tell except the things reported, which are these:—Hecataios on the one hand, the son of Hegesander, said in his history that it was done unjustly; for he said that when the Athenians saw the land which extends below Hymettos, which they had themselves given them to dwell in, as payment for the wall built round the Acropolis in former times, when the Athenians, I say, saw that this land was made good by cultivation, which before was bad and worthless, they were seized with jealousy and with longing to possess the land, and so drove them out, not alleging any other pretext: but according to the report of the Athenians themselves they drove them out justly; for the Pelasgians being settled under Hymettos made this a starting-point and committed wrong against them as follows:—the daughters and sons of the Athenians were wont ever to go for water to the spring of Enneacrunos; for at that time neither they nor the other Hellenes as yet had household servants; and when these girls came, the Pelasgians in wanton contempt of the Athenians would assault them. And it was not enough for them even to do this, but at last they were found in the act of plotting an attack upon the city: and the narrators say that they herein proved themselves better men than the Pelasgians, inasmuch as when they might have slain the Pelasgians, who had been caught plotting against them, they did not choose to do so, but ordered them merely to depart out of the land: and thus having departed out of the land, the Pelasgians took possession of several other places and especially of Lemnos. The former story is that which was reported by Hecataios, while the latter is that which is told by the Athenians. **138.** These Pelasgians then, dwelling after that in Lemnos, desired to take vengeance on the Athenians; and having full knowledge also of the festivals of the Athenians, they got fifty-oared galleys and laid wait for the women of the Athenians when they were keeping festival to Artemis in Brauron; and having carried off a number of them from thence, they departed and sailed away home, and taking the women to Lemnos they kept them as concubines. Now when these women had children, they made it their practise to teach their sons both the Attic tongue and the manners of the Athenians. And these were not willing to associate with the sons of the Pelasgian women, and moreover if any of them were struck by any one of those, they all in a body came to the rescue and helped one another. Moreover the boys claimed to have authority over the other boys and got the better of them easily. Perceiving these things the Pelasgians considered the matter; and when they took counsel together, a fear came over them and they thought, if the boys were indeed resolved now to help one another against the sons of the legitimate wives, and were endeavouring already from the first to have authority over them, what would they do when they were grown up to be men? Then they determined to put to death the sons of the Athenian women, and this they actually did; and in addition to them they slew their mothers also. From this deed and from that which was done before this, which the women did when they killed Thoas and the rest, who were their own husbands,* it has become a custom in Hellas that all deeds of great cruelty should be called "Lemnian deeds." **139.** After the Pelasgians had killed their own sons and wives, the earth did not bear fruit for them, nor did their women or their cattle bring forth young as they did before; and being hard pressed by famine and by childlessness, they sent to Delphi to ask for a release from the evils which were upon them; and the Pythian prophetess bade them pay such penalty to the Athenians as the Athenians themselves should appoint. The Pelasgians came accordingly to Athens and professed that they were willing to pay the penalty for all the wrong which they had done: and the Athenians laid a couch in the fairest possible manner in the City Hall, and having set by it a table covered with all good things, they bade the Pelasgians deliver up to them their land in that condition. Then the Pelasgians answered and said: "When with a North Wind in one single day a ship shall accomplish the voyage from your land to ours, then we will deliver it up," feeling assured that it was impossible for this to happen, since Attica lies far away to the South of Lemnos. **140.** Such were the events which happened then: and very many years later, after the Chersonese which is by the Hellespont had come to be under the Athenians, Miltiades the son of Kimon, when the Etesian Winds blew steadily, accomplished the voyage in a ship from Elaius in the Chersonese to Lemnos, and proclaimed to the Pelasgians that they should depart out of the island, reminding them of the oracle, which the Pelasgians had never expected would be accomplished for them. The

*A reference to the myth of Lemnian women who assassinated their spouses and other men. Hypsipyle uniquely saved one, her father Thoas.

men of Hephaistia accordingly obeyed; but those of Myrina, not admitting that the Chersonese was Attica, suffered a siege, until at last these also submitted. Thus it was that the Athenians and Miltiades took possession of Lemnos.

BOOK VII

XERXES' EXPEDITION INTO GREECE, BATTLE OF THERMOPYLAE

1. Now WHEN THE REPORT came to Dareios the son of Hystaspes of the battle which was fought at Marathon, the king, who even before this had been greatly exasperated with the Athenians on account of the attack made upon Sardis, then far more displayed indignation, and was far more desirous of making a march against Hellas. Accordingly at once he sent messengers to the various cities and ordered that they should get ready a force, appointing to each people to supply much more, and not only ships of war, but also horses and provisions and transport vessels; and when these commands were carried round, all Asia was moved for three years, for all the best men were being enlisted for the expedition against Hellas, and were making preparations. In the fourth year however the Egyptians,* who had been reduced to subjection by Cambyses, revolted from the Persians; and then he was even more desirous of marching against both these nations.

2. While Dareios was thus preparing to set out against Egypt and against Athens, there arose a great strife among his sons about the supreme power; and they said that he must not make his expeditions until he had designated one of them to be king, according to the custom of the Persians. For to Dareios already before he became king three sons had been born of his former wife the daughter of Gobryas, and after he became king four other sons of Atossa the daughter of Cyrus: of the first the eldest was Artobazanes, and of those who had been born later, Xerxes. These being not of the same mother were at strife with one another, Artobazanes contending that he was the eldest of all the sons, and that it was a custom maintained by all men that the eldest should have the rule, and Xerxes arguing that he was the son of Atossa the daughter of Cyrus, and that Cyrus was he who had won for the Persians their freedom. **3.** Now while Dareios did not as yet declare his judgment, it chanced that Demaratos also, the son of Ariston, had come up to Susa at this very same time, having been deprived of the kingdom in Sparta and having laid upon himself a sentence of exile from Lacedemon. This man, hearing of the difference between the sons of Dareios, came (as it is reported of him) and counselled Xerxes to say in addition to those things which he was wont to say, that he had been born to Dareios at the time when he was already reigning as king and was holding the supreme power over the Persians, while Artobazanes had been born while Dareios was still in a private

---

*The revolt of Egypt took place in 486 B.C.

345

station: it was not fitting therefore nor just that another should have the honour before him; for even in Sparta, suggested Demaratos, this was the custom,* that is to say, if some of the sons had been born first, before their father began to reign, and another came after, born later while he was reigning, the succession of the kingdom belonged to him who had been born later. Xerxes accordingly made use of the suggestion of Demaratos; and Dareios perceiving that he spoke that which was just, designated him to be king. It is my opinion however that even without this suggestion Xerxes would have become king, for Atossa was all-powerful. **4.** Then having designated Xerxes to the Persians as their king, Dareios wished to go on his expeditions. However in the next year after this and after the revolt of Egypt, while he was making his preparations, it came to pass that Dareios himself died, having been king in all six-and-thirty years;† and thus he did not succeed in taking vengeance either upon the revolted Egyptians or upon the Athenians.

5. Dareios being dead the kingdom passed to his son Xerxes. Now Xerxes at the first was by no means anxious to make a march against Hellas, but against Egypt he continued to gather a force. Mardonios however, the son of Gobryas, who was a cousin of Xerxes, being sister's son to Dareios, was ever at his side, and having power with him more than any other of the Persians, he kept saying: "Master, it is not fitting that the Athenians, after having done to the Persians very great evil, should not pay the penalty for that which they have done. You should at this present time do what you have in hand; and when you have tamed the land of Egypt, which has broken out insolently against us, then march an army against Athens, that a good report may be made of you by men, and that in future every one may beware of making expeditions against your land." Thus far his speech had to do with vengeance, and to this he would add, saying that Europe was a very fair land and bore all kinds of trees that are cultivated for fruit, and was of excellent fertility, and such that the king alone of all mortals was worthy to possess it. **6.** These things he was wont to say, since he was one who had a desire for perilous enterprise and wished to be himself the governor of Hellas under the king. So in time he prevailed upon Xerxes and persuaded him to do this; for other things also assisted him and proved helpful to him in persuading Xerxes. In the first place there had come from Thessaly messengers sent by the Aleuadai, who were inviting the king to come against Hellas and were showing great zeal in his cause, (now these Aleuadai were kings of Thessaly): and then secondly those of the sons of Peisistratos who had come up to Susa were inviting him also, holding to the same arguments as the Aleuadai; and moreover they offered him yet more inducement in addition to these; for there was one Onomacritos an Athenian, who both uttered oracles and also had collected and arranged the oracles of Musaios; and with this man they had come up, after they had first

---

*No evidence for this custom exists, and Herodotus exaggerates this example of a wise adviser's influence in Persian affairs.
†Dareios died in 486 B.C., after a reign of 35 years.

reconciled the enmity between them. For Onomacritos had been driven forth from Athens by Hipparchos the son of Peisistratos, having been caught by Lasos of Hermiōn interpolating in the works of Musaios an oracle to the effect that the islands which lie off Lemnos should disappear under the sea. For this reason Hipparchos drove him forth, having before this time been very much wont to consult him. Now however he had gone up with them; and when he had come into the presence of the king, the sons of Peisistratos spoke of him in magnificent terms, and he repeated some of the oracles; and if there was in them anything which imported disaster to the Barbarians, of this he said nothing; but choosing out of them the most fortunate things he told how it was destined that the Hellespont should be yoked with a bridge by a Persian, and he set forth the manner of the march. He then thus urged Xerxes with oracles, while the sons of Peisistratos and the Aleuadai pressed him with their advice.

7. So when Xerxes had been persuaded to make an expedition against Hellas, then in the next year after the death of Dareios he made a march first against those who had revolted. Having subdued these and having reduced all Egypt to slavery much greater than it had suffered in the reign of Dareios,[*] he entrusted the government of it to Achaimenes his own brother, a son of Dareios. Now this Achaimenes being governor of Egypt was slain afterwards by Inarōs the son of Psammetichos, a Libyan. **8.** Xerxes then after the conquest of Egypt, being about to take in hand the expedition against Athens, summoned a chosen assembly of the best men among the Persians, that he might both learn their opinions and himself in the presence of all declare that which he intended to do; and when they were assembled, Xerxes spoke to them as follows: (*a*) "Persians, I shall not be the first to establish this custom in your nation, but having received it from others I shall follow it: for as I am informed by those who are older than myself, we never yet have kept quiet since we received this supremacy in succession to the Medes, when Cyrus overthrew Astyages; but God thus leads us, and for ourselves it tends to good that we are busied about many things.[†] Now about the nations which Cyrus and Cambyses and my father Dareios subdued and added to their possessions there is no need for me to speak, since you know well: and as for me, from the day when I received by inheritance this throne upon which I sit I carefully considered always how in this honourable place I might not fall short of those who have been before me, nor add less power to the dominion of the Persians: and thus carefully considering I find a way by which not only glory may be won by us, together with a land not less in extent nor worse than that which we now possess, (and indeed more varied in its productions), but also vengeance and retribution may be brought about. Wherefore I have assembled you together now, in order that I may communicate to you that which I have it in my mind to do. (*b*) I design to yoke the Hellespont with a bridge, and to

---

[*]Xerxes returned Egypt to subjection in 484 B.C.
[†]Herodotus has Xerxes claim a Persian "manifest destiny."

march an army through Europe against Hellas, in order that I may take
vengeance on the Athenians for all the things which they have done both
to the Persians and to my father. You saw how my father Dareios also was
purposing to make an expedition against these men; but he has ended his
life and did not succeed in taking vengeance upon them. I however, on
behalf of him and also of the other Persians, will not cease until I have
conquered Athens and burnt it with fire; seeing that they did wrong unprovoked to me and to my father. First they went to Sardis, having come
with Aristagoras the Milesian our slave, and they set fire to the sacred
groves and the temples; and then secondly, what things they did to us
when we disembarked in their land, at the time when Datis and Artaphrenes were commanders of our army, you all know well, as I think.
(c) For these reasons I have resolved to make an expedition against them,
and reckoning I find in the matter so many good things as you shall
hear:—if we shall subdue these and the neighbours of these, who dwell in
the land of Pelops the Phrygian, we shall cause the Persian land to have
the same boundaries as the heaven of Zeus; since in truth upon no land
will the sun look down which borders upon ours, but I with your help shall
make all the lands into one land, having passed through the whole extent
of Europe. For I am informed that there is no city of men nor any race of
human beings remaining, which will be able to come to a contest with us,
when those whom I just now mentioned have been removed out of the
way. Thus both those who have committed wrong against us will have the
yoke of slavery, and also those who have not committed wrong. (d) And
you will please me best if you do this:—whensoever I shall signify to you
the time at which you ought to come, you must appear every one of you
with zeal for the service; and whosoever shall come with a force best
equipped, to him I will give gifts such as are accounted in our land to be
the most honourable. Thus must these things be done: but that I may not
seem to you to be following my own counsel alone, I propose the matter
for discussion, bidding any one of you who desires it, declare his opinion."

Having thus spoken he ceased; **9,** and after him Mardonios said: "Master, you do surpass not only all the Persians who were before you, but also
those who shall come after, since you did not only attain in your words to
that which is best and truest as regards other matters, but also you will not
permit the Ionians who dwell in Europe to make a mock of us, having no
just right to do so: for a strange thing it would be if, when we have subdued
and keep as our servants Sacans, Indians, Ethiopians, Assyrians, and other
nations many in number and great, who have done no wrong to the Persians, because we desired to add to our dominions, we should not take
vengeance on the Hellenes who committed wrong against us unprovoked.
(a) Of what should we be afraid?—what gathering of numbers, or what resources of money? for their manner of fight we know, and as for their resources, we know that they are feeble; and we have moreover subdued
already their sons, those I mean who are settled in our land and are called
Ionians, Aiolians and Dorians. Moreover I myself formerly made trial of
marching against these men, being commanded thereto by your father; and

although I marched as far as Macedonia, and fell but little short of coming to Athens itself, no man came to oppose me in fight. (*b*) And yet it is true that the Hellenes make wars, but (as I am informed) very much without wise consideration, by reason of obstinacy and want of skill: for when they have proclaimed war upon one another, they find out first the fairest and smoothest place, and to this they come down and fight; so that even the victors depart from the fight with great loss, and as to the vanquished, of them I make no mention at all, for they are utterly destroyed.* They ought however, being men who speak the same language, to make use of heralds and messengers and so to take up their differences and settle them in any way rather than by battles; but if they must absolutely war with one another, they ought to find out each of them that place in which they themselves are hardest to overcome, and here to make their trial. Therefore the Hellenes, since they use no good way, when I had marched as far as the land of Macedonia, did not come to the resolution of fighting with me. (*c*) Who then is likely to set himself against you, O king, offering war, when you are leading both all the multitudes of Asia and the whole number of the ships? I for my part am of opinion that the power of the Hellenes has not attained to such a pitch of boldness: but if after all I should prove to be deceived in my judgment, and they stirred up by inconsiderate folly should come to battle with us, they would learn that we are the best of all men in the matters of war. However that may be, let not anything be left untried; for nothing comes of itself, but from trial all things come to men."

10. Mardonios having thus dressed up the resolution expressed by Xerxes had ceased speaking: and when the other Persians were silent and did not venture to declare an opinion contrary to that which had been proposed, then Artabanos the son of Hystaspes, being father's brother to Xerxes and having reliance upon that, spoke as follows: (*a*) "O king, if opinions opposed to one another be not spoken, it is not possible to select the better in making the choice, but one must accept that which has been spoken; if however opposite opinions be uttered, this is possible; just as we do not distinguish the gold which is free from alloy when it is alone by itself, but when we rub it on the touchstone in comparison with other gold, then we distinguish that which is the better. Now I gave advice to your father Dareios also, who was my brother, not to march against the Scythians, men who occupied no abiding city in any part of the earth. He however, expecting that he would subdue the Scythians who were nomads, did not listen to me; but he made a march and came back from it with the loss of many good men of his army. But you, O king, are intending to march against men who are much better than the Scythians, men who are reported to be excellent both by sea and on land: and the thing which is to be feared in this matter it is right that I should declare to you. (*b*) You say that you will yoke the

---

*A humorous if uncomprehending critique of Hellenic modes of warfare and political disunity. A *hoplite* was a heavily armed warrior who fought alongside others in a compact formation called a *phalanx*.

Hellespont with a bridge and march an army through Europe to Hellas. Now supposing we are worsted either by land or by sea, or even both, for the men are reported to be valiant in fight, (and we may judge for ourselves that it is so, since the Athenians by themselves destroyed that great army which came with Datis and Artaphrenes to the Attic land),—suppose however that they do not succeed in both, yet if they shall attack with their ships and conquer in a sea-fight, and then sail to the Hellespont and break up the bridge, this of itself, O king, will prove to be a grave peril. (c) Not however by any native wisdom of my own do I conjecture that this might happen: I am conjecturing only such a misfortune as all but came upon us at the former time, when your father, having yoked the Bosphorus of Thracia and made a bridge over the river Ister, had crossed over to go against the Scythians. At that time the Scythians used every means of entreaty to persuade the Ionians to break up the passage, to whom it had been entrusted to guard the bridges of the Ister. At that time, if Histiaios the despot of Miletos had followed the opinion of the other despots and had not made opposition to them, the power of the Persians would have been brought to an end. Yet it is a fearful thing even to hear it reported that the whole power of the king had come to depend upon one human creature. (d) Do not therefore propose to go into any such danger when there is no need, but do as I say:—at the present time dissolve this assembly; and afterwards at whatever time it shall seem good to you, when you have considered prudently with yourself, proclaim that which seems to you best: for good counsel I hold to be a very great gain; since even if anything shall prove adverse, the counsel which has been taken is no less good, though it has been defeated by fortune; while he who took counsel badly at first, if good fortune should go with him has lighted on a prize by chance, but none the less for that his counsel was bad. (e) You see how God strikes with thunderbolts the creatures which stand above the rest and suffers them not to make a proud show; while those which are small do not provoke him to jealousy: you see also how he hurls his darts ever at those buildings which are the highest and those trees likewise; for God is wont to cut short all those things which stand out above the rest. Thus also a numerous army is destroyed by one of few men in some such manner as this, namely when God having become jealous of them casts upon them panic or thundering from heaven, then they are destroyed utterly and not as their worth deserves; for God suffers not any other to have high thoughts save only himself. (f) Moreover the hastening of any matter breeds disasters, whence great losses are wont to be produced; but in waiting there are many good things contained, as to which, if they do not appear to be good at first, yet one will find them to be so in course of time. (g) To you, O king, I give this counsel: but you son of Gobryas, Mardonios, cease speaking foolish words about the Hellenes, since they in no way deserve to be spoken of with slight; for by uttering slander against the Hellenes you are stirring up the king himself to make an expedition, and it is to this very end that I think you are straining all your endeavour. Let not this be so; for slander is a most grievous thing: in it the wrongdoers are two, and the person who suffers wrong is one. The slanderer does a wrong in that he speaks against one who is not present, the other in that he is persuaded of the thing before he gets certain knowledge of it, and he who is not present when the words are spoken suffers wrong in the matter thus,—both because he has been slandered by the one and because he has been believed to be bad by the other. (*h*) However, if it be absolutely needful to make an expedition against these men, come, let the king himself remain behind in the abodes of the Persians, and let us both set to the wager our sons; and then lead an army by yourself, choosing for yourself the men whom you desire, and taking an army as large as you think good: and if matters turn out for the king as you sayest, let my sons be slain and let me also be slain in addition to them; but if in the way which I predict, let your sons suffer this, and with them yourself also, if you shall return back. But if you are not willing to undergo this proof, but will by all means lead an army against Hellas, then I say that those who are left behind in this land will hear that Mardonios, after having done a great mischief to the Persians, is torn by dogs and birds, either in the land of the Athenians, or else perchance you will be in the land of the Lacedemonians (unless indeed this should come to pass even before that upon the way), and that you have at length been made aware against what kind of men you are persuading the king to march."

11. Artabanos thus spoke; and Xerxes enraged by it made answer as follows: "Artabanos, you are my father's brother, and this shall save you from receiving any recompense such as your foolish words deserve. Yet I attach to you this dishonour, seeing that you are a coward and spiritless, namely that you do not march with me against Hellas, but remain here together with the women; and I, even without your help, will accomplish all the things which I said: for I would I might not be descended from Dareios, the son of Hystaspes, the son of Arsames, the son of Ariaramnes, the son of Teïspes, or from Cyrus, the son of Cambyses, the son of Teïspes, the son of Achaimenes, if I take not vengeance on the Athenians; since I know well that if we shall keep quiet, yet they will not do so, but will even march against our land, if we may judge by the deeds which have been done by them to begin with, since they both set fire to Sardis and marched upon Asia. It is not possible therefore that either side should retire from the quarrel, but the question before us is whether we shall do or whether we shall suffer; whether all these regions shall come to be under the Hellenes or all those under the Persians: for in our hostility there is no middle course. It follows then now that it is well for us, having suffered wrong first, to take revenge, that I may find out also what is this terrible thing which I shall suffer if I lead an army against these men,—men whom Pelops the Phrygian, who was the slave of my forefathers, so subdued that even to the present day both the men themselves and their land are called after the name of him who subdued them."*

---

*Reference to the peninsula of the Peloponnese, home of the Corinthians, Argives, Spartans, etc.

12. Afterwards when darkness came on, the opinion of Artabanos tormented Xerxes continually; and making night his counsellor he found that it was by no means to his advantage to make the march against Hellas. So when he had thus made a new resolve, he fell asleep, and in the night he saw, as is reported by the Persians, a vision as follows:—Xerxes thought that a man tall and comely of shape came and stood by him and said: "Are you indeed changing your counsel, O Persian, of leading an expedition against Hellas, now that you have made proclamation that the Persians shall collect an army? You do not well in changing your counsel, nor will he who is here present with you excuse you for it; but as you did take counsel in the day to do, by that way go." **13.** After he had said this, Xerxes thought that he who had spoken flew away; and when day had dawned he made no account of this dream, but gathered together the Persians whom he had assembled also the former time and said to them these words: "Persians, pardon me that I make quick changes in my counsel; for in judgment not yet am I come to my prime, and they who advise me to do the things which I said, do not for any long time leave me to myself. However, although at first when I heard the opinion of Artabanos my youthful impulses burst out, so that I cast forth unseemly words against a man older than myself; yet now I acknowledge that he is right, and I shall follow his opinion. Consider then I have changed my resolve to make a march against Hellas, and remain still."

14. The Persians accordingly when they heard this were rejoiced and made obeisance: but when night had come on, the same dream again came and stood by Xerxes as he lay asleep and said: "Son of Dareios, it is manifest then that you have resigned this expedition before the assembly of the Persians, and that you have made no account of my words, as if you had heard them from no one at all. Now therefore be well assured of this:—if you do not make your march immediately, there shall thence spring up for you this result, namely that, as you did in short time become great and mighty, so also you shall speedily be again brought low." **15.** Xerxes then, being very greatly disturbed by fear of the vision, started up from his bed and sent a messenger to summon Artabanos; to whom when he came Xerxes spoke thus: "Artabanos, at the first I was not discreet, when I spoke to you foolish words on account of your good counsel; but after no long time I changed my mind and perceived that I ought to do these things which you did suggest to me. I am not able however to do them, although I desire it; for indeed, now that I have turned about and changed my mind, a dream appears haunting me and by no means approving that I should do so; and just now it has left me even with a threat. If therefore it is God who sends it to me, and it is his absolute will and pleasure that an army should go against Hellas, this same dream will fly to you also, laying upon you a charge such as it has laid upon me; and it occurs to my mind that this might happen thus, namely if you should take all my attire and put it on, and then seat yourself on my throne, and after that lie down to sleep in my bed."

16. Xerxes spoke to him thus; and Artabanos was not willing to obey the command at first, since he did not think himself worthy to sit upon the royal throne; but at last being urged further he did that which was commanded, first having spoken these words: (*a*) "It is equally good in my judgment, O king, whether a man has wisdom himself or is willing to follow the counsel of him who speaks well: and you, who have attained to both these good things, are caused to err by the communications of evil men; just as they say that the Sea, which is of all things the most useful to men, is by blasts of winds falling upon it prevented from doing according to its own nature. I however, when I was denigrated by you, was not so much stung with pain for this, as because, when two opinions were laid before the Persians, the one tending to increase wanton insolence and the other tending to check it and saying that it was a bad thing to teach the soul to endeavour always to have something more than the present possession,—because, I say, when such opinions as these were laid before us, you did choose that one which was the more dangerous both for yourself and for the Persians. (*b*) And now that you have turned to the better counsel, you say that when you are disposed to let go the expedition against the Hellenes, a dream haunts you sent by some god, which forbids you to abandon your enterprise. Nay, but here too you err, my son, since this is not divine, for the dreams of sleep which come roaming about to men, are of such nature as I shall inform you, being by many years older than you. The visions of dreams are wont to hover before us in such form for the most part as the things of which we are thinking during the day; and we in the days preceding were very much occupied with this campaign. (*c*) If however after all this is not such a thing as I interpret it to be, but is something which is concerned with God, you have summed the matter up in that which you have said: let it appear, as you sayest, to me also, as to you, and give commands. But supposing that it desires to appear to me at all, it is not bound to appear to me any the more if I have your garments on me than if I have my own, nor any more if I take my rest in your bed than if I am in my own; for assuredly this thing, whatever it may be, which appears to you in your sleep, is not so foolish as to suppose, when it sees me, that it is you, judging so because the garments are yours. That however which we must find out now is this, namely if it will hold me in no account, and not think fit to appear to me, whether I have my own garments or whether I have yours, but continue still to haunt you; for if it shall indeed haunt you perpetually, I shall myself also be disposed to say that it is of the Deity. But if you have resolved that it shall be so, and it is not possible to turn aside your resolution, but I must go to sleep in your bed, then let it appear to me also, when I perform these things: but until then I shall hold to the opinion which I now have."

17. Artabanos, expecting that he would prove that Xerxes was speaking folly, did that which was commanded him; and having put on the garments of Xerxes and seated himself in the royal throne, he afterwards went to bed: and when he had fallen asleep, the same dream came to him which used to come to Xerxes, and standing over Artabanos spoke these words: "Are you indeed he who endeavours to dissuade Xerxes from making a march against Hellas, pretending to have a care of him? However, neither in the future nor now at the present shall you escape unpunished for trying to turn away that which is destined to come to pass: and as for Xerxes, that which he must suffer if he disobeys, has been shown already to the man himself." **18.** Thus it seemed to Artabanos that the dream threatened him, and at the same time was just about to burn out his eyes with hot irons; and with a loud cry he started up from his bed, and sitting down beside Xerxes he related to him throughout the vision of the dream, and then said to him as follows: "I, O king, as one who has seen before now many great things brought to their fall by things less, urged you not to yield in all things to the inclination of your youth, since I knew that it was evil to have desire after many things; remembering on the one hand the march of Cyrus against the Massagetai, what fortune it had, and also that of Cambyses against the Ethiopians; and being myself one who took part with Dareios in the campaign against the Scythians. Knowing these things I had the opinion that you were to be envied of all men, so long as you should keep still. Since however there comes a divine impulse, and, as it seems, a destruction sent by heaven is taking hold upon the Hellenes, I for my part am both changed in myself and also I reverse my opinions; and signify to the Persians the message which is sent to you from God, bidding them follow the commands which were given by you at first with regard to the preparation to be made; and endeavour that on your side nothing may be wanting, since God delivers the matter into your hands." Both were excited to confidence by the vision, and so soon as it became day, Xerxes communicated the matter to the Persians, and Artabanos, who before was the only man who came forward to dissuade him, now came forward to urge on the design.

19. Xerxes being thus desirous to make the expedition, there came to him after this a third vision in his sleep, which the Magians, when they heard it, explained to have reference to the dominion of the whole Earth and to mean that all men should be subject to him; and the vision was this:— Xerxes thought that he had been crowned with a wreath of an olive-branch and that the shoots growing from the olive-tree covered the whole Earth; and after that, the wreath, placed as it was about his head, disappeared. When the Magians had thus interpreted the vision, immediately every man of the Persians who had been assembled together departed to his own province and was zealous by all means to perform the commands, desiring each one to receive for himself the gifts which had been proposed: and thus Xerxes was gathering his army together, searching every region of the continent. **20.** During four full years from the conquest of Egypt he was preparing the army and the things that were of service for the army, and in the course of the fifth year he began his campaign with a host of great multitude. For of all the armies of which we have knowledge this proved to be by far the greatest; so that neither that led by Dareios against the Scythians appears anything as compared with it, nor the Scythian host, when the Scythians pursuing the Kimmerians made invasion of the Median land and subdued and occupied nearly all the upper parts of Asia, for which invasion afterwards Dareios attempted to take vengeance, nor that led by the sons of Atreus to Ilion, to judge by that which is reported of their expedition, nor that of the Mysians and Teucrians, before the Trojan war, who passed over into Europe by the Bosphorus and not only subdued all the Thracians, but came down also as far as the Aegean Sea and marched southwards to the river Peneios. **21.** All these expeditions put together, with others, if there be any, added to them, are not equal to this one alone. For what nation did Xerxes not lead out of Asia against Hellas? and what water was not exhausted, being drunk by his host, except only the great rivers? For some supplied ships, and others were appointed to serve in the land-army; to some it was appointed to furnish cavalry, and to others vessels to carry horses, while they served in the expedition themselves also; others were ordered to furnish ships of war for the bridges, and others again ships with provisions.

22. Then in the first place, since the former fleet had suffered disaster in sailing round Athōs, preparations had been going on for about three years past with regard to Athōs: for triremes lay at anchor at Elaius in the Chersonese, and with this for their starting-point men of all nations belonging to the army worked at digging, compelled by the lash; and the men worked regularly in succession: moreover those who dwelt round about Athōs worked also at the digging: and Bubares the son of Megabazos and Artachaies the son of Artaios, Persians both, were set over the work. Now Athōs is a mountain great and famous, running down to the sea and inhabited by men: and where the mountain ends on the side of the mainland the place is like a peninsula with an isthmus about one and one-third miles across. Here it is plain or hills of no great size, extending from the sea of the Acanthians to that which lies off Toronē; and on this isthmus, where Athōs ends, is situated a Hellenic city called Sanē: moreover there are others before Sanē and within the peninsula of Athōs, all which at this time the Persian had resolved to make into cities of an island and no longer of the mainland; these are, Dion, Olophyxos, Acrothōon, Thyssos, Cleonai.

23. These are the cities which occupy Athōs: and they dug as follows, the country being divided among the Barbarians by nations for the work:—at the city of Sanē they drew a straight line across the isthmus, and when the channel became deep, those who stood lowest dug, while others delivered the earth as it was dug out to other men who stood above, as upon steps, and they again to others when it was received, until they came to those that were highest; and these bore it away and cast it forth. Now the others except the Phenicians had double toil by the breaking down of the steep edges of their excavation; for since they endeavoured to make the opening at the top and that at the bottom both of the same measure, some such thing was likely to result, as they worked: but the Phenicians, who are apt to show ability in their works generally, did so in this work also; for when they had had assigned to them by lot their share, they proceeded to dig, making the opening of the excavation at the top twice as wide as the channel itself was to be; and as the work went forward, they kept contracting the width; so that, when they came to the bottom, their

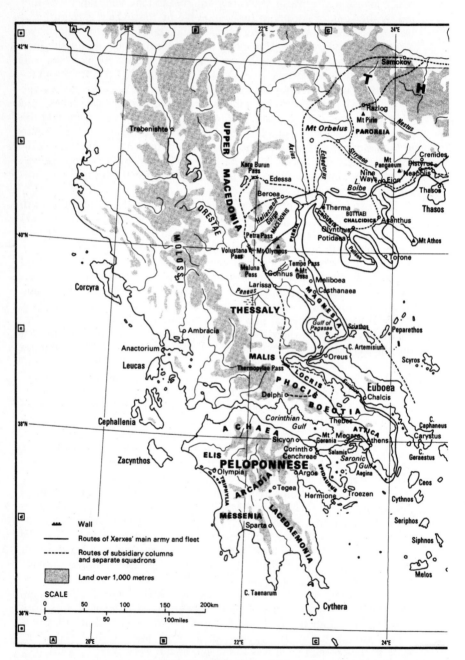

MAP 4. GREECE AND THE AEGEAN SEA.

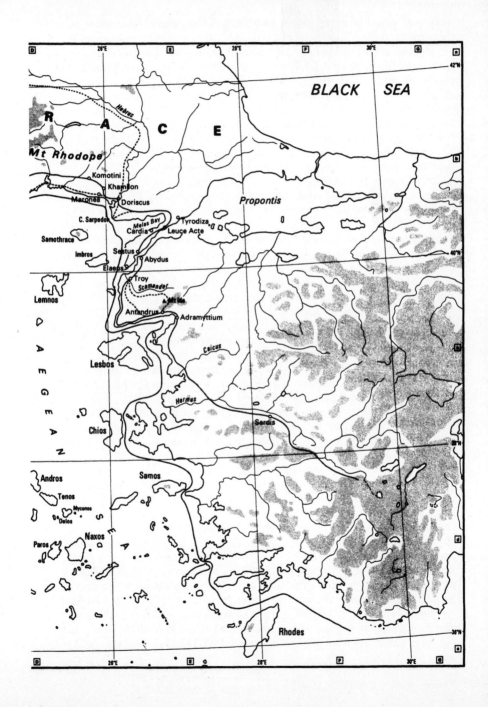

work was made of equal width with that of the others. Now there is a meadow there, in which there was made for them a market and a place for buying and selling; and great quantities of grain came for them regularly from Asia, ready ground. **24.** It seems to me that Xerxes when he ordered this to be dug was moved by a love of magnificence and by a desire to make a display of his power and to leave a memorial behind him; for though they might have drawn the ships across the isthmus with no great labour, he bade them dig a channel for the sea of such breadth that two triremes might sail through, propelled side by side. To these same men to whom the digging had been appointed, it was appointed also to make a bridge over the river Strymon, yoking together the banks.

25. Xerxes meanwhile caused ropes also to be prepared for the bridges, made of papyrus and of white flax, appointing this to the Phenicians and Egyptians; and also he was making preparations to store provisions for his army on the way, that neither the army itself nor the baggage animals might suffer from scarcity, as they made their march against Hellas. Accordingly, when he had learnt by inquiry of the various places, he bade them make stores where it was most convenient, carrying supplies to different parts by merchant ships and ferry-boats from all the countries of Asia. So they conveyed the greater part of the grain to the place which is called Leukē Actē in Thrace, while others conveyed stores to Tyrodiza of the Perinthians, others to Doriscos, others to Eïon on the Strymon, and others to Macedonia, the work being distributed between them.

26. During the time that these were working at the task which had been proposed to them, the whole land-army had been assembled together and was marching with Xerxes to Sardis, setting forth from Critalla in Cappadokia;* for there it had been ordered that the whole army should assemble, which was to go with Xerxes himself by the land: but which of the governors of provinces brought the best equipped force and received from the king the gifts proposed, I am not able to say, for I do not know that they even came to a competition in this matter. Then after they had crossed the river Halys and had entered Phrygia, marching through this land they came to Kelainai, where the springs of the river Maiander come up, and also those of another river not less than the Maiander, whose name is Catarractes; this rises in the market-place itself of Kelainai and runs into the Maiander: and here also is hanging up in the city the skin of Marsyas the Silen, which is said by the Phrygians to have been flayed off and hung up by Apollo. **27.** In this city Pythios the son of Atys, a Lydian, was waiting for the king and entertained his whole army, as well as Xerxes himself, with the most magnificent hospitality: moreover he professed himself ready to supply money for the war. So when Pythios offered money, Xerxes asked those of the Persians who were present, who Pythios was and how much money he possessed, that he made this offer. They said: "O king, this is he who presented your father Dareios with the golden

---

*Xerxes marched to Sardis in 481 B.C.

plane-tree and the golden vine; and even now he is in wealth the first of all men of whom we know, excepting you only." **28.** Marvelling at the conclusion of these words Xerxes himself asked of Pythios then, how much money he had; and he said: "O king, I will not conceal the truth from you, nor will I allege as an excuse that I do not know my own substance, but I will enumerate it to you exactly, since I know the truth: for as soon as I heard that you were coming down to the Sea of Hellas, desiring to give you money for the war I ascertained the truth, and calculating I found that I had of silver two thousand talents, and of gold four million daric staters* short seven thousand: and with this money I present you. For myself I have sufficient livelihood from my slaves and from my estates of land." **29.** Thus he said; and Xerxes was pleased by the things which he had spoken, and replied: "Lydian host, ever since I went forth from the Persian land I have encountered no man up to this time who was desirous to entertain my army, or who came into my presence and made offer of his own free will to contribute money to me for the war, except only you: and you not only did entertain my army magnificently, but also now offer great sums of money. To you therefore in return I give these rewards,—I make you my guest-friend, and I will complete for you the four million staters by giving from myself the seven thousand, in order that your four million may not fall short by seven thousand, but you may have a full sum in your reckoning, completed thus by me. Keep possession of that which you have got for yourself, and be sure to act always thus; for if you doest so, you will have no cause to repent either at the time or afterwards."

30. Having thus said and having accomplished his promise, he continued his march onwards; and passing by a city of the Phrygians called Anaua and a lake whence salt is obtained, he came to Colossai, a great city of Phrygia, where the river Lycos falls into an opening of the earth and disappears from view, and then after an interval of about 3,000 feet it comes up to view again, and this river also flows into the Maiander. Setting forth from Colossai towards the boundaries of the Phrygians and Lydians, the army arrived at the city of Kydrara, where a squared pillar is fixed, set up by Crœsus, which declares by an inscription that the boundaries are there. **31.** From Phrygia then he entered Lydia; and here the road parts into two, and that which goes to the left leads towards Caria, while that which goes to the right leads to Sardis; and travelling by this latter road one must needs cross the river Maiander and pass by the city of Callatebos, where men live whose trade it is to make honey of the tamarisk-tree and of wheat-flour. By this road went Xerxes and found a plane-tree, to which for its beauty he gave an adornment of gold, and appointed that some one should have charge of it always in undying succession; and on the next day he came to the city of the Lydians. **32.** Having

---

*See 4.166, on their purity; this "standard" coin, named for Dareios, weighed more than half an ounce (129 grains). Dareios ("the shopkeeper"; see 3.89) introduced coinage, taxes, and tribute to the vast Eastern realm.

come to Sardis he proceeded first to send heralds to Hellas, to ask for earth and water, and also to give notice beforehand to prepare meals for the king; except that he sent neither to Athens nor Lacedemon to ask for earth, but to all the other States: and the reason why he sent the second time to ask for earth and water was this,—as many as had not given at the former time to Dareios when he sent, these he thought would certainly give now by reason of their fear: he desired to have certain knowledge, and he sent accordingly.

33. After this he made his preparations intending to march to Abydos: and meanwhile they were bridging over the Hellespont from Asia to Europe. Now there is in the Chersonese of the Hellespont between the city of Sestos and Madytos, a broad headland running down into the sea right opposite Abydos; this is the place where no long time afterwards* the Athenians under the command of Xanthippos the son of Ariphron, having taken Artaÿctes a Persian, who was the governor of Sestos, nailed him alive to a board with hands and feet extended, (he was the man who was wont to take women with him to the temple of Protesilaos at Elaius and to do things there which are not lawful). **34.** To this foreland they on whom this work was laid were making their bridges, starting from Abydos, the Phenicians constructing the one with ropes of white flax, and the Egyptians the other, which was made with papyrus rope. Now from Abydos to the opposite shore is a distance of eight-tenths of a mile. But when the strait had been bridged over, a great storm came on and dashed together all the work and broke it up. **35.** Then when Xerxes heard it he was exceedingly enraged, and bade them scourge the Hellespont with three hundred strokes of the lash and let down into the sea a pair of fetters. Nay, I have heard further that he sent branders also with them to brand the Hellespont. However this may be, he enjoined them, as they were beating, to say Barbarian and presumptuous words as follows: "Bitter water, your master lays upon you this penalty, because you did wrong him not having suffered any wrong from him: and Xerxes the king will pass over you whether you be willing or no; but with right, as it seems, no man sacrifices to you, seeing that you are a treacherous and briny stream." The sea he enjoined them to chastise thus, and also he bade them cut off the heads of those who were appointed to have charge over the bridging of the Hellespont. **36.** Thus then the men did, to whom this ungracious office belonged; and meanwhile other chief-constructors proceeded to make the bridges; and thus they made them:—They put together fifty-oared galleys and triremes, three hundred and sixty to be under the bridge towards the Euxine Sea, and three hundred and fourteen to be under the other, the vessels lying in the direction of the stream of the Hellespont (though crosswise in respect to the Pontus), to support the tension of the ropes. They placed them together thus, and let down very large anchors, those on the one side towards the Pontus because of the winds which blow from within

---

*More than two years later, as described at 9.115–120.

outwards, and on the other side, towards the West and the Egean, because of the South-East and South Winds. They left also an opening between the fifty-oared galleys and triremes in three places for a passage through, so that any who wished might be able to sail into the Pontus with small vessels, and also from the Pontus outwards. Having thus done, they proceeded to stretch tight the ropes, straining them with wooden windlasses, not now appointing the two kinds of rope to be used apart from one another, but assigning to each bridge two ropes of white flax and four of the papyrus ropes. The thickness and beauty of make was the same for both, but the flaxen ropes were heavier in proportion, and of this rope a foot and one-half weighed fifty-seven pounds. When the passage was bridged over, they sawed up logs of wood, and making them equal in length to the breadth of the bridge they laid them above the stretched ropes, and having set them thus in order they again fastened them above. When this was done, they carried on brushwood, and having set the brushwood also in place, they carried on to it earth; and when they had stamped down the earth firmly, they built a barrier along on each side, so that the baggage-animals and horses might not be frightened by looking out over the sea.

37. When the construction of the bridges had been finished, and the works about Athōs, both the embankments about the mouths of the channel, which were made because of the breaking of the sea upon the beach, that the mouths of it might not be filled up, and the channel itself, were reported to be fully completed, then, after they had passed the winter at Sardis, the army set forth from thence fully equipped, at the beginning of spring, to march to Abydos; and when it had just set forth, the Sun left his place in the heaven and was invisible, though there was no gathering of clouds and the sky was perfectly clear; and instead of day it became night.* When Xerxes saw and perceived this, it became a matter of concern to him; and he asked the Magians what the appearance meant to portend. These declared that the god was foreshowing to the Hellenes a "leaving" of their cities, saying that the Sun was the foreshower of events for the Hellenes, but the Moon for the Persians. Having been thus informed, Xerxes proceeded on the march with very great joy. **38.** Then as he was leading forth his army on its march, Pythios the Lydian, being alarmed by the appearance in the heavens and elated by the gifts which he had received, came to Xerxes, and said: "Master, I would desire to receive from you a certain thing at my request, which, as it chances, is for you an easy thing to grant, but a great thing for me, if I obtain it." Then Xerxes, thinking that his request would be for anything rather than that which he actually asked, said that he would grant it, and bade him speak and say what he desired. He then, when he heard this, was encouraged and spoke: "Master, I have, as it chances, five sons, and it is their fortune to be all going together with you on the march against Hellas. O king, have compassion upon me, who have

---

*The army marched from Sardis in April of 480 B.C., but there is no record of an eclipse, a word that also means "leaving."

come to so great an age, and release from serving in the expedition one of my sons, the eldest, in order that he may be caretaker both of myself and of my wealth: but the other four take along, and after you have accomplished that which you have in your mind, have a safe return home." **39.** Then Xerxes was angry and answered: "Wretched man, do you dare, when I am going on a march myself against Hellas, and am taking my sons and my brothers and my relations and friends, do you dare to make any mention of a son of yours, seeing that you are my slave, who ought to have been accompanying me yourself with your whole household and your wife as well? Now therefore be assured of this, that the passionate spirit of man dwells within the ears; and when it has heard good things, it fills the body full of delight, but when it has heard the opposite things to this, it swells up with anger. As then you can not boast of having surpassed the king in conferring benefits formerly, when you did to us good deeds and offered to do more of the same kind, so now that you have turned to shamelessness, you shall receive not your desert but less than you deserve: for your gifts of hospitality shall rescue from death yourself and the four others of your sons, but you shall pay the penalty with the life of the one, him to whom you do cling most." Having answered thus, he straightaway commanded those to whom it was appointed to do these things, to find out the eldest of the sons of Pythios and to cut him in two in the middle; and having cut him in two, to dispose the halves, one on the right hand of the road and the other on the left, and that the army should pass between them by this way.

40. Then the army proceeded to pass between; and first the baggage-bearers led the way together with their horses, and after these the host composed of all kinds of nations mingled together without distinction: and when more than the half had gone by, an interval was left and these were separated from the king. For before him went first a thousand horsemen, chosen out of all the Persians; and after them a thousand spearmen chosen also from all the Persians, having the points of their spears turned down to the ground; and then ten sacred horses, called "Nesaian," with the fairest possible trappings. Now the horses are called Nesaian for this reason:— there is a wide plain in the land of Media which is called the Nesaian plain, and this plain produces the great horses of which I speak. Behind these ten horses the sacred chariot of Zeus was appointed to go, which was drawn by eight white horses; and behind the horses again followed on foot a charioteer holding the reins, for no human creature mounts upon the seat of that chariot. Then behind this came Xerxes himself in a chariot drawn by Nesaian horses, and by the side of him rode a charioteer, whose name was Patiramphes, son of Otanes a Persian.

41. Thus did Xerxes march forth out of Sardis; and he used to change, whenever he was so disposed, from the chariot to a carriage. And behind him went spearmen, the best and most noble of the Persians, a thousand in number, holding their spear-points up in the customary way; and after them another thousand horsemen chosen out from the Persians; and after the horsemen ten thousand men chosen out from the remainder of the Persians. This body went on foot; and of these a thousand had upon their spears pomegranates of gold instead of the spikes at the butt-end, and these enclosed the others round, while the remaining nine thousand were within these and had silver pomegranates. And those also had golden pomegranates who had their spear-points turned towards the earth, while those who followed next after Xerxes had golden apples. Then to follow the ten thousand there was appointed a body of ten thousand Persian cavalry; and after the cavalry there was an interval of as much as 1,200 feet. Then the rest of the host came marching without distinction.

42. So the army proceeded on its march from Lydia to the river Caïcos and the land of Mysia; and then setting forth from the Caïcos and keeping the mountain of Canē on the left hand, it marched through the region of Atarneus to the city of Carenē. From this it went through the plain of Thebē, passing by the cities of Adramytteion and Antandros of the Pelasgians; and taking Mount Ida on the left hand, it came on to the land of Ilion. And first, when it had stopped for the night close under mount Ida, thunder and bolts of lightning fell upon it, and destroyed here in this place a very large number of men. **43.** Then when the army had come to the river Scamander,—which of all rivers to which they had come, since they set forth from Sardis and undertook their march, was the first where the stream failed and was not sufficient for the drinking of the army and of the animals with it,—when, I say, Xerxes had come to this river, he went up to the Citadel of Priam, having a desire to see it all; and having seen it and learnt by inquiry of all the events of the Trojan War, he sacrificed a thousand heifers to Athenē of Ilion, and the Magians poured libations in honour of the heroes: and after they had done this, a fear fell upon the army in the night. Then at break of day he set forth from thence, keeping on his left hand the cities of Rhoition and Ophryneion and Dardanos, which last borders upon Abydos, and having on the right hand the Gergith Teucrians.

44. When Xerxes had come into the midst of Abydos, he had a desire to see all the army; and there had been made for him beforehand upon a hill in this place a raised seat of white stone, which the people of Abydos had built at the command of the king. Here he took his seat, and looking down upon the shore he gazed both upon the land-army and the ships; and gazing upon them he had a longing to see a contest take place between the ships; and when the Phenicians of Sidon were victorious, he was delighted both with the contest and with the whole armament. **45.** And seeing all the Hellespont covered over with the ships, and all the shores and the plains of Abydos full of men, then Xerxes pronounced himself a happy man, and after that he fell to weeping.

46. Artabanos his uncle therefore perceiving him,—the same who at first boldly declared his opinion advising Xerxes not to march against Hellas,—this man, having observed that Xerxes wept, asked as follows: "O king, how far different from one another are the things which you have done now and a short while before now! for having pronounced yourself a happy man, you are now shedding tears." He said: "True, for after I had reckoned up, it came into my mind to feel pity at the thought how brief was the whole life of man, seeing that of these multitudes not one will be alive when a hundred years have gone by." He then made answer and said: "To another evil more pitiful than this we are made subject in the course of our life; for in the period of life, short as it is, no man, either of these here or of others, is made by nature so happy, that there will not come to him many times, and not once only, the desire to be dead rather than to live; for misfortunes falling upon us and diseases disturbing our happiness make the time of life, though short indeed, seem long: thus, since life is full of trouble, death has become the most acceptable refuge for man; and God, having given him to taste of the sweetness of life, is discovered in this matter to be full of jealousy."

47. Xerxes made answer saying: "Artabanos, of human life, which is such as you define it to be, let us cease to speak, and not remember evils when we have good things in hand: but declare to me this:—If the vision of the dream had not appeared with so much evidence, would you still be holding your former opinion, endeavouring to prevent me from marching against Hellas, or would you have changed from it? Come, tell me this exactly." He answered saying: "O king, may the vision of the dream which appeared have such fulfilment as we both desire! but I am even to this moment full of apprehension and cannot contain myself, taking into account many things besides, and also seeing that two things, which are the greatest things of all, are utterly hostile to you." **48.** To this Xerxes made answer in these words: "Strangest of men, of what nature are these two things which you sayest are utterly hostile to me? Is it that the land-army is to be found fault with in the matter of numbers, and that the army of the Hellenes appears to you likely to be many times as large as ours? or do you think that our fleet will fall short of theirs? or even that both of these things together will prove true? For if you think that in these respects our power is deficient, one might make gathering at once of another force."

49. Then he made answer and said: "O king, neither with this army would any one who has understanding find fault, nor with the number of the ships; and indeed if you shall assemble more, the two things of which I speak will be made thereby yet more hostile: and these two things are—the land and the sea. For neither in the sea is there, as I suppose, a harbour anywhere large enough to receive this fleet, if a storm should arise, and to ensure the safety of the ships till it be over; and yet not one alone ought this harbour to be, but there should be such harbours along the whole coast of the continent by which you sail; and if there are not harbours to receive your ships, know that accidents will rule the men and not men the accidents. Now having told you of one of the two things, I am about to tell you of the other. The land, I say, becomes hostile to you in this way:—if nothing shall come to oppose you, the land is hostile to you by so much the more in proportion as you shall advance more, always lured further and further, for there is no satiety of good fortune felt by men: and this I say, that with no one to stand against you the country traversed, growing more and more as time goes on, will produce for you famine. Man, however, will be in the best condition, if when he is taking counsel he feels fear, reckoning to suffer everything that can possibly come, but in doing the deed he is bold."

50. Xerxes made answer in these words: "Artabanos, reasonably do you set forth these matters; but do not fear everything nor reckon equally for everything: for if you should set yourself with regard to all matters which come up at any time, to reckon for everything equally, you would never perform any deed. It is better to have good courage about everything and to suffer half the evils which threaten, than to have fear beforehand about everything and not to suffer any evil at all: and if, while contending against everything which is said, you omit to declare the course which is safe, you incur in these matters the reproach of failure equally with him who says the opposite to this. This then, I say, is evenly balanced: but how should one who is but man know the course which is safe? I think, in no way. To those then who choose to act, for the most part gain is wont to come; but to those who reckon for everything and shrink back, it is not much wont to come. You see the power of the Persians, to what great might it has advanced: if then those who came to be kings before me had had opinions like to yours, or, though not having such opinions, had had such counsellors as you, you would never have seen it brought forward to this point. As it is however, by running risks they conducted it on to this: for great power is in general gained by running great risks. We therefore, following their example, are making our march now during the fairest season of the year; and after we have subdued all Europe we shall return back home, neither having met with famine anywhere nor having suffered any other thing which is unpleasant. For first we march bearing with us ourselves great store of food, and secondly we shall possess the crops of all the peoples to whose land and nation we come; and we are making a march now against men who plough the soil, and not against nomad tribes."

51. After this Artabanos said: "O king, since you urge us not to have fear of anything, I pray you accept a counsel from me; for when speaking of many things it is necessary to extend speech to a greater length. Cyrus the son of Cambyses subdued all Ionia except the Athenians, so that it was tributary to the Persians. These men therefore I counsel you by no means to lead against their parent stock, seeing that even without these we are able to get the advantage over our enemies. For supposing that they go with us, either they must prove themselves doers of great wrong, if they join in reducing their mother city to slavery, or doers of great right, if they join in freeing her: now if they show themselves doers of great wrong, they bring to us no very large gain in addition; but if they show themselves doers of great right, they are able then to cause much damage to your army. Therefore lay to heart also the ancient saying, how well it has been said that at the beginning of things the end does not completely appear." **52.** To this Xerxes made answer: "Artabanos, of all the opinions which you have uttered, you are mistaken most of all in this; seeing that you fear lest the Ionians should change sides, about whom we have a most sure proof, of which you are a witness yourself and also the rest are witnesses who went with Dareios on his march against the Scythians,—namely this, that the whole Persian army then came to be dependent upon these men, whether they would destroy or whether they would save it, and they displayed

righteous dealing and trustworthiness, and nought at all that was un-
friendly. Besides this, seeing that they have left children and wives and
wealth in our land, we must not even imagine that they will make any rebellion. Fear not then this thing either, but have a good heart and keep
safe my house and my government; for to you of all men I entrust my sceptre of rule."

53. Having sent Artabanos back to Susa, next Xerxes summoned to his
presence the men of most repute among the Persians, and he spoke to them
as follows: "Persians, I assembled you together desiring this of you, that you
should show yourselves good men and should not disgrace the deeds done
in former time by the Persians, which are great and glorious; but let us each
one of us by himself, and all together also, be zealous in our enterprise; for
this which we labour for is a common good for all. And I exhort you that
you persevere in the war without relaxing your efforts, because, as I am informed, we are marching against good men, and if we shall overcome them,
there will not be any other army of men which will ever stand against us.
Now therefore let us begin the crossing, after having made prayer to those
gods who have the Persians for their allotted charge."

54. During this day then they were making preparation to cross over;
and on the next day they waited for the Sun, desiring to see him rise, and
in the meantime they offered all kinds of incense upon the bridges and
strewed the way with branches of myrtle. Then, as the Sun was rising,
Xerxes made libation from a golden cup into the sea, and prayed to the
Sun, that no accident might befall him such as should cause him to cease
from subduing Europe, until he had come to its furthest limits. After having thus prayed he threw the cup into the Hellespont and with it a golden
mixing-bowl and a Persian sword, which they call *akinakēs:* but whether
he cast them into the sea as an offering dedicated to the Sun, or whether
he had repented of his scourging of the Hellespont and desired to present
a gift to the sea as amends for this, I cannot for certain say. **55.** When Xerxes
had done this, they proceeded to cross over, the whole army both the infantry and the horsemen going by one bridge, namely that which was on
the side of the Pontus, while the baggage-animals and the attendants went
over the other, which was towards the Egean. First the ten thousand Persians led the way, all with wreaths, and after them came the mixed body of
the army made up of all kinds of nations: these on that day; and on the
next day, first the horsemen and those who had their spear-points turned
downwards, these also wearing wreaths; and after them the sacred horses
and the sacred chariot, and then Xerxes himself and the spear-bearers and
the thousand horsemen; and after them the rest of the army. In the meantime the ships also put out from shore and went over to the opposite side.
I have heard however another account which says that the king crossed
over the very last of all.

56. When Xerxes had crossed over into Europe, he gazed upon the
army crossing under the lash; and his army crossed over in seven days and
seven nights, going on continuously without any pause. Then, it is said,
after Xerxes had now crossed over the Hellespont, a man of that coast

exclaimed: "Why, O Zeus, in the likeness of a Persian man and taking for yourself the name of Xerxes instead of Zeus, are you proposing to lay waste Hellas, taking with you all the nations of men? for it was possible for you to do so even without the help of these."

57. When all had crossed over, after they had set forth on their way a great portent appeared to them, of which Xerxes made no account, although it was easy to conjecture its meaning,—a mare gave birth to a hare. Now the meaning of this was that Xerxes was about to march an army against Hellas very proudly and magnificently, but would come back again to the place whence he came, running for his life. There happened also a portent of another kind while he was still at Sardis,—a mule brought forth young and gave birth to a mule which had organs of generation of two kinds, both those of the male and those of the female, and those of the male were above. Xerxes however made no account of either of these portents, but proceeded on his way, and with him the land-army. **58.** The fleet meanwhile was sailing out of the Hellespont and coasting along, going in the opposite direction to the land-army; for the fleet was sailing towards the West, making for the promontory of Sarpedon, to which it had been ordered beforehand to go, and there wait for the army; but the land-army meanwhile was making its march towards the East and the sunrising, through the Chersonese, keeping on its right the tomb of Hellē the daughter of Athamas, and on its left the city of Cardia, and marching through the midst of a town named Agora. Thence bending round the gulf called Melas and having crossed over the river Melas, the stream of which did not suffice at this time for the army but failed,—having crossed, I say, this river, from which the gulf also has its name, it went on Westwards, passing by Ainos a city of the Aiolians, and by the lake Stentoris, until at last it came to Doriscos. **59.** Now Doriscos is a sea-beach and plain of great extent in Thrace, and through it flows the great river Hebros: here a royal fortress had been built, the same which is now called Doriscos, and a garrison of Persians had been established in it by Dareios, ever since the time when he went on his march against the Scythians. It seemed then to Xerxes that the place was convenient to order his army and to number it throughout, and so he proceeded to do. The commanders of the ships at the bidding of Xerxes had brought all their ships, when they arrived at Doriscos, up to the sea-beach which adjoins Doriscos, on which there is situated both Salē a city of the Samothrakians, and also Zonē, and of which the extreme point is the promontory of Serreion, which is well known; and the region belonged in ancient time to the Kikonians. To this beach then they had brought in their ships, and having drawn them up on land they were letting them get dry: and during this time he proceeded to number the army at Doriscos.

60. Now of the number which each separate nation supplied I am not able to give certain information, for this is not reported by any persons; but of the whole land-army taken together the number proved to be 1,700,000 and they numbered them throughout in the following manner:—they gathered together into one place a body of ten thousand men, and packing them together as closely as they could, they drew a circle round outside: and thus having drawn a circle round and having let the ten thousand men go from it, they built a wall of rough stones round the circumference of the circle, rising to the height of a man's navel. Having made this, they caused others to go into the space which had been built round, until they had in this manner numbered them all throughout: and after they had numbered them, they ordered them separately by nations.

61. Now those who served were as follows:*—The Persians with this equipment:—about their heads they had soft felt caps called *tiaras,* and about their body tunics of various colours with sleeves, presenting the appearance of iron scales like those of a fish, and about the legs trousers; and instead of the ordinary shields they had shields of wicker-work, under which hung quivers; and they had short spears and large bows and arrows of reed, and moreover daggers hanging by the right thigh from the girdle: and they acknowledged as their commander Otanes the father of Amestris the wife of Xerxes. Now these were called by the Hellenes in ancient time Kephenes; by themselves however and by their neighbours they were called Artaians: but when Perseus, the son of Danaē and Zeus, came to Kepheus the son of Belos and took to wife his daughter Andromeda, there was born to them a son to whom he gave the name Perses, and this son he left behind there, for it chanced that Kepheus had no male offspring: after him therefore this race was named. **62.** The Medes served in the expedition equipped in precisely the same manner; for this equipment is in fact Median and not Persian: and the Medes acknowledged as their commander Tigranes an Achaimenid. These in ancient time used to be generally called Arians; but when Medea the Colchian came from Athens to these Arians, they also changed their name. Thus the Medes themselves report about themselves. The Kissians served with equipment in other respects like that of the Persians, but instead of the felt caps they wore fillets: and of the Kissians Anaphes the son of Otanes was commander. The Hyrcanians were armed like the Persians, acknowledging as their leader Megapanos, the same who after these events became governor of Babylon. **63.** The Assyrians served with helmets about their heads made of bronze or plaited in a Barbarian style which it is not easy to describe; and they had shields and spears, and daggers like the Egyptian knives, and moreover they had wooden clubs with knobs of iron, and corslets of linen. These are by the Hellenes called Syrians, but by the Barbarians they have been called always Assyrians: [among these were the Chaldeans]:† and the commander of them was Otaspes the son of Artachaies. **64.** The Bactrians served wearing about their heads nearly the same covering as the Medes, and having native bows of reed and short spears. The Sacan Scythians had

---

*This catalog of armies has analogues in the sculptures at Persepolis and may be based on a Persian source, geographically arranged, that followed a traveler's itinerary; the catalog proceeds from the heartland to the east, south, and west.
†Probably an interpolation; compare 1.181 on the caste of priests of Belos.

about their heads caps which were carried up to a point and set upright and stiff; and they wore trousers, and carried native bows and daggers, and besides this axes of the kind called *sagaris*. These were called Amyrgian Sacans, being in fact Scythians; for the Persians call all the Scythians Sacans: and of the Bactrians and Sacans the commander was Hystaspes, the son of Dareios and of Atossa the daughter of Cyrus. **65.** The Indians wore garments made of tree-wool [cotton], and they had bows of reed and arrows of reed with iron points. Thus were the Indians equipped; and serving with the rest they had been assigned to Pharnazathres the son of Artabates. **66.** The Arians were equipped with Median bows, and in other respects like the Bactrians: and of the Arians Sisamnes the son of Hydarnes was in command. The Parthians and Chorasmians and Sogdians and Gandarians and Dadicans served with the same equipment as the Bactrians. Of these the commanders were, Artabazos the son of Pharnakes of the Parthians and Chorasmians, Azanes the son of Artaios of the Sogdians, and Artyphios the son of Artabanos of the Gandarians and Dadicans. **67.** The Caspians served wearing coats of skin and having native bows of reed and short swords: thus were these equipped; and they acknowledged as their leader Ariomardos the brother of Artyphios. The Sarangians were conspicuous among the rest by wearing dyed garments; and they had boots reaching up to the knee, and Median bows and spears: of these the commander was Pherendates the son of Megabazos. The Pactyans were wearers of skin coats and had native bows and daggers: these acknowledged as their commander Artaÿntes the son of Ithamitres. **68.** The Utians and Mycans and Paricanians were equipped like the Pactyans: of these the commanders were, Arsamenes the son of Dareios of the Utians and Mycans, and of the Paricanians Siromitres the son of Oiobazos. **69.** The Arabians wore loose mantles girt up, and they carried at their right side backstrung bows of great length. The Ethiopians had skins of leopards and lions tied upon them, and bows made of a slip of palm-wood, which were of great length, not less than six feet, and for them small arrows of reed with a sharpened stone at the head instead of iron, the same stone with which they engrave seals: in addition to this they had spears, and on them was the sharpened horn of a gazelle by way of a spear-head, and they had also clubs with knobs upon them. Of their body they used to smear over half with white chalk, when they went to battle, and the other half with red ochre. Of the Arabians and the Ethiopians who dwelt above Egypt the commander was Arsames, the son of Dareios and of Artystonē the daughter of Cyrus, whom Dareios loved most of all his wives, and had an image made of her of beaten gold. **70.** Of the Ethiopians above Egypt and of the Arabians the commander, I say, was Arsames; but the Ethiopians from the direction of the sunrising (for the Ethiopians were in two bodies) had been appointed to serve with the Indians, being in no way different in appearance from the other Ethiopians, but in their language and in the nature of their hair only; for the Ethiopians from the East are straight-haired, but those of Libya have hair more thick and woolly than that of any other men. These Ethiopians from

Asia were armed for the most part like the Indians, but they had upon
their heads the skin of a horse's forehead flayed off with the ears and the
mane, and the mane served instead of a crest, while they had the ears of
the horse set up straight and stiff: and instead of shields they used to make
defences to hold before themselves of the skins of cranes. **71.** The Libyans
went with equipments of leather, and they used javelins burnt at the
point. These acknowledged as their commander Massages the son of
Oarizos. **72.** The Paphlagonians served with plaited helmets upon their
heads, small shields, and spears of no great size, and also javelins and
daggers; and about their feet native boots reaching up to the middle of
the shin. The Ligyans and Matienians and Mariandynoi and Syrians
served with the same equipment as the Paphlagonians: these Syrians
are called by the Persians Cappadokians. Of the Paphlagonians and Matienians the commander was Dotos the son of Megasidros, and of the
Mariandynoi and Ligyans and Syrians, Gobryas, who was the son of
Dareios and Artystonē. **73.** The Phrygians had an equipment very like
that of the Paphlagonians with some slight difference. Now the Phrygians, as the Macedonians say, used to be called Brigians during the time
that they were natives of Europe and dwelt with the Macedonians; but
after they had changed into Asia, with their country they changed also
their name and were called Phrygians. The Armenians were armed just
like the Phrygians, being settlers from the Phrygians. Of these two together the commander was Artochmes, who was married to a daughter
of Dareios. **74.** The Lydians had arms very closely resembling those of the
Hellenes. Now the Lydians were in old time called Meonians, and they
were named again after Lydos the son of Atys, changing their former
name. The Mysians had upon their heads native helmets, and they bore
small shields and used javelins burnt at the point. These are settlers from
the Lydians, and from mount Olympos they are called Olympienoi. Of the
Lydians and Mysians the commander was Artaphrenes the son of Artaphrenes, he who invaded Marathon together with Datis. **75.** The Thracians served having fox-skins upon their heads and tunics about their
body, with loose mantles of various colours thrown round over them; and
about their feet and lower part of the leg they wore boots of deerskin; and
besides this they had javelins and round bucklers and small daggers. These
when they had crossed over into Asia came to be called Bithynians, but
formerly they were called, as they themselves report, Strymonians, since
they dwelt upon the river Strymon; and they say that they were driven out
of their abode by the Teucrians and Mysians. Of the Thracians who lived
in Asia the commander was Bassakes the son of Artabanos. **76.** The [Pisid-
ians] had small shields of raw ox-hide, and each man carried two hunting-
spears of Lykian workmanship. On their heads they wore helmets of
bronze, and to the helmets the ears and horns of an ox were attached, in
bronze, and upon them also there were crests; and the lower part of their
legs was wrapped round with red-coloured strips of cloth. Among these
men there is an Oracle of Ares. **77.** The Meonian Cabelians, who are
called Lasonians, had the same equipment as the Kilikians, and what this

was I shall explain when in the course of the catalogue I come to the array of the Kilikians. The Milyans had short spears, and their garments were fastened on with buckles; some of them had Lykian bows, and about their heads they had caps made of leather. Of all these Badres the son of Hystanes was in command. **78.** The Moschoi had wooden caps upon their heads, and shields and small spears, on which long points were set. The Tibarenians and Macronians and Mossynoicoi served with equipment like that of the Moschoi, and these were arrayed together under the following commanders,—the Moschoi and Tibarenians under Ariomardos, who was the son of Dareios and of Parmys, the daughter of Smerdis son of Cyrus; the Macronians and Mossynoicoi under Artaÿctes the son of Cherasmis, who was governor of Sestos on the Hellespont. **79.** The Mares wore on their heads native helmets of plaited work, and had small shields of hide and javelins; and the Colchians wore wooden helmets about their heads, and had small shields of raw ox-hide and short spears, and also knives. Of the Mares and Colchians the commander was Pharandates the son of Teaspis. The Alarodians and Saspeirians served armed like the Colchians; and of these the commander was Masistios the son of Siromitres. **80.** The island tribes which came with the army from the Erythraian Sea, belonging to the islands in which the king settles those who are called the "Removed,"* had clothing and arms very like those of the Medes. Of these islanders the commander was Mardontes the son of Bagaios, who in the year after these events was a commander of the army at Mykalē and lost his life in the battle.

81. These were the nations which served in the campaign by land and had been appointed to be among the foot-soldiers. Of this army those who have been mentioned were commanders; and they were the men who set it in order by divisions and numbered it and appointed commanders of thousands and commanders of tens of thousands, but the commanders of hundreds and of tens were appointed by the commanders of ten thousands; and there were others who were leaders of divisions and nations. **82.** These, I say, who have been mentioned were commanders of the army; and over these and over the whole army together that went on foot there were in command Mardonios the son of Gobryas, Tritantaichmes the son of that Artabanos who gave the opinion that they should not make the march against Hellas, Smerdomenes the son of Otanes (both these being sons of brothers of Dareios and so cousins of Xerxes), Masistes the son of Dareios and Atossa, Gergis the son of Ariazos, and Megabyzos the son of Zopyros. **83.** These were generals of the whole together that went on foot, excepting the ten thousand; and of these ten thousand chosen Persians the general was Hydarnes the son of Hydarnes; and these Persians were called "Immortals," because, if any one of them made the number incomplete, being overcome either by death or disease, another man was chosen to his place, and they were never either more or fewer than ten thousand. Now

---

*Mentioned at 3.93 in the catalog of tribute-payers.

of all the nations, the Persians showed the greatest splendour of ornament
and were themselves the best men. They had equipment such as has been
mentioned, and besides this they were conspicuous among the rest for
great quantity of gold freely used; and they took with them carriages, and
in them concubines and a multitude of attendants well furnished; and provisions for them apart from the soldiers were borne by camels and beasts
of burden.

84. The nations who serve as cavalry are these; not all however supplied
cavalry, but only as many as here follow:—the Persians equipped in the
same manner as their foot-soldiers, except that upon their heads some of
them had beaten-work of metal, either bronze or iron. **85.** There are also
certain nomads called Sagartians, Persian in race and in language and having a dress which is midway between that of the Persians and that of the
Pactyans. These furnished eight thousand horse, and they are not accustomed to have any arms either of bronze or of iron excepting daggers, but
they use ropes twisted of thongs, and trust to these when they go into war:
and the manner of fighting of these men is as follows:—when they come to
conflict with the enemy, they throw the ropes with nooses at the end of
them, and whatsoever the man catches by his throw, whether horse or
man, he draws to himself, and they being entangled in toils are thus destroyed. **86.** This is the manner of fighting of these men, and they were arrayed next to the Persians. The Medes had the same equipment as for their
men on foot, and the Kissians likewise. The Indians were armed in the
same manner as those of them who served on foot, and they both rode
horses and drove chariots, in which were harnessed horses or wild asses.
The Bactrians were equipped in the same way as those who served on
foot, and the Caspians likewise. The Libyans too were equipped as those
who served on foot, and these also all drove chariots. So too the Caspians
and Paricanians were equipped like those who served on foot. The Arabians had the same equipment as those of them who served on foot, and
they all rode on camels, which in swiftness were not inferior to horses.
87. These nations alone served as cavalry, and the number of the cavalry
proved to be 80,000, apart from the camels and the chariots. Now the rest
of the cavalry was arrayed in squadrons, but the Arabians were placed after them and last of all, for the horses could not endure the camels, and
therefore they were placed last, in order that the horses might not be
frightened. **88.** The commanders of the cavalry were Harmamithras and
Tithaios sons of Datis, but the third, Pharnuches, who was in command of
the horse with them, had been left behind at Sardis sick: for as they were
setting forth from Sardis, an accident befell him of an unwished-for
kind,—as he was riding, a dog ran up under his horse's feet, and the horse
not having seen it beforehand was frightened, and rearing up he threw
Pharnuches off his back, who falling vomited blood, and his sickness
turned to a consumption. To the horse however they at once did as he
commanded, that is to say, the servants led him away to the place where he
had thrown his master and cut off his legs at the knees. Thus was Pharnuches removed from his command.

89. Of the triremes the number proved to be one thousand two hundred and seven, and these were they who furnished them:—the Phenicians together with the Syrians who dwell in Palestine furnished three hundred; and they were equipped thus, that is to say, they had about their heads leathern caps made very nearly in the Hellenic fashion, and they wore corslets of linen, and had shields without rims and javelins. These Phenicians dwelt in ancient time, as they themselves report, upon the Erythraian Sea, and thence they passed over and dwell in the country along the sea coast of Syria; and this part of Syria and all as far as Egypt is called Palestine. The Egyptians furnished two hundred ships: these men had about their heads helmets of plaited work, and they had hollow shields with the rims large, and spears for sea-fighting, and large axes: the greater number of them wore corslets, and they had large knives. **90.** These men were thus equipped; and the Cyprians furnished a hundred and fifty ships, being themselves equipped as follows,—their kings had their heads wound round with turbans, and the rest had tunics, but in other respects they were like the Hellenes. Among these there are various races as follows,—some of them are from Salamis and Athens, others from Arcadia, others from Kythnos, others again from Phenicia and others from Ethiopia, as the Cyprians themselves report. **91.** The Kilikians furnished a hundred ships; and these again had about their heads native helmets, and for shields they carried targets made of raw ox-hide: they wore tunics of wool and each man had two javelins and a sword, this last being made very like the Egyptian knives. These in old time were called Hypachaians, and they got their later name from Kilix the son of Agenor, a Phenician. The Pamphylians furnished thirty ships and were equipped in Hellenic arms. These Pamphylians are of those who were dispersed from Troy together with Amphilochos and Calchas. **92.** The Lykians furnished fifty ships; and they were wearers of corslets and greaves, and had bows of cornel-wood and arrows of reeds without feathers and javelins and a goat-skin hanging over their shoulders, and about their heads felt caps wreathed round with feathers; also they had daggers and sickle-swords. The Lykians were formerly called Termilai, being originally of Crete, and they got their later name from Lycos the son of Pandion, an Athenian. **93.** The Dorians of Asia furnished thirty ships; and these had Hellenic arms and were originally from the Peloponnese. The Carians supplied seventy ships; and they were equipped in other respects like Hellenes but they had also sickle-swords and daggers. What was the former name of these has been told in the first part of the history.* **94.** The Ionians furnished a hundred ships, and were equipped like Hellenes. Now the Ionians, so long time as they dwelt in the Peloponnese, in the land which is now called Achaia, and before the time when Danaos and Xuthos came to the Peloponnese, were called, as the Hellenes report, Pelasgians of the Coast-land, and then Ionians after Ion the son of Xuthos. **95.** The islanders furnished seventeen

---

*See 1.171; a cross-reference to the Leleges.

ships, and were armed like Hellenes, this also being a Pelasgian race,
though afterwards it came to be called Ionian by the same rule as the Ionians of the twelve cities, who came from Athens. The Aiolians supplied
sixty ships; and these were equipped like Hellenes and used to be called
Pelasgians in the old time, as the Hellenes report. The Hellespontians,
excepting those of Abydos (for the men of Abydos had been appointed
by the king to stay in their place and be guards of the bridges), the rest, I
say, of those who served in the expedition from the Pontus furnished a
hundred ships, and were equipped like Hellenes: these are colonists of
the Ionians and Dorians.

96. In all the ships there served as fighting-men Persians, Medes, or
Sacans: and of the ships, those which sailed best were furnished by the
Phenicians, and of the Phenicians the best by the men of Sidon. Over all
these men and also over those of them who were appointed to serve in
the land-army, there were for each tribe native chieftains, of whom, since
I am not compelled by the course of the inquiry,* I make no mention by
the way; for in the first place the chieftains of each separate nation were
not persons worthy of mention, and then moreover within each nation
there were as many chieftains as there were cities. These went with the
expedition too not as commanders, but like the others serving as slaves;
for the generals who had the absolute power and commanded the various
nations, that is to say those who were Persians, have already been mentioned by me. **97.** Of the naval force the following were commanders,—
Ariabignes the son of Dareios, Prexaspes the son of Aspathines, Megabazos
the son of Megabates, and Achaimenes the son of Dareios; that is to say,
of the Ionian and Carian force Ariabignes, who was the son of Dareios
and of the daughter of Gobryas; of the Egyptians Achaimenes was commander, being brother of Xerxes by both parents; and of the rest of the
armament the other two were in command: and galleys of thirty oars and
of fifty oars, and light vessels, and long ships to carry horses had been assembled together, as it proved, to the number of three thousand. **98.** Of
those who sailed in the ships the men of most note after the commanders
were these,—of Sidon, Tetramnestos son of Anysos; of Tyre, Matten
son of Siromos; of Arados, Merbalos son of Agbalos; of Kilikia, Syennesis son of Oromedon; of Lykia, Kyberniscos son of Sicas; of Cyprus,
Gorgos son of Chersis and Timonax son of Timagoras; of Caria, Histiaios
son of Tymnes, Pigres son of Hysseldomos, and Damasithymos son of
Candaules. **99.** Of the rest of the officers I make no mention by the way
(since I am not bound to do so), but only of Artemisia, at whom I marvel
most that she joined the expedition against Hellas, being a woman;† for
after her husband died, she holding the power herself, although she had

---

*A rare indication that history already has some parameters and guidelines; see
also 4.30.
†Hometown pride perhaps affects Herodotus' portrait of Halicarnassos' despot;
her gender tweaks the nose of the invader (compare 9.107).

a son who was a young man, went on the expedition impelled by high spirit and manly courage, no necessity being laid upon her. Artemisia was the daughter of Lygdamis, and by descent she was of Halicarnassos on the side of her father, but of Crete by her mother. She was ruler of the men of Halicarnassos and Cos and Nisyros and Calydna, furnishing five ships; and she furnished ships which were of all the fleet reputed the best after those of the Sidonians, and of all his allies she set forth the best counsels to the king. Of the States of which I said that she was leader I declare the people to be all of Dorian race, those of Halicarnassos being Troizenians, and the rest Epidaurians. So far then I have spoken of the naval force.

100. Then when Xerxes had numbered the army, and it had been arranged in divisions, he had a mind to drive through it himself and inspect it; and driving through in a chariot by each nation, he inquired about them and his scribes wrote down the names, until he had gone from end to end both of the horse and of the foot. When he had done this, the ships were drawn down into the sea, and Xerxes changing from his chariot to a ship of Sidon sat down under a golden canopy and sailed along by the prows of the ships, asking of all just as he had done with the land-army, and having the answers written down. And the captains had taken their ships out to a distance of about four hundred feet from the beach and were staying them there, all having turned the prows of the ships towards the shore in an even line and having armed all the fighting-men as for war; and he inspected them sailing between the prows of the ships and the beach.

101. Now when he had sailed through these and had disembarked from his ship, he sent for Demaratos the son of Ariston, who was marching with him against Hellas; and having called him he asked as follows: "Demaratos, now it is my pleasure to ask you somewhat which I desire to know. You are not only a Hellene, but also, as I am informed both by you and by the other Hellenes who come to speech with me, of a city which is neither the least nor the feeblest of Hellas. Now therefore declare to me this, namely whether the Hellenes will endure to raise hands against me: for, as I suppose, even if all the Hellenes and the remaining nations who dwell towards the West should be gathered together, they are not strong enough to endure my attack, especially since they are not united. I desire however to be informed also of your opinion, what you say about these matters." He inquired thus, and the other made answer and said: "O king, shall I utter the truth in speaking to you, or that which will give pleasure?" and he bade him utter the truth, saying that he should suffer nothing unpleasant in consequence of this, any more than he suffered before.

102. When Demaratos heard this, he spoke as follows: "O king, since you bid me by all means utter the truth, and so speak as one who shall not be afterwards convicted by you of having spoken falsely, I say this:—with Hellas poverty is ever a companion from birth, while enterprising valour has been driven in later, being acquired by intelligence and the force of law; and of it Hellas makes use ever to avert from herself not only poverty but also servitude to a master. Now I commend all the Hellenes who are settled in those Dorian lands, but this which I am about to say has regard not to all, but to the Lacedemonians alone: of these I say, first that it is not possible that they will ever accept your terms, which carry with them servitude for Hellas; and next I say that they will stand against you in fight, even if all the other Hellenes shall be of your party: and as for numbers, ask not how many they are, that they are able to do this; for whether it chances that a thousand of them have come out into the field, these will fight with you, or if there be less than this, or again if there be more."

103. Xerxes hearing this laughed, and said: "Demaratos, what a speech is this which you have uttered, saying that a thousand men will fight with this vast army! Come tell me this:—you say that you were yourself king of these men; will you therefore consent immediately to fight with ten men? and yet if your State is such throughout as you describe it, you their king ought by your laws to stand in array against double as many as another man;* that is to say, if each of them is a match for ten men of my army, I expect of you that you should be a match for twenty. Thus would be confirmed the report which is made by you: but if you, who boast thus greatly are such men and in size so great only as the Hellenes who come commonly to speech with me, yourself included, then beware lest this which has been spoken prove but an empty vaunt. For come, let me examine it by all that is probable: how could a thousand or ten thousand or even fifty thousand, at least if they were all equally free and were not ruled by one man, stand against so great an army? since, as you know, we shall be more than a thousand coming about each one of them, supposing them to be in number five thousand. If indeed they were ruled by one man after our fashion, they might perhaps from fear of him become braver than it was their nature to be, or they might go compelled by the lash to fight with greater numbers, being themselves fewer in number; but if left at liberty, they would do neither of these things: and I for my part suppose that, even if equally matched in numbers, the Hellenes would hardly dare to fight with the Persians taken alone. With us however this of which you speak is found in a few men, but rarely; for there are Persians of my spearmen who will consent to fight with three men of the Hellenes at once: but you have had no experience of these things and therefore you babble nonsense."

104. To this Demaratos replied: "O king, from the first I was sure that if I uttered the truth I should not speak that which was pleasing to you; since however you did compel me to speak the very truth, I told you of the matters which concern the Spartans. And yet how I am at this present time attached to them by affection you know better than any; seeing that first they took away from me the rank and privileges which came to me from

*The logic suits their doubled portions of food; compare 6.57.

my fathers, and then also they have caused me to be without native land and an exile; but your father took me up and gave me livelihood and a house to dwell in. Surely it is not to be supposed likely that the prudent man will thrust aside friendliness which is offered to him, but rather that he will accept it with full contentment. And I do not profess that I am able to fight either with ten men or with two, nay, if I had my will, I would not even fight with one;* but if there were necessity or if the cause which urged me to the combat were a great one, I would fight most willingly with one of these men who says that he is a match for three of the Hellenes. So also the Lacedemonians are not inferior to any men when fighting one by one, and they are the best of all men when fighting in a body: for though free, yet they are not free in all things, for over them is set Law as a master,† whom they fear much more even than your people fear you. It is certain at least that they do whatsoever that master commands; and he commands ever the same thing, that is to say, he bids them not flee out of battle from any multitude of men, but stay in their post and win the victory or lose their life. But if when I say these things I seem to you to be speaking rubbish, of other things for the future I prefer to be silent; and at this time I spake only because I was compelled. May it come to pass however according to your mind, O king."

105. He thus made answer, and Xerxes turned to laughter and felt no anger, but dismissed him with kindness. Then after he had conversed with him, and had appointed Mascames son of Megadostes to be governor at this place Doriscos, removing the governor who had been appointed by Dareios, Xerxes marched his army through Thrace to invade Hellas. 106. And Mascames, whom he left behind here, proved to be a man of such qualities that to him alone Xerxes used to send gifts, considering him the best of all the men whom either he himself or Dareios had appointed to be governors,—he used to send him gifts, I say, every year, and so also did Artoxerxes the son of Xerxes to the descendants of Mascames. For even before this march governors had been appointed in Thrace and everywhere about the Hellespont; and these all, both those in Thrace and in the Hellespont, were conquered by the Hellenes after this expedition, except only the one who was at Doriscos; but Mascames at Doriscos none were ever able to conquer, though many tried. For this reason the gifts are sent continually for him from the king who reigns over the Persians. 107. Of those however who were conquered by the Hellenes Xerxes did not consider any to be a good man except only Boges, who was at Eïon: him he never ceased commending, and he honoured very highly his children who survived him in the land of Persia. For in truth Boges proved himself worthy of great commendation, seeing that when he was besieged

---

*Herodotus here quietly undercuts the false image of Spartan belligerence at all levels.

†Only a genius would dare put his highest praise of some Greeks in the mouth of a traitor and exile.

by the Athenians under Kimon the son of Miltiades,* though he might
have gone forth under a truce and so returned home to Asia, he preferred
not to do this, for fear that the king should think that it was by cowardice
that he survived; and he continued to hold out till the last. Then when
there was no longer any supply of provisions within the wall, he heaped
together a great pyre, and he cut the throats of his children, his wife, his
concubines and his servants, and threw them into the fire; and after this he
scattered all the gold and silver in the city from the wall into the river Strymon, and having so done he threw himself into the fire. Thus he is justly
commended even to this present time by the Persians.

108. Xerxes from Doriscos was proceeding onwards to invade Hellas;
and as he went he compelled those who successively came in his way, to
join his march: for the whole country as far as Thessaly had been reduced
to subjection, as has been set forth by me before,† and was tributary under
the king, having been subdued by Megabazos and afterwards by Mardonios. And he passed in his march from Doriscos first by the Samothrakian
strongholds, of which situated furthest towards the West is a city called
Mesambria. Next to this follows Strymē, a city of the Thasians, and mid-
way between them flows the river Lisos, which at this time did not suffice
when supplying its water to the army of Xerxes, but the stream failed. This
country was in old time called Gallaïkē, but now Briantikē; however by
strict justice this also belongs to the Kikonians. **109.** Having crossed over
the bed of the river Lisos after it had been dried up, he passed by these
Hellenic cities, namely Maroneia, Dicaia and Abdera, and also the following lakes of note lying near them,—the Ismarian lake, lying between
Maroneia and Strymē; the Bistonian lake near Dicaia, into which two
rivers pour their waters, the Trauos and the Compsantos; and at Abdera no
lake indeed of any note was passed by Xerxes, but the river Nestos, which
flows there into the sea. Then after passing these places he went by the
[Thasian] cities of the mainland, near one of which there is, as it chances, a
lake of somewhere about three and one-half miles in circumference,
abounding in fish and very brackish; this the baggage-animals alone dried
up, being watered at it: and the name of this city is Pistyros. **110.** These
cities, I say, lying by the sea coast and belonging to Hellenes, he passed by,
leaving them on the left hand; and the tribes of Thracians through whose
country he marched were as follows, namely the Paitians, Kikonians, Bistonians, Sapaians, Dersaians, Edonians, Satrians. They who were settled
along the sea coast accompanied him with their ships, and those of them
who dwelt inland and have been enumerated by me, were compelled to
accompany him on land, except the Satrians: **111,** the Satrians however
never yet became obedient to any man, so far as we know, but they remain
up to my time still free, alone of all the Thracians; for they dwell in lofty
mountains, which are covered with forest of all kinds and with snow, and

---

*He was captured c.475 B.C.
†See 5.1, 5.26, and 6.44, for earlier European achievements.

also they are very skilful in war. They possess the Oracle of Dionysos on their most lofty mountains. Of the Satrians those who act as prophets of the temple are the Bessians; it is a prophetess who utters the oracles, as at Delphi, and nothing more bizarre.

112. Xerxes next after this passed the strongholds of the Pierians, of which the name of the one is Phagres and of the other Pergamos. He made his march, going close by the walls of these, and keeping Mount Pangaion on the right hand, which is both great and lofty and in which are mines both of gold and of silver possessed by the Pierians and Odomantians, and especially by the Satrians. **113.** Thus passing by the Paionians, Doberians and Paioplians, who dwell beyond Pangaion towards the North Wind, he went on Westwards, until at last he came to the river Strymon and the city of Eïon, of which, so long as he lived, Boges was commander, about whom I was speaking a short time back. This country about Mount Pangaion is called Phyllis, and it extends Westwards to the river Angites, which flows into the Strymon, and Southwards it stretches to the Strymon itself; and at this river the Magians sacrificed for good omens, slaying white horses. **114.** Having done this and many other things in addition to this, as charms for the river, at the Nine Ways in the land of the Edonians, they proceeded by the bridges, for they had found the Strymon already yoked with bridges; and being informed that this place was called the Nine Ways, they buried alive in it that number of boys and maidens, children of the natives of the place. Now burying alive is a Persian custom; for I am informed that Amestris also, the wife of Xerxes, when she had grown old, gave thanks for her own life to the god who is said to be beneath the earth by burying twice seven children of Persians who were men of renown.

115. As the army proceeded on its march from the Strymon, it found after this a sea-beach stretching westerly, and passed by a Hellenic city, Argilos. This region and that which lies above it is called Bisaltia. Thence, keeping on the left hand the gulf which lies off Posideion, he went through the plain which is called the plain of Syleus, passing by Stageiros a Hellenic city, and so came to Acanthos, taking with him as he went each one of these tribes and also of those who dwell about Mount Pangaion, just as he did those whom I enumerated before, having the men who dwelt along the sea coast to serve in the ships and those who dwelt inland to accompany him on foot. This road by which Xerxes the king marched his army, the Thracians do not disturb nor sow crops over, but pay very great reverence to it down to my own time. **116.** Then when he had come to Acanthos, Xerxes proclaimed a guest-friendship with the people of Acanthos and also presented them with the Median dress and commended them, perceiving that they were zealous to serve him in the war and hearing of that which had been dug. **117.** And while Xerxes was in Acanthos, it happened that he who had been set over the making of the channel, Artachaies by name, died of sickness, a man who was highly esteemed by Xerxes and belonged to the Achaimenid family; also he was in stature the tallest of all the Persians, eight feet in height, and he had a voice the loudest of all men; so that Xerxes was greatly grieved at the loss of him, and carried him forth

and buried him with great honour, and the whole army joined in building
a mound for him. To this Artachaies the Acanthians by the bidding of an
oracle do sacrifice as a hero, calling upon his name in worship.

118. Meanwhile the Hellenes who were entertaining his army and providing Xerxes with dinners had been brought to utter ruin, so that they
were being driven from house and home; seeing that when the Thasians,
for example, entertained the army of Xerxes and provided him with a dinner on behalf of their towns upon the mainland, Antipater the son of
Orgeus, who had been appointed for this purpose, a man of repute among
the citizens equal to the best, reported that four hundred talents* of silver
had been spent upon the dinner. **119.** Just so or nearly so in the other cities
also those who were set over the business reported the reckoning to be:
for the dinner was given as follows, having been ordered a long time beforehand, and being counted by them a matter of great importance:—In
the first place, so soon as they heard of it from the heralds who carried
round the proclamation, the citizens in the various cities distributed grain
among their several households, and all continued to make wheat and barley meal for many months; then they fed cattle, finding out and obtaining
the finest animals for a high price; and they kept birds both of the land and
of the water, in cages or in pools, all for the entertainment of the army.
Then again they had drinking-cups and mixing-bowls made of gold and of
silver, and all the other things which are placed upon the table: these were
made for the king himself and for those who ate at his table; but for the
rest of the army only the things appointed for food were provided. Then
whenever the army came to any place, there was a tent pitched ready
wherein Xerxes himself made his stay, while the rest of the army remained
out in the open air; and when it came to be time for dinner, then the en-
tertainers had labour; but the others, after they had been satiated with
food and had spent the night there, on the next day tore up the tent and
taking with them all the movable furniture proceeded on their march,
leaving nothing, but carrying all away with them. **120.** Then was uttered a
word well spoken by Megacreon, a man of Abdera, who advised those of
Abdera to go in a body, both themselves and their wives, to their temples,
and to sit down as suppliants of the gods, entreating them that for the future
also they would ward off from them the half of the evils which threatened;
and he bade them feel great thankfulness to the gods for the past events, because king Xerxes had not thought good to take food twice in each day; for
if it had been ordered to them beforehand to prepare breakfast also in like
manner as the dinner, it would have remained for the men of Abdera either
not to await the coming of Xerxes, or if they stayed, to be crushed by misfortune more than any other men upon the Earth.

121. They then, I say, though hard put to it, yet were performing that
which was appointed to them; and from Acanthos Xerxes, having commanded the generals to wait for the fleet at Therma, let the ships take their

---

*Nearly 23,000 pounds.

t im-
only,
had
and
often
nd is
n the
the
ould
the
be-

here;
a no
nia it
n the
their
were
ated,
cient

ssaly,
g in-
nnel,
there
out-
road
ne
as
l

self, (now this Therma is that which is situated on
which also this gulf has its name); and thus he did
d that this was the shortest way: for from Doriscos
rmy had been making its march thus:—Xerxes had
army into three divisions, and one of them he had
accompanying the fleet, of which division Mardo-
commanders; another third of the army had been
inland way, and of this the generals in command
l Gergis; and meanwhile the third of the divisions,
self went, marched in the middle between them,
commanders Smerdomenes and Megabyzos.
was let go by Xerxes and had sailed right through
os (which went across to the gulf on which are sit-
Piloros, Singos and Sartē), having taken up a con-
s also, sailed thence with a free course to the
ng round Ampelos the headland of Toronē, it left
ng Hellenic cities, from which it took up contin-
namely Toronē, Galepsos, Sermylē, Mekyberna,
called Sithonia. **123.** And the fleet of Xerxes, cut-
a d land of Ampelos to that of Canastron, which runs
all Pallenē, took up there contingents of ships and
Aphytis, Neapolis, Aigē, Therambo, Skionē, Mendē
are the cities which occupy the region which now is
was formerly called Phlegra. Then sailing along the
y also the fleet continued its course towards the place
entioned before, taking up contingents also from the
next after Pallenē and border upon the Thermaïc gulf;
them are these,—Lipaxos, Combreia, Lisai, Gigonos,
ineia; and the region in which these cities are is called
ent day Crossaia. Then sailing from Aineia, with which
list of the cities, at once the fleet came into the Thermaïc
region of Mygdonia, and so it arrived at the aforesaid
the cities of Sindos and Chalestra upon the river Axios.
e boundary between the land of Mygdonia and Bottiaia, of
the narrow region which lies on the sea coast is occupied by
hnai and Pella.
while his naval force was encamped about the river Axios
of Therma and the cities which lie between these two, waiting
ing of the king, Xerxes and the land-army were proceeding
thos, cutting through the middle by the shortest way with a
aching Therma: and he was proceeding through Paionia and
to the river Cheidoros, which beginning from the land of the
ns, runs through the region of Mygdonia and comes out along-
e marsh which is by the river Axios. **125.** As he was proceeding,
cked the camels which carried his provisions; for the lions used
down regularly by night, leaving their own haunts, but they
nothing else, neither beast of burden nor man, but killed the

camels only: and I marvel what was the cause, and what it was tha
pelled the lions to abstain from all else and to attack the camels
creatures which they had never seen before, and of which they ha
no experience. **126.** Now there are in these parts both many lion
also wild oxen, those that have the very large horns which are
brought into Hellas: and the limit within which these lions are fo
on the one side the river Nestos, which flows through Abdera, and (
other the Acheloös, which flows through Acarnania; for neither
East of the Nestos, in any part of Europe before you come to this,
you see a lion, nor again in the remaining part of the continent
West of the Acheloös, but they are produced in the middle spa
tween these rivers.

127. When Xerxes had reached Therma he established the army
and his army encamping there occupied of the land along by the
less than this,—beginning from the city of Therma and from Mygd
extended as far as the river Lydias and the Haliacmon, which fo
boundary between the lands of Bottiaia and Macedonia, minglin;
waters together in one and the same stream. The Barbarians, I sa
encamped in these regions; and of the rivers which have been enume
only the river Cheidoros flowing from the Crestonian land was insu
for the drinking of the army and failed in its stream.

128. Then Xerxes seeing from Therma the mountains of Th
Olympos and Ossa, that they were of very great height, and be
formed that in the midst between them there was a narrow cl
through which flows the Peneios, and hearing also that by this wa
was a road leading to Thessaly, desired to sail thither and look at t
let of the Peneios, because he was meaning to march by the uppe
through the land of the Macedonians who dwell inland, until he c
the Perraibians, passing by the city of Gonnos; for by this way he
formed that it was safest to go. And so he proceeded; he embark
Sidonian ship, the same in which he always embarked when he wi
do anything of this kind, and he displayed a signal for the others
out to sea also, leaving there the land-army. Then when Xerx
looked at the outlet of the Peneios, he marvelled greatly, and sumn
his guides he asked them whether it was possible to turn the rive
and bring it out to the sea by another way. **129.** Now it is said tha
saly was in old time a lake, being enclosed on all sides by very lofty
tains: for the parts of it which lie towards the East are shut in
ranges of Pelion and Ossa, which join one another in their lower
the parts towards the North by Olympos, those towards the West
dos and those towards the mid-day and the South by Othrys; and
gion in the midst, between these mountains which have been na
Thessaly, forming as it were a hollow. Whereas then many rivers fl
it and among them these five of most note, namely Peneios, Ap
Onochonos, Enipeus and Pamisos, these, which collect their wate
the mountains that enclose Thessaly round, and flow into this plai
their outflow to the sea by one channel and that a narrow one, fir

gling their waters all together in one and the same stream; and so soon as they are mingled together, from that point onwards the Peneios causes the others to lose their separate names. And it is said that in ancient time, there not being yet this channel and outflow between the mountains, these rivers, and besides these rivers the lake Boibeïs also, had no names as they have now, though they flowed just as much as they do now, but by their waters they made Thessaly to be all sea. The Thessalians themselves say that Poseidon made the channel through which the Peneios flows; and reasonably they report it thus, because whosoever believes that it is Poseidon who shakes the Earth and that the partings asunder produced by earthquake are the work of this god, would say, if he saw this, that it was made by Poseidon; for the parting asunder of the mountains is the work of an earthquake, as is evident to me. **130.** So the guides, when Xerxes asked whether there was any other possible outlet to the sea for the Peneios, said with exact knowledge of the truth: "O king, for this river there is no other outgoing which extends to the sea, but this alone; for all Thessaly is circled about with mountains as with a crown." To this Xerxes is said to have replied: "The Thessalians then are prudent men. They long ago protected themselves by giving way, realizing that they had a country which, it appears, is easy to conquer and may quickly be taken: for it would have been necessary only to let the river flow over their land by making an embankment to keep it from going through the narrow channel and so diverting the course by which now it flows, in order to put all Thessaly under water except the mountains." This he said in reference to the sons of Aleuas, because they, being Thessalians, were the first of the Hellenes to join the king;* for Xerxes thought that they offered him friendship on behalf of their whole nation. Having said thus and having looked at the place, he sailed back to Therma.

131. He then was staying in the region of Pieria many days, for the road over the mountains of Macedonia was being cut meanwhile by a third part of his army, that all the host might pass over by this way into the land of the Perraibians: and now the heralds returned who had been sent to Hellas to demand the gift of earth, some empty-handed and others bearing earth and water. **132.** And among those who gave that which was demanded were the following, namely the Thessalians, Dolopians, Enianians, Perraibians, Locrians, Magnesians, Malians, Achaians of Phthiotis, and Thebans, with the rest of the Bœotians also excepting the Thespians and Plataians. Against these the Hellenes who took up war with the Barbarian made an oath; and the oath was this,†—that whosoever being Hellenes had given themselves over to the Persian, not being compelled, these, if their own affairs should come to a good conclusion, they would dedicate as an offering to the god at Delphi. **133.** Thus ran the oath which was taken by the Hellenes.

---

*There is some conflict here with 7.174, but compare 7.6.
†An inscription of doubtful authenticity records this oath; see Fornara 57.

Xerxes however had not sent to Athens or to Sparta heralds to demand the gift of earth,* and for this reason, namely because at the former time when Dareios had sent for this very purpose, the one people threw the men who made the demand into the pit† and the others into a well, and bade them take from thence earth and water and bear them to the king. For this reason Xerxes did not send men to make this demand. And what evil thing came upon the Athenians for having done this to the heralds, I am not able to say, except indeed that their land and city were laid waste; but I do not think that this happened for that cause: **134,** on the Lacedemonians however the wrath fell of Talthybios, the herald of Agamemnon; for in Sparta there is a temple of Talthybios, and there are also descendants of Talthybios called Talthybiads, to whom have been given as a right all the missions of heralds which go from Sparta; and after this event it was not possible for the Spartans when they sacrificed to obtain favourable omens. This was the case with them for a long time; and as the Lacedemonians were grieved and regarded it as a great misfortune, and general assemblies were repeatedly gathered together and proclamation made, asking if any one of the Lacedemonians was willing to die for Sparta, at length Sperthias the son of Aneristos and Bulis the son of Nicolaos, Spartans of noble birth and in wealth attaining to the first rank, voluntarily submitted to pay the penalty to Xerxes for the heralds of Dareios which had perished at Sparta. Thus the Spartans sent these to the Medes to be put to death.

135. And not only the courage then shown by these men is worthy of admiration, but also the following sayings in addition: for as they were on their way to Susa they came to Hydarnes (now Hydarnes was a Persian by race and commander of those who dwelt on the sea coasts of Asia), and he offered them hospitality and entertained them; and while they were his guests he asked them as follows: "Lacedemonians, why is it that you flee from becoming friends to the king? for you may see that the king knows how to honour good men, when you look at me and at my fortunes. So also you, Lacedemonians, if you gave yourselves to the king, since you have the reputation with him already of being good men, would have rule over Hellenic land by the gift of the king." To this they made answer thus: "Hydarnes, your counsel with regard to us is not based on experience, for you give counsel having made trial indeed of the one thing, but being without experience of the other: you know well what it is to be a slave, but you have never yet made trial of freedom, whether it is pleasant to the taste or no; for if you should make trial of it, you would then counsel us to fight for it not with spears only but also with any blade." **136.** Thus they answered Hydarnes; and then, after they had gone up to Susa and had come into the presence of the king, first when the spearmen of the guard commanded them and endeavoured to compel them by force to do obeisance to the

---

*See 6.48.
†The Athenian place of public execution; see 6.48 for Dareios' earlier demand.

king by falling down before him,* they said that they would not do any such deed, though they should be pushed down by them head foremost; for it was not their custom to do obeisance to a man, and it was not for this that they had come. Then when they had resisted this, next they spoke these words or words to this effect: "O king of the Medes, the Lacedemonians sent us in place of the heralds who were slain in Sparta, to pay the penalty for their lives." When they said this, Xerxes moved by a spirit of magnanimity replied that he would not be like the Lacedemonians; for they had violated the rules which prevailed among all men by slaying heralds, but he would not do that himself which he blamed them for having done, nor would he free the Lacedemonians from their guilt by slaying these in return. **137.** Thus the wrath of Talthybios ceased for the time being, even though the Spartans had done no more than this and although Sperthias and Bulis returned back to Sparta; but a long time after this it was roused again during the war between the Peloponnesians and Athenians, as the Lacedemonians report. This I believe to have been most supernatural: for in that the wrath of Talthybios fell upon messengers and did not cease until it had been fully satisfied, so much was but in accordance with justice; but that it happened to come upon the sons of these men who went up to the king on account of the wrath, namely upon Nicolaos the son of Bulis and Aneristos the son of Sperthias (the same who conquered the men of Halieis, who came from Tiryns, by sailing into their harbour with a merchant ship filled with fighting men),—by this it is evident to me that the matter came to pass by supernatural plan. For these men, sent by the Lacedemonians as envoys to Asia, having been betrayed by Sitalkes the son of Teres king of the Thracians and by Nymphodoros the son of Pythes a man of Abdera, were captured at Bisanthē on the Hellespont;† and then having been carried away to Attica they were put to death by the Athenians, and with them also Aristeas the son of Adeimantos the Corinthian. These things happened many years after the expedition of the king; and I return now to the former narrative.

138. Now the march of the king's army was in name against Athens, but in fact it was going against all Hellas: and the Hellenes being informed of this long before were not all equally affected by it; for some of them having given earth and water to the Persian had confidence, supposing that they would suffer no hurt from the Barbarian; while others not having given were in great terror, seeing that there were not ships existing in Hellas which were sufficient in number of receiving the invader in fight, and seeing that the greater part of the States were not willing to take up the war, but adopted readily the side of the Medes.

---

*The standard greeting for any superior, as 1.134 states.
†The Spartan ambassadors were captured in 430 B.C.; this is one of the latest events recorded in the *Histories*. See also the references to Delos at 6.98, Cythera at 7.235, and Deceleia at 9.73 for mention of other events in the later Peloponnesian War.

139. And here I am compelled by necessity to declare an opinion which in the eyes of most men will seem to be invidious, but nevertheless I will not abstain from saying that which I see evidently to be the truth.[*] If the Athenians had been seized with fear of the danger which threatened them and had left their land, or again, without leaving their land, had stayed and given themselves up to Xerxes, none would have made any attempt by sea to oppose the king. If then none had opposed Xerxes by sea, it would have happened on the land somewhat thus:—even if many mail-coated walls had been thrown across the Isthmus by the Peloponnesians, the Lacedemonians would have been deserted by their allies, not voluntarily but of necessity, since these would have been conquered city after city by the naval force of the Barbarian, and so they would have been left alone: and having been left alone and having displayed great deeds of valour, they would have met their death nobly. Either they would have suffered this fate, or before this, seeing the other Hellenes also taking the side of the Medes, they would have made an agreement with Xerxes; and thus in either case Hellas would have come to be under the rule of the Persians: for as to the good to be got from the walls thrown across the Isthmus, I am unable to discover what it would have been, when the king had command of the sea. As it is however, if a man should say that the Athenians proved to be the saviours of Hellas, he would not fail to hit the truth; for to whichever side these turned, to that the balance was likely to incline: and these were they who, preferring that Hellas should continue to exist in freedom, roused up all of Hellas which remained, so much, that is, as had not gone over to the Medes, and (after the gods at least) these were they who repelled the king. Nor did fearful oracles, which came from Delphi and cast them into dread, induce them to leave Hellas, but they stayed behind and endured to receive the invader of their land. **140.** For the Athenians had sent men to Delphi to inquire and were preparing to consult the Oracle; and after these had performed the usual rites in the sacred precincts, when they had entered the sanctuary and were sitting down there, the Pythian prophetess, whose name was Aristonikē, uttered to them this oracle:

> "Why do ye sit, ye wretched? Flee to the uttermost limits,
> Leaving your home and the heights of the wheel-round city behind you!
> Lo, there remaineth now nor the head nor the body in safety,—
> Neither the feet below nor the hands nor the middle are left thee,—
> All are destroyed together; for fire and the passionate War-god,
> Urging the Assyrian car to speed, hurl them to ruin.
> Not thine alone, he shall cause many more great strongholds to perish,
> Yea, many temples of gods to the ravening fire shall deliver,—

---

[*]Herodotus' analysis of alternative outcomes is noteworthy and sound; his reluctance reflects the unpopularity of the Athenian Empire in his own day.

Temples which stand now surely with sweat of their terror down-
   streaming,
Quaking with dread; and lo! from the topmost roof to the pavement
Dark blood trickles, forecasting the dire unavoidable evil.
Forth with you, forth from the shrine, and steep your soul in the
   sorrow!"

141. Hearing this the men who had been sent by the Athenians to consult the Oracle were very greatly distressed: and as they were despairing
by reason of the evil which had been prophesied to them, Timon the son of
Androbulos, a man of the Delphians in reputation equal to the first, counselled them to take a suppliant's bough and to approach the second time
and consult the Oracle as suppliants. The Athenians did as he advised and
said: "Lord, we pray you utter to us some better oracle about our native
land, having respect to these suppliant boughs which we have come to you
bearing; otherwise surely we will not depart away from the sanctuary, but
will remain here where we are now, even until we bring our lives to an
end." when they spoke these words, the prophetess gave them a second oracle as follows:

"Pallas cannot prevail to appease great Zeus in Olympos,
   Though she with words very many and wiles close-woven entreat
      him.
   But I will tell thee this more, and will clench it with steel adamantine:
   Then when all else shall be taken, whatever the boundary of Kecrops
   Holdeth within, and the dark ravines of divinest Kithairon,
   A bulwark of wood at the last Zeus grants to the Trito-born goddess
   Sole to remain unwasted, which thee and thy children shall profit.
   Stay not there for the horsemen to come and the footmen
      unnumbered;
   Stay not still for the host from the mainland to come, but retire
      thee,
   Turning thy back to the foe, for yet thou shall face him hereafter.
   Salamis, the divine, thou shalt cause sons of women to perish,
   Either when the grain is scattered or when it is gathered together."

142. This seemed to them to be (as in truth it was) a milder utterance than
the former one; therefore they had it written down and departed with it to
Athens: and when the messengers after their return made report to the
people, many various opinions were expressed by persons inquiring into
the meaning of the oracle, and among them these, standing most in opposition to one another:—some of the elder men said they thought that the god
had prophesied to them that the Acropolis should survive; for the Acropolis
of the Athenians was in old time fenced with a thorn hedge; and they
conjectured accordingly that this saying about the "bulwark of wood" referred to the fence: others on the contrary said that the god meant by this
their ships, and they advised to leave all else and get ready these. Now they

who said that the ships were the bulwark of wood were shaken in their interpretation by the two last verses which the prophetess uttered:

"Salamis, the divine, thou shalt cause sons of women to perish,
Either when the grain is scattered or when it is gathered together."

In reference to these verses the opinions of those who said that the ships were the bulwark of wood were disturbed; for the interpreters of oracles took these to mean that it was fated for them, having got ready for a sea-fight, to suffer defeat round about Salamis. **143.** Now there was one man of the Athenians who had lately been coming forward to take a place among the first, whose name was Themistocles, called son of Neocles. This man said that the interpreters of oracles did not make right conjecture of the whole, and he spoke as follows, saying that if these words that had been uttered referred really to the Athenians, he did not think it would have been so mildly expressed in the oracle, but rather thus, "Salamis, the merciless," instead of "Salamis, the divine," at least if its settlers were destined to perish round about it: but in truth the oracle had been spoken by the god with reference to the enemy, if one understood it rightly, and not to the Athenians: therefore he counselled them to get ready to fight a battle by sea, for in this was their bulwark of wood. When Themistocles declared his opinion thus, the Athenians judged that this was to be preferred by them rather than the advice of the interpreters of oracles, who bade them not make ready for a sea-fight, nor in short raise their hands at all in opposition, but leave the land of Attica and settle in some other.*

144. Another opinion too of Themistocles before this one proved the best at the right moment, when the Athenians, having got large sums of money in the public treasury, which had come in to them from the mines which are at Laureion, were intending to share it among themselves, taking each in turn the sum of ten drachmas. Then Themistocles persuaded the Athenians to give up this plan of division and to make for themselves with this money two hundred ships for the war, meaning by that the war with the Eginetans: for this war proved in fact the salvation of Hellas at that time, by compelling the Athenians to become a naval power. And the ships, not having been used for the purpose for which they had been made, thus proved of service to Hellas at need. These ships the Athenians had already, having built them beforehand, and it was necessary to construct others. They resolved then, when they took counsel after the oracle was given, to receive the Barbarian invading Hellas with their ships in full force, following the commands of the god, in combination with those of the Hellenes who were willing to join them.

145. These oracles had been given before to the Athenians: and when

---

*A decree of contested authenticity and date offers details and some conflicting information; see Fornara 55.

those Hellenes who had the better mind about Hellas came together to one place,* and considered their affairs and interchanged assurances with one another, then deliberating together they thought it well first to reconcile the enmities and bring to an end the wars which they had with one another. Now there were wars engaged between others also, but the greatest was between the Athenians and the Eginetans. After this, being informed that Xerxes was with his army at Sardis, they determined to send spies to Asia to make observation of the power of the king; and moreover they resolved to send envoys to Argos to form an alliance against the Persian, and to send others to Sicily to Gelon the son of Deinomenes and also to Corcyra, to urge them to come to the assistance of Hellas, and others again to Crete; for they made it their aim that if possible the Hellenic race might unite in one, and that they might join all together and act towards the same end, since dangers were threatening all the Hellenes equally. The power of Gelon was said to be great, far greater than any other Hellenic power.

146. When they had thus resolved, they reconciled their enmities and then sent first three men as spies to Asia. These having come to Sardis and having got knowledge about the king's army, were discovered, and after having been examined by the generals of the land-army were being led off to die. For these men, I say, death was the sentence; but Xerxes, being informed of this, found fault with the decision of the generals and sent some of the spearmen of his guard, enjoining them, if they should find the spies yet alive, to bring them to his presence. So having found them yet surviving they brought them into the presence of the king; and upon that Xerxes, being informed for what purpose they had come, commanded the spearmen to lead them round and to show them the whole army both foot and horse, and when they should have had their fill of looking at these things, to let them go unhurt to whatsoever land they desired. **147.** Such was the command which he gave, saying that if the spies had been put to death, the Hellenes would not have been informed beforehand of his power, how far beyond description it was; while on the other hand by putting to death three men they would not very greatly have damaged the enemy; but when these returned back to Hellas, he thought it likely that the Hellenes, hearing of his power, would deliver up their peculiar freedom to him themselves, before the expedition took place which was being set in motion; and thus there would be no need for them to have the labour of marching an army against them. This opinion of his is like his manner of thinking at other times; for when Xerxes was in Abydos, he saw vessels which carried grain from the Pontus sailing out through the Hellespont on their way to Egina and the Peloponnese. Those then who sat by his side, being informed that the ships belonged to the enemy, were prepared to capture them, and were looking to the king to see when he would give the word; but Xerxes asked about them whither the men were sailing, and they replied: "Master, to your foes, conveying to them grain": he then made answer and said: "Are we not also sailing to the same place as these

---

*At Corinth in 481 B.C.

men, furnished with grain as well as with other things necessary? How then do these wrong us, since they are conveying provisions for our use?"

148. The spies then, having thus looked at everything and after that having been dismissed, returned back to Europe: and meanwhile those of the Hellenes who had sworn alliance against the Persian, after the dispatch of the spies proceeded to send envoys next to Argos. Now the Argives report that the matters concerning themselves took place as follows:—They were informed, they say, at the very first of the movement which was being set on foot by the Barbarian against Hellas; and having been informed of this and perceiving that the Hellenes would endeavour to get their alliance against the Persian, they had sent messengers to inquire of the god at Delphi, and to ask how they should act in order that it might be best for themselves: because lately there had been slain of them six thousand men by the Lacedemonians and by Cleomenes the son of Anaxandrides,* and this in fact was the reason that they were sending to inquire: and when they inquired, the Pythian prophetess made answer to them as follows:

> "Thou to thy neighbours a foe, by the gods immortal beloved,
>   Keep thy spear within bounds, and sit well-guarded behind it :
>   Guard well the head, and the head shall preserve the limbs and the
>   body."

Thus, they say, the Pythian prophetess had replied to them before this; and afterwards when the messengers of the Hellenes came, as I said, to Argos, they entered the Council-chamber and spoke that which had been enjoined to them; and to that which was said the Council replied that the Argives were ready to do as they were requested, on condition that they got peace made with the Lacedemonians for thirty years and that they had half the leadership of the whole confederacy: and yet by strict right (they said) the - whole leadership fell to their share, but nevertheless it was sufficient for them to have half. **149.** Thus they report that the Council made answer, although the oracle forbade them to make the alliance with the Hellenes; and they were anxious, they say, that a truce from hostilities for thirty years should be made, although they feared the oracle, in order, as they allege, that their sons might grow to manhood in these years; whereas if a truce did not exist, they had fear that, supposing another disaster should come upon them in fighting against the Persian in addition to that which had befallen them already, they might be for all future time subject to the Lacedemonians. To the Council's response those of the envoys who were of Sparta replied, that as to the truce they would refer the matter to their public assembly, but as to the leadership they had themselves been commissioned to make reply, and did in fact say this, namely that they had two kings, while the Argives had one; and it was not possible to remove either of the two who were of Sparta from the leadership, but there was nothing to prevent the Argive king from

---

*At 6.77, Herodotus recounts the battle of Sepeia, about 14 years earlier.

having an equal vote with each of their two. Then, say the Argives, they could not endure the grasping selfishness of the Spartans, but chose to be ruled by the Barbarians rather than to yield at all to the Lacedemonians; and they gave notice to the envoys to depart out of the territory of the Argives before sunset, or, if not, they would be dealt with as enemies.

150. The Argives themselves report so much about these matters: but there is another story reported in Hellas to the effect that Xerxes sent a herald to Argos before he set forth to make an expedition against Hellas, and this herald, they say, when he had come, spoke as follows: "Men of Argos, king Xerxes says to you these things:—We hold that Perses, from whom we are descended, was the son of Perseus, the son of Danaē, and was born of the daughter of Kepheus, Andromeda; and according to this it would seem that we are descended from you. It is not fitting then that we should go forth on an expedition against those from whom we trace our descent, nor that you should set yourselves in opposition to us by rendering assistance to others; but it is fitting that you keep still and remain by yourselves: for if things happen according to my mind, I shall not esteem any people to be of greater consequence than you." Having heard this the Argives, it is said, considered it a great matter; and therefore at first they made no offer of help nor did they ask for any share; but afterwards, when the Hellenes tried to get them on their side, then, since they knew well that the Lacedemonians would not give them a share in the command, they asked for this merely in order that they might have a pretext for remaining still. **151.** Also some of the Hellenes report that the following event, in agreement with this account, came to pass many years after these things:—there happened, they say, to be in Susa the city of Memnon* envoys of the Athenians come about some other matter, namely Callias the son of Hipponicos and the others who went up with him; and the Argives at that very time had also sent envoys to Susa, and these asked Artoxerxes the son of Xerxes, whether the friendship which they had formed with Xerxes still remained unbroken, if they themselves desired to maintain it, or whether they were esteemed by him to be enemies; and king Artoxerxes said that it most certainly remained unbroken, and that there was no city which he considered to be more his friend than Argos. **152.** Now whether Xerxes did indeed send a herald to Argos saying that which has been reported, and whether envoys of the Argives who had gone up to Susa inquired of Artoxerxes concerning friendship, I am not able to say for certain; nor do I declare any opinion about the matters in question other than that which the Argives themselves report: but I know this much, that if all the nations of men should bring together into one place the evils which they have suffered themselves, desiring to make exchange with their neighbours, each people of them, when they had examined closely the evils suffered by their fellows,

---

*See 5.53 on the name; 9.12 on Argive collaboration; and 1.82 on the Argive—Spartan contention. The Athenians may have made a treaty with Persia c.450 B.C., to which an allusion appears here.

would gladly carry away back with them those which they had brought. Thus not even the Argives have done the worst. I however am bound to report that which is reported, though I am not bound altogether to believe it; and let this saying be considered to hold good as regards every narrative in the history:* for I must add that this also is reported, namely that the Argives were actually those who invited the Persian to invade Hellas, because their war with the Lacedemonians had had an evil issue, being willing to suffer anything whatever rather than the trouble then upon them.

153. Meanwhile envoys had come to Sicily from the allies, to confer with Gelon, among whom was also Syagros from the Lacedemonians. Now the ancestor of this Gelon, he who was at Gela as a settler, was a native of the island of Telos, which lies off Triopion; and when Gela was founded by the Lindians of Rhodes and by Antiphemos, he was not left behind. Then in course of time his descendants became and continued to be priests of the mysteries of the Earth goddesses, an office which was acquired by Telines one of their ancestors in the following manner:—certain of the men of Gela, being worsted in a party struggle, had fled to Mactorion, the city which stands above Gela: these men Telines brought back to Gela from exile with no force of men but only with the sacred rites of these goddesses; but from whom he received them, or whether he obtained them for himself, this I am not able to say; trusting in these however, he brought the men back from exile, on the condition that his descendants should be priests of the mysteries of the goddesses. To me it has caused wonder also that Telines should have been able to perform so great a deed, considering that which I am told; for such deeds, I think, are not apt to proceed from every man, but from one who has a brave spirit and manly vigour, whereas Telines is said by the dwellers in Sicily to have been on the contrary a man of effeminate character and rather poor spirit.

154. He then had thus obtained the privilege of which I speak: and when Cleander the son of Pantares brought his life to an end, having been despot of Gela for seven years and being killed at last by Sabyllos a man of Gela, then Hippocrates succeeded to the monarchy, who was brother of Cleander. And while Hippocrates was despot, Gelon, who was a descendant of Telines the priest of the mysteries, was spearman of the guard to Hippocrates with many others and Ainesidemos the son of Pataicos. Then after no long time he was appointed by reason of valour to be commander of the whole cavalry; for when Hippocrates besieged successively the cities of Callipolis, Naxos, Zanclē, Leontini, and also Syracuse and many towns of the Barbarians, in these wars Gelon showed himself a most brilliant warrior; and of the cities which I just now mentioned, not one except Syracuse escaped being reduced to subjection by Hippocrates: the Syracusans however, after they had been defeated in battle at the river Eloros, were rescued by the Corinthians and Corcyreans; these rescued them and brought the quarrel to a settlement on this condition, namely that the

---

*A caveat that many critics ignore or forget.

Syracusans should deliver up Camarina to Hippocrates. Now Camarina used in ancient time to belong to the men of Syracuse.

155. Then when it was the fate of Hippocrates also, after having been despot for the same number of years as his brother Cleander, to be killed at the city of Hybla, whither he had gone on an expedition against the Sikelians, then Gelon made a pretence of helping the sons of Hippocrates, Eucleides and Cleander, when the citizens were no longer willing to submit; but actually, when he had been victorious in a battle over the men of Gela, he robbed the sons of Hippocrates of the power and was ruler himself. After this stroke of fortune Gelon restored those of the Syracusans who were called "land-holders," after they had been driven into exile by the common people and by their own slaves, who were called Kyllyrians, these, I say, he restored from the city of Casmenē to Syracuse, and so got possession of this last city also, for the common people of Syracuse, when Gelon came against them, delivered up to him their city and themselves. **156.** So after he had received Syracuse into his power,* he made less account of Gela, of which he was ruler also in addition, and he gave it in charge to Hieron his brother, while he proceeded to strengthen Syracuse; and Syracuse was for him the place of sole importance. So immediately that city rose and shot up to prosperity; for in the first place he brought all those of Camarina to Syracuse and made them citizens, and razed to the ground the city of Camarina; then secondly he did the same to more than half of the men of Gela, as he had done to those of Camarina: and as regards the Megarians of Sicily, when they were besieged and had surrendered by capitulation, the well-to-do men of them, though they had stirred up war with him and expected to be put to death for this reason, he brought to Syracuse and made them citizens, but the common people of the Megarians, who had no share in the guilt of this war and did not expect that they would suffer any evil, these also he brought to Syracuse and sold them as slaves to be carried away from Sicily: and the same thing he did moreover to the men of Euboia in Sicily, making a distinction between them: and he dealt thus with these two cities because he thought that a body of commons was a most unpleasant element in the State.

157. In the manner then which has been described Gelon had become a powerful despot; and at this time when the envoys of the Hellenes had arrived at Syracuse, they spoke to him as follows: "The Lacedemonians and their allies sent us to get you to be on our side against the Barbarian; for we suppose that you are certainly informed of him who is about to invade Hellas, namely that a Persian is designing to bridge over the Hellespont, and to make an expedition against Hellas, leading against us out of Asia all the armies of the East, under colour of marching upon Athens, but in fact meaning to bring all Hellas to subjection under him. Therefore, seeing that you have attained to a great power and have no small portion of Hellas for your share, being the ruler of Sicily, come to the assistance of those who are

---

*Gelon was despot of Syracuse 485–478 B.C.

endeavouring to free Hellas, and join in making her free; for if all Hellas be gathered together in one, it forms a great body, and we are made a match in fight for those who are coming against us; but if some of us go over to the enemy and others are not willing to help, and the sound portion of Hellas is consequently small, there is at once in this a danger that all Hellas may fall to ruin. For do not hope that if the Persian shall overcome us in battle he will not come to you, but guard yourself against this beforehand; for in coming to our assistance you are helping yourself; and the matter which is wisely planned has for the most part a good issue afterwards." **158.** The envoys spoke thus; and Gelon was very vehement with them, speaking to them as follows: "Hellenes, a selfish speech is this, with which you have ventured to come and invite me to be your ally against the Barbarian; whereas you yourselves, when I in former time requested of you to join with me in fighting against an army of Barbarians, contention having arisen between me and the Carthaginians, and when I charged you to exact vengeance of the men of Egesta for the death of Dorieus the son of Anaxandrides,* while at the same time I offered to help in setting free the trading-places, from which great advantages and gains have been reaped by you,—you, I say, then neither for my own sake came to my assistance, nor in order to exact vengeance for the death of Dorieus; and, so far as you are concerned, all these parts are even now under the rule of Barbarians. But since it turned out well for us and came to a better issue, now that the war has come round and reached you, there has at last arisen in your minds a recollection of Gelon. However, though I have met with contempt at your hands, I will not act like you; but I am prepared to come to your assistance, supplying two hundred triremes and twenty thousand hoplites, with two thousand horsemen, two thousand bowmen, two thousand slingers and two thousand light-armed men to run beside the horsemen; and moreover I will undertake to supply grain for the whole army of the Hellenes, until we shall have finished the war. These things I engage to supply on this condition, namely that I shall be commander and leader of the Hellenes against the Barbarian; but on any other condition I will neither come myself nor will I send others."

159. Hearing this Syagros could not contain himself but spoke these words: "Deeply would Agamemnon son of Pelops lament,† if he heard that the Spartans had had the leadership taken away from them by Gelon and by the Syracusans. Nay, but make no further mention of this condition, namely that we should deliver the leadership to you; but if you are desirous to come to the assistance of Hellas, know that you will be under the command of the Lacedemonians; and if you do indeed claim not to be under command, come not to our help at all."

160. To this Gelon, seeing that the speech of Syagros was adverse, set forth to them his last proposal thus: "Stranger from Sparta, reproaches

---

*See 5.44–46, on the Spartan disaster.

†See, for the original referent of Syagros' allusion, *Iliad* 7.125, the hexameter in full where Nestor speaks of the advice of Peleus, Achilles' father.

sinking into the heart of a man are wont to rouse his spirit in anger against them; you however, though you have uttered insults against me in your speech, will not bring me to show myself unseemly in my reply. But whereas you so strongly lay claim to the leadership, it were fitting that I should lay claim to it more than you, seeing that I am the leader of an army many times as large and of ships many more. Since however this condition is so distasteful to you, we will recede somewhat from our former proposal. Suppose that you should be leaders of the land-army and I of the fleet; or if it pleases you to lead the sea-forces, I am willing to be leader of those on land; and either you must be contented with these terms or go away without the alliance which I have to give."

161. Gelon, I say, made these offers; and the envoy of the Athenians, answering before that of the Lacedemonians, replied to him as follows: "O king of the Syracusans, it was not of a leader that Hellas was in want when it sent us to you, but of an army. You however do not set before us the hope that you will send an army, except you have the leadership of Hellas; and you are striving how you may become commander of the armies of Hellas. So long then as it was your demand to be leader of the whole army of the Hellenes, it was sufficient for us Athenians to keep silence, knowing that the Lacedemonian would be able to make defence even for us both; but now, since being repulsed from the demand for the whole you are requesting to be commander of the naval force, we tell you that thus it is:—not even if the Lacedemonian shall permit you to be commander of it, will we permit you; for this at least is our own, if the Lacedemonians do not themselves desire to have it. With these, if they desire to be the leaders, we do not contend; but none others beside ourselves shall we permit to be in command of the ships: for then to no purpose should we be possessors of a sea-force larger than any other which belongs to the Hellenes, if, being Athenians, we should yield the leadership to Syracusans, we who boast of a race which is the most ancient of all and who are of all the Hellenes the only people who have not changed from one land to another; to whom also belonged a man who Homer the Epic poet said was the best of all who came to Ilion in drawing up an army and setting it in array.* Thus we are not justly to be reproached if we say these things." **162.** To this Gelon made answer thus: "Stranger of Athens, it would seem that you have the commanders, but that you will not have the men to be commanded. Since then you will not at all give way, but desire to have the whole, it were well that you should depart home as quickly as possible and report to the Hellenes that the spring has been taken out of their year." Now this is the meaning of the saying:—evidently the spring is the noblest part of the year; and so he meant to say that his army was the noblest part of the army of the Hellenes: for Hellas therefore, deprived of his alliance, it was, he said, as if the spring had been taken out of the year.

163. The envoys of the Hellenes, having thus had conference with

---

*See *Iliad* 2.552, the 'catalogue of ships'.

Gelon, sailed away; and Gelon upon this, fearing on the one hand about the Hellenes, lest they should not be able to overcome the Barbarian, and on the other hand considering it monstrous and not to be endured that he should come to Peloponnesus and be under the command of the Lacedemonians, seeing that he was despot of Sicily, gave up the thought of this way and followed another: for so soon as he was informed that the Persian had crossed over the Hellespont, he sent Cadmos the son of Skythes, a man of Cos, with three fifty-oared galleys to Delphi, bearing large sums of money and friendly proposals, to wait there and see how the battle would fall out: and if the Barbarian should be victorious, he was to give him the money and also to offer him earth and water from those over whom Gelon had rule; but if the Hellenes should be victorious, he was bidden to bring it back. **164.** Now this Cadmos before these events, having received from his father in a prosperous state the government of the people of Cos, had voluntarily and with no danger threatening, but moved merely by uprightness of nature, placed the government in the hands of the people of Cos and had departed to Sicily, where he took from the Samians and newly colonised the city of Zanclē, which had changed its name to Messenē. This same Cadmos, having come thither in such manner as I have said, Gelon was now sending, having selected him on account of the integrity which in other matters he had himself found to be in him; and this man, in addition to the other upright acts which had been done by him, left also this to be remembered, not the least of them: for having got into his hands that great sum of money which Gelon entrusted to his charge, though he might have taken possession of it himself he did not choose to do so; but when the Hellenes had got the better in the sea-fight and Xerxes had marched away and departed, he also returned to Sicily bringing back with him the whole sum of money.

165. The story which here follows is also reported by those who dwell in Sicily, namely that, even though he was to be under the command of the Lacedemonians, Gelon would have come to the assistance of the Hellenes, but that Terillos, the son of Crinippos and despot of Himera, having been driven out of Himera by Theron the son of Ainesidemos the ruler of the Agrigentines, was just at this very time bringing in an army of Phenicians, Libyans, Iberians, Ligurians, Elisycans, Sardinians and Corsicans, to the number of 300,000, with Amilcas the son of Annon king of the Carthaginians as their commander, whom Terillos had persuaded partly by reason of his own guest-friendship, and especially by the zealous assistance of Anaxilaos the son of Cretines, who was despot of Rhegion, and who to help his father-in-law endeavoured to bring in Amilcas to Sicily, and had given him his sons as hostages; for Anaxilaos was married to the daughter of Terillos, whose name was Kydippē. Thus it was, they say, that Gelon was not able to come to the assistance of the Hellenes, and sent therefore the money to Delphi. **166.** In addition to this they report also that, as it happened, Gelon and Theron were victorious over Amilcas the Carthaginian on the very same day when the Hellenes were victorious at

Salamis over the Persian.* And this Amilcas, who was a Carthaginian on the father's side but on the mother's a Syracusan, and who had become king of the Carthaginians by merit, when the engagement took place and he was being worsted in the battle, disappeared, as I am informed; for neither alive nor dead did he appear again anywhere upon the earth, though Gelon used all diligence in the search for him. **167.** Moreover there is also this story reported by the Carthaginians themselves, who therein relate that which is probable in itself, namely that while the Barbarians fought with the Hellenes in Sicily from the early morning till late in the afternoon (for to such a length the combat is said to have been protracted), during this time Amilcas was remaining in the camp and was making sacrifices to get good omens of success, offering whole bodies of victims upon a great pyre: and when he saw that there was a rout of his own army, he being then, as it chanced, in the act of pouring a libation over the victims, threw himself into the fire, and thus he was burnt up and disappeared. Amilcas then having disappeared, whether it was in such a manner as this, as it is reported by the Phenicians, or in some other way, the Carthaginians both offer sacrifices to him now, and also they made memorials of him then in all the cities of their colonies, and the greatest in Carthage itself.

168. So far of the affairs of Sicily: and as for the Corcyreans, they made answer to the envoys as follows, afterwards acting as I shall tell: for the same men who had gone to Sicily endeavoured also to obtain the help of these, saying the same things which they said to Gelon; and the Corcyreans at the time engaged to send a force and to help in the defence, declaring that they must not permit Hellas to be ruined without an effort on their part, for if it should suffer disaster, they would be reduced to subjection from the very first day; but they must give assistance so far as lay in their power. Thus speciously they made reply; but when the time came to send help, they manned sixty ships, having other intentions in their minds, and after making much difficulty they put out to sea and reached Peloponnese; and then near Pylos and Tainaron in the land of the Lacedemonians they kept their ships at anchor, waiting, as Gelon did, to see how the war would turn out: for they did not expect that the Hellenes would overcome, but thought that the Persian would gain the victory over them with ease and be ruler of all Hellas. Accordingly they were acting of set purpose, in order that they might be able to say to the Persian some such words as these: "O king, when the Hellenes endeavoured to obtain our help for this war, we, who have a power which is not the smallest of all, and could have supplied a contingent of ships in number not the smallest, but after the Athenians the largest, did not choose to oppose you or to do anything which was not to your mind." By speaking thus they hoped that they would obtain some advantage over the rest, and so it would have happened,

---

*The battle of Himera was fought in 480 B.C. Fornara 54 records Gelon's tripod (a large, metal, three-footed stand on an inscribed stone base) dedicated at Delphi.

as I am of opinion: while they had for the Hellenes an excuse ready made, that namely of which they actually made use: for when the Hellenes reproached them because they did not come to help, they said that they had manned sixty triremes, but had not been able to get past Malea owing to the Etesian Winds; therefore it was that they had not come to Salamis, nor was it by any want of courage on their part that they had been left out of the sea-fight.

169. These then evaded the request of the Hellenes thus: but the Cretans, when those of the Hellenes who had been appointed to deal with these endeavoured to obtain their help, did thus, that is to say, they joined together and sent men to inquire of the god at Delphi whether it would be better for them if they gave assistance to Hellas: and the Pythian prophetess answered: "You fools, do you think those woes too few, which Minos sent upon you in his wrath, because of the assistance that you gave to Menelaos? seeing that, whereas they did not join with you in taking vengeance for his death in Camicos, you nevertheless joined with them in taking vengeance for the woman who by a Barbarian was carried off from Sparta." When the Cretans heard this answer reported, they abstained from the giving of assistance.

170. For the story goes that Minos, having come to Sicania, which is now called Sicily, in search of Daidalos, died there by a violent death; and after a time the Cretans, urged thereto by a god, all except the men of Polichnē and Praisos, came with a great armament to Sicania and besieged for seven years the city of Camicos, which in my time was occupied by the Agrigentines; and at last not being able either to capture it or to remain before it, because they were hard pressed by famine, they departed and went away. And when, as they sailed, they came to be off the coast of Iapygia, a great storm seized them and cast them away upon the coast; and their vessels being dashed to pieces, they, since they saw no longer any way of coming to Crete, founded there the city of Hyria; and there they stayed and were changed so that they became instead of Cretans, Messapians of Iapygia, and instead of islanders, dwellers on the mainland: then from the city of Hyria they founded those others settlements which the Tarentines long afterwards endeavoured to destroy and suffered great disaster in that enterprise, so that this in fact proved to be the greatest slaughter of Hellenes that is known to us, and not only of the Tarentines themselves but of those citizens of Rhegion who were compelled by Mikythos the son of Choiros to go to the assistance of the Tarentines, and of whom there were slain in this manner three thousand men: of the Tarentines themselves however, who were slain there, there was no numbering made. This Mikythos, who was a servant of Anaxilaos, had been left by him in charge of Rhegion; and he it was who after being driven out of Rhegion took up his abode at Tegea of the Arcadians and dedicated those many statues at Olympia.

171. This of the men of Rhegion and of the Tarentines has been a footnote in my narrative: in Crete however, as the men of Praisos report, after it had been thus stripped of inhabitants, settlements were made by various

nations, but especially by Hellenes; and in the next generation but one after the death of Minos came the Trojan war, in which the Cretans proved
not the most contemptible of those who came to assist Menelaos. Then after this, when they had returned home from Troy, famine and pestilence
came upon both the men and their cattle, until at last Crete was stripped
of its inhabitants for the second time, and a third population of Cretans
now occupy it together with those which were left of the former inhabitants. The Pythian prophetess, I say, by calling these things to their minds
stopped them from giving assistance to the Hellenes, though they desired
to do so.

172. As for the Thessalians, they at first had taken the side of the Persians against their will, and they gave proof that they were not pleased by
that which the Aleuadai were designing; for so soon as they heard that the
Persian was about to cross over into Europe, they sent envoys to the Isthmus: now at the Isthmus were assembled representatives of Hellas chosen
by the cities which had the better mind about Hellas: having come then to
these, the envoys of the Thessalians said: "Hellenes, you must guard the
pass by Olympos, in order that both Thessaly and the whole of Hellas may
be sheltered from the war. We are prepared to join with you in guarding it,
but you must send a large force as well as we; for if you shall not send, be
assured that we shall make agreement with the Persian; since it is not right
that we, standing as outposts so far in advance of the rest of Hellas, should
perish alone in your defence: and not being willing to come to our help, you
cannot apply to us any force to compel us, for force never was strong
enough to compel inability; but we shall endeavour to devise some means
of safety for ourselves." **173.** Thus spoke the Thessalians; and the Hellenes
upon this resolved to send to Thessaly by sea an army of men on foot to
guard the pass: and when the army was assembled it set sail through Euripos, and having come to Alos in the Achaian land, it disembarked there
and marched into Thessaly leaving the ships behind at Alos, and arrived at
Tempē, the pass which leads from lower Macedonia into Thessaly by the
river Peneios, going between the mountains of Olympos and Ossa. There
the Hellenes encamped, being assembled to the number of about ten thousand hoplites, and to them was added the cavalry of the Thessalians; and
the commander of the Lacedemonians was Euainetos the son of Carenos,
who had been chosen from the Spartan polemarchs, not being of the royal
house, and of the Athenians Themistocles the son of Neocles. They remained however but few days here, for envoys came from Alexander the
son of Amyntas the Macedonian, who advised them to depart thence and
not to remain in the pass and be trodden under foot by the invading host,
signifying to them at the same time both the great numbers of the army and
the ships which they had. When these gave them this counsel, they followed
the advice, for they thought that the counsel was good, and the Macedonian was evidently well-disposed towards them. Also, as I think, it was fear
that persuaded them to it, when they were informed that there was another
pass besides this to the Thessalian land by upper Macedonia through the
Perraibians and by the city of Gonnos, the way by which the army of

Xerxes did in fact make its entrance. So the Hellenes went down to their ships again and made their way back to the Isthmus.

174. Such was the expedition to Thessaly, which took place when the king was about to cross over from Asia to Europe and was already at Abydos. So the Thessalians, being stripped of allies, upon this took the side of the Medes with a good will and no longer half-heartedly, so that in the course of events they proved very serviceable to the king.

175. When the Hellenes had returned to the Isthmus, they deliberated, having regard to that which had been said by Alexander, where and in what regions they should set the war on foot: and the opinion which prevailed was to guard the pass at Thermopylai; for it was seen to be narrower than that leading into Thessaly, and at the same time it was single, and nearer also to their own land; and as for the path by means of which some of the Hellenes were taken at Thermopylai, they did not even know of its existence until they were informed by the people of Trachis after they had come to Thermopylai. This pass then they resolved to guard, and not permit the Barbarian to enter Hellas; and they resolved that the fleet should sail to Artemision in the territory of Histiaia: for these points are near to one another, so that each division of their forces could have information of what was happening to the other.* And the places are so situated as I shall describe. **176.** As to Artemision first, coming out of the Thracian Sea the space is contracted from great width to that narrow channel which lies between the island of Skiathos and the mainland of Magnesia; and after the strait there follows at once in Eubœa the sea-beach called Artemision, upon which there is a temple of Artemis. Then secondly the passage into Hellas by Trachis is, where it is narrowest, but fifty feet wide: it is not here however that the narrowest part of this whole region lies, but in front of Thermopylai and also behind it, consisting of a single wheel-track only† both by Alpenoi, which lies behind Thermopylai, and again by the river Phoinix near the town of Anthela there is no space but a single wheel-track only: and on the West of Thermopylai there is a mountain which is impassable and precipitous, rising up to a great height and extending towards the range of Oitē, while on the East of the road the sea with swampy pools succeeds at once. In this passage there are hot springs, which the natives of the place call the "Pots," and an altar of Heracles is set up near them. Moreover a wall had once been built at this pass, and in old times there was a gate set in it; which wall was built by the Phokians, who were struck with fear because the Thessalians had come from the land of the Thesprotians to settle in the Aiolian land, the same which they now possess. Since then the Thessalians, as they supposed, were attempting to subdue them, the Phokians guarded themselves against this beforehand; and at that time they let the water of the hot springs run over the passage, that the place might be converted into a ravine, and devised every means

---

*Herodotus glances here at the Greeks' amphibious strategy.
†The bradyseismic rising of the land now leaves 2 miles of level ground.

that the Thessalians might not make invasion of their land. Now the ancient wall had been built long before, and the greater part of it was by that time in ruins from lapse of time; the Hellenes however resolved to set it up again, and at this spot to repel the Barbarian from Hellas: and very near the road there is a village called Alpenoi, from which the Hellenes counted on getting supplies.

177. These places then the Hellenes perceived to be such as their purpose required; for they considered everything beforehand and calculated that the Barbarians would not be able to take advantage either of superior numbers or of cavalry, and therefore they resolved here to receive the invader of Hellas: and when they were informed that the Persian was in Pieria, they broke up from the Isthmus and set forth for the campaign, some going to Thermopylai by land, and others making for Artemision by sea.

178. The Hellenes, I say, were coming to the rescue with speed, having been appointed to their several places: and meanwhile the men of Delphi consulted the Oracle of the god on behalf of themselves and on behalf of Hellas, being struck with dread; and a reply was given them that they should pray to the Winds, for these would be powerful helpers of Hellas in fight. So the Delphians, having accepted the oracle, first reported the answer which had been given them to those of the Hellenes who desired to be free; and having reported this to them at a time when they were in great dread of the Barbarian, they laid up for themselves an immortal store of gratitude: then after this the men of Delphi established an altar for the Winds in Thuia, where is the sacred enclosure of Thuia the daughter of Kephisos, after whom moreover this place has its name; and also they approached them with sacrifices.

179. The Delphians then according to the oracle even to this day make propitiatory offerings to the Winds: and meanwhile the fleet of Xerxes setting forth from the city of Therma had passed over with ten of its ships, which were those that sailed best, straight towards Skiathos, where three Hellenic ships, a Troizenian, an Eginetan and an Athenian, were keeping watch in advance. When the crews of these caught sight of the ships of the Barbarians, they set off to make their escape: **180,** and the ship of Troizen, of which Prexinos was in command, was pursued and captured at once by the Barbarians; who upon that took the man who was most distinguished by beauty among the fighting-men on board and cut his throat at the prow of the ship, making a good omen for themselves of the first and handsomest of the Hellenes whom they had captured. The name of this man who was sacrificed was Leon, and perhaps his name brought about what befell him.

181. The ship of Egina however, of which Asonides was master, gave them some trouble to capture it, seeing that Pytheas the son of Ischenoös served as a fighting-man on board of her, who proved himself a most valiant man on this day; for when the ship was being taken, he held out fighting until he was hacked all to pieces: and as when he had fallen he did not die, but had still breath in him, the Persians who served as fighting-men on board the ships, because of his valour used all diligence to save his life, both applying unguents of myrrh to heal his wounds and also wrapping him up in bands of the finest linen; and when they came back to their own main body, they showed him to all the army, making a marvel of him and giving him good treatment; but the rest whom they had taken in this ship they treated as slaves. **182.** Two of the three ships, I say, were captured thus; but the third, of which Phormos an Athenian was master, ran ashore in its flight at the mouth of the river Peneios; and the Barbarians got possession of the vessel but not of the crew; for so soon as the Athenians had run the ship ashore, they leapt out of her, and passing through Thessaly made their way to Athens.

183. Of these things the Hellenes who were stationed at Artemision were informed by fire-signals from Skiathos; and being informed of them and being struck with fear, they removed their place of anchorage from Artemision to Chalkis, intending to guard the Euripos, but leaving at the same time watchers by day on the heights of Eubœa. Of the ten ships of the Barbarians three sailed up to the reef called Myrmex, which lies between Skiathos and Magnesia; and when the Barbarians had there erected a stone pillar, which for that purpose they brought to the reef, they set forth with their main body from Therma, the difficulties of the passage having now been cleared away, and sailed thither with all their ships, having let eleven days go by since the king set forth on his march from Therma. Now of this reef lying exactly in the middle of the fairway they were informed by Pammon of Skyros. Sailing then throughout the day the Barbarians accomplished the voyage to Sepias in Magnesia and to the sea-beach which is between the city of Casthanaia and the headland of Sepias.

184. So far as this place and so far as Thermopylai the army was exempt from calamity; and the number was then still, as I find by computation, this:—Of the ships which came from Asia, which were one thousand two hundred and seven, the original number of the crews supplied by the several nations I find to have been 240,000 and also in addition to them one thousand four hundred, if one reckons at the rate of two hundred men to each ship: and on board of each of these ships there served as fighting-men, besides the fighting-men belonging to its own nation in each case, thirty men who were Persians, Medes, or Sacans; and this amounts to thirty-six thousand two hundred and ten in addition to the others. I will add also to this and to the former number the crews of the fifty-oared galleys, assuming that there were eighty men, more or less, in each one. Of these vessels there were gathered together, as was before said, three thousand: it would follow therefore that there were in them 240,000 men. This was the naval force which came from Asia, amounting in all to 517,610 men. Then of the footmen there had been found to be 1,700,000, and of the horsemen 80,000. I will add also to these the Arabian camel-drivers and the Libyan drivers of chariots, assuming them to amount to twenty thousand men. The result is then that the number of the ships' crews combined with that of the land-army amounts to 2,317,610 men. This is the statement of the army which was brought up out of Asia itself, without counting the attendants which accompanied it or the corn-transports and the men who sailed in these.

185. There is still to be reckoned, in addition to all this which has been summed up, the force which was being led from Europe; and of this we must give a probable estimate. The Hellenes of Thrace and of the islands which lie off the coasts of Thrace supplied a hundred and twenty ships; from which ships there results a sum of twenty-four thousand men: and as regards the land-force which was supplied by the Thracians, Paionians, Eordians, Bottiaians, the race which inhabits Chalkidikē, the Brygians, Pierians, Macedonians, Perraibians, Enianians, Dolopians, Magnesians, Achaians, and all those who dwell in the coast-region of Thrace, of these various nations I estimate that there were 300,000 men. These forces then added to those from Asia make a total sum of 2,641,610 men. **186.** Such being the number of this body of fighting men, the attendants who went with these and the men who were in the small vessels which carried grain, and again in the other vessels which sailed with the army, these I suppose were not less in number but more than the fighting men. I will assume them to be equal in number with these, and neither at all more nor less; and so, they make up the same number as they. Thus 5,283,220 was the number of men whom Xerxes son of Dareios led as far as Sepias and Thermopylai.* **187.** This is the number of the whole army of Xerxes; but of the women who made bread for it, and of the concubines and eunuchs no man can state any exact number, nor again of the draught-animals and other beasts of burden or of the Indian hounds, which accompanied it, could any one state the number by reason of their multitude: so that it does not occur to me to wonder that the streams of some rivers should have failed them, but I wonder rather how the provisions were sufficient to feed so many myriads; for I find on computation that if each man received a daily allowance of a quart of wheat every day and nothing more, there would be expended each day 110,340 *medimnoi* besides:† and here I am not reckoning anything for the women, eunuchs, baggage-animals, or dogs. Of all these men, amounting to so many, not one was for beauty and stature more worthy than Xerxes himself to possess this power.

188. The fleet, I say, set forth and sailed: and when it had put in to land in the region of Magnesia at the beach which is between the city of Casthanaia and the headland of Sepias, the first of the ships which came lay moored by the land and the others rode at anchor behind them; for, as the beach was not large in extent, they lay at anchor with prows projecting towards the sea in an order which was eight ships deep. For that night they lay thus; but at early dawn, after clear sky and windless calm, the sea began to be violently agitated and a great storm fell upon them with a strong North-East Wind, that wind which they who dwell about those parts call

---

*These numbers are absurd, though in fact the Persians and their allies far outnumbered the Greeks. Perhaps the Persian army had a force of 300,000, though this remains a speculative calculation.

†The arithmetic is slightly high here; the *medimnos* was a dry measure of 1½ bushels or 11.4 gallons, so approximately 1,257,876 gallons per day is calculated.

Hellespontias. Now as many of them as perceived that the wind was rising and who were so moored that it was possible for them to do so, drew up their ships on land before the storm came, and both they and their ships escaped; but as for those of the ships which it caught out at sea, some it cast away at the place called "Ovens" in Pelion and others on the beach, while some were wrecked on the headland of Sepias itself, others at the city of Meliboia, and others were thrown up on shore at Casthanaia: and the violence of the storm could not be resisted. **189.** There is a story reported that the Athenians had called upon Boreas to aid them, by suggestion of an oracle, because there had come to them another utterance of the god bidding them call upon their brother by marriage to be their helper. Now according to the story of the Hellenes Boreas has a wife who is of Attica, Oreithuia the daughter of Erechtheus. By reason of this affinity, I say, the Athenians, according to the tale which has gone abroad, conjectured that their "brother by marriage" was Boreas, and when they perceived the wind rising, as they lay with their ships at Chalkis in Euboea, or even before that, they offered sacrifices and called upon Boreas and Oreithuia to assist them and to destroy the ships of the Barbarians, as they had done before round about mount Athōs. Whether it was for this reason that the wind Boreas fell upon the Barbarians while they lay at anchor, I am not able to say; but however that may be, the Athenians report that Boreas had come to their help in former times, and that at this time he accomplished those things; and when they had returned home they set up a temple dedicated to Boreas by the river Ilissos.

190. In this disaster the number of the ships which were lost was not less than four hundred, according to the report of those who state the number which is lowest, with men innumerable and an immense quantity of valuable things; insomuch that to Ameinocles the son of Cretines, a Magnesian who held lands about Sepias, this shipwreck proved very gainful; for he picked up many cups of gold which were thrown up afterwards on the shore, and many also of silver, and found treasure-chests which had belonged to the Persians, and made acquisition of other things of gold more than can be described. This man however, though he became very wealthy by the things which he found, yet in other respects was not fortunate; for he too suffered misfortune, being troubled by the slaying of a child. **191.** Of the grain-slaying transports and other vessels which perished there was no numbering made; and so great was the loss that the commanders of the fleet, being struck with fear lest the Thessalians should attack them now in their plight, threw round their camp a lofty palisade built of the fragments of wreck. For the storm continued during three days; but at last the Magians, making sacrifice of victims and singing incantations to appease the Wind by enchantments, and in addition to this, offering to Thetis and the Nereïds, caused it to cease on the fourth day,—or else for some other reason it abated of its own will.* Now they offered sacrifice to Thetis, being informed by the Ionians of the story

---

*Herodotus gives three supernatural "explanations" but then undercuts them all.

that she was carried off from this place by Peleus, and that the whole headland of Sepias belonged to her and to the other Nereïds. **192.** The storm then had ceased on the fourth day; and meanwhile the day-watchers had run down from the heights of Eubœa on the day after the first storm began, and were keeping the Hellenes informed of all that had happened as regards the shipwreck. They then, being informed of it, prayed first to Poseidon the Saviour and poured libations, and then they hastened to go back to Artemision, expecting that there would be but a very few ships of the enemy left to come against them. **193.** They, I say, came for the second time and lay with their ships about Artemision: and from that time even to this they preserve the use of the surname "Saviour" for Poseidon. Meanwhile the Barbarians, when the wind had ceased and the swell of the sea had calmed down, drew their ships into the sea and sailed on along the shore of the mainland, and having rounded the extremity of Magnesia they sailed straight into the gulf which leads towards Pagasai. In this gulf of Magnesia there is a place where it is said that Heracles was left behind by Jason and his comrades, having been sent from the Argo to fetch water, at the time when they were sailing for the fleece to Aia in the land of Colchis: for from that place they designed, when they had taken in water, to loose their ship into the open sea; and from this the place has come to have the name Aphetai or "Send-off". Here then the fleet of Xerxes took up its moorings.

194. Now it chanced that fifteen of these ships put out to sea a good deal later than the rest, and they happened to catch sight of the ships of the Hellenes at Artemision. These ships the Barbarians supposed to be their own, and they sailed thither accordingly and fell among the enemy. Of these the commander was Sandokes the son of Thamasios, the governor of Kymē in Aiolia, whom before this time king Dareios had taken and crucified (he being one of the Royal Judges) for this reason,[*] namely that Sandokes had pronounced judgment unjustly for money. So then after he was hung up, Dareios reckoned and found that more good services had been done by him to the royal house than his offences; and having found this, and perceived that he had himself acted with more haste than wisdom, he let him go. Thus he escaped from king Dareios, and survived; now, however, when he sailed in toward the Hellenes, he was destined not to escape the second time; for when the Hellenes saw them sailing up, perceiving the mistake they put out against them and captured them without difficulty. **195.** Sailing in one of these ships Aridolis was captured, the despot of Alabanda in Caria, and in another the Paphian commander Penthylos son of Demonoös, who brought twelve ships from Paphos, but had lost eleven of them in the storm which had come on by Sepias, and now was captured sailing in towards Artemision with the one which had escaped. These men the Hellenes sent away in bonds to the Isthmus of the Corinthians, after having inquired of them that which they desired to learn of the army of Xerxes.

196. The fleet of the Barbarians then, except the fifteen ships of which I

---

*See also 3.35 and 5.25.

said that Sandokes was in command, had arrived at Aphetai; and Xerxes meanwhile with the land-army, having marched through Thessalia and Achaia, had already entered the land of the Malians two days before, after having held in Thessaly a contest for his own horses, making trial also of the Thessalian cavalry, because he was informed that it was the best of all among the Hellenes; and in this trial the horses of Hellas were far surpassed by the others. Now of the rivers in Thessalia the Onochonos alone failed to suffice by its stream for the drinking of the army; but of the rivers which flow in Achaia even that which is the largest of them, namely Epidanos, even this, I say, held out but barely.

197. When Xerxes had reached Alos of Achaia, the guides who gave him information of the way, wishing to inform him fully of everything, reported to him a legend of the place, the things, namely, which have to do with the temple of Zeus Laphystios; how Athamas the son of Aiolos contrived death for Phrixos, having taken counsel with Ino, and after this how by command of an oracle the Achaians propose to his descendants the following tasks to be performed:—whosoever is the eldest of this race, on him they lay as an injunction that he is forbidden to enter the City Hall, and they themselves keep watch; now the City Hall is called by the Achaians the "Hall of the People"; and if he enter it, he shall not come forth until he is about to be sacrificed. They related moreover in addition to this, that many of these who were about to be sacrificed had before now run away and departed to another land, because they were afraid; and if afterwards in course of time they returned to their own land and were caught, they were placed in the City Hall: and they told him how the man is sacrificed all thickly covered with wreaths, and with what form of procession he is brought forth to the sacrifice. This is done to the descendants of Kytissoros the son of Phrixos, because, when the Achaians were making of Athamas the son of Aiolos a victim to purge the sins of the land according to the command of an oracle, and were just about to sacrifice him, this Kytissoros coming from Aia of the Colchians rescued him; and having so done he brought the wrath of the god upon his own descendants. Having heard these things, Xerxes, when he came to the sacred grove, both abstained from entering it himself, and gave the command to his whole army to do so likewise; and he paid reverence both to the house and to the sacred enclosure of the descendants of Athamas.

198. These then are the things which happened in Thessalia and in Achaia; and he proceeded to the Malian land, going along by a gulf of the sea, in which there is an ebb and flow of the tide every day. Round about this gulf there is a level space, which in parts is broad but in other parts very narrow; and mountains lofty and inaccessible surrounding this space enclose the whole land of Malis and are called the rocks of Trachis. The first city upon this gulf as one goes from Achaia is Antikyra, by which the river Spercheios flowing from the land of the Enianians runs out into the sea. At a distance of two and one-third miles or thereabouts from this river there is another, of which the name is Dyras; this is said to have appeared that it might bring assistance to Heracles when he was burning: then again at a distance of two and one-third miles from this there is another river called

Melas. **199.** From this river Melas the city of Trachis is distant half a mile; and here, in the parts where Trachis is situated, is even the widest portion of all this district, as regards the space from the mountains to the sea; for the plain has an extent of five thousand acres. In the mountain-range which encloses the land of Trachis there is a cleft to the South of Trachis itself; and through this cleft the river Asopos flows, and runs along by the foot of the mountain. **200.** There is also another river called Phoinix, to the South of the Asopos, of no great size, which flowing from these mountains runs out into the Asopos; and at the river Phoinix is the narrowest place, for here has been constructed a road with a single wheel-track only. Then from the river Phoinix it is a distance of one and three-quarter miles to Thermopylai; and in the space between the river Phoinix and Thermopylai there is a village called Anthela, by which the river Asopos flows, and so runs out into the sea; and about this village there is a wide space in which is set up a temple dedicated to Demeter of the Amphictyons, and there are seats for the Amphictyonic councillors and a temple dedicated to Amphictyon himself.*

201. King Xerxes, I say, was encamped within the region of Trachis in the land of the Malians, and the Hellenes within the pass. This place is called by the Hellenes in general Thermopylai, but by the natives of the place and those who dwell in the country round it is called Pylai. Both sides then were encamped hereabout, and the one had command of all that lies beyond Trachis in the direction of the North, and the others of that which tends towards the South and the mainland on this side of the continent.

202. These were the Hellenes who awaited the attack of the Persian in this place:—of the Spartans three hundred hoplites; of the men of Tegea and Mantineia a thousand, half from each place, from Orchomenos in Arcadia a hundred and twenty, and from the rest of Arcadia a thousand,—of the Arcadians so many; from Corinth four hundred, from Phlius two hundred, and of the men of Mykenē eighty: these were they who came from Peloponnese; and from the Bœotians seven hundred of the Thespians, and of the Thebans four hundred. **203.** In addition to these the Locrians of Opus had been summoned to come in their full force, and of the Phokians a thousand: for the Hellenes had of themselves sent a summons to them, saying by messengers that they had come as forerunners of the others, that the rest of the allies were to be expected every day, that their sea was safely guarded, being watched by the Athenians and Eginetans and by those who had been appointed to serve in the fleet, and that they need fear nothing: for he was not a god, they said, who was coming to attack Hellas, but a man; and there was no mortal, nor would be any, with whose fortunes evil had not been mingled at his very birth, and the greatest evils for the greatest men; therefore he also who was marching against them, being mortal, would be destined to fail of his expectation. They accordingly, hearing this, came to the assistance of the others at Trachis.

---

*This religious body for governing the Delphi sanctuary met twice a year, once at Thermopylai (the "Hot Gates").

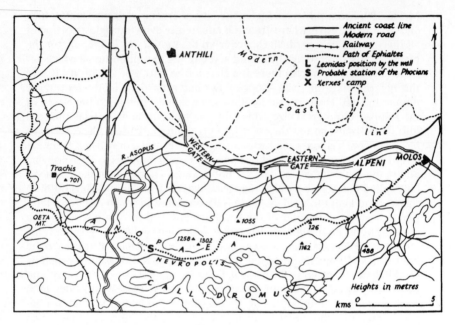

MAP 5. THERMOPYLAE.

204. Of these troops, although there were other commanders also according to the State to which each belonged, yet he who was most held in regard
and who was leader of the whole army was the Lacedemonian Leonidas
son of Anaxandrides, son of Leon, son of Eurycratides, son of Anaxander,
son of Eurycrates, son of Polydoros, son of Alcamenes, son of Teleclos, son
of Archelaos, son of Hegesilaos, son of Doryssos, son of Leobotes, son of
Echestratos, son of Agis, son of Eurysthenes, son of Aristodemos, son of
Aristomachos, son of Cleodaios, son of Hyllos, son of Heracles. Leonidas
had obtained the kingdom of Sparta contrary to expectation. **205.** For as he
had two brothers each older than himself, namely Cleomenes and Dorieus,
he had been far removed from the thought of becoming king. Since however
Cleomenes had died without male child, and Dorieus was then no longer
alive, but he also had brought his life to an end in Sicily, thus the kingdom
came to Leonidas, both because he was of elder birth than Cleombrotos (for
Cleombrotos was the youngest of the sons of Anaxandrides) and also because he had in marriage the daughter of Cleomenes. He then at this time
went to Thermopylai, having chosen the three hundred who were appointed
by law who chanced to have sons; and he took up with him besides, before he
arrived, those Thebans whom I mentioned when I reckoned them in the
number of the troops, of whom the commander was Leontiades the son of
Eurymachos: and for this reason Leonidas was anxious to take up these with
him of all the Hellenes, namely because accusations had been strongly

brought against them that they were taking the side of the Medes; therefore he summoned them to the war, desiring to know whether they would send troops with them or whether they would openly renounce the alliance of the Hellenes; and they sent men, having other thoughts in their mind.

206. These with Leonidas the Spartans had sent out first, in order that seeing them the other allies might join in the campaign, and for fear that they also might take the side of the Medes, if they heard that the Spartans were putting off action. Afterwards however, when they had kept the festival, (for the festival of the Carneia stood in their way), they intended then to leave a garrison in Sparta and to come to help in full force with speed: and just so also the rest of the allies had thought of doing themselves; for it chanced that the Olympic festival fell at the same time as these events. Accordingly, since they did not suppose that the fighting in Thermopylai would so soon be decided, they sent only the forerunners of their force. **207.** Meanwhile the Hellenes at Thermopylai, when the Persian had come near to the pass, were in dread, and deliberated about making retreat from their position. To the rest of the Peloponnesians then it seemed best that they should go to the Peloponnese and hold the Isthmus in guard; but Leonidas, when the Phokians and Locrians were indignant at this opinion, gave his vote for remaining there, and for sending at the same time messengers to the several States bidding them come up to help them, since they were but few to repel the army of the Medes.

208. As they were thus deliberating, Xerxes sent a scout on horseback to see how many they were in number and what they were doing; for he had heard while he was yet in Thessaly that there had been assembled in this place a small force, and that the leaders of it were Lacedemonians together with Leonidas, who was of the race of Heracles. And when the horseman had ridden up towards their camp, he looked upon them and had a view not indeed of the whole of their army, for of those which were posted within the wall, which they had repaired and were keeping in guard, it was not possible to have a view, but he observed those who were outside, whose station was in front of the wall; and it chanced at that time that the Lacedemonians were they who were posted outside. So then he saw some of the men practising athletic exercises and some combing their long hair: and as he looked upon these things he marvelled, and at the same time he observed their number: and when he had observed all exactly, he rode back unmolested, for no one attempted to pursue him and he found himself treated with much indifference. And when he returned he reported to Xerxes all that which he had seen. **209.** Xerxes was not able to conjecture the truth about the matter, namely that they were preparing themselves to die and to deal death to the enemy so far as they might; but it seemed to him that they were acting in a manner merely ridiculous; and therefore he sent for Demaratos the son of Ariston, who was in his camp, and when he came, Xerxes asked him, desiring to discover what the Lacedemonians were doing. Demaratos said: "You heard from my mouth at a former time, when we were setting forth to go against Hellas, the things concerning these men; and having heard them you made me an object of laughter, because I told you of these things which I perceived would come to pass; for to me it is the greatest of all ends to speak the truth continually before you, O king. Hear then now also: these men have come to fight with us for the passage, and this it is that they are preparing to do; for they have a custom which is as follows;—whenever they are about to put their lives in peril, then they attend to the arrangement of their hair. Be assured however, that if you shall subdue these and the rest of them which remain behind in Sparta, there is no other race of men which will await your onset, O king, or will raise hands against you: for now you are about to fight against the noblest kingdom and city of those which are among the Hellenes, and the best men." To Xerxes that which was said seemed to be utterly incredible, and he asked again a second time in what manner being so few they would fight with his host. He said: "O king, deal with me as with a liar, if you find not that these things come to pass as I say."

210. He did not convince Xerxes, who let four days go by, expecting always that they would take to flight; but on the fifth day, when they did not depart but remained, being obstinate, as he thought, in impudence and folly, he was enraged and sent against them the Medes and the Kissians, charging them to take the men alive and bring them into his presence. Then when the Medes moved forward and attacked the Hellenes,* there fell many of them, and others kept coming up continually, and they were not driven back, though suffering great loss: and they made it evident to every man, and to the king himself not least of all, that human beings are many but men are few. This combat went on throughout the day: **211,** and when the Medes were being roughly handled, then these retired from the battle, and the Persians, those namely whom the king called "Immortals," of whom Hydarnes was commander, took their place and came to the attack, supposing that they at least would easily overcome the enemy. When however these also engaged in combat with the Hellenes, they gained no more success than the Median troops but the same as they, seeing that they were fighting in a place with a narrow passage, using shorter spears than the Hellenes, and not being able to take advantage of their superior numbers. The Lacedemonians meanwhile were fighting in a memorable fashion, and besides other things of which they made display, being men perfectly skilled in fighting opposed to men who were unskilled, they would turn their backs to the enemy and make a pretence of taking to flight; and the Barbarians, seeing them thus taking to flight, would follow after them with shouting and clashing of arms: then the Lacedemonians, when they were being caught up, turned back and faced the Barbarians; and thus turning round they would slay innumerable multitudes of the Persians; and there fell also at these times a few of the Spartans themselves. So, as the Persians were not able to obtain any success by making trial of the entrance and attacking it by divisions and every way, they retired back.

212. And during these onsets it is said that the king, looking on, three times leapt up from his seat, struck with fear for his army. On the following day the Barbarians strove with no better result; for because the men op-

---

*Battles at Thermopylai were fought in June or July of 480 B.C.

posed to them were few in number, they engaged battle with the expectation that they would be found to be disabled and would not be capable any longer of raising their hands against them in fight. The Hellenes however were ordered by companies as well as by nations, and they fought successively each in turn, excepting the Phokians, for these were posted upon the mountain to guard the path. So the Persians, finding nothing different from that which they had seen on the former day, retired from the fight.

213. Then when the king was in a strait as to what he should do in the matter before him, Epialtes the son of Eurydemos, a Malian, came to speech with him, supposing that he would win a very great reward from the king; and this man told him of the path which leads over the mountain to Thermopylai, and brought about the destruction of those Hellenes who remained in that place. Afterwards from fear of the Lacedemonians he fled to Thessaly, and when he had fled, a price was proclaimed for his life by the Deputies, when the Amphictyons met for their assembly at Pylai. Then some time afterwards having returned to Antikyra he was slain by Athenades a man of Trachis. Now this Athenades killed Epialtes for another cause, which I shall set forth in the following part of the history,* but he was honoured for it none the less by the Lacedemonians. **214.** Thus Epialtes after these events was slain: there is however another tale told, that Onetes the son of Phanagoras, a man of Carystos, and Corydallos of Antikyra were those who held this speech to the king and who showed the Persians the way round the mountain; but this I can by no means accept: for first we must judge by this fact, namely that the Deputies of the Hellenes did not proclaim a price for the lives of Onetes and Corydallos, but for that of Epialtes the Trachinian, having surely obtained the most exact information of the matter; and secondly we know that Epialtes was an exile from his country to avoid this charge. True it is indeed that Onetes might know of this path, even though he were not a Malian, if he had had much intercourse with the country; but Epialtes it was who led them round the mountain by the path, and him therefore I write down as the guilty man.

215. Xerxes accordingly, being pleased by that which Epialtes engaged to accomplish, at once with great joy proceeded to send Hydarnes and the men of whom Hydarnes was commander; and they set forth from the camp about the time when the lamps are lit. This path of which we speak had been discovered by the Malians who dwell in that land, and having discovered it they led the Thessalians by it against the Phokians, at the time when the Phokians had fenced the pass with a wall and thus were sheltered from the attacks upon them: so long ago as this had the pass been proved by the Malians to be of no value. **216.** And this path lies as follows:—it begins from the river Asopos, which flows through the cleft, and the name of this mountain and of the path is the same, namely Anopaia; and this Anopaia stretches over the ridge of the mountain and ends by the town of Alpenos, which is the first town of the Locrians towards Malis, and by the stone called Black

---

*One of Herodotus' few unfulfilled promises.

Buttocks and the seats of the Kercopes, where is the very narrowest part.
217. By this path thus situated the Persians after crossing over the Asopos proceeded all through the night, having on their right hand the mountains of the Oitaians and on the left those of the Trachinians: and when dawn appeared, they had reached the summit of the mountain. In this part of the mountain there were, as I have before shown, a thousand hoplites of the Phokians keeping guard, to protect their own country and to keep the path: for while the pass below was guarded by those whom I have mentioned, the path over the mountain was guarded by the Phokians, who had undertaken the business for Leonidas by their own offer. **218.** While the Persians were ascending they were concealed from these, since all the mountain was covered with oak-trees; and the Phokians became aware of them after they had made the ascent as follows:—the day was calm, and not a little noise was made by the Persians, as was likely when leaves were lying spread upon the ground under their feet; upon which the Phokians started up and began to put on their arms, and by this time the Barbarians were close upon them. These, when they saw men arming themselves, fell into wonder, for they were expecting that no one would appear to oppose them, and instead of that they had met with an armed force. Then Hydarnes, seized with fear lest the Phokians should be Lacedemonians, asked Epialtes of what people the force was; and being accurately informed he set the Persians in order for battle. The Phokians however, when they were hit by the arrows of the enemy, which flew thickly, fled and got away at once to the topmost peak of the mountain, fully assured that it was against them that the enemy had come, and here they were ready to meet death. The Persians meanwhile with Epialtes and Hydarnes made no account of the Phokians, but descended the mountain with all speed.

219. To the Hellenes who were in Thermopylai first the soothsayer Megistias, after looking into the victims which were sacrificed, declared the death which was to come to them at dawn of day; and afterwards deserters brought the report of the Persians having gone round. These signified it to them while it was yet night, and thirdly came the day-watchers, who had run down from the heights when day was already dawning. Then the Hellenes deliberated, and their opinions were divided; for some urged that they should not desert their post, while others opposed this counsel. After this they departed from their assembly, and some went away and dispersed each to their several cities, while others of them were ready to remain there together with Leonidas. **220.** However it is reported also that Leonidas himself sent them away, having a care that they might not perish, but thinking that it was not seemly for himself and for the Spartans who were present to leave the post to which they had come at first to keep guard there. I am inclined rather to be of this latter opinion, namely that because Leonidas perceived that the allies were out of heart and did not desire to face the danger with him to the end, he ordered them to depart, but held that for himself to go away was not honourable, whereas if he remained, a great fame of him would be left behind, and the prosperity of Sparta would not be blotted out: for an oracle had been given by the Pythian prophetess to the Spartans, when they consulted about this war at the beginning, to the effect that either Lacedemon must be destroyed by the Barbarians, or their king must lose his life. This reply the prophetess gave them in hexameter verses, and it ran thus:

"But as for you, ye men who in wide-spaced Sparta inhabit,
Either your glorious city is sacked by the children of Perses,
Or, if it be not so, then a king of the stock Heracleian
Dead shall be mourned for by all in the boundaries of broad
        Lacedemon.
The Persian neither the might of bulls nor the raging of lions shall
        hinder;
For he hath might as of Zeus; and I say he shall not be restrained,
Till one or other of these he have utterly torn and divided."

I am of opinion that Leonidas considering these things and desiring to lay up for the Spartans glory above all the other nations, dismissed the allies, rather than that those who departed did so in such disorderly fashion, because they were divided in opinion. **221.** Of this the following has been to my mind a proof as convincing as any other, namely that Leonidas is known to have endeavoured to dismiss the soothsayer also who accompanied this army, Megistias the Acarnanian, who was said to be descended from Melampus, that he might not perish with them after he had declared from the victims that which was about to come to pass for them. He however when he was bidden to go would not himself depart, but sent away his son who was with him in the army, besides whom he had no other child.

222. The allies then who were dismissed departed and went away, obeying the word of Leonidas, and only the Thespians and Thebans remained behind with the Lacedemonians. Of these the Thebans stayed against their will and not because they desired it, for Leonidas kept them, counting them as hostages; but the Thespians very willingly, for they said that they would not depart and leave Leonidas and those with him, but they stayed behind and died with them. The commander of these was Demophilos the son of Diadromes.

223. Xerxes meanwhile, having made libations at sunrise, stayed for some time, until about the hour when the market fills, and then made an advance upon them; for thus it had been enjoined by Epialtes, seeing that the descent of the mountain is shorter and the space to be passed over much less than the going round and the ascent. The Barbarians accordingly with Xerxes were advancing to the attack; and the Hellenes with Leonidas, feeling that they were going forth to death, now advanced out much further than at first into the broader part of the defile; for when the fence of the wall was being guarded, they on the former days fought retiring before the enemy into the narrow part of the pass; but now they engaged with them outside the narrows, and very many of the Barbarians fell: for behind them the leaders of the divisions with scourges in their hands were striking each man, ever urging them on to the front. Many of them then were driven into the sea and perished, and many more still were trodden down while yet alive by one another, and there was no reckoning of the number that perished: for knowing the death which was about to come upon them by reason of those who were going round the mountain, the Lacedemonians displayed all the strength which they had, to its greatest extent, disregarding danger and acting as if possessed by a spirit of recklessness. **224.** Now by this time the spears of the greater number of them were broken, so it chanced, in this combat, and they were slaying the Persians with their swords; and in this fighting fell Leonidas, having proved himself a very good man, and others also of the Spartans with him, men of note, of whose names I was informed as of men who had proved themselves worthy, and indeed I was told also the names of all the three hundred. Moreover of the Persians there fell here, besides many others of note, especially two sons of Dareios, Abrocomes and Hyperanthes, born to Dareios of Phratagunē the daughter of Artanes: now Artanes was the brother of king Dareios and the son of Hystaspes, the son of Arsames; and he in giving his daughter in marriage to Dareios gave also with her all his substance, because she was his only child. **225.** Two brothers of Xerxes, I say, fell here fighting; and meanwhile over the body of Leonidas there arose a great struggle between the Persians and the Lacedemonians, until the Hellenes by valour dragged this away from the enemy and turned their opponents to flight four times. This conflict continued until those who had gone with Epialtes came up; and when the Hellenes learnt that these had come, from that moment the nature of the combat was changed; for they retired backwards to the narrow part of the way, and having passed by the wall they went and placed themselves upon the hillock, all in a body together except only the Thebans: now this hillock is in the entrance, where now the stone lion is placed for Leonidas. On this spot while defending themselves with daggers, that is those who still had them left, and also with hands and with teeth, they were overwhelmed by the missiles of the Barbarians, some of these having followed directly after them and destroyed the wall, while others had come round and stood about them on all sides.

226. Such were the proofs of valour given by the Lacedemonians and Thespians; yet the Spartan Dienekes is said to have proved himself the best man of all, the same who, as they report, uttered this saying before they engaged battle with the Medes:—being informed by one of the men of Trachis that when the Barbarians discharged their arrows they obscured the light of the sun by the multitude of the arrows, so great was the number of their host. He was not dismayed by this, but making small account of the number of the Medes, he said that their guest from Trachis brought them very good news, for if the Medes obscured the light of the sun, the battle against them would be in the shade and not in the sun. **227.** This and other sayings of this kind they report that Dienekes the Lacedemonian left as memorials of himself; and after him the bravest they say of the Lacedemonians were two brothers Alpheos and Maron, sons of Orsiphantos. Of the Thespians the man who gained most honour was named Dithyrambos son of Harmatides.

228. The men were buried where they fell; and for these, as well as for those who were slain before their fellows had been sent away by Leonidas, there is an inscription which runs thus:

"Here once, facing in fight three hundred myriads of foemen,
    Thousands four did contend, men of the Peloponnese."

This is the inscription for the whole body; and for the Spartans separately there is this:

"Stranger, report this word, we pray, to the Spartans, that lying
    Here in this spot we remain, faithfully still keeping their laws."

This, I say, for the Lacedemonians; and for the soothsayer as follows:

"This is the tomb of Megistias renowned, whom the Median foemen,
    Where Spercheios doth flow, slew when they forded the stream;
Soothsayer he, who then knowing clearly the fates that were coming,
    Did not endure in the fray Sparta's good leaders to leave."

The Amphictyons it was who honoured them with inscriptions and memorial pillars, excepting only in the case of the inscription to the soothsayer; but that of the soothsayer Megistias was inscribed by Simonides the son of Leoprepes on account of guest-friendship.

229. Two of these three hundred, it is said, namely Eurytos and Aristodemos, who, if they had made agreement with one another, might either have come safe home to Sparta together (seeing that they had been dismissed from the camp by Leonidas and were lying at Alpenoi with disease of the eyes, suffering extremely), or again, if they had not wished to return home, they might have been slain together with the rest,—when they might, I say, have done either one of these two things, would not agree together; but the two being divided in opinion, Eurytos, it is said, when he was informed that the Persians had gone round, asked for his arms and having put them on ordered his Helot to lead him to those who were fighting; and after he had led him thither, the man who had led him ran away and departed, but Eurytos plunged into the thick of the fighting, and so lost his life: but Aristodemos was left behind fainting. Now if either Aristodemos had been ill alone, and so had returned home to Sparta, or the men had both of them come back together, I do not suppose that the Spartans would have displayed any anger against them; but in this case, as the one of them had lost his life and the other, clinging to an excuse which the first also might have used, had not been willing to die, it necessarily happened that the Spartans had great indignation against Aristodemos. **230.** Some say that Aristodemos came safe to Sparta in this manner, and on a pretext such as I have said; but others, that he had been sent as a messenger from the camp, and when he might have come up in time to find the battle going on, was not willing to do so, but stayed upon the road and so saved his life, while his fellow-messenger reached the battle and was slain. **231.** When Aristodemos, I say, had returned home to Lacedemon, he had reproach and dishonour; and that which he suffered by way of dishonour was this,—no one of the Spartans would either give him light for a fire or speak with him, and he had reproach in that he was called Aristodemos the "trembling" coward.* **232.** He however in the battle at Plataia repaired all the guilt that was charged against him: but it is reported that another man also survived of these three hundred, whose name was Pantites, having been sent as a messenger to Thessaly, and this man, when he returned back to Sparta and found himself dishonoured, is said to have hanged himself.

233. The Thebans however, of whom the commander was Leontiades, being with the Hellenes had continued for some time to fight against the king's army, constrained by necessity; but when they saw that the fortunes of the Persians were prevailing, then and not before, while the Hellenes with Leonidas were making their way with speed to the hillock, they separated from these and holding out their hands came near to the Barbarians, saying at the same time that which was most true, namely that they were on the side of the Medes and that they had been among the first to give earth and water to the king; and moreover that they had come to Thermopylai constrained by necessity, and were blameless for the loss which had been inflicted upon the king: so that thus saying they preserved their lives, for they had also the Thessalians to bear witness to these words. However, they did not altogether meet with good fortune, for some had even been slain as they were approaching, and when they had come and the Barbarians had them in their power, the greater number of them were branded by command of Xerxes with the royal marks, beginning with their leader Leontiades, the same whose son Eurymachos was afterwards slain by the Plataians, when he had been made commander of four hundred Thebans and had seized the city of the Plataians.†

234. Thus did the Hellenes at Thermopylai contend in fight; and Xerxes summoned Demaratos and inquired of him: "Demaratos, you are a good man; and this I conclude by the truth of your words, for all that you said turned out as you said. Now, however, tell me how many in number are the remaining Lacedemonians, and of them how many are like these in matters of war; or are they so even all of them?" He said: "O king, the number of all the Lacedemonians is great and their cities are many, but that which you desire to learn, you shall know. There is in Lacedemon the city of Sparta, having about eight thousand men; and these are all equal to those who fought here: the other Lacedemonians are not equal to these, but they are good men too." To this Xerxes said: "Demaratos, in what manner shall we with least labour get the better of these men? Come set forth to us this; for you know the courses of their counsels, seeing that you were once their king." **235.** He made answer: "O king, if you seriously take

---

*See 9.71; the ferocious Spartan social system does not attract Herodotus' sympathy.

†The attempt on Plataia was made in 431 B.C., early in the Peloponnesian War.

counsel with me, it is right that I declare to you the best thing. What if you should send three hundred ships from your fleet to attack the Laconian land? Now there is lying near it an island named Kythera, about which Chilon, who was a very wise man among us, said that it would be a greater gain for the Spartans that it should be sunk under the sea than that it should remain above it; for he always anticipated that something would happen from it of such a kind as I am now setting forth to you: not that he knew of your armament beforehand, but that he feared equally every armament of men. Let your forces then set forth from this island and keep the Lacedemonians in fear; and while they have a war of their own close at their doors, there will be no fear for you from them that when the remainder of Hellas is being conquered by the land-army, they will come to the rescue there. Then after the remainder of Hellas has been reduced to subjection, from that moment the Lacedemonian power will be left alone and therefore feeble. If however you shall not do this, I will tell you what you must look for. There is a narrow isthmus leading to the Peloponnese, and in this place you must look that other battles will be fought more severe than those which have taken place, seeing that all the Peloponnesians have sworn to a league against you: but if you shall do the other thing of which I spoke, this isthmus and the cities within it will come over to your side without a battle." **236.** After him spoke Achaimenes, brother of Xerxes and also commander of the fleet, who chanced to have been present at this discourse and was afraid lest Xerxes should be persuaded to do this: "O king," he said, "I see that you are admitting the speech of a man who envies your good fortune, or is even a traitor to your cause: for in truth the Hellenes delight in such a temper as this; they envy a man for his good luck, and they hate that which is stronger than themselves. And if, besides the other misfortunes which we have upon us, seeing that four hundred of our ships have suffered wreck, you shall send away other three hundred from the station of the fleet to sail round Peloponnese, then your antagonists become a match for you in fight; whereas while it is all assembled together our fleet is hard for them to deal with, and they will not be at all a match for you: and moreover the whole sea-force will support the land-force and be supported by it, if they proceed onwards together; but if you shall divide them, neither will you be of service to them nor they to you. My determination is rather to set your affairs in good order and not to consider the affairs of the enemy, either where they will set on foot the war or what they will do or how many in number they are; for it is sufficient that they should themselves take thought for themselves, and we for ourselves likewise: and if the Lacedemonians come to stand against the Persians in fight, they will assuredly not heal the wound from which they are now suffering." **237.** To him Xerxes made answer as follows: "Achaimenes, I think that you speak well, and so will I do; but Demaratos speaks that which he believes to be best for me, though his opinion is defeated by yours: for I will not certainly admit that which you said; namely that he is not well-disposed to my cause, judging both by what was said by him before this, and also by that which is the truth, namely that though one citizen envies another for his good fortune and shows enmity to him by his silence, nor would a citizen when a fellow-citizen consulted him suggest that which seemed to him the best, unless he had attained to a great height of virtue, and such men doubtless are few; yet guest-friend to guest-friend in prosperity is well-disposed as nothing else on earth, and if his friend should consult him, he would give him the best counsel. Thus then as regards the evil-speaking against Demaratos, that is to say about one who is my guest-friend, I bid every one abstain from it in the future."

238. Xerxes passed in review the bodies of the dead; and as for Leonidas, hearing that he had been the king and commander of the Lacedemonians he bade them cut off his head and crucify him. And it has been made plain to me by many proofs besides, but by none more strongly than by this, that king Xerxes was enraged with Leonidas while alive more than with any other man on earth; for otherwise he would never have done this outrage to his corpse; since of all the men whom I know, the Persians are accustomed most to honour those who are good men in war. They then to whom it was appointed, proceeded to do so.

239. I will return now to that point of my narrative where it remained unfinished. The Lacedemonians had been informed before all others that the king was preparing an expedition against Hellas; and thus it happened that they sent to the Oracle at Delphi, where that reply was given them which I reported shortly before this. And they got this information in a strange manner; for Demaratos the son of Ariston after he had fled for refuge to the Medes was not friendly to the Lacedemonians, as I am of opinion and as likelihood suggests supporting my opinion; but it is open to any man to make conjecture whether he did this thing which follows in a friendly spirit or in malicious triumph over them. When Xerxes had resolved to make a campaign against Hellas, Demaratos, being in Susa and having been informed of this, had a desire to report it to the Lacedemonians. Now in no other way was he able to signify it, for there was danger that he should be discovered, but he contrived thus, that is to say, he took a folding tablet and scraped off the wax which was upon it, and then he wrote the king's plan upon the wood of the tablet, and having so done he melted the wax and poured it over the writing, so that the tablet (being carried without writing upon it) might not cause any trouble to be given by the keepers of the road. Then when it had arrived at Lacedemon, the Lacedemonians were not able to make conjecture of the matter; until at last, as I am informed, Gorgo, the daughter of Cleomenes and wife of Leonidas, suggested a plan of which she had herself thought, bidding them scrape the wax and they would find writing upon the wood; and doing as she said they found the writing and read it, and after that they sent notice to the other Hellenes. These things are said to have happened.

BOOK VIII

BATTLE OF ARTEMISION, ATHENS ABANDONED, BATTLE OF SALAMIS

1. THE HELLENES APPOINTED TO serve in the fleet were these:—the Athenians furnished a hundred and twenty-seven ships, and the Plataians moved by valour and zeal for the service, although they had had no practise in seamanship, joined with the Athenians in manning their ships. The Corinthians furnished forty ships, the Megarians twenty; the Chalkidians manned twenty ships with which the Athenians furnished them;* the Eginetans furnished eighteen ships, the Sikyonians twelve, the Lacedemonians ten, the Epidaurians eight, the Eretrians seven, the Troizenians five, the Styrians two, the Keïans two triremes and two fifty-oared galleys, while the Locrians of Opus came also to the assistance of the rest with seven fifty-oared galleys.

2. These were those who joined in the expedition to Artemision, and I have mentioned them according to the number of the ships which they severally supplied: so the number of the ships which were assembled at Artemision was (apart from the fifty-oared galleys) two hundred and seventy-one. The commander who had the supreme power was furnished by the Spartans, namely Eurybiades son of Eurycleides, since the allies said that they would not follow the lead of the Athenians. Unless a Lacedemonian were leader they would break up the expedition which was to be made: **3.** for it had come to be said at first, even before they sent to Sicily to obtain allies, that the fleet ought to be placed in the charge of the Athenians. So as the allies opposed this, the Athenians yielded, having it much at heart that Hellas should be saved, and perceiving that if they should have disagreement with one another about the leadership, Hellas would perish. Herein they judged rightly, for disagreement between those of the same race is worse than war undertaken with one consent by as much as war is worse than peace. Being assured then of this truth, they did not contend, but gave way for so long time as they were urgently in need of the allies; and that this was so their conduct proved. When, after repelling the Persian from themselves, they were now contending for his land and no longer for their own, they alleged the insolence of Pausanias as a pretext and took away the leadership from the Lacedemonians. This however took place afterwards.† **4.** But at this time these Hellenes who after all had come to Artemision, when they saw that a great number of ships had put in to Aphetai and that everything was

---

*At 5.77, Herodotus reports an Athenian settlement in Chalkis.
†A reference to 478 B.C. and material recounted by Thucydides 1.128–134.

filled with their armament, were struck with fear, because the fortunes of the Barbarians had different issue from that which they expected, and they deliberated about retreating from Artemision to the inner parts of Hellas. And the Eubœans perceiving that they were so deliberating, asked Eurybiades to stay there by them for a short time, until they should have removed out of their land their children and their households; and as they did not persuade him, they went elsewhere and persuaded Themistocles the commander of the Athenians by a payment of thirty talents, the condition being that the fleet should stay and fight the sea-battle in front of Eubœa. **5.** Themistocles then caused the Hellenes to stay in the following manner:—to Eurybiades he imparted five talents of this sum with the pretence that he was giving it from himself; and when Eurybiades had been persuaded by him to change his resolution, Adeimantos son of Okytos, the Corinthian commander, was the only one of all the others who still made a struggle, saying that he would sail away from Artemision and would not stay with the others: to him therefore Themistocles said with an oath: "You at least shall not leave us, for I will give you greater gifts than the king of the Medes would send to you, if you should desert your allies." Thus he spoke, and at the same time he sent to the ship of Adeimantos three talents of silver. So these had been persuaded, touched by gifts, to change their resolution, and at the same time the request of the Eubœans had been gratified and Themistocles himself gained money; and it was not known that he had the rest of the money, but those who received a share of this money were fully persuaded that it had come from the Athenian State for this purpose.

6. Thus they remained in Eubœa and fought a sea-battle; and it came to pass as follows:—when the Barbarians had arrived at Aphetai about the beginning of the afternoon, having been informed even before they came that a few ships of the Hellenes were stationed about Artemision and now seeing them for themselves, they were eager to attack them, to see if they could capture them. Now they did not think it good yet to sail against them directly for this reason,—for fear namely that the Hellenes, when they saw them sailing against them, should set forth to take flight and darkness should come upon them in their flight; and so they were likely (thought the Persians) to get away; whereas it was right, according to their calculation, that "not even the sacrosanct fire-bearer should escape and save his life." **7.** With a view to this then they contrived as follows:—of the whole number of their ships they delegated two hundred and sent them round to sail by Caphereus and round Geraistos to the Euripos, going outside Skiathos so that they might not be sighted by the enemy as they sailed round Eubœa: and their purpose was that with these coming up by that way, and blocking the enemies' retreat, and themselves advancing against them directly, they might surround them on all sides. Having formed this plan they proceeded to send off the ships which were appointed for this, and they themselves had no design of attacking the Hellenes on that day nor until the signal agreed upon should be displayed to them by those who were sailing round, to show that they had arrived. Meanwhile they were numbering the rest at Aphetai.

8. During this time, there was in that camp a man of Skionē named Skyllias, the best diver of that time, who also in the shipwreck which took place by Pelion had saved for the Persians many of their goods and many of them also he had acquired for himself. This Skyllias it appears had had an intention even before this of deserting to the side of the Hellenes, but it had not been possible for him to do so then. In what manner after this attempt he did actually come to the Hellenes, I am not able to say with certainty, but I marvel if the reported tale is true; for it is said that he dived into the sea at Aphetai and did not come up till he reached Artemision, having traversed here somewhere about nine miles under the sea. Now there are told about this man several other tales which seem likely to be false, but some also which are true: about this matter however let it be stated as my opinion that he came to Artemision in a boat. Then when he had come, he immediately informed the commanders about the shipwreck, how it had come to pass, and of the ships which had been sent away to go round Eubœa. **9.** Hearing this the Hellenes considered the matter with one another; the prevailing opinion was that they should remain there that day and encamp on shore, and then, when midnight was past, they should set forth and go to meet those ships which were sailing round. After this however, as no one sailed out to attack them, they waited for the coming of the late hours of the afternoon and sailed out themselves to attack the Barbarians, desiring to make a trial both of their manner of fighting and of the manoeuvre of breaking their line.*

10. And seeing them sailing thus against them with few ships, not only the others in the army of Xerxes but also their commanders judged them to be moved by mere madness, and they themselves also put out their ships to sea, supposing that they would easily capture them: and their expectation was reasonable enough, since they saw that the ships of the Hellenes were few, while theirs were many times as numerous and sailed better. They came round and enclosed them in the middle. Then so many of the Ionians as were kindly disposed to the Hellenes and were serving in the expedition against their will, counted it a matter of great grief to themselves when they saw them being surrounded and felt assured that not one of them would return home, so feeble did they think the power of the Hellenes to be; while those to whom this event was a source of pleasure, were vying with one another, each one endeavouring to be the first to take an Athenian ship and receive gifts from the king: for in their camps there was more report of the Athenians than of any others. **11.** The Hellenes meanwhile, when the signal was given, first set themselves with prows facing the Barbarians and drew the sterns of their ships together in the middle; and when the signal was given a second time, although shut off in a small space and prow against prow, they set to work vigorously; and they captured thirty ships of the Barbarians and also Philaon the son of Chersis, the brother of Gorgos king of the Salaminians, who was a man of great repute in the army. Now the first of the Hellenes

---

*The tactic that Dionysios of Phocaia wished to practice; see 6.12.

who captured a ship of the enemy was an Athenian, Lycomedes the son of Aischraios, and he received the prize for valour. So these, as they were contending in this sea-fight with doubtful result, were parted from one another by the coming on of night. The Hellenes accordingly sailed away to Artemision and the Barbarians to Aphetai, the contest having been widely different from their expectation. In this sea-fight Antidoros of Lemnos alone of the Hellenes who were with the king deserted to the side of the Hellenes, and the Athenians on account of this deed gave him a piece of land in Salamis.

12. When the darkness had come on, although the season was the middle of summer, yet there came on very abundant rain, which lasted through the whole of the night, with crashing thunder from Mount Pelion; and the dead bodies and pieces of wreck were cast up at Aphetai and became entangled round the prows of the ships and struck against the blades of the oars: and the men of the army who were there, hearing these things became afraid, expecting that they would certainly perish, to such troubles had they come; for before they had had even breathing space after the shipwreck and the storm which had arisen off Mount Pelion, there had come upon them a hard sea-fight, and after the sea-fight a violent storm of rain and strong streams rushing to the sea and crashing thunder. **13.** These then had such a night as I have said; and meanwhile those of them who had been appointed to sail round Eubœa experienced the very same night, but against them it raged much more fiercely, inasmuch as it fell upon them while they were making their course in the open sea. And the end proved nasty for them; for when the storm and the rain together came upon them as they sailed, being then off the "Hollows" of Eubœa, they were borne by the wind not knowing by what way they were carried, and were cast away upon the rocks. And all this was being brought about by God in order that the Persian force might be made more equal to that of the Hellenes and might not be by very much the larger.

14. Meanwhile the Barbarians at Aphetai, when day had dawned upon them, of which they were glad, were keeping their ships quiet, and were satisfied in their evil plight to remain still for the present time; but to the Hellenes there came as a reinforcement three-and-fifty Athenian ships. The coming of these gave them more courage, and at the same time they were encouraged also by a report that those of the Barbarians who had been sailing round Eubœa had all been destroyed by the storm that had taken place. They waited then for the same time of day as before, and then they sailed and fell upon some Kilikian ships; and having destroyed these, they sailed away when the darkness came on, and returned to Artemision.

15. On the third day the commanders of the Barbarians, being exceedingly indignant that so small a number of ships should thus do them damage, and fearing what Xerxes might do, did not wait this time for the Hellenes to begin the fight, but passed the word of command and put out their ships to sea about the middle of the day. Now it so happened that these battles at sea and the battles on land at Thermopylai took place on the same days; and for those who fought by sea the whole aim of the fighting was concerned with the channel of Euripos, just as the aim of Leonidas and of his band was to guard the pass: the Hellenes accordingly exhorted one another not to let the Barbarians go by into Hellas; while these cheered one another on to destroy the fleet of the Hellenes and to get possession of the straits. **16.** Now while the forces of Xerxes were sailing in order towards them, the Hellenes kept quiet at Artemision; and the Barbarians, having made a crescent of their ships that they might enclose them, were endeavouring to surround them. Then the Hellenes put out to sea and engaged battle with them; and in this battle the two sides were nearly equal to one another; for the fleet of Xerxes by reason of its great size and numbers suffered damage from itself, since the ships were thrown into confusion and ran into one another: nevertheless it stood out and did not give way, for they disdained to flee so few ships. Many ships therefore of the Hellenes were destroyed and many men perished, but many more ships and men of the Barbarians. Thus contending they parted and went each to their own place. **17.** In this sea-fight the Egyptians did best of the men who fought for Xerxes; and these, besides other great deeds which they displayed, captured five ships of the Hellenes together with their crews: while of the Hellenes those who did best on this day were the Athenians, and of the Athenians Cleinias the son of Alkibiades, who was serving with two hundred men and a ship of his own, furnishing the expense at his own cost.

18. Having parted, both sides gladly hastened to their moorings; and after they had separated and got away out of the sea-fight, although the Hellenes had possession of the bodies of the dead and of the wrecks of the ships, yet having suffered severely (and especially the Athenians, of whose ships half had been disabled), they were deliberating now about retreating deeper into Hellas. **19.** Themistocles however had conceived that if there should be detached from the force of the Barbarians the Ionian and Carian nations, they would be able to overcome the rest; and when the people of Eubœa were driving their flocks down to that sea, he assembled the generals and said to them that he thought he had a device by which he hoped to cause the best of the king's allies to leave him. This matter he revealed to that extent only; and with regard to their present circumstances, he said that they must do as follows:—every one must slaughter of the flocks of the Eubœans as many as he wanted, for it was better that their army should have them than the enemy; moreover he advised that each one should command his own men to kindle a fire: and as for the time of their departure he would see to it in such wise that they should come safe to Hellas. This they were content to do, and immediately when they had kindled a fire they turned their attention to the flocks. **20.** For in fact the Eubœans, neglecting the oracle of Bakis as if it had no meaning at all, had neither carried away anything from their land nor laid in any store of provisions with a view to war coming upon them, and by their conduct moreover they had brought a reversal and trouble upon themselves. For the oracle uttered by Bakis about these matters runs as follows:

"Mark, when a man, a Barbarian, shall yoke the Sea with papyrus,
   Then do thou plan to remove the loud-bleating goats from Eubœa."

In the hard times which were either upon them or soon to be expected they might feel very sorry that they had paid no attention to these lines.

21. While these were thus engaged, there came to them the scout from Trachis: for there was at Artemision a scout named Polyas, by birth of Antikyra, to whom it had been appointed, if the fleet should be disabled, to signify this to those at Thermopylai, and he had a vessel equipped and ready for this purpose; and similarly there was with Leonidas Abronichos son of Lysicles, an Athenian, ready to carry news to those at Artemision with a thirty-oared galley, if any disaster should happen to the land-army. This Abronichos then had arrived, and he proceeded to signify to them that which had come to pass about Leonidas and his army; and they when they were informed of it no longer put off their retreat, but set forth as they were severally posted, the Corinthians first and the Athenians last.

22. Themistocles however selected those ships of the Athenians which sailed best, and went round to the springs of drinking-water, cutting inscriptions on the stones there, which the Ionians read when they came to Artemision on the following day. These inscriptions ran thus: "Ionians, you act not rightly in making expedition against the fathers of your race and endeavouring to enslave Hellas.* Best of all were it that you should come and be on our side; but if that may not be done by you, stand aside even now from the combat against us and ask the Carians to do the same as you. If however neither of these two things is possible to be done, and you are bound down by too strong compulsion to be able to make revolt, then in the action, when we engage battle, be purposely slack, remembering that you are descended from us and that our quarrel with the Barbarian took its rise at the first from you." Themistocles wrote thus, having, as I suppose, two things together in his mind, namely that either the inscriptions might elude the notice of the king and cause the Ionians to change and come over to the side on which he was, or that having been reported and denounced to Xerxes they might cause the Ionians to be distrusted by him, and so he might keep them apart from the sea-fights.

23. Themistocles then had set these inscriptions: and to the Barbarians there came immediately after these things a man of Histiaia in a boat bringing word of the retreat of the Hellenes from Artemision. They however, not believing it, kept the messenger under guard and sent swift-sailing ships to look on before. Then these having reported the facts, at last as daylight was spreading over the sky, the whole armament sailed in a body to Artemision; and having stayed at this place till mid-day, after this they sailed to Histiaia, and there arrived they took possession of the city of Histiaia and overran all the villages which lie along the coast in the region of Ellopia, which is the land of Histiaia.

24. While they were there, Xerxes, after he had made his dispositions with regard to the bodies of the dead, sent a herald to the fleet: and the

---

*The story of the multiple, rapid inscriptions is not credible; Herodotus describes the ethnic bond at 1.147.

dispositions which he made beforehand were as follows:—for all those of his army who were lying dead at Thermopylai, (and there were twenty thousand in all), with the exception of about a thousand whom he left, he dug trenches and buried them, laying over them leaves and heaping earth upon them, that they might not be seen by the men of the fleet. Then when the herald had gone over to Histiaia, he gathered an assembly of the whole force and spoke these words: "Allies, king Xerxes grants permission to any one of you who desires it, to leave his post and to come and see how he fights against those most senseless men who looked to overcome the power of the king." 25. When the herald had proclaimed this, then boats were in great request, so many were they who desired to see this sight; and when they had passed over they went through the dead bodies and looked at them: and every one supposed that those who were lying there were all Lacedemonians or Thespians, though the Helots also were among those that they saw: however, they who had passed over did not fail to perceive that Xerxes had done that which I mentioned about the bodies of his own dead; for in truth it was even laughable: on the one side there were seen a thousand dead bodies lying, while the others lay all gathered together in the same place, four thousand of them. During this day then they busied themselves with looking, and on the day after this they sailed back to the ships at Histiaia, while Xerxes and his army set forth upon their march.

26. There had come also to them a few deserters from Arcadia, men in want of livelihood and desiring to be employed. These the Persians brought into the king's presence and inquired about the Hellenes, what they were doing; and one man it was who asked them. They told them that the Hellenes were keeping the Olympic festival and were looking on at a contest of athletics and horsemanship. He then inquired again, what was the prize proposed to them, for the sake of which they contended; and they told them of the wreath of olive which is given. Then Tigranes the son of Artabanos uttered a thought which was most noble, though thereby he incurred from the king the reproach of cowardice: for hearing that the prize was a wreath and not money, he could not endure to keep silence, but in the presence of all he spoke these words: "Ah! Mardonios, what kind of men are these against whom you have brought us to fight, who make their contest not for money but for honour!"

27. In the meantime, so soon as the disaster at Thermopylai had come about, the Thessalians sent a herald immediately to the Phokians, against whom they had a grudge always, but especially because of the latest disaster which they had suffered: for when both the Thessalians themselves and their allies had invaded the Phokian land not many years before this expedition of the king, they had been defeated by the Phokians and handled roughly. For the Phokians had been shut up in Mount Parnassos having with them a soothsayer, Tellias the Eleian; and this Tellias contrived for them a device of the following kind:—he took six hundred men, the best of the Phokians, and whitened them over with chalk, both themselves and their armour, and then he attacked the Thessalians by night, telling the Phokians beforehand to slay every man whom they should see not coloured

over with white. So not only the sentinels of the Thessalians, who saw these first, were terrified by them, supposing it to be something portentous and other than it was, but also after the sentinels the main body of their army; so that the Phokians remained in possession of four thousand bodies of slain men and shields; of which last they dedicated half at Abai and half at Delphi; and from the tithe of the booty got by this battle were made the large statues which are contending for the tripod in front of the temple at Delphi, and others similar to these are dedicated as an offering at Abai. **28.** Thus had the Phokians done to the Thessalian footmen, when they were besieged by them; and they had done irreparable hurt to their cavalry also, when this had invaded their land: for in the pass which is by Hyampolis they had dug a great trench and laid down in it empty wine-jars; and then having carried earth and laid it on the top and made it like the rest of the ground, they waited for the Thessalians to invade their land. These supposing that they would make short work with the Phokians, riding in full course fell upon the wine-jars; and there the legs of their horses were utterly crippled. **29.** Bearing then a grudge for both of these things, the Thessalians sent a herald and addressed them thus: "Phokians, we advise you to be more disposed now to change your minds and to admit that you are not on a level with us: for in former times among the Hellenes, so long as it pleased us to be on that side, we always had the preference over you, and now we have such great power with the Barbarian that it rests with us to cause you to be deprived of your land and to be sold into slavery also. We however, though we have all the power in our hands, do not bear malice, but let there be paid to us fifty talents of silver in return for this, and we will engage to avert the dangers which threaten to come upon your land." **30.** Thus the Thessalians proposed to them; for the Phokians alone of all the people in those parts were not taking the side of the Medes, and this for no other reason, as I conjecture, but only because of their enmity with the Thessalians; and if the Thessalians had supported the cause of the Hellenes, I am of opinion that the Phokians would have been on the side of the Medes. When the Thessalians proposed this, they said that they would not give the money, and that it was open to them to take the Median side just as much as the Thessalians, if they desired it for other reasons; but they would not with their own will be traitors to Hellas.

31. When these words were reported, then the Thessalians, moved with anger against the Phokians, became guides to the Barbarian to show him the way: and from the land of Trachis they entered Doris; for a narrow strip of the Dorian territory extends this way, about three and one-half miles in breadth, lying between Malis and Phokis, the region which was in ancient time called Dryopis; this land is the mother-country of the Dorians in Peloponnese. Now the Barbarians did not lay waste Doris when they entered it, for the people of it were taking the side of the Medes, and also the Thessalians did not desire it. **32.** When however from Doris they entered Phokis, they did not indeed capture the Phokians themselves; for some of them had gone up to the heights of Parnassos,—and that summit of Parnassos is very convenient to receive a large number, which lies by itself near the city of Neōn, the name of it being Tithorea,—to this, I say, some of them had carried up their goods and gone up themselves; but most of them had conveyed their goods out to the Ozolian Locrians, to the city of Amphissa, which is situated above the Crissaian plain. The Barbarians however overran the whole land of Phokis, for so the Thessalians led their army, and all that they came to as they marched they burned or cut down, and delivered to the flames both the cities and the temples: **33,** for they laid everything waste, proceeding this way by the river Kephisos, and they destroyed the city of Drymos by fire, and also the following, namely Charadra, Erochos, Tethronion, Amphikaia, Neōn, Pedieis, Triteis, Elateia, Hyampolis, Parapotamioi and Abai, at which last-named place there was a temple of Apollo, wealthy and furnished with treasuries and votive offerings in abundance; and there was then, as there is even now, the seat of an Oracle there: this temple they plundered and burnt. Some also of the Phokians they pursued and captured upon the mountains, and some women they did to death by repeated rape.

34. Passing by Parapotamioi the Barbarians came to Panopeus, and from this point onwards their army was separated and went different ways. The largest and strongest part of the army, proceeding with Xerxes himself against Athens, entered the land of the Bœotians, coming into the territory of Orchomenos. Now the general body of the Bœotians was taking the side of the Medes, and their cities were being kept by Macedonians appointed for each, who had been sent by Alexander;* and they were keeping them with this aim, namely in order to make it plain to Xerxes that the Bœotians were disposed to be on the side of the Medes. **35.** These, I say, of the Barbarians took their way in this direction; but others of them with guides had set forth to go to the temple at Delphi, keeping Parnassos on their right hand: and all the parts of Phokis over which these marched they ravaged; for they set fire to the towns of Panopeus and Daulis and Aiolis. And for this reason they marched in that direction, divided from the rest of the army, namely in order that they might plunder the temple at Delphi and deliver over the treasures there to king Xerxes: and Xerxes was well acquainted with all that there was in it of any account, better, I am told, than with the things which he had left in his own house at home, seeing that many constantly reported of them, and especially of the votive offerings of Crœsus the son of Alyattes.

36. Meanwhile the Delphians, having been informed of this, had been brought to extreme fear; and being in great terror they consulted the Oracle about the sacred things, whether they should bury them in the earth or carry them forth to another land; but the god forbade them to meddle with these, saying that he was able by himself to take care of his own. Hearing this they began to take thought for themselves, and they sent their children and women over to Achaia on the other side of the sea, while most of the

---

*King of Macedonia (see 5.17–22 and 7.173); sometimes he acted as a mediator (8.136 and 8.140), and sometimes he played a double game, as at 9.45.

men themselves ascended up towards the summits of Parnassos and carried their property to the Corykian cave, while others departed for refuge to Amphissa of the Locrians. In short the Delphians had all left the town excepting sixty men and the interpreter-prophet of the Oracle. **37.** When the Barbarians had come near and could see the temple, then the prophet, whose name was Akeratos, saw before the cell arms lying laid out, having been brought forth out of the sanctuary, which were sacred and on which it was not permitted to any man to lay hands. He then was going to announce the portent to those of the Delphians who were still there, but when the Barbarians pressing onwards came opposite the temple of Athenē Pronaia, portents yet greater than before occurred: Although that too was a great marvel, that arms of war should appear of themselves laid forth outside the cell, yet this, which happened straightway after that, is worthy of marvel beyond all other prodigies. When the Barbarians in their approach were opposite the temple of Athenē Pronaia, at this time from the heaven there fell thunderbolts upon them, and from Parnassos two crags were broken away and rushed down upon them with a great crashing noise falling upon many of them, while from the temple of Pronaia there was heard a shout, and a battle-cry was raised. **38.** All these things having come together, there fell fear upon the Barbarians; and the Delphians having perceived that they were flying, came down after them and slew a great number of them; and those who survived fled straight to Bœotia. These who returned of the Barbarians reported, as I am informed, that in addition to this which we have said they saw also other miraculous things; for two men (they said) in full armour and of stature more than human followed them slaying and pursuing. **39.** These two the Delphians say were the native heroes Phylacos and Autonoös, whose sacred enclosures are about the temple, that of Phylacos being close by the side of the road above the temple of Pronaia and that of Autonoös near Castalia under the peak called Hyampeia. Moreover the rocks which fell from Parnassos were still preserved even to my time, lying in the sacred enclosure of Athenē Pronaia, into which they fell when they rushed through the ranks of the Barbarians. Such was these men's departure from the temple.

40. Meanwhile the fleet of the Hellenes after leaving Artemision put in to land at Salamis at the request of the Athenians: and for this reason, in order that they might remove out of Attica to a place of safety their children and their wives, and also deliberate what they would have to do; for they meant to take counsel afresh, because they had been deceived in their expectation. For they had thought to find the Peloponnesians in full force waiting for the Barbarians in Bœotia; they found however nothing of this, but they were informed on the contrary that the Peloponnesians were fortifying the Isthmus with a wall, valuing above all things the safety of the Peloponnese and keeping this in guard; and that they were disposed to let all else go. Being informed of this, the Athenians therefore made request of them to put in to Salamis.

41. The others then landed at Salamis, but the Athenians went over to their own land; and after their coming they made a proclamation that every one of the Athenians should endeavour to save his children and household as best he could. So the greater number sent them to Troizen, but others to Egina, and others to Salamis, and they were urgent to put these out of danger, both because they desired to obey the oracle and also especially for another reason, which was this:—the Athenians say that a great serpent lives in the temple of Athena Polias and guards the Acropolis; and they not only say this, but also they set forth for it monthly offerings, as if it were really there; and the offering consists of a honey-cake. This honey-cake, which before used always to be consumed, was at this time left untouched. When the priestess had signified this, the Athenians left the city much more and with greater eagerness than before, seeing that the goddess also had (as they supposed) left the Acropolis. Then when all their belongings had been removed out of danger, they sailed to the encampment of the fleet.

42. When those who came from Artemision had landed their ships at Salamis, the remainder of the naval force of the Hellenes, being informed of this, came over gradually to join them from Troizen: for they had been ordered beforehand to assemble at Pogon, which is the harbour of the Troizenians. There were assembled accordingly now many more ships than those which were in the sea-fight at Artemision, and from more cities. Over the whole was set as admiral the same man as at Artemision, namely Eurybiades the son of Eurycleides, a Spartan but not of the royal house; the Athenians however supplied by far the greatest number of ships and those which sailed the best. **43.** The following were those who joined the muster:—From Peloponnese the Lacedemonians furnishing sixteen ships, the Corinthians furnishing the same complement as at Artemision, the Sikyonians furnishing fifteen ships, the Epidaurians ten, the Troizenians five, the men of Hermiōn three, these all, except the Hermionians, being of Doric and Makednian race and having made their last migration from Erineos and Pindos and the land of Dryopis; but the people of Hermiōn are Dryopians, driven out by Heracles and the Malians from the land which is now called Doris. **44.** These were the Peloponnesians who joined the fleet, and those of the mainland outside the Peloponnese were as follows:—the Athenians, furnishing a number larger than all the rest, namely one hundred and eighty ships, and serving alone, since the Plataians did not take part with the Athenians in the sea-fight at Salamis, because when the Hellenes were departing from Artemision and come near Chalkis, the Plataians disembarked on the opposite shore of Bœotia and proceeded to the removal of their households. So being engaged in saving these, they had been left behind. As for the Athenians, in the time when the Pelasgians occupied that which is now called Hellas, they were Pelasgians, being named Cranaoi, and in the time of king Kecrops they came to be called Kecropidai; then when Erechtheus had succeeded to his power, they had their name changed to Athenians; and after Ion the son of Xuthos became commander of the Athenians, they got the name from him of Ionians. **45.** The Megarians furnished the same complement as at Artemision; the Amprakiots came to the assistance of the rest with seven ships, and the Leucadians with three, these being by race Dorians from Corinth. **46.** Of the islanders the Eginetans furnished thirty; these had also other ships manned, but with them they were guarding their own land, while with the thirty which sailed best they joined in the sea-fight at Salamis. Now the Eginetans are Dorians from Epidauros, and their island had formerly the name Oinonē. After the Eginetans came the Chalkidians with the twenty ships which were at Artemision, and the Eretrians with their seven: these are Ionians. Next the Keïans, furnishing the same as before and being by race Ionians from Athens. The Naxians furnished four ships, they having been sent out by the citizens of their State to join the Persians, like the other islanders; but neglecting these commands they had come to the Hellenes, urged thereto by Democritos, a man of repute among the citizens and at that time commander of a trireme. Now the Naxians are Ionians coming originally from Athens. The Styrians furnished the same ships as at Artemision, and the men of Kythnos one ship and one fifty-oared galley, these both being Dryopians. Also the Seriphians, the Siphnians and the Melians served with the rest; for they alone of the islanders had not given earth and water to the Barbarian. **47.** These all who have been named dwelt south-east of the land of the Thesprotians and the river Acheron; for the Thesprotians border upon the land of the Amprakiots and Leucadians, and these were they who came from the greatest distance to serve: but of those who dwell outside these limits the men of Crotōn were the only people who came to the assistance of Hellas in her danger; and these sent one ship, of which the commander was Phaÿllos, a man who had three times won victories at the Pythian games. Now the men of Crotōn are by descent Achaians. **48.** All the rest who served in the fleet furnished triremes, but the Melians, Siphnians and Seriphians fifty-oared galleys: the Melians, who are by descent from Lacedemon, furnished two, the Siphnians and Seriphians, who are Ionians from Athens, each one. And the whole number of the ships, apart from the fifty-oared galleys, was three hundred and seventy-eight.*

49. When the commanders had assembled at Salamis from the States which have been mentioned, they began to deliberate, Eurybiades having proposed that any one should declare his opinion as to where he thought it most convenient to fight a sea-battle in those regions of which they had command; for Attica had already been let go, and he was now proposing the question about the other regions. And the opinions of the speakers for the most part agreed that they should sail to the Isthmus and there fight a sea-battle in defence of the Peloponnese, arguing that if they should be defeated in the sea-battle, supposing them to be at Salamis they would be blockaded in an island, where no help would come to them, but at the Isthmus they would be able to land where their own men were. **50.** While the commanders from the Peloponnese argued thus, an Athenian had come in reporting that the Barbarians were arrived in Attica and that all the land

---

*Only 366, from Herodotus' previous report of contingents; the addition of the Eginetan coastguard may have produced the total given here.

was being laid waste with fire. For the army which directed its march through Bœotia in company with Xerxes, after it had burnt the city of the Thespians (the inhabitants having left it and gone to the Peloponnese) and that of the Plataians likewise, had now come to Athens and was laying waste everything in those regions. Now he had burnt Thespiai and Plataia because he was informed by the Thebans that these were not taking the side of the Medes. **51.** So in three months from the crossing of the Helles- pont, whence the Barbarians began their march, after having stayed there one month while they crossed over into Europe, they had reached Attica, in the year when Calliades was archon of the Athenians.* And they took the lower city, which was deserted, and then they found still a few of the Athenians left in the temple, either stewards of the temple or needy per- sons, who had barred the entrance to the Acropolis with doors and with a palisade of timber and endeavoured to defend themselves against the at- tacks of the enemy, being men who had not gone out to Salamis partly be- cause of their poverty, and also because they thought that they alone had discovered the meaning of the oracle which the Pythian prophetess had uttered to them, namely that the "bulwark of wood" should be impreg- nable, and supposed that this was in fact the safe refuge according to the oracle, and not the ships.

52. So the Persians taking their post upon the rising ground opposite the Acropolis, which the Athenians call the Hill of Ares, proceeded to be- siege them in this fashion, that is they put tow round about their arrows and lighted it, and then shot them against the palisade. The Athenians who were besieged continued to defend themselves nevertheless, although they had come to the extremity of distress and their palisade had played them false; nor would they accept proposals for surrender, when the sons of Pei- sistratos brought them forward: but endeavouring to defend themselves they devised several contrivances against the enemy, and among the rest they rolled down large stones when the Barbarians approached the gates; so that for a long time Xerxes faced difficulty capturing them. **53.** In time however there appeared for the Barbarians a way of approach, since by the oracle it was destined that all of Attica which is on the mainland should come to be under the Persians. On the North side of the Acropolis behind the gates and the way up to the entrance, in a place where no one was keeping guard, nor would one have supposed that any man could as- cend by this way, here men ascended by the temple of Aglauros the daughter of Kecrops, although indeed the place is precipitous: and when the Athenians saw that they had ascended up to the Acropolis, some of them threw themselves down from the wall and perished, while others took refuge in the sanctuary of the temple. Then those of the Persians who had ascended went first to the gates, and after opening these they proceeded to kill the suppliants; and when all had been slain by them, they plundered the temple and set fire to the whole of the Acropolis.

---

*Mid-September of 480 B.C.

54. Then Xerxes, having fully taken possession of Athens, sent to Susa a mounted messenger to report to Artabanos the good success which they had. And on the next day after sending the herald he called together the exiles of the Athenians who were accompanying him, and bade them go up to the Acropolis and sacrifice the victims after their own manner; whether it was that he had seen some vision of a dream which caused him to give this command, or whether perchance he had a scruple in his mind because he had set fire to the temple.

The Athenian exiles did what was commanded them: **55,** and the reason why I made mention of this I will here declare:—there is in this Acropolis a shrine of Erechtheus, who is said to have been born of the Earth, and in this there is an olive-tree and a sea, which (according to the story told by the Athenians) Poseidon and Athenē, when they contended for the land, set as witnesses of themselves. Now this olive-tree was set on fire with the rest of the temple by the Barbarians; and on the next day after the conflagration those of the Athenians who were commanded by the king to offer sacrifice, saw when they had gone up to the temple that a shoot had run up from the stock of the tree about eighteen inches in length. These reported this.

56. The Hellenes meanwhile at Salamis, when they learned how the Acropolis of the Athenians was taken, were disturbed so greatly that some of the commanders did not even wait for the question to be decided which had been proposed, but began to go hastily to their ships and to put up their sails, meaning to make off with speed; and by those of them who remained behind it was finally decided to fight at sea in defence of the Isthmus. So night came on, and dismissed from the council they were going to their ships. **57.** When Themistocles had come to his ship, Mnesiphilos an Athenian asked him what they had resolved; and being informed by him that it had been determined to take out the ships to the Isthmus and fight a battle by sea in defence of the Peloponnese, he said: "Then, if they set sail with the ships from Salamis, you will not fight any more sea-battles at all for the fatherland, for they will all take their way to their several cities and neither Eurybiades nor any other man will be able to detain them or to prevent the fleet from being dispersed: and Hellas will perish by reason of evil counsels. But if there be any means, go and try to unsettle that which has been resolved, if perchance you may persuade Eurybiades to change his plans, so as to stay here." **58.** This advice very much commended itself to Themistocles; and without making any answer he went to the ship of Eurybiades. Having come thither he said that he desired to communicate to him a matter which concerned the common good; and Eurybiades bade him come into his ship and speak, if he desired to say anything. Then Themistocles sitting down beside him repeated to him all those things which he had heard Mnesiphilos say, making as if they were his own thoughts, and adding to them many others; until at last by urgent request he persuaded him to come out of his ship and gather the commanders together to the council.

59. So when they were gathered together, before Eurybiades proposed the discussion of the things for which he had assembled the commanders,

Themistocles spoke with much vehemence being very eager to gain his end; and as he was speaking, the Corinthian commander, Adeimantos the son of Okytos, said: "Themistocles, at the games those who stand forth for the contest before the due time are beaten with rods." He justifying himself said: "Yes, but those who remain behind are not crowned." **60.** At that time he made answer mildly to the Corinthian; and to Eurybiades he said not now any of those things which he had said before, to the effect that if they should set sail from Salamis they would disperse in different directions; for it was not seemly for him to bring charges against the allies in their presence: but he held to another way of reasoning, saying: "Now it is in your power to save Hellas, if you will follow my advice, which is to stay here and here to fight a sea-battle, and if you will not follow the advice of those among these men who bid you remove the ships to the Isthmus. For hear both ways, and then set them in comparison. If you engage battle at the Isthmus, you will fight in an open sea, into which it is by no means convenient for us that we go to fight, seeing that we have ships which are heavier and fewer in number than those of the enemy. Then secondly you will give up to destruction Salamis and Megara and Egina, even if we have success in all else; for with their fleet will come also the land-army, and thus you will yourself lead them to the Peloponnese and will risk the safety of all Hellas. If however you shall do as I say, you will find therein all the advantages which I shall tell you of:—in the first place by engaging in a narrow place with few ships against many, if the fighting has that issue which it is reasonable to expect, we shall have very much the better; for to fight a sea-fight in a narrow place is for our advantage, but to fight in a wide open space is for theirs. Then again Salamis will be preserved, whither our children and our wives have been removed for safety; and moreover there is this also secured thereby, to which you are most of all attached, namely that by remaining here you will fight in defence of the Peloponnese as much as if the fight were at the Isthmus; and you will not lead the enemy to Peloponnese, if you are wise. Then if that which I expect come to pass and we gain a victory with our ships, the Barbarians will not come to you at the Isthmus nor will they advance further than Attica, but they will retire in disorder; and we shall be the gainers by the preservation of Megara and Egina and Salamis, at which place too an oracle tells us that we shall get the victory over our enemies. Now when men take counsel reasonably for themselves, reasonable issues are wont as a rule to come, but if they do not take counsel reasonably, then God does not generally attach himself to the judgment of men."

61. When Themistocles thus spoke, the Corinthian Adeimantos inveighed against him for the second time, bidding him be silent because he had no native land, and urging Eurybiades not to put to the vote the proposal of one who was a citizen of no city; for he said that Themistocles might bring opinions before the council if he could show a city belonging to him, but otherwise not. This objection he made against him because Athens had been taken and was held by the enemy. Then Themistocles said many evil things of him and of the Corinthians both, and declared also that he himself and his countrymen had in truth a city and a land larger than that of the Corinthians, so long as they had two hundred ships fully manned; for none of the Hellenes would be able to repel the Athenians if they came to fight against them. **62.** Signifying this he turned then to Eurybiades and spoke yet more urgently: "If you will remain here, and remaining here show yourself a good man, well; but if not, you will bring about the overthrow of Hellas, for upon the ships depends all our power in the war. Nay, but do as I advise. If, however, you shall not do so, we shall immediately take up our households and voyage to Siris in Italy, which is ours already of old and the oracles say that it is destined to be colonised by us; and you, when you are left alone and deprived of allies such as we are, will remember my words." **63.** When Themistocles thus spoke, Eurybiades was persuaded to change his mind; and, as I think, he changed his mind chiefly from fear lest the Athenians should depart and leave them, if he should take the ships to the Isthmus; for if the Athenians left them and departed, the rest would be no longer able to fight with the enemy. He chose then this counsel, to stay in that place and decide matters there by a sea-fight.

64. Thus those at Salamis, after having skirmished with one another in speech, were making preparations for a sea-fight there, since Eurybiades had so determined: and as day was coming on, at the same time when the sun rose there was an earthquake felt both on the land and on the sea: and they determined to pray to the gods and to call upon the sons of Aiacos to be their helpers. And so also they did; for when they had prayed to all the gods, they called Ajax and Telamon to their help from Salamis, where the fleet was, and sent a ship to Egina to bring Aiacos himself and the rest of the sons of Aiacos.

65. Moreover Dicaios the son of Theokydes, an Athenian, who was an exile and had become of great repute among the Medes at this time, declared that when the Attic land was being ravaged by the land-army of Xerxes, having been deserted by the Athenians, he happened then to be in company with Demaratos the Lacedemonian in the Thriasian plain; and he saw a cloud of dust going up from Eleusis, as if made by a company of about thirty thousand men, and they wondered at the cloud of dust, by what men it was caused. Then immediately they heard a sound of voices, and Dicaios perceived that the sound was the mystic cry *Iacchos;* but Demaratos, having no knowledge of the sacred rites which are done at Eleusis, asked him what this was that uttered the sound, and he said: "Demaratos, it cannot be but that some great destruction is about to come to the army of the king: for as to this, it is very manifest, seeing that Attica is deserted, that this which utters the sound is of the gods, and that it is going from Eleusis to help the Athenians and their allies: if then it shall come down in the Peloponnese, there is danger for the king himself and for the army which is upon the mainland, but if it shall direct its course towards the ships which are at Salamis, the king will be in danger of losing his fleet. This feast the Athenians celebrate every year to the Mother and the Daughter;* and he that desires it, both of them and of the other Hellenes, is initiated in the mysteries; and the sound of voices which you hearest is the cry *Iacchos* which they utter at this feast."

To this Demaratos said: "Keep silence and tell not this tale to any other man; for if your words be reported to the king, you will lose your head, and neither I nor any other man upon earth will be able to save you: but keep quiet, and about this expedition the gods will provide." He then thus advised, and after the cloud of dust and the sound of voices there came a mist which was borne aloft and carried towards Salamis to the camp of the Hellenes: and thus they learnt (said he) that the fleet of Xerxes was destined to be destroyed. Such was the report made by Dicaios the son of Theokydes, appealing to Demaratos and others also as witnesses.

66. Meanwhile those who were appointed to serve in the fleet of Xerxes, having gazed in Trachis upon the disaster of the Lacedemonians and having passed over from thence to Histiaia, after staying three days sailed through Euripos, and in another three days they had reached Phaleron. And, as I suppose, they made their attack upon Athens not fewer in number both by land and sea than when they arrived at Sepias and at Thermopylai: for against those of them who perished by reason of the storm and those who were slain at Thermopylai and in the sea-fights at Artemision, I will set those who at that time were not yet accompanying the king, the Malians, Dorians, Locrians, and Bœotians (who accompanied him in a body, except the Thespians and Plataians), and moreover those of Carystos, Andros, and Tenos, with all the other islanders except the five cities of which I mentioned the names before; for the more the Persian advanced towards the centre of Hellas, the more nations accompanied him.

67. So then, when all these had come to Athens except the Parians, (now the Parians had remained behind at Kythnos waiting to see how the war would turn out),—when all the rest, I say, had come to Phaleron, then Xerxes himself came down to the ships desiring to visit them and to learn the opinions of those who sailed in them: and when he had come and was set in a conspicuous place, then those who were despots of their own nations or commanders of divisions being sent for came before him from their ships, and took their seats as the king had assigned rank to each one, first the king of Sidon, then he of Tyre, and after them the rest: and when they were seated in due order, Xerxes sent Mardonios and inquired, making trial of each one, whether he should fight a battle by sea. **68.** So when Mardonios went round asking them, beginning with the king of Sidon, the others gave their opinions all to the same effect, advising him to fight a battle by sea, but Artemisia spoke these words:—(*a*) "Tell the king for me, Mardonios, that I, who have proved myself to be not the worst in the sea-fights which have been fought near Eubœa, and have displayed deeds not inferior to those of others, speak to him thus: Master, it is right that I set forth the opinion which I really have, and say that which I happen to think best for your cause: and this I say,—spare your ships and do not make a sea-fight; for the men are as much stronger than your men by sea, as men are stronger than

---

*Demeter and Persephone enjoyed a sanctuary, mystery cult, and an annual festival at Eleusis, 14 miles west of Athens.

women. And why do you need to run the risk of sea-battles? have you not Athens in your possession, for the sake of which you did set forth on your march, and also the rest of Hellas? and no man stands in your way to resist, but those who did stand against you came off as it was fitting that they should. (*b*) Now the manner in which I think the affairs of your adversaries will have their issue, I will declare. If you do not hasten to make a sea-fight, but keep your ships here by the land, either remaining here yourself or even advancing on to the Peloponnese, that which you have come to do, O master, will easily be effected; for the Hellenes are not able to hold out against you for any long time, but you will soon disperse them and they will take flight to their several cities: since neither have they provisions with them in this island, as I am informed, nor is it probable that if you shall march your land-army against the Peloponnese, they who have come from thence will remain still; for these will have no care to fight a battle in defence of Athens. (*c*) If however you hasten to fight soon, I fear that damage done to the fleet may ruin the land-army also. Moreover, O king, consider also this, that the servants of good men are apt to grow bad, but those of bad men good; and you, who are of all men the best, have bad servants, namely those who are reckoned as allies, Egyptians and Cyprians and Kilikians and Pamphylians, in whom there is no profit." **69.** When she thus spoke to Mardonios, those who were friendly to Artemisia were grieved at her words, supposing that she would suffer some evil from the king because she urged him not to fight at sea; while those who had envy and jealousy of her, because she had been honoured above all the allies, rejoiced at the opposition, supposing that she would now be ruined. When however the opinions were reported to Xerxes, he was greatly pleased with the opinion of Artemisia; and whereas even before this he thought her excellent, he commended her now yet more. Nevertheless he gave orders to follow the advice of the greater number, thinking that when they fought by Eubœa they were purposely slack, because he was not himself present with them, whereas now he had made himself ready to look on while they fought a sea-battle.

70. So when they passed the word to put out to sea, they brought their ships out to Salamis and quietly ranged themselves along the shore in their several positions. At that time the daylight was not sufficient for them to engage battle, for night had come on; but they made their preparations to fight on the following day. Meanwhile the Hellenes experienced fear and dismay, especially those who were from Peloponnese: and these were dismayed because remaining in Salamis they were to fight a battle on behalf of the land of the Athenians, and being defeated they would be cut off from escape and blockaded in an island, leaving their own land unguarded. And indeed the land-army of the Barbarians was marching forward during that very night towards the Peloponnese. **71.** Yet every means had been taken that the Barbarians might not be able to enter Peloponnesus by land: for as soon as the Peloponnesians heard that Leonidas and his company had perished at Thermopylai, they came together quickly from the cities and took post at the Isthmus, and over them was set as commander Cleombrotos, the son of Anaxandrides and brother of Leonidas. These being posted at the Isthmus had destroyed the Skironian way, and after this (having so determined in counsel with one another) they began to build a wall across the Isthmus; and as they were many thousands and every man joined in the work, the work proceeded fast; for stones and bricks and pieces of timber and baskets full of sand were carried to it continually, and they who had thus come to help paused not at all in their work either by night or by day. **72.** Now those of the Hellenes who came in full force to the Isthmus to help were these,— the Lacedemonians, the Arcadians of every division, the Eleians, Corinthians, Sikyonians, Epidaurians, Phliasians, Troizenians and Hermionians. These were they who came to the help of Hellas in her danger and who had apprehension for her, while the rest of the Peloponnesians showed no care: and the Olympic and Carneian festivals had by this time gone by. **73.** Now Peloponnesus is inhabited by seven races; and of these, two are natives of the soil and are settled now in the place where they dwelt of old, namely the Arcadians and the Kynurians; and one race, that of the Achaians, though it did not remove from Peloponnese, yet removed in former time from its own land and dwells now in that which was not its own. The remaining races, four in number, have come in from without, namely the Dorians, Aitolians, Dryopians and Lemnians. Of the Dorians there are many cities and of great renown; of the Aitolians, Elis alone; of the Dryopians, Hermiōn and Asinē, which latter is opposite Cardamylē in the Laconian land; and of the Lemnians, all the Paroreatai. The Kynurians, who are natives of the soil, seem alone to be Ionians, but they have become Dorians completely because they are subject to the Argives and by lapse of time, being originally citizens of Orneai or the dwellers in the country round Orneai. Of these seven nations the remaining cities, except those which I enumerated just now, stood aside and did nothing; and if one may be allowed to speak freely, in thus standing aside they were in fact taking the side of the Medes.

74. Those at the Isthmus were struggling with the labour which I have said, since now they were running a race in which their very being was at stake, and they did not look to have any brilliant success with their ships: while those who were at Salamis, though informed of this work, were yet dismayed, not fearing so much for themselves as for Peloponnesus. For some time then they spoke of it in private, one man standing by another, and they marvelled at the ill-counsel of Eurybiades; but at last it broke out publicly. A meeting accordingly was held, and much was spoken about the same points as before, some saying that they ought to sail away to Peloponnesus and run the risk in defence of that, and not stay and fight for a land which had been captured by the enemy, while the Athenians, Eginetans and Megarians urged that they should stay there and defend themselves. **75.** Then Themistocles, when his opinion was like to be defeated by the Peloponnesians, secretly went forth from the assembly, and having gone out he sent a man to the encampment of the Medes in a boat, charging him with that which he must say: this man's name was Sikinnos, and he was a slave of Themistocles and tutor to his children; and after these events Themistocles entered him as a Thespian citizen, when the Thespians were admitting new citizens, and made him a wealthy man. He at this time came with a boat and said to the commanders of the Barbarians these words: "The commander of the Athenians sent me privately without the knowledge of the other Hellenes (for he is disposed to the cause of the king, and desires that your side should gain the victory rather than that of the Hellenes), to inform you that the Hellenes are planning to take flight, having been struck with dismay; and now it is possible for you to execute a most noble work, if you do not permit them to flee away: for they are not of one mind with one another and they will not stand against you in fight, but ye shall see them fighting a battle by sea with one another, those who are disposed to your side against those who are not."

76. He then having signified to them this, departed; and they, thinking that the message deserved credit, landed first a large number of Persians in the small island of Psyttaleia, which lies between Salamis and the mainland; and then, as midnight came on, they put out the Western wing of their fleet to sea, circling round towards Salamis, and also those stationed about Keos and Kynosura put out their ships to sea; and they occupied all the passage with their ships as far as Munychia. And for this reason they put out their ships, namely in order that the Hellenes might not be permitted to get away, but being cut off in Salamis might pay the penalty for the contests at Artemision: and they disembarked men of the Persians on the small island called Psyttaleia for this reason, namely that when the fight should take place, these might save the men of the one side and destroy those of the other, since there especially it was likely that the men and the wrecks of ships would be cast up on shore, for the island lay in the way of the coming sea-fight. These things they readied in silence, that the enemy might not learn of them.

[**77.** They then were making their preparations thus in the night without having taken any sleep at all: and with regard to oracles, I am not able to make objections against them that they are not true, for I do not desire to attempt to overthrow the credit of them when they speak clearly, looking at such matters as these:

"But when with ships they shall join the sacred strand of the goddess,
  Artemis golden-sword-girded, and thee, wave-washed Kynosura,
  Urged by a maddening hope, having given rich Athens to plunder,
  Then shall Justice divine quell Riot, of Insolence first-born,
  Longing to overthrow all things and terribly panting for bloodshed:
  Brass shall encounter with brass, and Ares the sea shall empurple,
  Tinging its waves with the blood: then a day of freedom for Hellas
  Cometh from wide-seeing Zeus and from Victory, lady and mother."*

Looking to such things as this, and when Bakis speaks so clearly, I do not venture myself to make any objections about oracles, nor can I admit them from others.]

78. Now the commanders at Salamis were greatly contending in speech

---

*Good critics reject chapter 77 as a later interpolation. See 8.20 for more oracles from Bakis; also 8.96 and 9.43.

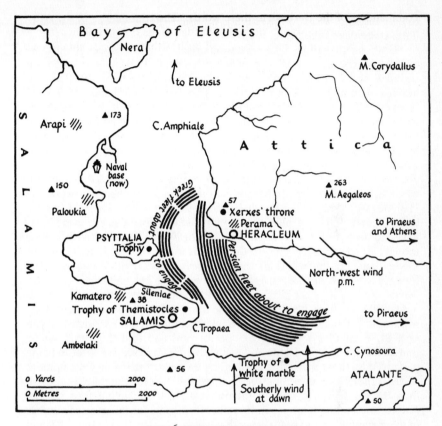

MAP 6. THE BATTLE OF SALAMIS.

and they did not yet know that the Barbarians were surrounding them
with their ships, but they thought that they were still in their place as they
saw them disposed in the day. **79.** Then while the commanders were engaged in strife, there came over from Egina Aristeides the son of Lysimachos, an Athenian who had been ostracised by the people, a man whom I
hold (according to that which I hear of his character) to have been the
best and most upright of all Athenians.* This man came into the council
and called forth Themistocles, who was to him not a friend, but a bitter
enemy; but because of the greatness of the present troubles he let those
matters be forgotten and called him forth, desiring to communicate with
him. Now he had heard beforehand that the Peloponnesians were pressing

---

*See Plutarch's anecdotal life of this aristocrat; also see Fornara 41 for ostracism
at Athens.

to take the ships away to the Isthmus. So when Themistocles came forth to him, Aristeides spoke these words:

"Both at other times when occasion arises, and also especially now we ought to carry on rivalry as to which of us shall do more service to our country. And I tell you now that it is indifferent whether the Peloponnesians say many words or few about sailing away from hence; for having been myself an eye-witness I tell you that now not even if the Corinthians and Eurybiades himself desire to sail out, will they be able; for we are encompassed round by the enemy. Go in then, and signify this to them." **80.** He made answer as follows: "You advise very well, and also the news which you have brought is good, since you are come having witnessed with your own eyes that which I desired might come to pass: for know that this which is being done by the Medes is of my suggestion; because, when the Hellenes would not come to a battle of their own will, it was necessary to bring them over to us against their will. However, since you are come bearing good news, report it to them yourself; for if I say these things, I shall be thought to speak that which I have myself invented, and I shall not persuade them, but they will think that the Barbarians are not doing so. Come forward to speak, and declare to them how things are; and when you have declared this, if they are persuaded, that will be the best thing; but if this is not credible to them, it will be the same thing so far as concerns us, for they will no longer be able to flee, if we are encompassed on all sides, as you say." **81.** Aristeides accordingly came forward and told them this, saying that he had come from Egina and had with difficulty escaped without being perceived by those who were blockading them; for the whole encampment of the Hellenes was encompassed by the ships of Xerxes; and he counselled them to get ready to defend themselves. He then having thus spoken retired, and among them again there arose dispute, for the greater number of the commanders did not believe that which was reported to them: **82,** and while these were doubting, there came a trireme manned by Tenians, deserting from the enemy, of which the commander was Panaitios the son of Sosimenes, which brought them the whole truth. For this deed the Tenians were inscribed at Delphi on the tripod among those who had conquered the Barbarians.* With the ship which deserted at Salamis and the Lemnian ship which deserted before and came to Artemision, the naval force of the Hellenes was completed to the number of three hundred and eighty ships, for before this two ships were yet wanting to make up this number.

83. The Hellenes then, since they believed that which was said by the Tenians, were preparing for a sea-fight:† and as the dawn appeared, they made an assembly of those who fought on board the ships and addressed them, Themistocles making a speech which was eloquent beyond the rest; and the substance of it was to set forth all that is better as opposed to that

---

*See 9.81 and the footnote there.
†The battle of Salamis was fought on September 20 of 480 B.C.; Aeschylus' tragedy *Persians* furnishes a combatant's account.

which is worse, of the several things which arise in the nature and constitution of man; and having exhorted them to choose the better, and thus having wound up his speech, he bade them embark in their ships. These then proceeded to embark, and there came in meanwhile the trireme from Egina which had gone away to bring the sons of Aiacos. **84.** Then the Hellenes put out all their ships, and while they were putting out from shore, the Barbarians attacked them right away. Now the other Hellenes began backing their ships and were about to run them aground, but Ameinias of Pallenē, an Athenian, put forth with his ship and charged one of the enemy; and his ship being entangled in combat and the men not being able to get away, the others joined in the fight to assist Ameinias. The Athenians say that the beginning of the battle was made thus, but the Eginetans say that the ship which went away to Egina to bring the sons of Aiacos was that which began the fight. It is also reported that an apparition of a woman was seen by them, and that having appeared she encouraged them to the fight so that the whole army of the Hellenes heard it, first having reproached them in these words: "Strange men, how far will you yet back your ships?"

85. Opposite the Athenians had been ranged the Phenicians, for these occupied the wing towards Eleusis and the West, and the opposite the Lacedemonians were the Ionians, who occupied the wing which extended to the East and to Piræus. Of them however a few were purposely slack in the fight according to the injunctions of Themistocles, but the greater number were not so. I might mention now the names of many captains of ships who destroyed ships of the Hellenes, but I will mention only Theomestor the son of Androdamas and Phylacos the son of Histiaios, of Samos both. For this reason I make mention of these, because Theomestor on account of this deed became despot of Samos, appointed by the Persians, and Phylacos was recorded as a benefactor of the king and received much land as a reward. Now the benefactors of the king are called in the Persian tongue *orosangai.* **86.** Thus it was with these; but the greater number of their ships were disabled at Salamis, being destroyed some by the Athenians and others by the Eginetans: for since the Hellenes fought in order and ranged in their places, while the Barbarians were no longer ranged in order nor did anything with design, it was likely that there would be some such result as in fact followed. Yet on this day they surpassed themselves much more than when they fought by Euboea, every one being eager and fearing Xerxes, and each man thinking that the king was looking especially at him.

87. As regards the rest I cannot speak of them separately, or say precisely how the Barbarians or the Hellenes individually contended in the fight; but with regard to Artemisia this happened, whence she gained yet more esteem than before from the king.—When the affairs of the king had come to great confusion, at this crisis the ship of Artemisia was being pursued by an Athenian ship; and as she was not able to escape, for in front of her were other ships of her own side, while her ship, as it chanced, was furthest advanced towards the enemy, she resolved what she would do, and it proved also much to her advantage to have done so. While she was being pursued by the Athenian ship she charged in full career against a ship of

her own side manned by Calyndians and in which the king of the Calyndians Damasithymos was embarked. Now, even though it be true that she
had had some strife with him before, while they were still about the Hellespont, yet I am not able to say whether she did this by intention, or whether
the Calyndian ship by chance fell in her way. Having charged against it
however and sunk it, she enjoyed good fortune and got for herself good in
two ways; for first the captain of the Athenian ship, when he saw her charge
against a ship manned by Barbarians, turned away and went after others,
supposing that the ship of Artemisia was either a Hellenic ship or was deserting from the Barbarians and fighting for the Hellenes, **88,**—first, I say, it
was her fortune to escape and not suffer destruction; and then secondly it
happened that though she had done mischief, she yet gained great reputation by this thing with Xerxes. For it is said that the king looking on at the
fight perceived that her ship had charged the other; and one of those present
said: "Master, do you see Artemisia, how well she is fighting and how she
sank even now a ship of the enemy?" He asked whether this was in truth the
deed of Artemisia, and they said that it was; for (they declared) they knew
very well the sign of her ship: and that which was destroyed they thought
surely was one of the enemy; for besides other things which happened fortunately for her, as I have said, there was this also, namely that not one of
the crew of the Calyndian ship survived to become her accuser. And Xerxes
in answer to that which was said to him is reported to have uttered these
words: "My men have become women, and my women men." **89.** And
meanwhile in this struggle there was slain the commander Ariabignes, son
of Dareios and brother of Xerxes, and there were slain too many others of
note of the Persians and Medes and also of the allies; and of the Hellenes
on their part a few; for since they knew how to swim, those whose ships
were destroyed and who were not slain in hand-to-hand conflict swam
over to Salamis; but of the Barbarians the greater number perished in the
sea, not being able to swim. And when the first ships turned to flight, then
it was that the largest number perished, for those who were stationed behind, while endeavouring to pass with their ships to the front in order that
they also might display some deed of valour for the king to see, ran into
the ships of their own side as they fled.

90. It happened also in this confusion that some of the Phenicians,
whose ships had been destroyed, came to the king and accused the Ionians, saying that by means of them their ships had been lost, and that they
had been traitors to the cause. Now not only the commanders of the Ionians did not lose their lives, but the Phenicians who accused them received
this reward. While these men were yet speaking thus, a Samothrakian
ship charged against an Athenian ship: and as the Athenian ship was being sunk by it, an Eginetan ship came up against the Samothrakian vessel
and ran it down. Then the Samothrakians, being skilful javelin-throwers,
by hurling cleared off the fighting-men from the ship which had wrecked
theirs and then embarked upon it and took possession of it. This event
saved the Ionians from punishment; for when Xerxes saw that they had
performed a great exploit, he turned to the Phenicians (for he was

exceedingly vexed and disposed to find fault with all) and bade cut off their heads, in order that they might not, after having been cowards themselves, accuse others who were better men than they. For whensoever Xerxes (sitting just under the mountain opposite Salamis, which is called Aigaleōs) saw any one of his own side display a deed of valour in the sea-fight, he inquired about him who had done it, and the scribes recorded the name of the ship's captain with that of his father and the city from whence he came. Moreover also Ariaramnes, a Persian who was present, shared the fate of the Phenicians, being their friend. They then proceeded to deal with the Phenicians.

91. In the meantime, as the Barbarians turned to flight and were sailing out towards Phaleron, the Eginetans waited for them in the passage and displayed memorable actions: for while the Athenians in the confused tumult were disabling both those ships which resisted and those which were fleeing, the Eginetans were destroying those which attempted to sail away; and whenever any escaped the Athenians, they went in full course and fell among the Eginetans. **92.** Then the ship of Themistocles, which was pursuing a ship of the enemy, met that of Polycritos the son of Crios the Eginetan. This last had charged against a ship of Sidon, the same that had taken the Eginetan vessel which was keeping watch in advance at Skiathos,* and in which sailed Pytheas the son of Ischenoös, whom the Persians kept in their ship, all cut to pieces as he was, making a marvel of his valour. The Sidonian ship then was captured bearing with it this man as well as the Persians of whom I spoke, so that Pytheas thus came safe to Egina. Now when Polycritos looked at the Athenian vessel he recognised when he saw it the sign of the admiral's ship, and shouting out he addressed Themistocles with mockery about the accusation brought against the Eginetans of taking the side of the Medes, and reproached him. This taunt Polycritos threw out against Themistocles after he had charged against the ship of Sidon. And meanwhile those Barbarians whose ships had escaped destruction fled and came to Phaleron for protection from the land-army.

93. In this sea-fight the Eginetans were of all the Hellenes the best reported of, and next to them the Athenians; and of the individual men the Eginetan Polycritos and the Athenians Eumenes of Anagyrus and Ameinias of Pallenē, the man who had pursued Artemisia. Now if he had known that Artemisia was sailing in this ship, he would not have ceased until either he had taken her or had been taken himself; for orders had been given to the Athenian captains, and moreover a prize was offered of ten thousand drachmas for the man who should take her alive; since they thought it intolerable that a woman should make an expedition against Athens. She then, as has been said before, had made her escape; and the others also, whose ships had escaped destruction, were at Phaleron.

94. As regards Adeimantos the commander of the Corinthians, the Athenians say that as soon as the ships were engaging in the fight, being

---

*See 7.179–181.

struck with panic and terror he put up his sails and fled away; and the Corinthians, when they saw the admiral's ship fleeing, departed likewise: and after this, as the story goes, when they came in their flight opposite to the temple of Athenē Skiras in the land of Salamis, there fell in with them by divine guidance a small vessel, which no one was ever found to have sent, and which approached the Corinthians at a time when they knew nothing of that which was happening with the fleet. And by this the Athenians conjectured that the matter was of the Deity; for when they came near to the ships, the men in the light vessel said these words: "Adeimantos, you have turned your ships away and have set forth to flee, deserting the cause of the Hellenes, while they are in truth gaining a victory and getting the better of their foes as much as they desired." When they said this, since Adeimantos doubted of it, they spoke a second time and said that they might be taken as hostages and slain, if the Hellenes should prove not to be gaining the victory. Then he turned his ship back, he and the others with him, and they reached the camp when the work was finished. Such is the report spread by the Athenians against these: the Corinthians themselves however do not allow this to be so, but hold that they were among the first in the sea-fight; and the rest of Hellas also bears witness on their side.*

95. Aristeides moreover the son of Lysimachos, the Athenian, of whom I made mention also shortly before this as a very good man, he in this tumult which had arisen about Salamis did as follows:—taking with him a number of the hoplites of Athenian race who had been ranged along the shore of Salamis, with them he disembarked on the island of Psyttaleia; and these slew all the Persians who were on this islet.

96. When the sea-fight had been broken off, the Hellenes towed in to Salamis so many of the wrecks as chanced to be still about there, and held themselves ready for another sea-fight, expecting that the king would yet make use of the ships which remained unhurt; but many of the wrecks were taken by the West Wind and borne to that beach in Attica called Colias; so as to fulfil not only all that other oracle which was spoken about this sea-fight by Bakis and Musaios, but also especially, with reference to the wrecks cast up here, that which had been spoken in an oracle many years before these events by Lysistratos, an Athenian who uttered oracles, and which had not been observed by any of the Hellenes:

"Then shall the Colian women with firewood of oars roast barley."

This was destined to come to pass after the king had marched away.

97. When Xerxes perceived the disaster which had come upon him, he feared lest some one of the Ionians should suggest to the Hellenes, or they should themselves form the idea, to sail to the Hellespont and break up the bridges; and so he might be cut off in Europe and run the risk of perishing

---

*Fornara 21 preserves their epitaph found on Salamis.

utterly: therefore he began to consider taking flight. He desired however that his intention should not be perceived either by the Hellenes or by those of his own side; therefore he attempted to construct a mole going across to Salamis, and he bound together Phenician merchant vessels in order that they might serve him both for a bridge and a wall, and made preparations for fighting as if he were going to have another battle by sea. Seeing him do so, all the rest were convinced that he had got himself ready in earnest and intended to stay and fight; but Mardonios did not fail to perceive the true meaning of all these things, being by experience very well versed in his way of thinking.

98. While Xerxes was doing thus, he sent a messenger to the Persians, to announce the calamity which had come upon them. Now there is nothing mortal which accomplishes a journey with more speed than these messengers, so skilfully has this been devised by the Persians: for they say that according to the number of the days of which the entire journey consists, so many horses and men are set at intervals, each man and horse appointed for a day's journey. These neither snow nor rain nor heat nor darkness of night prevents from accomplishing each one the task proposed to him, with the very utmost speed. The first then rides and delivers the message with which he is charged to the second, and the second to the third; and after that it goes through them handed from one to the other, as in the torch-race among the Hellenes, which they perform for Hephaistos. This kind of running of their horses the Persians call *angareion*. **99.** The first message then which came to Susa, announcing that Xerxes had Athens in his possession, so greatly rejoiced the Persians who had been left behind, that they strewed all the ways with myrtle boughs and offered incense perpetually, and themselves continued in sacrifices and feasting. The second message however, which came to them after this, so greatly disturbed them that they all tore their garments and gave themselves up to crying and lamentation without stint, laying the blame upon Mardonios: and this the Persians did not so much because they were grieved about the ships, as because they feared for Xerxes himself.

100. The Persians grieved for all the time which intervened, until the coming of Xerxes himself caused them to cease: and Mardonios seeing that Xerxes was greatly troubled by the sea-fight, and suspecting that he was meaning to take flight from Athens, considered with regard to himself that he would have to suffer punishment for having persuaded the king to make an expedition against Hellas, and that it was better for him to run the risk of either subduing Hellas or ending his own life honourably, placing his safety in suspense for a great end, though his opinion was rather that he would subdue Hellas. He addressed the king as follows: "Master, do not grieve, or feel great trouble on account of this thing which has come to pass; for it is not upon a contest of timbers that all our fortunes depend, but of men and of horses: and none of these who suppose now that all has been achieved by them will attempt to disembark from the ships and stand against you, nor will any in this mainland do so; but those who did stand against us paid the penalty. If therefore you think this good to do, let us now attempt the Peloponnese, or if you think good to hold back, we may do that. Do not despond however, for there is no way for the Hellenes to avoid being your slaves, after they have first given an account of that which they did to you both now and at former times. Thus it were best to do; but if you have indeed resolved to retire and to withdraw your army, I have another counsel to offer for that case too. Do not, king, let the Persians be an object of laughter to the Hellenes; for none of your affairs have suffered by means of the Persians, nor will you be able to mention any place where we proved ourselves cowards: but if Phenicians or Egyptians or Cyprians or Kilikians proved themselves cowards, the calamity which followed does not belong to the Persians in any way. Now therefore, since it is not the Persians who are guilty towards you, follow my counsel. If you have determined not to remain here, retire to your own abode, taking with you the main body of the army, and it must then be for me to deliver over to you Hellas reduced to subjection, choosing for this purpose three hundred thousand men from the army."

101. Hearing this Xerxes was rejoiced and delighted so far as he might be after his misfortunes, and to Mardonios he said that when he had taken counsel he would reply and say which of these two things he would do. So when he was taking counsel with those of the Persians who were called to be his advisers, it seemed good to him to send for Artemisia also to give him counsel, because at the former time she alone had showed herself to have perception of that which ought to be done. So when Artemisia had come, Xerxes removed all the rest, both the Persian councillors and also the spearmen of the guard and spoke to her thus: "Mardonios bids me stay here and make an attempt on the Peloponnese, saying that the Persians and the land-army are not guilty of any share in my calamity, and that they would gladly give me proof of this. He bids me therefore either do this or, if not, he desires himself to choose three hundred thousand men from the army and to deliver over to me Hellas reduced to subjection; and he bids me withdraw with the rest of the army to my own abode. As you did well advise about the sea-fight which was fought, urging that we should not bring it on, so also now advise me which of these things I shall do, that I may succeed in determining well." **102.** He thus consulted her, and she spoke these words: "O king, it is hard for me to succeed in saying the best things when one asks me for counsel; yet it seems good to me at the present that you should retire back and leave Mardonios here, if he desires it and undertakes to do this, together with those whom he desires to have: for on the one hand if he subdue those whom he says that he desires to subdue, and if those matters succeed well which he has in his mind when he thus speaks, the deed will after all be yours, master, seeing that your slaves achieved it: and on the other hand if the opposite shall come to pass of that which Mardonios intends, it will be no great misfortune, seeing that you will yourself remain safe, and also the power in those parts, Asia, which concerns your house: for if you shall remain safe with your house, many contests many times over repeated will the Hellenes have to pass through for their own existence. Of Mardonios however, if he suffer any disaster, no account will be made; and if the Hellenes conquer they gain a victory which is no victory, having destroyed one who is but your slave. You however will retire having done that for which you made your march, that is to say, having delivered Athens to the fire."

103. With this advice Xerxes was greatly delighted, since she succeeded in saying that very thing which he himself was meaning to do: for not even if all the men and all the women in the world had been counselling him to remain, would he have done so, as I think, so much had he been struck with terror. He commended Artemisia therefore and sent her away to conduct his sons to Ephesos, for there were certain bastard sons of his which accompanied him. **104.** With these sons he sent Hermotimos to have charge of them, who was by race of Pedasa and was in the estimation of the king second to none of the eunuchs. [Now the Pedasians dwell above Halicarnassos, and at this Pedasa a thing happens as follows:—whenever to the whole number of those who dwell about this city some trouble is about to come within a certain time, then the priestess of Athenē in that place gets a long beard; and this has happened to them twice before now. **105.** Of these Pedasians was Hermotimos.]* And this man of all persons whom we know up to this time obtained the greatest revenge for a wrong done to him. For he had been captured by enemies and was being sold, and Panionios a man of Chios bought him, one who had set himself to gain his livelihood by the most impious practises; for whenever he obtained boys who possessed some beauty, he would make eunuchs of them, and then taking them to Sardis or Ephesos sold them for large sums of money, since with the Barbarians eunuchs are held to be of more value for all matters of trust than those who are not eunuchs. Panionios then, I say, made eunuchs of many others, since by this he got his livelihood, and also of this man. Hermotimos, being not in everything unfortunate, was sent from Sardis to the king with other gifts, and as time went on he come to be honoured more than all the other eunuchs in the sight of Xerxes.

106. And when the king, being at that time in Sardis, was setting the Persian army in motion to march against Athens, then Hermotimos, having gone down for some business to that part of Mysia which the Chians occupy and which is called Atarneus, found there Panionios: and having recognised him he spoke to him many friendly words, first recounting to him all the good things which he had by his means, and next making promises in return for this, and saying how many good things he would do for him, if he would bring his household and dwell in that land; so that Panionios gladly accepting his proposals brought his children and his wife. Then, when he had caught him together with his whole house, Hermotimos spoke as follows: "O you, who of all men that ever lived up to this time did gain your substance by the most impious deeds, what evil did either I myself or any of my forefathers do either to you or to any of yours, that you

---

*Much here repeats 1.175 and so has been suspected as interpolation.

made me a nothing instead of a man? Did you suppose that you would escape the notice of the gods for such things? They however following the
rule of justice delivered you into my hands, since you had done impious
deeds; so that you shall not have reason to find fault with the penalty
which shall be inflicted upon you by me." When he had thus reproached
him, the man's sons were brought into his presence and Panionios was
compelled to cut off [all] the genitals of his own sons, who were four in
number, and being compelled he did so. When he had so done, the sons
were compelled to cut the same from him. Thus vengeance and Hermotimos came around and overtook Panionios.

107. When Xerxes had entrusted his sons to Artemisia to carry them
back to Ephesos, he called Mardonios and bade him choose from the army
whom he would, and make his deeds, if possible, correspond to his words.
That night on the command of the king the leaders of the fleet began to
withdraw their ships from Phaleron to the Hellespont, as quickly as possible, to guard the bridges for the king to pass over. And when the Barbarians were near Zoster as they sailed, seeing the small points of rock which
stretch out to sea from the mainland, they thought that these were ships
and fled for a good distance. In time however, perceiving that they were
only points of rock, they assembled together again and continued on their
voyage.

108. When day dawned, the Hellenes, seeing that the land-army was
still in its place, supposed that the ships also were about Phaleron; and
thinking that they would fight another sea-battle, they made preparations
to repel them. When however they were informed that the ships had departed, they thought it good to pursue them. They pursued therefore as far
as Andros, but did not get a sight of the fleet of Xerxes; and when they had
come to Andros, they deliberated. Themistocles then declared as his opinion
that they should sail through the islands and pursue the ships, and afterwards sail straight to the Hellespont to break up the bridges; but Eurybiades expressed the opposite opinion, saying that if they should break up
the floating-bridges, they would therein do the greatest possible evil to Hellas. If the Persian should be cut off and compelled to remain in Europe, he
would endeavour not to remain still, since if he remained still, neither could
any of his affairs go forward, nor would any way of returning home appear;
but his army would perish of hunger: whereas if he made the attempt and
persevered in it, all Europe might be brought over to him, city by city and
nation by nation, the inhabitants being either conquered or surrendering
on terms before they were conquered: moreover they would have for food
the crops of the Hellenes which grew year by year. He thought however
that conquered in the sea-fight the Persian would not stay in Europe,
and therefore he must be allowed to flee until in his flight he came to his
own land. Then after that they might begin the contest for the land which
belonged to the Persian. To this opinion the commanders of the other Peloponnesians adhered.

109. When Themistocles perceived that he would not be able to persuade
them, or at least the greater number of them, to sail to the Hellespont, he

changed his counsel and turning to the Athenians (for these were grieved most at the escape of the enemy and were anxious to sail to the Hellespont even by themselves alone, if the others were not willing) to them he spoke as follows: "I myself also have been present before now on many occasions, and have heard of many more, on which something of this kind came to pass, namely that men who were forced into great straits, after they had been defeated fought again and repaired their former disaster: and as for us, since we have won as a prize from fortune the existence of ourselves and of Hellas by repelling from our land so great a cloud of men, let us not pursue enemies who flee from us: for of these things not we were the doers, but the gods and heroes, who grudged that one man should become king both of Asia and of Europe, and he a man sacrilegious and presumptuous, one who made no difference between things sacred and things profane, burning and casting down the images of the gods, and who also scourged the Sea and sank shackles into it. But as things are at present, it is well that we should now remain in Hellas and look after ourselves and our households; and let each man repair his house, and have a care for sowing his land, after he has completely driven away the Barbarian: and then at the beginning of the spring let us sail down on the Hellespont and Ionia." Thus he spoke, intending to lay up for himself a store of gratitude with the Persian, in order that if after all any evil should come upon him at the hands of the Athenians, he might have a place of refuge: and this in fact came to pass.

110. Themistocles then speaking thus endeavoured to deceive them, and the Athenians followed his advice: for he had had the reputation even in former times of being a man of ability and he had now proved himself to be in truth both able and of good judgment; therefore they were ready in every way to follow his advice when he spoke. So when these had been persuaded by him, then and there Themistocles sent men with a vessel, whom he trusted to keep silence, to whatever torture they might be brought. He himself charged them to tell the king, and of them Sikinnos his servant again was one. When these came to Attica, the rest stayed behind in the ship, while Sikinnos went up to Xerxes and spoke these words: "Themistocles the son of Neocles sent me, who is commander of the Athenians, and of all the allies the best and the ablest man, to tell you that Themistocles the Athenian, desiring to be of service to you, held back the Hellenes when they were desirous to pursue after your ships and to destroy the bridges on the Hellespont. Now therefore you may make your way home quite undisturbed." They having signified this sailed back.

111. The Hellenes meanwhile, having resolved not to pursue after the ships of the Barbarians further, nor to sail to the Hellespont to break up the passage, were investing Andros intending to take it: for the Andrians were the first of the islanders who, being asked by Themistocles for money, refused to give it. When Themistocles made proposals to them and said that the Athenians had come having on their side two great deities, Persuasion and Compulsion, and therefore they must by all means give them money, they replied to this that not without reason, as it now appeared, was Athens great and prosperous, since the Athenians were well supplied with serviceable deities. As for the Andrians, they were poor, having in this respect attained to the greatest eminence, and there were two unprofitable deities which never left their island but always remained attached to the place, Poverty and Helplessness: and the Andrians being possessed of these deities would not give money; for never could the power of the Athenians get the better of their inability. **112.** These, having refused to give the money, were being besieged: and Themistocles not ceasing in his desire for gain sent threatening messages to the other islands and asked them for money by the same envoys, employing those whom he had before sent to the king; and he said that if they did not give that which was demanded of them, he would bring the fleet of the Hellenes against them to besiege and take them. Thus saying he collected great sums of money from the Carystians and the Parians, who being informed how Andros was besieged, because it had taken the side of the Medes, and how Themistocles was held in more regard than any of the other commanders, sent money for fear of this. Whether any others of the islanders also gave money I am not able to say, but I think so. Yet to the Carystians at least there was no respite from the evil on this account, but the Parians escaped the attack, because they propitiated Themistocles with money. Thus Themistocles with Andros as his starting-point was acquiring sums of money for himself from the men of the islands without the knowledge of the other commanders.*

113. Xerxes meanwhile with his army stayed for a few days after the sea-fight, and then they all began to march forth towards Bœotia by the same way by which they had come: for Mardonios thought both that it was well for him to escort the king on his way, and also that it was now too late in the year to carry on the war; it was better, he thought, to winter in Thessaly and then at the beginning of spring to attempt the Peloponnese. When he came to Thessaly, then Mardonios chose out for himself first all those Persians who are called "Immortals," except only their commander Hydarnes (for Hydarnes said that he would not be left behind by the king), and after them of the other Persians those who wore cuirasses, and the body of a thousand horse: also the Medes, Sacans, Bactrians and Indians, foot and horsemen both. These nations he chose in the mass, but from the other allies he selected a few at a time, choosing those who had fine appearance or those of whom he knew that they had done good service. From the Persians he chose more than from any other single nation, and these wore collars of twisted metal and bracelets; and after them came the Medes, who in fact were not inferior in number to the Persians, but only in bodily strength. The result was that there were thirty myriads, or 300,000, in all, including cavalry.

---

*Herodotus paints an inconsistent portrait of the brilliant Athenian politician and strategist, who was ostracized in 471 B.C. See also Plutarch's life of him and the portrait in Thucydides 1.135–138.

114. During this time, while Mardonios was selecting his army and Xerxes was in Thessaly, there had come an oracle from Delphi to the Lacedemonians, bidding them ask satisfaction from Xerxes for the murder of Leonidas and accept that which should be given by him. The Spartans therefore sent a herald as quickly as possible, who having found the whole army still in Thessaly came into the presence of Xerxes and spoke these words: "O king of the Medes, the Lacedemonians and the sons of Heracles of Sparta demand satisfaction for murder, because you killed their king, fighting in defence of Hellas." He laughed and then kept silence some time, and after that pointing to Mardonios, who happened to be standing by him, he said: "Then Mardonios here shall give them satisfaction, such as is fitting for them to have." **115.** The herald accordingly accepted the utterance and departed; and Xerxes leaving Mardonios in Thessaly went on himself in haste to the Hellespont and arrived at the passage where the crossing was in forty-five days, bringing back next to nothing, as one may say, of his army: and wherever they came on the march and to whatever nation, they seized the crops of that people and used them for provisions; and if they found no crops, then they took the grass which was growing up from the earth, and stripped off the bark from the trees and plucked down the leaves and devoured them, alike of the cultivated trees and of those growing wild; and they left nothing behind them: thus they did by reason of famine. Then plague too seized upon the army and dysentery, which destroyed them by the way, and some of them also who were sick the king left behind, laying charge upon the cities where he was in his march, to take care of them and support them: of these he left some in Thessaly, and some at Siris in Paionia, and some in Macedonia. In these parts too he had left behind him the sacred chariot of Zeus, when he was marching against Hellas; but on his return he did not receive it back: for the Paionians had given it to the Thracians, and when Xerxes asked for it again, they said that the mares while at pasture had been carried off by the Thracians of the upper country, who dwelt about the source of the Strymon.

116. Here also a Thracian, the king of the Bisaltians and of the Crestonian land, did a deed of surpassing horror; for he had said that he would not himself be subject to Xerxes with his own will and had gone away up to Mount Rhodopē, and also he had forbidden his sons to go on the march against Hellas. They however, either because they cared not for his command, or else because a desire came upon them to see the war, went on the march with the Persian: and when they returned all unhurt, six in number, their father plucked out their eyes for this cause. **117.** When the Persians passing on from Thrace came to the passage, they crossed over the Hellespont in haste to Abydos by means of the ships,[*] for they did not find the floating-bridges still stretched across but broken

---

*Xerxes passed back over to Asia in November of 480 B.C.; he has traveled about 550 miles toward home in 45 days—not excessive haste.

up by a storm. While staying there for a time they had distributed to them
an allowance of food more abundant than they had had by the way, and
from satisfying their hunger without restraint and also from the changes
of water there died many of those in the army who had remained safe till
then. The rest arrived with Xerxes at Sardis.

118. There is also another story reported as follows, namely that when
Xerxes on his march away from Athens came to Eïon on the Strymon,
from that point he did not continue further to make marches by road, but
delivered his army to Hydarnes to lead back to the Hellespont, while he
himself embarked in a Phenician ship and set forth for Asia; and as he
sailed he was seized by a wind called the Strymonian, violent and raising
great waves; and since he was tossed by the storm more and more, the
ship being heavily laden (for there were upon the deck great numbers of
Persians who went with Xerxes), the king upon that falling into fear
shouted aloud and asked the pilot whether there were for them any
means of safety. He said: "Master, there are none, unless some way be
found of freeing ourselves of the excessive number of passengers." Then
it is said that Xerxes, when he heard this, spoke thus: "Persians, now let
each one of you show that he has care for the king; for my safety, as it
seems, depends upon you." He, they say, thus spoke, and they prostrated
themselves before him and leapt out into the sea; and so the ship being
lightened came safe to Asia. As soon as they had landed Xerxes, they say,
first presented the pilot with a wreath of gold, because he had saved the
life of the king, and then cut off his head, because he had caused the
death of many of the Persians. **119.** This other story, I say, is reported
about the return of Xerxes, but I for my part can by no means believe it,*
what is said to have happened to the Persians; for if the pilot spoke thus
to Xerxes, not one person's opinion in ten thousand will differ from mine
that the king would have done something like this. He would have caused
those who were upon the deck to go down into the hold of the ship, seeing that they were Persians and of the highest rank among the Persians;
and of the rowers, who were Phenicians, he would have thrown out into
the sea an equal number. In fact however, as I have said before, he made
his return to Asia together with the rest of the army by road. **120.** And
this also which follows is a strong witness that it was so; for Xerxes is
known to have come to Abdera on his way back, and to have made with
them a guest-friendship and presented them with a Persian sword of gold
and a gold-spangled tiara. The men of Abdera themselves say (though I
can by no means believe it), he took off his belt there for the first time
during his flight back from Athens, considering himself to be in security.
Now Abdera is situated further towards the Hellespont than the river
Strymon and Eïon, from which place the story says that he embarked in
the ship.

---

*The story displays the twisted logic that the Hellenes attributed to despots, es-
pecially barbarian potentates.

121. The Hellenes meanwhile, when it proved that they were not able to conquer Andros, turned towards Carystos, and having laid waste the land of that people they departed and went to Salamis. Then for the gods they chose out first-fruits from the spoils, and among them three Phenician triremes, one to be dedicated as an offering at the Isthmus, which remained there still up to my time, another at Sunion, and the third to Ajax in Salamis where they were. After this they divided the spoil among themselves and sent the tithe of first-fruits to Delphi, of which was made a statue holding in its hand the beak of a ship and in height measuring eighteen feet. This statue stood in the same place with the golden statue of Alexander the Macedonian. **122.** Then when the Hellenes had sent first-fruits to Delphi, they asked the god on behalf of all whether the first-fruits which he had received were fully sufficient and acceptable to him. He said that from the other Hellenes he had received enough, but not from the Eginetans, and from them he demanded the offering of their prize of valour for the sea-fight at Salamis. Hearing this the Eginetans dedicated golden stars, three in number, upon a ship's mast of bronze, which are placed in the corner of the temple-entrance close to the mixing-bowl of Crœsus.

123. After the division of the spoil the Hellenes sailed to the Isthmus, to give the prize of valour to him who of all the Hellenes had proved himself the most worthy during this war: and when they had come thither and the commanders distributed their votes at the altar of Poseidon, selecting from the whole number the first and the second in merit, then every one of them gave in his vote for himself, each man thinking that he himself had been the best; but for the second place the greater number of votes came out in agreement, assigning that to Themistocles. They then were left alone in their votes, while Themistocles in regard to the second place surpassed the rest by far. **124.** Although the Hellenes would not give decision of this by reason of envy, but sailed away each to their own city without deciding, yet Themistocles was loudly reported and was esteemed throughout Hellas to be the man who was the ablest brain by far of the Hellenes. Since he had not received honour from those who had fought at Salamis, although he was the first in the voting, he went immediately after this to Lacedemon, desiring to receive honour there; and the Lacedemonians received him well and gave him great honours. As a prize of valour they gave to Eurybiades a wreath of olive; and for ability and skill they gave to Themistocles also a wreath of olive, and presented him besides with the chariot judged to be the best in Sparta. So having much commended him, they escorted him on his departure with three hundred picked men of the Spartans, the same who are called the "horsemen," as far as the boundaries of Tegea: and he is the only man of all we know to whom the Spartans ever gave escort on his way.

125. When however he had come to Athens from Lacedemon, Timodemos of Aphidnai, one of the opponents of Themistocles, but otherwise undistinguished, maddened by envy attacked him, bringing against him his going to Lacedemon, and saying that it was on account of Athens that he had those marks of honour which he had from the Lacedemonians, and not on his own account. Then, as Timodemos continued ceaselessly to repeat this, Themistocles said: "This is how it is:—if I had been a native of Belbina* I should never have been thus honoured by the Spartans; but neither would you, my friend, for all that you are an Athenian."

126. Artabazos meanwhile the son of Pharnakes, a man who was held in esteem among the Persians even before this and came to be so yet more after the events about Plataia, was escorting the king as far as the passage with sixty thousand men of that army which Mardonios had selected for himself; and when the king was in Asia and Artabazos on his march back came near to Pallenē, finding that Mardonios was wintering in Thessaly and Macedonia and was not at present urgent with him to come and join the rest of the army, he thought it not good to pass by without reducing the Potidaians to slavery, whom he had found in revolt: for the men of Potidaia, when the king had marched by them and when the fleet of the Persians had departed in flight from Salamis, had openly made revolt from the Barbarians; and so also had the others done who occupy Pallenē.†

127. So upon this Artabazos began to besiege Potidaia, and suspecting that the men of Olynthos also were intending revolt from the king, he began to besiege this city too, which was occupied by Bottiaians who had been driven away from the Thermaian gulf by the Macedonians. So when he had taken these men by siege, he brought them forth to a lake and cut their throats there; and the city he delivered to Critobulos of Toronē to have in charge, and to the natives of Chalkidikē; and thus it was that the Chalkidians got possession of Olynthos. **128.** Having taken this city Artabazos set himself to attack Potidaia with vigour, and as he was setting himself earnestly to this work, Timoxeinos the commander of the troops from Skionē concerted with him to give up the town by treachery. Now in what manner he did this at the first, I for my part am not able to say, for this is not reported; at last however it happened as follows. Whenever either Timoxeinos wrote a paper wishing to send it to Artabazos, or Artabazos wishing to send one to Timoxeinos, they wound it round by the little feather-slits of an arrow, and then, putting feathers over the paper, they shot it to a place agreed upon between them. It was found out that Timoxeinos was attempting to betray Potidaia; for Artabazos, shooting an arrow at the place agreed upon, missed this spot and struck a man of Potidaia in the shoulder; and when he was struck, a crowd came about him, as is apt to happen when there is fighting, and they immediately took the arrow and having discovered the paper carried it to the commanders. Now there was present an allied force of the other men of Pallenē also. Then when the commanders had read the paper and detected who was guilty of the treachery, they resolved not openly to strike down Timoxeinos

---

*An insignificant islet off the southern coast of Attica.
†Western finger of the Chalkidic peninsula, east of Thessalonika.

for treachery, for the sake of the city of Skionē, lest the men of Skionē should be esteemed traitors for all time to come.

129. He then had been discovered; three months later while Artabazos was besieging the town, there came a great ebb of the sea backwards, which lasted for a long time; and the Barbarians, seeing that shallow water had been produced, endeavoured to get by into the peninsula of Pallenē, but when they had passed through two fifths of the distance, and three-fifths remained, which they must pass through before they were within Pallenē, then there came upon them a great flood-tide higher than ever before, as the natives of the place say, though high tides come often. So those of them who could not swim perished, and those who could were slain by the men of Potidaia who put out to them in boats. The cause of the high tide and flood and of that which befell the Persians was this, as the Potidaians say, namely that these same Persians who perished by means of the sea had committed impiety towards the temple of Poseidon and his image in the suburb of their town; and in saying that this was the cause, in my opinion they say well. The survivors of his army Artabazos led away to Thessaly to join Mardonios. Thus it fared with these who escorted the king.

130. The fleet of Xerxes, so much of it as remained, when it had touched Asia in its flight from Salamis, and had conveyed the king and his army over from the Chersonese to Abydos, passed the winter at Kymē: and when spring dawned,* it assembled early at Samos, where some of the ships had even passed the winter; and most of the Persians and Medes still served as fighting-men on board of them. To be commanders of them there came Mardontes the son of Bagaios, and Artaÿntes the son of Artachaies, and with them also Ithamitres was in joint command, who was brother's son to Artaÿntes and had been added by the choice of Artaÿntes himself. They then, since they had suffered a heavy blow, did not advance further up towards the West, nor did any one compel them to do so; but they remained still in Samos and kept watch over Ionia, lest it should revolt, having three hundred ships including those of the Ionians; and they did not expect that the Hellenes on their part would come to Ionia, but thought that it would satisfy them to guard their own land, judging from the fact that they had not pursued after them in their flight from Salamis but were well contented then to depart homewards. As regards the sea their spirit was broken, but on land they thought that Mardonios would get much the advantage. So they being at Samos were taking counsel to do some damage if they could to their enemies, and at the same time they were listening for news how the affairs of Mardonios would fall out.

131. The Hellenes on their part were roused both by the coming on of spring and by the presence of Mardonios in Thessaly. Their land-army had not yet begun to assemble, when the fleet arrived at Egina, in

---

*This date is March of 479 B.C.

number one hundred and ten ships, and the commander and admiral
was Leotychides, who was the son of Menares, the son of Hegesilaos,
the son of Hippocratides, the son of Leotychides, the son of Anaxilaos,
the son of Archidemos, the son of Anaxandrides, the son of Theopompos, the son of Nicander, the son of Charilaos, the son of Eunomos, the
son of Polydectes, the son of Prytanis, the son of Euryphon, the son of
Procles, the son of Aristodemos, the son of Aristomachos, the son of
Cleodaios, the son of Hyllos, the son of Heracles, being of the other
royal house. These all, except the seven enumerated first after Leotychides, had been kings of Sparta. And of the Athenians the commander
was Xanthippos the son of Ariphron. **132.** When all the ships had arrived at Egina, there came Ionian envoys to the camp of the Hellenes,
who also came a short time before this to Sparta and asked the Lacedemonians to set Ionia free; and of them one was Herodotos the son of
Basileides. These had banded themselves together and had plotted to
put to death Strattis the despot of Chios, being originally seven in number; but when one of those who took part with them gave information
of it and they were discovered to be plotting against him, then the remaining six escaped from Chios and came both to Sparta and also at
this time to Egina, asking the Hellenes to sail over to Ionia: but they
with difficulty brought them forward as far as Delos; for the parts beyond this were all fearful to the Hellenes, since they were without experience of those regions and everything seemed to them to be filled with
armed force, while their persuasion was that it was as long a voyage to
Samos as to the Pillars of Heracles.* Thus at the same time it so chanced
that the Barbarians dared sail no further up towards the West than
Samos, being smitten with fear, and the Hellenes no further down towards the East than Delos, when the Chians made request of them. So
fear guarded the space which lay between them.

133. The Hellenes, I say, sailed to Delos; and Mardonios meanwhile had
been wintering in Thessaly. From thence he sent round a man, a native of
Europos, whose name was Mys, to the various Oracles, charging him to go
everywhere to consult, wherever they were able to consult the Oracles.
What he desired to find out from the Oracles when he gave this charge, I
cannot say, for that is not reported; but I conceive that he sent to consult
about his present affairs. **134.** This Mys is known to have come to Lebadeia
and to have persuaded by payment one of the natives of the place to go
down to Trophonios, and also he came to the Oracle at Abai of the
Phokians; and moreover when he came for the first time to Thebes, he not
only consulted the Ismenian Apollo,—there one may consult just as at
Olympia with victims,—but also by payment he persuaded a stranger who
was not a Theban, and induced him to lie down to sleep in the temple of

---

*An example of Herodotus' and the Ionians' sense of humor at mainland ex-
pense (compare 6.112). The reduction to absurdity equates 100 miles to approximately 1,900 miles; the joke confuses caution with timidity.

Amphiaraos. In this temple no one of the Thebans is permitted to seek divination for the following reason:—Amphiaraos dealing by oracles bade them choose which they would of these two things, either to have him as a diviner or else as an ally in war, abstaining from the other use; and they chose that he should be their ally in war: for this reason it is not permitted to Thebans to sleep in that temple. **135.** A very great marvel to me is said by the Thebans later to have come to pass:—it seems that this man Mys of Europos, as he journeyed round to all the Oracles, came also to the sacred enclosure of the Ptōan Apollo. This temple is called "Ptōon," and belongs to the Thebans, and it lies above the lake Copaïs at the foot of the mountain, close to the town of Acraiphia. When the man called Mys came to this temple with three men chosen from the citizens in his company, who were sent by the public authority to write down that which the god should utter in his divination, immediately it is said the prophet of the god began to give the oracle in a Barbarian tongue; and while those of the Thebans who accompanied him were full of wonder, hearing a Barbarian instead of the Hellenic tongue, and did not know what to make of the matter before them, it is said that the man of Europos, Mys, snatched from them the tablet which they bore and wrote upon it that which was being spoken by the prophet; and he said that the prophet was giving his answer in the Carian tongue: and then when he had written it, he went away and departed to Thessaly.

136. Mardonios having read that which the Oracles uttered, whatever that was, after this sent as an envoy to Athens Alexander the son of Amyntas, the Macedonian, both because the Persians were connected with him by marriage, (for Gygaia the sister of Alexander and daughter of Amyntas had been married to a Persian Bubares, and from her had been born to him that Amyntas who lived in Asia, having the name of his mother's father, to whom the king gave Alabanda, a great city of Phrygia, to possess), and also Mardonios was sending him because he was informed that Alexander was a public guest-friend and benefactor of the Athenians. By this means he thought that he would be most likely to gain over the Athenians to his side, about whom he heard that they were a numerous people and brave in war, and of whom he knew moreover that these were they who more than any others had brought about the disasters which had befallen the Persians by sea. Therefore if these should be added to him, he thought that he should easily have command of the sea (and this in fact would have been the case), while on land he supposed himself to be already much superior in force. Thus he reckoned that his power would be much greater than that of the Hellenes. Perhaps also the Oracles told him this beforehand, counselling him to make the Athenian his ally, and so he was sending persuaded by their advice.

137. Now of this Alexander the seventh ancestor was that Perdiccas who first became despot of the Macedonians in this manner:—From Argos there fled to the Illyrians three brothers of the descendants of Temenos, Gauanes, Aëropos, and Perdiccas; and passing over from the Illyrians into the upper parts of Macedonia they came to the city of Lebaia.

There they became farm-servants for pay in the household of the king, one pasturing horses, the second oxen, and the youngest of them, namely Perdiccas, the smaller kinds of cattle; and the wife of the king cooked for them their food herself. In ancient times even those who were rulers over men were poor in money, and not the common people only. And whenever she baked, the loaf of the boy their servant, namely Perdiccas, became twice as large. When this happened constantly in the same manner, she told it to her husband, and he when he heard it conceived immediately that this was a portent and tended to something great. He summoned the farm-servants therefore, and gave notice to them to depart out of his land; and they said that it was right that before they went forth they should receive the wages which were due. Now it chanced that the sun was shining into the house down through the opening which received the smoke, and the king when he heard about the wages said, being infatuated by a divine power: "I pay you then this for wages, and it is such as you deserve," pointing to the sunlight. So then Gauanes and Aëropos the elder brothers stood struck with amazement when they heard this, but the boy, who happened to have in his hand a knife, said these words: "We accept, king, that which you give;" and he traced a line with his knife round the sunlight on the floor of the house, and having traced the line round he thrice drew the sunlight into his bosom, and after that he departed both himself and his fellows. **138.** To the king one of those who sat by him at table told what the boy had done, and how the youngest of them had taken that which was given with some design: and he being angered, sent after them horsemen to slay them. Now there is a river in this land to which the descendants of these men from Argos sacrifice as a saviour. This river, so soon as the sons of Temenos had passed over it, began to flow with such great volume of water that the horsemen could not pass over. So the brothers, having come to another region of Macedonia, took up their dwelling near the so-called gardens of Midas the son of Gordias, where roses grow wild which have each one sixty petals and excel all others in perfume. In these gardens too Silenos was captured, as is reported by the Macedonians: and above the gardens is situated a mountain called Bermion, which is inaccessible by reason of the cold.* Having taken possession of that region, they made this their starting-point, and proceeded to subdue also the rest of Macedonia. **139.** From this Perdiccas the descent of Alexander was as follows:—Alexander was the son of Amyntas, Amyntas was the son of Alketes, the father of Alketes was Aëropos, of him Philip, of Philip Argaios, and of this last the father was Perdiccas, who first obtained the kingdom.

140. Thus then, I say, Alexander the son of Amyntas was descended; and when he came to Athens sent from Mardonios, he spoke as follows: (*a*) "Athenians, Mardonios speaks these words:—There has come to me

---

*This Macedonian mountain rises to 5,249 feet and has perpetual snow.

a message from the king which speaks in this manner:—To the Athenians I remit all the offences which were committed against me: and now, Mardonios, thus do,—first give them back their own land; then let them choose for themselves another in addition to this, whichsoever they desire, remaining independent; and set up for them again all their temples, which I set on fire, provided that they consent to make a treaty with me. This message having come to me, it is necessary for me to do so, unless by your means I am prevented: and thus I speak to you now:— Why are you so mad as to raise up war against the king? since neither will you overcome him, nor are you able to hold out against him for ever: for you saw the multitude of the host of Xerxes and their deeds, and you are informed also of the power which is with me at the present time; so that even if you overcome and conquer us (of which you can have no hope if you are rational), another power will come many times as large. Do not then desire to match yourselves with the king, and so to be both deprived of your land and for ever running a course for your own lives; but make peace with him: and you have a most honourable occasion to make peace, since the king has himself set out upon this road: agree to a league with us then without fraud or deceit, and remain free. (*b*) These things Mardonios charged me to say to you, O Athenians; and as for me, I will say nothing of the goodwill towards you on my part, for you would not learn that now for the first time; but I ask of you to do as Mardonios says, since I perceive that you will not be able to war with Xerxes for ever,—if I perceived in you ability to do this, I should never have come to you speaking these words,—for the power of the king is above that of a man and his arm is very long. If therefore you do not make an agreement immediately, when they offer you great things as the terms on which they are willing to make a treaty, I have fear on your behalf, seeing that you dwell more upon the path of danger than any of your allies, and are exposed ever to destruction alone, the land which you possess being parted off from the rest and lying between the armies which are contending together. Nay, but be persuaded, for this is a matter of great consequence to you, that to you alone of the Hellenes the great king remits the offences committed and desires to become a friend."

141. Thus spoke Alexander; and the Lacedemonians having been informed that Alexander had come to Athens to bring the Athenians to make a treaty with the Barbarians, and remembering the oracles, how it was destined that they together with the other Dorians should be driven out of the Peloponnese by the Medes and the Athenians combined, had been very greatly afraid lest the Athenians should make a treaty with the Persians; and immediately they had resolved to send envoys. It happened moreover that they were introduced with Alexander; for the Athenians had waited for them, protracting the time, because they were well assured that the Lacedemonians would hear that an envoy had come from the Barbarians to make a treaty, and that having heard it they would themselves send envoys with all speed. They acted therefore of set purpose, so as to let the Lacedemonians see their inclination.

142. So when Alexander had ceased speaking, the envoys from Sparta followed him directly and said: "As for us, the Lacedemonians sent us to ask of you not to make any change in that which concerns Hellas, nor to accept proposals from the Barbarian; since this is not just in any way nor honourable for any of the Hellenes to do, but least of all for you, and that for many reasons. You were they who stirred up this war, when we by no means willed it; and the contest came about for your dominion, but now it extends even to the whole of Hellas. Besides this it is by no means to be endured that you Athenians, who are the authors of all this, should prove to be the cause of slavery to the Hellenes, seeing that you ever from ancient time also have been known as the liberators of many. We feel sympathy however with you for your sufferings and because you were deprived of your crops twice and have had your substance ruined now for a long time. In compensation for this the Lacedemonians and their allies make offer to support your wives and all those of your households who are unfitted for war, so long as this war shall last: but let not Alexander the Macedonian persuade you, making smooth the speech of Mardonios; for these things are fitting for him to do, since being himself a despot he is working in league with a despot: for you however they are not fitting to do, if you happen to be thinking straight; for you know that in Barbarians there is neither faith nor truth at all."

Thus spoke the envoys: **143,** and to Alexander the Athenians made answer thus: "Even of ourselves we know so much, that the Mede has a power many times as numerous as ours; so that there is no need for you to cast this up against us. Nevertheless because we long for liberty we shall defend ourselves as we may be able: and do not endeavour to persuade us to make a treaty with the Barbarian, for we on our part shall not be persuaded. And now report to Mardonios that the Athenians say thus:—So long as the Sun goes on the same course by which he goes now, we will never make an agreement with Xerxes; but we will go forth to defend ourselves against him, trusting in the gods and the heroes as allies, for whom he had no respect when he set fire to their houses and to their sacred images. And in the future do not appear before the Athenians with any such proposals as these, nor think that you are rendering them good service in advising them to do that which is not lawful; for we do not desire that you should suffer anything unpleasant at the hands of the Athenians, who are their public guest and friend."

144. To Alexander they thus made answer, but to the envoys from Sparta as follows: "That the Lacedemonians should be afraid lest we should make a treaty with the Barbarian was very human no doubt; but it seems to be an unworthy fear for men who knew so well the spirit of the Athenians, namely that there is neither so great quantity of gold anywhere upon the earth, nor any land so much excelling in beauty and goodness, that we should be willing to accept it and enslave Hellas by taking the side of the Medes. For many and great are the reasons which hinder us from doing this, even though we should desire it; first and greatest the images and houses of the gods set on fire or reduced to ruin, which we must necessarily avenge to the very utmost rather than make an agreement with him who did these deeds; then secondly there is the bond of Hellenic race, by which we are of one blood and of one speech, the common temples of the gods and the common sacrifices, the manners of life which are the same for all; to these it would not be well that the Athenians should become traitors.* And be assured of this, if by any chance you were not assured of it before, that so long as one of the Athenians remains alive, we will never make an agreement with Xerxes. We admire however the forethought which you had with regard to us, in that you took thought for us who have had our substance destroyed, and are willing to support the members of our households; and so far as you are concerned, the kindness has been fully performed: but we shall continue to endure as we may, and not be a trouble in any way to you. Now therefore, with full conviction that this is so, send out an army as speedily as you may: for, as we conjecture, the Barbarian will be here invading our land at no far distant time but so soon as he shall be informed of the message sent, namely that we shall do none of those things which he desired of us. Therefore before he arrives here in Attica, it is fitting that you come to our rescue quickly in Bœotia." Thus the Athenians made answer, and upon that the envoys went away back to Sparta.

---

*Herodotus often puts his understanding of motivating forces into his protagonists' speeches. Hellenism, a nascent dynamic produced in part by invasion, here is defined as bonds of religion, ethnic relation, language, and customs. The speech forms a fitting coda to the naval victory at Salamis and an overture for the infantry victory at Plataia.

BOOK IX

BATTLES OF PLATAIA AND
MYCALE; EPILOGUES

1. MARDONIOS, WHEN ALEXANDER HAD returned and signified to him what the Athenians said, set forth from Thessaly and began to lead his army with all diligence towards Athens: and to whatever land he came, he took up with him the people of that land. The leaders of Thessaly meanwhile did not repent at all of that which had been done already, but on the contrary they urged on the Persian yet much more; and Thorax of Larissa had joined in escorting Xerxes in his flight and at this time he openly offered Mardonios passage to invade Hellas. **2.** Then when the army in its march came to Bœotia, the Thebans endeavoured to detain Mardonios, and counselled him saying that there was no region more convenient for him to place his encampment than that; and they urged him not to advance further, but to sit down there and endeavour to subdue the whole of Hellas without fighting: for to overcome the Hellenes by open force when they were united, since, as before, they were of one accord, was a difficult task even for the whole world combined, "but," they proceeded, "if you will do that which we advise, with little labour you will have in your power all their plans of resistance. Send money to the men who have power in their cities, and thus sending you will divide Hellas into two parties: after that you will with ease subdue by the help of your party those who are not inclined to your side." **3.** Thus they advised, but he did not follow their counsel; for there had instilled itself into him a great desire to take Athens for the second time, partly from obstinacy* and partly because he meant to signify to the king in Sardis that he was in possession of Athens, by beacon-fires through the islands. However he did not even at this time find the Athenians there when he came to Attica; but he was informed that the greater number were either in Salamis or in the ships, and he captured the city finding it deserted. Now the capture of the city by the king had taken place ten months before the later expedition of Mardonios against it. **4.** When Mardonios had come to Athens, he sent to Salamis Morychides a man of the Hellespont, bearing the same proposals as Alexander the Macedonian had brought over to the Athenians. These he sent for the second time, being aware beforehand that the dispositions of the Athenians were not friendly, but hoping that they would give way and leave their obstinacy, since the Attic land had been captured by the enemy and was in his power. **5.** For this reason he sent Morychides to Salamis; and he came

---

*Mardonios arrived at Athens in June of 479 B.C.

before the Council and reported the words of Mardonios. Then one of the Councillors, Lykidas, expressed the opinion that it was better to receive the proposal which Morychides brought before them and refer it to the assembly of the people. He, I say, uttered this opinion, whether because he had received money from Mardonios, or because this was his own inclination: however the Athenians immediately, both those of the Council and those outside, when they heard of it, were very indignant, and they came about Lykidas and stoned him to death; but the Hellespontian Morychides they dismissed unhurt. Then when there had arisen much uproar in Salamis about Lykidas, the women of the Athenians heard of that which was being done, and one woman passing the word to another and one taking another with her, they went of their own accord to the house of Lykidas and stoned his wife and his children to death.*

6. The Athenians had passed over to Salamis as follows:—So long as they were expecting that an army should come from the Peloponnese to help them, they remained in Attica; but as those in Peloponnesus acted very slowly and with much delay, while the invader was said to be already in Bœotia, they accordingly removed everything out of danger, and themselves passed over to Salamis; and at the same time they sent envoys to Lacedemon to reproach the Lacedemonians for having permitted the Barbarian to invade Attica and for not having gone to Bœotia to meet him in company with them, and also to remind them how many things the Persian had promised to give the Athenians if they changed sides; bidding the envoys warn them that if they did not help the Athenians, the Athenians would find some shelter for themselves. **7.** For the Lacedemonians in fact were keeping a feast during this time, and celebrating the Hyakinthia;† and they held it of the greatest consequence to provide for the things which concerned the god, while at the same time their wall which they had been building at the Isthmus was just at this moment being completed with battlements. And when the envoys from the Athenians came to Lacedemon, bringing with them also envoys from Megara and Plataia, they came in before the Ephors and said as follows: "The Athenians sent us saying that the king of the Medes not only offers to give us back our land, but also desires to make us his allies on fair and equal terms without deceit or treachery,‡ and is desirous moreover to give us another land in addition to our own, whichsoever we shall ourselves choose. We however, having respect for Zeus of the Hellenes and disdaining to be traitors to Hellas, did not agree but refused, although we were unjustly dealt with by the other Hellenes and left to destruction, and although we knew that it was more profitable to make a treaty with the Persian than to carry on war: nor shall we make a treaty at any future time, if we have our own will. Thus sincerely is our duty done towards the Hellenes: but as for you, after having come then to great

---

*This extirpation of the line recalls Leotychides' fable about Glaucos at 6.86.
†Spartan religious delay, as at 6.106, before the battle of Marathon.
‡As described at 8.140a.

dread lest we should make a treaty with the Persian, so soon as you learnt certainly what our spirit was, namely that we should never betray Hellas, and because your wall across the Isthmus is all but finished, now you make no account of the Athenians, but having agreed with us to come to Bœotia to oppose the Persian, you have now deserted us, and you permitted the Barbarian moreover to make invasion of Attica. For the present then the Athenians are incensed with you, for you did not act fittingly: and now they bid you with all speed send out an army together with us, in order that we may receive the Barbarian in the land of Attica; for since we failed of Bœotia, the most suitable place to fight in our land is the Thriasian plain."

8. When the Ephors heard this they deferred their reply to the next day, and then on the next day to the succeeding one; and this they did even for ten days, deferring the matter from day to day, while during this time the whole body of the Peloponnesians were building the wall over the Isthmus with great diligence and were just about to complete it. Now I am not able to say why, when Alexander the Macedonian had come to Athens, they were so very anxious lest the Athenians should take the side of the Medes, whereas now they had no care about it, except indeed that their wall over the Isthmus had now been built, and they thought they had no need of the Athenians any more; whereas when Alexander came to Attica the wall had not yet been completed, but they were working at it in great dread of the Persians. **9.** At last however the answer was given and the going forth of the Spartans took place in the following manner:— on the day before that which was appointed for the last hearing of the envoys, Chileos a man of Tegea, who of all strangers had most influence in Lacedemon, heard from the Ephors all that which the Athenians were saying; and he, it seems, said to them these words: "Thus the matter stands, Ephors:—if the Athenians are not friendly with us but are allies of the Barbarian, then though a strong wall may have been built across the Isthmus, yet a wide door has been opened for the Persian into Peloponnesus. Listen to their request, before the Athenians resolve upon something else tending to the fall of Hellas." **10.** Thus he counselled them, and they immediately took his words to heart; and saying nothing to the envoys who had come from the cities, while yet it was night they sent out five thousand Spartans, with no less than seven of the Helots set to attend upon each man of them, appointing Pausanias the son of Cleombrotos to lead them forth. Now the leadership belonged to Pleistarchos the son of Leonidas; but he was yet a boy, and the other was his guardian and cousin: for Cleombrotos, the father of Pausanias and son of Anaxandrides, was no longer alive, but soon after he had led home from the Isthmus the army which had built the wall, he died. Now the reason why Cleombrotos led home the army from the Isthmus was this:—as he was offering sacrifice for fighting against the Persian, the sun was darkened in the heaven.* And

---

*This solar eclipse occurred on October 2 of 480 B.C.—the preceding year, after the battle of Salamis.

Pausanias chose as commander in addition to himself Euryanax the son of Dorieus, a man of the same house.

11. So Pausanias with his army had gone forth out of Sparta; and the envoys, when day had come, not knowing anything of this going forth, came in before the Ephors meaning to depart also, each to his own State: and when they had come in before them they said these words: "You, O Lacedemonians, are remaining here and celebrating the Hyakinthia and enjoying yourselves, having left your allies to destruction; and the Athenians being wronged by you and for want of allies will make peace with the Persians on such terms as they can: and having made peace, evidently we become allies of the king, and therefore we shall join with him in expeditions against any land to which the Persians may lead us; and you will learn then what shall be the issue for you of this matter." When the envoys spoke these words, the Ephors said and confirmed it with an oath, that they supposed by this time the men were at Orestheion on their way against the strangers: for they used to call the Barbarians "strangers." So they, not knowing of the matter, asked the meaning of these words, and asking they learnt all the truth; so that they were struck with amazement and set forth as quickly as possible in pursuit; and together with them five thousand chosen hoplites of the Lacedemonian *perioikoi,* or "dwellers in the country round," did the same thing also.

12. They then were hastening towards the Isthmus; and the Argives so soon as they heard that Pausanias with his army had gone forth from Sparta, sent as a herald to Attica the best whom they could find of the long-distance runners, because they had before of their own motion engaged for Mardonios that they would stop the Spartans from going forth: and the herald when he came to Athens spoke as follows: "Mardonios, the Argives sent me to tell you that the young men have gone forth from Lacedemon, and that the Argives are not able to stop them from going forth: with regard to this therefore may it be your fortune to take measures well." **13.** He having thus spoken departed and went back; and Mardonios was by no means anxious any more to remain in Attica when he heard this message. Before he was informed of this he had been waiting, because he desired to know the news from the Athenians as to what they were about to do; and he had not been injuring or laying waste the land of Attica, because he hoped always that they would make a treaty with him; but as he did not persuade them, being now informed of everything he began to retire out of the country before the force of Pausanias arrived at the Isthmus, having first set fire to Athens and cast down and destroyed whatever was left standing of the walls, houses or temples. Now he marched away for this cause, namely first because Attica was not a land suited to horsemen, and also because, if he should be defeated in a battle in Attica, there was no way of retreat except by a narrow pass, so that a few men could stop them. He intended therefore to retreat to Thebes, and engage battle near to a friendly city and to a country where cavalry could act freely.

14. Mardonios then was retiring, and when he was already upon the road a message came to him saying that another body of troops in advance of the rest had come to Megara, consisting of a thousand Lacedemonians. Being thus informed he took counsel with himself, desiring if possible first to capture these. Therefore he turned back and proceeded to lead his army towards Megara, and the cavalry going in advance of the rest overran the Megarian land: this was the furthest land in Europe towards the sun-setting to which this Persian army came. **15.** After this a message came to Mardonios that the Hellenes were assembled at the Isthmus; therefore he marched back by Dekeleia, for the Boeotarchs, the chiefs of Bœotia, had sent for those of the Asopians who dwelt near the line of march, and these were his guides along the road to Sphendaleis and thence to Tanagra. So having encamped for the night at Tanagra and on the next day having directed his march to Scolos, he was within the land of the Thebans. Then he proceeded to cut down the trees in the lands of the Thebans, although they were on the side of the Medes, moved not at all by enmity to them, but pressed by urgent necessity both to make a defence for his camp, and also a refuge, in case that when he engaged battle things should not turn out for him as he desired. Now the encampment of his army extended from Erythrai along by Hysiai and reached down to the Plataian land, being ranged along the banks of the river Asopos: he was not however making the wall to extend so far as this, but with each face measuring somewhere about ten stades or a little over a mile.

16. While the Barbarians were engaged upon this work, Attaginos the son of Phrynon, a Theban, having made magnificent preparations invited to an entertainment Mardonios himself and fifty of the Persians who were of most account; and these being invited came; and the dinner was given at Thebes. Now this which follows I heard from Thersander, an Orchomenian and a man of very high repute in Orchomenos. This Thersander said that he too was invited by Attaginos to this dinner, and there were invited also fifty men of the Thebans, and their host did not place them to recline separately each nation by themselves, but a Persian and a Theban upon every couch. Then when dinner was over, as they were drinking pledges to one another, the Persian who shared a couch with him speaking in the Hellenic tongue asked him of what place he was, and he answered that he was of Orchomenos. The other said: "Since now you have become my table-companion and the sharer of my libation, I desire to leave behind with you a memorial of my opinion, in order that you yourself also may know beforehand and be able to take such counsels for yourself as may be profitable. Do you see these Persians who are feasting here, and the army which we left behind encamped upon the river? Of all these, when a little time has gone by, you shall see but very few surviving." While the Persian said these words he shed many tears, as Thersander reported; and he marvelling at the speech said to him: "Surely then it is right to tell this to Mardonios and to those of the Persians who after him are held in regard." He upon this said: "Friend, that which is destined to come from God, it is impossible for a man to avert; for no man is willing to follow counsel, even when one speaks that which is reasonable. And these things which I say many of us Persians know well; yet we go with the rest being bound in the bonds of necessity: and the most hateful grief of all human griefs is this, to have knowledge of the truth but no power over the event." These things I heard from Thersander of Orchomenos, and in addition to them this also, namely that he told them to various persons immediately, before the battle took place at Plataia.

17. Mardonios then being encamped in Bœotia, the rest of the Hellenes who lived in these parts and took the side of the Medes were all supplying troops and had joined in the invasion of Attica, but the Phokians alone had not joined in the invasion,—the Phokians I say, for these too were now actively taking the side of the Medes, not of their own will however, but by compulsion. Not many days however after the arrival of Mardonios at Thebes, there came of them a thousand hoplites, and their leader was Harmokydes, the man who was of most repute among their citizens. When these too came to Thebes, Mardonios sent horsemen and bade the Phokians take up their position by themselves in the plain. After they had so done, immediately the whole cavalry appeared; and upon this there went a rumour through the army of Hellenes which was with the Medes that the cavalry was about to shoot them down with javelins, and this same report went through the Phokians themselves also. Then their commander Harmokydes exhorted them, speaking as follows: "Phokians, it is manifest that these men are meaning to deliver us to a death which we may plainly foresee, because we have been falsely accused by the Thessalians, as I conjecture: now therefore it is right that every one of you prove himself a good man; for it is better to bring our lives to an end doing deeds of valour and defending ourselves, than to be destroyed by a dishonourable death offering ourselves for the slaughter. Let each man of them learn that they are Barbarians and that we, against whom they contrived murder, are Hellenes." **18.** While he was thus exhorting them, the horsemen having encompassed them round were riding towards them as if to destroy them; and they were already aiming their missiles as if about to discharge them, nay some perhaps did discharge them: and meanwhile the Phokians stood facing them gathered together and with their ranks closed as much as possible every way. Then the horsemen turned and rode away back. Now I am not able to say for certain whether they came to destroy the Phokians at the request of the Thessalians, and then when they saw them turn to defence they feared lest they also might suffer some loss, and therefore rode away back, for so Mardonios had commanded them; or whether on the other hand he desired to make trial of them and to see if they had in them any war-like spirit. Then, when the horsemen had ridden away back, Mardonios sent a herald and spoke to them as follows: "Be of good courage, Phokians, for you proved yourselves good men, and not as I was informed. Now therefore carry on this war with zeal, for you will not surpass in benefits either myself or the king." Thus far it happened as regards the Phokians.

19. When the Lacedemonians came to the Isthmus they encamped

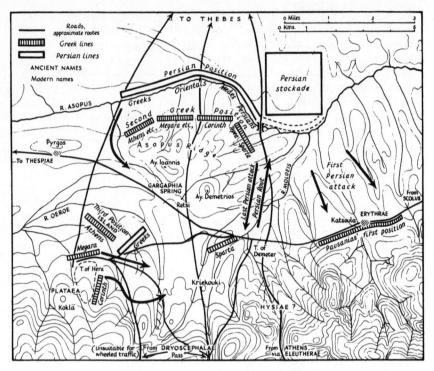

MAP 7. THE BATTLE OF PLATAEA (PLATAIA).

upon it, and hearing this the rest of the Peloponnesians who favoured the
better cause, and some also because they saw the Spartans going out, did
not think it right to be left behind the Lacedemonians. So from the Isthmus, when the sacrifices had proved favourable, they marched all together
and came to Eleusis; and having performed sacrifices there also, when the
signs were favourable they marched onwards, and the Athenians together
with them, who had passed over from Salamis and had joined them at
Eleusis. And when they had come to Erythrai in Bœotia, then they learnt
that the Barbarians were encamping on the Asopos, and having perceived
this they ranged themselves over against them on the lower slopes of
Kithairon. **20.** Then Mardonios, as the Hellenes did not descend into the
plain, sent towards them all his cavalry, of which the commander was Masistios (by the Hellenes called Makistios), a man of reputation among the
Persians, who had a Nesaian horse with a bridle of gold and in other respects finely caparisoned. So when the horsemen had ridden up to the
Hellenes they attacked them by squadrons, and attacking they did them
much mischief, and moreover in contempt they called them women.
21. Now it happened by chance that the Megarians were posted in the

place which was the most assailable of the whole position and to which the cavalry could best approach: so as the cavalry were making their attacks, the Megarians being hard pressed sent a herald to the commanders of the Hellenes, and the herald having come spoke these words: "The Megarians say:—we, O allies, are not able by ourselves to sustain the attacks of the Persian cavalry, keeping this position where we took post at the first; nay, even hitherto by endurance and valour alone have we held out against them, hard pressed as we are: and now unless you shall send some others to take up our position in succession to us, know that we shall leave the position in which we now are." The herald brought report to them thus; and upon this Pausanias made trial of the Hellenes, whether any others would voluntarily offer to go to this place and post themselves there in succession to the Megarians: and when the rest were not desirous to go, the Athenians undertook the task, and of the Athenians those three hundred picked men of whom Olympiodoros the son of Lampon was captain.

22. These were they who undertook the task and were posted at Erythrai in advance of the other Hellenes who were there present, having chosen to go with them the bow-men also. For some time then they fought, and at last an end was set to the fighting in the following manner:—while the cavalry was attacking by squadrons, the horse of Masistios, going in advance of the rest, was struck in the side by an arrow, and feeling pain he reared upright and threw Masistios off; and when he had fallen, the Athenians immediately pressed upon him; and his horse they took and himself, as he made resistance, they slew, though at first they could not, for his equipment was of this kind,—he wore a cuirass of gold scales underneath, and over the cuirass he had put on a crimson tunic. So as they struck upon the cuirass they could effect nothing, until some one, perceiving what the matter was, thrust into his eye. Then at length he fell and died; and by some means the other men of the cavalry had not observed this take place, for they neither saw him when he had fallen from his horse nor when he was slain, and while the retreat and the turn [for another charge] were being made, they did not perceive that which was happening; but when they had stopped their horses, then at once they missed him, since there was no one to command them; and when they perceived what had happened, they passed the word to one another and all rode together, that they might recover the body. **23.** The Athenians, seeing that the cavalry were riding to attack them no longer by squadrons but all together, shouted to the rest of the army to help them. Then while the whole number of those on foot were coming to their help, there arose a sharp fight for the body;* and so long as the three hundred were alone they had much the worse and were about to abandon the body, but when the mass of the army came to their help, then the horsemen no longer sustained the fight, nor did they succeed in recovering the body; and besides him they lost others of their number also. Then they drew off about one-quarter mile

---

*There are reminiscences here of Homeric attempts to recover corpses; see also, in the *Iliad*, the catalog of troops, at 9.28–30, and the breach of the wall, at 9.70.

away and deliberated what they should do; and it seemed good to them, as they had no commander, to ride back to Mardonios. **24.** When the cavalry arrived at the camp, the whole army and also Mardonios made great mourning for Masistios, cutting off their own hair and that of their horses and baggage-animals and giving way to lamentation without stint; for all Bœotia was filled with the sound of it, because one had perished who after Mardonios was of the most account with the Persians and with the king. **25.** The Barbarians then were paying honours in their own manner to Masistios slain: but the Hellenes, when they had sustained the attack of the cavalry and had driven them back, were much more encouraged; and first they put the dead body in a cart and conveyed it along their ranks; and the body was a sight worth seeing for its size and beauty, wherefore also the men left their places in the ranks and went one after the other to gaze upon Masistios. After this they resolved to come down further towards Plataia; for the region of Plataia was seen to be much more convenient for them to encamp in than that of Erythrai, for other reasons and because it is better watered. To this region then and to the spring Gargaphia, which is in this region, they resolved that they must come, and encamp in their several posts. So they took up their arms and went by the lower slopes of Kithairon past Hysiai to the Plataian land; and having there arrived they posted themselves according to their several nations near the spring Gargaphia and the sacred enclosure of Androcrates the hero, over low hills or level ground.

26. Then in the arranging of the several posts there arose a contentious argument between the Tegeans and the Athenians; for they each claimed to occupy the other, left, wing of the army themselves, alleging deeds both new and old. The Tegeans on the one hand said as follows: "We have been always judged worthy of this post by the whole body of allies in all the common expeditions which the Peloponnesians have made before this, whether in old times or but lately, ever since that time when the sons of Heracles endeavoured after the death of Eurystheus to return to the Peloponnese. This honour we gained at that time by reason of the following event:—When with the Achaians and the Ionians who were then in Peloponnesus we had come out to the Isthmus to give assistance and were encamped opposite to these who desired to return, then it is said that Hyllos made a speech saying that it was not right that the one army should risk its safety by engaging battle with the other, and urging that that man of the army of the Peloponnesians whom they should judge to be the best of them should fight in single combat with himself on terms concerted between them. The Peloponnesians then resolved that this should be done; and they made oath with one another on this condition,—that if Hyllos should conquer the leader of the Peloponnesians, then the sons of Heracles should return to their father's heritage; but if he should be conquered, then on the other hand the sons of Heracles should depart and lead away their army, and not within a hundred years attempt to return to the Peloponnese. There was selected then of all the allies, he himself making a voluntary offer, Echemos the son of Aëropos, the son of Phegeus, who was our commander and king: and he fought a single combat and slew Hyllos.

By reason of this deed we obtained among the Peloponnesians of that time, besides many other great privileges which we still possess, this also of always leading the other wing of the army, when a common expedition is made. To you, Lacedemonians, we make no opposition, but we give you freedom of choice, and allow you to command whichever wing you desire; but of the other we say that it belongs to us to be the leaders as in former time: and apart from this deed which has been related, we are more worthy than the Athenians to have this post; for in many glorious contests have we contended against you, O Spartans, and in many also against others. Therefore it is just that we have the other wing rather than the Athenians; for they have not achieved deeds such as ours, either new or old."

27. Thus they spoke, and the Athenians replied as follows: "Though we know that this gathering was assembled for battle with the Barbarian and not for speech, yet since the Tegean has proposed to us as a task to speak of things both old and new, the deeds of merit namely which by each of our two nations have been achieved in all time, it is necessary for us to point out to you whence it comes that to us, who have been brave men always, it belongs as a heritage rather than to the Arcadians to have the chief place. First as to the sons of Heracles, whose leader they say that they slew at the Isthmus, these in the former time, when they were driven away by all the Hellenes to whom they came flying from slavery under those of Mykenē, we alone received; and joining with them we subdued the insolence of Eurystheus, having conquered in fight those who then dwelt in Peloponnesus. Again when the Argives who with Polyneikes marched against Thebes, had been slain and were lying unburied, we declare that we marched an army against the Cadmeians and recovered the dead bodies and gave them burial in our own land at Eleusis. We have moreover another glorious deed performed against the Amazons who invaded once the Attic land, coming from the river Thermodon: and in the toils of Troy we were not inferior to any. But it is of no profit to make mention of these things; for on the one hand, though we were brave men in those times, we might now have become worthless, and on the other hand even though we were then worthless, yet now we might be better. Let it suffice therefore about ancient deeds; but if by us no other deed has been displayed (as many there have been and glorious, not less than by any other people of the Hellenes), yet even by reason of the deed wrought at Marathon alone we are worthy to have this privilege and others besides this, seeing that we alone of all the Hellenes fought in single combat with the Persian, and having undertaken so great a deed we overcame and conquered six-and-forty nations.* Are we not worthy then to have this post by reason of that deed alone? However, since at such a time as this it is not fitting to contend for post, we are ready to follow your saying, O Lacedemonians, as to where you think it most convenient that we should stand and opposite to whom; for wheresoever we are

---

*This is the total derived from 7.61–80.

posted, we shall endeavour to be brave men. Prescribe to us therefore and we shall obey." They made answer thus; and the whole body of the Lacedemonians shouted aloud that the Athenians were more worthy to occupy the wing than the Arcadians. Thus the Athenians obtained the wing, and overcame the Tegeans.

28. After this the Hellenes were ranged as follows, both those of them who came in continually afterwards and those who had come at the first. The right wing was held by ten thousand Lacedemonians; and of these the five thousand who were Spartans were attended by thirty-five thousand Helots serving as light-armed troops, seven of them appointed for each man. To stand next to themselves the Spartans chose the Tegeans, both to do them honour and also because of their valour; and of these there were one thousand five hundred hoplites. After these were stationed five thousand Corinthians, and they had obtained permission from Pausanias that the three hundred who were present of the men of Potidaia in Pallenē should stand by their side. Next to these were stationed six hundred Arcadians of Orchomenos; and to these three thousand Sikyonians. Next after these were eight hundred Epidaurians: by the side of these were ranged a thousand Troizenians: next to the Troizenians two hundred Lepreates: next to these four hundred of the men of Mykenē and Tiryns; and then a thousand Phliasians. By the side of these stood three hundred Hermionians; and next to the Hermionians were stationed six hundred Eretrians and Stryians; next to these four hundred Chalkidians; and to these five hundred men of Amprakia. After these stood eight hundred Leucadians and Anactorians; and next to them two hundred from Palē in Kephallenia. After these were ranged five hundred Eginetans; by their side three thousand Megarians; and next to these six hundred Plataians. Last, or if you will first, were ranged the Athenians, occupying the left wing, eight thousand in number, and the commander of them was Aristeides the son of Lysimachos. **29.** These all, excepting those who were appointed to attend the Spartans, seven for each man, were hoplites, being in number altogether thirty-eight thousand and seven hundred. This was the whole number of hoplites who were assembled against the Barbarian; and the number of the light-armed was as follows:—of the Spartan division thirty-five thousand men, reckoning at the rate of seven for each man, and of these every one was equipped for fighting; and the light-armed troops of the rest of the Lacedemonians and of the other Hellenes, being about one for each man, amounted to thirty-four thousand five hundred. **30.** Of the light-armed fighting men the whole number then was sixty-nine thousand and five hundred; and of the whole Hellenic force which assembled at Plataia the number (including both the hoplites and the light-armed fighting men) was one hundred ten thousand less one thousand eight hundred men; and with the Thespians who were present the number of one hundred ten thousand myriads was fully made up; for there were present also in the army those of the Thespians who survived, being in number about one thousand eight hundred, and these too were without heavy arms. These then having been ranged in order were encamped on the river Asopos.

31. Meanwhile the Barbarians with Mardonios, when they had sufficiently mourned for Masistios, being informed that the Hellenes were at Plataia came themselves also to that part of the Asopos which flows there; and having arrived there, they were ranged against the enemy by Mardonios thus:—against the Lacedemonians he stationed the Persians; and since the Persians were much superior in numbers, they were arrayed in deeper ranks than those, and notwithstanding this the Persian line extended in front of the Tegeans also: and he ranged them in this manner,—all the strongest part of that body he selected from the rest and stationed it opposite to the Lacedemonians, but the weaker part he ranged by their side opposite to the Tegeans. This he did on the information and suggestion of the Thebans. Then next to the Persians he ranged the Medes; and these extended in front of the Corinthians, Potidaians, Orchomenians and Sikyonians. Next to the Medes he ranged the Bactrians; and these extended in front of the Epidaurians, Troizenians, Lepreates, Tirynthians, Mykenians and Phliasians. After the Bactrians he stationed the Indians; and these extended in front of the Hermionians, Eretrians, Styrians and Chalkidians. Next to the Indians he ranged the Sacans, who extended in front of the men of Amprakia, the Anactorians, Leucadians, Palians and Eginetans. Next to the Sacans and opposite to the Athenians, Plataians and Megarians, he ranged the Bœotians, Locrians, Malians, Thessalians, and the thousand men of the Phokians: for not all the Phokians had taken the side of the Medes, but some of them were even supporting the cause of the Hellenes, being shut up in Parnassos; and setting out from thence they plundered from the army of Mardonios and from those of the Hellenes who were with him. He ranged the Macedonians also and those who dwell about the borders of Thessaly opposite to the Athenians. **32.** These which have been named were the greatest of the nations who were arrayed in order by Mardonios, those, I mean, which were the most renowned and of greatest consideration: but there were in his army also men of several other nations mingled together, of the Phrygians, Thracians, Mysians, Paionians, and the rest; and among them also some Ethiopians, and of the Egyptians those called Hermotybians and Calasirians, carrying knives, who of all the Egyptians are the only warriors. These men, while he was yet at Phaleron, he had caused to disembark from the ships in which they served as fighting-men; for the Egyptians had not been appointed to serve in the land-army which came with Xerxes to Athens. Of the Barbarians then there were thirty myriads,* as has been declared before; but of the Hellenes who were allies of Mardonios no man knows what the number was, for they were not numbered; but by conjecture I judge that these were assembled to the number of five myriads. These who were placed in array side by side were on foot; and the cavalry was ranged apart from them in a separate body. **33.** When all had been drawn up by nations and by divisions, then on

---

*300,000, as noted at 8.113.

the next day they offered sacrifice on both sides. For the Hellenes
Tisamenos the son of Antiochos was he who offered sacrifice, for he it
was who accompanied this army as diviner. This man the Lacedemonians
had made to be one of their own people, being an Eleian and of the race
of the Iamidai: for when Tisamenos was seeking divination at Delphi concerning issue, the Pythian prophetess made answer to him that he should
win five of the greatest contests. He accordingly, missing the meaning of
the oracle, began to attend to athletic games, supposing that he should
win contests of athletics; and he practised for the pentathlon or "five contests" and came within one fall of winning a victory at the Olympic
games, being set to contend with Hieronymos of Andros. The Lacedemonians however perceived that the oracle given to Tisamenos had reference not to athletic but to martial contests, and they endeavoured to
persuade Tisamenos by payment of money, and to make him a leader in
their wars together with the kings of the race of Heracles. He then, seeing
that the Spartans set much store on gaining him over as a friend, having
perceived this, I say, he raised his price and signified to them that he
would do as they desired, if they would make him a citizen of their State
and give him full rights, but for no other payment. The Spartans at first
when they heard this displayed indignation and altogether gave up their
request, but at last, when great terror was hanging over them of this Persian armament, they gave way and consented. He then perceiving that
they had changed their minds, said that he could not now be satisfied
even so, nor with these terms alone; but it was necessary that his brother
Hegias also should be made a Spartan citizen on the same terms as he
himself became one.

34. By saying this he followed the example of Melampus in his request,
if one may compare royal power with mere citizenship; for Melampus on
his part, when the women in Argos had been seized by madness, and the
Argives endeavoured to hire him to come from Pylos and to cause their
women to cease from the malady, proposed as payment for himself the half
of the royal power; and the Argives did not suffer this, but departed: and afterwards, when more of their women became mad, at length they accepted
that which Melampus had proposed, and went to offer him this: but he then
seeing that they had changed their minds, increased his demand, and said
that he would not do that which they desired unless they gave to his
brother Bias also one-third share in the royal power. And the Argives, being driven into straits, consented to this also. **35.** Just so the Spartans also,
being very much in need of Tisamenos, agreed with him on any terms which
he desired: and when the Spartans had agreed to this demand also, then Tisamenos the Eleian, having become a Spartan, had part with them in winning five of the greatest contests as their diviner: and these were the only
men who ever were made fellow-citizens with the Spartans. Now the five
contests were these: one and the first of them was this at Plataia; and after
this the contest at Tegea, which took place with the Tegeans and Argives;
then that at Dipaieis against all the Arcadians except the Mantineians;
after that the contest with the Messenians at Ithomē; and last of all that

which took place at Tanagra against the Athenians and Argives. This, I say, was accomplished last of the five contests.*

36. This Tisamenos was acting now as diviner for the Hellenes in the Plataian land, being brought by the Spartans. Now to the Hellenes the sacrifices were of good omen if they defended themselves only, but not if they crossed the Asopos and began a battle; **37,** and Mardonios too, who was eager to begin a battle, found the sacrifices not favourable to this design, but they were of good omen to him also if he defended himself only; for he too used the Hellenic manner of sacrifice, having as diviner Hegesistratos an Eleian and the most famous of the Telliadai, whom before these events the Spartans had taken and bound, in order to put him to death, because they had suffered much mischief from him. He then being in trouble, seeing that he was fighting for his life and was likely moreover to suffer much torment before his death, had done a deed such as may hardly be believed. Being made fast in a block bound with iron, he obtained an iron tool, which had in some way been brought in, and contrived immediately a deed the most courageous of any that we know: for having first calculated how the remaining portion of his foot might be got out of the block, he cut away the flat end of his own foot, and after that, since he was guarded still by warders, he broke through the wall and so ran away to Tegea, travelling during the nights and in the daytime entering a wood and resting there; so that, though the Lacedemonians searched for him in full force, he arrived at Tegea on the third night; and the Lacedemonians were possessed by great wonder both at his courage, when they saw the piece of the foot that was cut off lying there, and also because they were not able to find him. So he at that time having thus escaped them took refuge at Tegea, which then was not friendly with the Lacedemonians; and when he was healed and had procured for himself a wooden foot, he became an open enemy of the Lacedemonians. However in the end the enmity into which he had fallen with the Lacedemonians was not to his advantage; for he was caught by them while practising divination in Zakynthos, and was put to death.

38. However the death of Hegesistratos took place later than the events at Plataia, and he was now at the Asopos, having been hired by Mardonios for no mean sum, sacrificing and displaying zeal for his cause both on account of his enmity with the Lacedemonians and on account of the gain which he got: but as the sacrifices were not favourable for a battle either for the Persians themselves or for those Hellenes who were with them (for these also had a diviner for themselves, Hippomachos a Leucadian), and as the Hellenes had men constantly flowing in and were becoming more in number, Timagenides the son of Herpys, a Theban, counselled Mardonios to set a guard on the pass of Kithairon, saying that the Hellenes were constantly flowing in every day and that he would thus

*These were battles fought between 475 and 456 B.C. The end forms a "ring composition" with 9.33.

cut off large numbers. **39.** Eight days had now passed while they had been sitting opposite to one another, when he gave this counsel to Mardonios; and Mardonios, perceiving that the advice was good, sent the cavalry when night came on to the pass of Kithairon leading towards Plataia, which the Bœotians call the "Three Heads" and the Athenians the "Oak Heads." The cavalry did not come without effect, for they caught five hundred baggage-animals coming out into the plain, which were bearing provisions from Peloponnesus to the army, and also the men who accompanied the carts: and having taken this prize the Persians proceeded to slaughter them without sparing either beast or man; and when they were satiated with killing they surrounded the rest and drove them into the camp to Mardonios.

40. After this deed they spent two days more, neither side wishing to begin a battle; for the Barbarians advanced as far as the Asopos to make trial of the Hellenes, but neither side would cross the river. However the cavalry of Mardonios made attacks continually and did damage to the Hellenes; for the Thebans, being very strong on the side of the Medes, carried on the war with vigour, and always directed them up to the moment of fighting; and after this the Persians and Medes took up the work and displayed valour in their turn.

41. For ten days then nothing more was done than this; but when the eleventh day had come, while they still sat opposite to one another at Plataia, the Hellenes having by this time grown much more numerous and Mardonios being greatly vexed at the delay of action, then Mardonios the son of Gobryas and Artabazos the son of Pharnakes, who was esteemed by Xerxes as few Persians were, came to speech; the opinions which they expressed were these,—that of Artabazos, that they must put the whole army in motion as soon as possible and go to the wall of the Thebans, whither great stores of grain had been brought in for them and fodder for their beasts; and that they should settle there quietly and get their business done as follows:—they had, he said, great quantities of gold, both coined and uncoined, and also of silver and of drinking-cups; and these he advised that they should send about to the Hellenes without any stint, more especially to those of the Hellenes who were leaders in their several cities; and these, he said, would speedily deliver up their freedom: and he advised that they should not run the risk of a battle. His opinion then was the same as that of the Thebans,* for he as well as they had some true foresight: but the opinion of Mardonios was more vehement and more obstinate, and he was by no means disposed to yield; for he said that he thought their army far superior to that of the Hellenes, and he gave as his opinion that they should engage battle as quickly as possible and not allow them to assemble in still greater numbers than were already assembled; and as for the sacrifices of Hegesistratos, they should leave them alone and not endeavour to force a good sign, but follow the custom of the Persians and

---

*Reference to their strategy noted at 9.2.

engage battle. **42.** When he so expressed his judgment, none opposed him, and thus his opinion prevailed; for he and not Artabazos had the command of the army given him by the king. He summoned therefore the commanders of the divisions and the generals of those Hellenes who were with him, and asked whether they knew of any oracle regarding the Persians, which said that they should be destroyed in Hellas; and when those summoned to council were silent, some not knowing the oracles and others knowing them but not considering it safe to speak, Mardonios himself said: "Since then you either know nothing or do not venture to speak, I will tell you, since I know very well. There is an oracle saying that the Persians are destined when they come to Hellas to plunder the temple at Delphi, and having plundered it to perish every one of them. We therefore, just because we know this, will not go to that temple nor will we attempt to plunder it; and for this cause we shall not perish. So many of you therefore as wish well to the Persians, have joy so far as regards this matter, and be assured that we shall overcome the Hellenes." Having spoken to them thus, he next commanded to prepare everything and to set all in order, since at dawn of the next day a battle would be fought.

43. Now this oracle, which Mardonios said referred to the Persians, I know for my part was composed with reference to the Illyrians and the army of the Enchelians, and not with reference to the Persians at all. However, the oracle which was composed by Bakis with reference to this battle,

"The gathering of Hellenes together and cry of Barbarian voices,
Where the Thermodon flows, by the banks of grassy Asopos;
Here very many shall fall ere destiny gave them to perish,
Medes bow-bearing in fight, when the fatal day shall approach them,"—

these sayings, and others like them composed by Musaios, I know had reference to the Persians. Now the river Thermodon flows between Tanagra and Glisas.

44. After the inquiry about the oracles and the exhortation given by Mardonios night came on and the guards were set: and when night was far advanced, and it seemed that there was quiet everywhere in the camps, and that the men were in their deepest sleep, then Alexander the son of Amyntas, commander and king of the Macedonians, rode his horse up to the guard-posts of the Athenians and requested that he might have speech with their generals. So while the greater number of the guards stayed in their posts, some ran to the generals, and when they reached them they said that a man had come riding on a horse out of the camp of the Medes, who discovered nothing further, but only named the generals and said that he desired to have speech with them. **45.** Having heard this, immediately they accompanied the men to the guard-posts, and when they had arrived there, Alexander thus spoke to them: "Athenians, I lay up these words of mine as a trust with you, charging you to keep them secret and tell them to no one except only to Pausanias, lest you bring me to ruin: for I should not utter them if I did not care greatly for the general safety of Hellas, seeing that I am a Hellene myself by original descent and I should not wish to see Hellas enslaved instead of free. I say then that Mardonios and his army cannot get the sacrifices that they would like, for otherwise you would long ago have fought. Now however he has resolved to let the offerings alone and to bring on a battle at dawn of day; for, as I conjecture, he fears lest you should assemble in greater numbers. Therefore prepare yourselves; and if after all Mardonios should put off the battle and not bring it on, stay where you are and hold out patiently; for they have provisions only for a few days remaining. And if this war shall have its issue according to your mind, then each one of you ought to remember me also concerning liberation, since I have done for the sake of the Hellenes so hazardous a deed by reason of my zeal for you, desiring to show you the design of Mardonios, in order that the Barbarians may not fall upon you when you are not yet expecting them: and I am Alexander the Macedonian." Thus having spoken he rode away back to the camp and to his own position.

46. Then the generals of the Athenians came to the right wing and told Pausanias that which they had heard from Alexander. Struck with fear of the Persians, he spoke as follows: "Since then at dawn the battle comes on, it is right that you, Athenians, should take your stand opposite to the Persians, and we opposite to the Bœotians and those Hellenes who are now posted against you; and for this reason, namely because you are acquainted with the Medes and with their manner of fighting, having fought with them at Marathon, whereas we have had no experience of these men and are without knowledge of them; for not one of the Spartans has made trial of the Medes in fight, but of the Bœotians and Thessalians we have had experience. It is right therefore that you should take up your arms and come to this wing of the army, and that we should go to the left wing." In answer to this the Athenians spoke as follows: "To ourselves also long ago at the very first, when we saw that the Persians were being ranged opposite to you, it occurred to say these very things, which you now bring forward before we have uttered them; but we feared lest these words might not be pleasing to you. Since however you yourselves have made mention of this, know that your words have caused us pleasure, and that we are ready to do this which you say." **47.** Both then were content to do this, and as dawn appeared they began to change their positions with one another: and the Bœotians perceiving that which was being done reported it to Mardonios, who, when he heard it, immediately himself also endeavoured to change positions, bringing the Persians along so as to be against the Lacedemonians: and when Pausanias learnt that this was being so done, he perceived that he was not unobserved, and he led the Spartans back again to the right wing; and just so also did Mardonios upon his left.

48. When they had been thus brought to their former positions, Mardonios sent a herald to the Spartans and said as follows: "Lacedemonians, you are alleged by those who are here to be very good men, and they admire you because you do not flee in war nor leave your post, but stay there and either destroy your enemies or perish yourselves. In this however, as it now appears, there is no truth; for before we engaged battle and came to hand-to-hand conflict we saw you already flee and leave your station, desiring to make the trial with the Athenians first, while you ranged yourselves opposite to our slaves. These are not at all the deeds of good men in war, but we were deceived in you very greatly; for we expected by reason of your renown that you would send a herald to us, challenging us and desiring to fight with the Persians alone; but though we on our part were ready to do this, we did not find that you said anything of this kind, but rather that you cowered with fear. Now therefore since you were not the first to say this, we are the first. Why do we not now fight, you on behalf of the Hellenes, since you have the reputation of being the best, and we on behalf of the Barbarians, with equal numbers on both sides? and if we think it good that the others should fight also, then let them fight afterwards; and if on the other hand we should not think it good, but think it sufficient that we alone should fight, then let us fight it out to the end, and whichsoever of us shall be the victors, let these be counted as victorious with their whole army."

49. The herald having thus spoken waited for some time, and then, as no one made him any answer, he departed and went back; and having returned he signified to Mardonios that which had happened to him. Mardonios then being greatly rejoiced and elated by his empty victory, sent the cavalry to attack the Hellenes: and when the horsemen had ridden to attack them, they did damage to the whole army of the Hellenes by hurling javelins against them and shooting with bows, being mounted archers and hard therefore to fight against: and they disturbed and choked up the spring Gargaphia, from which the whole army of the Hellenes was drawing its water. Now the Lacedemonians alone were posted near this spring, and it was at some distance from the rest of the Hellenes, as they chanced to be posted, while the Asopos was near at hand; but when they were kept away from the Asopos, then they used to employ this spring; for they were not permitted by the horsemen and archers to fetch water from the river. **50.** The generals of the Hellenes, since the army had been cut off from its water and was being harassed by the cavalry, assembled to consult about these and other things, coming to Pausanias upon the right wing: for other things too troubled them yet more than these of which we have spoken, since they no longer had provisions, and their attendants who had been sent to Peloponnese for the purpose of getting them had been cut off by the cavalry and were not able to reach the camp. **51.** It was resolved then by the generals in council with one another, that if the Persians put off the battle for that day, they would go to the Island. This is distant a mile and a quarter from the Asopos and the spring Gargaphia, where they were then encamped, and is in front of the city of the Plataians: and if it be asked how there can be an island on the mainland, thus it is:—the river parts in two above, as it flows from Kithairon down to the plain, keeping a distance of about 1800 feet between its streams, and after that it joins again in one stream; and the name of it is Oëroē, said by the natives of the country to be the daughter of Asopos. To this place they determined to remove, in order that they might be able to get an abundant supply of water and that the cavalry might not do them damage, as now when they were right opposite. And they proposed to remove when the second watch of the night should have come, so that the Persians might not see them set forth and harass them with the cavalry pursuing. They proposed also, after they had arrived at this place, round which, as I say, Oëroē the daughter of Asopos flows, parting as she runs from Kithairon, to send half of the army to Kithairon during this same night, in order to take up their attendants who had gone to get the supplies of provisions; for these were cut off from them in Kithairon.

52. Having thus resolved, during the whole of that day they had trouble unceasingly, while the cavalry pressed upon them; but when the day drew to a close and the attacks of the cavalry had ceased, then as it was becoming night and the time had arrived at which it had been agreed that they should retire from their place, the greater number of them set forth and began to retire, not however keeping it in mind to go to the place which had been agreed upon; but on the contrary, when they had begun to move, they readily took occasion to flee from the cavalry towards the city of the Plataians, and in their flight they came as far as the temple of Hera, which temple is in front of the city of the Plataians at a distance of two and a half miles from the spring Gargaphia; and when they had there arrived they halted in front of the temple. **53.** These then were encamping about the temple of Hera; and Pausanias, seeing that they were retiring from the camp, gave the word to the Lacedemonians also to take up their arms and go after the others who were preceding them, supposing that these were going to the place to which they had agreed to go. Then, when all the other commanders were ready to obey Pausanias, Amompharetos the son of Poliades, the commander of the Pitanate division, said that he would not flee from the strangers, nor with his own will would he disgrace Sparta; and he expressed wonder, not having been present at the former discussion. And Pausanias and Euryanax were greatly disturbed that he did not obey them and still more that they should be compelled to leave the Pitanate division behind, since he thus refused; for they feared that if they should leave it in order to do that which they had agreed with the other Hellenes, both Amompharetos himself would perish and also the men with him. With this thought they kept the Lacedemonian force from moving, and meanwhile they endeavoured to persuade him that it was not right for him to do so.

54. They then were exhorting Amompharetos, who had been left behind alone of the Lacedemonians and Tegeans; and meanwhile the Athenians were keeping themselves quiet in the place where they had been posted, knowing the spirit of the Lacedemonians, that they were apt to say otherwise than they really meant; and when the army began to move, they sent a horseman from their own body to see whether the Spartans were attempting to set forth, or whether they had in truth no design at all to retire; and they bade him ask Pausanias what they ought to do.

55. So when the herald came to the Lacedemonians, he saw that they were still in their place and that the chiefs of them had come to strife with one another: for when Euryanax and Pausanias both exhorted Amompharetos not to run the risk of remaining behind with his men, alone of all the Lacedemonians, they did not at all persuade him, and at last they had come to open quarrel; and meanwhile the herald of the Athenians had arrived and was standing by them. And Amompharetos in his dispute took a rock in both his hands and placed it at the feet of Pausanias, saying that with this pebble* he gave his vote not to fly from the "strangers," meaning the Barbarians. Pausanias then, calling him a madman and one who was not in his right senses, bade the Athenian herald report the state of their affairs. He was asking that which he had been charged to ask; and at the same time Pausanias requested the Athenians to come towards the Lacedemonians and to do in regard to the retreat the same as they did. **56.** He then went away back to the Athenians; and as the dawn of day found them yet disputing with one another, Pausanias, who had remained still throughout all this time, gave the signal and led away all the rest over the low hills, supposing that Amompharetos would not stay behind when the other Lacedemonians departed (in which he was in fact right); and with them also went the Tegeans. Meanwhile the Athenians, following the commands which were given them, were going in the direction opposite to that of the Lacedemonians; for these were clinging to the hills and the lower slope of Kithairon from fear of the cavalry, while the Athenians were marching below in the direction of the plain. **57.** As for Amompharetos, he did not at first believe that Pausanias would ever venture to leave him and his men behind, and he stuck to it that they should stay there and not leave their post; but when Pausanias and his troops were well in front, then he perceived that they had actually left him behind, and he made his division take up their arms and led them slowly towards the main body. This, when it had got away about a mile and a quarter, stayed for the division of Amompharetos, halting at the river Moloeis and the place called Argiopion, where also there stands a temple of the Eleusinian Demeter: and it stayed there for this reason, namely in order that if Amompharetos and his division should not leave the place where they had been posted, but should remain there, it might be able to come back to their assistance. So Amompharetos and his men were coming up to join them, and the cavalry also of the Barbarians was at the same time beginning to attack them in full force: for the horsemen did on this day as they had been wont to do every day; and seeing the place vacant in which the Hellenes had been posted on the former days, they rode their horses on continually further, and as soon as they came up with them they began to attack them.

58. Then Mardonios, when he was informed that the Hellenes had

---

*The Greeks used pebbles as voting tokens; thus we have a Spartan pun.

departed during the night, and when he saw their place deserted, called Thorax of Larissa and his brothers Eurypylos and Thrasydeios, and said: "Sons of Aleuas, will you yet say anything more, now that you see these places deserted? For you who dwell near them were wont to say that the Lacedemonians did not fly from a battle, but were men unsurpassed in war; and these men you not only saw before this changing from their post, but now we all of us see that they have run away during the past night; and by this they showed clearly, when the time came for them to contend in battle with those who were in truth the best of all men, that after all they were men of no worth, who had been making a display of valour among Hellenes, a worthless race. As for you, since you had had no experience of the Persians, I for my part was very ready to excuse you when you praised these, of whom after all you knew something good; but much more I marvelled at Artabazos that *he* should have been afraid of the Lacedemonians, and that having been afraid he should have uttered that most cowardly opinion, namely that we ought to move our army away and go to the city of the Thebans to be besieged there,—an opinion about which the king shall yet be informed by me. Of these things we will speak in another place; now however we must not allow them to act thus, but we must pursue them until they are caught and pay the penalty to us for all that they did to the Persians in time past."

59. Thus having spoken he led on the Persians at a run, after they had crossed the Asopos, on the track of the Hellenes,* supposing that these were running away from him; and he directed his attack upon the Lacedemonians and Tegeans only, for the Athenians, whose march was towards the plain, he did not see by reason of the hills. Then the rest of the commanders of the Barbarian divisions, seeing that the Persians had started to pursue the Hellenes, immediately all raised the signals for battle and began to pursue, each as fast as they could, not arranged in any order or succession of post.

60. These then were coming on with shouting and confused numbers, thinking to make short work of the Hellenes; and Pausanias, when the cavalry began to attack, sent to the Athenians a horseman and said thus: "Athenians, now that the greatest contest is set before us, namely that which has for its issue the freedom or the slavery of Hellas, we have been deserted by our allies, we Lacedemonians and you Athenians, seeing that they have run away during the night that is past. Now therefore it is determined what we must do upon this, namely that we must defend ourselves and protect one another as best we may. If then the cavalry had set forth to attack you at the first, we and the Tegeans, who with us refuse to betray the cause of Hellas, should have been bound to go to your help; but as it is, since the whole body has come against us, it is right that you should come to that portion of the army which is hardest pressed, to give aid. If however anything has happened to you which makes it impossible for you

---

*The battle of Plataia was fought in September of 479 B.C.

to come to our help, then do us a kindness by sending to us the archers; and we know that you have been in the course of this present war by far the most zealous of all, so that you will listen to our request in this matter also." **61.** When the Athenians heard this they were desirous to come to their help and to assist them as much as possible; and as they were already going, they were attacked by those of the Hellenes on the side of the king who had been ranged opposite to them, so that they were no longer able to come to the help of the Lacedemonians, for the force that was attacking them gave them much trouble. Thus the Lacedemonians and Tegeans were left alone, being in number, together with light-armed men, the former fifty thousand and the Tegeans three thousand; for these were not parted at all from the Lacedemonians: and they began to offer sacrifice, meaning to engage battle with Mardonios and the force which had come against them. Then since their offerings did not prove favourable, and many of them were being slain during this time and many more wounded,—for the Persians had made a palisade of their wicker-work shields and were discharging their arrows in great multitude and without sparing,—Pausanias, seeing that the Spartans were hard pressed and that the offerings did not prove favourable, fixed his gaze upon the temple of Hera of the Plataians and called upon the goddess to help, praying that they might by no means be cheated of their hope: **62,** and while he was yet calling upon her thus, the Tegeans started forward before them and advanced against the Barbarians, and immediately after the prayer of Pausanias the offerings proved favourable for the Lacedemonians as they sacrificed. So when this at length came to pass, then they also advanced against the Persians; and the Persians put away their bows and came against them. Then first there was fighting about the wicker-work shields, and when these had been overturned, after that the fighting was fierce by the side of the temple of Demeter, and so continued for a long time, until at last they came to hand-to-hand combat; for the Barbarians would take hold of the spears and break them off. Now in courage and in strength the Persians were not inferior to the others, but they were without defensive armour, and moreover they were unversed in war and unequal to their opponents in skill; and they would dart out one at a time or in groups of about ten together, some more and some less, and fall upon the Spartans and perish.

63. In the place where Mardonios himself was, riding on a white horse and having about him the thousand best men of the Persians, here, I say, they pressed upon their opponents most of all: and so long as Mardonios survived, they held out against them, and defending themselves they cast down many of the Lacedemonians; but when Mardonios was slain and the men who were ranged about his person, which was the strongest portion of the whole army, had fallen, then the others too turned and gave way before the Lacedemonians; for their manner of dress, without defensive armour, was a very great cause of destruction to them, since in truth they were contending light-armed against hoplites. **64.** Then the satisfaction for the murder of Leonidas was paid by Mardonios according to the oracle given to the Spartans,* and the most famous victory of all those about which we have knowledge was gained by Pausanias the son of Cleombrotos, the son of Anaxandrides; of his ancestors above this the names have been given for Leonidas,† since, as it happens, they are the same for both. Now Mardonios was slain by Arimnestos, a man of consideration in Sparta, who afterwards, when the Median wars were over, with three hundred men fought a battle against the whole army of the Messenians, then at war with the Lacedemonians, at Stenycleros, and he and the three hundred were slain. **65.** When the Persians were turned to flight at Plataia by the Lacedemonians, they fled in disorder to their own camp and to the palisade which they had made in the Theban territory. It is a marvel to me that, whereas they fought by the side of the sacred grove of Demeter, not one of the Persians was found to have entered the enclosure or to have been slain within it, but round about the temple in the unconsecrated ground fell the greater number of the slain. I suppose (if one ought to suppose anything about divine things) that the goddess herself refused to receive them, because they had set fire to the temple, that is to say the "lordly palace" at Eleusis.

66. Thus far then had this battle proceeded: but Artabazos the son of Pharnakes had been displeased at the very first because Mardonios remained behind after the king was gone; and afterwards he had been bringing forward objections continually and doing nothing, but had urged them always not to fight a battle: and for himself he acted as follows, not being pleased with the things which were being done by Mardonios.— The men of whom Artabazos was commander (and he had with him no small force but one which was in number as much as four myriads of men), these, when the fighting began, being well aware what the issue of the battle would be, he led carefully, having first given orders that all should go by the way which he should lead them and at the same pace at which they should see him go. Having given these orders he led his troops on pretence of taking them into battle; and when he was well on his way, he saw the Persians already taking flight. Then he no longer led his men in the same order as before, but set off at a run, taking flight by the quickest way not to the palisade nor yet to the wall of the Thebans, but towards Phokis, desiring as quickly as possible to reach the Hellespont. **67.** These, I say, were thus directing their march: and in the meantime, while the other Hellenes who were on the side of the king were purposely slack in the fight, the Bœotians fought with the Athenians for a long space; for those of the Thebans who took the side of the Medes had no small zeal for the cause, and they fought and were not slack, so that three hundred of them, the first and best of all, fell there by the hands of the Athenians: and when these also turned to flight, they fled to

---

*At 8.114 Xerxes makes this ominous promise in response to a Spartan, oracle-driven request.
†At 7.204, before the battle of Thermopylai.

Thebes, not to the same place as the Persians: and the main body of the other allies fled without having fought constantly with any one or displayed any deeds of valour.

68. And this is an additional proof to me that all the fortunes of the Barbarians depended upon the Persians, namely that at that time these men fled before they had even engaged with the enemy, because they saw the Persians doing so. Thus all were in flight except only the cavalry, including also that of the Bœotians; and this rendered service to the fugitives by constantly keeping close to the enemy and separating the fugitives of their own side from the Hellenes. **69.** The victors then were coming after the troops of Xerxes, both pursuing and slaughtering them; and during the time when this panic arose, the report was brought to the other Hellenes who had posted themselves about the temple of Hera and had been absent from the battle, that a battle had taken place and that the troops of Pausanias were gaining the victory. When they heard this, then without ranging themselves in any order the Corinthians and those near them turned to go by the skirts of the mountain and by the low hills along the way which led straight up to the temple of Demeter, while the Megarians and Phliasians and those near them went by the plain along the smoothest way. When however the Megarians* and Phliasians came near to the enemy, the cavalry of the Thebans caught sight of them from a distance hurrying along without any order, and rode up to attack them, the commander of the cavalry being Asopodoros the son of Timander; and having fallen upon them they slew six hundred of them, and the rest they pursued and drove to Kithairon.

70. These then perished thus ingloriously; and meanwhile the Persians and the rest of the throng, having fled for refuge to the palisade, succeeded in getting up to the towers before the Lacedemonians came; and having got up they strengthened the wall of defence as best they could. Then when the Lacedemonians came up to attack it, there began between them a rather vigorous fight for the wall: for while the Athenians were away, they defended themselves and had much the advantage over the Lacedemonians, since these did not understand the art of fighting against walls; but when the Athenians came up to help them, then there was a fierce fight for the wall, lasting for a long time, and at length by valour and endurance the Athenians mounted up on the wall and made a breach in it, through which the Hellenes poured in. Now the Tegeans were the first who entered the wall, and these were they who plundered the tent of Mardonios, taking, besides the other things which were in it, also the manger of his horse, which was all of bronze and a sight worth seeing. This manger of Mardonios was dedicated by the Tegeans as an offering in the temple of Athenē Alea, but all the other things which they took, they brought to the common stock of the Hellenes. The Barbarians however, after the wall had been captured, no longer formed themselves into any close body, nor did any of them think of making resistance, but they were utterly at a loss, as

---

*Fornara 60 translates a stone Megarian memorial of their service.

you might expect from men who were in a panic with many thousands of them shut up together in a small space: and the Hellenes were able to slaughter them so that out of an army of 300,000 if those four be subtracted which Artabazos took with him in his flight, of the remainder not three thousand men survived. Of the Lacedemonians from Sparta there were slain in the battle ninety-one in all, of the Tegeans sixteen, and of the Athenians two-and-fifty.

71. Among the Barbarians those who proved themselves the best men were, of those on foot the Persians, and of the cavalry the Sacans, and for a single man Mardonios it is said was the best. Of the Hellenes, though both the Tegeans and the Athenians proved themselves good men, yet the Lacedemonians surpassed them in valour. Of this I have no other proof (for all these were victorious over their opposites), but only this, that they fought against the strongest part of the enemy's force and overcame it. And the man who proved himself in my opinion by much the best was that Aristodemos who, having come back safe from Thermopylai alone of the three hundred, had reproach and dishonour. After him the best were Poseidonios and Philokyon and Amompharetos the Spartans. However, when there came to be conversation as to which of them had proved himself the best, the Spartans who were present gave it as their opinion that Aristodemos had evidently wished to be slain in consequence of the charge which lay upon him, and so, being as it were in a frenzy and leaving his place in the ranks, he had displayed great deeds, whereas Poseidonios had proved himself a good man although he did not desire to be slain; and so far he was the better man of the two. This however they perhaps said from ill-will; and all these whose names I mentioned among the men who were killed in this battle, were specially honoured; but Aristodemos, since he desired to be slain on account of the before-mentioned charge, was not honoured.

72. These obtained the most renown of those who fought at Plataia, for as for Callicrates, the most beautiful who came to the camp, not of the Lacedemonians alone, but also of all the Hellenes of his time, he was not killed in the battle itself; but when Pausanias was offering sacrifice, he was wounded by an arrow in the side, as he was sitting down in his place in the ranks; and while the others were fighting, he having been carried out of the ranks was dying a lingering death: and he said to Arimnestos a Plataian that it did not grieve him to die for Hellas, but it grieved him only that he had not proved his strength of hand, and that no deed of valour had been displayed by him worthy of the spirit which he had to perform great deeds.

73. Of the Athenians the man who gained most glory is said to have been Sophanes the son of Eutychides of the deme of Dekeleia,—a deme of which the inhabitants formerly did a deed that was of service to them for all time, as the Athenians themselves report. For when of old the sons of Tyndareus invaded the Attic land with a great host, in order to bring home Helen, and were laying waste the demes, not knowing to what place of hiding Helen had been removed, then they say that the men of Dekeleia, or as some say Dekelos himself, being aggrieved by the insolence of Theseus and fearing for all the land of the Athenians, told them the whole matter and led them to Aphidnai, which Titakos who was sprung from the soil delivered up by treachery to the sons of Tyndareus. In consequence of this deed the Dekeleians have had continually freedom from dues in Sparta and front seats at the games, privileges which exist still to this day; insomuch that even in the war which many years after these events arose between the Athenians and the Peloponnesians, when the Lacedemonians laid waste all the rest of Attica, they abstained from injury to Dekeleia.* **74.** To this deme belonged Sophanes, who showed himself the best of all the Athenians in this battle; and of him there are two different stories told: one that he carried an anchor of iron bound by chains of bronze to the belt of his corslet; and this he threw whensoever he came up with the enemy, in order, they say, that the enemy when they came forth out of their ranks might not be able to move him from his place; and when a flight of his opponents took place, his plan was to take up the anchor first and then pursue after them. This story is reported thus; but the other of the stories, disputing the truth of that which has been told above, is reported as follows, namely that upon his shield, which was ever moving about and never remaining still, he bore an anchor as a device, and not one of iron bound to his corslet. **75.** There was another illustrious deed done too by Sophanes; for when the Athenians besieged Egina he challenged to a fight and slew Eurybates the Argive, one who had been victor in the pentathlon, or five contests, at the games. To Sophanes himself it happened after these events that when he was general of the Athenians together with Leagros the son of Glaucon, he was slain after proving himself a good man by the Edonians at Daton, fighting for the gold-mines.

76. When the Barbarians had been laid low by the Hellenes at Plataia, a woman approached, the concubine of Pharandates the son of Teaspis a Persian, coming over of her own will from the enemy. When she perceived that the Persians had been destroyed and that the Hellenes were the victors, she descended from her carriage and came up to the Lacedemonians while they were yet engaged in the slaughter. This woman had adorned herself with many ornaments of gold, and her attendants likewise, and she had put on the fairest robe she had; and when she saw that Pausanias was directing everything there, being well acquainted before with his name and with his lineage, because she had heard it often, she recognised Pausanias and taking hold of his knees she said: "O king of Sparta, deliver me your suppliant from the slavery of the captive: for you have also done me service hitherto in destroying these, who have regard neither for demigods nor yet for gods. I am by race of Cos, the daughter of Hegetorides the son of Antagoras; and the Persian took me by force in Cos and kept me a prisoner." He made answer in these words: "Woman, be of good courage, both

---

*Dekeleia was spared in 431 B.C. and later in the Peloponnesian War; this reference is an important *terminus post quem* for dating the publication of the *Histories.*

because you are a suppliant, and also if in addition to this it chances that you are speaking the truth and are the daughter of Hegetorides the Coan, who is bound to me as a guest-friend more than any other of the men who dwell in those parts." Having thus spoken, for that time he gave her in charge to those of the Ephors who were present, and afterwards he sent her away to Egina, whither she herself desired to go.

77. After the arrival of the woman, immediately upon this arrived the Mantineians, when all was over; and having learnt that they had come too late for the battle, they were greatly grieved and said that they deserved to be punished: and being informed that the Medes with Artabazos were in flight, they pursued after them as far as Thessaly, though the Lacedemonians endeavoured to prevent them from pursuing after fugitives. Then returning back to their own country they sent the leaders of their army into exile from the land. After the Mantineians came the Eleians; and they, like the Mantineians, were greatly grieved by it and so departed home; and these also when they had returned sent their leaders into exile. So much of the Mantineians and Eleians.

78. At Plataia among the troops of the Eginetans was Lampon the son of Pytheas, one of the leading men of the Eginetans, who was moved to go to Pausanias with a most impious proposal, and when he had come with haste, he said as follows: "Son of Clembrotos, you have done a deed of marvellous greatness and glory, and to you God has permitted by rescuing Hellas to lay up for yourself the greatest renown of all the Hellenes about whom we have any knowledge. Then perform also that which remains, in order that you may gain yet greater reputation, and also that in future every one of the Barbarians may beware of beginning presumptuous deeds towards the Hellenes. For when Leonidas was slain at Thermopylai, Mardonios and Xerxes cut off his head and crucified him: to him therefore repay like with like, and you shall have praise first from all the Spartans and then secondly from the other Hellenes also; for if you impale the body of Mardonios, you will then have taken vengeance for Leonidas your father's brother." **79.** He said this thinking to give pleasure; but the other made him answer again in these words: "Stranger of Egina, I admire your friendly spirit and your forethought for me, but you have failed of a good opinion nevertheless: for having exalted me on high and my family and my deed, you then cast me down to nought by advising me to do outrage to a dead body, and by saying that if I do this I shall be better reported of. These things it is more fitting for Barbarians to do than for Hellenes; and even with them we find fault for doing so. However that may be, I do not desire in any such manner as this to please either Eginetans or others who like such things; but it is enough for me that I should keep from unholy deeds, and even from unholy speech also, and so please the Spartans. As for Leonidas, whom you bid me avenge, I declare that he has been greatly avenged already, and by the unnumbered lives which have been taken of these men he has been honoured, and not he only but also the rest who brought their lives to an end at Thermopylai. As for you however, come not again to me with such a proposal, nor give me such advice; and be thankful moreover that you have no punishment for it now."

80. He having heard this went his way; and Pausanias made a proclamation that none should lay hands upon the spoil, and he ordered the Helots to collect the things together. They accordingly dispersed themselves about the camp and found tents furnished with gold and silver, and beds overlaid with gold and overlaid with silver, and mixing-bowls of gold, and cups and other drinking vessels. They found also sacks laid upon waggons, in which there proved to be caldrons both of gold and of silver; and from the dead bodies which lay there they stripped bracelets and collars, and also their Persian swords if they were of gold, for as to embroidered raiment, there was no account made of it. Then the Helots stole many of the things and sold them to the Eginetans, but many things also they delivered up, as many of them as they could not conceal; so that the great wealth of the Eginetans first came from this, that they bought the gold from the Helots making pretence that it was brass. **81.** Then having brought the things together, and having set apart a tithe for the god at Delphi, with which the offering was dedicated of the golden tripod which rests upon the three-headed serpent of bronze and stands close by the altar,* and also for the god at Olympia, with which they dedicated the offering of a bronze statue of Zeus fifteen feet high, and finally for the god at the Isthmus, with which was made a bronze statue of Poseidon ten and one-half feet high,— having set apart these things, they divided the rest, and each took that which they ought to have, including the concubines of the Persians and the gold and the silver and the other things, and also the beasts of burden. How much was set apart and given to those of them who had proved themselves the best men at Plataia is not reported by any, though for my part I suppose that gifts were made to these also; Pausanias however had ten of each thing set apart and given to him, that is women, horses, talents, camels, and so also of the other things.

82. It is said moreover that Xerxes in his flight from Hellas had left to Mardonios the furniture of his own tent, and Pausanias accordingly seeing the furniture of Mardonios decorated with gold and silver and hangings of different colours, ordered the bakers and the cooks to prepare a meal as they were used to do for Mardonios. Then when they did this as they had been commanded, it is said that Pausanias seeing the couches of gold and of silver with luxurious coverings, and the tables of gold and of silver, and the magnificent apparatus of the feast, was astonished at the good things set before him, and for sport he ordered his own servants to prepare a Laconian meal; and as, when the banquet was served, the difference between the two was great, Pausanias laughed and sent for the commanders of the Hellenes; and when these had come together, Pausanias said,

---

*Once at Delphi, the remains of the Serpent Column now stand in the Byzantine hippodrome in Istanbul; see Fornara 59.

pointing to the preparation of the two meals severally: "Hellenes, for this reason I assembled you together, because I desired to show you the sense-lessness of this leader of the Medes, who having such fare as this, came to us who have such sorry fare as you see here, in order to take it away from us." Thus it is said that Pausanias spoke to the commanders of the Hellenes.

83. However, after these events many of the Plataians also found chests of gold and of silver and of other treasures; and moreover after-wards this which follows was seen in the case of the dead bodies here, af-ter the flesh had been stripped off from the bones; for the Plataians brought together the bones all to one place:—there was found, I say, a skull with no suture but all of one bone, and there was seen also a jaw-bone, that is to say the upper part of the jaw, which had teeth joined to-gether and all of one bone, both the teeth that bite and those that grind; and the bones were seen also of a man seven and a half feet high. **84.** The body of Mardonios however had disappeared on the day after the battle, taken by whom I am not able with certainty to say, but I have heard the names of many men of various cities who are said to have buried Mardo-nios, and I know that many received gifts from Artontes the son of Mar-donios for having done this: who he was however who took up and buried the body of Mardonios, I am not able for certain to discover, but Dionyso-phanes an Ephesian is reported with some show of reason to have been he who buried Mardonios. **85.** He then was buried in some such manner as this: and the Hellenes when they had divided the spoil at Plataia pro-ceeded to bury their dead, each nation apart by themselves. The Spar-tans made for themselves three burial-places, one in which they buried the younger Spartans, of whom also were Poseidonios, Amompharetos, Philokyon and Callicrates,—in one of the graves, I say, were laid the younger men, in the second the rest of the Spartans, and in the third the Helots. These then thus buried their dead; but the Tegeans buried theirs all together in a place apart from these, and the Athenians theirs to-gether; and the Megarians and Phliasians those who had been slain by the cavalry. Of all these the burial-places had bodies laid in them, but as to the burial-places of other States which are to be seen at Plataia, these, as I am informed, are all mere mounds of earth without any bodies in them, raised by the several peoples on account of posterity, because they were ashamed of their absence from the fight; for among others there is one there called the burial-place of the Eginetans, which I hear was raised at the request of the Eginetans by Cleades the son of Autodicos, a man of Plataia who was their public guest-friend, no less than ten years after these events.

86. When the Hellenes had buried their dead at Plataia, immediately they determined in common council to march upon Thebes and to ask the Thebans to surrender those who had taken the side of the Medes, and among the first of them Timagenides and Attaginos, who were leaders equal to the first; and if the Thebans did not give them up, they deter-mined not to retire from the city until they had taken it. Having thus resolved, they came accordingly on the eleventh day after the battle and began to besiege the Thebans, bidding them give the men up: and as the Thebans refused to give them up, they began to lay waste their land and also to attack their wall. **87.** So then, as they did not cease their ravages, on the twentieth day Timagenides spoke as follows to the Thebans: "Thebans, since it has been resolved by the Hellenes not to retire from the siege until either they have taken Thebes or you have delivered us up to them, now therefore let not the land of Bœotia suffer any more for our sakes, but if they desire to have money and are demanding our surrender as a colour for this, let us give them money taken out of the treasury of the State; for we took the side of the Medes together with the State and not by ourselves alone: but if they are making the siege truly in order to get us into their hands, then we will give ourselves up for trial." In this it was thought that he spoke very well and seasonably, and the Thebans immediately sent a herald to Pausanias offering to deliver up the men. **88.** After they had made an agreement on these terms, Attaginos escaped out of the city; and when his sons were delivered up to Pausanias, he released them from the charge, saying that the sons had no share in the guilt of taking the side of the Medes. As to the other men whom the Thebans delivered up, they supposed that they would get a trial, and they trusted moreover to be able to repel the danger by payment of money; but Pausanias, when he had received them, suspecting this very thing, first dismissed the whole army of allies, and then took the men to Corinth and put them to death there. These were the things which happened at Plataia and at Thebes.

89. Artabazos meanwhile, the son of Pharnakes, in his flight from Plataia was by this time well on his way: and the Thessalians, when he came to them, offered him hospitality and inquired concerning the rest of the army, not knowing anything of that which had happened at Plataia; and Artabazos knowing that if he should tell them the whole truth about the fighting, he would run the risk of being destroyed, both himself and the whole army which was with him, (for he thought that they would all set upon him if they were informed of that which had happened),— reflecting, I say, upon this he had told nothing of it to the Phokians, and now to the Thessalians he spoke as follows: "I, as you see, Thessalians, am earnest to march by the shortest way to Thracia; and I am in great haste, having been sent with these men for a certain business from the army; moreover Mardonios himself and his army are shortly to be looked for here, marching close after me. To him give entertainment and show yourselves serviceable, for you will not repent of so doing." Having thus said he continued to march his army with haste through Thessaly and Macedonia straight for Thracia, being in truth earnest to proceed and going through the land by the shortest possible way: and so he came to Byzantion, having left behind him great numbers of his army, who had either been cut down by the Thracians on the way or had struggled with hunger and fatigue; and from Byzantion he passed over in ships. He himself then thus made his return back to Asia.

90. Now on the same day on which the defeat took place at Plataia, another took place also, as fortune would have it, at Mycalē in Ionia. For when the Hellenes who had come in the ships with Leotychides the Lacedemonian, were lying at Delos, there came to them as envoys from Samos Lampon the son of Thrasycles and Athenagoras the son of Archestratides and Hegesistratos the son of Aristagoras, who had been sent by the people of Samos without the knowledge either of the Persians or of the despot Theomestor the son of Androdamas, whom the Persians had set up to be despot of Samos. When these had been introduced before the commanders, Hegesistratos spoke at great length using arguments of all kinds, and saying that so soon as the Ionians should see them they would at once revolt from the Persians, and that the Barbarians would not wait for their attack; and if after all they did so, then the Hellenes would take a prize such as they would never take again hereafter; and appealing to the gods worshipped in common he endeavoured to persuade them to rescue from slavery men who were Hellenes and to drive away the Barbarian: and this he said was easy for them to do, for the ships of the enemy sailed badly and were no match for them in fight. Moreover if the Hellenes suspected that they were endeavouring to bring them on by fraud, they were ready to be taken as hostages in their ships. **91.** Then as the stranger of Samos was urgent in his prayer, Leotychides inquired thus, either desiring to hear for the sake of the omen or perhaps by a chance which Providence brought about: "Stranger of Samos, what is your name?" He said "Hegesistratos" [which means "Expedition-Leader"]. The other cut short the rest of the speech, stopping all that Hegesistratos had intended to say further, and said: "I accept the augury given in Hegesistratos, stranger of Samos. See that you give us assurance, you and the men who are with you, that the Samians will without fail be our zealous allies, and after that sail away home."

92. Thus he spoke and to the words he added the deed; for immediately the Samians gave assurance and made oaths of alliance with the Hellenes, and having so done the others sailed away home, but Hegesistratos he bade sail with the Hellenes, considering the name to be an augury of good success. Then the Hellenes after staying still that day made sacrifices for success on the next day, their diviner being Deïphonos the son of Euenios an Apolloniate, of that Apollonia which lies in the Ionian gulf.

93. To this man's father Euenios the following happened:—There are at this place Apollonia sheep sacred to the Sun, which during the day feed by a river running from Mount Lacmon through the land of Apollonia to the sea by the haven of Oricos; and by night they are watched by men chosen for this purpose, who are the most highly considered of the citizens for wealth and noble birth, each man having charge of them for one year; for the people of Apollonia set great store on these sheep by reason of an oracle: and they are protected in a cave at some distance from the city. Here at the time of which I speak this man Euenios was keeping watch over them, having been chosen for that purpose; and it happened one night that he fell asleep during his watch, and wolves came into the cave and killed about sixty of the sheep. When he perceived this, he kept it secret and told no one, meaning to buy others and substitute them in the place of those that were killed. It was discovered however by the people of Apollonia that this had happened; and when they were informed of it, they brought him up before a court and condemned him to be deprived of his eyesight for having fallen asleep during his watch. But when they had blinded Euenios, immediately after this their flocks ceased to bring forth young and their land to bear crops as before. Then prophesyings were uttered to them both at Dodona and also at Delphi, when they asked the prophets the cause of the evil which they were suffering, and they told them that they had unjustly deprived of his sight Euenios the watcher of the sacred sheep, for the gods of whom they inquired had themselves sent the wolves to attack the sheep; and they would not cease to take vengeance for him till the men of Apollonia should have paid to Euenios such satisfaction as he himself should choose and deem sufficient: and this being fulfilled, the gods would give to Euenios a gift of such a kind that many men would think him happy in that he possessed it.

94. These oracles then were uttered to them, and the people of Apollonia, making a secret of it, proposed to certain men of the citizens to manage the affair; and they managed it for them thus:—when Euenios was sitting on a seat in public, they came and sat by him, and conversed about other matters, and at last they came to sympathising with him in his misfortune; and thus leading him on they asked what satisfaction he should choose, if the people of Apollonia should undertake to give him satisfaction for that which they had done. He then, not having heard the oracle, made choice and said that if there should be given him the lands belonging to certain citizens, naming those whom he knew to possess the two best lots of land in Apollonia, and a dwelling-house also with these, which he knew to be the best house in the city,—if he became possessor of these, he said, he would have no anger against them for the future, and this satisfaction would be sufficient for him if it should be given. Then as he was thus speaking, the men who sat by him said interrupting him: "Euenios, this satisfaction the Apolloniates pay to you for blinding you in accordance with the oracles which have been given to them." Upon this he was angry, being thus informed of the whole matter and considering that he had been deceived; and they bought the property from those who possessed it and gave him that which he had chosen. And immediately after this he had a natural gift of divination, so that he became very famous. **95.** Of this Euenios, I say, Deïphonos was the son, and he was acting as diviner for the army, being brought by the Corinthians. I have heard however also that Deïphonos wrongly made use of the name of Euenios, and undertook work of this kind about Hellas, not being really the son of Euenios.

96. Now when the sacrifices were favourable to the Hellenes, they put their ships to sea from Delos to go to Samos; and having arrived off Calamisa in Samos, they moored their ships there opposite the temple of Hera which is at this place, and made preparations for a sea-fight; but the Persians, being informed that they were sailing thither, put out to sea also and went over to the mainland with their remaining ships, (those of the Phenicians having been already sent away to sail home): for deliberating of

the matter they thought it good not to fight a battle by sea, since they did
not think that they were a match for the enemy. And they sailed away to
the mainland in order that they might be under the protection of their
land-army which was in Mycalē, a body which had stayed behind the rest of
the army by command of Xerxes and was keeping watch over Ionia: of this
the number was sixty thousand and the commander of it was Tigranes, who
in beauty and stature excelled the other Persians. The commanders of the
fleet then had determined to take refuge under the protection of this army,
and to draw up their ships on shore and put an enclosure round as a protection for the ships and a refuge for themselves. **97.** Having thus determined they began to put out to sea; and they came along by the temple of
the "Revered goddesses" to the Gaison and to Scolopoeis in Mycalē, where
there is a temple of the Eleusinian Demeter, which Philistos the son of Pasicles erected when he had accompanied Neileus the son of Codros for the
founding of Miletos; and there they drew up their ships on shore and put an
enclosure round them of stones and timber, cutting down fruit-trees for
this purpose, and they fixed stakes round the enclosure and made their
preparations either for being besieged or for gaining a victory, for in making their preparations they reckoned for both chances.

98. The Hellenes however, when they were informed that the Barbarians had gone away to the mainland, were vexed because they thought
that they had escaped; and they were in a difficulty what they should do,
whether they should go back home, or sail down towards the Hellespont.
At last they resolved to do neither of these two things, but to sail on to the
mainland. Therefore when they had prepared as for a sea-fight both
boarding-bridges and all other things that were required, they sailed towards Mycalē; and when they came near to the camp and no one was seen
to put out against them, but they perceived ships drawn up within the wall
and a large land-army ranged along the shore, then first Leotychides, sailing along in his ship and coming as near to the shore as he could, made
proclamation by a herald to the Ionians, saying: "Ionians, those of you who
chance to be within hearing of me, attend to this which I say: for the Persians will not understand anything at all of that which I enjoin to you.
When we join battle, each one of you must remember first the freedom of
all, and then the watchword 'Hebē'; and this let him also who has not
heard know from him who has heard." The design in this act was the same
as that of Themistocles at Artemision; for it was meant that either the
words uttered should escape the knowledge of the Barbarians and persuade the Ionians, or that they should be reported afterwards to the Barbarians and make them distrustful of the Hellenes.

99. After Leotychides had thus suggested, then next the Hellenes proceeded to bring their ships up to land, and they disembarked upon the
shore. These then were ranging themselves for fight; and the Persians, when
they saw the Hellenes preparing for battle and also that they had given exhortation to the Ionians, in the first place deprived the Samians of their
arms, suspecting that they were inclined to the side of the Hellenes; for
when the Athenian prisoners, the men whom the army of Xerxes had

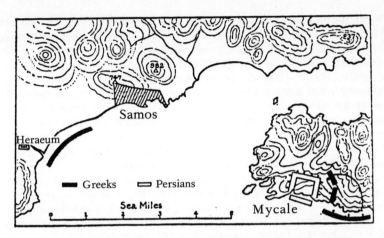

MAP 8. MYCALE, SAMOS STRAIT, AND HERAEUM (TEMPLE TO HERA).
LOOKING NORTH: ■■ GREEKS. ▭ PERSIANS.

found left behind in Attica, had come in the ships of the Barbarians, the Samians had ransomed all these and sent them back to Athens, supplying them with means for their journey; and for this reason especially they were suspected, since they had ransomed five hundred persons of the enemies of Xerxes. Then secondly the Persians appointed the Milesians to guard the passes which lead to the summits of Mycalē, on the pretext that they knew the country best, but their true reason for doing this was that they might be out of the camp. Against these of the Ionians, who, as they suspected, would make some hostile move if they found the occasion, the Persians sought to secure themselves in the manner mentioned; and they themselves then brought together their wicker-work shields to serve them as a fence.

100. Then when the Hellenes had made all their preparations, they proceeded to the attack of the Barbarians; and as they went, a rumour came suddenly to their whole army, and at the same time a herald's staff was found lying upon the beach; and the rumour went through their army to this effect, namely that the Hellenes were fighting in Bœotia and conquering the army of Mardonios. Now by many signs is the divine power seen in earthly things, and by this among others, namely that now, when the day of the defeat at Plataia and of that which was about to take place at Mycalē happened to be the same, a rumour came to the Hellenes here, so that the army was encouraged much more and was more eagerly desirous to face the danger. **101.** Moreover this other thing by coincidence happened besides, namely that there was a sacred enclosure of the Eleusinian Demeter close by the side of both the battle-fields; for not only in the Plataian land did the fight take place close by the side of the temple of Demeter, as I have before said, but also in Mycalē it was to be so likewise. And whereas the rumour which came to them said that a victory had been already gained by the

Hellenes with Pausanias, this proved to be a true report; for that which was done at Plataia came about while it was yet early morning, but the fighting at Mycalē took place in the afternoon; and that it happened on the same day of the same month as the other became evident to them not long afterwards, when they inquired into the matter. Now they had been afraid before the rumour arrived, not for themselves so much as for the Hellenes generally, lest Hellas should stumble and fall over Mardonios; but when this report had come suddenly to them, they advanced on the enemy much more vigorously and swiftly than before. The Hellenes then and the Barbarians were going with eagerness into the battle, since both the islands and the Hellespont were placed before them as prizes of the contest.*

102. Now for the Athenians and those who were ranged next to them, to the number perhaps of half the whole army, the road lay along the sea-beach and over level ground, while the Lacedemonians and those ranged in order by these were compelled to go by a ravine and along the mountain side: so while the Lacedemonians were yet going round, those upon the other wing were already beginning the fight; and as long as the wicker-work shields of the Persians still remained upright, they continued to defend themselves and had rather the advantage in the fight; but when the troops of the Athenians and of those ranged next to them, desiring that the achievement should belong to them and not to the Lacedemonians, with exhortations to one another set themselves more vigorously to the work, then from that time forth the fortune of the fight was changed; for these pushed aside the wicker-work shields and fell upon the Persians with a rush all in one body, and the Persians sustained their first attack and continued to defend themselves for a long time, but at last they fled to the wall; and the Athenians, Corinthians, Sikyonians and Troizenians, for that was the order in which they were ranged, followed close after them and rushed in together with them to the space within the wall: and when the wall too had been captured, then the Barbarians no longer betook themselves to resistance, but began at once to take flight, excepting only the Persians, who formed into small groups and continued to fight with the Hellenes as they rushed in within the wall. Of the commanders of the Persians two made their escape and two were slain; Artaÿntes and Ithamitres commanders of the fleet escaped, while Mardontes and the commander of the land-army, Tigranes, were slain. **103.** Now while the Persians were still fighting, the Lacedemonians and those with them arrived, and joined in carrying through the rest of the work; and of the Hellenes themselves many fell there and especially many of the Sikyonians, together with their commander Perilaos. And those of the Samians who were serving in the army, being in the camp of the Medes and having been deprived of their arms, when they saw that from the very first the battle began to be doubtful, did as much as they could, endeavouring to give assistance to the Hellenes; and the other Ionians seeing that the Samians had set the example, themselves

---

*The battle of Mycalē was fought in September of 479 B.C.

also upon that made revolt from the Persians and attacked the Barbarians.
104. The Milesians too had been appointed to watch the passes for the Persians in order to secure their safety, so that if any defeat should after all come upon them, which actually came, they might have guides and so get safe away to the summits of Mycalē,—the Milesians, I say, had been appointed to do this, not only for that end but also for fear that, if they were present in the camp, they might make some hostile move: but they did in fact the opposite of that which they were appointed to do; for they not only directed them in the flight by other than the right paths, by paths indeed which led towards the enemy, but also at last they themselves became their worst foes and began to slay them. Thus then for the second time Ionia revolted from the Persians.*

105. In this battle, of the Hellenes the Athenians were the best men, and of the Athenians Hermolycos the son of Euthoinos, a man who had trained for the *pancration* the 'no holds barred' fight. This Hermolycos after these events, when there was war between the Athenians and the Carystians, was killed in battle at Kyrnos in the Carystian land near Geraistos, and there was buried. After the Athenians the Corinthians, Troizenians and Sikyonians were the best.

106. When the Hellenes had slain the greater number of the Barbarians, some in the battle and others in their flight, they set fire to the ships and to the whole of the wall, having first brought out the spoil to the sea-shore; and among the rest they found some stores of money. So having set fire to the wall and to the ships they sailed away; and when they came to Samos, the Hellenes deliberated about removing the inhabitants of Ionia, and considered where they ought to settle them in those parts of Hellas of which they had command, leaving Ionia to the Barbarians: for it was evident to them that it was impossible on the one hand for them to be always stationed as guards to protect the Ionians, and on the other hand, if they were not stationed to protect them, they had no hope that the Ionians would escape with impunity from the Persians. Therefore it seemed good to those of the Peloponnesians who were in authority that they should remove the inhabitants of the trading ports which belonged to those peoples of Hellas who had taken the side of the Medes, and give that land to the Ionians to dwell in; but the Athenians did not think it good that the inhabitants of Ionia should be removed at all, nor that the Peloponnesians should consult about Athenian colonies; and as these vehemently resisted the proposal, the Peloponnesians gave way. So the end was that they joined as allies to their league the Samians, Chians, Lesbians, and the other islanders who chanced to be serving with the Hellenes, binding them by assurance and by oaths to remain faithful and not withdraw from the league: and having bound these by oaths they sailed to break up the bridges, for they supposed they would find them still stretched over the straits.

These then were sailing towards the Hellespont; **107,** and meanwhile

---

*Reference to the Ionian Revolt described at 5.30 ff.

those Barbarians who had escaped and had been driven to the heights of
Mycalē, being not many in number, were making their way to Sardis: and
as they went by the way, Masistes the son of Dareios, who had been present at the disaster which had befallen them, was saying many evil things of
the commander Artaÿntes, and among other things he said that in respect
of the generalship which he had shown he was worse than a woman, and
that he deserved every kind of evil for having brought evil on the house of
the king. Now with the Persians to be called worse than a woman is the
greatest possible reproach. So he, after he had been much reviled, at length
became angry and drew his sword upon Masistes, meaning to kill him; and
as he was running upon him, Xeinagoras the son of Prexilaos, a man of
Halicarnassos, perceived it, who was standing just behind Artaÿntes; and
this man seized him by the middle and lifting him up dashed him upon the
ground; and meanwhile the spearmen of Masistes came in front to protect
him. Thus did Xeinagoras, and thus he laid up thanks for himself both with
Masistes himself and also with Xerxes by saving the life of his brother; and
for this deed Xeinagoras became ruler of all Kilikia by the gift of the king.
Nothing further happened than this as they went on their way, but they arrived at Sardis.

Now at Sardis, as it chanced, king Xerxes had been staying ever since
that time when he came thither in flight from Athens, after suffering defeat in the sea-fight. **108.** At that time, while he was at Sardis, he had a passionate desire, as it seems, for the wife of Masistes, who was also there: and
as she could not be bent to his will by his messages to her, and he did not
wish to employ force because he had regard for his brother Masistes (and
the same consideration withheld the woman also, for she well knew that
force would not be used towards her), then Xerxes abstained from all else,
and endeavoured to bring about the marriage of his own son Dareios with
the daughter of this woman and of Masistes, supposing that if he should do
so he would obtain her more easily. Then having made the betrothal and
done all the customary rites, he went away to Susa; and when he had arrived there and had brought the woman into his own house for Dareios,
then he ceased from attempting the wife of Masistes and changing his
inclination he conceived a desire for the wife of Dareios, who was daughter of Masistes, and obtained her: now the name of this woman was Artaÿntē. **109.** However as time went on, this became known in the following
manner:—Amestris the wife of Xerxes had woven a mantle, large and of
various work and a sight worthy to be seen, and this she gave to Xerxes.
He then being greatly pleased put it on and went to Artaÿntē; and being
greatly pleased with her too, he bade her ask what she would to be given
to her in return for the favours which she had granted to him, for she
should obtain, he said, whatsoever she asked: and she, since it was destined
that she should perish miserably with her whole house, said to Xerxes
upon this: "Will you give me whatsoever I shall ask?" and he, supposing
that she would ask anything rather than that which she did, promised this
and swore to it. Then when he had sworn, she boldly asked for the mantle;

and Xerxes tried every means of persuasion, not being willing to give it to her, and that for no other reason but only because he feared Amestris, lest by her, who even before this had some inkling of the truth, he should thus be discovered in the act; and he offered her cities and gold in any quantity, and an army which no one else should command except herself. Now this of an army is a thoroughly Persian gift. Since however he did not persuade her, he gave her the mantle; and she being overjoyed by the gift wore it and prided herself upon it. **110.** And Amestris was informed that she had it; and having learnt that which was being done, she was not angry with this woman, but supposing that her mother was the cause and that she was bringing this about, she planned destruction for the wife of Masistes. She waited then until her husband Xerxes had a royal feast set before him:— this feast is served up once in the year on the day on which the king was born, and the name of this feast is in Persian *tycta,* which in the tongue of the Hellenes means "complete"; also on this occasion alone the king anoints his head, and he makes gifts then to the Persians:—Amestris, I say, waited for this day and then asked of Xerxes that the wife of Masistes might be given to her. And he considered it a strange and untoward thing to deliver over to her his brother's wife, especially since she was innocent of this matter; for he understood why she was making the request.

111. At last however as she continued to entreat urgently and he was compelled by the rule, namely that it is impossible among them that he who makes request when a royal feast is laid before the king should fail to obtain it, at last very much against his will consented; and in delivering her up he bade Amestris do as she desired, and meanwhile he sent for his brother and said these words: "Masistes, you are the son of Dareios and my brother, and moreover in addition to this you are a man of worth. I say to you, live no longer with this wife with whom you now live, but I give you instead of her my daughter; with her live as your wife, but the wife whom you now have, do not keep; for it does not seem good to me that you should keep her." Masistes then, marvelling at that which was spoken, said these words: "Master, how unprofitable a speech is this which you utter to me, in that you bid me send away a wife by whom I have sons who are grown up to be young men, and daughters one of whom even you yourself did take as a wife for your son, and who is herself, as it chances, very much to my mind,—that you bid me, I say, send away her and take to wife your daughter! I, O king, think it a very great matter that I am judged worthy of your daughter, but nevertheless I will do neither of these things: and do not urge me by force to do such a thing as this. For your daughter another husband will be found not in any wise inferior to me, and let me, I pray, live still with my own wife." He returned answer in some such words as these; and Xerxes being stirred with anger said as follows: "This then, Masistes, is your case, —I will not give you my daughter for your wife, nor yet shall you live any longer with that one, in order that you may learn to accept that which is offered you." He then when he heard this went out, having first said these words: "Master, you have not surely brought ruin upon me?" **112.** During this interval of time, while Xerxes was conversing with his brother, Amestris had sent the spearmen of Xerxes to bring the wife of Masistes, and she was doing to her shameful outrage; for she cut away her breasts and threw them to dogs, and she cut off her nose and ears and lips and tongue, and sent her back home thus outraged. **113.** Then Masistes, not yet having heard any of these things, but supposing that some evil had fallen upon him, came running to his house; and seeing his wife thus mutilated, immediately upon this he took counsel with his sons and set forth to go to Bactria together with his sons and doubtless some others also, meaning to make the province of Bactria revolt and to do the greatest possible injury to the king: and this in fact would have come to pass, as I imagine, if he had got up to the land of the Bactrians and Sacans before he was overtaken, for they were much attached to him, and also he was the governor of the Bactrians: but Xerxes being informed that he was doing this, sent after him an army as he was on his way, and slew both him and his sons and his army. So far of that which happened about the passion of Xerxes and the death of Masistes.

114. Now the Hellenes who had set forth from Mycalē to the Hellespont first moored their ships about Lecton, being stopped by winds; and thence they came to Abydos and found that the bridges had been broken up, which they thought to find still stretched across, and on account of which especially they had come to the Hellespont. So the Peloponnesians with Leotychides resolved to sail back to Hellas, while the Athenians and Xanthippos their commander determined to stay behind there and to make an attempt upon the Chersonese. Those then sailed away, and the Athenians passed over from Abydos to the Chersonese and began to besiege Sestos. **115.** To this town of Sestos, since it was the greatest stronghold of those in that region, men had come together from the cities which lay round it, when they heard that the Hellenes had arrived at the Hellespont, and especially there had come from the city of Cardia Oiobazos a Persian, who had brought to Sestos the ropes of the bridges. The inhabitants of the city were Aiolians, natives of the country, but there were living with them a great number of Persians and also of their allies. **116.** And of the province Artaÿctes was despot, as governor under Xerxes, a Persian, but a man of desperate and reckless character, who also had practised deception upon the king on his march against Athens, in taking away from Elaius the things belonging to Protesilaos the son of Iphiclos. For at Elaius in the Chersonese there is the tomb of Protesilaos with a sacred enclosure about it, where there were many treasures, with gold and silver cups and bronze and raiment and other offerings, which things Artaÿctes carried off as plunder, the king having granted them to him. And he deceived Xerxes by saying to him some such words as these: "Master, there is here the house of a man, a Hellene, who made an expedition against your land and met with his deserts and was slain: this man's house I ask you to give to me, that every one may learn not to make expeditions against your land." By saying this it was likely that he would easily enough persuade Xerxes to give him a man's house, not suspecting what was in his mind: and when he said that Protesilaos had made expedition against the land of the king, it must be understood that the Persians consider all Asia to be theirs and to belong to their reigning king. So when the things had been given him, he brought them from Elaius to Sestos, and he sowed the sacred enclosure for crops and occupied it as his own; and he himself, whenever he came to Elaius, had sex with women in the inner sanctuary of the temple. And now he was being besieged by the Athenians, when he had not made any preparation for a siege nor had been expecting that the Hellenes would come; for they fell upon him, as one may say, off his guard. **117.** When however autumn came and the siege still went on, the Athenians began to be vexed at being absent from their own land and at the same time not able to conquer the fortress, and they requested their commanders to lead them home; but these said that they would not do so, until either they had taken the town or the public authority of the Athenians sent for them home: and so they endured their present state.

118. Those however who were within the walls had now come to the greatest misery, so that they boiled down the straps of their beds and used them for food; and when they no longer had even these, then the Persians and with them Artaÿctes and Oiobazos ran away and departed in the night, climbing down by the back part of the wall, where the place was left most unguarded by the enemy; and when day came, the men of the Chersonese signified to the Athenians from the towers concerning that which had happened, and opened the gates to them. So the greater number of them went in pursuit, and the rest occupied the city.* **119.** Now Oiobazos, as he was escaping to Thrace, was caught by the Apsinthian Thracians and sacrificed to their native god Pleistoros with their rites, and the rest who were with him they slaughtered in another manner: but Artaÿctes with his companions, who started on their flight later and were overtaken at a little distance above Aigospotamoi, defended themselves for a considerable time and some of them were killed and others taken alive: and the Hellenes had bound these and were bringing them to Sestos, and among them Artaÿctes also in bonds together with his son. **120.** Then, it is said by the men of the Chersonese, as one of those who guarded them was frying dried fish, a portent occurred as follows,—the dried fish when laid upon the fire began to leap and struggle just as if they were fish newly caught: and the others gathered round and were marvelling at the portent, but Artaÿctes seeing it called to the man who was frying the fish and said: "Stranger of Athens, be not at all afraid of this portent, seeing that it has not appeared for you but for me. Protesilaos who dwells at Elaius signifies thereby that though he is dead and his body is dried like those fish, yet he has power given him by the gods to exact vengeance from the man who does him wrong. Now therefore I desire to impose this penalty for him,— that in place of the things which I took from the temple I should pay down a hundred talents to the god, and moreover as ransom for myself and my

---

*Sestos was taken at the end of 479 B.C.

son I will pay two hundred talents to the Athenians, if my life be spared."
Thus he engaged to do, but he did not prevail upon the commander Xanthippos; for the people of Elaius desiring to take vengeance for Protesilaos asked that he might be put to death, and the inclination of the
commander himself tended to the same conclusion. They brought him
therefore to that headland to which Xerxes made the passage across, or as
some say to the hill which is over the town of Madytos, and there they
nailed him to boards and hung him up; and they stoned his son to death
before the eyes of Artaÿctes himself. **121.** Having so done, they sailed
away to Hellas, taking with them, besides other things, the ropes also of
the bridges, in order to dedicate them as offerings in the temples: and for
that year nothing happened further than this.

122. Now a forefather of this Artaÿctes who was hung up, was that
Artembares who set forth to the Persians a proposal which they took up
and brought before Cyrus, being to this effect: "Seeing that Zeus grants to
the Persians leadership, and of all men to you, O Cyrus, by destroying
Astyages, come, since the land we possess is small and also rugged, let us
change from it and inhabit another which is better: and there are many
near at hand, and many also at a greater distance, of which if we take one,
we shall have greater reverence and from more men. It is reasonable too
that men who are rulers should do such things; for when will there ever be
a fairer occasion than now, when we are rulers of many nations and of the
whole of Asia?" Cyrus, hearing this and not being surprised at the proposal, bade them do so if they would; but he exhorted them and bade them
prepare in that case to be no longer rulers but subjects; "For," said he,
"from lands which are not rugged men who are not rugged are apt to
come forth, since it does not belong to the same land to bring forth fruits
of the earth which are admirable and also men who are good in war." So
the Persians acknowledged that he was right and departed from his presence, having their opinion defeated by that of Cyrus; and they chose
rather to dwell on poor land and be rulers, than to sow crops in a level
plain and be slaves to others.

The End

APPENDIX

A REPERTORY OF ENGLISH TRANSLATIONS OF HERODOTUS

B. R. (1584). Books I and II only. The first version in English, mostly from Valla's Latin. B.R.'s identity has not been established. Reprinted in 1924.

Isaac Littlebury (1709; second edition, 1737). Translates still from the Latin. Attractive prose.

William Beloe (1791). Translated from the Greek, though largely adapted from a French version; later editions (starting with 1806) include many of Paul Larcher's good notes. Beloe's sixth and last edition was revised in 1826.

John Lemprière (1792). Books I–III only. Lemprière later published a long-celebrated classical dictionary.

P. E. Laurent (1827). Translated from Thomas Gaisford's text; clumsy and poor.

Isaac Taylor (1829). Elegant, inaccurate; sometimes squeamishly omits sexual and other details.

Henry Carey (1847). Bohn Classical Series. Pleasant and usually accurate, but in some passages ridiculous.

George Rawlinson (1858–1860; second edition, 1862; third edition, 1875). The translator was the brother of Near Eastern archaeologist Henry Creswicke Rawlinson. "Prosaic, dull," according to David Grene; archaic; sludgy. The first three editions have very full annotations. The translation stripped of its annotations has been reprinted more than any other, though for no good philological reason. This translation is the source of most English speakers' awareness of Herodotus.

G. C. Macaulay (1890). Lively, yet, following the original, appropriately formal. Accurate beyond any competitor, good poetic coloring; the best indexes ever produced, and now with maps. Macaulay (1852–1915) was a fellow of Trinity College, Cambridge, an assistant master at the Rugby School, and later Professor of English at Aberystwyth. He also translated

Jean Froissart, chronicler of the Crusades, and edited John Gower, Matthew Arnold, and James Thompson.

A. D. Godley (1920–1924). Loeb Classical Library. Archaic, with a few maps. Less accurate than Macaulay, lacking that text's dramatic color; plodding, despite the charming peculiarities of this translator, who is best known for light verse he composed while at Oxford University.

J. E. Powell (1949). An eccentric, intentionally archaic style that consciously imitates the prose of the Authorized Version of the English Bible; produced by an outstanding Herodotus scholar who also edited book VIII and compiled the invaluable *A Lexicon to Herodotus* (1938). Powell—a longtime, somewhat notoriously conservative member of the British Parliament—provides a useful introductory note on many earlier translations.

Aubrey de Sélincourt (1952; revised edition, 1972; revised edition by John Marincola, 1996). Chatty, somewhat journalistic in tone, flat to some ears; now with extensive and useful annotations.

Harry Carter (1958). Elegantly rendered and pleasantly illustrated (by Edward Bawden) American and European book-club edition. An excellent informal translation, with drawings suited to the text.

Kenneth Cavander (1959). This edition presents only books VII–IX and omits some material therein. Another elegant book-club edition, with two-color engravings and an introduction by the delightful Russell Meiggs.

David Grene (1987). Lively, less lucid, consciously archaic version that misses the driving Herodotean idiolect, which uniquely combines Ionic and Attic Greek with Homeric tinges.

Walter Blanco, with Jennifer Roberts, editor (1992). One complete book, the others represented by brief and long excerpts in a free and colloquial American English. Includes a useful supplementary selection of recent scholarly essays.

R. Waterfield, with Carolyn Dewald's introduction and notes (1998). This sometimes superior and always fluent translation remains most valuable for its impressive annotations and recent bibliography.

INSPIRED BY THE *HISTORIES* OF HERODOTUS

All the great historians, Herodotus, Plutarch, Livy, were poets.

—Percy Bysshe Shelley

Over the last 2,500 years, Herodotus has eclipsed many of his successors. His impact has been immense. In addition to establishing the discipline of history, Herodotus and his work have inspired paintings, works of fiction, operas, films, and travel guides.

As soon as the *Histories* first appeared, artists began incorporating aspects of the text into their work. Herodotus' friend Sophocles adapted passages from the *Histories* in two of his plays: *Oedipus at Colonus* and *Antigone*. Before Herodotus' death, Aristophanes parodied his work in the play *The Acharnians,* which opens with the conflict between Athens and Megara. Because of the accuracy of the travel routes and other points of interest described in the *Histories,* explorers from the time of Herodotus to the early twentieth century have used the book as a guide. One such traveler was Gustave Flaubert, best known for his novel *Madame Bovary* (1857). Using a volume of Herodotus as his only guide, Flaubert visited Egypt in search of a setting for the novel that became *Salammbô* (1862), which he ultimately set instead in Carthage.

Herodotus' language—the first still complete recorded prose text in Western literature—serves as the slogan for the United States Postal Service. Inscribed into the classical architecture of the main post office building in Manhattan is this phrase, adapted from Herodotus: "Neither snow, nor rain, nor heat, nor gloom of night stays these couriers from the swift completion of their appointed rounds."

Father of History, Father of Lies

The Roman statesman and man of letters Cicero dubbed Herodotus the "Father of History." Expanding the role of the early logographers— "recorders of stories and legends," who attempted to synthesize divergent local legends into coherent accounts and who traced the roots of families and cities to uncover their roots in mythical times—Herodotus was the first to connect cause and effect in a historical account. In a time when annals were mere lists of unconnected facts, it was an act of revolution for Herodotus to assert that the origins of the Persian Wars could be traced far into the past to events in Assyria, India, and other distant countries. Perhaps most significant, Herodotus, along with Hecataios, pioneered the practice of traveling to obtain firsthand data, rather than relying on unsubstantiated reports and myth. His continuing, if often flawed, attempt at objectivity in describing foreign peoples also earned him the titles "Father of Ethnography" and "Father of Anthropology," among others.

Thucydides, who lived a generation after Herodotus and wrote *History of the Peloponnesian War,* was probably the first to follow in Herodotus' footsteps. Some literary scholars, connecting the few dots available, believe that Thucydides saw Herodotus recite the *Histories* in Athens and came away inspired to become a historian. But Thucydides later alleged that his own method was more accurate than that of Herodotus. Indeed, Herodotus' early reputation was plagued by allegations that he distorted facts. Some writers claimed to correct the "lies" of Herodotus, among them Ctesias, who in the early fourth century B.C. wrote *Persica,* a history of the Assyrians and the Persians. Ctesias was in fact the scoundrel; he copied information from Herodotus and made obvious factual errors. The second-century writer Plutarch, in his essay "The Malice of Herodotus," complained that Herodotus represented the Theban Greeks unfairly; he also took issue with Herodotus' opinion that Greek religion had roots in Egypt.

Comments regarding Herodotus' veracity have become more varied since ancient times. In *A Horse's Tale* (1906), Mark Twain writes, "Along through the book I have distributed a few anachronisms and unborn historical incidents and such things, so as to help the tale over the difficult places. This idea is not original with me; I got it out of Herodotus. Herodotus says, 'Very few things happen at the right time, and the rest do not happen at all: the conscientious historian will correct these defects.'"

Painting

Scenes from the *Histories* have filled many artists' canvases, among them seventeenth-century Dutch painter Peter Paul Rubens' *Queen Tomyris before the Head of Cyrus,* in which a man kneels before Tomyris, lifting the head of Cyrus, dripping, from a bowl of blood. Female attendants flank the Queen, as she grimly views the dead shell of her son's murderer, and proud soldiers look on, vengeance finally achieved. In the sixteenth century Jodocus van Winghe had portrayed the same scene, and the fifteenth-century Italian painter Andrea del Castagno included Queen Tomyris in his series *Famous Men and Women.*

Neoclassical French painter Jacques Louis David portrayed Spartan soldiers before their noble death in *Leonidas at Thermopylae* (1814). Leonidas, leader of the Spartans, sits coolly at the center of the enormous canvas, awaiting the arrival of the Persian army, his heroism in the face of certain death represented by light shining on him from above. Behind Leonidas masses of young troops prepare to defend the narrow pass. Edwin Long's *Babylonian Marriage Market* (1875) depicts what Herodotus calls the wisest custom of the Babylonians: a complicated annual auction of eligible townswomen. The most beautiful women were offered first, the rest following in descending order of beauty. The painting portrays the auction from behind the stage, where women waiting to be auctioned sit side by side on the floor. On the stage a woman stands before a crowd, lifting her finely detailed veil while an auctioneer points out her charms. Interest in foreign cultures was widespread in the Victorian era, and the painstaking historical and anthropological accuracy of *Babylonian Marriage Market* accounted for its great popularity; the painting was the highest-priced work sold by a living artist in the nineteenth century. Thomas Holloway, one of England's richest men, purchased it—ironically, for a women's college he endowed. It hangs in a building at the University of London.

Poetry

In the Victorian era many poets drew inspiration from scenes and places described in the *Histories* of Herodotus. The nineteenth-century English Romantic poet Lord Byron mourned the Greeks who died in the battle of Thermopylai in "The Isles of Greece." One of Elizabeth Barrett Browning's first published poems was *The Battle of Marathon* (1820). Later, her husband, Robert Browning, amalgamated several versions of that battle in his poem "Pheidippides" (1879) and returned to it again in "Echetlos" (1880), the story of an unnamed soldier who slew a multitude of Persians. Matthew Arnold composed "Mycerinus" (1849) based on section 2.133 of the *Histories,* in which an oracle tells a king that the gods have granted him only six years more to live. Hoping to expand his six years to twelve, he lights lamps and carouses day and night.

Perhaps the most popular among poems inspired by the *Histories* is "The Oracles," by A. E. Housman, published in his collection *Last Poems* (1922). The poem's final lines describe the doomed Greeks at Thermopylai, where such a vast number of Persians approach that one messenger believes their arrows will blot out the sun.

The Oracles

'Tis mute, the word they went to hear on high Dodona mountain
    When winds were in the oakenshaws and all the cauldrons tolled,
And mute's the midland navel-stone beside the singing fountain,
    And echoes list to silence now where gods told lies of old.

I took my question to the shrine that has not ceased from speaking,
    The heart within, that tells the truth and tells it twice as plain;
And from the cave of oracles I heard the priestess shrieking
    That she and I should surely die and never live again.

Oh priestess, what you cry is clear, and sound good sense I think it;
    But let the screaming echoes rest, and froth your mouth no more.

508 Inspired by the *Histories* of Herodotus

'Tis true there's better boose than brine, but he that drowns must
drink it;
And oh, my lass, the news is news that men have heard before.

The King with half the East at heel is marched from lands of morning;
Their fighters drink the rivers up, their shafts benight the air,
And he that stands will die for nought, and home there's no returning.
The Spartans on the sea-wet rock sat down and combed their hair.

The English Patient

In this 1992 novel, after a plane crash over the Sahara Desert disfigures him and erases his memory, a man who becomes known as the English patient finds the only intimation of his identity in his copy of Herodotus' *Histories*. Taken from the wreckage of the crash, it is his sole remaining possession, "the book he brought with him through the fire." While convalescing he discovers among the pages photographs, drawings, and objects, as well as notes and quotations scribbled in the margins. These artifacts, in addition to the passages from the *Histories* itself, stir the patient's memory, recalling his past as a Hungarian explorer mapping the Sahara in the early years of World War II and his affair with a British woman, Katharine Clifton. In the novel's denouement, the English patient's nurse, Hana, finds inscribed in the margins Katharine's final words, which Hana recites to the dying man.

Canadian writer Michael Ondaatje shines a contemporary light on many of the issues Herodotus examines: the role of the individual in the tide of great events, particularly war; the complications of nationality, nationhood, and empire; the explorations of Europeans in Africa; and the subjectivity of historical practice. Ondaatje's text mirrors the *Histories* in casually leaping back and forth in time in a nonlinear narrative that often digresses or shifts into anecdote. The English patient's copy of the *Histories*, with its collage of quotations and images, reflects the manner in which Herodotus' work is constructed from the accounts of witnesses from around the world. *The English Patient* won the Booker Prize in 1992. In 1996 Anthony Minghella directed a film version of *The English Patient* that won nine Academy Awards, including Best Picture. Ralph Fiennes stars as the title character, Juliette Binoche plays Hana, and Kristin Scott Thomas portrays Katharine Clifton.

COMMENTS & QUESTIONS

In this section, we aim to provide the reader with an array of perspectives on the text, as well as questions that challenge those perspectives. The commentary has been culled from literary criticism of later generations and subsequent appreciations. Following the commentary, a series of questions seeks to filter Herodotus's the Histories *through a variety of points of view and bring about a richer understanding of this enduring work.*

Comments

THUCYDIDES

Finding the facts involved great effort because eye-witnesses did not report the same events in the same way but according to partisanship or memory. My result, by avoiding patriotic storytelling, may perhaps seem less enjoyable for listening, but I hope it will be judged useful by those who wish to know the truth about past events and those in future times. . . . The Persian War was the greatest action in the past, but it had a quick resolution in two battles on sea and two on land.

—translated by Donald Lateiner,
from *History of the Peloponnesian War* (fifth century B.C.)

ARISTOTLE

It is not the function of the poet to relate what has happened, but what might happen. . . . The poet and the historian differ not by writing verse or prose. If you put the work of Herodotus into verse, it would no less be history, metrical or not. . . . Poetry therefore is more philosophical and serious than history. Poetry speaks of the universal while history reports events one by one.

—translated by S. H. Butcher, from *Poetics* (fourth century B.C.)

CICERO

Indeed, although in history all things should be judged by truth, in poetry most things should be judged by pleasure; however, in both Herodotus, the father of history, and in Theopompus there are innumerable tall-tales.

—translated by Lateiner, from *On Laws* 1.1.5 (first century B.C.)

PLUTARCH

1. On behalf of his Boeotian ancestors, Plutarch must expose Herodotus as a base flatterer, a slanderer, a liar, and a fabricator. . . . 12: Herodotus

prefers the barbarians to the Greeks, whom he often mocks. . . . 31: He tried but failed to extort money from the Thebans to present them more favorably [taken from Aristophanes the Boeotian]. . . . 32: He is full of unedifying and obscene material because of his venomous malice.

—summary by Lateiner of sections
from *On the Vices of Herodotus* (first–second centuries A.D.)

LUCIAN
There is no one who does not write history; in fact, in our time all are Thucydideses and Herodotuses and Xenophons.

—translated by Lateiner, from *How to Write History*
(second century A.D.)

JUAN LUIS VIVES
You could more truly say [Herodotus] is the father of lies than, as many call him, the father of history.

—translated by Lateiner, from *On Discipline,* book 12 (1531)

EDWARD GIBBON
There is not any writer who describes in so lively a manner as Herodotus the true genius of polytheism. . . . Herodotus sometimes writes for children and sometimes for philosophers.

—from *The History of the Decline and Fall of the
Roman Empire* (1776–1788)

THE *TIMES* OF LONDON
Who does not remember the old Halicarnassian? the father of history, in whose pages, as an example of the Latin grammar tells little boys, "there are innumerable stories." Some, it is true, render the word "lies." Heaven forbid! Herodotus a liar! the most truthful and simple-minded of men a liar!—who went everywhere, and saw every thing, and heard every thing, jotting it all down as he went along in his easy-flowing Ionic! A storyteller, if you please; but no relater of fibs. How the whole book tumbles at once into the mind, head over heels, digression after digression, episode on episode, as it were in a royal game of historical leapfrog, or sacks-in-the-mill. "The strife of the barbarians and Greeks," indeed! Why, the book tells of the quarrels of the whole world,—Cimmerians, Scythians, Egyptians, Medes, Persians, Assyrians, Indians,—every tribe and kindred on earth, rush one after the other on the scene, and tell their story, or have it told for them in the same delightful long-winded way. And yet the work does not tire—why? Because it is pervaded by a profoundly religious idea, which distinguishes Herodotus from every other ancient historian. It justifies the ways of Providence with men. It tells how the Persians, having subdued the Medes and swallowed up the kingdoms of Crœsus and the Assyrians, having made Egypt and India tributary, waxed haughty and insolent with the wealth and magnificence of the East, and lusted for Greece also, the favoured land of the gods, stretching forth impious hands against

the treasures of her fanes. "Pride goes before a fall," saith the proverb, and so it was with the armies of Darius and Xerxes. The indignation and vengeance of Heaven waited on the swelling power of the barbarians, and marked them for its own, so soon as they should have reached their pitch of pride. Tomyris and her Scythians taught Cyrus a lesson, but he neglected the warning; the slaughter of Marathon was wasted on Darius; his son, Xerxes, renewed the impious struggle. Then the patience of Olympus was exhausted, and the blessed powers passed the fatal word that the Greeks "should pull down the Mede." Founding his work on this idea, Herodotus pursues his way, and never loses sight of it in his widest digressions; they are only the tributary streams which feed the great river of his story, and are, one after the other, absorbed by it, until it flows alone in the breadth and depth of its majesty.

—January 31, 1848

THOMAS DE QUINCEY

Few, even amongst literary people, are aware of the true place occupied by Herodotus in universal literature; secondly, scarce here and there a scholar up and down a century is led to reflect upon the *multiplicity* of his relations to the whole range of civilization. We endeavor in these words to catch, as in a net, the gross prominent faults of his appreciation; on which account, first, we say pointedly, *universal* literature, not Grecian— since the primary error is, to regard Herodotus merely in relation to the literature of Greece; secondly, on which account we notice the circuit, the numerical amount, of his collisions with science—because the second and greater error is, to regard him exclusively as an historian. But now, under a juster allocation of his rank, as the general father of prose composition, Herodotus is nearly related to all literature whatsoever, modern not less than ancient; and as the father of what may be called ethnographical geography, as a man who speculated most ably on all the *humanities* of science—that is, on all the scientific questions which naturally interest our human sensibilities.

—from *Historical and Critical Essays* (1853)

GEORGE C. SWAYNE

[Herodotus] is traveller, archæologist, natural philosopher, and historian combined in one. He appears scarcely ever to have concluded his visit to a country without exhausting every available source of information. Personal inquiry alone seems to have satisfied him, wherever it could be made; though he consulted carefully all written materials within his reach, records public and private, sacred and secular. He rightly calls his work a "History," for the Greek word "history" means really "investigation," though it has passed into a different use with us. . . .

In Herodotus we perceive the dawning of that criticism which finds its full expression in Thucydides, who was in mind a modern historian, though less fastidious as to the evidence of facts than a man of our century would be. The incredulity of Herodotus, when it shows itself, seems rather evoked by the suspected veracity of his informant, or some contradiction in phenomena, than by the incredible nature of the facts themselves. He has been most found fault with for ascribing effects to inadequate causes, but we ought rather to feel grateful to him, considering the mould in which the mind of his time was cast, for endeavouring to trace the connection between cause and effect at all.

—from *Herodotus* (1870)

BASIL L. GILDERSLEEVE
An Alexandrian scholar of some note denied that Herodotus wrote the preface of his work, but every word in it is significant, and, if properly studied, the preface gives the key to the whole. It gives the authorship. It tells us that it is a setting forth of investigation, that its object is to prevent the history of the world from being effaced by the lapse of time. The great and marvellous deeds wrought by Greeks and non-Greeks are not to be left unfamoused, and the cause of the war between them is to be set down. Thucydides is satisfied with *how?* Herodotus demands *why?* Thucydides looks to history as a lesson for future generations drawn from experience. Herodotus looks to history as a record of the dealings of a higher power. For the wrath of Achilles substitute the envy of the gods, and we have a movement like that of the "Iliad." . . .

Immeasurably superior to his predecessors in breadth of theme and unity of purpose, Herodotus was superior to them in critical faculty, and it has justly been said that he may be called the Father of Criticism as well as the Father of History. He does not deal with his material according to modern methods; he does not even set up the standard of his younger contemporary, Thucydides. His history is to a great extent a story-book, and as such it has no peer, but it is much more than a story-book. It is a picture of the world, not a mere series of sketches. It is a panorama full of moral significance. This moralizing makes us suspicious, but, after all, modern historiography is not much more honest, and, if we exclude tendency and partisanship, we exclude the light and shade that are necessary to literary performance. To be sure, we do not believe in dreams and signs, as did Herodotus; we do not couch the philosophy of history in speeches, nor sum up the verdict of posterity in the words of some convenient sage, but we, too, are apt to doctor facts and to manufacture epigrams. Herodotus is no credulous child, no garrulous old man. He is a thinker, whose thoughts are as sane as the expression is clear, and a Herodotean calendar with its daily words of wisdom might be framed as well as a Shakespearian calendar. He is a critic of far greater acumen than was once supposed, and the assaults on his honesty have not demolished the importance of his evidence. Of course, we must carefully distinguish between the facts for which he vouches and the reports that he simply repeats, but in the vast number of details it is not always clear when he is giving mere hearsay. The trouble we have found in establishing his itinerary recurs when we follow the historian along the track of events. Those who study Herodotus critically must be content to put every narrative to the test, to tap every wheel on which the train runs so smoothly. But no historian can escape this scrutiny, and the good faith of Thucydides himself, who claims so much greater accuracy than does Herodotus, has been mercilessly impugned. Even in antiquity the untrustworthiness of Herodotus was a jest, and the frivolous scepticism of a later age selected for ridicule the very points on which the testimony of Herodotus has been sustained by recent exploration. Travellers' tales are proverbial, and Herodotus may have contributed currency to the proverb.

—from his introduction to the *Histories* (1899)

R. G. COLLINGWOOD
Herodotus [was] one of the great innovating geniuses of the fifth century. . . . Herodotus had no successors. . . . Herodotus triumphed over that [Greek anti-historical] tendency.

—from *The Idea of History* (1946)

J. D. DENNISTON
Herodotus is an unaccountable phenomenon in the history of literature. . . . He had a technique at once effortless and adequate to any demands he chose to make upon it. Nor were these demands so small. . . . His achievement, measured by what we know of his predecessors, marks, I believe, a greater advance than any other Greek prose writer achieved.

—from *Greek Prose Style* (1952)

ARNALDO MOMIGLIANO
But we must admit that if we had to give an *a priori* estimate of the chances of success in writing history by Herodotus' method, we should probably shake our heads in sheer despondency. Herodotus' success in touring the world and handling oral traditions is something exceptional by any standard—something that we are not yet in a position to explain fully. The secrets of his workshop are not yet all out.

—from "The Place of Herodotus in the History of Historiography," in *Studies in Historiography* (1958)

Questions

1. An anonymous reviewer for the London *Times* writes that Herodotus's work "is pervaded by a profoundly religious idea. . . . It justifies the ways of Providence with men." Is this claim justified by the text? If so, is that a good or a bad thing?

2. Herodotus does some things that modern historians avoid, and he neglects to do some things that are important to modern historians. Can you name some of the differences—and say whether Herodotus's method or that of a modern historian is preferable, and why?

3. Does Herodotus admire the Egyptians, Persians and other non-Greeks, called barbarians without prejudice, as well as the Greeks? Does he admire all Greeks or some? Finally, what does he find to admire in the various peoples he mentions?

4. Imagine that all written, audio, video, and electronic records have been destroyed, yet you want to write a history of World War II or the Vietnam War. How will you go about it?

FOR FURTHER READING

Historical Contexts: The Late Archaic Age of Greece

General Reference

Boardman, J. N., N. G. L. Hammond, D. M. Lewis, and M. Ostwald, eds. *Persia, Greece, and the Western Mediterranean c.525 to 479 B.C.* Vol. 4 of *The Cambridge Ancient History.* Second edition. Cambridge: Cambridge University Press, 1988. Recent, thorough survey that includes art and archaeological research.

Connolly, Peter, and Hazel Dodge. *The Ancient City.* Oxford: Oxford University Press, 1998. Useful, well-illustrated introduction to daily life in ancient (classical) Athens and Rome.

Hornblower, Simon, and Antony Spawforth, eds. *The Oxford Classical Dictionary.* Third edition. Oxford and New York: Oxford University Press, 1996. Excellent first resource for people, places, and concepts.

Levi, Peter, ed. *The Greek World.* Oxford: Phaidon, 1980. Useful atlas with essays and maps on special topics, such as raw materials and manufacturing.

Talbert, Richard, and Roger Bagnall, eds. *Barrington Atlas of the Greek and Roman World.* Princeton, NJ: Princeton University Press, 2000. The only entirely modern atlas of the ancient world.

Studies of Particular Historical Topics

Andrewes, Antony. *The Greek Tyrants.* London: Hutchinson's University Library, 1956. Good brief introduction to the era that produced the wealth and attitudes of Herodotus' subjects.

Boardman, John. *The Greeks Overseas: Their Early Colonies and Trade.* Fourth edition. London and New York: Thames and Hudson, 1999. Sound introduction to Greek expansion into the Black Sea and the southern and western Mediterranean.

Burkert, Walter. *Greek Religion.* Translated by John Raffan. Cambridge, MA: Harvard University Press, 1985. Magisterial survey of the history, sources, and phenomena of Greek belief, ritual, and religious equipment.

Burn, A. R. *Persia and the Greeks: The Defence of the West, c.546–478 B.C.* London: Edward Arnold, 1962. The historical background, expansion of the Persians, literary environment, and battles; good maps.

Camp, John M. *Archaeology of Athens.* New Haven, CT: Yale University Press, 2001. Well-illustrated introduction to the topography, architecture, and artifacts of a leading city of the Archaic Age.

Carradice, Ian. *Greek Coins.* Austin: University of Texas Press, 1995. Introduction to the development and role of coinage in Greek life and numismatics as evidence for the historian.

Cook, J. M. *The Persian Empire.* London: Dent, 1983. Good introduction to the leading power for two centuries of Greek history.

Dillon, Matthew, and Lynda Garland, eds. *Ancient Greece: Social and Historical Documents from Archaic Times to the Death of Socrates (c.800–399 B.C.).* Second edition. London and New York: Routledge, 2000. Fuller selection than Fornara's *Archaic Times to the End of the Peloponnesian War* (see below), with more elementary commentary.

Fontenrose, Joseph. *The Delphic Oracle: Its Responses and Operations.* Berkeley: University of California Press, 1978. Skeptical examination of the historical and literary evidence.

Fornara, Charles. *Archaic Times to the End of the Peloponnesian War.* Vol. 1 in *Translated Documents of Greece and Rome.* Second edition. Cambridge: Cambridge University Press, 1983. Translates and annotates documentary, nonliterary sources, chiefly inscriptions; in this edition of the *Histories,* references to "Fornara" in the notes are to document numbers in *Archaic Times.*

Forrest, William George Grieve. *A History of Sparta 950–192 B.C.* London: Hutchinson, 1968. Sober introduction to a poorly documented but important topic.

Garland, Robert. *The Greek Way of Life: From Conception to Old Age.* Ithaca, NY: Cornell University Press, 1990. Informed introduction to secular and sacred rituals and attitudes towards stages in human development.

Green, Peter. *Xerxes at Salamis.* 1970. Revised edition reissued as *The Greco-Persian Wars.* Berkeley: University of California Press, 1996. A rethinking of the events recounted in Herodotus' final books; includes useful maps.

Hall, Edith. *Inventing the Barbarian: Greek Self-definition through Tragedy.* Oxford and New York: Oxford University Press, 1989. How did the Greeks conceptualize others? What did they admire, and what did they despise?

Hignett, Charles. *Xerxes' Invasion of Greece.* Oxford: Clarendon Press, 1963. Thorough British examination of the last books of Herodotus and the ancillary written sources.

Huxley, George Leonard. *The Early Ionians.* London: Faber and Faber, 1966. Survey of Ionia, a relatively unknown area of the Greek world that was Herodotus' home and a center for conflicts with the Persians.

Lazenby. J. F. *The Defence of Greece, 490–479 B.C.* Warminster, England: Aris and Phillips, 1993. Focus on the military logistics and encounters.

Morris, Ian, ed. *Classical Greece: Ancient Histories and Modern Archaeologies.* Cambridge: Cambridge University Press, 1994. What artifacts can tell us about ancient Greek history.

Osborne, Robin. *Greece in the Making, 1200–479 B.C.: The Greek City un-der Construction.* London: Routledge, 1996. Revisionist reconsidera-tion of the history based on the archaeological evidence.

———. *Archaic and Classical Greek Art.* Oxford: Oxford University Press, 1998. A historian's consideration of directions and concerns in Greek art in Herodotus' period.

Powell, Anton, ed. *Classical Sparta: Techniques behind Her Success.* Lon-don: Routledge, 1989. Essays on an esoteric, xenophobic culture.

Pritchett, W. Kendrick. *The Greek State at War.* 5 vols. Berkeley: University of California Press, 1971–1991. Essential for many aspects of Greek hoplite and other forms of warfare and skirmishing.

Salmon, J. B. *Wealthy Corinth: A History of the City to 338 B.C.* Oxford: Clarendon Press, 1984. Study of the most important colonizing *polis* in ancient Greece and its economic development.

Snodgrass, A. *Archaic Greece: The Age of Experiment.* Berkeley: Univer-sity of California Press, 1980. Essay examining the results of archaeo-logical surface surveys and "big digs."

Tandy, David W. *Warriors into Traders: The Power of the Market in Early Greece.* Berkeley: University of California Press, 1997. Movement of goods and economic development in archaic Greece.

Wees, Hans van. *War and Violence in Ancient Greece.* London: Duckworth Publishing, 2000. Collection of essays on the nature of personal and po-litical force employed against individuals and groups.

Whatley, Norman. "On the Possibility of Reconstructing Marathon and Other Ancient Battles." 1929. *Journal of Hellenic Studies* 84 (1964), pp. 119–139. Reconstructing ancient military logistics, strategy, and tac-tics in engagements.

Herodotus: The Man, His Life and Historiographic Antecedents: Collections of Essays

Bakker, Egbert J., Irene de Jong, and Hans van Wees, eds. *Brill's Compan-ion to Herodotus.* Leiden and Boston: Brill, 2002. Twenty-five essays on the *Histories* and Herodotus' sources and methods.

Boedeker, Deborah, ed. *Herodotus and the Invention of History. Arethusa* 20 (1987). Seventeen philologists and historians examine Herodotus' unique qualities.

Derow, Peter, and Robert Parker, eds. *Herodotus and His World.* Oxford and New York: Oxford University Press, 2003. Nineteen essays on nar-rative technique, ethnography, religion, and Athens.

Luraghi, Nino, ed. *The Historian's Craft in the Age of Herodotus.* Oxford and New York: Oxford University Press, 2001. Fourteen essays on earlier and contemporary prose authors—for example, Hecataios and Hellanicus.

Books, Commentaries, Monographs, and Articles

Asheri, D., A. Corcella., G. Nenci, M. Lombardo, and A. Masaracchia. *Erodoto: Le Storie.* Florence: Mondadori, 1989–. The latest line-by-line commentary, in Italian.

Bury, John Bagnall. *The Ancient Greek Historians.* 1909. Reprint: New York: Dover, 1958. Useful introductory survey.

Dewald, Carolyn. "Introduction." In *Herodotus: The Histories,* translated by Robin Waterfield. Oxford and New York: Oxford University Press, 1998, pp. ix–xli. A leading student of Herodotus' text concisely summarizes recent scholarship; for greater detail on many of the same topics, see Bakker et al., *Brill's Companion to Herodotus.*

Drews, Robert. *The Greek Accounts of Eastern History.* Washington, D.C.: Center for Hellenic Studies, 1973. Examines the very limited in extent and few fragments of antecedent historians.

Fornara, Charles. *Herodotus: An Interpretative Essay.* Oxford: Clarendon Press, 1971. Herodotus seen as commenting on his own age, especially on the consequences of the Athenian Empire.

How, W. W., and J. Wells. *A Commentary on Herodotus.* Oxford: Oxford University Press, 1912. 2 vols. Obsolete but as yet unreplaced examination of nearly every paragraph; the unacknowledged source for many editions' comments.

Lloyd, Alan B. *Herodotus, Book II.* 3 vols. Leiden: E. J. Brill, 1975–1988. Dependable commentary on the peculiar problems of Herodotus' detailed description of Egypt.

Macan, Reginald W., ed. *Herodotus: The Fourth, Fifth, and Sixth Books.* 1895. New York: Arno Press, 1973. *Herodotus: The Seventh, Eighth, and Ninth Books.* 1908. 2 vols. New York: Arno Press, 1973. The sharpest, wittiest, and most delightfully digressive commentary on the middle and late books.

Myres, John. *Herodotus, Father of History.* Oxford: Clarendon Press, 1953. Fine and loving introduction, with special attention to geographical elements.

Redfield, James. "Herodotus the Tourist." *Classical Philology* 80 (1985), pp. 97–118. What Herodotus did in Egypt and elsewhere as he collected his materials.

Sélincourt, Aubrey de. *The World of Herodotus.* Boston: Little, Brown, 1962. Elementary but comprehensive introduction by a translator of the full text.

Stadter, Philip. "Herodotus and the North Carolina Oral Narrative Tradition." *Histos* 1 (1997), pp. 1–23. Useful study of the oral elements in Herodotus' sources and his own rhetoric; compare Evans and Murray in Luraghi, *The Historian's Craft in the Age of Herodotus,* and Slings in Bakker et al., *Brill's Companion to Herodotus.*

Contemporary Social, Intellectual, Artistic, and Literary Contexts for Herodotus' Histories, and his Later Influence

Bowersock, G. W. "Herodotus, Alexander, and Rome." *The American Scholar* 58 (1989), pp. 407–414. A survey of Herodotus' place in Hellenistic and Roman antiquity and historiography.

Easterling, P. E., and J. V. Muir, eds. *Greek Religion and Society*. Cambridge and New York: Cambridge University Press, 1985. The place of religion in classical Greek life.

Flory, Stewart. "Who Read Herodotus' *Histories*?" *American Journal of Philology* 101 (1980), pp. 12–28. Investigation of the intended audience and the original format.

Fornara, Charles. *The Nature of History in Ancient Greece and Rome*. Berkeley: University of California Press, 1983. Survey of the genre over a period of a thousand years.

Hunter, Virginia. *Past and Process in Herodotus and Thucydides*. Princeton, NJ: Princeton University Press, 1982. Comparative study of myth, cause, explanation, etc. in the two historians.

Immerwahr, Henry R. *Form and Thought in Herodotus*. Cleveland: Published for the American Philological Association by the Press of Western Reserve University, 1966. Path-breaking, influential survey of how Herodotus organizes his presentation of material.

Lateiner, Donald. *The Historical Method of Herodotus*. Toronto and London: University of Toronto Press, 1989. Comprehensive explanations and analyses of specific passages: how and why Herodotus thought about history and wrote historical narrative as he did.

Marincola, John. *Authority and Tradition in Ancient Historiography*. Cambridge: Cambridge University Press, 1997. Comparison of the attitudes of Herodotus and those of other historians toward the past and its recorders.

Momigliano, Arnaldo. "The Place of Herodotus in the History of Historiography." 1958. Reprinted in his *Studies in Historiography*. New York: Harper and Row, 1966. Essential, influential study of the originality and significance of Herodotus.

Munson, Rosaria. *Telling Wonders: Ethnographic and Political Discourse in the Work of Herodotus*. Ann Arbor: University of Michigan Press, 2001. "Otherness" and the exotic in the first anthropologist.

Lloyd, G. E. R. *Polarity and Analogy: Two Types of Argumentation in Early Greek Thought*. Cambridge: Cambridge University Press, 1966. Essential elements of human comprehension in early Greek thought, including that of Herodotus.

Pearson, L. I. C. *Early Ionian Historians*. Oxford: Clarendon Press, 1939. Survey of Herodotus' predecessors.

Quincey, Thomas de. "The Philosophy of Herodotus." 1842. In his *Historical and Critical Essays*. Boston: Ticknor, Reed, and Fields, 1864. "Of all writers, Herodotus is the most cautious not to trespass on his reader's patience."

Raaflaub, K. "Philosophy, Science, Politics: Herodotus and the Intellectual Trends of his Time." In Bakker et al., *Brill's Companion to Herodotus,* pp. 149–186. Herodotus' relationship to contemporary political theory and other intellectual trends of a cutting-edge age.

Romm, J. S. *The Edges of the Earth in Ancient Thought: Geography, Exploration, and Fiction.* Princeton, NJ: Princeton University Press, 1992. Original study of how the Greeks thought about their immediate world and distant neighbors.

Solmsen, Friedrich. *Intellectual Experiments of the Greek Enlightenment.* Princeton, NJ: Princeton University Press, 1975. Thucydides' and other intellectuals' responses to the sophistic and scientific trends that had already stimulated the mind of Herodotus.

Thomas, Rosalind. *Herodotus in Context: Ethnography, Science and the Art of Persuasion.* Cambridge and New York: Cambridge University Press, 2000. Herodotus' connections to contemporary intellectual activities in rhetoric, the medical writers (theorists and practitioners), and the life and physical sciences.

Vermeule, Emily. *Aspects of Death in Early Greek Art and Poetry.* Berkeley: University of California Press, 1979. Sensitive investigation of the Greek archaic age's literature and art on the theme of death.

Wells, Joseph. "Herodotus in English Literature." In his *Studies in Herodotus.* Oxford: Basil Blackwell, 1923, pp. 205–228. Sketch of later treatments of material presented in the *Histories.*

Selected Themes and Topics in the Histories

Benardete, Seth. *Herodotean Inquiries.* The Hague: Martinus Nijhoff, 1969. A reading of Herodotus as the most complete pre-Socratic text extant and a meditative study of his concept of "Greekness."

Boedeker, D. "The Two Faces of Demaratus." In her collection, *Herodotus and the Invention of History* (1987), pp. 185–201. Study of the peculiar Spartans in Herodotus' work.

———. "Epic Heritage and Mythical Patterns in Herodotus." In Bakker et al., *Brill's Companion to Herodotus,* pp. 97–116. Homer's influence and that of Greek legend.

Cartledge, P., and E. Greenwood. "Herodotus as a Critic: Truth, Fiction, Polarity." In Bakker et al., *Brill's Companion to Herodotus,* pp. 351–372. How Herodotus sorted out evidence and testimonies.

Dewald, Carolyn. "Women and Culture in Herodotus' *Histories.*" *Women's Studies* 8 (1981), pp. 93–127. Thorough investigation of the major role of women in the work of the first historian.

———. "Narrative Surface and Authorial Voice in Herodotus' *Histories.*" In Boedeker, *Herodotus and the Invention of History,* pp. 147–170. Pioneering study of the narrator's presence in and absence from his text.

———. " 'I didn't give my own genealogy': Herodotus and the Authorial Personality." In Bakker et al., *Brill's Companion to Herodotus,* pp. 267–289. A look at intrusions of the narrator into the text.

Harrison, Thomas. *Divinity and History: The Religion of Herodotus.* Oxford and New York: Clarendon Press, 2000. Controversial monograph that argues for a very conventional-thinking Herodotus.

Hornblower, S. "Panionios of Chios and Hermotimos of Pedasa (Hdt. 8.104–6)." In Derow and Parker, *Herodotus and His World,* pp. 37–57. Study of an incident of castration that is arguably central for Herodotean conceptions of retaliation and balance.

Lang, Mabel L. *Herodotean Narrative and Discourse.* Cambridge, MA: Published for Oberlin College by Harvard University Press, 1984. Patterns and oral antecedents of Herodotus' style.

Lateiner, D. "Nonverbal Communication in the Histories of Herodotus." In Boedeker, *Herodotus and the Invention of History,* pp. 83–119. The contribution of gesture and the display of affect to the historian's dramatic and psychological dimensions.

———. "Deceptions and Delusions in Herodotus." *Classical Antiquity* 9 (1990), pp. 230–246. Tricksters, frauds, and their dupes, especially Athenian, in anecdotes and legends.

Mikalson, Jon D. *Herodotus and Religion in the Persian Wars.* Chapel Hill: University of North Carolina Press, 2003. Survey of the role of the supernatural, including the gods of Olympus, in the first Greek historian.

Murray, O. "Herodotus and Oral History." 1987. In Luraghi, *The Historian's Craft in the Age of Herodotus,* pp. 16–44. How does one relate local traditions to Herodotus' more removed presentation?

Pritchett, W. Kendrick. *The Liar School of Herodotos.* Amsterdam: J. C. Gieben, 1993. Thorough refutation of the "liar and fraud" approach to the *Histories* of Fehling and others.

West, S. "Herodotus' Epigraphical Interests." *Classical Quarterly* 35 (1985), pp. 278–305. Skeptical account of the author's knowledge and use of Hellenic and oriental inscriptions.

Other Works Cited in the Introduction

Collingwood, Robin. *The Idea of History.* Oxford: Clarendon Press, 1946. A philosopher and archaeologist examines the emergence and problems of the historical discipline.

Creasy, Edward. *The Fifteen Decisive Battles of the World.* 1851. Reprint: New York, Military Heritage Press, 1987. Contains a chapter on the battle of Marathon and its significance for Greek and world history.

Denniston, John D. *Greek Prose Style.* Oxford: Clarendon Press, 1965. A master of Greek briefly dissects the achievement of Herodotus the writer.

Evans, J. A. S. *Herodotus: Explorer of the Past.* Princeton, NJ: Princeton

University Press, 1991. Three essays discuss imperialism, individuals, and the oral tradition in Herodotus.

Fehling, Detlev. *Herodotus and His "Sources."* Translated from the German by J. G. Howie. Leeds, Great Britain: Francis Cairns, 1989. Remarkable if misguided deconstruction of historical value in the *Histories*.

Gould, John. *Herodotus*. London: Weidenfeld and Nicolson, 1989. Highly regarded introduction to basic aspects of the historian's efforts and achievements.

Hartog, François. *The Mirror of Herodotus: The Representation of the Other in the Writing of History*. Translated by Janet Lloyd. Berkeley: University of California Press, 1988. Influential French structuralist interpretation of the ethnographies, especially the Scythians.

Jacoby, Felix. "Herodot." In A. Pauly, G. Wissowa, and W. Kroll, eds., *Real-Encyclopaedie der klassischen Altertumswissenschaft*. Stuttgart: Neue Bearbeitung, 1893–. *Suppl. II* (1913), cols. 205–520. Thorough, dependable, and encyclopedic review in German of extractable facts of Herodotus' life and work.

INDEX OF PROPER NAMES

(A General Index follows on page 572.)

Note.—The names printed in square brackets are readings not adopted in the text of this translation.

The system of reference is this:—First come references to all the places where the name occurs, given in the order of the text, distinction being made however of those cases in which the name of a person is introduced only as an appendage of another name (*e.g.* as a patronymic), and in which the name of a place is merely attached to an individual person, or applied in some other special manner. Then (if necessary) there follow classified references selected from those already given. Thus under the heading Cyrus (1) there is first a list of all the places in which the name occurs independently; then of the places where Cyrus is mentioned only as father of Cambyses, Smerdis, Atossa, etc. Next come the classified references, repeating to a great extent those already given.

The orthography adopted is in most cases that of the original language; but (to avoid the use of k as far as possible) k is written as c wherever the English c has a hard sound, as in Cleisthenes, and ch is used to represent χ; υ is represented by y, except where it occurs in combination with other vowels as in ευ, αυ, υι, which are written eu, au, ui, while ου is represented by u. The long vowels η and ω are given as ē, ō, where the name occurs in its alphabetical place in the index, and occasionally elsewhere.

In cases where Latin or other forms of names are fully established in the English language, these have been generally retained, and in such cases the orthography which more nearly resembles that of the original, is given in the index in round brackets after the name, *e.g.* Esop (Aisōpos).

The names in which such forms are admitted are these:—Æschylus, Agrigentine, Ajax, Bœotia, Carthage, Chaldean, Corcyra, Crœsus, Cyclades, Cyprus, Cyrus, Egean, Egina, Egypt, Esop, Ethiopia, Eubœa, Jason, Lacedemon, Macedonia, Medea, Nineveh, OEdipus, Phenicia, Phœbus, Piræus, Sardinia, Scythia, Sicily, Thrace, with their derivatives, *e.g.* Carthaginian, Lacedemonian.

Other slight variations (of termination chiefly) may be left unnoticed here.

ABAI, town, i. 46; viii. 27, 33, 134
Abantians of Eubœa, i. 146
Abaris, iv. 36
Abdēra, city, i. 168; vi. 46, 47: vii. 109, 126; viii. 120—
    Men of Abdēra, vii. 120; viii. 120;

Megacreon, vii. 120; Pythes, Nymphodoros, vii. 137
Abrocomēs, son of Dareios, vii. 224
Abrōnichos, son of Lysicles, Athenian scout at Thermopylai, viii. 21

Abydos, city, v. 117; vii. 33, 34, 37, 43, 44, 147, 174; viii. 117, 130; ix, 114
  Men of Abydos, vii. 44, 95; Daphnis, iv. 138; Apollophanes, Bisaltes, vi. 26: plains of Abydos, vii. 45
Acanthos, city, vi. 44; vii. 115–117, 121, 124: Acanthian, of Acanthos, vii. 116, 117: sea of the Acanthians, vii. 22
Acarnania, ii. 10; vii. 126: Acarnanians, Amphilytos, i. 62; Megistias, vii. 221
Achaia (1) of Peloponnese, vii. 94; viii. 36
  Achaian, of Achaia, i. 145; ii. 120 (in Homeric sense); viii. 47; ix. 26; Cleomenes v. 72: Achaian race, viii. 73; twelve cities of the Achaians, i. 145
  (2) of Phthiotis, vii. 173, 196–198: Achaian, of Achaia, vii. 132, 185, 197
Achaia, Demeter, at Athens, v. 61
Achaimenēs (1), father of Teïspes, iii. 75; vii. II
  (2), son of Dareios, iii. 12; vii. 7, 97, 236, 237
Achaimenidai, Achaimenid, i. 125; iii. 65; Hystaspes, i. 209; Pharnaspes, iii. 2; Sataspes, iv. 43; Megabates, v. 32; Tigranes, vii. 62; Artachaies, vii. 117. See also vii. II
Achaios, father of Phthios, ii. 98
Achelōos, river, ii. 10; vii. 126
Acherōn, river, v. 92g; vii. 47
Achilleion, city, v. 94
Achillēs, racecourse of, iv. 55, 76
Acraiphia, town, viii. 135
Acrisios, father of Danaē, vi. 53, 54
Acropolis of Athens, v. 71, 72, 74, 77, 90; vi. 105, 137; vii. 142; viii. 41, 51–56
Acrothōon, town in Athos, vii. 22
Adeimantos, son of Okytos, Corinthian commander, viii. 5, 59, 61, 94; (father of Aristeas) vii. 137
Adicran, king of the Libyans about Kyrene, iv. 159
Adramytteion, city, vii. 42
Adrastos (1), Phrygian, son of Gordias, i. 35, 41–43, 45
  (2), Argive, son of Talaos, v. 67, 68
Adriatic Sea, i. 163; iv. 33; v. 9
Adyrmachidai, Libyans iv. 168
[Aeimnēstos]. See Arimnestos (1)
Aëropos (1) (Ēëropos), father of Echemos, king of Tegea, ix. 26
  (2), Argive, brother of Gauanes and Perdiccas, viii. 137
  (3), son of Philip, in genealogy of Macedonian kings viii. 139

Aëtiōn (Ēëtiōn), Corinthian, son of Echecrates and father of Kypselos, i. 14; v. 92 b-e
Æschylus (Aischylos), the poet, son of Euphorion, ii. 156
Agaios, father of Onomastos, vi. 127
Agamemnōn, vii. 159: (father of Orestes) i. 67; (of Iphigeneia) iv. 103; Talthybios his herald, vii. 134
Agaristē (1), daughter of Cleisthenes of Sikyon, vi. 126, 130, 131
  (2), daughter of Hippocrates the Athenian, vi. 131
Agasiclēs (1), of Halicarnassos, i. 144
  (2), king of Sparta. See Hegesicles
Agathyrsians, iv. 49, 100, 102, 104, 125: king of the Agathyrsians, iv. 78, 119
Agathyrsos, son of Heracles, iv. 10
Agbalos, father of Merbalos of Arados, vii. 98
Agbatana (1), in Media, i. 98, 110, 153; iii. 64, 92
  (2), in Syria, iii. 62, 64
Agēnōr, father of Cadmos and Europa, iv. 147; vii. 91
Agēsilaos. See Hegesilaos
Agētos, Spartan, son of Alkeides, vi. 61, 62
Agis (1) (Ēgis), son of Eurysthenes, in genealogy of Leonidas, vii. 204
  (2), son of Hippocratides, in genealogy of Leotychides, vi. 65 (cp. viii. 131)
Aglauros daughter of Kecrops, temple of, viii. 53
Aglōmachos, of Kyrene, iv. 164
Agora, town, vii. 58
Agoraios, Zeus, at Selinus, v. 46
Agrianēs, river, iv. 90
Agrianians, v. 16
Agrigentines (Acragantinoi), vii. 170; Theron, son of Ainesidemos, king of the Agrigentines, vii. 165
Agrōn, son of Ninos, king of Sardis, i. 7
Agylla, men of, i. 167
Aia in Colchis, i. 2; vii. 193, 197
Aiacos, v. 89; vi. 35; viii. 64: sons of Aiacos, v. 80, 81; viii. 64, 83, 84
Aiakēs (1), father of Polycrates, ii. 182; iii. 39, 139; vi. 13
  (2), son of Syloson, iv. 138; vi. 13, 14, 22, 25
Aias. See Ajax
Aigai, town, i. 145
Aigaiai, town, i. 149
Aigaleos, mountain, viii. 90
Aigē, town, vii. 123
Aigeidai, Spartan clan, iv. 149

Aigeira, town, i. 145
Aigeus (1), Athenian, son of Pandion, i.
　173
　(2), Spartan, son of Oiolycos, iv. 149
Aigialeis (1), tribe of Sikyon, v. 68
　(2), Pelasgians "of the coastland," vii.
　94
Aigialeus, son of Adrastos of Sikyon, v.
　68
Aigicoreus, son of Ion, v. 66
Aigilea, town in Eretrian land, vi. 101
[Aigileia.] See Aigleia
Aigina. See Egina
Aigion, town, i. 145
Aigiroëssa, town, i. 149
Aigleia, island, vi. 107
Aigloi, iii. 92
Aigos-potamoi, ix. 119
Aigyptos, brother of Danaos, ii. 182; see
　also ii. 43 (note)
Aineia, town, vii. 123
Ainēsidēmos, son of Pataicos, vii. 154, 165
[Ainianians.] See Enianians
Ainos, town in Thrace, iv. 90; vii. 58
Ainyra, in Thasos, vi. 47
Aiolia, v. 123; Aiolian land, afterwards
　called Thessaly, vii. 176; cities of
　Aiolia or of the Aiolians, i. 149–151;
　vii. 58, 194
Aiolians, i. 6, 26, 28, 141, 149–152, 157,
　171; ii. 1, 178; iii. 1, 90; iv. 89, 138; v.
　94, 122, 123; vi. 8, 28, 98; vii. 9a, 95; ix.
　115
　Aiolians originally Pelasgians, vii. 95;
　description of their cities, i. 149–151;
　lose Smyrna, i. 150; conquered by
　Crœsus, i. 26; offer submission to
　Cyrus, i. 141; send to Sparta with
　Ionians, i. 151, 152; serve under
　Harpagos, i. 171; under Cambyses, ii.
　1; iii. 1; included in the 1st satrapy by
　Dareios, iii. 90; with Scythian
　expedition, iv. 89; subdued by
　Hymaies, v. 122; at Ladē, vi. 8; with
　Histiaios, vi. 28; with Datis, vi. 98;
　with Xerxes, vii. 95
Aiolis (city of the Aiolidai), in Phokis,
　viii. 35
Aiolos, father of Athamas, vii. 197
Aisanios, father of Grinnos, of Thera, iv.
　150
Aischinēs, son of Nothon, of Eretria, vi.
　100
Aischraios, Athenian, father of
　Lycomedes, viii. 11
Aischriōnian tribe in Samos, iii. 26
Aisōpos. See Esop.

Aitōlia, vi. 127: Aitolians, viii. 73;
　Titormos, vi. 127
Ajax (Aias), v. 66; vi. 35 (father of
　Philaios), viii. 64, 121
Akēratos, prophet at Delphi, viii. 37
Akēs, river, iii. 117
Alabanda, city (1), in Caria, vii. 195
　(2), in Phrygia, viii. 136
Alalia, city of Corsica, i. 165, 166
Alarodians, iii. 94; vii. 79
Alazeir, king of Barca, iv. 164
Alazonians, iv. 17, 52
Alcaios (1), son of Heracles, i. 7
　(2), poet, v. 95
Alcamenēs, king of Sparta and ancestor
　of Leonidas, vii. 204
Alcanōr. See Alkenor
Alcmaiōn (Alcmeōn), Athenian, father
　of Megacles, i. 59; vi. 125, 127, 130
Alcmaiōnidai, sons of Alcmaiōn, i. 61, 64;
　v. 62, 66, 70, 71, 90; vi. 115, 121, 123,
　125, 131
　Early history, vi. 125, 126, 131; under
　the curse, v. 70, 71; cp. i. 61; exiles
　under the Peisistratids, i. 64; v. 62, 63;
　accused of treachery after the battle
　of Marathon, vi. 115, 121, 123, 124
Alcmēnē, mother of Heracles, ii. 43, 145
Alcōn, Molossian, suitor of Agaristē, vi.
　127
Alea, Athenē, of Tegea, i. 66; ix. 70
Alēïan plain, in Kilikia, vi. 95
Aleuadai, sons of Aleuas, vii. 6, 130, 172;
　ix. 58
Alexander (1), son of Priam, i. 3; ii.
　113–118, 120
　(2), son of Amyntas, king of the
　Macedonians, v. 17, 19–22; vii. 173,
　175; viii. 34, 121, 136, 137, 139–144; ix.
　1, 4, 8, 44–46
　Hellenic origin, v. 22; viii. 137–139;
　destroys Persian embassy, v. 19–21;
　envoy of Mardonios to Athens, viii.
　136, 140–144; at Plataia, ix. 44, 45
Alilat, Arabian name of (Aphroditē)
　Urania, iii. 8
Alitta, Arabian name of Aphroditē, i.
　131. See note
Alkeidēs, Spartan, father of Agetos, vi.
　61
Alkēnōr, Argive, i. 82
Alketēs, king of the Macedonians, in
　genealogy of Alexander, viii. 139
Alkibiadēs, Athenian, father of Cleinias,
　viii. 17
Alkimachos, Eretrian, father of
　Euphorbos, vi. 101

[Allēsos.] See *Anysos*

Alōpecai, in Attica, v. 63

Alos, in Thessaly, vii. 173, 197

Alpēnos, town, vii. 216; called also Alpēnoi (village), vii. 176, 229

Alpheos, Spartan distinguished at Thermopylai, vii. 227

Alpis, river, iv. 49

Alyattēs, king of the Lydians, father of Croesus, i. 6, 16, 18–22, 25, 26, 73, 74, 92, 93; iii. 48; viii. 35

His war with the Milesians, i. 17–22; with Kyaxares, i. 16, 73, 74; tomb, i. 93

Amasis (1), king of Egypt, i. 30, 77; ii. 43, 134, 145, 154, 162, 163, 169, 172, 174–178, 180–182; iii. 1–4, 10, 14, 16, 39–41, 43, 47, 126

Revolt against Apries, ii. 162, 163, 169; character and habits, 172–174; buildings and offerings to temples, ii. 175, 176, 182; favour to Hellenes, ii. 178, 180–182; friendship with Polycrates, iii. 39–43; quarrel with Cambyses, iii. 1–4; death, iii. 10; insults to his body, iii. 16

(2), Persian commander against Barca, iv. 167, 201, 203

Amathūs, city in Cyprus, v. 105, 114

Amathusians, men of Amathus, v. 104, 108, 114, 115

Amazons, iv. 110, 112, 114, 115, 117; ix. 27

Their connection with the Sauromatai, iv. 110–117

Ameinias, Athenian distinguished at Salamis, viii. 84, (87), 93

Ameinoclēs, Magnesian enriched by Persian shipwrecks, vii. 190

Amēstris, wife of Xerxes, vii. 61, 114; ix. 109–112

Her cruelty, vii. 114; ix. 112

Amiantos, Arcadian of Trapezus, suitor of Agaristē, vi. 127

Amilcas, king of the Carthaginians, vii. 165–167

Ammōn, Zeus, i. 46; ii. 18, 32, 55; (iv. 181). See also *Amun*

Ammōnian(s), ii. 32, 33, 42; iii. 17, 25, 26; iv. 181, 182; Etearchos, ii. 33

Expedition of Cambyses, iii. 26; description of oasis, iv. 181

Amompharetos, Spartan, ix. 53–57, 71, 85

Amorgēs, Persian commander, v. 121

Ampē, city on Persian gulf, vi. 20

Ampelos, headland near Toronē, vi. 122, 123

Amphiaraos, father of Amphilochos, iii. 91; Oracle of Amphiaraos, i. 46, 49, 52, 92; viii. 134

Amphicaia, town of the Phokians, viii. 33

Amphicratēs, king of Samos, iii. 59

Amphictyon, temple of, vii. 200

Amphictyons, Amphictyonic councillors, ii. 180; v. 62; vii. 200, 213, 228; Demeter of the Amphictyons, vii. 200

Amphilochos, son of Amphiaraos, iii. 91; vii. 91

Amphilytos, Acarnanian diviner, i. 62

Amphimnēstos, of Epidamnos, suitor of Agaristē, vi. 127

Amphiōn, Corinthian, father of Labda, v. 92*b*

Amphissa, city, viii. 32, 36

Amphitryōn, father of Heracles, ii. 43, 44, 146; v. 59; vi. 53

Amprakiōt, of Amprakia, viii. 45, 47; ix. 28, 31

Amūn, Zeus, ii. 42. Cp. *Ammon*

Amyntas (1), king of the Macedonians, v. 17–20, 94; (father of Alexander) vii. 173; viii. 136, 139, 140; ix. 44

(2), grandson of the above, son of Bubares, viii. 136

Amyrgian Sacans, vii. 64

Amyris, of Siris, father of Damasos, vi. 127

Amyrtaios, ii. 140; iii. 15

Amytheōn, father of Melampus, ii. 49

Anacharsis, Scythian, iv. 46, 76, 77

Anacreōn of Teos, iii. 121

Anactorians, ix. 28, 31

Anagyrūs, deme of Attica, viii. 93

Anaphēs, Persian, son of Otanes, vii. 62

Anaphlystos, deme of Attica, iv. 99

Anaua, city of Phrygia, vii. 30

Anaxander, Spartan king in genealogy of Leonidas, vii. 204

Anaxandridēs (1), son of Theopompos, in genealogy of Leotychides, viii. 131

(2), son of Leon, king of Sparta, i. 67; v. 39, 40, 42; his sons, vii. 205; (father of Cleomenes) iii. 148; v. 64; vi. 50, 108; vii. 148; (of Dorieus) vii. 158; (of Leonidas) vii. 204; (of Cleombrotos) viii. 71; ix. 10, 64

Anaxilaos (1), Spartan, in genealogy of Leotychides, viii. 131

(2), despot of Rhegion, vi. 23; vii. 165, 170

Anchimolios, Spartan commander, v. 63

Andreas, ancestor of Cleisthenes of Sikyon, vi. 126

Androbūlos, Delphian, father of Timon, vii. 141

Androcratēs, hero, ix. 25

Androdamas, Samian, father of Theomestor, viii. 85; ix. 90

Andromeda, daughter of Kepheus, vii. 61, 150

Androphagoi, iv. 18, 100, 102, 106, 119, 125

Andros, island, iv. 33; v. 31; viii. 108, 111, 112, 121

    Andrians, men of Andros, viii. 66, 111; Hieronymos, ix. 33

    Besieged by Themistocles, viii. 111

Anēristos, Spartan (1), father of Sperthias, vii. 134

    (2), son of Sperthias, vii. 137

Angitēs, river, vii. 113

Angros, river, iv. 49

Annōn, father of Amilcas, vii. 165

Anopaia, mountain and path, vii. 216

Ant rock. See Myrmex

Antagoras, father of Hegetorides, ix. 76

Antandros, city in Troas, v. 26; vii. 42

Anthēla, town or village, vii. 176, 200

Anthemūs, city, v. 94

Anthylla, city of Egypt, ii. 97, 98

Anticharēs of Eleon, v. 43

Antidōros of Lemnos, viii. 11

Antikyra, city, vii. 198, 213

    Men of Antikyra, Corydallos, vii. 214; Polyas, viii. 21

Antiochos, father of Tisamenes, ix. 33

Antipater of Thasos, vii. 118

Antiphēmos of Lindos, vii. 153

Anysis (1), city of Egypt, ii. 137

    (2), blind king of Egypt, ii. 137; his return from the marshes, ii. 140

Anysos, father of Tetramnestos, vii. 98

Anytis or Anysis, district of, ii. 166

Aparytai, in 7th satrapy, iii. 91

Apatūria, feast of, i. 147

Aphetai, place in Magnesia, vii. 193, 196; viii. 4, 6–8, 11, 12, 14

    Origin of name, vii. 193

Aphidnai, deme of Attica, ix. 73

    Callimachos of Aphidnai, vi. 109; Timodemos, viii. 125

Aphrodisias, island, iv. 169

Aphroditē, i. 105, 131, 199; ii. 41, 112, 181; iv. 59, 67

    In Ascalon, Cyprus, Kythera, i. 105; in Arabia, i. 131; iii. 8; in Persia (Mitra), i. 131; in Scythia (Argimpasa), iv. 59, 67; at Babylon (Mylitta), i. 131, 199; at Atarbechis, ii. 41; Memphis ("foreign"), ii. 112; Kyrenē, ii. 181. See also Urania.

Aphthis, district (nome) of, in Egypt, ii. 166

Aphytis, town of Chalkidikē, vii. 123

Api, Scythian name for the goddess Earth, iv. 59

Apidanos, river, vii. 129, 196

Apis (1), god, ii. 153; iii. 27–29, 33, 64; marks of, iii. 28

    (2), city, ii. 18

Apollo, i. 52, 69, 87, 92, 144; ii. 83, 144, 155, 156, 159, 178; iii. 52; iv. 15, 59, 155, 158; v. 59–61; vi. 57, 80, 118; vii. 26; viii. 33, 134, 135

    At Thebes (Ismenian), i. 52, 92; v. 59–61; Thornax, i. 69; Triopion, i. 144; in Egypt (Oros), ii. 83, 144, 155, 156; at Branchidai, ii. 159; Naucratis, ii. 178; Metapontion, iv. 15; in Scythia (Oitosyros), iv. 59; at Delphi, iv. 155; vi. 80; Kyrenē (fountain of Apollo), iv. 158; Sparta, vi. 57; Delion, vi. 118; Abai, viii. 33; "Ptoan" Apollo, viii. 135; Oracle in Egypt, ii. 83. See also Branchidai, Delos, Delphi, Loxias, Patara, Phœbus

Apollōnia (1), city on the Euxine, iv. 90, 93

    (2), city on the Ionian gulf, people of, ix. 92–94; Euenios, Deïphonos, ix. 92

Apollophanēs, father of Bisaltes, vi. 26

Apriēs, king of Egypt, ii. 161–163, 169, 172; iii. 1, 2; iv. 159

    His war with Kyrenē, ii. 161; iv. 159; revolt of his subjects, ii. 162, 163; his defeat and death, ii. 169

Apsinthians, in Thrace, vi. 34, 36, 37; ix. 119

Arabia, Arabian land, ii. 8, 11, 12, 15, 19, 73, 75, 124, 158; iii. 9, 107, 109, 113; iv. 39

    Arabian(s), i. 131, 198; ii. 30, 75, 141, 158; iii. 4, 8, 9, 88, 91, 97, 107, 109–112; vii. 69, 70, 86, 97, 184; Arabian king, iii. 5, 7, 9; Arabian gulf, ii. 11 (measurement), 102, 158; iv. 39, 42, 43; Arabian mountains, ii. 8, 124; Soil of Arabia, ii. 12; products, iii. 107–113; customs of Arabians, iii. 8; gifts to Dareios, iii. 97; Arabians serve under Xerxes, vii. 69, 86 (with camels); Sanacharib, king of, ii. 141

Arados, city of Phenicia, vii. 98; Agbalos, Merbalos

Araros, river, iv. 48

Araxēs, river, i. 201, 202, 205, 209, 211, 216; iii. 36; iv. 11, 40

[Arbalos]. See Agbalos

Arcadia, Arcadian land, i. 66, 67; vi. 74,
    83, 127; vii. 90, 202; viii. 26
Arcadian(s), men of Arcadia, i. 66; ii.
    171; iv. 161; v. 49; vi. 74, 127
    (Amiantos); vii. 170, 202; viii. 72, 73;
    ix. 27, 28, 35; Pelasgians of Arcadia, i.
    146; Demonax, Cleander, Amiantos,
    Lycurgos (3)
Archander, son of Phthios, ii. 98; City of
    Archander (Archandrūpolis), ii. 97,
    98
Archelaoi, tribe at Sikyon, v. 68
Archelaos, Spartan king, in genealogy of
    Leonidas, vii. 204
Archestratidēs, father of Athenagoras, ix.
    90
Archias (1), Spartan, father of Samios, iii.
    55
    (2) son of Samios, iii. 55
Archidēmos (1), Spartan, in genealogy of
    Leotychides, viii. 131
    (2), Spartan king, son of Zeuxidemos,
    vi. 71
Archidikē, courtesan of Naucratis, ii. 135
Archilochos the Parian, i. 12. See note
Ardericca (1), village on the Euphrates, i.
    185
    (2), place in Kissia, vi. 119
Ardys, son of Gyges, king of the Lydians,
    i. 15, 16, 18
Areians, in 16th satrapy, iii. 93. See vii. 66
    (note)
Arēs, ii. 59, 63, 83; iv. 59, 62; v. 7; vii. 76,
    140 (war-god); viii. 77
    In Egypt at Papremis, ii. 59, 63, 83; in
    Scythia, iv. 59–62; Thrace, v. 7;
    Oracles of Arēs, ii. 83; vii. 76
    Hill of Arēs (Areopagus) at Athens,
    viii. 52
Argadēs, son of Ion, v. 66
Argaios, king of the Macedonians, in
    genealogy of Alexander, viii. 139
Arganthōnios, king of Tartessos, i. 163, 165
Argē, maiden from the Hyperboreans, iv.
    35
Argeia, wife of Aristodemos, vi. 52
Argilos, town in Bisaltia, vii. 115
Argimpasa, Scythian Aphroditē, iv. 59
Argiopion, place near Plataia, ix. 57
Argippaians, iv. 23
Argō, ship, iv. 145, 179; vii. 193
Argos (1), hero, sanctuary of, vi. 75, 78,
    80, 82
    (2), city, i. 1, 5, 82; v. 67, 113; vi. 76, 80,
    82, 83; vii. 145, 148, 150–152; viii. 137,
    138; ix. 34; Land of Argos (Argolis),
    i. 82; vi. 92

Argives, men of Argos, i. 31, 61, 82; iii.
    131; v. 49, 57, 61, 67, 68, 86–89; vi. 19,
    75–79, 83, 84, 92, 127; vii. 148–153;
    viii. 73; ix. 12, 27, 34, 35; Argive
    women, i. 31; iii. 134; v. 94; Biton,
    Cleobis, i. 31; Alkenor, Chromios, i.
    82; Alexander, v. 22; Adrastos, v. 67;
    Pheidon, Leokedes, vi. 127;
    Eurybates, ix. 75; Argive tribes, v. 68;
    Argolic mixing-bowl, iv. 152
War with Sparta, i. 82; Argives help
    Eginetans, v. 86–88; Cleomenes at
    Argos, vi. 76–82; conduct at the time
    of the Persian invasion, vii. 148–152;
    ix. 12
Ariabignēs, Persian, son of Dareios, vii.
    97; viii. 89
Arians (1), former name of Medes, vii.
    62
    (2) (or Areians), vii. 66
Ariantas, king of the Scythians, iv. 81
Ariapeithēs, father of Skyles, king of the
    Scythians, iv. 76, 78
Ariaramnēs (1), Achaimenid, son of
    Teïspēs, vii. 11
    (2), Persian with Xerxes, viii. 90
Ariazos, father of Gergis, vii. 82
Aridōlis, despot of Alabanda, vii. 195
Arimaspeia, poem of Aristeas, iv. 14
Arimaspians, iii. 116; iv. 13, 27; derivation
    of the name, iv. 27
Arimnēstos (1), Spartan, ix. 64
    (2), Plataian, ix. 72
Ariomardos (1), Persian, son of
    Artabanos, vii. 67
    (2), son of Dareios, vii. 78
Ariōn of Methymna, i. 23, 24
Ariphrōn, Athenian, father of
    Xanthippos, vi. 131, 136; vii. 33; viii.
    131
Arisba, city of Lesbos, i. 151
Aristagoras (1), despot of Kyzicos, iv. 138
    (2), despot of Kymē, iv. 138; v. 37, 38
    (3), of Miletos, v. 30–38, 49–51, 54, 55,
    65, 97–99, 103, 105, 124, 126; vi. 1, 3,
    5, 9, 13, 18; vii. 8b
    Expedition to Naxos, v. 30–34; mission
    to Sparta, v. 49–51; to Athens, v. 97,
    march on Sardis, v. 99–102; death, v.
    126
    (4), father of Hegesistratos, ix. 90
Aristeas (1), of Proconnesos, iv. 13–16
    (2), Corinthian, son of Adeinantos, vii.
    137
Aristeidēs, Athenian, viii. 79, 81, 95; ix. 28
Aristocratēs, father of Casamebos,
    Eginetan, vi. 73

Aristodēmos (1), father of Eurythenes
    and Procles, iv. 147; vi. 52; vii. 204;
    viii. 131
    (2), Spartan, survivor of Thermopylai,
    vii. 229–231; ix. 71
Aristodicos of Kymē, i. 158, 159
Aristogeitōn, Gephyraian of Athens, v.
    55; vi. 109, 123
Aristokypros, king of the Solians in
    Cyprus, v. 113
Aristolaidēs, Athenian, father of
    Lycurgos, i. 59
Aristomachos, father of Aristodēmos (1),
    vi. 52; vii. 204; viii. 131
Aristōn (1), king of Sparta, i. 67; (father
    of Demaratos) v. 75; vi. 51, 61–66, 68,
    69; vii. 3, 101, 209, 239
    (2), despot of Byzantion, iv. 138
Aristonikē, Pythian prophetess, vii. 140
Aristōnymos, father of Cleisthenes of
    Sikyon, vi. 126
Aristophantos, Delphian, vi. 66
Aristophilidēs, king of the Tarentines, iii.
    136
Arizantians, tribe of the Medes, i. 101
[Arizos.] See Ariazos
Arkesilaos, name of kings of Kyrenē, iv.
    163
    (1), son of Battos the founder of
    Kyrenē, iv. 159
    (2), son of Battos "the Prosperous," ii.
    181; iv. 160, 161
    (3), son of Battos "the Lame" and of
    Pheretimē, iv. 162–165, 167, 200
Armenia, v. 52
    Armenians, i. 180, 194; iii. 93; v. 49, 52;
    vii. 73; mountains of Armenia, i. 72
Arpoxaïs, Scythian, son of Targitaos, iv. 5, 6
Arsamenēs, son of Dareios, vii. 68
Arsamēs (1), Achaimenid, father of
    Hystaspes, i. 209; vii. 11, 224
    (2), son of Dareios, vii. 69, 70
Artabanos, son of Hystaspes, uncle of
    Xerxes, iv. 83, 143; vii. 10–13, 15–18,
    46, 47, 50–53, (father of Artyphios)
    66, (of Bassakes) 75, (of
    Tritantaichmes) 82; (of Tigranes) viii.
    26
Artabatēs, father of Pharnazathres, vii. 65
Artabazos (1), Persian, son of Pharnakes,
    vii. 66; viii. 126–129; ix. 41, 42, 58, 66,
    70, 77, 89
    Operations against Potidaia, vii.
    126–129; conduct at Plataia, ix. 41,
    66; return to Asia, ix. 89
    (2), Persian, father of Tritantaichmes
    (1), i. 192

Artachaiēs, Persian, son of Artaios, vii.
    22, 117, 118; (father of Otaspes) vii.
    63; (father of Artaÿntes) viii. 130
Artaioi, ancient name of the Persians, vii.
    61
Artaios, Persian, (father of Artachaiēs)
    vii. 22, (of Azanes) 66
Artakē, town near Kyzicos, iv. 14; vi. 33
Artanēs (1), Persian, son of Hystaspes,
    vii. 224
Artanēs (2), river, iv. 49
Artaphrenēs (1), Persian, son of
    Hystaspes, v. 25, 30–33, 35, 73, 96,
    100, 123; vi. 1, 2, 4, 30, 42; (father of
    Artaphrenēs) vi. 94; vii. 74
    Satrap of Sardis, v. 25; helps
    Aristagoras, v. 30, 34; enemy of
    Histiaios, vi. 1–4, 30
    (2), son of Artaphrenēs (1), vi. 94, 119;
    vii. 8b, 10b, 74; expedition to
    Marathon, vi. 94
Artaxerxes. See Artoxerxes
Artaÿctēs, Persian at Sestos, vii. 33, 78; ix.
    116, 118–120, 122
    His sacrilege, ix. 116; capture and
    death, 118–120
Artaÿntē, daughter of Masistes, ix. 108, 109
Artaÿntēs (1), Persian, son of Artachaies,
    viii. 130; ix. 102, 107
    (2), Persian, son of Ithamitres, vii. 67
Artembarēs (1), Mede, i. 114–116
    (2), Persian, ix. 122
Artemis, i. 26; ii. 59, 83, 137, 155, 156; iii.
    48, iv. 33–35, 87; v. 7; vi. 138; vii. 176;
    viii. 77
    At Ephesos, i. 26; in Egypt, (Bubastis)
    at Bubastis, ii. 59, 83, 137, 156; at
    Buto, ii. 155, 156; in Samos, iii. 48; in
    Thrace, iv. 33; v. 7; at Delos, temple
    of, iv. 34, 35; at Byzantion (Orthosia),
    iv. 87; at Brauron, vi. 138; at
    Artemision, vii. 176; "the sacred
    strand of Artemis," viii. 77; Oracle of
    Artemis in Egypt, ii. 83
Artemisia queen of Halicarnassos, vii. 99;
    viii. 68, 69, 87, 88, 93, 101, 103, 107
    At Salamis, viii. 87, 88, 93
Artemision, strand in Eubœa, vii.
    175–177, 182, 192–195; viii. 2, 4–6, 8,
    11, 14, 16, 21–23, 40, 42–46, 66, 76, 82
    Description of Artemision, vii. 176;
    battles of, viii. 6–11, 14, 15–18;
    retreat from, viii. 21, 22
Artēscos, river, iv. 92
[Artimpasa.] See Argimpasa
Artobazanēs, Persian, son of Dareios, vii.
    2, 3

Artochmēs, Persian commander, vii.
  73
Artontēs (1), Persian, father of Bagaios,
  iii. 128
  (2), Persian, son of Mardonios, ix. 84
Artoxerxēs, son of Xerxes, king of the
  Persians, vi. 98; vii. 106, 151, 152
Artozōstra, daughter of Dareios and wife
  of Mardonios, vi. 43
Artybios, Persian commander in Cyprus,
  v. 108, 110–113
Artyphios, Persian, son of Artabanos, vii.
  66, 67
Artystonē, daughter of Cyrus, iii. 88; vii.
  69, 72
Arÿandēs, Persian governor of Egypt, iv.
  165–167, 200, 203; Arÿandic silver, iv.
  166
Arÿēnis, daughter of Alyattes, i. 74
Asbystai, iv. 170, 171
Ascalōn, city of Syria, i. 105
Asia, (1) continent, i. 4, 6, 15, 16, 27, 72,
  79, 95, 102–104, 106–108, 130, 177,
  192, 209; ii. 16, 17, 103; iii. 56, 67, 88,
  90, 94, 96, 98, 115, 117, 137, 138; iv. 1,
  4, 11, 12, 36, (37), 38, 40, 41, 42, 44,
  45, 143, 198; v. 12, 15, 17, 30, 49, 50,
  96, 97, 119; vi. 24, 43, 45, 58, 70, 116,
  118, 119; vii. 1, 9c, 11, 20, 21, 23, 25,
  33, 70, 73, 75, 107, 135, 137, 145, 146,
  157, 174, 184, 185; viii. 109, 118, 119,
  126, 136; ix. 89, 116, 122
  Geography of Asia, iv. 37–40, 44; name,
    iv. 45; Upper Asia (above Halys), i.
    95, 103, 130, 177; iv. 1; vii: 20; Lower
    Asia, i. 72; seacoasts of Asia, v. 30;
    vii. 135; Hellenes of Asia, i. 6, 27;
    Ethiopians of Asia, iii. 94; vii. 70;
    Thracians of Asia, vii. 75;
    Magnesians of Asia, iii. 90; Amyntas
    of Asia, viii. 136
  (2), wife of Prometheus, iv. 45
Asian tribe at Sardis, iv. 45
Asias, son of Cotys, iv. 45
Asinē, city of the Dryopians in
  Peloponnese, viii. 73
Asmach, the "Deserters," ii. 30
Asōnidēs, Eginetan, vii. 181
Asōpians, ix. 15
Asōpodōrus, Theban, son of Timander, ix.
  69
Asōpos (1), river of Bœotia, v. 80; vi. 108;
  ix. 15, 19, 30, 31, 36, 38, 40, 43, 49, 51,
  59; daughters of Asopos, Egina,
  Thebē, v. 80; Oëroē, ix. 51
  (2), river of Trachinia, vii. 199, 200, 216,
  217

Aspathinēs, father of Prexaspes, iii. 70,
  78; vii. 97
Assa, city of Chalkidikē, vii. 122
Assēsos, in territory of Miletos, i. 19, 22:
  Athenē of Assēsos, i. 19, 22
Assyria, i. 1, 178, 185; ii. 17; iii. 92; iv. 39;
  Assyrian land, i. 192
  Assyrian(s) i. 95, 102, 103, 106, 131, 178,
    188, 192–194, 199; ii. 17, 30, 141, 150;
    iii. 155; vi. 54 (Perseus); vii. 9, 63;
    Assyrian wares, i. 1; Assyrian history,
    i. 184; Assyrian characters, iv. 87
  Assyria and its cities described, i.
    178–187, 192–200; Sanacharib, ii. 141;
    wars with Medes, i. 102, 103, 106;
    conquest by Cyrus, i. 188–191;
    equipment when serving under
    Xerxes, vii. 63
Astacos, Theban, father of Melanippos, v.
  67
Aster, Spartan, father of Anchimolios, v. 63
Astrabacos (or Astrobacos), hero at
  Sparta, vi. 69
Astyagēs, king of the Medes, i. 46, 73–75,
  91, 107–112, 114–130, 162; iii. 62; vii.
  8a; ix. 122
  Married to the daughter of Alyattes, i.
    74; his dreams, i. 107; discovery of
    Cyrus and revenge on Harpagos, i.
    114–119; deposition, i. 127–129
Asychis, king of Egypt, ii. 136
Atarantians, iv. 184
Atarbēchis, city of Egypt, ii. 41
Atarneus, region of Mysia, i. 160; vi. 28,
  29; vii. 42; viii. 106; Hermippos of
  Atarneus, vi. 4
Athamas, father of Phrixos and Hellē, vii.
  58, 197
Athēnadēs of Trachis, vii. 213
Athēnagoras, Samian envoy, ix. 90
Athēnē, i. 19, 22, 60, 62, 66, 92, 160, 175; ii.
  28, 59, 83, 169, 170, 175, 182; iii. 47, 59;
  iv. 180, 188, 189; v. 45, 77, 82, 95; vii.
  43, (141); viii. 37, 39, 55, 94, 104; ix. 70
  At Assēsos, i. 19, 22; at Athens, i. 60; v.
    77, 82; viii. 55; at Pallenē, i. 62; at
    Tegea (Alea), i. 66; ix. 76; at Delphi
    (Pronaia), i. 92; viii. 37, 39; in Chios
    (Poliuchos), i. 160; of the Pedasians,
    i. 175; viii. 104; in Egypt at Saïs, ii. 28,
    59, 83, 169, 170, 175; at Lindos, ii. 182;
    iii. 47; in Egina, iii. 59; in Libya
    (daughter of lake Tritonis), iv. 180,
    188, 189; cp. vii. 141; "of the Crathis"
    at Sybaris, v. 45; in Sigeion, v. 95; of
    Ilion, vii. 43; in Salamis (Skiras), viii.
    94; Oracle in Egypt, ii. 83

Athens (Athēnai), i. 60, 64, 98, 143, 146, 147, 173; ii. 7; iii. 160; v. 55, 57, 61–66, 70–72, 76, 77, 82, 87, 88, 91, 96, 97; vi. 34, 35, 39, 41, 43, 85, 86, 94, 99, 103, 107, 109, 120, 121, 123, 125, 127, 128, 133, 139; vii. 2, 5, 6, 8, 9, 32, 62, 90, 95, 133, 138, 142, 157, 162, 182; viii. 34, 46, 48, 50, 54, 61, 66–68, 77, 93, 99, 100, 102, 106, 111, 118, 120, 125, 136, 140, 141; ix. 1, 3, 4, 8, 12, 13, 32, 99, 107, 116, 120

Athenian(s) i. 29, 30, 32, 56, 57, 59, 60, 62–65, 86 (Solon), 143; ii. 51, 177; iii. 131, 134 (women), 160; iv. 99, 137 (Miltiades), 145; v. 55, 57, 61–66, 69–74, 76–79, 81, 82, 84–91, 93–97, 99, 103, 105, 113 (Solon); vi. 21, 35, 36, 49, 50, 73, 75, 86–90, 92–94, 100, 102–106, 108, 109, 111–117, 120, 121, [122], 124, 127, 130–132, 135–140; vii. 1, 4, 5, 6 (Onomacritos), 8, 10 11, 33, 51, 92 (Lycos), 107, 133, 137, 139–145, 151, 161, 168, 173, 182, 189, 203; viii. 1–5, 10, 11, 17, 18, 21, 22, 40–42, 44, 50–56, 57 (Mnesiphilos), 61, 63, 65, 70, 74, 75, 79, 84–86, 91, 93–95, 96 (Lysistratos), 109–111, 125, 136, 140–144; ix. 1, 3–9, 11, 13, 19, 21–23, 26–28, 31, 35, 39, 44–46, 48, 54–56, 59–61, 67, 70, 71, 73, 74, 75, 85, 99, 102, 105, 106, 114, 116–118, 120; Athenian women in Lemnos, vi. 138; Athenian ship(s), vii. 179; viii. 10, 14, 87, 90, 92; Cyprians from Athens, vii. 90; Ionians from Athens, i. 146

Origin and ancient names of Athenians, i. 57; viii. 44; never changed land, i. 56; vii. 161; religious rites, ii. 51; of Ionic race but ashamed of the name, i. 143; ancient tribes, v. 66; early exploits, vii. 161; ix. 27; Theseus, ix. 73; quarrel with Pelasgians, vi. 137; attempt of Kylon, v. 71; Peisistratos despot, i. 59–64; assassination of Hipparchos, v. 55, 56, Hippias expelled, v. 62–65; Cleisthenes, v. 66, 69–73; wars with Spartans, Bœotians, and Chalkidians, v. 74–81; feud with Egina, v. 82–89; vi. 49, 50, 73, 86–94; Aristagoras at Athens, v. 97; Athenian expedition to Sardis, v. 99–103; cause of the Ionians given up, v. 103; grief at the capture of Miletos, vi. 21; ambassadors put to death at Athens, vii. 133, 137; help to Eretria, vi. 100; Marathon, vi. 102–117; expedition to

Paros, vi. 132–136; oracles to the Athenians, vii. 140–143; speech of the Athenian envoy to Gelon, vii. 161; at Artemision, viii. 1–22; fleet at Salamis, viii. 40–44; Athens deserted, viii. 41; Athens occupied by Xerxes, viii. 50–55; battle of Salamis, viii. 56–65, 74–97; Alexander at Athens, viii. 136, 140–144; Athenian envoys at Sparta, ix. 6–11; Athens occupied by Mardonios, ix. 13; Athenians at Plataia, ix. 19, 21–23, 26–28, 31, 44–47, 54–56, 59–61, 67, 70, 71, 73; at Mykalē, ix. 102, 105; at Sestos, ix. 115–121; reduction of Persian garrisons by the Athenians, vii. 107; circuit of walls, i. 98; Pelasgian wall, vi. 137; the "wheel-round city," vii. 140; wooden walls, vii. 141–143; viii. 51, 52; temple of Erechtheus, viii. 55; the serpent, viii. 41; number of Athenians, v. 97; dress of women, v. 87; services of Athens of Hellas, vii. 139; patriotism, viii. 3, 143, 144; increase of power on becoming free, v. 78; naval power, vii. 144, 161; viii. 1–3, 44

Athōs, mountain peninsula, vi. 44, 45, 95; vii. 22, 23, 37, 122, 189

Athribis, district of, in Egypt, ii. 166

Athrys, tributary of Ister, iv. 49

Atlantians, in Libya, iv. 184, 185

Atlantis, Sea, i. 203

Atlas (1), mountain, iv. 184
  (2), tributary of Ister, iv. 49

Atossa, daughter of Cyrus, iii. 68, 69, 88, 133, 134; vii. 2, 3, (mother of Hystaspes) 64, (of Masistes) 82

Atramytteion. See Adramytteion

Atreus, sons of, vii. 20

Attagīnos, Theban, ix. 16, 86, 88

Attica, Attic land, i. 62; iv. 99; v. 63, 64, 65, 74, 76, 81, 87, 89; vi. 73, 102, 120, 137, 139, 140; vii. 10b, 137, 143, 189; viii. 40, 49–51, 53, 60, 65, 96, 110, 144; ix. 3, 4, 6–8, 12, 13, 17, 27, 73, 99

Conformation, iv. 99; olive, v. 82; nature of ground, ix. 13; invasion of Attica by the sons of Tyndareus, ix. 73; by Dorians four times, v. 76. See also Athens. Attic race, i. 57, 59; Attic tongue, vi. 138; Attic dances, vi. 129; Attic measures mentioned, i. 192; demes of Attica mentioned, Alopecai, Anaphlystos, Aphidnai, Dekeleia, Hysiai, Oinoē, Paiania, Paionia, Sphendaleis, Thoricos

Atys (1), king of the Lydians, i. 7, 94; vii. 74
  (2), Lydian, son of Crœsus, i. 34
  (3), father of Pythios, vii. 27. Perhaps the same as (2)
Auchatai, Scythians, iv. 6
Augila, region of Libya, iv. 172, 182, 183
Auras, tributary of the Ister, iv. 49
Auschisai, Libyans, iv. 171, 172
Auseans, Libyans, iv. 180, 191
Autesiōn, father of Theras and Argeia, iv. 147; vi. 52
Autodicos, Plataian, father of Cleades, ix. 85
Autonoös, hero at Delphi, viii. 39
Auxēsia, goddess in Epidauros and Egina, v. 82, 83
Avenging deities (Erinyes), iv. 149
Axios, river, vii. 123, 124
[Axos.] See Oaxos
Azanēs, Persian commander, vii. 66
Azanian, vi. 127
Aziris in Libya, iv. 157, 169
Azōtos, city of Syria, ii. 157

BABYLŌN, i. 153, 178–180, 183–185, 187, 189–194; iii. 92, 151, 153–160; iv. 1; vii. 62; land or district of Babylon, i. 106, 192, 193; iv. 198 Babylonians, men of Babylon, i. 77, 186, 190–192, 196, 198–200; ii. 109; iii. 150–153, 155–159; Labynetos the Babylonian, i. 74; the Babylonian queen (Nitocris), ii. 100; Babylonian works, i. 93; talent, iii. 89, 95; shoes, i. 195
  Description and early history of Babylon, i. 178–187; ruled by Labynētos, i. 77; captured by Cyrus, i. 188–191; besieged and captured by Dareios, iii. 150–159; Babylonian land and its productions, i. 192, 193; dress and manners of Babylonians, i. 195–200; boats on the Euphrates, i. 194
Bacalēs, Libyans, iv. 171
Bacchiadai, v. 92b, 92c
Bacchus, iv. 79; rite of Bacchus, iv. 79, 108; Bacchic observances, ii. 81. See Dionysos
Bactra, city, vi. 9; ix. 113; Bactria, country (or province) of Bactria, iv. 204; ix. 113: Bactrians, iii. 92, 102; vii. 64, 66, 86; viii. 113; ix. 31, 113; Bactrian race, i. 153
Badrēs (1), Persian commander against Barca, iv. 167, 203
  (2), Persian, son of Hystanes, vii. 77

Bagaios, Persian, son of Artontes, iii. 128; (father of Mardontes) vii. 80; viii. 130
Bakis, oracles of, viii. 20, 77, 96; ix. 43
Barbarian(s), i, pref., 2, 4, 6, 10, 14, 57, 58, 60, 173, 214; ii. 50, 52, 57, 158, 167; iii. 115, 139; iv. 12; v. 22, 23, 49, 58, 97; vi. 9, 31, 58, 99, 106, 107, 112, 113, 115–117, 121; vii. 6, 23, 35, 63, 127, 132, 138, 139, 144, 148, 149, 154, 157, 158, 163, 167, 169, 175–180, 182, 183, 189, 193, 194, 196, 211, 212, 218, 220, 223, 225, 226, 233; viii. 4, 6, 9, 11, 14–16, 19, 20, 22, 23, 29, 31, 32, 34, 35, 37–40, 46, 50–53, 55, 60, 70, 71, 75, 78, 80, 82, 84, 86, 87, 89, 91, 92, 105, 107, 109, 111, 126, 129, 132, 135, 141–144; ix. 6, 7, 9, 11, 16, 17, 19, 25, 27, 29, 31, 32, 40, 43, 45, 48, 55, 57, 59, 62, 68, 70, 71, 76, 78, 79, 90, 98–103, 106, 107
  Pelasgians were Barbarians, i. 57, 58; Barbarians in Crete, i. 173; Hellenic gods come from the Barbarians, ii. 50; Barbarian words, vii. 35; voices, ix. 43; tongue, ii. 57; iii. 115; viii. 135; style of work, vii. 63; manner of burying kings, vi. 58; Egyptians call foreigners Barbarians, ii. 158; Alexander objected to at Olympia as a Barbarian, v. 22
Barca (1), in Libya, iii. 91; iv. 160, 165, 167, 171, 200, 203
  Barcaians, men of Barca, iii. 13; iv. 164, 167, 186, 200–205
  (2) village in Bactria, iv. 204
[Barēs.] See Badres
Basileidēs, father of Herodotos, viii. 132
Bassakēs, Persian, son of Artabanos, vii. 75
Battiadai, house of Battos, iv. 202
Battos, name of kings of Kyrenē, iv. 163
  (1), son of Polymnestos, founder of Kyrenē, iv. 150, 153–157, 159
  (2), son of Arkesilaos, "the Prosperous," ii. 181; iv. 159, 160
  (3), "the Lame," iv. 161, 162, 205
Belbina, island near Attica; of Belbina, viii. 125
Bēlos (1), son of Alcaios, i. 7; vii. 61
  (2), Zeus Belos, i. 181; iii. 158; temple of Belos at Babylon, i. 181–183; gate of Belos, iii. 155, 158. See Zeus
Bermion, mountain, viii. 138
Bēssians, in Thrace, vii. 111
Bias (1), brother of Melampus, ix. 34
  (2) of Priene, i. 27, 170
Bisaltēs of Abydos, vi. 26
Bisaltia, vii. 115; Bisaltians, viii. 116
Bisanthē, town of the Hellespont, vii. 137

Bistonians, in Thrace, vii. 110; Bistonian lake, vii. 109
Bithynian Thracians, i. 28; vii. 75
Bitōn, Argive, brother of Cleobis, i. 31
Black Buttocks, near Thermopylai, vii. 216
Blessed, Isle of the, (Oasis), iii. 26
Bœōtia (Boiōtia), ii. 49; v. 57; viii. 40, 44, 144; ix. 2, 6, 7, 17, 19, 24, 87; Thebes of Bœotia, i. 92; v. 59, 67; chiefs of Bœotia (Bœotarchs), ix. 15
Bœotians, i. 92; v. 57, 59, 61, 74, 77, 81, 89, 91; vi. 34, 108; vii. 132, 202; viii. 34, 38, 50, 66, 113; ix. 31, 39, 46, 47, 67, 68, 100; Bœotian shoes, i. 195
Bœotians drive out Cadmeians, v. 57; war with Athens, v. 74–81; join the Persians, vii. 132; viii. 34, 66; conduct at Plataia, ix. 67, 68
Bogēs, Persian, vii. 107, 113
Boibēïs, lake, vii. 129
Bolbinitic, mouth of the Nile, ii. 17
Boreas, vii. 189
Borysthenēs (1), river, iv. 5, 18, 24, 47, 53, 54, 56, 71, 81, 101; description of river, iv. 53
(2), town, iv. 78; trading-station of the Borysthenēs, iv. 24; Borysthenites, iv. 18, 53, 78, 79; trading-station of the Borysthenites, iv. 17; city of the Borysthenites, iv. 78
Bosphorus (1), Thracian, iv. 83, 85–89, 118; vii. 10c, 20; measurement, iv. 85
(2), Kimmerian, iv. 12, 28, 100
Bottiaia, vii. 123, 127; Bottiaians, vii. 185; viii. 127
Branchidai (1), in the Milesian land, i. 46, 92, 157, 159; ii. 159; v. 36
(2), the people of the place, priests of the temple, i. 158
Braurōn, in Attica, iv. 145; vi. 138
Brentesion, Brundusium, in Italy, iv. 99
Briantikē, region in Thrace, vii. 108
Brigians, old name of Phrygians, vii. 73
Brongos, tributary of the Ister, iv. 49
Brygian Thracians, vi. 45; vii. 185
Bubarēs, son of Megabazos, v. 21; vii. 22; viii. 136
Bubastis (1), city of Egypt, ii. 59, 60, 67, 137, 154, 158, 166; district (nome) of Bubastis, ii. 166
Description, ii. 137, 138; festival of Artemis, ii. 60; cats buried there, ii. 67
(2), name of Artemis in Egypt, ii. 137, 156. See Artemis
Bucolic mouth of the Nile, ii. 17
Budians, tribe of the Medes, i. 101

Budinoi, iv. 21, 22, 102, 105, 108, 109, 119, 120, 122, 123, 136
Bulis, Spartan, vii. 134, 137
Bura, city of the Achaians, i. 145
Busai, tribe of the Medes, i. 101
Busiris, city of Egypt, ii. 59, 61; district (nome) of, ii. 165
Butakidēs of Croton, father of Philip, v. 47
Butō, city of Egypt, ii. 59, 63, 67, 75, 83, 111, 133, 152, 155, 156; iii. 64
Description of temple, ii. 155, 156; oracles from Butō, ii. 83, 111, 133, 152; iii. 64; hawks and shrew-mice buried there, ii. 67
Bybassos, peninsula of, i. 174
Byzantion, city, iv. 87, 144; v. 103; vi. 5, 26, 33; ix. 89
Byzantines, iv. 87, 144; v. 26; vi. 33; Ariston of Byzantion, iv. 138; Position of Byzantion, iv. 144; Histiaios at Byzantion, vi. 5, 26; Byzantines leave their city, vi. 33

[CABALES.] See Bacales
Cabalians, iii. 90. Cp. Cabelians
Cabeiroi, at Memphis, iii. 37; in Samothrakē, ii. 51
Cabēlians, Maionian, vii. 77. Cp. Cabalians
Cadmeians, sons of Cadmos, i. 56, 146; v. 57, 61; ix. 27; Theras, iv. 147; Cadmeian victory, i. 166; Cadmeian characters, v. 59
Cadmos (1), son of Agenor, ii. 49, 145; iv. 147; v. 57–59
(2), of Cos, son of Skythēs, vii. 163, 164
Cadytis, city of Syria, ii. 159; iii. 5
Caïcos, river, vii. 42; plain of the Caïcos, vi. 28
Caineus, son of, v. 92b
Calamisa in Samos, ix. 96
Calasirians, warrior class of Egypt, ii. 164, 166, 168; ix. 32
Calchas, vii. 91
Calchēdōn, territory of, iv. 85: men of Calchedon, iv. 144; v. 26; vi. 33
Calē Actē, in Sicily. See Fair Strand
Callantian Indians, iii. 97
Callatēbos, city, vii. 31
Callatian Indians, iii. 38
Calliadēs, archon at Athens for the year 480 B.C., viii. 51
Callias (1), Athenian, son of Hipponicos, vii. 151
(2), Athenian, son of Phainippos, vi. 121, [122]
(3), Eleian diviner, v. 44, 45

Callicratēs, Spartan, ix. 72, 85
Callimachos, Athenian polemarch, vi. 109–111, 114
Calliphōn, father of Demokedes, iii. 125
Callipidai (or Callippidai), iv. 17
Callipolis, in Sicily, vii. 154
Callista, ancient name of Thera, iv. 147
Calydna, people of, vii. 99
Calyndians, viii. 87; Calyndian ship, viii. 88; borders of the Calyndians, i. 172
Camarina, city of Sicily, vii. 154, 156
Cambysēs (1), son of Teïspes, father of Cyrus, i. 46, 73, 107, 108, 111, 122, 124, 207; iii. 69; vii. 11, 51
(2), son of Cyrus, i. 208; ii. 1, 181; iii. 1–4, 7, 9, 10, 13–17, 19–21, 25, 27, 29–34, 36, 38, 39, 44, 61–68, 73–75, 80, 88, 89, 97, 120, 122, 126, 139, 140; iv. 165, 166; v. 25; vii. 1, 8a, 18
March against Egypt, iii. 1, etc.; against Ethiopians, iii. 25; against Ammonians, iii. 26; outrages and madness, iii. 16, 27–38; death, iii. 64–66; character of his rule, iii. 89; physical state, iii. 33; love of wine, iii. 34; dealing with a corrupt judge, v. 25
Cameiros, city, i. 144
Camicos, town in Sicily, vii. 169, 170
Camp of the Tyrians at Memphis, ii. 112; "Camps" (of the Ionians or Carians), ii. 154
Campsa, town near Pallenē, vii. 123
Canastra, promontory of (Canastraion), vii. 123
Candaulēs (1), king of the Lydians, i. 7, 8, 10–13
(2), Carian, father of Damasithymos, vii. 98
Canē, mountain of, vii. 42
Canōbos, city of Egypt, ii. 15, 97; Canobic mouth of the Nile, ii. 17, 113, 179
Caphēreus, promontory of Eubœa, viii. 7
Cappadokia, i. 71–73, 76; v. 52; vii. 26
Cappadokians, i. 72; v. 49; vii. 72
Car, father of the Carians, i. 171
Carchēdōn. See Carthage
Cardamylē in Laconia, viii. 73
Cardia, city of the Chersonese, vi. 34, 36, 41; vii. 58; ix. 115
Carēnē, town near Atarneus, vii. 42
Carēnos, father of Euainetos, vii. 173
Caria, i. 142, 175; v. 103, 117, 122; vi. 25; vii. 31, 195
Carian(s), people of Caria, i. 28, 171, 172, 174; ii. 61, 152, 154, 163; iii. 11, 90; v. 111, 112, 117–121; vi. 20; vii. 93, 97, 98; viii. 22; Carian women, i. 92,

146; Carian race, i. 171, 172; Carian nation, viii. 19; Carian dress, v. 88; equipment, vii. 93; tongue, i. 171; viii. 135; Carian force, vii. 97; customs, i. 173; Hellenes in Caria, i. 142; Carian Zeus, v. 66
Origin and ancient name, i. 171; inventions, i. 171; Carians in Egypt, ii. 61, 152, 154, 163; iii. 11; Carian women at Miletos, i. 146; Carians submit to Harpagos, i. 174; join Ionians in revolt, v. 117–121; in army of Xerxes, vii. 93; Carian ships, vii. 97
Carkinītis, city of Scythia, iv. 55, 99
Carneia, Carneian festival, of the Lacedemonians, vii. 206; viii. 72
Carpathos, island, iii. 45
Carpis, tributary of Ister, iv. 49
Carthage (Carchēdōn), city, iii. 19; vii. 167
Carthaginians, i. 166, 167; (ii. 32); iii. 17, 19; iv. 43, 195, 196, (197); v. 42; vi. 17; vii. 158, 165–167; Annōn, Amilcas, vii. 165
Circumnavigation of Libya, iv. 43; war with Phocaians of Alalia, i. 166, 167; invasion of Sicily, vii. 165–167
Carÿanda, man of, iv. 44
Carystos, city of Eubœa, iv. 33; vi. 99; viii. 121
Carystians, men of Carystos, iv. 33; vi. 99; viii. 66, 112; ix. 105; Phanagoras, Onetes, vii. 214; Carystian land, ix. 105
Casambos, Eginetan, vi. 73
Casion, Mount, ii. 6, 158; iii. 5
Casmenē, town of Sicily, vii. 155
Caspatyros, city, iii. 102; iv. 44
Caspian Sea, i. 202–204; iv. 40
Caspians (1), in 11th satrapy, iii. 92
(2), in 15th satrapy, iii. 93; vii. 67, 86. See also vii. 86 note
Cassandanē, mother of Cambyses, ii. 1 ; iii. 2, 3
Cassiteridĕs, "Tin islands," iii. 115
Castalia, spring, viii. 39
Casthanaia, town near Sepias, vii. 183, 188
Cataract (Catadupa) of the Nile, ii. 17
Catarractēs, river of Asia Minor, vii. 26
Catiaroi, Scythians, iv. 6
Caucasa, in Chios, v. 33
Caucasus, mountains, i. 104, 203, 204; iii. 97; iv. 12
Caucōnians, i. 147; iv. 148
Caunos, city, i. 176; v. 103 : Caunians, men of Caunos, i. 171, 172, 176; Caunian race (language and customs), i. 172

"Cave-dwelling" Ethiopians, iv. 183
Caÿster, river, v. 100
Caÿstrobios of Proconnesos, father of
  Aristeas, iv. 13
Chaldeans, i. 181, 183; vii. 63; gate of the
  Chaldeans, iii. 155
  Quoted as authorities, i. 181, 183
Chalestra, town upon the Axios, vii. 123
Chalkidikē, race dwelling in, natives of,
  vii. 185; viii. 127; Chalkidians of
  Thrace, viii. 127
Chalkis, city of Euboea, vi. 118; vii. 183,
  189; viii. 44
  Chalkidians, men of Chalkis, v. 74, 77,
  91, 99; vi. 100; viii. 1, 46; ix. 28, 31;
  Hippobatai, v. 77; vi. 100
Chalybians, i. 28
Charadra, town of Phokis, viii. 33
Charaxos, brother of Sappho, ii. 135
Charilaos (1), king of Sparta, in
  genealogy of Leotychides, viii. 131
  (2), Samian, brother of Maiandrios, iii.
  145, 146
Charitěs, ii. 50: Hill of the Charitěs, iv. 175
Charopīnos, brother of Aristagoras, v. 99
Chemmis (1), island, ii. 156
  (2), city of Egypt, ii. 91; people of
  Chemmis, ii. 91; district (nome) of
  Chemmis, ii. 165
Cheops, king of Egypt, ii. 124, 126, 127,
  129
Chephrēn, king of Egypt, ii. 127
Cherasmis, Persian, father of Artaÿctes,
  vii. 78
Chersis, Salaminian, father of Gorgos and
  Onesilos, v. 104, 113; vii. 98; viii. 11
Chersonese (1), Thracian, iv. 143; vi. 33,
  34, 36, 37, 39–41, 103, 104, 140; vii. 22,
  33, 58; viii. 130; ix. 114, 116: men of
  Chersonese, iv. 137; vi. 38, 39; ix. 118,
  120
  Ruled by family of Miltiades, vi. 34–40,
  103, 104, 140; Athenian operations
  there, ix. 114–121
  (2), "rugged," in Tauris, iv. 99
Chileos of Tegea, ix. 9
Chilōn (1), Spartan, one of the seven
  Sages, i. 59; vii. 235
  (2), Spartan, son of Demarmenos, vi. 65
Chios, island, i. 142, 160, 164; ii. 178; v. 33,
  34, 98; vi. 25, 26, 31; viii. 132; Chian
  land, vi. 26
  Chians, men of Chios, i. 18, 142, 160,
  161, 165; ii. 135; v. 98; vi. 2, 5, 8, 15, 16,
  26, 27; viii. 106, 132; ix. 106; Glaucos,
  i. 25; Strattis, iv. 138; Panionios, viii.
  105

Race and language, i. 142; Chians help
  Miletos against the Lydians, i. 18; in
  battle of Ladē, vi. 8, 15, 16;
  conquered by Histiaios, vi. 26, 27;
  Chian envoys to Leotychides, viii.
  132; altar at Delphi, ii. 135
Choaspēs, river, i. 188; v. 49, 52
Choireai, in Euboea, vi. 101
Choireātai, tribe of Sikyon, v. 68
Choiros, father of Mikythos, vii. 170
[Chōn], river, ix. 93 note
Chorasmians, iii. 93, 117; vii. 66
Chromios, Argive, i. 82
Chthoniai. See Earth goddesses
Chytroi. See Pots
Clazomenai, city, i. 16, 142; ii. 178; v. 123: men
  of Clazomenai, i. 51; Timesios, i. 168
Cleadēs, Plataian, ix. 85
Cleander (1), son of Pantares, despot of
  Gela, vii. 154, 155
  (2), son of Hippocrates, vii. 155
  (3), Phigalian diviner, vi. 83
Cleinias, Athenian, son of Alkibiades, viii.
  17
Cleisthenēs (1), despot of Sikyon, v. 67,
  68, 69; vi. 126, 128–131
  (2), Athenian, son of Megacles, v. 66,
  67, 69, 70, 72, 73; vi. 131
Cleobis, Argive, brother of Biton, i. 31
Cleodaios, son of Hyllos, vi. 52; vii. 204;
  viii. 131
Cleombrotos, Spartan, son of
  Anaxandrides, v. 41; vii. 205; viii. 71;
  ix. 10; (father of Pausanias) iv. 81; v.
  32; ix. 64, 78
Cleomenēs, son of Anaxandrides, king of
  Sparta, iii. 148; v. 39, 41, 42, 48–51, 54,
  64, 70, 72–76, 90, 97; vi. 50, 51, 61,
  64–66, 73–76, 78–82, 84, 85, 92, 108;
  vii. 148, 205, 239 (father of Gorgo)
  Birth, v. 41; accession, v. 39; madness, v.
  42; vi. 75; advice to the Plataians, vi.
  108; dealings with Maiandrios, iii.
  148; at Athens, v. 64, 72; in Attica, v.
  74, 75; Aristagoras, v. 49–51; war with
  Argos, vi. 76–83; in Egina, vi. 50;
  deposes Demaratos, vi. 61, 65, 66;
  second expedition to Egina, vi. 73;
  flight from Sparta, vi. 74; return, vi.
  75; death, vi. 75
Cleōnai, town in Athōs, vii. 22
Cliffs. See Cremnoi
[Clytiadai], ix. 33 note
Cnidos, city, i. 144; ii. 178; iii. 138; land of
  Cnidos, i. 174: iv. 164
  Cnidians, men of Cnidos, i. 174; iii. 138;
  iv. 164

Cnoithos, father of Nicodromos, vi. 88
Cnōssian, iii. 122
Coast-land, Pelasgians of the, vii. 94
Cobōn, Delphian, vi. 66
Codros, king of Athens, i. 147; v. 65, 76; ix.
    97 (father of Neileus)
Cōēs of Mytilenē, iv. 97; v. 11, 37, 38
Coilē, in Attica, vi. 103
Coinyra, in Thasos, vi. 47
Cōlaios, Samian, iv. 152
Colaxaïs, Scythian, son of Targitaos, iv. 5, 7
Colchis, i. 104: Colchians, people of
    Colchis, i. 2, 104; ii. 104, 105; iii. 97; iv.
    37, 40; vii. 79; Medea the Colchian,
    vii. 62; the Phasis in Colchis, iv. 45;
    Aia of Colchis, i. 2; vii. 193, 197; linen
    of Colchis, ii. 105
Cōlias, strand in Attica, viii. 96; Colian
    women, viii. 96
Colophōn, city, i. 14, 16, 142: men of
    Colophōn, i. 147, 150
Colossai, city of Phrygia, vii. 30
Cōmbreia, town near Pallenē, vii. 123
Compsantos (or Compsatos), river in
    Thrace, vii. 109
Conion, of, v. 63
Contadesdos, river of Thrace, iv. 90
Cōpaïs, lake, viii. 135
Corcyra (Kerkyra), iii. 48, 52, 53; vii. 145:
    Corcyreans, men of Corcyra, iii.
    48–50, 53; vii. 145, 154, 168
Corēssos, near Ephesos, v. 100
Corinth, city, i. 23, 24; iii. 50, 52, 53; v. 92,
    93; vi. 128; vii. 202; viii. 45; ix. 88
    Corinthians, i. 14, 23, 24, 50, 51; ii. 167;
    iii. 48, 49; iv. 162; v. 75, 76, 92, 93; vi.
    89, 108; vii. 137 (Aristeas), 154, 195;
    viii. 1, 5 (Adeimantos), 21, 43, 61, 72,
    79, 94; ix. 28, 31, 69, 95, 102, 105;
    Periander, Lycophron, Aëtion,
    Amphion, Echecrates, Kypselos,
    Socles, Aristeas, Okytos,
    Adeimantos; Corinthian women, iii.
    134; v. 92g; Melissa, Labda;
    Corinthian helmet, iv. 180; dress, v. 87
    Bacchiadai at Corinth, v. 92b, c;
    Kypselos, v. 92; Periander, i. 20, 23,
    24; iii. 50–53; v. 92f, g; Corinthians go
    against Samos, iii. 48; oppose war
    with Athens, v. 75, 92; help
    Athenians, vi. 89; at Thermopylai, vii.
    202; at Artemision, viii. 1; at Salamis,
    viii. 94; at Plataia, ix. 28, 31, 69; at
    Mycalē, ix. 102, 105; respect for
    mechanic arts, ii. 167
Corōbios, purple-fisher of Crete, iv.
    151–153

Corōneia, men of, v. 79
Corsica. See Kyrnos
Corydallos of Antikyra, vii. 214
Cōrykian cave, viii. 36
Corys, river in Arabia, iii. 9
Cōs, island, i. 144; ix. 76: Cōans, men of
    Cōs, vii. 99, 164; Coan (woman), ix.
    76; Cadmos, vii. 163; Antagoras,
    Hegetorides, ix. 76
Cotys, father of Asias, iv. 45
Cranaoi, ancient name of Athenians, viii.
    44
Cranaspēs, Persian, father of Mitrobates,
    iii. 126
Crannōn, of, vi. 127
Crathis (1), river of Achaia in
    Peloponnese, i. 145
    (2), river at Sybaris in Italy, v. 45;
    Athenē of the Crathis, v. 45
Crēmnoi (cliffs), in Scythia, iv. 20, 110
Crēstōn, city, i. 57: Crēstōnians, men of
    Creston, i. 57; v. 3, 5; vii. 124, 127;
    Crestonian land, viii. 116. See note
    on i. 57
Crete, i. 65, 172, 173; iii. 44, 59; iv. 45, 151,
    154; vii 92, 145, 170, 171
    Cretans, i. 2, 171; iii. 59; iv. 151, 161; vii.
    99 (Artemisia), 169–171; Minos,
    Corobios, Etearchos; Phronimē,
    Artemisia
    Relation to Carians, Lykians, etc., i.
    171, 173; expedition of Minos to
    Sicily; vii. 170; disasters of Crete, vii.
    170, 171; Cretan pirates, i. 2; refuse to
    help against Xerxes, vii. 169; Spartan
    constitution taken from Crete, i. 65
Crētinēs (1), father of Anaxilaos of
    Rhegion, vii. 165
    (2), father of Ameinocles, vii. 190
Crinippos, father of Terillos of Himera,
    vii. 165
Crios, Eginetan, vi. 50, 73; viii. 92
Crisaian plain, viii. 32
Critalla, in Cappadokia, vii. 26
Critobulos (1), of Kyrenē, ii. 181
    (2), of Toronē, viii. 127
Crobyzian Thracians, iv. 49
Crocodiles, City of, ii. 148
Crœsus (Croisos), i. 6, 7, 26–28, 30–38, 40,
    41, 43–49, 51, 53–56, 59, 65, 67, 69–71,
    73, 75–81, 83–93, 95, 130, 141, 153,
    155, 156, 207, 208, 211; iii. 14, 34, 36,
    47; v. 36; vi. 37, 38, 125, 127; vii. 30;
    viii. 35, 122
    His wars with Ionians, i. 26, 27;
    conquests, i. 28; Solon, i. 29–33; helps
    Miltiades, vi. 37; Atys and Adrastos,

i. 34–45; consults Oracles, i. 46–49,
53–55; enriches Alcmaion, vi. 125;
offerings at Delphi, i. 51; viii. 35, 122;
to Amphiaraos, i. 52; other offerings,
i. 92; v. 36; alliance with Sparta, i. 69,
70; war with Cyrus, i. 71, 73, 75–86;
saved from death, i. 86–88;
reproaches Oracle, i. 90, 91; advice to
Cyrus, i. 89, 90, 155, 156, 207; advice
to Cambyses, iii. 36; his liberality, i.
69; vi. 125
Cronidēs, *note* on viii. 77
Crōphi, mountain, ii. 28
Crossaia, region near Pallenē, vii. 123
Crotōn (1) city in the south of Italy, iii.
131, 136–138; v. 44, 47; land of
Croton, v. 45
  Crotoniates, men of Croton, iii. 137; v.
  44, 45; vi. 21; viii. 47; physicians of
  Croton, iii. 131; Calliphon,
  Demokedes, iii. 125; Butakides,
  Philip, v. 47; Phaÿllos
  (2) [in Etruria]. See *note* on i. 57
Cuphagoras, Athenian, father of
  Epizelos, vi. 117
Curion, city, v. 113: Curians, Stesenor, v.
  113
Cyclades, islands, v. 30, 31
Cyprian Epic, ii. 117, 118
Cyprus (Kypros), i. 72, 105, 199, ii. 79, 182;
  iii. 91; iv. 162, 164, v. 31, 49, 108, 109,
  113, 115
  Cyprians, men of Cyprus, i. 105; iii. 19;
  v. 9, 104, 109, 110, 113, 115, 116; vi. 6;
  vii. 90, 98; viii. 68c, 100; Euelthon,
  Siromos, Chersis, Gorgos, Onesilos,
  Timagoras, Timonax
  Races in Cyprus, vii. 90; conquered by
  Amasis, ii. 182; submission to
  Persians, iii. 19; revolt, v. 104,
  108–116; with Persians against
  Histiaios, vi. 6; with Xerxes, vii. 90;
  equipment, vii. 90
  "Keys of Cyprus," v. 108
Cyrus (Kyros) (1) son of Cambyses, i. 46,
  54, 71–73, 75–77, 79, 80, 84, 86–91, 95,
  108, 113–116, 120–130, 141, 152–157,
  160, 162, 169, 177, 178, 183, 188–191,
  201, 202, 204–214; ii. 1; iii. 1–3, 32, 34,
  36, 69, 75, 88, 89, 120, 152, 159, 160; v.
  52; vii. 2, 8a, 11, 18, 51; ix. 122; (father
  of Cambyses) i. 208; ii. 1; iii. 1, 14, 34,
  44, 61, 64, 66, 139; iv. 165; (father of
  Smerdis) iii. 61, 63, 65–69, 71, 74, 75,
  88; vii. 78; (father of Atossa) iii. 88,
  133; vii. 2, 64; (father of Artystonē)
  iii. 88; vii. 69

Birth and early life, i. 107–122; leader
of the Persians against the Medes, i.
123–130; war with Crœsus, i. 75–91;
receives envoys from Ionians and
Aiolians, i. 141; from Sparta, i. 152,
153; sends Mazares to reduce Lydian
revolt, i. 156; then Harpagos, i. 162;
conquests, i. 177; war on Babylon, i.
188–191; on the Massagetai, i.
201–214; death, i. 214; character as
ruler, iii. 89; regard for his memory,
iii. 160; his reply to Artembares, ix.
122
  (2), grandfather of the above, i. 111

DADICANS, in 7th satrapy, iii. 91; vii. 66
Daidalos, vii. 170
Damasithymos, Carian, vii. 98; king of the
  Calyndians, viii. 87
Damasos of Siris, suitor of Agaristē, vi.
  127
Damia, goddess in Epidauros and Egina,
  v. 82, 83
Danaē, mother of Perseus, ii. 91; vi. 53;
  vii. 61, 150
Danaos, ii. 91, 98; vii. 94; daughters of
  Danaos, ii. 171, 182
Daoi, tribe of Persians, i. 125
Daphnai, town in Egypt, ii. 30, 107
Daphnis of Abydos, iv. 138
Dardanians, above Assyria, i. 189
Dardanos, city, v. 117; vii. 43
Dareios (1), son of Hystaspes, i. 130, 183,
  187, 209–211; ii. 110, 158; iii. 38,
  70–73, 76–78, 82, 85–90, 95, 96, 101,
  119, 126–130, 132–135, 137–141, 147,
  151, 152, 154–160; iv. 1, 4, 7, 39, 44, 46,
  83–85, 87–89, 91–93, 97, 98, 102, 105,
  121, 124–126, 128, 129, 131–137, 141,
  143, 166, 167, 204; v. 1, 2, 11–14, 17,
  18, 23–25, 27, 30, 36, 37, 65, 73, 96, 98,
  103, 105–108, 124; vi. 1–3, 9, 13, 20,
  24, 25, 30, 40, 41, 43, 46, 48, 49, 70, 84,
  94, 95, 98, 101, 119; vii. 1–5, 7, 8, 10a,
  18, 20, 27, 32, 52, 59, 69, 105, 106, 133,
  134, 194; (father of Achaimenes) iii.
  12; vii. 97; (of Xerxes) vii. 2, 11, 14,
  186; ix. 111; (of Hystaspes) vii. 64; (of
  Arsamenes) vii. 68; (of Arsames) vii.
  69; (of Gobryas) vii. 72; (of Masistes)
  vii. 82; ix. 107, 111; (of Ariomardos)
  vii. 78; (of Ariabignes) vii. 97; viii. 89;
  (of Abrocomes and Hyperanthes)
  vii. 224; (brother of Artaphrenes) v.
  30; (of Artanes) vii. 224; (uncle of
  Mardonios) vii. 5; (of Tritantaichmes
  and Smerdomenes) vii. 82; (cousin of

Dareios (1) (continued)
  Megabates), v. 32; daughters of
  Dareios mentioned, v. 116; vii. 73;
  sister of Dareios, iv. 43; daric staters,
  vii. 28
  Suspected by Cyrus, i. 209, 210; the
  cloak of Syloson, iii. 139; conspiracy
  against Magians, iii. 70–79; Dareios
  becomes king, iii. 80–88; his satrapies
  and tribute, iii. 89–97; revolt of
  Medes, i. 130; dealings of Dareios
  with Intaphrenes, iii. 118, 119; with
  Oroites, iii. 126–128; with
  Demokedes, iii. 129–132; suggestion
  of Atossa, iii. 134; sends exploring
  ship to Hellas, iii. 135–138;
  expedition to Samos, iii. 139–149; the
  revolt and capture of Babylon, iii.
  150–160; Dareios opens tomb of
  Nitocris, i. 187; Scythian expedition,
  iv. 1, 83–98, 102, 118–144; vii. 10, 18,
  20, 52; treatment of Oiobazos, iv. 84;
  dealings with Histiaios, v. 11, 23–25;
  vi. 30; with the Paionians, v. 12–15;
  anger against Athenians, v. 105;
  completes canal to Arabian gulf, ii.
  158; iv. 39; attempts to set up a statue
  at Memphis, ii. 110; treatment of
  Metiochos, vi. 41; of Aryandes, iv.
  166; sends Mardonios to the coast,
  vi. 43; demands earth and water of
  Hellenes, vi. 48; receives Demaratos,
  vi. 70; appoints Datis and
  Artaphrenes to command, vi. 94;
  treatment of Eretrians, vi. 119;
  preparations against Hellas and
  Egypt, vii. 1; settlement of
  succession, vii. 2, 3; death, vii. 4;
  character as a ruler, iii. 89; treatment
  of a corrupt judge, vii. 194; questions
  Indians and Hellenes, iii. 38; coinage
  of darics, vii. 166; presents from
  Pythios, vii. 27; geographical
  discoveries, iv. 44
  (2), son of Xerxes, ix. 108
Dareitai, in 11th satrapy, iii. 92
Daskyleion, city (giving name to the 3d
  satrapy), iii. 120, 126; vi. 33
Daskylos, father of Gyges, i. 8
Datis, Mede, vi. 94, 97, 98, 118, 119; vii. 8b,
  10b, 74; father of Harmamithras and
  Tithaios, vii. 88
Daton, town in Thrace, ix. 75
Daughter (Corē), at Eleusis, viii. 65
Daulis, in Phokis, viii. 35
Daurisēs, Persian commander, v. 116–118,
  121, 122

Deinomenēs, father of Gelon, vii. 145
Dēïokēs, king of the Medes, i. 16, 73,
  96–99, 101–103
Dēïphonos, diviner of Apollonia, ix. 92, 95
Dekeleia, in Attica, ix. 15, 73; men of
  Dekeleia, ix. 73; Sophanes, vi. 92
Dekelos, hero, ix. 73
Dēlion, in Bœotia, vi. 118
Dēlos, island, i. 64; ii. 170; iv. 33–35; vi.
  97–99, 118; viii. 132, 133; ix. 90, 96
  Delians, men of Delos, iv. 33, 34; vi. 97,
  98, 118
Delphi, i. 13, 14, 19, 25, 31, 46–52, 65–67,
  85, 90, 92, 167, 174; ii. 135, 180; iii. 57;
  iv. 15, 150, 155–157, 161–163, 179; v.
  42, 43, 62, 63, 67, 82, 89, 92; vi. 19, 27,
  34, 35, 52, 57, 66, 70, 76, 86c, 135, 139;
  vii. 111, 132, 139, 140, 148, 163, 165,
  169, 239; viii. 27, 35, 82, 114, 121, 122;
  ix. 33, 42, 81, 93
  Delphians, men of Delphi, i. 14, 20, 51,
  54, 55; ii. 134, 180; vi. 66; vii. 141, 178,
  179; viii. 36–39; Timesitheos, v. 72;
  Aristophantos, Cobon, Perialla,
  Timon, Akeratos
  Temple burnt and rebuilt, ii. 180; v. 62;
  Oracle consulted by Lydians about
  Gyges, i. 13; by Alyattes, i. 19; by
  Crœsus, i. 47, 48, 53–55, 85; by
  Lycurgus, i. 65; by the Spartans, i. 66,
  67; v. 63; vi. 52, 66; vii. 220; viii. 114;
  by the men of Agylla, i. 167; by the
  Cnidians, i. 174; by the Sīphnians, iii.
  57; by the Metapontines, iv. 15; by
  the Theraians, iv. 150, 157; by Battos,
  iv. 155; by the Kyrenians, iv. 161; by
  Arkesilaos, iv. 164; by Cleisthenes of
  Sikyon, v. 67; by the Thebans, v. 79;
  by the Epidaurians, v. 82; by the
  Athenians, v. 89; vii. 140, 141, 189; by
  Aëtion, by the Bacchiadai, and by
  Kypselos, v. 92; by the Argives, vi. 19;
  cp. vi. 77; by the Dolonkians, vi. 34;
  by Cleomenes, vi. 76; by Glaucos, vi.
  86: by the Parians, vi. 135; by the
  Pelasgians of Lemnos, vi. 139; by the
  Argives, vii. 148; by the Cretans, vii.
  169; by the Delphians, vii. 178; viii.
  36; by Tisamenos, ix. 33; by the
  people of Apollonia, ix. 93;
  reproached by Crœsus, i. 90, 91;
  bribed by the Alcmaionidai, v. 63;
  influenced by Cleomenes, vi. 66;
  offerings of Midas and Gyges, i. 14;
  of Crœsus, i. 50, 51, cp. 92; of
  Rhodopis, ii. 135, of the Phokians,
  viii. 27; of the Hellenes after Salamis,

viii. 121, 122; after Plataia, ix. 81; attempt of the Persians upon Delphi, viii. 35–39. See also *Pythian prophetess*

Delta of Egypt, ii. 13, 15–19, 41, 59, 97, 179

Dēmarātos, king of Sparta, v. 75; vi. 50, 51, 61–67, 70–75, 84; vii. 3, 101–104, 209, 234–237, 239; viii. 65

Birth, vi. 61–63, 68, 69; becomes king, vi. 64; quarrel with Cleomenes, v. 75; vi. 51, 61; deposed, vi. 65, 66; leaves Sparta, vi. 67, 70; with Dareios, vi. 70; vii. 3; informs Spartans of the coming invasion, vii. 239; with Xerxes at Doriscos, vii. 101–104; at Thermopylai, vii. 209, 234–237, 239; in Attica, viii. 65

Dēmarmenos, father of Prinetades and Chilon, v. 41; vi. 65

Dēmētēr, ii. 156; "Giver of Laws" (Thesmophoros), ii. 171; in Egina, vi. 91; in Paros, vi. 134: "Achaia," of the Gephyraians, v. 61: Eleusinian, at Eleusis (vi. 75; viii. 65); at Plataia, ix. 57, 62, 65, 69, 101; at Mykalē, ix. 97, 101: of the Amphictyons at Thermopylai, vii. 200: in Egypt, equivalent to Isis, ii. 59, 122, 123, 156: [in Scythia, see *note* on iv. 53]: fruit of Demeter, i. 193; iv. 198; cp. vii. 141, 142

Dēmocritos of Naxos, viii. 46

Dēmokēdēs, physician of Croton, iii. 125, 129–137

Dēmōnax of Mantineia, iv. 161, 162

Dēmonoös, father of Penthylos, vii. 195

Dēmophilos, Thespian, vii. 222

Dersaians in Thrace, vii. 110

Derusiaians, tribe of Persians, i. 125

Deserters, ii. 30, 31

Destinies, i. 91

Deucaliōn, i. 56

Diactoridēs (1), of Crannon, suitor of Agaristē, vi. 127

(2), Spartan, vi. 71

Diadromēs, father of Demophilos, vii. 222

Dicaia, town of Thrace, vii. 109

Dicaios, Athenian, viii. 65

Dictyna, iii. 59. See *note*

Didyma, *i.e.* Branchidai, vi. 19

Diēnekēs, Spartan, vii. 226, 227

Dindymos, mountain, i. 80

Diomede, in the Iliad, ii. 116

Dion, town in Athōs, vii. 22

Dionysios of Phocaia, vi. 11, 12, 17

Dionysophanēs of Ephesos, ix. 84

Dionysos, ii. 49, 52, 145, 146; iii. 111: of the Egyptians (Osiris), ii. 42, 47, 48, 123, 144, 145, 156; of the Ethiopians, ii. 29; iii. 97; of the Thracians, v. 7; vii. 111; of the Budinoi, iv. 108; of the Borysthenites (Bacchus), iv. 79; of the Arabians (Orotalt), iii. 8; at Smyrna, i. 150; at Sikyon, v. 67; at Byzantion, iv. 87; Oracle of, vii. 111

Dioscuroi, ii. 43, 50; vi. 127. See *sons of Tyndareus*

Dipaieis, town in Arcadia, ix. 35

Dithyrambos, Thespian, distinguished at Thermopylai, vii. 227

Dobērians, in Thrace, v. 16; vii. 113

Dōdōna, i. 46; ii. 52, 57; ix. 93: people of Dodona, ii. 55, 57; iv. 33; priestesses, ii, 53, 55; prophetesses, ii. 55

Origin of the Oracle, ii. 54–57; consulted by Pelasgians, ii. 52; by Crœsus, i. 46; by people of Apollonia, ix. 93

Dolonkian Thracians, vi. 34–36, 40

Dolopians, vii. 132, 185

Dōrians, i. 57, 139, 171; v. 69, 72, 76; vi. 53, 55; vii. 95; viii. 31, 66, 73, 141; Dorians of Asia, i. 6, 28, 144; ii. 178; vii. 9a, 93, 99; of Lacedemon, iii. 56; from Corinth (the Leucadians), viii. 45; of Epidauros, i. 146; viii. 46

Doric (or Dorian) race, i. 56; vii. 99; viii. 43; Dorian dress, v. 87, 88; Dorian tribes, v. 68

Doris, Dorian land, viii. 31, 32, 43; Dorian land, *i.e.* Peloponnese, vii. 102

Dōrieus, Spartan, son of Anaxandrides, v. 41–48; vii. 158, 205; (father of Euryanax) ix. 10

Doriscos in Thrace, v. 98; vii. 25, 58, 59, 105, 106, 108, 121

Dōros, son of Hellen, i. 56

Doryssos, king of Sparta, in genealogy of Leonidas, vii. 204

Dōtos, Spartan commander, vii. 72

Dropicans, tribe of Persians, i. 125

Drymos, town in Phokis, viii. 33

Dryopis, i. 56; viii. 31, 43

Dryopians, i. 146; viii. 43, 46, 73

Dryos-Kephalai. See *Oak-heads*

Dwellers (in the country) round (perioicoi), of Lacedemon, vi. 58 (vii. 234), ix. 11; of Argos, viii. 73

Dymanatai, tribe of the Dorians, v. 68

Dymē, city of the Achaians, i. 145

Dyras, river of Trachis, vii. 198

Dysōron, mountain, v. 17

EARTH, worshipped by the Persians, i.
131; by the Scythians, iv. 59
Earth goddesses at Paros, vi. 134; at Gela,
vii. 153
Ecbatana. See *Agbatana*
Echecrates, father of Aëtiōn, v. 92*b*
[Echeidoros], vii. 124, *note*
Echemos, king of Tegea, ix. 26
Echestratos, king of Sparta, in genealogy
of Leonidas, vii. 204
Echinadĕs, islands, ii. 10
Ēdōnians in Thrace, v. 124; vii. 110, 114;
ix. 75; Myrkinos of the Edonians, v.
11
Egean Sea, (Aigaion), ii. 97, 113; iv. 85;
vii. 36, 55
Egesta, people of, v. 46, 47; vii. 158
Egina (1), daughter of Asopos, v. 80; vi. 35
(2), island, iii. 59, 131; v. 84, 85, 87; vi.
50, 61, 85, 88–90, 92; vii. 147; viii. 41,
60, 64, 79, 81, 83, 84, 92, 131, 132; ix.
75, 76; Eginĕtan land, v. 86
Eginĕtans (men) of Egina, ii. 178; iii.
59, 131; v. 80–84, 86–89; vi. 49, 50, 61,
64, 65, 73, 85, 87–94; vii. 144, 145, 203;
viii. 1, 46, 74, 84, 86, 91–93, 122; ix. 28,
31, 78–80, 85; Laodamas, Sostratos,
Polycritos, Crios, Aristocrates,
Casambos, Asonides, Ischenoös,
Pytheas, Lampon: Eginetan ships, vi.
92; vii. 179, 181; viii. 90, 92
The Eginetans were Dorians of
Epidauros, viii. 46; early history, v.
83; feud with Athenians, v. 82–89;
war with Samians in Crete, iii. 59;
they help the Thebans against
Athens, v. 80, 81, 89; give earth and
water to Dareios, vi. 49; Cleomenes
in Egina, vi. 50, 73; Eginetan
hostages at Athens, vi. 73, 85, 86;
renewed war with Athens, vi. 87–93;
peace made, vii. 105; ships at
Artemision, viii. 1; at Salamis, viii. 46;
in battle of Salamis, viii. 84, 86,
90–93; offerings at Delphi, viii. 122;
troops at Plataia, ix. 28, 31; wealth
and commerce of Eginetans, iv. 152;
ix. 80; mound at Plataia, ix. 85;
brooches of their women, v. 88
Egis. See *Agis*
Egypt, (Aigyptos), i. 1, 2, 5, 30, 77, 105,
140, 193, 198; ii. 1, 4–9, 11–13, 15–18,
22, 28, 31, 32, 34–36, 39, 43, 45, 47, 49,
50, 52, 55, 57, 61, 62, 65, 73, 75, 77, 79,
91, 94, 97, 97–99, 102, 105–109, 113,
116, 118, 119, 124, 129, 133, 135, 136,
137, 139–142, 144, 146, 147, 149–155,

157, 158, 160, 161, 171, 177–181; iii. 1,
3–7, 10, 11, 13–15, 19, 25, 30, 31, 34,
39, 42, 44, 45, 47, 61–63, 65, 88, 91, 97,
107, 126, 139, 140, 160; iv. 39, 41–43,
45, 47, 152, 159, 165–168, 180, 186,
200, 203–205; vii. 2, 4, 5, 7, 8, 20, 69,
89; Egyptian territory, i. 193
Egyptian(s), i. 77, 153, 182; ii. 2–5, 10,
13, 14, 15, 17–19, 28–30, 35–37, 39,
41–43, 45–51, 54, 57–59, 61–66, 69, 71,
75, 77, 79–82, 86, 90–92, 94, 98, 100,
103–105, 107–110, 119–124, 127–128,
132, 136, 137, 140–142, 145–148, 150,
152, 154, 156, 158, 160–163, 167–169,
171–173, 177; iii. 1, 2, 10–16, 24,
27–30, 32, 64, 129; iv. 42, 44, 141, 159,
181, 186; vi. 6, 53–55, 60; vii. 1, 4, 25,
34, 63, 89, 97; viii. 17, 68*c*, 100; ix. 32:
Egyptian wares, i. 1, works, i. 93;
measure of land, ii. 6; tongue, ii. 79;
writing, ii. (36), 106, 125; corslets, i.
135; cp. ii. 182; iii. 47; vii. 89; linen, ii.
105; equipment, ii. 106; customs, ii.
106; iv. 168; sea of Egypt, ii. 113;
Egyptian cubit, ii. 168; Egyptian
division (satrapy), iii. 91; physicians,
iii. (129), 132; armour, iv. 180; Nile of
Egypt, iv. 45, 53; daggers, knives, vii.
63, 91
Land of Egypt, measurements, ii. 6–9;
alluvial origin, ii. 5, 10–15; extent, ii.
15–19; river Nile and Upper Egypt,
ii. 19–34; discoveries of the
Egyptians, ii. 4; contrast of Egyptians
and other men, ii. 35, 36: Religion, ii.
37–65; ceremonial cleanliness, ii. 37;
priests, ii. 37; manner of sacrifice, ii.
38–42, 47, 48; mysteries, ii. 171;
divination, ii. 82, 83; influence of
Egyptians on Hellenes in religion, ii.
50–58; Hellenic rites in Egypt, ii. 91;
festivals and assemblies, ii. 59–64;
sacred animals, ii. 41, 42, 65–67, 69,
71–76; the crocodile, ii. 68–70; the
hippopotamus, ii. 71; fish of the Nile
and Delta, ii. 72, 93; winged serpents,
ii. 75; ibis, ii. 76: Habits of the
Egyptians, ii. 77–90; farming, ii. 14;
classes of the people, ii. 164–168; cp.
vi. 60; physicians, ii. 84; iii. 1, 130;
health and food, ii. 77, 84; coffin at
feasts, ii. 78; song of Linos, ii. 79;
respect to elders, ii. 80; dress, ii. 81;
equipment, vii. 89; divination, ii. 82,
83; funerals and embalming, ii.
85–90; aversion to foreign customs,
ii. 91; customs in the Delta, ii. 92, 94,

Ōlēn, Lykian, iv. 35

Ōlenos, city of the Achaians, i. 145

Oliatos, Mylasian, v. 37

Olophyxos, town of Athōs, vii. 22

Oloros, father of Hegesipylē, king of the Thracians, vi. 39, 41

Olympia, vii. 170; viii. 134; ix. 81: Olympic games (festival, victory, contest), games at Olympia, i. 59; ii. 160; v. 22 (Alexander), 47 (Philip), 71 (Kylon), vi. 36 (Miltiades), 70 (Demaratos), 103 (Kimon), [122, (Callias)], 125 (Alcmaion), 126 (Cleisthenes), 127 (usurpation of Pheidon), vii. 206; viii. 26 (games described to Xerxes), viii. 72; ix. 33 (Tisamenos)

Olympiodōros, Athenian, ix. 21

Olympos (1), in Thessaly, i. 56; vii. 128, 129, 173; pass by Olympos, vii. 172
    Zeus in Olympos, i. 65; vii. 141; Olympian Zeus, ii. 7; Heraclēs, ii. 44
    (2), in Mysia, i. 36, 43; vii. 74: Olympiēnoi, vii. 74

Olynthos, city of Chalkidikē, vii. 122; viii. 127: people of Olynthos, viii. 127

Ombricans, i.e. Umbrians, in Italy, i. 94; iv. 49

Oneātai, tribe of the Sikyonians, v. 68

Onēsilos of Salamis in Cyprus, v. 104, 105, 108, 110–115

Onētēs, Carystian, vii. 214

Onochōnos, river of Thessaly, vii. 129, 196

Onomacritos, oracle-monger, vii. 6

Onomastos, Eleian, suitor of Agaristē, vi. 127

Onūphis, district (nome) of, in Egypt, ii. 166

Ophryneion, town of Troas, vii. 43

Ōpis (1), city of Assyria, i. 189
    (2), maiden of the Hyperboreans, iv. 35

Opoia, wife of Ariapeithes, iv. 78

Opūs, Locrians of, vii. 203; viii. 1

Orbēlos, mountain, v. 16

Orchomenos (1), in Arcadia, vii. 202; Orchomenians, of Orchomenos, vii. 202; ix. 28, 31
    (2), in Bœotia, ix. 16: of Orchomenos, i. 146; viii. 34; Thersander, ix. 16

Ordēssos, tributary of the Ister, iv. 48

Oreithuia, daughter of Erechtheus, vii. 189

Orestēs, son of Agamemnon, i. 67, 68

Orestheion, town of Arcadia, ix. 11

[Orgempaians]. See Argippaians

Orgeus, father of Antipater, vii. 118

Oricos, Scythian, iv. 78

Ōricos, port of Apollonia, ix. 93

Orneates of Argos, viii. 73; (Orneai, viii. 73)

Oroitēs, Persian satrap, iii. 120–129, 140

Ōromedōn, Kilikian, father of Syennesis, vii. 98

Ōrōpos, in Attica, vi. 101

Ōros, Horus, Egyptian name of Apollo, ii. 144, 156

Orotalt, Arabian name of Dionysos, iii. 8

Orphic observances, ii. 81

Orsiphantos, father of Maron and Alpheos, vii. 227

Orthian measure, i. 24

Orthocorybantians, iii. 92

Orthōsia, Artemis, at Byzantion, iv. 87

Osiris, Egyptian name of Dionysos, ii. 42, 144, 156. Cp. ii. 86, 132, 171, and see also Dionysos

Ossa, mountain, i. 56; vii. 128, 129, 173

Otanēs (1), Persian, son of Pharnaspes, iii. 68–72, 76, 80, 81, 83, 84, 88, 141, 144, 147, 149; vi. 43
    His conspiracy, iii. 68–84; his speech for democracy, iii. 80; privileges given to him, iii. 84; sent to Samos, iii. 141
    (2), father of Amestris, vii. 40, 61, 62, 82
    (3), son of Sisamnes, v. 25, 26, (28), 116–123

Otaspēs, son of Artachaies, vii. 63

Othryadēs, Spartan, i. 82

Othrys, mountain, vii. 129

Ovens (Ipnoi), vii. 188

Ozolian Locrians, viii. 32. See Locrians

Pactōlos, river of Lydia, v. 101

Pactyans, vii. 67, 68; equipment of the Pactyans, vii. 85; land of Pactyïkē, iii. 102; iv. 44; (near Armenia), iii. 93

Pactyas, Lydian, i. 153–161

Pactyē, town of the Chersonese, vi. 36

Padaians, iii. 99

Pagasai, place in Magnesia, vii. 193

Paiania, deme of Attica, i. 60

Paionia (1), region of Thrace, v. 13, 14, 98; vii. 124; viii. 115; ix. 32
    Paionians, iv. 49; v. 1, 2, 12–15, 17, 23, 98; vii. 113, 124, 185; viii. 115; ix. 32; women of Paionia, iv. 33; v. 13; Mantyas, Pigres, v. 12
    Paionians removed by Dareios, v. 14, 15; return, v. 98
    (2), in Attica, v. 62

Paioplians, v. 15; vii. 113

Paios, town of the Azanians, vi. 127

Paisos, town on the Hellespont, v. 117

Paitians, vii. 110

Palace (anactoron) at Eleusis, ix. 65

Palestine, Syria, i. 105; ii. 106; iii. 91; iv. 39; vii. 89: Syrians of Palestine, ii. 104; iii. 5; vii. 89
Palians, men of Palē, ix. 28, 31
Pallas, (v. 77); vii. 141; statues of, iv. 189. See *Athenē*
Pallēnē (1), peninsula of Chalkidikē, vii. 123; viii. 126, 129; ix. 28; men of Pallēnē, viii. 128
 (2), deme of Attica, Ameinias of Pallenē, viii. 84, 93; Athenē of Pallenē, i. 62
Pamisos, river of Thessaly, vii. 129
Pammōn of Skyros, vii. 183
Pamphylians, i. 28; iii. 90; vii. 91; viii. 68c
Pamphyloi, a tribe of the Dorians, v. 68
Pan, ii. 145, 146; vi. 105, 106; of the Egyptians (Mendes), ii. (42), 46, 145
Panaitios, Tenian, viii. 82
Panathēnaia, festival at Athens, v. 56
Pandiōn, Athenian, i. 173; vii. 92
Pangaion, mountain, v. 16; vii. 112, 113, 115
Paniōnia, festival of the Ionians, i. 148
Paniōnion at Mycalē, i. 141–143, 148, 170; vi. 7
Paniōnios, Chian, viii. 105, 106
Panitēs, Messenian, vi. 52
Panopeus, town of Phokis, viii. 34, 35
Panormos, harbour near Miletos, i. 157
Pantagnōtos, Samian, brother of Polycrates, iii. 39
Pantaleōn, Lydian, son of Alyattes, i. 92
Pantarēs, father of Cleander, vii. 154
Panthialaians, tribe of the Persians, i. 125
Panticapēs, river of Scythia, iv. 18, 19, 47, 54
Pantimathoi, in the 11th satrapy, iii. 92
Pantitēs, Spartan, vii. 232
Papaios, Zeus of the Scythians, iv. 59
Paphlagonians, i. 6, 28, 72; iii. 90; vii. 72; equipment of the Paphlagonians, vii. 73
Paphos, city of Cyprus, vii. 195
 Paphians, Demonoös, Penthylos, vii. 195
Paprēis, city of Egypt, ii. 59, 63; iii. 12; district (nome) of Paprēmis, ii. 71, 165
Paraibatēs, Spartan, v. 46
Paralatai, Scythians, iv. 6
Parapotamioi, town of Phokis, viii. 33, 34
Parētakēnians, tribe of the Medes, i. 101
Paricanians, in 10th satrapy, iii. 92, 94; vii. 68, 86
Parion, town of the Hellespont, v. 117; Herophantos of Parion, iv. 136

Parmys, daughter of Smerdis, iii. 88; vii. 78
Parnassos, mountain, viii. 27, 32, 35–37, 39; ix. 31
Parōreatai, iv. 148; viii. 73
Paros, island, v. 31; vi. 133–136
 Parians, v. 28–30; vi. 133–136; viii. 67, 112; Archilochos, i. 12; Tisias, Lysagoras, vi. 133; Parian stone, iii. 57; v. 62
 Reform of Miletos by the Parians, v. 28, 29; Paros attacked by Miltiades, vi. 133–135; Themistocles bribes, viii. 112
Parthenion mountain, vi. 105
Parthenios, river, ii. 104
Parthians, iii. 93, 117; vii. 66
Pasargadai, tribe of the Persians, i. 125; Badres, iv. 167
Pasiclēs, father of Philistos, ix. 97
Pataicoi, of the Phenicians, iii. 37
Pataicos, father of Ainesidemos, vii. 154
Patara, city of Lykia, i. 182
Patarbēmis, Egyptian, ii. 162
Patiramphēs, son of Otanes, vii. 40
Patizeithēs, Magian, iii. 61, 63. See *Magian*
Patreis, city of the Achaians, i. 145
Patūmos, city of Arabia, ii. 158
Pausanias, son of Cleombrotos, iv. 81; v. 32; viii. 3; ix. 10–13, 21, 28, 45–47, 50, 53–57, 60–62, 64, 69, 72, 76, 78, 80–82, 87, 88, 101
 Position at Sparta, ix. 10; sets out for the Isthmus, ix. 10, 11; at Plataia, ix. 21–79; division of the spoil, ix. 80, 81; siege of Thebes, ix. 86–88; his later designs, v. 32
Pausicai, in the 11th satrapy, iii. 92
Pausiris, son of Amyrtaios, iii. 15
[Pausoi.] See *Pausicai*
Pēdasos, Pēdasa, city, v. 121; viii. 104: Pedasians, of Pedasa, i. 175, 176; vi. 20; viii. 104, 105; Hermotimos, viii. 104
Pedieis, town in Phokis, viii. 33
Peirēnē, fountain at Corinth, v. 92b
Peiros, river in Achaia, i. 145
Peisistratos (1), son of Nestor, v. 65
 (2), despot of Athens, i. 59–64; v. 65, 71, 94; vi. 35, 103, 121; son (sons, family) of Peisistratos, v. 55, 62, 63, 65, 70, 76, 90, 91, 93; vi. 39, 94, 102, 103, 107, 123; vii. 6; viii. 52. See also *Hipparchos, Hippias*
Peithagoras, despot of Selinus, v. 46
Pelasgians, i. 57; ii. 50–52; iv. 145; v. 26; vi. 136–140; viii. 44; Pelasgians of the

coast-land, vii. 94; of Arcadia, i. 146;
Pelasgian race, i. 56–58; vii. 95;
Pelasgian women, ii. 171; vi. 138;
Pelasgian cities, i. 57; Pelasgian wall,
v. 64; Antandros of the Pelasgians,
vii. 42; Hellas formerly called
Pelasgia, ii. 56
   Language, i. 57; religion, ii. 50–52;
   connexion with Athenians, i. 56–58;
   ii. 51; vi. 137–140; viii. 44; in Lemnos,
   vi. 138–140
Pēleus, vii. 191
Pēlion, mountain, iv. 179; vii. 129, 188; viii.
   8, 12
Pella, city, vii. 123
Pellēnē, city of the Achaians, i. 145
Peloponnesus, Peloponnese, i. 56, 61, 68,
   145; ii. 171; iii. 56, 59, 148; iv. 179; v.
   42, 74; vi. 86a, 127; vii. 93, 94, 147,
   163, 168, 202, 207, 228, 235, 236; viii.
   31, 40, 43, 44, 49, 50, 57, 60, 65, 68b,
   70, 71, 73, 74, 79, 100, 101, 113, 141;
   ix. 6, 9, 26, 27, 39, 50; land of Pelops,
   vii. 8c, 11
   Peloponnesians, ii. 171; iv. 77, 161; v. 74,
   76; vi. 79, 127; vii. 137, 139, 207, 235;
   viii. 40, 44, 71, 72, 75, 79, 108; ix. 8, 19,
   26, 73, 106, 114
   Peoples of Peloponnese, viii. 73;
   Dorian invasion, i. 56; ii. 171; ix. 26;
   Ionians in Peloponnese, i. 145; vii. 94;
   ix. 26; security of, vi. 86a;
   Peloponnesians at Salamis, viii. 43;
   Peloponnesian war referred to, ix.
   73. See also Isthmus
Pelops, vii. 8, 11; son of Pelops
   (Agamemnon), vii. 159
Pēlūsion, city of Egypt, ii. 15, 141;
   Pelusian mouth of the Nile, ii. 17
   154; iii. 10; salting-houses of
   Pelusion, ii. 15; Daphnai near
   Pelusion, ii. 30, 107
Pēneios, river, vii. 20, 128–130, 173, 182
Pēnelopē, mother of Pan, ii. 145, 146
Pentapolis, "Five Cities" of the Dorians, i.
   144
Penthylos, Paphian, vii. 195
Percalos, daughter of Chilon, vi. 65
Percōtē, city of the Hellespont, v. 117
Perdiccas, king of the Macedonians, v. 22;
   viii. 137, 139
Pergamos, stronghold of the Pierians, vii.
   112
Perialla, prophetess of Delphi, vi. 66
Periander, son of Kypselos, i. 20, 23, 24;
   iii. 48–53; v. 92, 95
Periclēs, son of Xanthippos, vi. 131

Perilaos of Sikyon, ix. 103
Perinthos, city, iv. 90; v. 2; vi. 33:
   Perinthians, men of Perinthos, v. 1, 2;
   vii. 25
Perphereës at Delos, iv. 33
Perraibians or Perrhaibians, vii. 128, 131,
   132, 173, 185
Persēs, son of Perseus, vii. 61, 150;
   children of Perses, vii. 220; Perseïd
   kings, i. 125
Perseus, ii. 91; vi. 53, 54; vii. 61, 150;
   "watch-tower of Perseus" (in
   Egypt), ii. 15
Persia, Persian land, i. 126, 208, 209, 211;
   iii. 1, 4, 30, 70, 72, 89, 97, 102; iv. 39,
   40, 143; vii. 8c, 29, [53 note], 107;
   (land of the Persians, i. 108, 121, 123,
   157, etc.)
Persian(s), i. 1, 2, 4, 5, 46, 53, 71, 72, 75, 77,
   80, 84–86, 88–91, 94, 95, 102, 107
   (Cambyses), 108, 120–135, 137, 141,
   143, 148, 153, 156–160, 164, 165, 191,
   192, 206–208, 210, 211, 214; ii. 30, 98,
   99, 110 (Dareios), 158 (Dareios),
   167; iii. 1, 2, 7, 11–16, 19, 21, 22, 26,
   30, 31, 34–37, 61, 63, 65–70, 73–77,
   79–81, 83, 84, 87–89, 91, 97, 102, 105,
   117, 120 (Oroites, Mitrobates),
   126–128, 134–138, 140, 144–147, 149,
   151, 154, 155, 156–158, 160; iv. 37, 39,
   84 (Oiobazos), 91, 97, 118, 119, 120,
   122–125, 127–136, 140, 142, 143
   (Megabazos), 200–204; v. 1, 2, 10, 15,
   17–22, 27, 32, 33 (Megabates), 34, 36,
   73, 96, 97, 101, 102, 108–110, 113,
   116–122; vi. 4, 7, 9–11, 13, 18–21, 24,
   25, 28 (Harpagos), 29, 30, 32, 33,
   41–43, 45, 49, 54, 59, 94, 96, 98–101,
   112–115, 119, 121, 133; vii. 1–6, 8–14,
   16, 18, 19, 22 (Bubares, Artachaies),
   27, 33 (Artaÿctes), 37, 40, 41, 50, 51,
   53, 55, 56, 59, 61, 62, 72, 83, 84, 85, 86,
   96, 103, 106, 107, 114, 117, 132, 135
   (Hydarnes), 138, 139, 145, 148, 149,
   152, 157, 163, 166, 168, 172, 177, 181,
   184, 190, 202, 207, 211, 212, 214;
   217–219, 224, 225, 229, 233, 236, 238;
   viii. 3, 6, 8, 26, 46, 52, 53, 66, 76, 85,
   89, 90 (Ariaramnes), 92, 95, 98–101,
   108, 109, 113, 116–119, 126, 129, 130,
   136, 141; ix. 1, 6–11, 16, 20, 21, 24, 27,
   31, 38–43, 46–48, 51, 58, 59, 61–63,
   65–68, 70, 71, 76, 81, 90, 96, 98, 99,
   102–104, 106, 107, 109 (gift), 110, 115
   (Oiobazos), 116, 118, 122; Persian
   women, iii. 3; Persian power, rule, iii.
   97, 101, 137; Persian army, force, iv.

Persia (continued)
136; vii. 52; viii. 13, 106; ix. 14, 33;
Persian fleet, vi. 31; Persian dress,
equipments, vii. 62, 85; Persian
sword, vii. 54, (viii. 120); Persian
language, tongue, vi. 29; viii. 85; ix.
110; Persian fashion, v. 12
Geographical position of Persia, iv.
37–40; Royal road, v. 52–54;
primitive character of the Persians, i.
71, 89; advice of Cyrus, ix. 122; tribes
of the Persians, i. 125; Persian claim
to Asia, i. 4; ix. 116; Persian customs,
i. 131–141; religion, i. 131, 132; iii. 16;
names, i. 139; vi. 98; birthdays, i. 133;
ix. 110; salutations, i. 134; education,
i. 136; ready adoption of foreign
customs, i. 135; have no markets, i.
153; long hair, vi. 19; respect for sons
of kings, iii. 15; for valour, vii. 238;
viii. 181; customs of succession to the
throne, iii. 2; vi. 59; vii. 2; water of
Choaspes, i. 188; kings above the law,
iii. 31; honourable gifts, iii. 84; gift of
an army, ix. 109; regard for services
rendered, iii. 153, 160; couriers, viii.
98; manner of fighting (described by
Aristagoras), v. 49, 97; burial, i. 140;
thinness of skulls, iii. 12: Revolt of
Persians against Medes, i. 123–130;
Crœsus alarmed by Persian power, i.
46; campaign against Crœsus, i.
76–85; Persian conquest of Ionia, i.
162–170; of Upper Asia and
Babylon, i. 177, 188, 191; expedition
against the Massagetai, i. 205–214;
expedition to Egypt, iii. 1–13; against
Ethiopians and Ammonians, iii. 25,
26; conspiracy of the seven Persians,
iii. 68–88; satrapies and revenue, iii.
89–97; Persians sent to explore
Hellas, iii. 135–138; conquest of
Samos, iii. 139–149; revolt and
capture of Babylon, iii. 150–159;
Scythian expedition, iv. 1, 83–144;
expedition against Barca, iv.
200–204; conquest of the coasts of
Thrace, iv. 144; v. 1, 14–16: embassy
to Macedonia, v. 17–21; expedition to
Cyprus, v. 108–116; Ionic revolt
suppressed, vi. 6–20; islands
conquered, vi. 31–33; pacification of
Ionia, vi. 42; expedition of
Mardonios, vi. 43–45; of Datis and
Artaphrenes, vi. 94–119;
appointment of a successor by
Dareios, vii. 2–4; expedition of

Xerxes, vii. 19–viii. 120; order of
march, vii. 41; crossing the
Hellespont, vii. 54–56; review at
Doriscos, vii. 59–100; equipment of
Persians, vii. 61, 83, 84; Persians
serving in ships, vii. 96; advance from
Doriscos to Thermopylai and
Artemision, vii. 108–132, 179–201;
Persians at Thermopylai, vii. 211,
215–219; fleet at Artemision, viii.
6–23; attack on Delphi, viii. 35–39;
occupation of Athens, viii. 50–54;
fleet at Phaleron, viii. 66; battle of
Salamis, viii. 84–95; return of Xerxes,
viii. 113–120; fleet at Samos, viii. 130;
army of Mardonios, viii. 113;
Mardonios in Thessaly, viii. 115, 133;
ix. 1; second occupation of Athens,
ix. 3; Persian army in Bœotia and
battle of Plataia, ix. 15–84;
marshalling of army at Plataia, ix. 31,
32; Persians defeated at Mycalē, ix.
96–107; Persian towns captured,
Sestos, ix. 114–121; Eïon, vii. 107;
relation of Persians with Argives, vii.
150–152; ix. 12; Persians cited as
authority, i. 2, 4, 5; iii. 1, 105; vi. 54.
See also *Barbarians, Medes, Cyrus,
Cambyses, Dareios, Xerxes,
Mardonios*
Persuasion personified (Peithō), viii. 111
Petra, deme of Corinth, v. 92*b, c*
Phagrēs, stronghold of the Pierians, vii. 112
Phaidymē, daughter of Otanes, iii. 68, 69
Phainippos, father of Callias, vi. 121
Phalēron in Attica, v. 63, 81, 85; vi. 116;
viii. 66, 67, 91–93, 107, 108; ix. 32;
plain of Phaleron, v. 63
Phanagoras, Carystian, father of Onetes,
vii. 214
Phanēs, of Halicarnassos, iii. 4, 11
Pharandatēs, Persian commander, vii. 79;
ix. 76
Pharbaïthos, district (nome) of, in Egypt,
ii. 166
Phareis, city of the Achaians, i. 145
Pharnakēs, father of Artabazos, vii. 66;
viii. 126; ix. 41, 66, 89
Pharnaspēs, (father of Cassandanē) ii. 1;
iii. 2, (of Otanes) 68
Pharnazathrēs, Persian commander, vii. 65
Pharnūchēs, Persian commander of
cavalry, vii. 88
Phasēlis, city of the Dorians, ii. 178
Phasis, river, i. 2, 104; ii. 103; iv. 37, 38, 45,
86; vi. 84
Phaÿllos, of Croton, viii. 47

Phēgeus, father of Aëropos of Tegea, ix. 26. See *note*.
Pheidippides, Athenian, vi. 105, 106
Pheidōn, despot of the Argives, vi. 127
Pheneos, city of Arcadia, vi. 74
Phenicia (Phoinikē), i. 2; ii. 44, 49, 79, 116; iii. 5, 6, 91, 136; iv. 38, 39, 45; vi. 3, 17; vii. 90
Phenicians (Phoinikes), i. 1, 5, 105, 143; ii. 32 (in Libya), 44, 54, 56, 104, 112, 116; iii. 19, 37, 107, 111; iv. 42, 44, 147, 197 (of Libya); v. 46 (of Libya), 57, 58, 108, 109, 112; vi. 3, 6, 14, 25, 28, 33, 34, 41, 47, 104; vii. 23, 25, 34, 44, 89, 96, 165, 167 (of Libya); viii. 85, 90, 100, 119; ix. 96; Thales, i. 170; Poikiles, Membliaros, iv. 147; Agenor, Kilix, vii. 91; also Agenor, Cadmos, Europa, Anysos, Tetramnestos, Agbalos, Merbalos, Siromos, Matten; Phenician ship, vi. 118; viii. 118, 121; merchant ships, viii. 97; "phenicians" (*i.e.* letters), v. 58; Phenician mines, vi. 47; Phenician "Pataicoi," iii. 37; Phenician lyre, iv. 192
Origin of the Phenicians, i. 1; they colonise Thera, iv. 147; Thasos, vi. 47; in Persian fleet, iii. 19; v. 108; vi. 6, 14, 28, 33, 41; equipment, vii. 89; at Salamis, viii. 85, 90; dismissed before Mycalē, ix. 96 : Voyages and commerce, i. 1; iii. 107; iv. 42; naval skill, iii. 19; vii. 44, 96; engineering, vii. 23, 34; introduce letters into Hellas, v. 58
Pherendatēs, Persian commander, vii. 67
Pheretimē, mother of Arkesilaos (3), iv. 162, 165, 167, 200, 202, 205
Pherōs, king of Egypt, ii. 111
Phigalian, Cleander, vi. 83
Philagros, Eretrian, vi. 101
Philaios, son of Ajax, vi. 35
Philaōn, Salaminian, son of Chersis, viii. 11
Philēs, father of Rhoicos, iii. 60
Philip (1), king of the Macedonians, viii. 139
(2), son of Butakides, v. 47
[Philippidēs.] See *Pheidippides*
Philistos, son of Pasicles, ix. 97
[Philitiōn.] See *Philitis*
Philitis, the shepherd, ii. 128. See *note*
Philokyōn, Spartan, ix. 71, 85
Philokypros, king of the Solians, v. 113
Phla, island in lake Tritonis, iv. 178
Phlegra, ancient name of Pallenē, vii. 123

Phliūs, city, vii. 202: Phliasians, men of Phlius, viii. 72; ix. 28, 31, 69, 85
Phōcaia, city, i. 80, 142, 152, 162, 164, 165, 168; ii. 106, 178; vi. 17
Phocaians, men of Phocaia, i. 163–167; vi. 8; Pythermos, i. 152; Laodamas, iv. 138; Dionysios, vi. 11, 17
Discoveries of the Phocaian voyagers, i. 163; abandonment of their city, i. 164–167; Ladē, vi. 8–17
Phœbus (Phoibos), iv. 155; possessed by Phœbus, iv. 13; temple of Phœbus at Sparta, vi. 61. See *Apollo*
Phoinikē, See *Phenicia*
Phoinix, river of Trachis, vii. 176, 200
Phōkians, i. 46, 146; vi. 34; vii. 176, 203, 207, 212, 215, 217, 218; viii. 27–33, 134; ix. 17, 18, 31, 89
Phōkis, Phōkian land, viii. (27), 31, 32, 35; (ix. 66)
Relations with Thessalians, vii. 176; viii. 27–30; at Thermopylai, vii. 203, 207; guarding the mountain path, vii. 212, 215, 217, 218; Phokis laid waste by the Persians, viii. 31–33; Phokians with Mardonios, ix. 17, 18, 31
Phormos, Athenian, vii. 182
Phraortēs (1), father of Deïokes, i. 96
(2), son of Deïokes, i. 73, 102, 103
Phratagūnē, daughter of Artanes, wife of Dareios, vii. 224
Phricōnis, *i.e.* Kymē, i. 149. See *Kymē*
Phrixai, city of the Minyai, iv. 148
Phrixos, son of Athamas, vii. 197
Phronimē, daughter of Etearchos (2), iv. 154, 155
Phrygia, i. 14, 35; v. 52, 98; vii. 26, 30, 31; viii. 136; Phrygian division (satrapy), iii. 127
Phrygians, i. 28, 72; ii. 2; iii. 90; v. 49 (Eastern); vii. 26, 30, 73; ix. 32; Gordias (1), Midas, i. 14; Gordias (2), Adrastos, i. 35; Pelops, vii. 8
Phrynichos, Athenian dramatist, vi. 21
Phrynōn, Theban, father of Attaginos, ix. 16
Phthios, son of Achaios, ii. 98
Phthiōtis, i. 56; Achaians of, vii. 132
Phya, Athenian woman, i. 60
Phylacos (1), hero at Delphi, viii. 39
(2), Samian, viii. 85
Phyllis, land of, vii. 113
Pieria, in Macedonia, vii. 131, 177; pitch of Pieria, iv. 195: Pierians, vii. 112, 185
Pigrēs (1), Carian, vii. 98
(2), Paionian, v. 12

Pilōros, town of Chalchidikē, vii, 122
Pindar, iii. 38
Pindos (1), mountain, vii. 129
(2), town i. 56; viii. 43
Piræus (Peiraieus), viii. 85
Pisa, city, ii. 7
Pistyros, city of Thrace, vii. 109
Pitanē (1), city of the Aiolians, i. 149
Pitanē (2), deme of Sparta, iii. 55;
Pitanate division (lochos), or
division of the Pitanates, ix. 53
Pittacos, of Mytilenē, i. 27
Pixōdaros, Kindyan, v. 118
Plakia, town on the Hellespont, i. 57; men of, i. 57
Plataia (or Plataiai), city, vii. 232; viii. 50;
ix. 7, 16, 25, 30, 31, 35, 39, 41, 65, 72,
76, 78, 81, 85, 86, 89, 90, 100, 101;
battle of Plataia, events about
Plataia, vii. 232; viii. 126; ix. 38
Men of Plataia, Plataians, vi. 108, 111,
113; vii. 132, 233; viii. 1, 44, 50, 66; ix.
28, 31, 51, 52 (city of), 61, 83;
Arimnestos, ix. 72; Autodicos,
Cleades, ix. 85; Plataian land, ix. 15,
25, 36, 101
Connexion with Athenians, ix. 108, 111;
Plataians at Marathon, vi. 108, 111,
113; ships manned by Plataians, viii.
1; return to Plataia, viii. 44; city burnt
by Persians, viii. 50; battle of Plataia,
ix. 28–85
Platea, island of Libya, iv. 151–153, 156, 169
Pleistarchos, son of Leonidas, ix. 10
Pleistōros, god of the Apsinthians, ix. 119
Plinthinē, gulf of, ii. 6
Plynos, harbour of Libya, iv. 168
Pōgōn, harbour of the Troizenians, viii. 42
Poikilēs, father of Membliaros, iv. 147
Poliadēs, father of Amompharetos, ix. 53
Polias (Athene), at Athens, v. 82
Polichnē (1), of the Chians, vi. 26
(2), in Crete, men of, vii. 170
Poliūchos (Athene), in Chios, i. 160
Polyas, of Antikyra, viii. 21
Polybos, king of Sikyon, v. 67
Polycratēs, despot of Samos, ii. 182; iii.
39–46, 54, 56, 57, 120–126, 128, 131,
132, 139, 140, 142
His successes, iii. 39; relations with
Amasis, iii. 40–43; war with
Lacedemonians and Corinthians, iii.
45–49, 54–56; death of Polycrates, iii.
120–125
Polycritos (1), Eginetan, father of Crios,
vi. 50, 73

Polycritos (2), son of Crios, viii. 92, 93
Polydamna, wife of Thon, ii. 116
Polydectēs, king of Sparta, in genealogy
of Leotychides, viii. 131
Polydōros (1), son of Cadmos, v. 69
(2), king of Sparta, in genealogy of
Leonidas, vii. 204
Polymnēstos, father of Battos (1), iv. 150,
155
Polyneikēs, father of Thersander, iv. 147;
vi. 52; ix. 27
Pontus, iv. 8, 10, 38, 46, 81, 85, 86, 87, 89,
95, 99; vi. 5, 26; vii. 36, 55, 95, 147. See
also Euxine
Measurement, iv. 85, 86; trading-
stations of the Pontic coast, iv. 24;
Hellenes of Pontus, iv. 8, 10, 95; vii. 95
Porata, tributary of the Ister, iv. 48
Poseidōn, ii. 43, 50; vii. 129; viii. 55; "the
Saviour," vii. 192, 193; at Mycalē
(Heliconios), i. 148; at the Isthmus,
viii. 123; ix. 81; at Potidaia, viii. 129;
of the Libyans, iv. 180, 188; of the
Scythians (Thagimasadas), iv. 59
Poseidōnia, of, i. 167
Poseidōnios, Spartan, ix. 71, 85
Posideion (1), border city of Syria, iii. 91
(2), town of Thrace, vii. 115
Potidaia, city, vii. 123; viii. 127, 128:
Potidaians, men of Potidaia, viii.
126–129; ix. 28, 31
Connexion with Corinth, ix. 28; revolt
from Persians and siege, viii. 126–129
Potniai, "Revered goddesses," ix. 97
Pots (Chytroi), at Thermopylai, vii. 176
Poverty, personified (Penia), viii. 111
Praisos, in Crete, men of, vii, 170–171
Prasias, lake, v. 15–17
Prēxaspēs (1), Persian, bearer of
messages for Cambyses, iii. 30, 34, 35,
62, 63, 65, 66, 74–76, 78
(2), son of Aspathines, Persian
commander, vii. 97
Prēxilaos, father of Xeinagoras, ix. 107
Prēxinos, Troizenian, vii. 180
Priam, i. 3, 4; ii. 120; Citadel of Priam, vii. 43
Priēnē, city, i. 142: Prienians, men of
Priēnē, i. 15, 161; vi. 8; Bias, i. 170
Prinētadēs, son of Demarmenos, Spartan,
v. 41
Proclēs (1), son of Aristodemos, king of
Sparta, iv. 147; vi. 52; viii. 131
(2), despot of Epidauros, iii. 50–52
Proconnēsos, city, iv. 14, 15; vi. 33: of
Proconnesos, Caÿstrobios, Aristeas,
iv. 13; Metrodoros, iv. 138

Promeneia, priestess at Dodona, ii. 55
Promētheus, husband of Asia, iv. 45
Pronaia (Athenē), at Delphi, i. 92; viii. 37, 39
Propontis, iv. 85; v. 122
Propylaia, at Athens, v. 77
Prosōpitis, island in the Delta of Egypt, ii. 41, 165
Prōtesilaos, hero at Elaius, vii. 33; ix. 116, 120
Prōteus, king of Egypt, ii. 112, 114–116, 118, 121
Protothyas, father of Madyas, i. 103
Prytaneion or City Hall, vi. 38; at Athens, vi. 103, 139; at Alos, vii. 197
Prytanis, king of Sparta, in genealogy of Leotychides, viii. 131
Psammēnitos, son of Amasis, king of Egypt, iii. 10, 14, 15
Psammētichos (1), son of Necos, king of Egypt, i. 105; ii. 2, 28, 30, 151–154, 157, 158, 161
  Twice exiled, ii. 151, 152; becomes sole king, ii. 152; reign, ii. 157; bribes the Scythians, i. 105; his experiments, ii. 2, 28; pursuit of the Deserters, ii. 30; most prosperous of all the Egyptian kings, ii. 161
  (2), father of Inaros, vii. 7
Psammis, son of Necos, king of Egypt, ii. 159–161
Psylloi, in Libya, iv. 173
Psyttaleia, island near Salamis, viii. 76, 95
Pteria, region of Cappadokia, i. 76: Pterians, i. 76
Ptōon, in Bœotia, viii. 135; Ptoan Apollo, viii. 135
Pylagoroi. See Pylai
Pylai, i.e. Thermopylai, vii. 201; assembly (of the Amphictyons) at Pylai (Pylaia), vii. 213; deputies at Pylai (Pylagoroi), vii. 213
Pylaia. See Pylai
Pylians, v. 65; Cauconians of Pylos, i. 147
Pylos (1), ix. 34. Cp. i. 147
  (2), in Laconia, vii. 168
Pyrēnē, city of Western Europe, ii. 33
Pyretos, tributary of Ister (Porata), iv. 48
Pyrgos, city of the Minyai, iv. 148
Pythagoras (1), Samian, son of Mnesarchos, iv. 95, 96; Pythagorean observances, ii. 81
  (2), Milesian, v. 126
Pytheas (1), Eginetan, son of Ischenoös, vii. 181: viii. 92
  (2), Eginetan, father of Lampon, ix. 78

Pythermos, Phocaian, i. 152
Pythēs, of Abdera, father of Nymphodoros, vii. 137
Pythian games, [vi. 122 (Callias)], viii. 47 (Phaÿllos)
Pythian prophetess at Delphi, i. 13, 19, 47, 48, 55, 65–67, 85, 91, 167, 174; iii. 57, 58; iv. 15, 150, 151, 155–157, 159, 161, 163, 164; v. 43, 63, 66, 67, 79, 82, 90, 92; vi. 34, 35, 52, 66, 75, 77, 86c, 123, 135, 136, 139; vii. 140, 142, 148, 169, 171, 220; viii. 51; ix. 33; Perialla, vi. 66; Aristonikē, vii. 140. See Delphi
Pythians at Sparta, vi. 57
Pythios, Lydian, son of Atys, vii. 27, 28, 38, 39
Pythō (i.e. Delphi), i. 54
Pythogenēs of Zanclē, vi. 23

"REMOVED" (Anaspastoi), in islands of Erythraian Sea, iii. 93; vii. 80
"Revered goddesses" (Potniai), ix. 97
Rhampsinitos, king of Egypt, ii. 121, 122, 124
Rhēgion, city, i. 166, 167; vi. 23: men of Rhegion, vii. 170, 171; Anaxilaos, Kydippē, vii. 165
Rhēnaia, island near Delos, vi. 97
Rhodes, island, i. 174; ii. 178; vii. 153
Rhodopē, mountains, iv. 49; viii. 116
Rhodōpis, courtesan, ii. 134, 135
Rhoicos, Samian, iii. 60
Rhoition, city of Troas, vii. 43
Rhypěs, city of the Achaians, i. 145
Riot (Coros) personified, viii. 77
Round Pool (Trochoeidēs) at Delos, ii. 170
Royal Judges, iii. 14, 31; v. 25; vii. 194
Royal Scythians, iv. 20, 22, 56, 59, 71, 110 (free Scythians)
Rugged Chersonese, iv. 99

SABACŌS, king of the Ethiopians, ii. 137, 139, 152
Sabyllos of Gela, vii. 154
Sacans, i. 153; iii. 93; vi. 113; vii. 9, 64 (Amyrgian), 96, 184; viii. 113; ix. 31, 71, 113
  of Scythian race, vii. 64; in 15th satrapy, iii. 93; serving in the fleet, vii. 96; viii. 113
Sacred way, vi. 34
Sadyattēs, king of the Lydians, i. 16, 18, 73
Sagartians, tribe of the Persians, i. 125; iii. 93; vii. 85 (as cavalry)
Saïs, city of Egypt, ii. 28, 59, 62, 130, 163, 169, 170, 175, 176; iii. 16: people of Saïs, ii. 169; Amasis, ii. 172; district

Saïs (continued)
   (nome) of Saïs, ii. 152, 165, 169, 172;
   Saïtic mouth of the Nile, ii. 17
Salamis (1), island, vii. 90, 141–143, 166,
   168; viii. 11, 40–42, 44, 46, 49, 51, 56,
   57, 60, 64, 65, 70, 74, 76, 78, 82, 86, 89,
   90, 94 (land of), 95–97, 121, 122, 124,
   126, 130; ix. 3–6, 19
   Mentioned in oracle, vii. 141; Hellenic
   fleet at Salamis, viii. 40–108;
   Athenians take refuge there from
   Mardonios, ix. 3–6
   (2), city in Cyprus, iv. 162; v. 104, 108,
   115; plain of Salamis, v. 110:
   Salaminians, people of Salamis, v.
   104, 110, 113, 115; viii. 11; Onesilos, v.
   108; also Siromos, Chersis, Gorgos,
   Philaon
   Persian attack on Salamis, v. 108–115
Salē, city of the Samothrakians, vii. 59
Salmoxis, god of the Getai, iv. 94–96
Salmydēssos, in Thrace, iv. 93
Samios, Spartan, son of Archias, iii. 55
Samos, island and city, i. 70, 142, 148; ii.
   148, 182; iii. 39, 40, 43–45, 47–49,
   54–56, 120–122, 131, 139, 140,
   142–144, 146, 148–150; iv. 43, 95,
   162–164; v. 27; vi. 13, 14, 25, 95; viii.
   85, 130, 132; ix. 90, 96, 106
   Samian(s), of Samos, i. 51 (Theodoros),
   70, 142; ii. 134 (Iadmon), 135
   (Xanthes), 178; iii. 26 (at Oasis), 41
   (Theorodos), 44–49, 54, 55, 57–60,
   120 (Polycrates), 125, 128
   (Polycrates), 142, 146, 147; iv. 43
   (Polycrates), 87 (Mandrocles), 88,
   152; v. 99, 112; vi. 8, 13, 14, 22–25; vii.
   164 (of Zanclē); viii. 85 (Theomestor
   and Phylacos); ix. 90, 91
   (Hegesistratos), 92, 99, 103, 106:
   Samian land, i. 70; ix. 96; ship of
   Samos, iv. 152; cubit of Samos, ii. 168;
   Aischrionian tribe, iii. 26
   Samos an Ionian settlement, i. 142;
   great works at Samos, iii. 60; Samian
   naval enterprise, iv. 152; ancient
   quarrel with Eginetans, iii. 59; with
   the Corinthians, iii. 48, 49; with the
   Lacedemonians, i. 70; iii. 47;
   Polycrates despot, iii. 39, etc., see
   Polycrates; Maiandrios despot, iii.
   142; Persians subdue Samos for
   Syloson, iii. 142–149; Samians and
   Aiakēs at Ladē, vi. 8, 13, 14;
   migration to Zanclē, vi. 22–25;
   Persian fleet at Samos, viii. 130;
   Theomestor despot, ix. 90; Samian

   embassy to Hellenic fleet, ix. 90–92;
   Samians at Mycalē distrusted by
   Persians, ix. 99, 103
Samothrakē, island, ii. 51; vi. 47:
   Samothrakians, ii. 51; viii. 90;
   Samothrakian ship, viii. 90;
   strongholds, vii. 108
Sanacharib, king of the Assyrians, ii. 141
Sandanis, Lydian, i. 71
Sandōkēs, Persian commander, vii. 194,
   196
Sanē (1), town near Athōs, vii. 22, 23
   (2), in Pallene, vii. 123
Sapaians, vii. 110
Sapphō, the poetess, ii. 135
Sarangians, iii. 93, 117; vii. 67
Sardanapallos, king of Nineveh, ii. 150
Sardinia (Sardō), i. 170; v. 106, 124; vi. 2:
   Sardinians, vii. 165; Sardinian Sea, i.
   166
Sardis, city, i. 7, 15, 22, 27, 30, 35, 43, 47,
   48, 69, 70, 73, 77–81, 84, 86, 91, 141,
   152–157; ii. 106; iii. 3, 5, 48, 50, 120,
   126, 128, 129; iv. 45; v. 11–13, 23–25,
   31, 53, 54, 73, 96, 99–103, 105, 106,
   108, 116, 122, 123; vi. 1, 4, 5, 30, 42,
   101, 125; vii. 1, 8b, 11, 26, 31, 32, 37,
   41, 43, 57, 88, 145, 146; viii. 105, 106,
   117; ix. 3, 107, 108; herald from
   Sardis, i. 22, 83
   Sardis taken by the Kimmerians, i. 15;
   visited by Solon, i. 30; taken by
   Cyrus, i. 84; besieged by Pactyas, i.
   154; Oroites governor, iii. 120;
   Artaphrenes, v. 25; Sardis burnt by
   the Ionians, v. 101; Xerxes at Sardis,
   vii. 31, 37; viii. 117; ix. 108; Hellenic
   spies at Sardis, vii. 146; name used for
   the 2d satrapy, iii. 120; v. 25; vi. 1, etc.
Sardōnic linen, ii. 105
Sarpedōn (1), son of Europa, i. 173
   (2), promontory of, vii. 58
Sartē, town of Chalkidikē, vii. 122
Saspeirians, i. 104, 110; iii. 94; iv. 37, 40; vii.
   79
Sataspēs, Persian, nephew of Dareios, iv. 43
Satrai, Thracians, vii. 110–112
Sattagydai, in 7th satrapy, iii. 91
Saulios, king of the Scythians, brother of
   Anacharsis, iv. 76
Sauromatai, iv. 21, 57, 102, 110, 116, 117,
   119, 120, 122, 123 (land of), 128
   Origin of the Sauromatai, iv. 110–117
Scaios, Theban, v. 60
Scamander, river, v. 65; vii. 43
Scamandrōnymos, father of Sappho and
   Charaxos, ii. 135

Scaptē Hylē or Scaptesylē, in Thrace, vi.
46
Scolopoeis, place in Mycalē, ix. 97
Scōlos, town in Bœotia, ix. 15
Scolotoi, Scythians, iv. 6
Scopadai, ruling family of Crannon, vi.
127
Scōpasis, king of the Scythians, iv. 120, 128
Scythia (Skythia), Scythian land, ii. 22; iv.
5, 8, 12, 17, 21, 28, 48, 49, 51, 52, 58,
61, 76, 81, 99–101, 105, 123–125, 129,
130, 139
Scythian(s) (Skythai), i. 15, 73, 74,
103–107, 130, 201, 216; ii. 103, 110,
167; iii. 134; iv. 1–8, 10–13, 17–20,
22–24, 27, 28, 31–33, 48, 49, 51, 58, 59,
64, 66–68, 70, 72, 73, 75–81, 83, 91, 97,
98, 100, 102, 105, 110, 111, 113,
118–122, 124–137, 139, 140, 142; v. 24,
27; vi. 40, 41, 84; vii. 10, 18, 20, 52, 59,
64 (Sacans); nomad Scythians, i. 15,
73; iv. 19, 55; vi. 40, 84; vii. 10;
agricultural Scythians, iv. 17–19,
52–54; "Royal" Scythians, iv. 20, 22,
56, 57, 59, 71, 110 (free); Hellenic
Scythians, iv. 17; Scythian race, iv. 46;
Scythian language, iv. 27, 52, 59, 108,
117; Scythian manner of life, iv. 78;
customs, iv. 105, 107; dress,
equipment, i. 215; iv. 23, 78, 106; gifts,
iv. 134; Scythian bowl, iv. 81; rivers, iv.
48, 49, 53; fashion (of drinking), vi. 84
Description of Scythia and its rivers, iv.
17–20, 46–58, 99; climate, 2, 28–31;
customs of the Scythians, nomad life,
46; religion, 59–63; war, 64–66;
divination, 67–69; oaths, 70; burial,
71–75; cosmetics, 75; abhorrence of
foreign customs, 76–80; population,
81; marvels of Scythia, 82: Origin of
the Scythians, iv. 5–12; Scythian
invasion of Asia, i. 103–106; iv. 1;
invasion of Dareios, iv. 1, 83–98, 102,
118–144; Scythian invasion of
Thrace, vi. 40; "saying of the
Scythians," iv. 127
Sebennytos, district (nome) of, in Egypt,
ii. 166; Sebennytic mouth of the Nile,
ii. 17, 155
[Seldōmos.] See Hysseldomos
Selēnē. See Moon
Selinūs, city, v. 46: people of Selinus, v. 46;
Peithagoras, v. 46
Sēlymbria, city of Hellespont, vi. 33
Semelē, daughter of Cadmos, ii. 145, 146
Semiramis, queen of Babylon, i. 184; gate
of Semiramis, iii. 155

[Sēpeia.] See Hesipeia
Sēpias, headland, vii. 183, 186, 188, 190,
191, 195; viii. 66
Serbōnian lake, ii. 6; iii. 5
Seriphians, viii. 46, 48
Sermylē, town near Toronē, vii. 122
Serreion, promontory of, vii. 59
Sesōstris, king of Egypt, ii. 102–104,
106–108, 110, 111, 137
His fleet, ii. 103; conquers Asia and
Scythia, ii. 103, 104; his return, ii. 107;
works in Egypt, ii. 108–110; figures
on rocks in Ionia, ii. 106
Sestos, city, iv. 143; vii. 33, 78; ix. 114–116,
119; siege of Sestos by the
Athenians, ix. 114–120
Sethōs, king of Egypt, ii. 141
Sicania, vii. 170
Sicas, father of Kyberniscos, vii. 98
Sicily (Sikelia), i. 24; v. 43, 46; vi. 17,
22–24; vii. 145, 153, 156, 157, 163–168,
170, 205; viii. 3. See also Sikelians
Expedition of Minos, vii. 170; history of
Gela, vii. 153–156; Dorieus, v. 43, 46;
the Phocaians, vi. 17; the Samians, vi.
22–24; vii. 164; embassy to Gelon, vii.
153, 157–163; Carthaginian invasion,
vii. 165–167
Sidōn, city, ii. 116, 161; iii. 136
Sidonian, of Sidon, vii. 44, 96, 99; viii.
67, 68; Anysos, Tetramnestos, vii. 98;
ships of Sidon, vii. (99), 100, 128; viii.
92
Sigeion, city, iv. 38; v. 65, 91, 94–96
Sigynnai, v. 9
Sikelia. See Sicily. Sikelians, vi. 22, 23; vii.
155
Sikinnos, servant of Themistocles, viii. 75,
110
Sikyōn, city, i. 145; v. 67; vi. 126
Sikyonians, of Sikyon, v. 67, 68, 69
(Cleisthenes); vi. 92, 129; viii. 1, 43,
72; ix. 28, 31, 102, 103, 105;
Cleisthenes and his predecessors, vi.
126; Perilaos, ix. 103
Rule of Cleisthenes, v. 67, 68; wooing
of Agaristē, vi. 126–130; Sikyonians
distinguished at Mykalē, ix. 103,
105
Silēnos, viii. 138; Marsyas the Silenos, vii.
26
Simōnides of Keos, v. 102; vii. 228
Sindians, iv. 28: land of, iv. 86
Sindos, city on the Thermaïc gulf, vii.
123
Singos, town of Chalkidikē, vii. 122
Sinōpē, city, i. 76; ii. 34; iv. 12

Siphnos, island, iii. 57, 58: Siphnians, iii.
57, 58; viii. 46, 48
Wealth of the Siphnians, iii. 57
Siris (1), city in Italy, viii. 62; Amyris,
Damasos, vi. 127
(2), city in Paionia, viii. 115
Siromitrēs, Persian commander, vii. 68,
(father of Masistios) 79
Sirōmos (1), Salaminian, father of
Chersis, v. 104
(2), Tyrian, father of Matten, vii. 98
Siropaionians, or Siriopaionians, v. 15
Sisamnēs (1), Persian judge, father of
Otanes (3), v. 25
(2), Persian, son of Hydarnes, vii. 66
Sisimakēs, Persian commander, v. 121
Sitalkēs, king of the Thracians, iv. 80; vii.
137
Sithōnia, region of Chalkidikē, vii. 122
Siūph, city in Egypt, ii. 172
Six Cities (Hexapolis), of the Dorians, i.
144
Skiathos, island, vii. 176, 179, 183; viii. 7,
92
Skidros, town of the Sybarites, vi. 20
Skiōnē, city, vii. 123: men of Skionē, viii.
128; Skyllias, viii. 8; Timoxeinos, viii.
128
[Skios.] See Kios (2)
Skiras, Athenē, viii. 94
Skirōnian Way, viii. 71
Skitōn, servant of Demokedes, iii. 130
Skylakē, town on the Hellespont, i. 57
Skylax (1), of Caryanda, iv. 44
(2), of Myndos, v. 33
Skylēs, king of the Scythians, iv. 76, 78–80
Skyllias, diver of Skionē, viii. 8
Skyros, of, vii. 183
Skythēs (1), son of Heracles, iv. 10
(2), ruler of Zanclē, vi. 23, 24; (father of
Cadmos) vii. 163
Skythia. See Scythia
Smerdis (1), son of Cyrus, iii. 30, 32,
61–69, 71, 74, 75, 88; vii. 78
His death, iii. 30
(2), the Magian, iii. 61, 63–65, 80. See
also Magian
Smerdomenēs, Persian commander, vii.
82, 121
Smila, town near Pallenē, vii. 123
Smindyridēs, of Sybaris, suitor of
Agaristē, vi. 127
Smyrna, city, i. 14, 16, 94, 149, 150; ii. 106:
people of Smyrna, i. 143, 150
Smyrna lost to the Aiolians, i. 150
Sōclēs, Corinthian, v. 92, 93
Sogdians, iii. 93; vii. 66

Soloeis, headland of Libya, ii. 32; iv. 43
Soloi, city of Cyprus, v. 115: Solians, v.
110, 113
Solōn, Athenian, i. 29–32, 34, 86; ii. 177; v.
113
Solymoi, i. 173
Sōphanēs, Athenian, vi. 92; ix. 73–75
[Sōsiclēs.] See Socles
Sōsimenēs, father of Panaitios, viii. 82
Sōstratos, Eginetan, iv. 152
Southern Sea, i.e. Erythraian, ii. 158; iv.
37, 42: Euxine, iv. 13
Spacō, foster-mother of Cyrus, i. 110
Spargapeithēs (1), king of the Scythians,
iv. 76
(2), king of the Agathyrsians, iv. 78
Spargapisēs, son of Tomyris, i. 211, 213
Sparta, i. 65, 68, 69, 82, 83, 141, 152; ii. 113,
117; iii. 46, 148; iv. 146, 147, 149; v. 39,
48, 49–51, 55, 65, 75, 76, 90, 92a, 97;
vi. 49, 51, 61, 63, 65, 67, 68, 70–72, 74,
75, 81, 84–86, 105, 106, 120; vii. 3, 133,
134, 136, 137, 149, 169, 204, 206, 209,
220, 228–230, 232, 234; viii. 114, 124,
131, 132, 142, 144; ix. 11, 12, 53, 64,
70, 73, 76
Spartan(s), i. 65–67, 82, 141, 152, 153;
iii. 148; iv. 146; v. 39–42, 46, 50, 63, 75,
91; vi. 50–52, 56, 58, 59, 61, 63, 65, 66,
71, 74–77, 82, 84, 85, 86; vii. 104, 134,
137, 149, 159, 160, 202, 206, 211, 220,
224, 226 (Dienekès), 228, 229, 231,
235; viii. 2, 42 (Eurybiades), 114, 124,
125; ix. 9, 10, 12, 19, 26, 28, 29, 33, 35,
36, 37, 46, 47, 48, 54, 61, 62, 64, 71, 78,
79, 85; Spartan State, vi. 58; Spartan
fashion, v. 40; Spartan division, ix. 29
Number of the Spartans, vii. 234;
Spartans distinguished from
Lacedemonians, vi. 58; vii. 234; ix. 10,
12, 28, 29; number of Spartans at
Thermopylai, vii. 202–205; Spartan
citizenship granted to Tisamenos
and his brother, ix. 35. See also
Lacedemon, Lacedemonian
Spercheios, river, vii. 198, 228
Sperthias, Spartan, vii. 134, (father of
Aneristos) 137
Sphendaleis, deme of Attica, ix. 15
Stageiros, city, vii. 115
Stentoris, lake, vii. 58
Stenyclēros, town in Messenia, ix. 64
Stēsagoras (1), Athenian, father of
Kimon (1), vi. 34, 103
(2), son of Kimon (1), vi. 38, 39, 103
Stēsēnor, despot of Curion, v. 113
Stēsilaos, Athenian, vi. 114

Stratios, Zeus, v. 119

Stratopeda. See *Camps*

Strattis, despot of Chios, iv. 138; viii. 132

Struchates, tribe of the Medes, i. 101

Strymē, town of the Thasians, vii. 108, 109

Strymōn, river, i. 64; v. 1, 13, 23, 98; vii. 24, 25, 75, 107, 113–115; viii. 115, 118, 120; wind from the Strymon (Strymonias), viii. 118

Strymonians, ancient name of the Bithynian Thracians, vii. 75

Strymonias, wind from the Strymon, viii. 118

Stymphalian lake, vi. 76

Styrians, vi. 107; viii. 1, 46; ix. 28, 31

Styx, water of, vi. 74

Summer, name of statue at Memphis, ii. 121

Sun (Hēlios), worshipped by the Persians, i. 131; vii. 54; by the Egyptians at Heliopolis, ii. 59, 73, 111; by the Massagetai, i. 212, 216; by the Libyans, iv. 188; by the people of Apollonia, ix. 93; cursed by the Atarantians, iv. 184; Polycrates anointed by the Sun, iii. 124, 125; table of the Sun, iii. 17–19, 23; fountain of the Sun, iv. 181

Sūnion, headland of Attica, vi. 87, 90, 115, 116; viii. 121; hill region of Sunion, iv. 99

Sūsa, city, i. 188; iii. 30, 64, 65, 70, 91, 129, 132, 140; iv. 83, 85; v. 24, 25, 30, 32, 35, 49, 52–54, 107; vi. 1, 20, 30, 119; vii. 3, 6, 53, 135, 136, 151, 152, 239; viii. 54, 99; ix. 108

Position described, v. 49; royal road to Susa, v. 52; Acropolis, iii. 68; treasures of, iii. 96; v. 49; reception of news from Xerxes, viii. 99

Syagros, Spartan, vii. 153, 159, 160

Sybaris, city, v. 44, 45; vi. 21, 127

Sybarites, of Sybaris, v. 44, 45; Telys, v. 47; Hippocrates, Smindyrides, vi. 127

Syēnē, city of Egypt, ii. 28

Syennesis (1), Kilikian, i. 74

(2), king of the Kilikians, v. 118; (son of Oromedon) vii. 98

Syleus, plain of, vii. 115

Sylosōn, brother of Polycrates, iii. 39, 139–141, 144, 146, 147, 149; (father of Aiakes) vi. 13, 25

His cloak, iii. 139; despot of Samos, iii. 149

Symē, island, i. 174

Syracuse, city, vii. 154–157

Syracusans, people of Syracuse, iii. 125;

vii. 154, 155, 159, 161, [167 *note*]; Amilcas a Syracusan on the mother's side, vii. 166

Surrendered to Gelon, vii. 155; growth, vii. 156; Hellenic envoys at Syracuse, vii. 157–163

Syrgis, iv. 123. Cp. *Hyrgis*

Syria, ii. 11, 12, 20, 116, 152, 157–159; iii. 6, 62, 64; vii. 89; Palestine Syria, i. 105; ii. 106; iii. 91; iv. 39

Syrians (Syroi), ii. 12, 159; iii. 91; of Palestine, ii. 104; iii. 5; vii. 89

Syrians (Syrioi), of Cappadokia, i. 6, 72, 76; ii. 104; iii. 90; v. 49; vii. 72: Name for Assyrians, vii. 63, cp. vii. 140 (Syrian car)

Boundaries of the Syrians of Palestine, iii. 5; of the Cappadokians, i. 6, 72; Syrians of Palestine serve with the Phenicians in the fleet of Xerxes, vii. 89

Syrtis, in Libya, ii. 32, 150; iv. 169, 173

TABALOS, Persian commander, i. 153, 154, 161

Tabiti, Scythian name for Hestia, iv. 59

Tachompsō, island in the Nile, ii. 29

Tainaron, headland in Laconia, i. 23, 24; vii. 168

Talaos, father of Adrastos, v. 67

Talthybios, herald of Agamemnon, vii. 134, 137; Talthybiads at Sparta, vii. 134

[Tamynai.] See *Temenos*

Tanagra, city, ix. 15, 35, 43: men of Tanagra, v. 79; district of Tanagra, v. 57

Tanaïs, river, iv. 20, 21, 45, 47, 57, 100, 115, 116, 120, 122, 123

Description, iv. 57

Tanis, district (nome) of, in Egypt, ii. 166

Taras, Tarentum, city, i. 24; iii. 136, 138; iv. 99: Tarentines, iii. 136, 138; vii. 170; Gillos, iii. 138

Targitaos, king of the Scythians, iv. 5, 7

Taricheiai, in Egypt, ii. 113

Tartēssos, city, i. 163; iv. 152: Tartēssians, i. 163; Arganthonios, i. 163; weasels of Tartessos, iv. 192

Taucheira, city of the Barcaians, iv. 171

Tauroi, iv. 99, 100, 102, 103, 119; Tauric race, iv. 99

Tauric land, iv. 20, 99, 100; Tauric mountains, iv. 3

Position described, iv. 99; customs of the Tauroi, iv. 103

Taxakis king of the Scythians, iv. 120

Taÿgetos, mountain, iv. 145, 146, 148
Tearos, river of Thrace, iv. 89–91
Teaspis, Persian, (father of Sataspes) iv.
    43; (of Pharandates) vii. 79; ix. 76
Tegea, city, i. 66–68; vi. 72, 105; vii. 170; ix.
    35, 37
  Tegeans, men of Tegea, i. 65–68; vii.
    202; ix. 26–28, 31, 35, 54, 56, 59–62,
    70, 71, 85; Chileos, ix. 9; Phegeus,
    Aëropos, Echemos; boundaries of
    Tegea, viii. 124
  Single combat of Echemos and Hyllos,
    ix. 26; wars of Spartans and Tegeans,
    i. 65–68; ix. 35; Hegesistratos fled to
    Tegea, ix. 37; Tegeans at Plataia, ix.
    26–28, 59–62, 70, 71; Leotychides at
    Tegea, vi. 72; Mikythos, vii. 170
Teispēs, Persian, son of Achaimenes, vii.
    11. See also note
Telamōn, hero at Salamis, viii. 64
Teleboan land, v. 59
Teleclēs, father of Theodoros, iii. 41
Teleclos, king of Sparta, in genealogy of
    Leonidas, vii. 204
Telemachos, ii. 116
Telesarchos, Samian, iii. 143
Telinēs, of Gela, vii. 153, 154
Telliadai, family of diviners in Elis, ix. 37
Tellias, Eleian diviner, viii. 27
Tellos, Athenian, i. 30
Telmēssians, i. 78, 84
Telos, island, vii. 153
Telys, king of Sybaris, v. 44, 47
Temenos, place near Eretria, vi. 101
Temenos, Argive, viii. 137; Temenidai,
    sons of Temenos, viii. 137
Temnos, city of the Aiolians, i. 149
Tempē, pass in Thessaly, vii. 173
Tenedos, island, i. 151; vi. 31, 41
Tēnos, island, iv. 33; vi. 97
  Tenians, men of Tenos, iv. 33, viii. 66, 82,
    83
  Tenians inscribed on the Delphic
    tripod, and why, viii. 82
Teōs, city, i. 142, 170; ii. 178
  Teïans, men of Teos, i. 168; vi. 8;
    Anacreon, iii. 121
  Teians leave their city and found
    Abdera, i. 168; Teos the centre of
    Ionia, i. 170
Tērēs, father of Sitalkes, iv. 80; vii. 137
Tērillos, despot of Himera, vii. 165
Termera, of, v. 37
Termilai, ancient name of the Lykians, i.
    173; vii. 92
Tethrōnion, town of Phokis, viii. 33
Tetramnēstos, Sidonian, vii. 98

Teucrians, ii. 118; v. 13, 122; vii. 20, 43, 75,
    Alexander, ii. 114, Teucrian land, ii
    118
  Invasion of Asia by Teucrians and
    Mysians referred to, vii. 20
Teuthrania, ii. 10
Thagimasidas, Scythian name of
    Poseidon, iv. 59
Thalēs, of Miletos, i. 74, 75, 170
Thamanaians, in the 14th satrapy, iii. 93,
    117
Thamasios, Persian, father of Sandokes,
    vii. 194
[Thamimasadas.] See Thagimasidas
Thannyras, son of Inaros, iii. 15
Thasos (1), Phenician, vi. 47
  (2), island, ii. 44; vi. 28, 44, 46, 47:
    Thasians, vi. 44, 46, 47; vii. 108, 118;
    Orgeus, Antipater, vii. 118; Thasian
    Heracles, ii. 44
  Wealth of the Thasians, vi. 46, 47
Theasidēs, Spartan, vi. 85
Thēbē, daughter of Asopos, v. 80
Thēbē, plain of, vii. 42
Thebes (Thēbai) (1), in Egypt, i. 182; ii. 3,
    9, 15, 54–57, 69, 74, 143; iii. 10, 25, 26;
    iv. 181; district of Thebes, ii. 4, 28, 42,
    91, 166
  Thebans, men of Thebes, ii. 42; iii. 10;
    Theban Zeus, ii. 42, 54; iv. 181; see
    Zeus
  Thebes visited by Herodotus, ii. 3;
    distance from Heliopolis, ii. 9;
    temple and oracle of Ammon, i. 182;
    ii. 42, 54–57; iv. 181; rain at Thebes,
    iii. 10
  (2), in Bœotia, i. 52, 92; v. 59, 67; viii.
    134; ix. 13, 16, 17, 27, (41), (58), 67,
    86–88; Theban temple, i. 52; Theban
    territory, ix. 65
  Thebans, i. 61, v. 67, 79, 81, 89; vi. 87,
    108, 118; vii. 132, 202, 205, 222, 225,
    233; viii. 50, 134, 135; ix. 2, 15, 16, 31,
    40, 41, 58 (city of), 66 (wall of), 67,
    69, 86–88; Phrynon, Attaginos, ix. 16;
    Herpys, Timagenides, ix. 38; also
    Eurymachos, Leontiades, Timander,
    Asopodoros
  Thebans help Peisistratos, i. 61;
    relations with the Plataians, vi. 108;
    vii. 233; viii. 50; war with Athens, v.
    74, 77, 79–81; alliance with the
    Eginetans, v. 79, 80, 89; Medism
    suspected, vii. 205; Thebans at
    Thermopylai, vii. 202, 205, 222, 225,
    233; Thebans guide the Persians, viii.
    50; advice to Mardonios, ix. 2 (cp.

41); banquet at Thebes, ix. 16;
Thebans at Plataia, ix. 31, 40, 69;
compelled to surrender their leaders,
ix. 86–88
Themis, ii. 50
Themiskyra, city on the Euxine, iv. 86
Themisōn of Thera, iv. 154
Themistoclēs, Athenian, son of Neocles,
vii. 143, 144, 173; viii. 4, 5, 19, 22, 23,
57–59, 61, 63, 75, 79, 83, 85, 92,
108–112, 123–125; ix. 98
Advice to the Athenians to build ships,
vii. 144; interpretation of the oracle,
vii. 143; in command of Athenians at
Tempe, vii. 173; at Artemision,
detains the fleet, viii. 4, 5;
endeavours to detach the Ionians
and Carians, viii. 19, 22, 23; at
Salamis, viii. 57–63, 75–83, 92; advice
to pursue the Persians, viii. 108;
change of tone, viii. 109; message to
Xerxes, viii. 110; behaviour to the
islanders, viii. 111, 112; the voting for
the prize of valour, viii. 123; visit to
Sparta, viii. 124, 125
Theodōros of Samos, i. 51; iii. 41
Theokydēs, father of Dicaios, viii. 65
Theomēstōr, despot of Samos, viii. 85; ix.
90
Theophania, feast at Delphi, i. 51
Theopompos, king of Sparta, in
genealogy of Leotychides, viii. 131
Thēra, island, iv. 147–152, 153–157, 164:
Theraians, men of Thera, iv. 150–156,
161; v. 42; Aisanios, Grinnos,
Polymnestos, Battos, iv. 150;
Themison, iv. 154
Ancient name, colonisation by the
Phenicians, iv. 147; by Theras, iv. 148,
149; Theraians sent to settle in
Libya, iv. 150–157
Therambō, town of Pallenē, vii. 123
Therapnē, near Sparta, vi. 61
Thēras, son of Autesion, iv. 147, 148,
150
Therma, city, vii. 121, 123, 124, 127, 128,
130, 179, 183: Thermaian gulf, vii.
121–123; viii. 127
Thermōdōn (1), river of Cappadokia, ii.
104; iv. 86, 110; ix. 27
(2), river of Bœotia, ix. 43
Thermopylai, vii. 175–177, 184, 186, 200,
201, 205–207, 213, 219, 233, 234; viii.
15, 21, 24, 27, 66, 71; ix. 71, 78, 79
Description of Thermopylai and the
neighbourhood, vii. 176, 198–201; the
Hellenes at Thermopylai, vii.

202–204, 206–233; monuments and
inscriptions, vii. 228; Amphictyonic
Council, vii. 200, 213
Thērōn, ruler of the Agrigentines, vii.
165, 166
Thersander (1), son of Polyneikes, iv. 147;
vi. 52
(2), of Orchomenos, ix. 16
Thēseus, ix. 73
Thesmophoria, ii. 171; vi. 16
Thespeia or Thespiai, city, viii. 50:
Thespians, men of Thespiai, v. 79; vii.
132, 202, 222, 226, 227; viii. 25, 50, 66,
75; ix. 30; Diadromes, Demophilos,
Harmatides, Dithyrambos
Refuse earth and water to Xerxes, vii.
132; at Thermopylai, vii. 202, 222,
226; city burnt, viii. 50; Thespians at
Plataia, ix. 30; receive new citizens,
viii. 75
Thesprōtians, ii. 56; v. 92g; vii. 176 (land
of), viii. 47
Position, viii. 47; Oracle of the dead in
Thesprotia, v. 92g
Thessalos, Spartan, v. 46
Thessaly, Thessalia, iii. 96; v. 63, 64; vi. 72,
74, 127; vii. 6, 108, 128–130, 172–175,
182, 196, 198, 208, 213, 232; viii.
113–115, 126, 129, 131, 133, 135; ix. 1,
31, 77, 89; Thessaliōtis, i. 57
Thessalians, v. 63, 64, 94; vii. 129, 130, 132,
172–174, 176, 191, 215, 233; viii.
27–32; ix. 17, 18, 31, 46, 89; Thessalian
cavalry, vii. 196
Physical features, vii, 128–130;
Thessalians help the Peisistratidai, v.
63, 64; offer Iolcos to Hippias, v. 94;
Aleuadai invite Xerxes, vii. 6;
Thessalians apply to the Hellenes
for defence, vii. 172; join Xerxes, vii.
174; Thessalians and Phokians, vii.
176, 215; viii. 27–32; ix. 17;
Mardonios in Thessaly, viii. 113, 115,
133, 136; ix. 1; Thessalians at Plataia,
ix. 31; Artabazos passes through
Thessaly, ix. 89; Leotychides in
Thessaly, vi. 72
Thestē, fountain in Libya, iv. 159
Thetis, vii. 191
Thmüïs, district (nome) of, in Egypt, ii.
166
Thoas, Lemnian, vi. 138
Thōn, king of Egypt, ii. 116
Thōnis, Egyptian, ii. 113–115
Thōrax, Aleuad of Larissa, ix. 1, 58
Thoricos, deme of Attica, iv. 99
Thornax, mountain in Laconia, i. 69

Thrace, Thracia (Thrakia), i, 168; ii. 134; iv. 80, 89, 99, 143; v. 2, 14, 23, 24, 126; vi. 33, 95; vii. 25, 59, 105, 106, 185; viii. 117; ix. 89, 119

Thracians, i. 168; ii. 103, 167; iv. 49, 74, 80, 93–95, 104, 118; v. 3–6, 8, 10, 126; vi. 34 (Dolonkian), 39, 45 (Brygian); vii. 20, 110, 115, 137 (king of), 185; viii. 115, 116; ix. 32, 89, 119 (Apsinthian); Thracian women, iv. 33: Thracians in Asia (Bithynian), i. 28; iii. 90; vii. 75; Thracian sea, vii. 176

Thracian Bosphorus, vii. 10c, see Bosphorus; strongholds on the Thracian border, vi. 33

Position of Thrace, iv. 99; animals (lions, etc.), vii. 126; Thracian peoples, v. 3; their customs, iv. 93, 96; v. 4–8; conquest by Sesostris, ii. 103; passage of Dareios through Thrace, iv. 89–92, 97; return, iv. 143; Megabazos in Thrace, iv. 143; v. 1, 2, 14–17; Histiaios in Thrace, v. 11, 23; Mardonios attacked by Thracians, vi. 45; passage of Xerxes, vii. 58, 59, 108–126; tribes by which he passed, vii. 110, 111; Thracians in his army, vii. 185; return, viii. 115–120; Artabazos in Thrace, ix. 89; Hellenes of Thrace assist Xerxes, vii. 185; equipment of the Asiatic Thracians, vii. 75

Thrasybūlos, despot of Miletos, i. 20–23; v. 92f, g

Thrasyclēs, father of Lampon, ix. 90

Thrasydeios, Aleuad of Larissa, ix. 58

Thrasylaos, father of Stesilaos, vi. 114

Three Heads (Treis Kephalai), pass of Kithairon, ix. 39

Thriasian plain, in Attica, viii. 65; ix. 7

Thuia (1), daughter of Kephisos, vii. 178 (2), place near Delphi, vii. 178

Thynian Thracians, i. 28

Thyreai, Thyrea, place in Argolis, i. 82; vi. 76

Thyssagetai, iv. 22, 123

Thyssos, town of Athōs, vii. 22

Tiarantos, tributary of the Ister, iv. 48

Tibarēnians, in the 19th satrapy, iii. 94; vii. 78

Tibisis, tributary of the Ister, iv. 49

Tigranēs, Persian, son of Artabanos, vii. 62; viii. 26; ix. 96, 102

Tigris (Tigrēs), river, i. 189, 193; ii. 150; v. 52; vi. 20

Timagenidēs, Theban, ix. 38, 86, 87

Timagoras, father of Timonax, vii. 98

Timander, father of Asopodoros, ix. 69

Timaretē, priestess at Dodona, ii. 55

Timēsios, of Clazomenai, i. 167

Timēsitheos, of Delphi, v. 72

[Timnēs.] See Tymnes

Timō, under-priestess at Paros, vi. 134, 135

Timodēmos, Athenian, viii. 125

Timōn, of Delphi, vii. 141

Timōnax, Cyprian, vii. 98

Timoxeinos of Skionē, viii. 128

Tin Islands (Cassiterides), iii. 115

Tiryns, city, vi. 77, 83; vii. 137: men of Tiryns, Tirynthians, ix. 28, 31; territory of Tiryns, vi. 76

Tisamenos (1), Theban, iv. 147; vi. 52 (2), Eleian, ix. 33, 35, 36

Tisander (1), father of Isagoras, v. 66 (2), father of Hippocleides, vi. 127–129

Tisias, father of Lysagoras, vi. 133

Titacos, Athenian, ix. 73

Tithaios, son of Datis, vii. 88

Tithorea, peak of Parnassos, viii. 32

Titormos, Aitolian, vi. 127

Tmōlos, mountain, i. 84, 93; v. 100, 101

Tomyris, queen of the Massagetai, i. 205–208, 213, 214

Torōnē, city, vii. 22, 122: Critobulos of Toronē, viii. 127

Trachis, land of, vii. 176, 199, 201, 203; viii. 21, 31, 66; city, vii. 199, 201

Trachinians, men of Trachis, vii. 175, 217 (mountains of), 226; Athenades, vii. 213; rocks of Trachis, viii. 198

Description of Trachis, vii. 198–201

Trapezūs, city of Arcadia, vi. 127

Traspians, tribe of Scythians, iv. 6

Trauos, river of Thrace, vii. 109

Trausians, Thracian tribe, v. 3, 4

Treis Kephalai, Three Heads, ix. 39

Triballian plain, in Thrace, iv. 49

Triopion, headland, i. 174; iv. 38; vii. 153: Temple of Triopion, i. 144; Triopian Apollo, i. 144

Tritaieis, city of the Achaians, i. 145

Tritantaichmēs (1), Persian, son of Artabazos, i. 192 (2), Persian, son of Artabanos, vii. 82, 121; viii. 26

Triteis, town of the Phokians, viii. 33

"Trito-born goddess" (Tritogeneia), vii. 141

Tritōn (1), god, iv. 179, 188 (2), river, iv. 178, 180, 191

Tritōnis, lake, iv. 178–180, 186–188

Trochoeidēs, "Round Pool," ii. 170

Trōglodytes, iv. 183, note

Troizēn, city, viii. 41, 42

Troizēnians, men of Troizen, iii. 59; vii.

99; viii. 1, 42, 43, 72; ix. 28, 31, 102, 105; Troizenian ship, vii. 179, 180

Athenian fugitives at Troizen, viii. 41; Troizenians distinguished at Mycalē, ix. 105

Trophōnios, worshipped at Lebadeia, i. 46; viii. 134

Troy, city, iv. 191; v. 13; vii. 91, 171: Trojans, ii. 120; wars of Troy, toils of Troy, Trojan war, ii. 145; vii. 20, 171; ix. 27: land of Troas, land of Troy, iv. 38; v. 26, 122. See also *Ilion*

Site of Troy visited by Xerxes, vii. 43

Tydeus, v. 67

Tymnēs (1), steward of Ariapeithes, iv. 76 (2), Carian, father of Histiaios (2), v. 37; vii. 98

Tyndareus, father of Helen, ii. 112; sons of Tyndareus, iv. 145; v. 75; ix. 73

Typhōn, god of the Egyptians, ii. 144, 156; iii. 5

Tyras, river of Scythia, iv. 11, 47, 51, 52, 82; Tyritai, iv. 51

Tyre, city, i. 2; ii. 44
   Tyrians, ii. 112; king of Tyre, ii. 161; viii. 67; Europa, iv. 45; Cadmos, ii. 49; Siromos, Matten, vii. 98
   Antiquity of Tyre, ii. 44; Tyrians at Memphis, ii. 112

Tyrītai, Hellenes on the Tyras, iv. 51

Tyrodiza, town of the Perinthians, vii. 25

Tyrrhēnia. See *Tyrsenia*

Tyrsēnia, i. 94, 163; vi. 22: Tyrsenians, i. 57 (see *note*), 94, 166, 167; vi. 17
   Lydian colonisation, i. 94; war with Phocaians of Alalia, i. 166, 167

Tyrsēnos, son of Atys, i. 94

UMBRIANS. See *Ombricans*

Urania, Aphroditē, i. 105, 131; iii. 8; (Argimpasa), iv. 59

Utians, in the 14th satrapy, iii. 93; vii. 68.

VICTORY (Nikē), viii. 77

WELL-DOERS (Agatho-ergoi), at Sparta, i. 67

White Fortress (Leucon teichos) at Memphis, iii. 91. Cp. iii. 13

White Pillars (Leucai stelai), in Caria, v. 118

Winds, worshipped, vii. 178

Winter, name of a statue at Memphis, ii. 121

XANTHēS, Samian, ii. 135

Xanthippos, Athenian, vi. 131, 136: vii. 33; viii. 131; ix. 114, 120

Prosecutes Miltiades, vi. 136; in command of Athenians, viii. 131; ix. 114

Xanthos, city of Lykia, i. 176: Xanthians, i. 176; plain of Xanthos, i. 176

Xeinagoras of Halicarnassos, ix. 107

Xerxēs, i. 183; iv. 43; vi. 98; vii. 2–8, 10–19, 21, 24–29, 31, 35, 37–41, 43–48, 50, 52–57, 59, 61 (wife of), 82, 97 (brother of), 100, 103, 105–109, 112, 114 (wife of), 115–124, 127, 128, 130, 133, 134, 136, 139, 145–147, 150–152, 164, 173, 179, 186, 187, 193, 195–197, 201, 208–210, 215, 223, 225 (brothers of), 233, 234, 236, 237–239; viii. 10, 15–17, 22, 24, 25, 34, 35, 50, 52, 54, 65, 66, 67, 69, 81, 86, 88, 89 (brother of), 90, 97–101, 103, 105, 107, 108, 110, 113–120, 130, 140, 143, 144; ix. 1, 32, 41, 69, 78, 82, 96, 99, 107–113, 116, 120

Genealogy, vii. 11; appointed successor to Dareios, vii. 2, 3; succeeds to the throne, vii. 5; his council, vii. 8–11; his dreams and changes of plan, vii. 12–19; prepares his host, vii. 19–21; supposed message to Argos, vii. 150; march to Sardis, vii. 26–31; anger at the destruction of the bridges, vii. 35; march to Abydos, vii. 37–43; views his army and fleet in the Hellespont, conversation with Artabanos, vii. 44–52; crosses the Hellespont, vii. 54–56; march to Doriscos, vii. 57, 58; numbering and review of army, vii. 59–100; conversation with Demaratos, vii. 101–105; march to Therma, vii. 108–126; visit to Tempe, vii. 128–131; advance to Alos and Trachis, vii. 196–198, 201; an estimate of the number of his host, vii. 184–187; Xerxes at Thermopylai, vii. 208–215, 223, 233–238; treatment of the body of Leonidas, vii. 238; display of the bodies at Thermopylai, viii. 24, 25; sends a detachment to plunder Delphi, viii. 35; occupies Athens, viii. 50–54; visits the fleet and holds a council, viii. 67–69; spectator at the battle of Salamis, viii. 86, 88, 90; inclination to retreat and council, viii. 97, 100–103; retreat, viii. 113–120; at Sardis, family relations, ix. 107–113; his violation of the temple of Belos, i. 183; character as a ruler, iii. 89; love of displaying power, vii. 24; severity, iv. 43;

Xerxēs (continued)
    passionate disposition, vii. 11, 35, 39;
    viii. 90; timidity, viii. 97, 118;
    magnanimity, vii. 146, 147
Xūthos, father of Ion, vii. 94; viii. 44

[Zabatos], river, v. 52 note
Zakynthos, island, iv. 195; vi. 70; ix. 37:
    Zakynthians, men of Zakynthos, iii.
    59; vi. 70
[Zalmoxis.] See Salmoxis
Zanclē, city in Sicily, vi. 23, 24; vii. 164:
    men of Zanclē, Zanclaians, vi. 22–24;
    vii. 154
    Zanclē captured by the Samians, vi. 23,
    24
Zauēkĕs, in Libya, iv. 193
Zeus, i. 65, 89, 174, 207; ii. 13, 116, 136,
    146; iii. 124, 125; (iv. 79); v. 49; vii. 56,
    61, 141, 221; (viii. 77); ix. 122: At
    Dodona, ii. 55; (ix. 93); of the
    Hellenes (Hellenios), ix. 7;
    Olympian, in Olympos, at Olympia,
    ii. 7; vii. 141; ix. 81; guardian of the
    household (Herkeios), at Sparta, vi.
    67, 68; Lakedaimon, at Sparta, vi. 56;
    Uranios, at Sparta, vi. 56; Liberator,
    at Samos, iii. 142; Lycaios, at Kyrenē,
    iv. 203; Agoraios, at Selinus, v. 46; of

the Eginetans, at Naucratis, ii. 178;
    Laphystios, at Alos, vii. 197; Carian
    Zeus, at Athens, v. 66; at Mylasa, i.
    171; Stratios, at Labraunda, v. 119;
    Cleanser, Protector of Suppliants,
    Guardian of Friendship, in Lydia, i.
    44: Zeus of the Persians, i. 131; v. 105;
    vii. 8c, 40; chariot of Zeus, vii. 40; viii.
    115: Of the Babylonians (Belos), i.
    181, 183; iii. 158: Of the Egyptians, ii.
    45; Theban Zeus, i. 182; ii. 42, 54, 56,
    74, 83 (oracle), 143; iv, 181 (see
    Ammon); of the Ammonians
    (Ammon), ii. 55; iii. 25; iv. 181 (see
    Ammon): Of the Ethiopians, ii. 29:
    Of the Libyans, iv. 180: Of the
    Scythians (Papaios), iv. 5, 59, 127:
    Oracle of Zeus at Thebes, ii. 56; of
    Ammon, i. 46; ii. 18, 32, 55; iii. 25; at
    Dodona, ii. 54–57 (see Dodona);
    among the Ethiopians, ii. 29; of
    (Zeus) Trophonios, at Lebadeia, i.
    46; viii. 134
Zeuxidēmos, son of Leotychides, vi. 71
Zōnē, town of the Samothrakians, vii. 59
Zōpyros (1), son of Megabyzos (1), iii.
    153, 156–158, 160; iv. 43; vii. 82
    (2), grandson of the above, iii. 160
Zōstēr, place in Attica, viii. 107

GENERAL INDEX

ABLUTIONS of the Egyptians, ii. 37
acacia, thorny, (acantha), ii. 96
acinaces. See akinakēs
ægis of Pallas, origin, iv. 189
agatho-ergoi at Sparta. See Welldoers in
    Index I
age, respect for, ii. 80
agriculture despised by Thracians, v. 6
akinakēs, iii. 118, 128; iv. 62 (Scythian);
    vii. 54, 61; ix. 80, 107
alabaster box of unguent, iii. 20
alphabet, early Hellenic, v. 58–61
alum, ii. 180
amber, where found, iii. 115

amphor. See measures
anactoron at Eleusis, ix. 65
anaspastoi. See Removed, Index I
Anaxagoras, probably alluded to, ii. 22
anchor of Sophanes, ix. 74
androsphinx, ii. 175
angareion, Persian system of couriers,
    viii. 98
animals of Egypt, ii. 38–42, 46, 47, 65–76,
    93; of India, iii. 106; of Libya, iv. 191,
    192
antacaioi, fish of the Borysthenes, iv. 53
antelopes in Libya, iv. 192
ant-gold, iii. 102–105

antiquity of the Egyptians and Phrygians, ii. 2; of the Tyrians, ii. 44; recent origin of the Scythians, iv. 5
apparition of Perseus, ii. 91; of Ariteas, iv. 15; of Pan to Pheidippides, vi. 105; apparition seen by Epizelos at Marathon, vi. 117; by the Hellenes at Salamis, viii. 84
Arabian words, ladanon, iii. 112; cassia, iii. 110; zeira, vii. 69
argonauts, iv. 145, 179
arima, Scythian word meaning "one," iv. 27
armour of the Hellenes derived from Egypt, iv. 180; bronze armour introduced into Egypt by Hellenes, ii. 152
army of Xerxes, unprecedented size, vii. 20, 21; estimates of, vii. 60, 184–187; viii. 66
army, gift of, ix. 109
arrow of Abaris, iv. 36; arrow shot by Dareios, v. 105; arrows carrying fire, viii. 52; arrow bearing a message, viii. 128; arrows pointed with stone, vii. 69; saying about the arrows of the Persians at Thermopylai, vii. 226
art, at Samos, i. 51; iv. 152; at Corinth, ii. 167
artabē, Persian measure, i. 192
arūra, measure of land in Egypt, ii. 141, 168
as-chy, drink of the Argippaians, iv. 23
asmach, ii. 30
assemblies, Egyptian, ii. 59–64
asses cannot live in Scythia, iv. 28, 129; wild asses in chariots, vii. 86; horned asses, iv. 191; wild asses which do not drink, iv. 192
astrology, Egyptian, ii. 82
astronomy, Egyptian, ii. 4; Babylonian, ii. 109
asylum for runaway slaves in Egypt, ii. 113
athletic games at Chemmis, ii. 91

BAG produced by the Samians at Sparta, iii. 46
baker of Crœsus, statue of, i. 51
bald-headed men, iv. 23
ball, games of, invented by Lydians, i. 94
bangles worn, iv. 168
banks cast up against cities, i. 162
banquet to the Persians at Thebes, ix. 16
barathron at Athens, vii. 133

"Barbarian words" used to the Hellespont, vii. 35
baris, Egyptian boat, ii. 41, 96
battlements of various colours at Agbatana, i. 98
battos, Libyan word meaning "king," iv. 155
beard of the priestess of Athenē among Pedasians, i. 175; viii. 104
bears in Egypt, ii. 67; in Libya, iv. 191
beauty in men, Philip, v. 47; Leon, vii. 180; Xerxes, vii. 187; Callicrates, ix. 72
beavers in the land of the Budinoi, iv. 109
becos, Phrygian word meaning "bread," ii. 2
beer in Egypt, ii. 77
bees beyond the Ister, v. 10
benefactors of the king, iii. 140; v. 11; viii. 85
birthdays of the Persians, i. 133; of the king of Persia, ix. 110
bitter stream flowing into the Hypanis, iv. 52, 81
bitumen of Babylon, i. 179; of Kissia, vi. 119
blind kings of Egypt, ii. 111, 137, 140; blind slaves of the Scythians, iv. 2; blinding of Epizelos, vi. 117; of Euenios, ix. 93
boars on the beaks of Samian ships, iii. 59
boat-procession to Bubastis, ii. 60
boats on the Euphrates, i. 194; Nile, ii. 29, 96
body of Amasis, iii. 16; of Leonidas, vii. 238; of Masistios, ix. 25; of Mardonios, ix. 84
Bœotarchs, ix. 15
borÿes in Libya, iv. 192
bow of the king of the Ethiopians, iii. 21, 30; bows in the army of Xerxes, vii. 61, 64–67, 69, 77, 92; bow bent backwards, vii. 69; Lykian bows, vii. 77; comparison used by Amasis, ii. 173
branding the Hellespont, vii. 35; branding of the Thebans at Thermopylai, vii. 233
breaking the line (diecplūs), vi. 12
"breeders of horses," v. 77; vi. 100
bribing the Delphic oracle, v. 63; bribing Persians, v. 21; bribes offered to Spartans, iii. 148; v. 51; vi. 72; viii. 5; bribes accepted by Themistocles, viii. 4, 112; advice of Artabazos to bribe the leaders of the Hellenes, ix. 41

bricks at Babylon, i. 179; brick pyramid, ii. 136
bridges, Euphrates at Babylon, i. 186; Bosphorus, iv. 87, 88; Ister, iv. 89, 97, 139–141; Hellespont, vii. 25, 36; viii. 117; Strymon, vii. 24, 113
bronze armour, ii. 152
brooches of Athenian women, v. 87; of Argive and Eginetan women, v. 88
buffaloes in Libya, iv. 192
bull's blood as a poison, iii. 15
burial customs, Persian, i. 140; Babylonian, i. 198; Egyptian, ii. 85–90; Long-lived Ethiopians, iii. 24; Scythian kings, iv. 71, 72; other Scythians, iv. 73; Nasamonians, iv. 190; Thracians, v. 4–8; Spartan kings, vi. 58
burying alive, a Persian custom, iii. 35; vii. 114
byssos used for wrapping mummies, ii. 86

CALASIRIS, Egyptian garment, ii. 81
camels, i. 80; iii. 102, 103; vii. 83, 86, 87
canals of Babylon, i. 193; of Egypt, ii. 108; canal from the Nile to the Erythraian Sea, ii. 158; iv. 39; canal of Athōs, vii. 22–24, 37
cannibalism, Massagetai, i. 216; army of Cambyses, iii. 25; Callatian Indians, iii. 38; Padaians, iii. 99; Issedonians, iv. 26; Androphagoi, iv. 106
cap, Persian, i. 132; iii. 12; v. 49; vii. 61; Sacan Scythian, vii. 64
cassia, how got, iii. 110
castor oil, ii. 94
cats in Egypt, ii. 66, 67
cattle feeding backwards, iv. 183
cauterisation of children's heads, iv. 187
cenotaphs at Plataia, ix. 85
cerastes at Thebes in Egypt, ii. 74; in Libya, iv. 192
ceremonies of the Median court, i. 99
chairs carried for the leading Persians, iii. 144
challenge of Hyllos, ix. 26; of Eurybates, ix. 75; of Mardonios, ix. 48
champsa, Egyptian name for the crocodile, ii. 69
chariot of Zeus, vii. 40; viii. 115; chariot given to Themistocles, viii. 124; chariot-driving among the Libyans, iv. 170, 183, 189; chariot-racing of Hellenes, vi. 35, 70, 103, 122
children sent as tribute by Colchians and Ethiopians, iii. 97; sold by Thracians,

v. 6; killed in a school in Chios, vi. 27; death of the children of the Aigeidai, iv. 149
choinix. See *measures*
chronology of Egypt, ii. 142–145
cinnamon, how got, iii. 111
circumcision, Egyptian, ii. 36, 104; other nations, ii. 104
citizens admitted by Athenians, v. 57; by Spartans, ix. 33; by Thespians, viii. 75
City Hall. See *Prytaneion* in Index I
classes of the Egyptians, ii. 164; vi. 60
cleansing from guilt of blood, i. 35
cleruchs, Athenian, in Euboea, v. 77
climate, its effect on character, ix. 122; climate of Hellas, iii. 106; of Ionia, i. 142; Aiolia, i. 149; Scythia, iv. 28–31
cloak of Syloson, iii. 139, 140
clothes burnt for the dead, v. 92g
coffin at feasts of the Egyptians, ii. 78
coined money first used by the Lydians, i. 94; coining of daries and aryandics, iv. 166
collection for the return of Peisistratos, i. 61; for rebuilding the temple at Delphi, ii. 180
colossal statues, i. 183; ii. 91, 110, 121, 130, 176
columns of the temple at Ephesos given by Croesus, i. 92
combing hair before battle, vii. 208
constitution of Lycurgos, i. 65; of Cleisthenes, v. 66, 69
convulsions, remedy for, iv. 187
cooking among the Scythians, iv. 61
corn-trade of Scythia, iv. 17; vii. 147
corslets, Egyptian, i. 135; vii. 89; corslets of linen, ii. 182; iii. 47; vii. 63, 89
cosmetics used by Scythian women, iv. 75
cotton. See *tree-wool*
cotylē. See *measures*
courageous deed of Hegesistratos, ix. 37
courier sent from Athens to Sparta, vi. 105; from the Argives to Mardonios, ix. 12; Persian couriers, viii. 98
courtesans at Naucratis, ii. 135
cow at Sais, ii. 129–132; cow's flesh avoided by the Egyptians, ii. 18, 41; by nomad Libyans and women of Kyrenē and Barca, iv. 186
crafts inherited at Sparta, vi. 60
crests of helmets invented by the Carians, i. 171
cries in religious ceremonies, iv. 189
crocodile described, ii. 68–71; crocodiles in central Africa, ii. 32; in the Indus, iv. 44; land-crocodiles, iv. 192

cubit. See *measures*
cup attached to Scythian belt, iv. 10;
    golden cup thrown by Xerxes into
    the Hellespont, vii. 54
cursing the sun, iv. 184
Cyprian word "sigynnai," v. 9

DANCING of Hippocleides, vi. 129
daric stater. See *stater*
date of the composition of this History,
    (the latest events mentioned),
    attempt on Plataia, vii. 233; capture
    of Peloponnesian ambassadors, vii.
    137; expulsion of the Eginetans, vi.
    91; Dekeleia spared by Archidamos,
    ix. 73; flight of Zopyros, iii. 160;
    cruelties of Amestris, vii. 114
date-palms, i. 193; iv. 172
daughters obliged to support their
    parents, ii. 35
day, division of, ii. 109
debt, Egyptian law of, ii. 136
democracy advocated by Otanes, iii. 80;
    established in Ionia by Mardonios,
    vi. 43; democracies easily deceived, v.
    97; advantage of democracy, v. 78
demotic writing, ii. 36
desert of Libya, ii. 31; iii. 26; iv. 173, 185;
    of Syria, iii. 5; of India, iii. 90; of
    Scythia, iv. 123, 124
despotism advocated by Dareios, iii. 82;
    spoken against by Otanes, iii. 80; by
    Socles, v. 92; advantages of, vii. 103
devices on shields invented by the
    Carians, i. 171; device on the shield
    of Sophanes, ix. 74
dice, game of, invented by the Lydians, i.
    94
dictÿes in Libya, iv. 192
dinners, Persian, i. 133; prepared for the
    army of Xerxes, vii. 119
disappearance of Aristeas, iv. 14; of
    Amilcas, vii. 167
dishonour at Sparta, vii. 231, 232; ix. 71
dithyramb invented by Arion, i. 23
divination in Egypt, ii. 83; in Scythia, iv.
    67–69; by victims at Olympia and at
    Thebes, viii. 134
diviners. See in Index I *Amphilytos,
    Tellias, Megistias, Tisamenos,
    Hegesistratos, Hippomachos,
    Euenios, Deïphonos*. See also
    Eleians
diving of Skyllias, viii. 8
division of land in Egypt, ii. 109; at
    Kyrenē, iv. 159; in Eubœa, v. 77
divisions of the world, ii. 16; iv. 42, 45

dog-headed men, iv. 191
dogs in Egypt, ii. 67; dogs kept by
    Tritantaichmes, i. 192. See also
    Indian hounds in Index I
doves, black, from Thebes in Egypt, ii.
    55–57; white, objected to by the
    Persians, i. 138
drama of Phrynichos, vi. 21
dreamless men, iv. 184
dreams, warning or prophetic, Crœsus, i.
    34; Astyages, i. 107, 108; Cyrus, i. 209;
    Cambyses, iii. 30; daughter of
    Polycrates, iii. 124; Hipparchos, v. 56;
    Hippias, vi. 107; Datis, vi. 118;
    Agaristē, vi. 134; Xerxes, vii. 12, 14,
    19; Artabanos, vii. 17; dream-oracle
    of Amphiaraos, viii. 134; opinion of
    Artabanos on dreams. vii. 16;
    interpreters of dreams, v. 56. See also
    Magians in Index I
dress of the Persians, i. 71, 135; v. 49; vii.
    61; Medes, i. 135; vii. 61, 62; Lydians,
    i. 155; Babylonians, i. 195; fish-eaters
    of the Araxes, i. 202; Egyptians, ii. 36,
    81; Egyptian priests, ii. 37; Indians of
    the Indus, iii. 98; Scythian dress
    referred to, i. 215; iv. 23, 78, 106;
    Melanchlainoi, iv. 107; Budinoi, iv.
    109; women of the Sauromatai, iv.
    116; Libyan women, iv. 189; Hellenes,
    v. 88
drinking among the Persians, i. 133;
    Caunians, i. 172; at Bubastis, ii. 60;
    "in Scythian fashion," vi. 84
ducks eaten salted in Egypt, ii. 77
dumb-trading, iv. 196
dwarfs in Africa, ii. 32; iv. 43

"EARTH and water," iv. 126, 127; v. 18; vi.
    48, 94; vii. 32, 131–133; viii. 64
earthquake in Egina, v. 85; at Delos, vi.
    98; effects of earthquake, vii. 129
ebony sent as tribute, iii. 97
eclipse of the sun, predicted by Thales, i.
    74; when Xerxes set out from Sardis,
    vii. 37; at the Isthmus, ix. 10
education among the Persians, i. 136
eels in the Nile, ii. 72
effeminate pursuits, i. 155
Egyptian words, asmach (?), ii. 30; baris,
    ii. 96; calasiris, ii. 81; champsa, ii. 69;
    kiki, ii. 94; kyllestis, ii. 77; lotos, ii. 92;
    mendes, ii. 46; piromis, ii. 143. See
    also *names of gods*
"eight gods" of the Egyptians, ii. 145
elemental religion of the Persians, i. 131,
    132

elephants in Libya, iv. 191; elephants' tusks as tribute, iii. 97

embalming in Egypt, reason of, iii. 16; process, ii. 86–89

embankments in Babylonia, i. 184, 185; in Egypt, ii. 99, 137; at the mouth of the Athos canal, vii. 37

emerald pillar at Tyre, ii. 44

enomoties at Sparta, i. 65

envy ascribed to the Hellenes, vii. 236

epilepsy of Cambyses, iii. 33

episodes sought after by Herodotus, iv. 30

epitaphs at Thermopylai, vii. 228

equality of rights, advantage of, iii. 80; v. 78

equipment of the army of Xerxes, vii. 61–95

escort of Themistocles from Sparta, viii. 124

etymology, ii. 52; iv. 189

eunuchs valued by Asiatics, viii. 105; among Medes, i. 117; sent to Lydia, iii. 48; among Persians, iii. 77; viii. 104, 105

experiments of Psammetichos, ii. 2, 28

expounder of oracles (prophet), at Delphi, viii. 36, 37

extremities of the earth produce the most excellent things, iii. 106–116

FABLE of Cyrus, i. 141

fabulous creatures of Libya, iv. 191

fatalism of Herodotus, i. 8; [?? 423];pd 161; iv. 79; v. 32, 92d; vi. 64; ix. 109; of the Delphic oracle, i. 91; vi. 135

father, name given to Cyrus, iii. 89

fathom. See measures

feathers in the air, iv. 7; gold-dust got from mud with feathers, iv. 195

female line of descent reckoned by the Lykians, i. 173

fertility of Babylonia, i. 193; of Libya, iv. 198; of Europe, vii. 5; of Aiolia, i. 149

festivals of the Hellenes, names end in the letter a, i. 148. See in Index I Apaturia, Brauron, Carneia, Kyzicos, Gymnopaidiai, Hyakinthia, Olympia, Panionia, Sunion, Theophania, Thesmophoria

fifty-oared galleys used by the Phocaians, i. 163

fillet (mitra), vii. 62, 90

fine to be paid to Apollo, iii. 52; fine imposed on Phrynichos, vi. 21; on Miltiades, vi. 136; fines for aggression, vi. 92

finger, as a measure, i. 60

fir-cones, eaters of, iv. 109

"fire-bearer," in Hellenic fleet, viii. 6

fire-signals, vii. 182; ix. 3

first-fruits of inheritance offered by Crœsus, i. 92; of victory, offered by the Hellenes, viii. 121, 122

fish of Egypt, ii. 72, 93, 149; of the Borysthenes, iv. 53; of lake Prasias, v. 16; revenue from the fish of lake Moiris, ii. 149; iii. 91; fish-eaters, i. 200, 202; ii. 92; iii. 19

fleet of Minos, i. 171; of Sesostris, ii. 102; of Necos, ii. 159; of Polycrates, iii. 39; of Cambyses, iii. 19; of the Persians at Ladē, vi. 6; of the Ionians, vi. 8; of the Thasians, vi. 46, 47;of Mardonios, vi. 44; of Datis and Artaphrenes, vi. 95; of the Athenians, vi. 89; vii. 144, 161; viii. 42, 44, 61; ix. 114; of the Eginetans, vi. 83, 92; viii. 46; of Xerxes, vii. 44, 45, 89–100, 184; viii. 66, 107; ix. 96; Hellenic fleet at Artemision, viii. 1, 2; at Salamis, viii. 42–48

flocks and herds of the Phrygians, v. 49; flocks of the Eubœans, viii. 19, 20

flutes male and female, i. 17

foot. See measures

foot-pan of Amasis, ii. 172

footprint of Heracles, iv. 82

foot race at Olympia, v. 22

foreign customs adopted readily by the Persians, i. 135; avoided by the Egyptians, ii. 79; by the Scythians, iv. 76

foreign words in Herodotus. See Arabian, Cyprian, Egyptian, Libyan, Ligurian, Median, Paionian, Persian, Phenician, Phrygian, Scythian. See also names of the gods

forgery of oracles, vii. 6

founder, honours paid to, at Abdera, i. 168; in Chersonese, vi. 38

fountain of the Long-lived Ethiopians, iii. 23; of Apollo at Kyrenē, iv. 158; of the sun, iv. 181; Enneacrunos, vi. 137; Castalia, viii. 39; Gargaphia, ix. 49

four-yearly festivals (pentetērides) of the Athenians, vi. 87, 111, 138

foxes in Libya, iv. 192

fox-goose, ii. 72

frankincense, how got, iii. 107; offered to Belos, i. 183; as tribute from Arabia, iii. 97; offered by Datis at Delos, vi. 97

fringes of the Egyptian calasiris, ii. 81; of the dress of women in Libya, iv. 189

full moon waited for by the
Lacedemonians, vi. 108
fumes, intoxicating, i. 202; iv. 75
furlong. See *measures*
furthest point reached by Sesostris, ii.
103; by Persians in Libya, iv. 204; by
Mardonios, ix. 14

GALL-FLY, i. 193
games invented by the Lydians, i. 94
gardens of Midas, viii. 138
garlands placed upon the object of love,
vi. 69; worn by Persians in crossing
the Hellespont, vii. 55, 56
garrison posts in Egypt, ii. 30
gates of Babylon, i. 179; iii. 155; destroyed
by Dareios, iii. 159; tomb over a gate,
i. 187
genealogy of Egyptian kings and priests,
ii. 142, 143; of Hecataios, ii. 143;
Lydian kings, i. 7; Xerxes, vii. 11;
Spartan kings, vi. 53; vii. 204; viii. 131;
Macedonian kings, viii. 139; Perseus,
ii. 91
genesia, commemoration of the dead, iv.
26
geography of Herodotus. See especially i.
72, 202–204; ii. 5–34; iii. 115, 116; iv.
36–45, 99–101
geology of Herodotus, ii. 8–12; vii. 129
geometry came from Egypt, ii. 109
gifts of honour among the Persians, iii.
84; vii. 106, 116; viii. 120; gifts for
tribute to Dareios, iii. 97; gifts of the
Scythian king to Dareios, iv. 131; of
Euelthon to Pheretimē, iv. 162
gnats in the Delta of Egypt, ii. 95
gnomon received from Babylon, ii. 109
goat-footed Pan in Egypt, ii. 46; goat-
footed men, iv. 25
goat-skins dyed red, iv. 189
gold in Lydia, i. 93; v. 101; among the
Massagetai, i. 215; in Ethiopia, iii. 23,
97, 114; in Siphnos, iii. 57; in India, iii.
102–106; in Northern Europe, iii.
116; in Libya (Kyrauis), iv. 195; in
Thasos, vi. 47, 48; in Thrace, Scaptē
Hylē, vi. 47; Mount Pangaion, vii.
112; Daton, ix. 75; offerings of gold
from Gyges, i. 14; from Crœsus, i. 50,
51, 52, 92; gold given to the
Lacedemonians by Crœsus, i. 69;
gold on the battlements of
Agbatana, i. 98; golden image of
Belos, etc., i. 183; cow at Saïs, ii. 129,
130; statue of Athenē, ii. 182; gold-
dust as tribute from the Indians, iii.

94; Ethiopians, iii. 97; gold given to
Demokedes, iii. 131; gold and silver
vessels of Maiandrios, iii. 148; sacred
gold of the Scythians, iv. 5, 7; gold
given to Alcmaion, vi. 125; golden
plane-tree and vine at Susa, vii. 27;
golden vessels thrown into the
Hellespont, vii. 54; golden
pomegranates on spears, vii. 41; gold
worn by the Persians, vii. 83; golden
vessels washed up near Cape Sepias,
vii. 190; gifts of gold to the men of
Abdera, viii. 120; golden stars
offered by the Eginetans, viii. 121;
cuirass of Masistios, ix. 22; spoils of
Plataia, ix. 80; golden tripod at
Delphi, ix. 81; gold reckoned by the
Euboïc talent, iii. 89; value of gold as
compared with silver, iii. 95; gold
tried by the touchstone, vii. 10a
grain in Babylonia, i. 193; in Egypt, ii. 36
griffins, as decoration, iv. 79; gold-
guarding griffins, iii. 116
guest-friend, public, ix. 85
gum-mastich, how got, iii. 112
gum used for glue in Egypt, ii. 86
gymnopaidiai at Sparta, vi. 67

HAIR of the Babylonians, i. 195; Egyptians,
ii. 36, 104; Colchians, ii. 104; Libyans,
iv. 175, 180, 191; Persians, vi. 19;
Ethiopians, vii. 70; Lacedemonians,
vii. 208, 209
handles of shields invented by the
Carians, i. 171
hare used to convey a letter, i. 123
harvests of Kyrenē, iv. 199
hawks in Egypt, ii. 67; hawks seen
pursuing vultures, iii. 76
headless men, iv. 191
health of the Egyptians, ii. 77; of the
Libyans, iv. 187
heat in India, iii. 104
Hecataios quoted as authority, iv. 137;
criticised, ii. 143; also probably, ii. 21,
23; iv. 36
helmet of Egyptian kings, ii. 151, (162)
hemp in Scythia, iv. 74; hemp vapour-
bath, iv. 75
heralds outraged, iii. 13; vii. 133–137
heroes not worshipped in Egypt, ii. 50
(but see ii. 91); heroes of Ilion, vii.
43. See also in Index I, *Kyrnos,
Timesios, Heracles, Onesilos, Philip*
(2), *Ajax, Aiacos, Adrastos,
Melanippos, Miltiades* (1),
Astrabacos, Argos, Artachaies,

heroes not worshipped in Egypt
  (continued)
  Talthybios, Amilcas, Amphictyon,
  Phylacos, Autonoös, Erechtheus,
  Amphiaraos, Androcrates, Dekelos,
  Protesilaos
hieroglyphic writing, ii. 36
hippobotai. See *breeders of horses*
hippopotamus described, ii. 71
honey, burial in, i. 198; artificial honey, iv.
  194; vii. 31
horns of snakes, ii. 74; iv. 192; horns used
  for lyres, iv. 192; large horns of wild
  oxen, vii. 126
horoscopes, ii. 82
horses eating serpents, i. 78; horse of
  Dareios, iii. 85–88; horses of
  Heracles, iv. 8, 9; horses in Scythia, iv.
  28; horses trained to lie down, iv. 22;
  small horses of the Sigynnai, v. 9;
  horses kept by Tritantaichmes, i. 192;
  horses trained to fight, v. 111; horses
  of Zeus, vii. 40; viii. 115; Pharnuches
  thrown from his horse, vii. 88; horse
  of Masistios, ix. 20, 22; white horse of
  Mardonios, ix. 63; horses afraid of
  camels, i. 80; vii. 87; mares winning
  three times at Olympia, vi. 103. See
  also *Nesaian* in Index I
human life, misery of, v. 4; vii. 46;
  shortness, vii. 46
human sacrifices, Tauroi, iv. 103; Getai, iv.
  94; Persian, vii. 180; at Alos, vii. 197;
  Apsinthians, ix. 119
hunting by the Scythians in Media, i. 73;
  accident to Dareios, iii. 129; method
  among the Iyrcai, iv. 22; hunting
  Troglodytes with four-horse chariots,
  iv. 183
hyenas in Libya, iv. 192

IACCHOS, cry of, viii. 65
iambic verse mentioned, i. 12
ibis described, ii. 75, 76
ichneumon, ii. 67
immortality, belief of the Getai, iv. 94–96
impaling as a punishment for rebels, iii.
  159; vi. 30
imprecations of the Egyptians, ii. 39
incest of Cambyses, iii. 31
inscriptions, tomb of Alyattes, i. 93; of
  Nitocris, i. 187; on pillars of Sesostris,
  ii. 102; on rock-cut figure of
  Sesostris, ii. 106; on pyramid of
  Cheops, ii. 125; on brick pyramid, ii.
  136; on statue of Sethos, ii. 141; set
  by Dareios near the Bosphorus, iv.

87; at the Tearos, iv. 91; on the
  picture dedicated by Mandrocles, iv.
  88; on tripods at Thebes, v. 59–61; on
  chariot by the Propylaia at Athens, v.
  77; at Thermopylai, vii. 228; on the
  Delphic tripod, viii. 82; inscriptions
  cut by Themistocles, viii. 22
intercalation, Hellenic, i. 32; Egyptian, ii. 4
intoxication among the Persians, i. 133; by
  vapour, i. 202; iv. 75
inundation of Egypt, see *Nile* in Index I;
  possible inundation of Thessaly, vii.
  130
irenĕs of Sparta, ix. 85
iron, welding of, i. 25; iron spits offered at
  Delphi, ii. 135; no iron among the
  Massagetai, i. 215
irrigation in Babylonia, i. 192
island, largest, i. 170; v. 106; islands in the
  Erythraian sea, iii. 93; vi. 140; vii. 168;
  island near Plataia, ix. 51: Athos
  made into an island, vii. 22; cp. i. 174

JACKALS in Libya, iv. 192
jealousy of the deity, i. 32, 34; iii. 39–43;
  vii. 10e, 46; viii. 109
judge punished for corruption by
  Cambyses, v. 25; by Dareios, vii. 194.
  See also *Royal Judges* in Index I

KERKUROI, vii. 97
kiki, Egyptian word, ii. 94
killed at Marathon, number, vi. 117; at
  Thermopylai, viii. 24, 25; at Plataia,
  ix. 70; greatest slaughter of Hellenes,
  vii. 170
king of the Long-lived Ethiopians, how
  chosen, iii. 20; kings of Sparta, see
  Lacedemon in Index I. See also
  genealogy in Index II
kneading with the feet, ii. 36
knives, Egyptian, vii. 63, 91
knots for reckoning days, iv. 98
knuckle-bones, game of, i. 94
kyllestis, Egyptian word, ii. 77
kyrbasia, v. 49; vii. 64

LABYRINTH in Egypt, ii. 148
lakes as sources of rivers in Scythia, iv. 51,
  52, 54, 55, 57
lampadephoria. See *torch-race*
lamps, feast of, ii. 62
language, most ancient, ii. 2; language of
  the Pelasgians, i. 57, (ii. 52); dialects
  of the Ionians, i. 142; languages of
  Scythia and beyond, iv. 24; of the
  Cave-dwellers, iv. 183

lash used by the Persians at the Athos canal, vii. 22; at the crossing of the Hellespont, vii. 56; at Thermopylai, vii. 223
lassoes used in war, vii. 85
"Law is their master," vii. 103
law, reign of, iii. 38
laws of Solon, i. 29; ii. 177
left wing contended for at Plataia, ix. 26–28
lepers abhorred by the Persians, i. 139
lepidotos in the Nile, ii. 103
letters, form of, v. 58
liberty, advantage of, vii. 135
Libya, regions of, iv. 181
Libyan words, battos, iv. 155; zegeris, iv. 192
life, length of, i. 32; long life among the Ethiopians, iii. 23; Arganthonios, i. 163
Ligurian word, sigynnai, v. 9
linden-bark used in divination, iv. 67
linen of Egypt and Colchis, ii. 105; linen worn by priests in Egypt, ii. 37; linen corslets, ii. 182; iii. 47; vii. 63
lion, birth of, iii. 108; lions in Libya, iv. 191; in Europe, vii. 125, 126; stone lion at Thermopylai, vii. 225
lizards eaten by the Cave-dwellers, iv. 183; large lizards in Libya, iv. 192
locusts as food, iv. 172
lotos, Egyptian, ii. 92; Libyan, iv. 177
lots drawn by the Lydians, i. 92
lychnocaia. See lamps
lying abhorred by the Persians, i. 139; advocated by Dareios, iii. 72

MADNESS of Cambyses, iii. 30–38; of Cleomenes, v. 42, 75
maidens, battle of, iv. 180
manger of the horse of Mardonios, ix. 70
"many-voiced," v. 79
march of Xerxes, duration of, viii. 51; return, viii. 115
mares winning at Olympia, vi. 103; mares lost by Heracles, iv. 8, 9; mares of the chariot of Zeus, viii. 115
"marked head," v. 65
marks of Apis, iii. 28
marriage customs, Lydian, i. 93; Persian, i. 135; Babylonian (marriage market), i. 196; of the Massagetai, i. 216; Egyptian, ii. 92; Adyrmachidai, iv. 168; Nasamonians, iv. 172; Auseans, Machlyans, iv. 180; Thracians, v. 6; Athenians (referred to), vi. 122
marsh-men of Egypt, ii. 92, 94, 95
meals, Persian and Lacedemonian, ix. 82; common meals at Sparta, i. 65; vi. 57

measures of length, fingerbreadth, i. 60; cubit, i. 178; ii. 149, 168; schoine, ii. 6; palm, foot, fathom, plethron, furlong, ii. 149; day and night's voyage, iv. 86; day's journey, v. 53; vi. 42; parasang, v. 53; vi. 42: square measures, yoke (arura), ii. 168; plethron, vii. 199; measures of capacity, artabē, choinix, medimnos, i. 192; amphor, i. 51; cotylē, tetartē, vi. 57
mechanical skill of the Phenicians, vii. 23, 25
Median word, spaca, i. 110
medicine in Egypt, ii. 77, 84, 107 (quotation); mild methods of the Hellenes, iii. 130
medimnos. See measures
mendes, Egyptian word meaning "goat," ii. 46
mice cause the retreat of the Assyrians, ii. 141; mice of three kinds in Libya, iv. 192; burial of shrew-mice in Egypt, ii. 67
migrations of the Dorians, i. 56; vii. 99; of the Ionians, i. 145, 146; vii. 94; of the Pelasgians, vi. 137; of the Phocaians, i. 164–167; of the Teians, i. 168; threatened migration of the Athenians, viii. 62; migration of birds, ii. 22
milking among the Scythians, iv. 2
mina, Euboïc, iii. 89
mines, silver, in Siphnos, iii. 57; Thrace, iv. 23; near lake Prasias, iv. 17; Mount Pangaion, vii. 112; Attica, vii. 144: gold, in Siphnos, iii. 57; Thasos and Scaptē Hylē, vi. 46, 47; Pangaion, vii. 112; Daton, ix. 75: mines under walls discovered by a shield, iv. 200
mitra. See fillet
mixing-bowls, offered by Gyges, i. 14; by Alyattes, i. 25; by Crœsus, i. 51; mixing-bowl sent by the Lacedemonians to Crœsus, i. 70; iii. 47; at the entrance of the Euxine, iv. 81; dedicated by Samian merchants, iv. 152; thrown into the Hellespont by Xerxes, vii. 54; Lesbian mixing-bowls, iv. 61; Argolic, iv. 152
mole of the harbour at Samos, iii. 60
monarchy denounced by Otanes, iii. 80; advocated by Dareios, iii. 82
monolith chamber, ii. 175
mourning in Egypt, ii. 36, 85; for Scythian kings, iv. 71; for birth among the Trausians, v. 4; for Spartan kings, vi. 58; for Masistios, ix. 24

movable dwellings, Scythian, iv. 46;
    Libyan, iv. 190
mule producing young, iii. 153; vii. 57;
    "mule shall be monarch of Media," i.
    55, 91
myrtle-boughs to wreathe caps, i. 132;
    used for getting pitch, iv. 195; strewn
    by the Persians, vii. 54; viii. 99
mysteries of the Cabeiroi, ii. 51;
    Egyptians, ii. 171; Thesmophoria, ii.
    171, etc., see Index I; Demeter
    Achaia at Athens, v. 61; Epidaurians,
    v. 83; Eleusis, viii. 65

NAMELESS men, iv. 184
names of the gods, Assyrian, i. 131, 181;
    Egyptian, ii. 42, 46, 137, 144, 156;
    Arabian, i. 131; iii. 8; Scythian, iv. 59;
    "naming" of the Hellenic gods, ii. 52
names of the Persians, i. 139
natron used for embalming, ii. 86
naucraries at Athens, v. 71
naval power of Athens, vii. 144, 161
nekyomanteia in Thesprotia, v. 92g
netting islands, iii. 149; vi. 31
night festival for the mother of the gods,
    iv. 76
nomes of Egypt, ii. 165, 166
number of the army and fleet of Xerxes,
    viii. 60, 184–187; viii. 66

OATHS, ceremonies of, Median and
    Lydian, i. 74; Arabian, iii. 8; Scythian,
    iv. 70; Nasamonian, iv. 172; oath of
    the Persians at Barca, iv. 201; oaths
    by the water of Styx, vi. 74
obeisance to Persian king, vii. 136
obelisks, ii. 111, 170
oior, Scythian word meaning "man," iv.
    110
oiorpata, Scythian word meaning "man-
    slayer," iv. 110
oligarchy advocated by Megabyzos, iii.
    81
olives in Attica, v. 82; olive in the
    Erechtheion, viii. 55
omens, iii. 76, 86; viii. 65
one-eyed men, iii. 116; iv. 27
oracles. See in Index I, *Delphi, Dodona,
    Branchidai, Abai, Trophonios,
    Ammon, Buto, Bakis, Musaios,
    Laïos*: misleading oracles, given to
    Crœsus, i. 53, 55; to the
    Lacedemonians, i. 66; to the men of
    Kymē, i. 158, 159; to Cambyses, iii.
    64; to Cleomenes, vi. 80; editor of
    oracles, vii. 6: Oracle of Zeus among

the Ethiopians, ii. 29; Oracle of Ares,
    vii. 76; of Bacchus, vii. 111; Oracles
    used for discovery of theft, ii. 174;
    oracles collected by the
    Peisistratidai, v. 90, 93; vii. 6;
    neglected by Dorieus, v. 42; oracle
    directing the Phocaians to Kyrnos, i.
    165; promising Siris to the
    Athenians, viii. 62; Oracles visited by
    Mys, viii. 134; oracle quoted by
    Mardonios, ix. 42
orosangai, Persian name for the
    benefactors of the king, viii. 85
oryxes in Libya, iv. 192
ostracism of Aristeides, viii. 79
ostriches in Libya, iv. 192
otters in the Nile, ii. 72; in the country of
    the Budinoi, iv. 109
"oven heated overmuch," iv. 164; cold, v.
    92g

PAIŌN, cry of, v. 1
paiderastia of the Persians, i. 135
painting, portrait, ii. 181; historical, iv. 88;
    painting the body, iv. 191, 194; vii. 69;
    viii. 27
Paionian words, paprax, tilon (names of
    fish), v. 16
palm, as a measure, i. 50
palm-tree. See *date-palms*
panthers in Libya, iv. 192
paprax, Paionian name of a fish, v. 16
papyrus, ii. 92; shoes, ii. 37
parasang, Persian word, ii. 6; v. 53; vi. 42
pata, Scythian word meaning "slay," iv.
    110
pentathlon, vi. 92; ix. 33
perioicoi. See *Dwellers (in the country)
    round* in Index I
Persian words, artabē, i. 192; parasang, ii.
    6; v. 53; vi. 42; rhadinakē, vi. 119;
    akinakes, vii. 54; orosangai, viii. 85;
    angareion, viii. 98; tycta, ix. 110;
    Persian names translated, vi. 98
petroleum well, vi. 119
phallos, ii. 48, 49, 51
Phenician words, pataicoi, iii. 37;
    kinnamomon, iii. 111
phœnix, ii. 73
Phrygian word, becos, ii. 2
physicians of Egypt, ii. 84; iii. 1, 129
pigmy images of Hephaistos, iii. 37
pigs to tread in corn and thresh, ii. 14;
    unclean in Egypt, ii. 47; not kept by
    the Scythians, iv. 63; nor by the
    nomad Libyans, iv. 186
pile-dwellings in lake Prasias, v. 16

pillars of Sesostris, ii. 102, 103, 106; of
    Dareios at the Bosphorus, iv. 87; at
    the Tearos, iv. 91
pine-tree, destroy like a, vi. 37
piracy of Dionysios the Phocaian, vi. 17
piromis, Egyptian word, ii. 143
pitch at Zakynthos, iv. 195
plaited helmets, vii. 63, 72, 79
plane-trees, sacred grove of, v. 119;
    keeper appointed for a plane-tree by
    Xerxes, vii. 31
pledging the family mummies, ii. 136;
    pledges of the Arabians, iii. 8
plethron. See measures
polemarch, Athenian, v. 109, 111; Spartan,
    vii. 173
pomegranate eaten by Dareios, iv. 143;
    pomegranates on spears, vii. 41
Pontic tree, iv. 23
population of India, iii. 94; Scythia, iv. 81;
    Athens, v. 97; Sparta, vii. 234
porcupines in Libya, iv. 192
pōrinos lithos, v. 62
pottery, Athenian, v. 88
prickly mouse in Libya, iv. 192
priests at Babylon, i. 180, etc.; in Egypt, ii.
    37; at Memphis, ii. 3, etc.; at Thebes,
    ii. 54, etc.
prize at Olympia, viii. 26; prize of valour
    for Salamis, viii. 123
prodigies observed by the Egyptians, ii.
    82; prodigy at Olympia
    (Hippocrates), i. 59; Sardis, i. 78, 84;
    Babylon (Zopyros), iii. 153; Thera, iv.
    151; Epidauros, v. 82; Egina, v. 85;
    Amathus, v. 114; Chios, vi. 27; Argos
    (Cleomenes), vi. 82; Delos, vi. 98;
    Marathon, vi. 117; Delphi, viii. 37;
    Salamis, viii. 64, 65; (Perdiccas), viii.
    137; (Artaÿctes), ix. 120
profit from voyages, iv. 152
promiscuous intercourse, i. 216; iii. 101; iv.
    180
prophētēs at Delphi, viii. 36, 37. Cp. vii. 111
prophetess at Delphi. See in Index I
    Pythian prophetess; at Patara, i. 182; at
    Dodona, ii. 55–57; among the
    Satrians, vii. 111
prostitution of Lydian girls, i. 93; religious
    prostitution, i. 199; daughter of
    Rhampsinitos, ii. 121; daughter of
    Cheops, ii. 126; Rhodopis, ii. 134
proverbs, iv. 127; vi. 129
Providence, contrivances of, iii. 108, 109;
    special providence, vii. 137
provisions required for the army of
    Xerxes, vii. 187

punishment falling on descendants, i. 91;
    vii. 134; punishments for killing
    sacred animals in Egypt, ii. 65; great
    punishments for great wrongs, ii. 120
purging of the Egyptians, ii. 77
purification of Delos, i. 64; purification
    after sexual intercourse, i. 198; after
    burials, iv. 73–75
purple, iii. 20, 21; purple-fisher, iv. 151
pyramids of Egypt, ii. 124–127, 134, 136

QUAILS, salted, ii. 77
queens of Babylon, i. 184–187; queen of
    Egypt, ii. 100

RACES in Libya (two native, two foreign),
    iv. 197
rain in Assyria, i. 193; in upper Egypt, iii.
    10; in Libya, iv. 185, 198; failure of
    rain in Thera, iv. 151
ram-headed Zeus at Thebes, ii. 42;
    Ammon, iv. 181
rams in Libya, iv. 192
raven accompanying Apollo, iv. 15
records, Persian, vii. 100; viii. 85, 90
Red Sea described, ii. 11; Red Sea canal.
    See canal
reeds used in building walls, i. 179
reform of Kyrenē, iv. 161; of Miletos, v.
    28, 29
relaxation, need of, ii. 173
replies of Themistocles, viii. 59, 125
retribution, i. 13, 91, 167; ii. 120; iii. 126; iv.
    205; vi. 83, 84, 86; vii. 133, 137; ix.
    116–121
revenues of Peisistratos, i. 64; of the
    satrap of Babylon, i. 192; of Dareios,
    iii. 89–97
review of the host of Xerxes, vii. 59–100
rhadinakē, Persian word, "petroleum," vi.
    119
rhapsodists banished from Sikyon, v. 67
riches of Rhampsinitos, ii. 121; of the
    Alcmaionidai, v. 62; vi. 125; of
    Pythios, vii. 27, 28; of the Eginetans,
    ix. 80
ring of Polycrates, iii. 41, 42
rivers diverted, i. 75, 189, 191; iii. 152 (cp.
    vii. 176); rivers running
    underground, Erasinos, vi. 78; Lycos,
    vii. 31
rogues and vagabonds, laws against, ii.
    178
ropes of the bridges over the Hellespont,
    vii. 34, 36; ix. 115, 121
roses near Mount Bermion, viii. 138
route of Xerxes held sacred, vii. 115

royal road to Susa, v. 52
rumour of victory before the battle of
    Mycalē, ix. 100, 101
rushes, clothing made of, iii. 98

SACRED and common writing in Egypt, ii.
    36
sacred disease, iii. 33
sacred road to Delphi, vi. 34
sacrifices, Persian, i. 132; Egyptian, ii.
    39–48; Scythian, iv. 60–63; Tauroi, iv.
    103; nomad Libyans, iv. 188
sacrilege of Cleomenes, vi. 79–81; of the
    Eginetans, vi. 91; of the Persians, viii.
    109, 129, 143; of Artaÿctes, ix. 116
sagaris, i. 215; iv. 70; vii. 64
salt in Libya, iv. 181–185
salutations of the Persians, i. 134; of the
    Egyptians, ii. 80
san, Dorian letter, i. 139
sandal of Perseus, ii. 125
sand-storms, ii. 26; iv. 173
satrapies, i. 192; iii. 89–94
saying of the Scythians, iv. 127; of
    Megabazos, iv. 144; of Megacreon,
    vii. 120; of Dienekēs, vii. 226; of
    Chilon, vii. 235; of Tritantaichmes,
    viii. 26; of Callicrates, ix. 72
scale-armour, vii. 61; ix. 22
scalping and similar usages, iv. 64, 65
schoine. See measures
scourging of the Hellespont, vii. 35
scurrilous choruses of women, v. 83
Scythian words, arima, spū, iv. 27; oior,
    pata, oiorpata, iv. 110
sea in the Erechtheion, viii. 55
sealing-earth, ii. 38
seals of the Babylonians, i. 195
seal-skins for dress, i. 202
seat of Xerxes at Abydos, vii. 44; at
    Thermopylai, vii. 212; at Salamis, viii.
    90
secretaries, royal, iii. 128
self-mutilation of Zopyros, iii. 154
senate of Sparta, i. 65
serpents in Egypt, ii. 74; in Libya, iv. 191,
    192; winged serpents in Arabia, ii. 75;
    iii. 108, 109; serpent of the Acropolis
    at Athens, viii. 41; serpent-maiden in
    Scythia, iv. 9
servants in ancient time, vi. 137; viii. 137
seven Persians, iii. 70–83
sheep in Arabia, iii. 113; "sheep among
    wolves," iv. 149; sheep of the
    Eubœans, viii. 19, 20; sheep of the
    Sun, ix. 93

shepherd Philitis, ii. 128
shield used for discovering mines, iv. 201;
    shield lost by Alcaios, v. 95; shield
    raised as a signal, vi. 115
ships of the Phocaians, i. 163; ships
    dedicated as offerings, viii. 121
shoes of the wife of the satrap of Egypt,
    ii. 74
"shopkeeper," name for Dareios, iii. 89
shrewmice in Egypt, ii. 67
siege of Azotos for twenty-nine years, ii.
    157
sigma, Ionic letter, i. 139
signet-ring for marking victim, ii. 38; of
    Polycrates, iii. 41; of the Persian king,
    iii. 128
sillikypria, ii. 94
silphion, iv. 169
silver, in Siphnos, iii. 57; Thrace, iv. 17, 23;
    Lydia, v. 49; Pangaion, vii. 112;
    Attica, vii. 144: silver offered by
    Gyges, i. 14; by Crœsus, i. 51; couches
    of silver or covered with silver, i. 51;
    ix. 82; silver on the battlements of
    Agbatana, i. 98; silver of
    Rhampsinitos, i. 121; value of silver
    as compared with gold, iii. 95; silver
    stored in the royal treasuries, iii. 96;
    silver coinage of Aryandes, iv. 166;
    silver in the spoils of Plataia, ix. 80
single combats at Perinthos, v. 1; in
    Thracian games, v. 8; Eurybates in
    Egina, v. 92; ix. 75; Hyllos and
    Echemos, ix. 26; (Marathon, ix. 27)
"skins," i.e. paper, v. 58
skulls of Persians and Egyptians
    compared, iii. 12; skulls as cups, iv.
    65
slain, number at Marathon, vi. 117;
    Thermopylai, viii. 24; Plataia, ix. 70
slander, evils of, vii, 10
slaughter of Hellenes, greatest known,
    vii. 170
slaves of the Scythians, iv. 1–4; slaves at
    Argos, vi. 83
sleeping men, iv. 25
solecism of speech, iv. 117
song of Linos (Maneros), ii. 79; songs
    sung at Delos, iv. 35
soothsayers, utterances of, i. 62; v. 44; viii.
    96; ix. 33, 37. See diviners, and also in
    Index I Bakis, Musaios
source of the Nile, see Index I (Nile); of
    the Ister, iv. 49; of the Borysthenes,
    iv. 53
spaca, Median word, "bitch," i. 110

sphinxes in Egypt, ii. 175; in Scythia, iv. 79
spices of Arabia, iii. 107–113
spits offered by Rhodopis, ii. 135
spoil at Plataia, ix. 80, 81
spū, Scythian word, "eye," iv. 27
stater, Lydian, i. 54; daric, iii. 130; (iv. 166); vii. 28
storax, iii. 107
storm at Mount Athos, vi. 44; off Cape Sepias, vii. 188; at Artemision and round Eubœa, viii. 12, 13
"strangers," i.e. Barbarians, ix. 11, 55
succession to Persian throne, vii. 2, 3
Sun, sin against, i. 139; table of, iii. 17, 18; cursing the Sun, iv. 184
sun-dials, ii. 109
sunrise in the west, ii. 142; libations at sunrise, vii. 54, 223
suppliant boughs, v. 51; vii. 141
swineherds in Egypt, ii. 47
swipe, used in Babylonia, i. 193
sword as symbol of Ares in Scythia, iv. 62
syssitia, instituted by Lycurgos, i. 65

TABLE of the Sun, iii. 17, 18; tables of gold and silver, ix. 82
tablet sent by Demaratos, vii. 239
talent, Babylonian and Euboïc, iii. 89
tall men, (i. 68); vii. 117; women, i. 60; iii. 1; v. 12
tallies, vi. 86
tattooing of Thracians, v. 6
tent of Xerxes, ix. 82
"theos," etymology of, ii. 52
thirty-oared ships, iv. 148; viii. 21
three-headed serpent at Delphi, ix. 81
tiara, i. 132; iii. 12; vii. 61; viii. 120
tide in Red Sea, ii. 11; Maliac Gulf, vii. 198; at Potidaia, viii. 128
tilōn, Paionian name of a fish, v. 16
tin, where got, iii. 115
tithes offered at Delphi, etc., viii. 27; ix. 81; "tithing" as a punishment, vii. 132
tomb of Alyattes, i. 93; of Nitocris, i. 187; of Cheops, ii. 127; of the daughter of Mykerinos, ii. 129–132; of kings and crocodiles in the Labyrinth, ii. 148; of Amasis, ii. 169; of Argē and Opis, iv. 35; of Philip, v. 47; of Anchimolios, v. 63; of Hellē, vii. 58; of Artachaies, vii. 117; of Protesilaos, ix. 116
torch-race, vi. 105; viii. 98
trade, contempt for, ii. 168
tragic choruses for Adrastos, v. 67
transmigration of souls, ii. 123
transparent coffins, iii. 24

travels of Herodotus, Babylon, i. 181; Egypt, ii. 3, 29; Scythia, iv. 81; Colchis, ii. 104; Dodona, ii. 52; Zakynthos, iv. 195; Proconnesos, Metapontion, iv. 51; Sparta, iii. 55
treasury of the Corinthians at Delphi, i. 14, 51; of the people of Clazomenai, i. 51; of the Siphnians, iii. 57
tree-wool, iii. 47, 106; vii. 65
tribes of the Medes, i. 101; of the Persians, i. 125; of the Scythians, iv. 6; of the Thracians, v. 3–6; of the Ionians, v. 66; of the Dorians, v. 68
triēcads, i. 65
tripod of Jason, iv. 179; tripods in the temple of Apollo Ismenios, v. 59, 60; Plataian tripod, ix. 81
trochilus, ii. 68
"tunics of walls," vii. 139
tunnel-aqueduct at Samos, iii. 60
tusks as tribute, iii. 97
twelve cities of the Ionians, i. 145; Achaians, i. 146; Aiolians, i. 149
twelve gods of Egypt, ii. 145; altar of the twelve gods at Athens, ii. 7; vi. 108; twelve kings of Egypt, ii. 147, 151, 152
"two-legged" mouse, iv. 192
tycta, Persian word, "complete," ix. 110

UNDERGROUND chamber of Nitocris, ii. 100; of Salmoxis, iv. 95
underground dwellings, iii. 97; iv. 183

VEGETARIANS, iii. 100; iv. 184
vine and plane-tree, golden, vii. 27; vines not grown in Egypt, ii. 77
vote given for the Spartan kings, vi. 57; vote of the Athenian pole-march, vi. 109
voyage round Africa, iv. 42, 43; of Skylax down the Indus, iv. 44; voyages of the Phenicians, i. 1; of the Phocaians, i. 163

WALKING-STICKS of the Babylonians, i. 195
walls of Agbatana, i. 98; of Babylon, i. 178–181; Pelasgian wall at Athens, v. 64; vi. 137
warnings of calamity, vi. 27
warrior class in Egypt, ii. 164–168
watchword at Mycalē, ix. 98
water of Choaspes, i. 188; water for irrigation taxed, iii. 117
wealth of Asia, v. 49
weasels, iv. 192

weaving in Egypt, ii. 35; Colchis, ii. 105
weights and measures for Peloponnesus
   introduced by Pheidon, vi. 127
welding of iron invented, i. 25
wheat-straw wrapped round offerings, iv.
   33
"wheel-round city," vii. 140
wickerwork shields, vii. 61; ix. 61, 99,
   102
wife buried with husband, v. 5
willow-rods used in divination, iv. 67
wine-jars in Egypt, iii. 6, 7
winged serpents, ii. 94; iii. 107, 109
wives of the Minyai, iv. 146
wolves in Egypt, ii. 122; men changed
   into wolves, iv. 105
women in Egypt, ii. 35; Issedonian, iv. 26;
   of Sauromatai, iv. 116; Libyan
   women, iv. 189; women driving

chariots in war, iv. 193; women
   sleeping in temples, i. 181, 182;
   madness of women at Argos, ix. 34;
   women's dress at Athens, v. 87
wooden statues, ii. 182; v. 82; wooden city
   of the Budinoi, iv. 108, 123; wooden
   helmets, vii. 78, 79
woollen garments excluded from sacred
   places in Egypt, ii. 81
worms, Pheretimē eaten by, iv. 205
writing, Egyptian, ii. 36; Phenician and
   Hellenic, v. 58–61

YEAR, course of, ii. 4
yoke of land (arūra), ii. 168

ZEGERIS, Libyan name for a kind of
   mouse, iv. 192
zeira, Arabian word, vii. 69